# THE LOOM SAGA

## COMPLETE SERIES

## ELISE KOVA

Silver Wing Press

# THE LOOM SAGA

### COMPLETE SERIES

## ELISE KOVA

Silver Wing Press

Omnibus Edition 2022
Published by Silver Wing Press



Cover Artwork by: HoangLap
Interior Illustrations & Additional Cover Backgrounds by: Nick D. Grey
Proofreading by: Christine Herman
Editing by: Rebecca Faith Heyman

eISBN: 978-1-949694-51-2
Paperback: 978-1-949694-53-6
Hardcover: 978-1-949694-52-9

# ALSO BY ELISE KOVA

———

**See the most up to date list of all of Elise's books, and find where to get them, on her website at:**

https://elisekova.com/books/

———

## THE LOOM SAGA

The Alchemists of Loom

The Dragons of Nova

The Rebels of Gold

## MARRIED TO MAGIC

A Deal with the Elf King

A Dance with the Fae Prince

A Duel with the Vampire Lord

A Duet with the Siren Duke

*(More to come)*

## AIR AWAKENS UNIVERSE

**Air Awakens Series**

Air Awakens

Fire Falling

Earth's End

Water's Wrath

Crystal Crowned

**Vortex Chronicles**

Vortex Visions

Chosen Champion

Failed Future

Sovereign Sacrifice

Crystal Caged

**Golden Guard Trilogy**

The Crown's Dog

The Prince's Rogue

The Farmer's War

**A Trial of Sorcerers**

A Trial of Sorcerers

A Hunt of Shadows

A Tournament of Crowns

*(More to Come)*

NEVER MISS A RELEASE.

**Get exclusive giveaways, review copies, and a <u>free gift</u> on sign up by subscribing to Elise Kova's newsletter:**

https://elisekova.com/subscribe/

The
Territories
of
LO
TER.0
TER.2
TER.1
Keel
Faroe
N
2.4
2.3
2.5
2.2
1.2
1.5
1.6
1.3
4.3

M
TER.5
Dortam
5.4
5.2
5.3
5.5
4.5
4.2
TER.4
Holx
4.4
3.5
3.3
3.6
TER.3
3.2
Garre
3.4
1.4

Lysip
the
Islands
of Nova

euri

TEMPLE
OF LORD
XIN

EASTWIN

NAPOLE

VENYS

ABILLA

XIN
MANOR

# Ruana

---

*Want to know even more about the world of Loom?*

Check out **Appendix: The World of Loom** at the end of the book for symbols, pronunciation guides, and more.

# ELISE KOVA

# THE ALCHEMISTS OF LOOM

LOOM SAGA · BOOK ONE

*for grandpa*
*the man who taught me the beauty in science*

# 1

## ARIANNA

Arianna had a bomb, three bullets, two refined daggers, a mental map of her heist, and a magic winch box. All she waited for now was darkness.

The refinery she stared down upon had been coughing up only wisps of smog from its spiraling smokestacks since sunset. Ari had been watching it dwindle for weeks until it finally all but wrote *"Tonight is the night, oh White Wraith"* in the sky. She'd been eager for this job; the pay was astounding. But that hadn't been what drew her to it. No, she loved the challenge of it, the way it dredged up patience and planning and calculation from her like rare minerals from a mine.

Weeks of preparation—listening in on grunts describing their rotations, lifting papers from refinery manager's homes, studying the logic behind the blackened, mammoth skeleton of steel and iron that was known as the refinery— had come down to this night. She looped her line through the stonework next to her and clipped it to itself. Dortam's infamous White Wraith was so very ready for what was coming next.

Moonlight streamed bright enough to cut her shape into the ground far below, making her presence known to any who bothered to take note. But Ari stood with relaxed shoulders and a slack posture. The grunts would be called into the refinery's core to provide extra protection when the reagents were switched. They wouldn't know they were a glint in her eye until it was far too late.

The refinery belched up a sudden stream of smoke. Thick, inky, *oppressive*. It sizzled across Ari's nose with the uncomfortable tang of magic turned sour. The reagents had been exhausted.

The moon's annoyingly attentive stare finally faltered in the clouding sky, and Ari stepped forward into welcoming blackness. The winch box on her hip sang as it funneled golden cabling from spools attached to her belt and through the harness strapped across her waist and chest. Seconds ticked by in her mind, sharp and precise. Ari knew how fast she would fall, and the exact height of the building where she'd perched just a moment ago. After that it was basic arithmetic to determine how long it'd take to reach the top of the iron-spiked wall that bordered the refinery.

Magic pulsed from her fingertips as she tapped the winch box. The gears within clicked smoothly, slowing her descent at her behest. Ari reached down and felt the top of one of the spikes just beneath her, exactly where she had expected. Vaulting off the wall, she pulled the linchpin of her line and tumbled onto the barren ground below.

Ari rested a hand on one of the two crossed daggers at the small of her back and summoned the line back into the spool on her hip. The metal cord shuddered and sprang to life at her silent magical command, slithering back to its home like a snake to its den. She turned on her heel and strode through the murky darkness without need of a light. The refined goggles that served to enhance her already-above-average eyesight made easy work of navigating the night.

A giant, ineffective padlock attempted to bar her entry. She'd taken apart her first Rivet lock when she was a toddler; the satisfying weight of the tumblers engaging with the soft *click* that followed filled her with a familiar delight.

Numbers remained consistent. Numbers and facts attempted to bring order from a chaotic world, to make sense of the impossible. They were the foundation for colossal structures and the tiniest of clockwork machines alike. Ari loved numbers, and not just because they saved her life by keeping her alert in her surroundings.

She knew that each of her long strides were about a peca. She knew the dimly lit workers' passage she went through was about twenty pecas long. And just for fun, she knew—based on the foreman's old schematics that she lifted from his home office a week earlier—that they placed tiny bioluminescent sconces about every two pecas.

She moved with the ease and purposefulness that came from being unafraid and unhindered by the concerns that clouded the emotional mind. It all vanished the moment she became the White Wraith. Like this, she was an extension of the will of her benefactors, an enemy to all Dragons, and more than just a Fenthri. She cast aside the mortal coil to become something...*more*. When Ari felt the tattered flaps at the bottom of her white coat hit her booted calves, she felt like a bloody god.

The slow beats of mechanical hearts grinding to a halt echoed up to her from deep within the refinery. Mechanisms that spun molten steel for final refining grew still. The room would cool, then Revo grunts would guard the Alchemists as they replenished the reagent chambers anew. Which meant that right now, two floors above her, they were preparing the next batch of reagents for refining.

They had been taken from a chilled stasis locker and were waiting, ripe for the taking. Ari's fingers twitched.

With impeccable timing, Ari reached the grated door of one of the refinery's four supply elevators. The New Dortam refinery could process four separate chambers of reagents, but the smokestacks on the north end had been cool for over a month. As expected, the elevator was still and silent, just waiting for her.

The motor glinted high above, at the top of the shaft. Its large wheels nearly glowed through the filter of her goggles. Ari focused on it carefully, willing it to life. The cogs obeyed, slowly churning in the darkness. She stepped onto the roof of the elevator as it eased by, and rode it two landings up.

When heists were this easy, it almost felt like she hadn't done anything to earn her infamy. The "impenetrable fortress" of New Dortam had presented a challenge no greater than the one posed by a standard bank vault.

The elevator put her just where she expected: a dark wing of Alchemist laboratories. Magic hung heavy in the air, nearly suffocating. It made her skin crawl with the sensation of *rot*. Experiments they had been working for far too long were locked away in some of these chambers.

She stopped at the twelfth door, spinning the map of the refinery in her head. Each room was five pecas wide. On the diagonal heading she'd made after entry, she should be just above the reagent preparation room.

The door lock was plain iron—not a trace of gold about it. Ari clicked her tongue against her teeth. *Unrefined and nonmagical.* She'd have to open it manually. It was trickier than the Rivet padlock, but just slightly, and equally ineffective at barring her entry.

The room was thick with the nearly visible haze of magic and chemicals. Worktables stood littered with records and research. Beakers sat out, some full, some empty. Ari reached into her inner breast pocket and pulled out the metal disk that had been digging into her chest all night beneath the straps of her harness. She tossed it into the center of the room haphazardly before strolling back out.

Some Alchemist was about to have a *really* bad morning.

With a thought, the gold at the center of the disk turned molten and the heat activated the powder packed around it. The bomb exploded with a *BANG* of satisfyingly epic proportions. With it, Ari's relatively quiet heist was thrown full steam ahead.

She started to run.

She clipped her line to the handle of the door that had just failed to keep her out, jumping through the now gaping hole in the floor. She landed on rubble and the remnants of half the reagent preparation room. The blood of an Alchemist oozed from underneath the pile, and Ari was careful not to step in it. Blood left tracks that were too easy to follow by Fenthri, Chimera, and Dragon alike. The other Alchemists were still reeling, coughing, wheezing—trying to figure out what was happening.

"Th-the reagents. . ." one wheezed.

"Have been so beautifully prepared," Ari praised brightly. "Still cold and encapsulated, their magic preserved just so... Perfection!"

She grabbed the three golden tubes from the floor where they'd landed after the explosion. Her prizes had been destined for refining, but now she would whisk them away from the hands of Dragon dogs.

"White Wraith, die!" one of the Alchemists shouted.

Ari scrutinized the woman. Her hands were long and bright red, a thin scar around her wrists where they met pale grey flesh. Ari's eyes fell on the woman's face. Two triangles—one pointing up and the other down, connected by a line that intersected their off-set points—were tattooed in black ink on the woman's cheek. A bold circle encased them. "You're young for a circle. Don't throw your life away."

The woman charged with a cry.

"I warned you," Ari sighed dramatically. In one swift movement, she stepped to the side, drew her dagger, and plunged it to the hilt in the woman's gut. Ari hated murdering talent; the world had such precious little of it. But the woman had been warned. Ari pulled her magic back, only lacing her dagger with enough to make the wound difficult to heal but not impossible. The Alchemist was a Chimera and, if her Dragon blood was strong enough, she'd manage to survive such a wound.

The doors to the room burst open, the grunts behind it freezing at the sight before them. Ari grinned wildly. Their cheeks bore the tattooed symbol of a revolver chamber, with one of the six holes filled. *Revo grunts*.

"Too late!" Ari gleefully withdrew her dagger from where it was still nestled in the woman's gut. The winch box on her hip jolted to life with a thought and she sprang upward, back through the hole and up onto the floor above.

Gunfire pelted the opening she'd just traversed, leaving singed and pitted marks.

"Incendiary rounds, for little old me? You shouldn't have." Ari pulled her head away just in time for another volley of shots to light up the ceiling above her. *Barely marked Revos*. It took nothing to goad them into wasting a precious canister on her taunting.

"Get her!" someone cried, rather unhelpfully.

Ari would've been nervous or scared by the proclamation if anyone actually competent was on her tail. She bounded down the hall, each long stride of her muscled legs carrying her toward freedom, success, and a tidy sum of dunca. She threw her shoulder into a door as she opened it, letting the momentum swing her around a corner to another access hall.

Footsteps were incoming from the left, but Ari was too fast. She ran with her life on the line and, instead of fear, she felt elation at the fact. Blood pumped through every inch of her, racing as fast as her feet. Her skin tingled with the magic that mended the tiny tears from exertion in her muscles as soon as they formed.

Ari bounded through a door at the end of the hall and was met with the early light of a gray dawn. With near mechanical precision, she clipped onto—and leapt from—the railing surrounding the suspended walkway. Ari fell harmlessly, slowing just before the ground rose to greet her.

"It won't work," she called up to the grunts trying to cut through her clip. "For working at a refinery, you're certainly imbecilic about gold."

With a touch that was befitting of the White Wraith's reputation, Ari snapped her fingers at the clip high above her. It unclipped itself and reared back before slapping across the grunts' faces like a barbed whip, leaving a sharp crimson line across their tattoos in its wake. She swung her arm and watched with curt satisfaction as the clip soared to a balcony on the other side of the refinery wall. The winch on her hip couldn't have moved faster; Ari didn't have time to properly brace herself and her head shot back with the force of the pull. It wiped the smug grin off her face.

Magic was electric in the air, sending tiny daggers prickling against her exposed skin.

The seconds she took to move her line were almost too long. The ground rattled right where Ari had been standing, imploding inward in what should have been a lethal attack. *Bloody, steaming, Chimera, circled Revo.*

This was not like the Chimera Alchemist Ari had encountered in the reagent preparation chamber. *This* Chimera was a hulking creature whose skin was a scarred patchwork of a dark Fenthri gray and Dragon rainbow. Ari turned, straining her neck in spite of the pain to get a good look at him. If he had been chasing her from the onset, she would've been in trouble. *He* hadn't been in any of her notes.

She braced herself, slammed into the balcony railing she'd chosen, and flipped over it. The Chimera roared, foaming at the mouth. *Imperfect, poor soul.* The powers that were at the refinery had taken a circled Revo—a master of his craft—and stuffed as many Dragon parts as they could into him. He was a Chimera in the worst of ways, and he wasn't long for the world now. No matter how many organs or how much blood the Alchemists pumped into that "experiment" of a creature, his core was still Fenthri. And that much magic was breaking down his body, starting with his brain.

Ari thought he might not see more than another dawn, but that was enough time to make trouble for her.

The Chimera raised a hulking weapon. A crackle of magic filled the air and Ari was off with barely enough time to fill her lungs again. She wasn't there to slay any forsaken Chimera—that was *way* above the pay-grade for this job, even at the insane amount she'd been contracted for. Ari was proud, but she wasn't stupid. She didn't fight battles she had a slim chance of winning if there wasn't a reward on the line.

The creature gave chase the second Ari was on the move. She bounded from rooftop to rooftop as more grunts poured out from the refinery. The stone and concrete skeleton of a building under construction had her skidding to a halt over roof shingles. She pulled a small canister from her belt, three notches marring the otherwise flawless exterior. Ari drew her revolver from its holster on her left leg and popped the canister into one of its open chambers.

*Malice.*

It surged through her, the will to destroy—the desire to burn and crash. The *want* to explode things into a million tiny pieces that could never have any hope of being put back together. Alchemical runes on the outside of her gun shone white as she pulled the trigger, and let go of it all.

Florence hadn't been lying. The girl had outdone herself with the canister, which demanded an exhausting amount of magic, but in turn shot a beam of pure power to the structure Ari had chosen. The explosion was as bright as sunlight and nearly blinded her with the magnification of her goggles.

The building shuddered and groaned, coming to life. Ari pushed herself as hard as she could, the Revos from the refinery still hot on her tail. But she was several steps ahead, literally and figuratively. She knew how the building would sway and fall. She knew the way to run to narrowly miss the first colossal beam collapsing. Once more, it all came down to numbers: the number of load-bearing pillars, the weight distribution of the structure, the probability of how the collapse would occur.

The second she crossed onto the other side of the smoke and chaos, Ari dropped down into an alleyway. She'd had her grand finale. Now it was time for her to do as her namesake and disappear like a wraith with the dawn.

Ari didn't have any safe houses in New Dortam. She could never feel safe in an area that worked so closely with the Dragons, their Royuk language was used as commonly as Fennish. Even if her eyes could make sense of the rectangles, lines, and dots, she avoided reading the Dragon notices and advertisements plastered on buildings.

Well, almost.

"That looks nothing like me." Ari squinted at the drawing of a lithe and long-haired woman on a wanted poster that had *White Wraith* written in bold Royuk below, along with an impressive sum of dunca. The reward for her head had gone up, Ari noted with pride. She tore the notice off the wall. Florence would find amusement in it as well.

An unnatural scream tore through the sky, followed by a fast *zip*. Wind rushed through the alleyways and fluttered the mostly folded paper in her hands. Ari scowled at the rainbow trail glittering through the pale morning clouds.

*Bloody Dragon Rider.* What in the Five Guilds was going on to get a Rider involved? Ari felt in her bag for the three tubes she'd swiped from the refinery. It was a capital offense to engage in the illegal transport or harvesting of reagents, but that shouldn't merit the *King's* Riders.

A second time, the heavens themselves sounded like they were being torn apart as a Dragon descended from the sky world of Nova. The Dragon's mechanical gliders swept arcs of magic across the impenetrable clouds that separated Loom and Nova as they darted over the city. Ari pressed the wanted poster into her breast pocket. She'd stick to the original plan. Now was not the time for panic or over-calculation.

The sewer systems of New Dortam funneled together into the older, original system in Old Dortam. Ari headed in a straight line, sticking to alleyways and hastening across the slowly crowding streets she couldn't avoid. Eventually, she knew she'd hit a main line access, or she'd run into Old Dortam. She'd lost the Revo grunts from the refinery. So long as she moved quickly and confidently, people wouldn't notice the unorthodox clockwork gearbox and chest harness she wore. People only ever saw what they expected, rarely what was actually there.

Ari rounded the corner of a back alley near her expected sewer entry, and came to a dead stop.

Shingles littered the ground, scattered underneath a prone Dragon. Ari's breathing quickened, her goggles flaring brightly with the Dragon's magical presence. Slowly, she reached for the sharper of her daggers.

The Dragon's steel blue flesh was covered in the shining glow of a corona. It looked like the scales of a sea serpent, sparkling with its own unnatural brightness, and would render even her sharpest golden dagger useless no matter how much magic she put behind it. Ari inched around the opposite wall, her eyes tracking the Dragon the entire time.

He didn't move. She couldn't even tell if he was breathing despite being only a short peca away. Ari dared to creep forward, and luck rewarded her.

Exhausted, the Dragon's corona flashed and disappeared as the golden bracers that sustained the protective magic cracked and fell from around his wrists. Still, the Dragon did not stir. His head and heart were intact, so no matter what state he appeared to be in, he was certainly going to wake soon. His Dragon blood was quickly pulsing through his body, healing him. When his mind caught up from the blackness his fall had created, he would be as well as if nothing had ever happened.

Ari passed the dagger hand to hand.

She didn't have time to harvest the body properly of all its useful parts. She had to be prepared for the Dragon to wake the second she began trying—if she tried at all. Ari slid her feet over until she was standing next to him. She'd have to cut out his heart in one motion.

It was reckless to the point of idiocy. Ari's mouth curled into a sinister smile. *Florence would scold her for it later*. But perhaps the tidy sum a Dragon heart could fetch would be enough to sway the girl.

Kneeling down beside the rainbow-colored eyesore, Ari raised her golden dagger. It was refined steel, and tempered to her magic and her will. It'd slow him if he woke. Ari could only imagine what a fresh Dragon heart was going to fetch in the seedy underground market of Old Dortam.

She plunged her weapon down.

In the same instant, the Dragon's hand shot up and caught her wrist, stopping her just short of his chest. He stared at her in surprise.

Ari snarled and bared her teeth in rage. *She'd been set up.* It was certainly too good to be true. A prone Dragon without his corona? Never.

Ari pulled one hand from the dagger and reached for the other. She sliced at the Dragon's wrist, cutting deep, but the blade was the duller of the two and it stuck in his hardened bones, turning into a spigot for golden blood to pour onto her knees.

The Dragon didn't move. He held her in place and stared through her attacks and her snarls. The black slit of his yellow eyes roved over her face.

Was this a ploy by the Riders to find out what she looked like?

Ari pushed off the ground with her feet, rotating in place. The Dragon was strong and could hold the sharp point of her dagger off its mark even with all her weight above it. But it took two hands for him to do so, which meant when Ari twisted, she was able to bring her feet down, *hard,* onto his unprotected face.

He finally let her go and she flipped backward, landing on the balls of her feet, a dagger in each hand. The Dragon stood, contemplating the wound on his arm. It was as though he'd never been cut by anything other than unrefined steel. His broken nose was already resetting itself and would be healed well in advance of the gash in his wrist.

She had a choice. On one shoulder, there was a very sensible little version of herself reminding her that this was not her prey or her job. She'd done what she came into the land of Dragon dogs to do. She should leave and collect her handsome pay. In short, she should stick to the plan.

On the other shoulder was a different tiny version of herself. This version was screaming bloody murder. *Cut out his heart!* It demanded over and over. It cried for her to do what she was made to do: slay Dragons.

It wasn't hard to pick which one to listen to. Ari darted forward. First stepping with her right foot, she drew his attention in one direction before jumping onto her left and bringing her right heel across his face.

The Dragon half-dodged, reaching out his foot to hook behind the heel of Ari's supporting leg. She bent backward, releasing the duller of her two daggers to tumble with one unarmed hand.

"I don't want to fight you." The Dragon held up his palms as though any gesture of his could be nonthreatening. Despite his words, his claws were out— wicked sharp and extending past the end of his fingers in points.

"So don't, and let me cut out your heart." Ari set in for another string of attacks. The Dragon dodged about half of them.

"Fenthri—" He sidestepped, narrowly missing a dagger point in his throat. "Listen to me!"

"Not a chance!" she almost sang, pushing him against the wall. His head hit hard and he was dazed a moment. "I have a very strong 'no negotiating with the enemy' policy."

Ari rotated her grip on the knife to an icepick hold and pulled back. His eyes regained clarity as she once more attempted to plunge the dagger into his chest. He grabbed her wrist again, but *still* didn't attack. His claws had retracted.

The magical *zing* of a Dragon Rider flying overhead piqued both their attentions. Fenthri and Dragon alike looked up as the Rider slowed not far from where they'd been brawling.

"I can give you something better than my heart." The Dragon's voice had taken on a thrumming intensity that burned with a fire Ari hadn't heard there previously. But if her feverish attacks hadn't inspired the change...what had?

"Something better than the satisfaction of killing a Dragon and the reward of a fresh heart?" She hummed. "I doubt it."

"I'll give you a boon."

Ari paused, considering this. She'd heard of boons before, but oh, they *were* rare. A Dragon rarely lowered himself to the point of giving a boon, and especially not to a Fenthri. Dragons saw the Fenthri as the servant, not the other way around. A boon would make him *hers*.

"Any one wish of me." The Dragon's eyes kept darting skyward. "You can demand anything of me as the terms of the boon."

"For letting you keep your heart?"

"For taking me to the Alchemists' Guild."

It really didn't matter to Ari what she had to do for the boon. *A wish.* There were so many things she could wish for. So many old wrongs she could right with the unquestioned help of a Dragon and his magic. It could be a chance for redemption—for vengeance.

Or, at the very least, she could always wish for him to cut out his own heart and give it to her. Then she'd get the satisfaction of watching him do it.

"*Fine*, Dragon." The agreement was an ugly smear of magic across her tongue as the boon was formed. It tasted of disgust peppered with loathing. "You have your deal."

# 2

## CVAREH

"We're not going in there, are we?" Cvareh made a scene of squinting into the dark manhole. He could actually see perfectly fine.

The woman shot him a dull look and pointed into the hole. "Go."

"It smells rancid." He scrunched his nose. He'd known he'd need a Fenthri's knowledge of Loom to escape the King's Riders, but he'd hoped for something or someone a little more...elegant.

"So don't breathe."

"You must be—" Cvareh never finished his statement. Her legs felt dense as lead and the sharp kick to his lower back had him pin-wheeling his arms to avoid falling forward.

He landed nearly headfirst, choosing to crack a few bones in his wrists over taking yet another assault on his face. The ground was covered in a thin, cold film that had him frantically rubbing his hands over the walls—no cleaner—the moment he stood. *Filthy, filthy, filthy.*

The woman pulled the manhole cover back into place and slowly descended the metal ladder cemented into the portal wall.

"Do you have a light?" he asked, massaging the newly knitted bones in each of his wrists.

"Afraid of the dark?" she called over her shoulder. She'd begun walking confidently along the narrow path that was the only thing keeping them from the flowing sludge of the sewer.

"Ah, my darling—"

"I am not your darling." She wheeled and the dagger point pressed into his neck, attempting to pop the words from his throat.

"Will you ever talk to me without brandishing a weapon?" Cvareh sighed.

They both knew the dagger would do nothing more than annoy him, even refined. Pointing it at his chest was at least threatening. The only way his neck would be a cause for worry was if she somehow planned to cut his head clean off.

"I'd rather not talk to you at all," she ground out through her flat teeth.

"Where are you from?" He tried a different question, trying to ease the ever-increasing tensions between them. She had no guild mark on her face. *An illegal.*

The woman twirled the dagger in her hand, slicing up his mouth. He licked his lips, tasting his blood and then the flavor of the magic on her blade. He didn't recognize it; whatever Dragon had given parts of their body to refine that steel was one Cvareh didn't know personally.

But the weapon wasn't just refined; it was tempered. There was a layer of her power embedded above the original Dragon's magic that told him the weapon would only respond to her will. He wouldn't be able to command it no matter how much magic he exhausted.

And that wasn't all he learned. Cvareh pulled his lower lip between his teeth, his sharper canines nearly drawing blood, and ran his tongue over it. He tasted *her*, and wasn't that the most interesting of flavors...

"What did you do that for?" He narrowed his eyes.

"A threat."

"Of what sort?" Dragons smeared blood as warnings. They communicated through trace amounts of magic left behind. Had she been intentionally communicating with him as a Dragon would?

"That I will cut you every time you show idiocy."

"You wouldn—"

He didn't finish before she had him slammed against the wall again, her dagger half into his mouth. He'd have to cut through his cheek to move, or cut his tongue to speak. This woman was really starting to annoy him.

"Listen, Dragon, I will not repeat myself." Her words were level and calm, but they had a wild timbre at their edges, like chaos was trying to pull them apart into raw cries of rage. "You set the terms of the boon. I didn't ask why you need me to take you to the Alchemists' Guild because I don't give a bloody cog about who you are or why you want to go there. I won't pretend to enjoy this. So do us both a favor and don't make this something it's not."

He stared through the darkness at the Fenthri's face. It was round, like a loaf of bread, or a pork rump. The goggles pressed over her eyes, leaving small indents on her ashen-colored cheeks at their edges. Scraggly-cut white hair fell over her ears in messy parts. Fenthri were hideous creatures, really.

Finally, she withdrew her blade, wiping it on her covered leg before sheathing it and starting forward again. Cvareh followed in her steps through the winding sewer passages. The path became even narrower, and the walls changed from stone and steel to red clay bricks.

"Where are we headed now?" He decided his options were to go crazy from silence or risk her stabbing him again.

She didn't answer.

"Have we left New Dortam?"

"We're headed for the Alchemists' Guild."

Whoever this woman was, she certainly harbored a deep hatred for Dragons. Cvareh knew he'd never come across her before, so it wasn't as though she could resent him personally. In fact, she was the first Fenthri he'd ever met in person, and what an impression she was making for her entire race.

"Yes but—"

"Dragon, how was I unclear?" she sighed.

"Cvareh Xin'Ryu Soh," he persisted. "If we're going to be traveling together, we should at least know each other's names, don't you think?"

"Not really." She paused. "Cva."

Cvareh curled and uncurled his long fingers one at a time, resisting the urge to unsheathe his claws. "Cvareh Xin'Ryu Soh."

"You can't possibly expect me to say the whole thing," she drawled with an annoying little smirk. "It's such a mouthful."

"It's actually quite important on Nova." *Patience*, Cvareh reminded himself. The Fenthri had likely never left the ground of Loom. She didn't know what was important above the clouds.

"Oh, I know it is." She smiled, and he barely contained a cringe at how her flat teeth made a perfect line in her mouth. "Come now, Cva, we're going to be late," she chided.

"You may call me just Cvareh Soh," he insisted.

"*Mmm*, Cva is easier."

"I must insist—"

"Don't push your luck, Dragon." A hand curled around one of the crossed blades at the small of her back. He was getting rather tired of seeing that golden steel. "We could always go back to the heart-cutting."

Cvareh looked her in the eyes, or, well, the goggles. She didn't tense and didn't shy away. Whoever this woman was, she certainly had no love for Dragons—and no fear of them either.

"I don't think you will." He took a step closer to her. "You want your boon."

"Ah, yes, a boon." Rather than shrinking away, the woman met his step with her own. She was almost as tall as he, and Cvareh was of average height for Dragon standards. He'd always been told the Fenthri were a smaller race. "They're quite rare for Dragons to give out. What could you possibly want at the Alchemists' Guild so badly that you'd surrender yourself to my whims?"

"You think I'll tell you?" He took another step toward her. His blood rushed at the feeling of her magic: wild and varying, a blend of many Dragons' powers combined into something all her own.

"I could make you." Her chest, flat and strapped under what appeared to be a harness, touched his.

Cvareh paused. *A harness.* Why did his mind tell him that was important?

She clicked her tongue against her teeth then stepped away when he didn't rise to her challenge. His failure to respond to her banter had disappointed her. So his options seemed to be allowing himself to be annoyed at her very apparent efforts, or pleasing her. Or swallowing his pride and letting her say what she wanted but not giving her the satisfaction of taking the bait.

He was growing to hate this hideous wench with every second.

Somehow, Cvareh managed silence. He followed her through the rank passage for what seemed like forever until the sewer vomited its sludge into a slime-covered river. The woman paused, glancing outside and back at his hands.

"Dragon, can you make illusions?"

"Not a skill I possess." Though he was glad she asked. The look of consideration she gave his clawed fingers let Cvareh know she was well aware of what Dragon parts held what magic. It further confirmed that, whoever she was, she truly knew about Dragons beyond the value of a heart.

"Of course you can't. That would be far too easy." She let out a sigh of utter disappointment. The woman thought for another long moment. "Very well, stay here."

"Wait, where are you going?"

"If you walk around Old Dortam looking like—" Her head moved up and down as her eyes raked over him. "*You*, you're going to cause a scene. Or someone else will harvest you. And then I'm out a Dragon heart as well as a boon."

Cvareh would appreciate it if she'd stop discussing cutting out his heart, but he knew better than to say so. He also knew she was right. Cvareh adjusted the wide sash around his waist, heavy with the beads and embellishments of his station. His shirt was done in a dark navy that highlighted the color of his powder blue skin just so. Its capped sleeves showed the strength in his arms—his physical ability to assert dominance. Dragons took note of the feature, which had helped ward off challenges for years.

He looked back at the woman in her heavy leather coat and worker's trousers. She was unfashionable and plain, a continued source of vexation for him. Certainly, she was poor and couldn't afford more than basic clothing. But why would anyone choose to wear white in this industrial wasteland?

"I suppose you're right," he admitted.

"Of course I am," she agreed confidently. "Now stay here like a good little Dragon and don't move."

Cvareh did as he was told.

Time was hard for him to tell on Loom and the seconds smeared into tedious minutes. The thick layer of clouds above hid the progression of the sun, filtering it into a bleak and neutral light. Cvareh cursed himself for forgetting his timepiece back on Nova. He hadn't really had time to pack anything.

He opened a small pouch at his waist and pulled the folded papers from it. They were old, or had been through a lot to find their way up to Nova. He expected the latter was more likely. The parchment was weathered and already delicate, the leaves beginning to tear at the folds. He didn't dare spend longer than a moment making sure all were accounted for.

The delicate lines made up schematics that meant little to Cvareh, but they would mean something to a Rivet. However, he wasn't headed for the Rivets' Guildhall. The engineers of Loom had long been under the close eye of the Dragon King and, seeing as how Cvareh had stolen the documents from under said King's nose, he didn't think heading toward anyone or anything that was notorious for being under his thumb was a good idea.

The woman reappeared.

"You actually made a line in the slime." She appraised where he'd been pacing. "That bored?"

"Well—" Cvareh didn't know why he tried to answer. She interrupted him by tossing the cloak she'd had folded over her arm at his face, leaving Cvareh scrambling to catch it before it fell onto the grime-coated path.

"Put that on, pull the hood, and keep your head down."

Cvareh did as instructed and followed her without needing to be told.

She led him up the hard dirt of the river's embankment and into soot-covered streets. Welders worked in a nearby factory, their torches lighting up the cobblestones under his feet. He heard the occasional crackle of magic, but the world on Loom was quiet compared to the splendor of Nova. Mostly normal, un-augmented Fenthri surrounded him.

It made the woman in front of him stand out all the more. She seared his senses as wildly as the strongest Dragon Rider he'd ever met. Why would someone who hated Dragons so much choose to become a Chimera?

He dared a glance up at her back. She didn't turn or slow, ignorant of his study. She may have been a Chimera, but she looked very much Fenthri. Her shoulder-length white hair, gray skin, broad shoulders, and dingy clothes fit in with the iron, brass, and sepia tones of the world around her. It was as though Loom itself had given birth to the woman.

He followed her down a side street and up a flight of stairs to a shut down, boarded up shop. She glanced at him from the corners of her eyes, wedging her body between him and the intricate door lock. Metal slid on metal and the door swung open.

"Welcome back, Arianna!" *Ah, so that was her name.* Another Fenthri woman—barely more than a girl, really—jumped over a sofa in a haste to meet them. She skidded to a halt as the Fenthri in white closed the door behind Cvareh. "Is this the one?"

"Would I be around a Dragon if it wasn't?" The woman who held his boon and still hadn't bothered to tell him her name herself unclipped her high boots and dropped them on the entryway tile.

Cvareh took in the room and was surprised to find it well styled, given his earlier assessments of the person he was now keeping company with. The floors were smoothed from being walked on for years—uneven in a way that seemed perfectly imperfect. Dark leather furniture was accented with heavy knit blankets around a crackling iron stove. Steam and water piping ran through the barren beams overhead, keeping the room warm and glinting in the midday sunlight let in by two tall, iron-framed windows.

"Did you draw the bath?" His boon-holder started for a side door.

"I did," the younger Fenthri replied.

"Lovely."

"Wait, what am I to do?" Cvareh asked, hovering uncertainly. "I'm filthy."

The woman in white paused in the tall doorframe, unclasping the harness and shrugging out of her white coat. She wore a loose cotton shirt with ruffles at the collar under a tight black vest.

"Why don't you just stand there, Dragon?" She pulled her goggles over her forehead.

The woman's eyes were bright purple, a dark slit that matched his own instead of the usual rounded Fenthri iris. If Cvareh had needed any further proof that she was a Chimera, there it was.

"Your magic already stinks. I don't want you dragging sewer sludge into my home too." The woman threw the verbal jab at him before disappearing into the side room, working on the first button of her vest as she disappeared.

Cvareh looked at the remaining Fenthri, who was failing to hide her amusement behind a dark gray palm. Rolling his eyes, he started for one of the sofas.

"I wouldn't do that." The woman's black eyes focused on where Cvareh's still-booted feet crossed onto the wood. "If you track mud into the house after she made her proclamation, I fear she really will kill you."

"Not if she wants her boon." Cvareh was getting tired of repeating the fact, but he couldn't take his offer back. She'd agreed; the magical contract was formed between them. He was at the mercy of this Fenthri woman until she delivered him to the Alchemists or willingly relinquished her contract with him.

"Then I may kill you, because I'm the one who cleans the floors."

"Are you her servant?" Cvareh didn't think Fenthri kept households. Judging by the woman's laugh, he was right.

"Grind my gears, of course not." She shook her rounded face, her boxy shoulders shaking from her mirth. "I'm her initiate."

"Initiate?" Cvareh frowned. The outline of a raven had been tattooed on her cheek in black, almost blending in with her granite-colored skin. "You're both Ravens then?"

"No." Her demeanor changed completely. The girl regarded him coolly when she had been almost welcoming prior. "I am a Revolver. And my master is a Rivet."

Now *that* made no sense. One of them was an unmarked illegal, out of place in the world, and the other was claiming to be something other than what she had been marked. "Assuming that's true, a Rivet couldn't teach a Revolver."

"Indeed she can. And she is certain to get me help when her knowledge has gaps. We're in the heart of the Revolvers' Guild, after all." The woman grinned. Cvareh continued to be unnerved by the image of flat teeth making a perfect line.

"It is against Dragon law to be taught outside your guild. Any marked who desert their duty could be punished by death. Going unmarked is no better." Cvareh didn't actually care. He was hardly about to uphold the laws when he was the one seeking out the Fenthri rebels at the Alchemists' Guild.

"No one in Old Dortam would turn either of us in," the girl hummed. "And people in New Dortam have more important things to worry about when the White Wraith shows up than the fact that she isn't marked."

The sun fell from Cvareh's sky at three words. "The White Wraith?"

The young woman paused her ministrations at a back table. "Who did you think you were traveling with?"

Cvareh honestly hadn't a clue. But his guess wouldn't have been New Dortam's most infamous criminal.

# 3
## FLORENCE

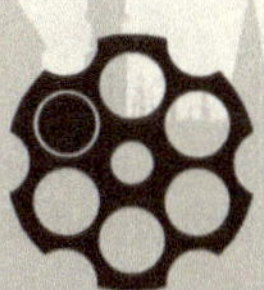



"I'M FLORENCE, BY THE WAY," SHE INTRODUCED HERSELF TO THE YET-HOVERING Dragon. "Take off your shoes and sit at the table. It'll be the easiest to wipe down."

The walking rainbow twisted off his ankle-length patent black boots and crossed over to the table in the corner of their flat by the small kitchen. At least he did as he was told. That would increase his chances of Ari not killing him before she got that boon.

Florence's master had stormed into their home like an engine off its tracks, demanding the largest cloak they owned and rambling something about a boon. It wasn't too long until Florence pieced together what exactly had her in such a tizzy. But by the time Ari had ranted off enough facts for her to do so, she had already left. Florence hadn't had much time to inquire deeply about the nature of this agreement, but whatever it was, she trusted her teacher implicitly. Ari always knew what she was doing.

Florence finished hanging Ari's harness and coat then crossed to the kitchen. She felt the Dragon's eyes on her as she rummaged through the upper cupboard.

"Here."

"What is it?" The Dragon inspected her peace offering skeptically.

"A cookie." Florence shoved one in her mouth for show. And then a second one, just because the first tasted so good.

"Why are you giving it to me?"

"Who questions a cookie?" She laughed, placed the confection on the table for the Dragon to decide if he wanted it or not, and started across the room. "But we will no longer be friends if you waste it."

"Are we friends?" There was genuine surprise in his inflection.

"That's your choice, Dragon," she called back. Florence left the truth of it—that if he did anything to hurt her Ari, all bets were off—unsaid.

"I'm Cvareh Xin'Ryu Soh," he replied quickly.

Florence glanced over her shoulder, looking at the man with the unreasonably long name. He wasn't so different from a Fenthri, really. Instead of gray, black, and white, he was colorful. Like the paintings she had seen of the foliage called flowers. There was his color, then, and his pointed ears, elongated canines, talons, *and* slits for eyes.

But he had two arms, two legs, and one head. He spoke with the same sounds they did and moved in similar ways. She gave him a small smile of acknowledgment.

Florence eased the bedroom door shut behind her. A giant bed greeted her, still a mess from when she'd woken not long ago. Florence turned right and focused on the footed copper bath that stood steaming under a large window.

Ari was submerged up to her neck, her white hair slicked back and shining in the light. Florence smiled, tiptoeing over.

"I hear you."

"I know you do." Florence laughed brightly.

"What is the Dragon doing?"

"Eating a cookie."

"You gave him a cookie?" Ari opened one eye. "That's generous of you."

"Is it?"

"You barely share your cookies with me," Ari muttered, closing her eyes again. "I'm going to think you like Dragons more than me."

"But you don't like cookies at all." Florence scooped salt scrub into her palms. She plucked Ari's hand from the bathwater and massaged it over her skin, soothing the calluses created by her gold lines.

Florence loved everything about the woman known as the White Wraith. Ari was sharp and witty. Her skin was the most lovely shade of gray and her face had a beautifully healthy curve to it. Arianna wasn't just pretty—she was strong too, broad shouldered and wonderfully stocky. Florence was of average build for a Fenthri, if a little too thin. Ari was perfect.

Florence kneaded stress out of the strong muscles that cut out from under Ari's skin. "So how did this all come to pass?" she asked.

"I was on my grand escape from the refinery and ran into a Dragon, unconscious, with an exhausted corona." Ari remained focused on the ceiling as she spoke. Florence could tell the woman was still debating with herself over the course of events that led them to having a Dragon in their home. The tension wasn't giving up on her shoulders. "So I decided to cut out his heart. He woke up and offered me a boon instead."

"You couldn't just leave him be?" she hummed playfully.

"If you want enough dunca to keep affording sugar for your confections, you don't want me to leave prone Dragons with all their organs intact."

"Wasn't that what the refinery job was for?" Florence waited with a drying cloth as Ari emerged from the bath.

"A little extra never hurts," her teacher reminded her.

"A little extra will get you killed." There was a heavy note to Florence's words, one she couldn't stop because it stemmed from a genuine fear of her master meeting an ill fate during one of her many dangerous jobs.

"Florence, look at me." Ari placed her fingertips under Florence's chin, guiding her gaze and giving her no other choice. Florence studied Ari's eyes, the unnatural purple striking an odd contrast with her skin. They had unnerved her at first, but she had learned to see past them. They may have been harvested from a Dragon, but they were Ari's now. "You know it would take a lot to kill me."

"I know," Florence mumbled, trying to look away.

Ari held her chin fast. "After all, I have some of the best canisters and explosives in Loom looking after me."

"Oh, what did you use? The bomb of course, but a canister? I saw number three was missing. It was number three, right?" Florence ran over to the bed, jumping on it as Ari began to rummage through her wardrobe, dropping clothes she decided against into a pile on the floor that Florence would likely be the one to tidy later.

"It was number three, and it was one of your best yet." Ari placed a tight-fitting white shirt onto the bed before returning to the wardrobe. "The disk had a nice blast radius. Incredibly effective but contained. Impressive destructive power."

"Tell me about it?" Florence dreamed of someday watching Ari on one of her little missions. She had no interest in actually fighting herself. But just once, she wanted to see one of her explosions in person, not just as calculations on paper.

"The canister? Flash of white, red at the edges, and then it turned yellow when it hit the target. There was black smoke too." Ari was awful at painting descriptions with words—she'd have had more success drawing it—but Florence hung on her every syllable all the same. "But it took a lot of energy and had a slow fire."

"If you want explosive canisters that large, it will." Florence picked at the white vest and silver necktie Ari had placed on the bed.

"You can do better, Flor. Make a canister like that, but designed for use with a refined gun by someone who isn't a Chimera, and you'll be a rich woman."

"I know, I know." Ari was right, as usual.

It had been two years since Florence had met Ari during her escape from the Ravens Guild and somehow convinced the woman to agree to be her teacher. In that time, Florence had been given ample opportunities to experiment with different ways to combine gunpowder, chemicals, refined metals, and even alchemical runes to create some of the best explosives Ari had ever seen. At least, that's what Ari told her. But the woman wouldn't lie, not even to spare her initiate's feelings.

Their life was unconventional and mostly outside the law, but it was a life Florence had come to love. Ari was an acolyte of the old ways, unmarked on her cheeks and firm in her belief that every guild was connected. That overlap between fields of study was essential. She let Florence explore, create, question for the sake of it. It had all made the terror of escaping the guild worthwhile.

"Speaking of." Ari adjusted the necktie, pinning it with a crossed wrench and bolt done in black iron—the symbol of a master in the Rivets' Guild. "How many canisters do we have in stock?"

"I think I have thirteen made. Why?"

"We may need more for the journey." Ari strapped the belt with her daggers and winch box high around her waist. "It's a three-day train ride to Ter.5.2. Then a week-long airship ride to Keel."

"We're going to ride an airship?" Florence bounced to sit at the edge of the bed.

"Fastest way to get to the Alchemists' Guild."

"I'll pick up materials in Mercury Town. But you better not blow up the first airship I ride on," Florence mock-scolded.

"You never know what wrench could get thrown into the machine along the way, Flor." Ari's grin was playful, but her words were serious. "Use the dunca from the reagents to get what we'll need for the trip. I trust your judgment. I'll fill in the Dragon on the plan and the rules for travel."

"He doesn't seem bad." Florence tried to smooth over the kinks she foresaw in their journey. After all the stories she'd heard of Dragons, she expected a horrible monster. While she wouldn't call the Dragon handsome by any stretch —his colors were borderline headache-inducing—she wouldn't call him evil incarnate, either.

Ari stilled. She crossed back to the bed and, with both hands, cradled Florence's face delicately.

"Listen to me," Arianna whispered. "None of them seem bad. But they are not what they seem. It's that thinking that killed Loom, Flor. *Don't trust him*. He will turn on you and kill you in a second if it suits him."

Florence swallowed. She knew Arianna had real memories of the time before the Dragons, when the Five Guilds were free and the world was run by the Vicar tribunal; when Fenthri didn't have to be marked—when they were free to study and learn as they wanted.

There was a terrifying lust for that time in Ari's heart.

"Do you understand?"

"I do." Florence nodded.

"Good." Ari let go of her face and started for the door again. "Now, get to Mercury Town before it gets too busy. The 'king' will want his reagents before they get warm."

Florence heard the muffled sounds of Ari and the Dragon talking on the other side of the door. She wondered if what her master said was true: if every Dragon was like the ones who had enslaved Loom and, if they were, why Ari had agreed to help one at all. But Ari would remain an enigma, and Florence knew better than to dig too deeply under her ashen skin. Florence said only quick goodbyes as she donned her favorite feathered top hat and grabbed Ari's bag, heading out for Mercury Town.

Old Dortam had woken and the streets were busy with men and women going about their business. Lace parasols shaded faces and pearl pins adorned ties. Storefronts glistened, freshly washed and still dripping. The air smelled sweetly of welding torches and gunpowder, creating a welcoming potpourri to complement the sounds of metal on metal that echoed over the conversation in the streets.

It was as perfect as a schematic.

Mercury Town, on the other hand, was a schematic of a very different sort. The narrow alleyways and curtained windows created a heavy atmosphere that only grew weightier every time someone opened a door to a parlor and released thick clouds of scented smoke on the backs of jacket-clad patrons. Men in long frock coats stood at some doors, watching those who passed warily, casting a careful eye over the street for any who might feel bold enough to try to put an end to the shadowy dealings that occurred in this tiny pocket of Old Dortam.

Florence wasn't uncomfortable. She'd been coming here for years now and most of the door guards gave her a nod as she passed. Two streets later, Florence stopped before a man with a shaved head.

"Ralph." She smiled. "Here for King Louie."

"Don't tell me the White Wraith actually did it."

"If you doubted she would, you shouldn't have sent her." Florence proudly flashed him the contents of Ari's bag. Long enough to tease, never long enough to give away the goods.

"Well, I'll be greased. Wait here."

The man disappeared by side-stepping into a narrow door. Florence rocked from her heels to the balls of her feet impatiently, spending the time by making a mental list of the supplies she'd need. She was only ten items down when Ralph reappeared, motioning for her to enter.

Louie was a scrawny, anemic Fenthri who positioned himself chiefly against the Dragons and at the head of Old Dortam's underworld by adopting the ironic title of "King". His patent velvet jacket was cutaway, set over another heavy velvet vest underneath. Long black hair, teased into ropes, pulled back tautly and tugged at the skin of his face, making his piercing black eyes look even sharper and more angular. It was all in stark contrast to the white of his skin, not a trace of gray on him.

Florence didn't let herself be intimidated. The man had more connections with powerful people than a refinery did slag, but that wasn't going to dissuade her. If this little man was the King of Old Dortam's underworld, then Ari was his champion knight—and that made Florence her page. The one thing that kings in stories never did was kill their champion's second.

"I have a delivery from the White Wraith." Florence slipped the bag off her shoulder, holding it out.

"Let's see what presents you bring me today." Louie hooked a bony finger and two men retrieved the bag from Florence. They placed it at the foot of Louie's wing-backed chair. With the toe of his pointed boot, he flipped open the satchel. His eyes lit up like sodium metal in water.

Louie reached forward, swooping down like a bird of prey. He held up one of the three gold canisters, still so cold it wafted mist into the dim and smoky air of his parlor.

"Aren't you a pretty thing?" He turned the canister before handing it to another one of his lackeys. The man had crimson eyes and the black symbol of two triangles, connected by a line, on his cheek—an Alchemist. "Well?"

"Prime reagents, in healthy condition," the man affirmed.

"Did you have any doubt?" Florence folded her arms over her chest.

"In my line of work, one must always check." Louie chuckled at her haughtiness. "I have another job for your master."

"My master has already accepted something."

He gasped in mock offense. At least, Florence *hoped* it was pretend. "Who is the White Wraith cheating on me with?"

"I didn't realize you two had become so serious," Florence replied in kind.

"Name this other upstart's price. I will double it." Louie settled back in his chair as the Alchemists ushered the reagents out of the room. It unnerved Florence, letting them out of her sight before they were paid for.

"I'm afraid that's something you can't do."

"Girl, do you know who I am?" He gripped the armrests of his chair as slowly and tightly as he enunciated his words.

"Louie, we've only been working together for a year now," Florence said brightly, so sweet it could give the man cavities. "I know well who you are. But this job is personal for the Wraith."

"I've never heard of a Wraith having feelings before." Louie squinted his eyes. "So Dortam's infamous thieving ghost is flesh and blood after all."

Florence needed to tread lightly now. Arianna was strict that no one should know her identity, or anything about her. The few times someone had decided to get cheeky and tail Florence back to the flat, Ari had intercepted them and quickly flayed them with her daggers, leaving the body in Mercury Town as a warning.

In truth, even Florence didn't know much about her benefactor. She couldn't say with confidence that "Arianna" was the White Wraith's real name. But unlike everyone else, the truth didn't matter to Florence. She wasn't trying to play detective. She was happy with her life, content to learn what the woman had to teach her. The only thing a person got when they stirred up a river was muck; Florence preferred clean hands.

"Ralph," Louie called across the room. "Have you heard of a Wraith needing to tend to personal matters?"

"I can't say I have," Ralph obliged. He knew who paid his checks, and that meant he had to play along.

"How interesting. So the Wraith really is Fenthri after all."

Florence didn't say anything, waiting for Louie to exhaust himself with his futile discourse.

"Perhaps, if he could come himself, we could strike a deal that would put him on my retainer." Louie hadn't tried this for a few weeks.

"I don't think the Wraith will be working for any one man or woman anytime soon," Florence responded, as she did almost every time. "Now, the three-hundred dunca?"

"I can see why the Wraith chooses you, Florence; you're quite stony when it comes to giving away his truths." Louie waved a hand with a smug little smirk. Florence didn't drive any bargains and they both knew it.

"My Master has taught me well." Florence watched as Louie's lackeys filled Ari's satchel with three paper wads. She knew fairly well what a stack of one-hundred dunca looked like, and she didn't think Louie would screw them. It wasn't in his best interest. And if there was one thing King Louie didn't do, it was anything that didn't directly benefit him in some way. "I'm afraid I can't be bought."

"That's the first rule, Florence: every man can be bought. What does he give you that I cannot?" Louie smiled, a somewhat sinister curve of the lips. There was an overtly sexual nature to the question.

Florence paid it no mind. Let them think she was the Wraith's lover. It made no difference to her and it helped maintain Louie's illusion that the Wraith was a man. The further he was from the truth, the better. Plus, her and Ari shared a bed anyway. "A certain type of knowledge."

She smirked and excused herself, focusing once more on giant explosions and guns. Louie was likely thinking of explosions of a different sort, judging by the look on his face. Ralph saw her out and the transaction was done. Overall, she liked working with King Louie the best of all Ari's patrons, and Florence had no doubt that helped Ari decide between jobs when it came down to choices.

It was as pleasant to look at Louie as it was a hairless anorexic cat, almost as bad as looking at a Dragon, and he had an equally appealing sense of humor. But the man paid on time, never backed out, and never wavered on the terms of the job. It made everyone's lives easier when Ari didn't have to go on any collection trips. The woman could hold a grudge.

Florence rested her hand on the pistol in her arm holster as she passed by some shady characters—and shady by Mercury Town's standards was saying a lot. The regular patrons gave her no cause to worry. They knew her, and they wouldn't risk the White Wraith's ire by harming Florence. It was the new lot that would set up shop in the dark overhangs and grimy alleys she needed to be wary of, those beneath King Louie who had yet to ingrain themselves in Old Dortam's illegal economy.

She made her way toward her favorite shop, the one that always had the things that made the biggest boom. This time, Ari had given her free permission to use the dunca as Florence saw fit to prepare for their trip, and she planned to see fit for quite a few things she'd been drooling over.

She was halfway to the shop when she heard the first Dragon Rider's glider scream through the sky.

# 4

## ARIANNA

In less than twelve hours he had managed to find Ari's last nerve, rip it out, step on it, throw it from the window, light it on fire, and bring it back to life, only to repeat the process twice over. She was half a breath away from telling the Dragon that his boon be damned, he had the choice of lying quietly while she tore out his heart...or struggling while she tore out his heart. And oh, how she hoped he picked the struggling if it came to that.

"Three Riders. There are *three* Riders now. There were two this morning— other than you. Now there are three, *here*, in Old Dortam." Ari peered out at the sky. The rainbow trails that tore through the clouds behind their gliders were still etched in her memory. The foreboding colors had long since vanished, glittering on the wind, but they remained burned into her eyes.

She'd cracked the window and stretched her Dragon sight, but the Riders were too far to be seen, even with her augmented goggles. And Ari couldn't make out their smell over the heavy aroma of oil, welders' tools, explosives, and the Dragon she had let into her home.

"Again, I'm sure she's—"

"Cva," Ari interrupted him with the grace of a gear falling off its axle. His eyes narrowed at her insistence on using a shortened version of his name. "Tell me something." She turned her gaze inward from the direction of Mercury Town, pulling off her goggles. The Dragon met her stare; he seemed more disturbed when she smiled than when she addressed him with outright malice. "These Riders, they wouldn't be looking for you, would they?"

"Why would you think that?" He sat back in his chair.

"Don't play me for a fool," Ari spat. "We can go a year without having

Riders descend once, even in New Dortam. Now, suddenly, we have two descents in one day? Or perhaps the same descent, and they haven't left yet? And that just so happens to be on the same day you seek passage to the Alchemists' Guild for some inexplicable reason."

Ari didn't remember crossing the room, but she now loomed over the Dragon. He looked up at her and she could almost smell his fearlessness. The man was confident in his ability to beat her, nearly to the point of arrogance. It was almost enough to make her scream. Almost enough to make her throw him down onto the floor and rip off an ear just to show him she could. Just to show him why he should be afraid.

"You didn't seem interested in asking me these questions before you accepted my offer of a boon." The blacks of his eyes narrowed to slits, his body responding to the challenge just as hers did.

"That was before Florence was gone for far too long."

"If you wish to relinquish the boon, perhaps you should get on with it so we can both move on." Where Ari's voice grew louder when faced with a confrontation, his lowered. It was the auditory equivalent of the velvet of his shirt. It was a contradiction that Ari couldn't explain. One that shouldn't be but was—something gentle and dangerous.

"No." She spoke the word like a curse. "No, I am not letting you go. You are going to be mine, Dragon. You are going to hang on the fact that I can call you at any time, on my whim, until I see fit to give you whatever command pleases me."

A low growl rumbled in the back of his throat. His magic spiked and brought Ari's up with it. The terms of the boon were only that she had to get him to the Alchemists' Guild. He'd said nothing about doing so without causing bodily harm in the process.

Magic cracked, strong enough to nearly be heard, and the rumble of an implosion followed. Ari raced to the window, her heart in her throat. Dust plumed up from Mercury Town, marring the horizon.

"We're leaving." She raced for her coat and harness, and grabbed the emergency satchel of basic supplies and weaponry she always left on a peg by the door.

Mercury Town was nearly two thousand peca away. It was close enough that if she used her winch box to propel her along her golden cords, she could cross the distance in a few breaths. Ari looked over the rooftops of Old Dortam, the buildings crumbling together to form a skyline of stone sentries no longer needed at their posts.

She could use her winch box *if* she could find places to loop her line. *If* she could do so without being noticed, or noticed as more than a blur. Her eyes turned inward and narrowed. *If* she didn't have a Dragon in tow.

Ari's mind whirred faster than a freshly struck flywheel. Eighty greca—or eight thousand peca—separated her from Flor and the Dragon Riders. She could run just under six hundred peca a minute, if she pushed and wasn't held up anywhere. Which meant, at best, it would take her just shy of fourteen minutes to reach Mercury Town.

A powerful Chimera could recharge an implosion gun in less than seven minutes. Ari suspected a Rider could do it in less than five. And all that was ignoring the havoc they could wreak with their claws and teeth in the meantime.

Every second she wasted was another second Flor was out there alone. The *one time* she hadn't trailed the girl into Mercury Town, and this happened. Arianna had no idea if Florence could take care of herself. Sure, she carried a revolver, but Ari had never seen her shoot it. She didn't even know if it was loaded or if Flor carried extra rounds. The girl had decent enough instinct, but no practice to back it up.

She needed time to get to Florence. Time she didn't have. Unless…

"Dragon." Arianna swallowed hard. It took two tries to get her pride down her throat and out of the way of her words. "Cvareh." Using his name got his attention, the sort of attention that implied he might actually be willing to listen to her. "Where does your power lie?"

He hesitated. The bloody Dragon wasted precious seconds as he sized up her inquiry.

"You infuriating monster, tell me!" Ari snarled.

"Going to sell my organs?" he replied, level. He'd known what she carried earlier. If she could sense the magic off the reagents, a Dragon would certainly be able to.

"If I wanted to turn you into a reagent farm, you'd already be in chains," she pointed out.

He considered this.

"Knowing what magic you wield will only help me fulfill your request."

"I have the ability to heal. To control minds and see long distances. To persuade others…"

*Blood, eyes, tongue.* Ari mentally listed off the parts where each of the magics resided in his body. He had nothing really special about him thus far. Rusty cogs, she was saddled with the most inept Dragon of them all. What was even the point of a boon if the Dragon delivering it barely had magic to speak of?

"And to slow time."

"What?" Ari focused on him with the attention of a wild dog on a bone. "Your lungs?" She was honestly surprised he'd confessed it to her.

"Yes, I can slow time." The Dragon was clearly uncomfortable with her naming off what body part the magic lived in.

No matter, she suddenly had the time she needed. "We're going to run for Mercury Town." Ari was talking even faster than she was moving. She grabbed an extra empty bag from the bedroom and a long frock coat that would cover up the Dragon's ghastly clothing. The former was slung over her shoulders and the latter she tossed to him. "I need you to stop time along the way. I want to get there in under five minutes."

"But that much magic—"

"Imbibe from me if you must."

His eyes widened and surprise stilled them both. The Dragon looked at her in shock as Ari once more swallowed down that sickening feeling she got from the prospect of working with a creature like him. Of helping him. Of doing anything that could make a Dragon stronger, not weaker.

It betrayed everything she stood for, and everything she worked for. But Ari had learned, the hard way, that fighting for an ideal meant nothing if the people it was meant to benefit died in the process. She was not a proud creature. She was a creature that did what must be done. Her coat was on now, and she was again the White Wraith. A Wraith was above nothing.

Shouts drifted up from the streets as Old Dortam continued to descend into chaos at the hands of the Dragon Riders, who were no doubt taking the opportunity to "impose the King's law" on the side of the city that was less than friendly toward their kind. Ari couldn't waste any more time. Nearly two minutes had passed since her count began. At this rate, they wouldn't make it there before there was another implosion.

She grabbed for the door handle. With or without the Dragon, she was leaving. Flor was more important than his indecision.

His hand closed around hers, and Ari felt his magic slipping over her skin. It wrapped itself around her like sentient, invisible ropes, tightening until she wondered how she was even breathing. She felt the magic build as pressure behind her eyes and a swarming in her ears like a thousand gnats. He remained focused on something beyond the physical world before them, oblivious to the discomfort he was causing her.

"Don't break contact," the Dragon whispered.

The world slowed, sand sliding through an hourglass underneath her feet and threatening to pull her down with it. Ari clutched onto his hand as though it were a lifeline thrown to her in a riptide. She fought against the current of time, fought for air, fought to break the bonds that chained her within space and time.

*You are the White Wraith*, Ari reminded herself. This would not stop her. Time itself would not stop her! Least of all when she was on a mission for Florence's sake. She was invincible, and she would be damned if something as small as magic and minutes got the better of her.

As though she were freeing her feet from mud, Ari pushed forward. She held onto the Dragon—onto her lifeline—and charged out the door. She threw herself into motion like a boulder down a hill. Time slowing had stunted her momentum, her world, but she had regained it with sheer will. Now she was like a locomotive, speeding weightlessly through the chaotic streets.

Men and women moved slowly, sounds were muffled; the fire from a welder's torch barely flickered. They were like the gradually turning pages of a flip-book, tiny shifts and changes only visible if one stared too closely. Ari darted through them, pulling the Dragon in tow. She may have been breaking the bones in his hand with how hard she was holding onto it, but she didn't care. Florence was out there alone, still.

A rumble shuddered through the world, rippling outward from the man at her side. The Dragon was quivering, his focus wavering. Ari pulled them into a side alley, then down a smaller, narrower walk. She got them out of sight before he lost his fragile control of time.

The Dragon collapsed against the wall as every clock crashed back into motion around them. Sound assaulted her senses as though it were the first time she'd heard it. Smells were sharper, light was brighter.

He slumped, coughing. Golden blood splattered the ground. *It was going to mark*, Ari noted, willing her senses back under her control. The Riders would know where they'd come from. Magic strong enough to send an organ into failure from one use would leave a trail, and the blood would set the Riders in the right direction. There was no going back now. They had to find Florence and get out of Dortam.

"Here!" Ari thrust her hand into his mouth. It raked against his teeth, their razor points cutting into her flesh and drawing blood. The Dragon shook his head in protest. *Arrogant beast,* he didn't even want her magic when he was so exhausted that his own was struggling to keep up the healing his body required. "The Riders will come. They will sense this magic. You knew that from the start." Gold streamed down over her wrist and onto the ground from his mouth. "We have no choice now but to get to Mercury Town so we can get Flor and leave. *So imbibe.*"

And he did. The lump in the Dragon's throat bobbed as he finally swallowed the blood that had been filling his mouth—her blood. Ari felt her magic leaving her, flowing into him. She felt it being leeched from her body, fading before it became his.

She'd understood the principle of imbibing before, but she'd never done it. His hand went up to hers, holding it to his mouth ravenously. His tongue was smoother than she expected as it lapped against the side of her thumb. His eyes met hers, seeking out validation for the understanding she was giving him—an understanding of her that was raw and base, impossible to gain from any other method.

Ari wrenched her hand away, covering it with her other palm. Golden blood still trailed down his chin as the Dragon panted softly, staring at her. The wound under Ari's fingers healed, leaving no remnant of his teeth on her flesh.

"Let's go," she whispered. A threat lay under the words that warned if he were to speak about what they'd just done, she would make sure it was the last thing he would ever say.

The Dragon wiped his face with the back of his hand, smearing away the blood that evaporated quickly in contact with the air. He stared at her with eyes the same color as that blood. Eyes that now seemed to look through her.

Ari felt exposed, mortal—even in her white coat and harness. It was terrible, and she hated him all the more for it.

There was that same slipping sensation as he took her hand again. This time, Ari was ready for it. She let the world pass through her fingers as the seconds slowed and everything stilled. Cvareh had that same faraway look on his face, one of brow-furrowing focus. Ari only waited long enough to know he had the magic under control before they were off again.

Just shy of eight minutes had passed when Arianna and Cvareh stepped into Mercury Town. They collapsed once more against a wall in some forsaken storage area packed with crates and barrels. She waited cautiously, until he coughed blood again, before shoving her hand into his mouth. The Dragon was no longer shy. Like a babe to a nipple he latched on, drawing life and magic alike from her veins.

Ari bit the insides of her cheeks, keeping herself focused when her eyes met his again and that same sensation took over. A sensation of seeing him as more than a Dragon, as more than a person—of seeing more than blue, and gold, and orange. It was as if skin and eyes and hair were blending together to make someone with as much will and heart as she possessed herself.

She would never let him imbibe from her again.

Footsteps, faster than a Fenthri's and closing in, echoed in her ears. Ari ripped her hand from Cvareh's bloody mouth and quickly hid it behind her back, grabbing a dagger while the marks from his teeth healed.

"Found you." A mint-skinned Dragon skidded to a stop at the entrance to their alley. He grinned wildly, flashing every one of his teeth.

Ari returned the expression, pushing her goggles over her eyes. Almost nonchalantly, she pulled cabling through her gearbox, clipping the end to a small loop at the end of the hilt of her dagger. "Yes, you did."

Her blood and half her organs might have been stolen from Dragons, but when Ari moved, it was like they had never belonged to anyone but her. The dagger flew out toward the leafy-colored monster at her mental behest. The Rider jumped, anticipating her attack.

Vaulting through the air, he swiped for her face and neck. Ari ducked and reached for her other dagger, then spun upward, slashing in reply. The gold of her dagger rang out against a bracer over his wrist as he twisted and fell behind her.

*Bloody corona.*

The Dragon's skin shone brightly as his magic was transformed into a barrier atop his flesh, keeping out her attacks. The one benefit of him activating a corona was that he could no longer expend mass amounts of energy on anything else. But when it came to removing it... There were only two options when a

Dragon activated a corona: wait for it to exhaust on its own, or force it to exhaust with attacks.

Ari wasn't the most innately patient of women.

Her dagger flew back toward her as the cord retracted. She arced it through the air and it rang harmlessly against the Rider's shoulder as he continued to advance on her. Ari flipped her grip on her other dagger, crouching for a flurry of small attacks designed to tire her opponent.

With a growl, Cvareh lunged past her. The two Dragons tumbled on the ground, blue and green. They were a jumble of claws and teeth, like two wolves fighting for the alpha position in the pack. There was no regard for etiquette or honor. Only the base desire to dominate.

Cvareh recovered on all fours, his claws scraping against the ground as the two broke apart.

"Cvareh Xin'Ryu Soh." The Rider's voice had gone deep and harsh, guttural. A heavy Royuk accent that wasn't there before bled into his vowels as he spoke. "More like Cvareh Xin."

Arianna only knew the overview of why titles were important on Nova. She had chosen to study other things than the hierarchy of Dragon nobility and the suffixes attached to every rank. She knew enough to know that it would annoy the Dragon when she'd dropped the ranks.

But Cvareh had clearly been making allowances for her as a Fenthri. When another Dragon chose to do the same, the rage was sudden. He roared and attacked faster than Ari's eyes could process. Golden blood exploded as Cvareh's hand plunged into the other man's chest and straight through the corona her steel had been useless against moments earlier.

The Rider coughed and sputtered, but Cvareh was more ruthless than Arianna had ever imagined—more than she had given the Dragon credit for after their first encounter. His hand closed, twisted, and pulled. In one motion, he ripped out the Rider's still beating heart, raised it to his mouth, and bit down with a snarl.

The Dragon Rider died instantly, the gaping wound in his chest still oozing gold that glittered and faded in the air. Cvareh stood and threw down the chewed remnants of the heart. "Dan *Tam*." He spit on the Rider's corpse. "All things were not made equal this day."

As if suddenly remembering she was there, Cvareh turned. This was the creature she had been expecting all along. Golden blood glistened on his face from where he had feasted on the heart of his fallen foe. He stood over the corpse like it was a prize—a trophy that illustrated what he was capable of. He was finally the monster she had been expecting.

But expectations had shifted, and they both looked at each other with new eyes. The Wraith and the Dragon had shared blood. It was a step toward something she hadn't expected—and certainly didn't want.

# 5
## FLORENCE

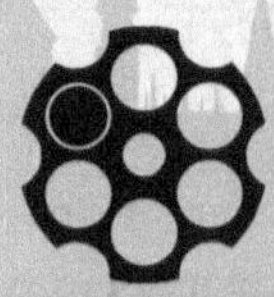


glanced up to see the rainbow of color arcing down toward the other end of
Mercury Town. Florence felt like she'd sprinted a hundred peca. Her heart raced
and her breathing quickened.

*Fight or flight*. Ari had explained the instinctual response time and again, but
Florence hadn't felt it much. Now, her mind was already clouding with the
choice to stay or run. A glider landed on a rooftop in the wake of her indecision.

The irony of Dragon gliders had never been lost on Florence. Dragon magic,
inherently, couldn't be used to manipulate anything tangible. But the moment the
Alchemists and Rivets had expanded the refining process for steel, the whole world
turned differently. Everything focused on the importance of gold: steel refined a final
time with the presence of reagents—Dragon organs and blood. Steel transformed
into gold was magic given form, and could be manipulated by Dragons and Chimera
alike. It wasn't long after that discovery that steam engines were replaced with magic
ones, and the first of the Dragons' gliders began to traverse the clouds.

The gliders were shaped to give Dragons the wings of their namesakes, a
surprisingly poetic choice by Loom's standards. True, the Dragons themselves
looked nothing like the mythical creatures in storybooks of old. They weren't
much different than the Fenthri in general form. But their gliders had wide,
fixed, pointed wings like a bat's, connected by a platform upon which the rider
could stand and steer the mechanical monster with a combination of handles and
mental—magical—commands.

Harnessing enough magic to use a glider was something not every Dragon
could do. Even Chimera—Fenthri outfitted with Dragon blood and organs—

stood no chance of using them; too much magic was required. That fact had been one of many that kept the Fenthri effectively grounded in the land below the clouds, solidly underneath the oppression of Dragon rule.

Florence was inclined to believe that even the strongest Chimera stood no chance of piloting a glider when the first Dragon Rider dismounted. Sparks of raw magic glittered into the air from underneath the contraption, fading into the haze that was Mercury Town's omnipresent tenant. Pure power seemed to ripple under every sculpted muscle.

It was easy to assess the Rider's physical prowess, as the woman hardly wore clothes. Her breasts were wrapped with a sash tied from shoulder to waist. Her midsection was on display for the world, the same bright vermilion as the rest of her. More wrappings around her legs disappeared under a short skirt made of fur that left little to curiosity other than wondering what animal had died for her to have it.

Her eyes shone like sapphires as they surveyed Mercury Town through her long bangs. A thick braid ran down her back and a single beaded strand dangled by her right ear. As if sensing Florence's stare, she turned suddenly; Florence pressed closer into the alcove.

The Rider issued some commands to the companion who landed next to her in the guttural sounds of Royuk. Florence leaned out once more and watched them with careful regard. They began walking along the rooftops with their long Dragon strides. She'd thought Cvareh had been a large creature, but these Dragons were virtual giants, nearly two times her size.

*Fight or flight.* She had never been in a scrap before and she didn't want her first experience to be with a Dragon Rider. She might be able to threaten some alleyway scum into leaving her alone, but a Dragon Rider would skin her alive. Florence stepped down out of the alcove and began to hurry for the nearest side alley that would lead out of Mercury Town. She wished she'd worn a shorter top hat.

"Fen." The Rider spoke the shortened slur for Fenthri with her thick Dragon accent to the assembled masses beneath her. "At the request of the Dragon King, we are looking for any who have knowledge of a Dragon that descended to Loom illegally earlier this morning. Those with information leading to his capture will be rewarded handsomely."

*She's talking about the Dragon Ari brought home.* He was on the run from the Dragon King? He didn't seem half as intimidating as the woman who addressed the alley beneath her. If it were true, it was no wonder he needed Ari's help.

The street slowed. Florence was forced to stop her flight so she didn't draw attention to herself as the only one not gawking at the Dragon addressing them from the rooftop.

"Permit me to rephrase." The Dragon tensed her hands, claws shooting from her fingertips. "Come forward with information, or I will extract it from you with necessary force."

Mercury Town was the lowest rung in Dortam, a small corner serving the necessities of many, though only a few would admit to traversing it. It would be a playground for the Riders, a place where they could reap whatever havoc they so chose without consequence. No one would come to the aid of illegals and dealers. The Riders could be as vicious as they wanted and hide behind the curtain of self-defense or upholding the law should any try to call them to task on the matter. They all knew it, and the Dragon wasted no time as a result.

The woman leapt from the rooftop, landing heavily on the ground. Crimson waterfalls poured from her fingertips, from the hearts she had ripped out of the two nearest Fenthri. Shocked onlookers wore masks of fight or flight for a brief moment, instinct surpassing all training. Half turned tail, fleeing. For the other half, conditioning won out as they boldly stood their ground.

Men and women reached for weapons concealed underneath their frock coats. Gun-barrels of varying sizes were hoisted parallel to the ground, aimed at the Dragon. The rider brought her wrists together, banging them with a sharp metallic noise.

The volleys would be useless against a corona. Florence knew it, and everyone else must have known it, too. But that didn't stop them from firing anyway.

Gunshots echoed over her hasty footsteps. She ignored the fighting and Dragons, focusing instead on turning down one narrow street, then another. Out of the flow of people, Florence tried to catch her breath and figure out her next move. She didn't want to risk going home. The chances of a Dragon actually following her specifically out of Mercury Town were infinitesimally small—a number Florence had no doubt Ari would have calculated in an instant and told her not to worry over. But any risk that would put Ari in needless danger as a direct result of her actions was too much for Florence. That woman was way too good at finding her own danger—she didn't need Florence's help.

The Dragon Ari had brought home didn't seem evil, not in the way Ari had painted him. Florence was willing to give him the benefit of the doubt, which meant these Riders were likely hunting him for some nefarious purpose. Florence constructed the story in her head and found it supported her decision not to go home.

That meant she had to head to the bunker.

The ground rumbled and the buildings shook with the crack of an implosion. The way the mortar and stone groaned was a symphony to Florence's ears, destruction of an epic nature the likes of which only pure Dragon magic could reap. It conveyed a clear message: the Riders had no qualms about leveling Mercury Town on their hunt for Cvareh.

Judging from the echo of the sound, Florence would have ranked it among one of the best implosions she'd ever heard. She was so enamored by it that she had to remind herself to be afraid. Her mental reminders were only partly successful, as she now harbored a secret desire to see one such implosion before they were done.

Florence pushed off, her breath nearly caught.

Ari had only taken her to their tiny safe room in Mercury Town once. It had been late at night, a time when oil burnt low and most seedy occupants were high on whatever the substance of the day was. Florence didn't have Ari's photographic memory; her muscles didn't remember every twist and turn as Ari's could.

But her mentor knew how Florence's mind worked. She had taken care to describe every step as they were taking it, utter every street name and point out every building flanking the alleyways on the way to the small room known to them as the bunker. The chaos and noise faded away and Florence focused only on where she was and where she was going. There was enough distance between her and the Dragons now that she didn't need to be worried.

Or so she thought.

An emerald-skinned Dragon seemed to fall from the sky just before her. Men and women scattered in all directions like rats from a flame. Florence skidded to a stop, shifting her weight from foot to foot to prevent herself from taking one more step closer to the Dragon or falling backward.

Her hand found the grip of her pistol as her heart raced. The option of flight had been taken from her. Now she could only fight or roll over for the Rider— and Florence, student of Arianna the White Wraith, would never roll over. Not for a Dragon, not for anyone.

"You're the one." The Dragon looked right at her with a sinister sort of smile. Even though he had the same elongated canines Cvareh had, they looked ten times sharper and more malicious in the Rider's mouth. "Girl—"

"I am not a girl." Her palm was too slick to get a good grip on her pistol.

The Dragon laughed. "You smell like Dragon."

He inhaled deeply, his eyes fluttering closed. Florence toed a step away before they opened again. The Dragon's eyes drifted to Ari's bag, so recently occupied by reagents.

"At least, *that* does. . ."

Florence finally got a grip on her pistol as another implosion rang out from afar.

"But whatever you had there wasn't *his*. Yet you still have that pungent scent of House Xin on you." The Dragon inhaled deeply. "Little organ trader, tell me, you wouldn't happen to know of the Dragon we're seeking, would you?"

"I don't know what you're talking about." That much was true. She didn't know anything about a House Xin. "But I wouldn't take another step closer."

Florence drew her pistol and targeted the man. She held it out with both hands, the skin on her fingers straining with the tightness of her grip. She wished her arms would stop shaking long enough for her to make a convincing threat.

But the truth was, Florence had never put the explosive end of a weapon toward any living creature before. For everything Ari had said, for all the Dragons had done, Florence couldn't help but wonder if it was right to kill the man before her. No, she'd be able to kill him to protect herself. What set her muscles to trembling was the idea of living with herself after.

"What do you think that'll do to me?" He roared with laughter. "You people are certainly determined little gnats."

"I'll shoot," she threatened.

"By all means, do. I'll even stand here and give you to three to do it."

Florence's forehead was dotted with sweat and her chest burned. She gulped down shallow breaths of air.

"One. . ."

Her eyes darted around for help. Everyone else had taken the Dragon's attention on her as an opportunity to clear the area. She would've done the same.

"Two. . ."

This was it. The clock had run out and it was time for her to make a stand. Even if the Dragon was about to tear her limb from limb, she couldn't go down without a fight—she wouldn't.

"Th—" The Dragon stopped himself short. His nostrils flared and his head jerked to attention over Florence's shoulder.

She instinctively glanced in the same direction, but saw nothing. The Dragon didn't lunge for her while she was distracted. Whatever he was seeing, it was something important—and something she could not.

With a roar and a triumphant flash of teeth, the Dragon bolted in the opposite direction. He led with his nose, pushing his feet into the ground as though pulled along by an invisible tether. Florence was completely forgotten. She spun, watching him go.

He was halfway down the alley when she lifted her gun again. Her finger ghosted over the trigger...but didn't squeeze. She returned the pistol to its holster. She'd been lucky the Dragon had been distracted by something and forgot about his quarrel with her. She didn't need to shoot him in the back just to prove that she could. Ari would never forgive her for taking a risk like that.

Florence continued her run in the direction opposite the Dragon. The bunker wasn't far and, if anything, she could be thankful that the Dragon's presence helped clear the streets of any potential witnesses. Through a narrow passage between two buildings, over a low wall, and down a decrepit flight of stairs, Florence found herself face to face with a soot-covered iron door.

Built into the door, in place of a knob, was a sort of circular lock. She had no confirmation, but likewise no doubt, that Arianna had been the one behind its design. Ari didn't like keys if she could avoid them. They were a security threat, too easy to replicate. No, Ari's locks were always a combination of numbers and shapes, turning wheels and timing sequences. They were numerical codes given shape in steel.

Florence spun the wheels until the shape Ari had shown her was made. The inner mechanisms of the door clicked in release and she pushed the portal open. The bunker got its name from being beneath a basement of a gambling hall. It was another flight of stairs down that would have been pitch black were it not for the electric lighting.

Only a building with as much money as a gambling hall would have the funds to outfit itself with electricity. The hum of the few solitary bulbs fascinated Florence every time. Rivets boasted that the lightning channeled through copper wire would be the future of Loom.

First steam had been 'the future of Loom.' Then the Dragons came, and magic was to be the future of Loom. Then, when magic could make machines accomplish things far beyond steam ever could, electricity was to be the future of Loom. In Florence's short life she'd heard people boast of three different futures. But no matter what future came, there'd always be something in it to blow up—which was what initially drew Florence to the studies of the Revolvers over the Ravens.

There was another door, and another lock, before she was in the actual bunker. One room, not much to consider by any stretch. It looked like more of a storeroom than any kind of living space. Shelves lined every wall and heavy boxes were piled on them, making the long planks sag in the middle. One bulb cast the room in a ghostly light, shadows haunting the corners of the various effects Ari had squirreled away here.

It was more than Florence had seen the first time, which meant Ari had been adding to it in secret. Florence sat herself on one of the boxes in the back corner, resting her timepiece next to her. Ari had told her to retreat here if ever there was a crisis. She'd wait for a good few hours before heading home. Either Ari would meet her here, or she had no idea what was happening in Mercury Town and would be waiting at home when Florence returned.

Florence pushed off the boxes, already unable to handle the boredom. She began poking around, looking for something to occupy her time. She had a sneaking suspicion she was waiting for Ari to come. There was no way an implosion of that size had gone unnoticed. And, if Florence knew anything about her mentor, it was that she wouldn't be physically able to keep herself from running head first into certain danger.

# 6

## CVAREH

"How did you do that?" Arianna demanded from over her shoulder. She led him through the winding alleyways of what he could now only assume was the infamous Mercury Town. It was filthier than the regular streets had been and he had no idea how living creatures could willingly choose to live in such squalor.

"Do what?"

"Break through a corona," she clarified, turning sharply and running backward a step or two for emphasis.

A man ahead of them froze in his tracks as they came barreling down the alley. Arianna didn't say anything, just shoved him out of the way as they tore past. The man blubbered, trying to find his thoughts. By the time he could even form the word "Dragon" they were already far enough away that the shout only echoed to them faintly.

"Corona are meant to keep out steel, bullets, blades, weak Chimera magic. . . My claws are none of those things."

"I see." It was the first time he'd witnessed her mind put to action when prejudice wasn't hindering the winds behind her mental sails. Arianna squinted at him thoughtfully. She kept using new eyes to give him looks he didn't yet comprehend.

"The other Riders will catch up soon," he warned.

"How soon?"

"I can't tell. I can sense their magic growing, but not how near or far." If they'd been bleeding, he would've been able to catch the smell or get a true taste of their power on the wind. But he wasn't exactly surprised that they had yet to be wounded. The only Fenthri whom Cvareh could see standing a chance against a Rider stood before him.

"Then I must assume the same is true of them and you?" He was surprised when her voice rose slightly on the last word, indicating a question. *She was actually asking him things.* Quite the sudden change from a few hours earlier.

"As long as we stay ahead of them. And I'm not coughing up more blood anytime soon." Cvareh wasn't pleased about her abuse of his powers. He should have known from the moment he told her about it that she would demand he use the ability for her ends, and it'd only taken her a minute to back him into a corner until he felt there was no other option. *Why had he told her?*

"I won't need you to stop time again." She vaulted over a railing and down into a tiny side stair. Cvareh walked around as she whirred dials on a strange looking lock built into the doorway. "We're here." Arianna paused, considering him for a long moment. "And you best hope that Florence is too."

Cvareh knew the outcome of her threat before he could respond. Arianna contained her emotions well. Her face remained impassive, swathed in the unnatural, terrible light of the electric bulbs that lined the tiny stairwell. But he could feel the relief about her, standing so close.

This was one of the many reasons why imbibing from the living was so taboo. If every person's mind was a locked chest, then their magic was the key. It was the way into a carefully guarded and illogical system, unique to each individual. Letting someone imbibe was allowing them to make a copy of that key. They could open you up and understand you without effort for a length of time after the imbibing. And really, once that understanding was imprinted on the mind, could it ever be forgotten?

Cvareh vowed to himself that he had no interest in understanding this woman as she opened the lock on the second door. She was equal parts intolerable, brash, harsh, improper, and—worst of all—unfashionable. But there was a counterweight to her heart. Something in her magic shone as brightly as starlight as she swept up her ward into a tight embrace. Something about it made the gray skinned Fenthri woman almost. . . glow.

"Flor! You had me more worried than a Harvester who can't find their mining pick."

"You know I can take care of myself." The girl patted the pistol that sat just under her arm for show. The motion was brave—false, but brave. "It's not like you to be so worried."

"There are Dragon Riders about and we're hiding in the bunker. This isn't normal. I think my worry is justified."

"Speaking of. . ." Florence's eyes drifted over to him. "They're looking for you, I think."

Cvareh wasn't surprised. His hand went to the folio strapped around his waist, checking to make sure the clasp hadn't come undone. The Dragon King would know what he'd stolen, and Cvareh had been expecting that he'd go to any measure to retrieve it.

"Yes. . . I don't believe we ever finished that conversation." Arianna stared at him with her stolen eyes. Cvareh wondered what Dragon had given them up. Had they been killed? Or were they harvested and left to suffer as the organs grew back in their empty sockets?

"I thought we had." He sighed, leaning against some of the boxes. The room was horribly dusty, but his clothes were already soiled past hope. Cvareh was distracted long enough to inwardly cringe at the notion of eventually being forced into some coverings like those they wore here on Loom.

"Dragons barely *lower themselves*—" her tone was sarcastic "—to come to Loom. Never Old Dortam and even less Mercury Town."

"Didn't you hear the doomsayers in the streets? They say Dragons are going to start raining from the sky and finally torch the gods' forsaken rock known as Loom." He returned her sarcasm with some of his own. Cvareh was tired of her mood swings, but could only seem to succeed in drawing them out.

She crossed the room in two long steps, almost as wide as his own. Her hands twisted around his collar as she pulled him onto his feet again. Cvareh met her halfway and kept his lips closed, resisting the urge to curl them back in a snarl.

"You're going to rip my shirt, and I quite like this shirt." So what if he'd already decided one of his favorite garments was forfeit? He'd already kicked the hornet's nest that was Arianna again; he may as well stomp on it too.

"I don't give a damn about your shirt." For a Fenthri, this woman could act like quite the Dragon.

"Then give no more care to who exactly I am, where I'm going, why I need to get there, or why the Riders want me." He narrowed his eyes, ignoring the hideous line of her teeth. "Care about getting me to the Alchemists' Guild hall. You think I'm any more thrilled at the idea of traveling with the White Wraith?"

Her eyebrows rose.

"Yes, I know you. Many have heard of you on Nova. The White Wraith is infamous for making organs disappear and helping traffic Dragons into illegal harvesting rings." *That's right*, he reminded himself, *I should hate this woman.* Whatever sparkle she had for her ward was overshadowed by the cloud of guilt she should bear for all the lives she had submitted to the torture of the harvesters. "Why do you think Dragons never—how did you put it?—*grace* Dortam?"

"Then it seems like I've done my job."

"Enough, both of you." The black-haired girl pushed herself between them, pulling Arianna away. "What's done is done. You said you'd get him to the Alchemists' Guild, Ari. There are King's Riders outside our door. I think we have more pressing matters than tallying up who's who and who's done what."

He didn't expect to find sense from the youngest among the three of them, but that was where it lay.

"Fine." Arianna pointed in his face, close enough that he could've bitten her finger clean off if he wanted. "Florence is right. It doesn't matter who we are. But I cannot take you to the Alchemists' Guild if you don't tell me what else I may be up against in getting you there."

"You seem to have the overview." He held out his palms in a 'nothing up my sleeves' gesture that was only half true. Cvareh still had the entire deck squirreled away. She just didn't need to know that.

"You're not being helpful." She pulled her hand from his face and began tearing through the room. Wood chips and shavings flew as she rummaged through crates. "Will I need a large revolver, or a small cannon?" Arianna stacked weaponry of varying shapes on the boxes as she continued her tirade. "Am I to assume they'll leave when they're done demolishing Mercury Town?"

"They could be at it for a while." The Riders would toy with Loom for a bit just because they could.

"Dragon—"

"They said they were after you because you descended illegally," Florence interjected before the argument spiraled out of control again.

"Flor." Arianna's voice audibly shifted when she addressed the girl. She went from ice to restorative broth within the space of a breath. "Descending illegally is a matter for their constabulary, not the King's Riders," she thought aloud. When she returned her attentions to him, the warmth completely vanished once more. "Why does the Dragon King want *you*?"

She continued to handle herself with an utter absence of grace and tact, but the question was sincere. She'd again put aside whatever grudge fueled her. Cvareh closed his eyes with a sigh.

He could have answered with a hundred things. He could've made up a lie, told a half truth, concocted almost any reason and—from what he knew of her— Arianna would've accepted it at face value just for the sake of ending the conversation. But Cvareh did none of those things. He told the truth.

"Because I want to help overthrow him."

"What?" The entire spectrum of color exploded across her magic.

"The Riders want me because I am working to overthrow the Dragon King."

"You lie," she whispered.

"Why else would the Riders be after me?" He sighed again, growing even more tired of the woman. He avoided her questions, and she throttled him. He was smart with her, and she drew her blades. He told her the truth, and she acted like he'd told the most boldfaced lie she'd ever heard. There was literally nothing he could say or do around her that didn't end with her maiming or insulting him.

"I could think of a number of reasons."

"And none are better than the explanation I just gave you," he insisted.

"Why would a Dragon want to overthrow his King?"

His cheek tensed as he struggled to keep his mouth from curving into a condescending smile. A Fenthri could never understand the plight of the Dragon houses. They saw all Dragons as one—one enemy, one overseer, one force to overtake. Even the most enlightened Fenthri would grapple with understanding nearly two thousand years of infighting and power struggles.

"Why are you the White Wraith?" Answering her question with a question annoyed her all the more.

Ari opened her mouth, rising to his challenge as he knew she would. And then her lips clamped shut, smothering the words she'd been about to say. She chewed them over and swallowed them along with every expectation he had for her reaction. Her face was as stony as her skin when she spoke, "Fine, we'll go with your earlier assessment, Dragon. We don't need to know anything real about each other."

Arianna stalked over to him. The woman was almost tall enough to look him in the eyes. She'd be average height for a Dragon, making her unnaturally tall among Fenthri. "But if you have some knowledge that will interfere with my ability to fulfill this boon. . ."

Cvareh took a sharp inhale, overwhelmed by her scent as she took one step closer and crossed the threshold into his personal space. Her magic assaulted his. It made him hungry for her. He'd had a taste of this woman and now all he could think of when she was so close was the feeling of her, the rush of power as her magic encapsulated his. Yes, there were so many reasons why imbibing from the living was an awful idea.

"If it's something that's going to put Flor in harm's way again..." She was talking. Cvareh struggled to focus on her words, to focus on anything other than the urge to grab her and sink his teeth into her flesh again. "I expect to know."

Every muscle in his body held him frozen with tension. Arianna was challenging his dominance, trying to overwhelm him, to stay in control of the unorthodox relationship they were forming. She was under his skin. In her he suddenly saw Petra in the most wonderful and heartbreaking way. He loathed it. He *loved* it.

"Well, now that that's settled. . ." Florence summoned both of their attentions once more, snapping them back to reality. She had an amused little glint to her eyes, as though they were more delightful than frightening to watch.

The woman eased away from him, and her magic with her. The powder kegs around them stacked taller, but for now remained dry and cool. Eventually, the only way out would be to forfeit everything they were and strike flint.

"Obviously I didn't have a chance to go shopping, but I still have the dunca."

"We have enough supplies here to get to Ter.5.2.," Arianna muttered. She seemed to look anywhere but him for the first few seconds following their confrontation.

"We're not going home, are we?" The girl seemed more intrigued than disappointed by the idea.

"Not until we've unsaddled ourselves from this one." Arianna's particular breed of tact had returned as she motioned rudely to him. "Speaking of. . ." She resumed rummaging through things, tossing rags in the shape of clothing his way. "You should change."

"You don't honestly expect me to wear *this*, do you?" He poked at the fabric with his toe as though the offending plain trousers were likely to attack him.

"We can't have you strolling around like a giant blueberry," Arianna drawled.

"My clothes are quite fashionable," he defended before he could stop himself. No doubt he'd just given her extra ammunition to attack him with later.

"I fail to see how *that*—" Ari stole his inflection on the word as she raked him up and down with her eyes, "could be construed as fashionable by anyone in their right mind."

The desire to rip out her throat was certainly more natural than whatever had been happening earlier.

"Come now, we don't have all day." She waved him on as though he were a lowly unranked. "We have a train to catch."

Cvareh scooped up the clothes along with the remnants of his pride. He waited for them to avert their eyes. "Are you going to turn around?"

"Oh he's modest," Arianna quipped to Florence. "Who knew? I didn't think anyone who could wear something so gaudy and revealing could have real modesty."

He was right. She had used the knowledge of his love of fashion against him at the first opportunity. But the two women finally obliged.

"If you think you can attack me while my back is turned, I'll—"

"I know, you'll cut me," he finished dryly.

Cvareh begrudgingly pulled the clothes from his frame, dressing instead in the dull rags that had been forced upon him. This was going to be a long trip to the Alchemists' Guild hall. A very, *very* long trip.

# 7
## LEONA

through beams of light like the tentacles of a hungry octopus. The windows were shades of blue, folded against splashes of gold and curves of iron. No two were alike. The stone arched over them like waves against a boat and cut each into a slightly different shape. Between them, mosaic was laid in abstract patches of color that had always reminded Leona of fish scales.

"Petra Xin'Oji To will arrive within the hour, Yveun Dono," a little man reported from her side of a large, circular screen. Wood the same shade as the floor outlined it, a base mirrored at the top and bottom creating the imagery of a sun rising through the clouds.

"See her to the red room," the Dragon King answered from the other side.

"Understood." The man gave a low bow before walking briskly from the room.

Leona narrowed her eyes to slits at the man's back, cautiously regarding him as he left. His skin was the standard jade of House Tam. They were loyal to the King—and generally smart enough not to challenge the fact. But she was always on alert when anyone was around her sovereign. It had been two decades since the last duel against the Yveun Dono, and she would see it to a third.

"Leona." The King's strong voice echoed across the space to her. Every time it formed her name, the muscles around Leona's pointed ears tensed, ever so slightly.

"Yveun Dono?" She bowed at the waist, holding the low pose of respect as he rounded the screen.

"Ease, Leona."

She stood straight at his command, retracting the claws that had been out on alert the entire time the man had been in her King's presence.

"Have you any word from your sister?"

She shook her head, a long strand of hair that extended past her bound breast clinking softly as the beads shifted.

"How many hours has it been?" The King walked over to the windows, near where she stood. Near enough that she could smell his skin as much as his magic. Near enough that he could strike her if he so chose.

"Since the theft it has been six, Dono." Leona stripped all emotion from her voice. She would betray no favoritism, no concern. She had been trained better. She had fought and killed and clawed her way up for twenty of her forty-six years to be the King's personal guard, and she would not let anything separate her from her lord for the remaining eighty her life should hold.

"Six hours, and three Riders." The sun lit fire in the King's red eyes as he studied its progression through the sky.

The Dono was a handsome man. His wine-colored skin brought out the purple tones of his hair that, in turn, contrasted with the brilliant fury of his eyes. He was over sixty-five, Leona knew that much. She suspected he could even be pushing eighty. But he looked not a day past fifty, a man still well in his prime.

"It seems too much to track down one lowly Xin Soh." He looked over to her, his stare ablaze with the same sort of quiet danger as lightning. Beautiful, enchanting even, from a distance. But it would strike and kill without warning.

"It does, Dono," Leona had to agree. Her sister or no, the fact was a fact.

"Your sister, Sybil, isn't it?"

She hated the way her sister's name rumbled the back of his throat. "Sybil Rok'Anh Soh," Leona specified for him.

They were both of house Rok, but Leona had the luck to be born of a Soh and a To, an upper common woman and a high noble. Her half-sister had not been so lucky. Their mother had chosen a life-mate who was also a Soh. Acceptable for their stature, but not so much in the way of getting Sybil ahead.

Leona didn't know who her father was. Her and her sister had both inherited their mother's crimson tinted skin, as the woman had been the alpha in both relationships. But, whoever he was, Leona thanked her sire silently most mornings as she stood next to the King.

"She seeks to be Sybil Rok'Anh Veh."

"She does." Leona couldn't deny it. Having a sister who was two ranks higher in society had been a strain on Sybil for many years. Leona didn't bother hiding her shadow; she cast it long and proud. Sybil would rise up and find her own light, or she would wither like a flower under the shade of a stronger tree.

"I gave her this as an opportunity to show me why she should be of my chosen nobility, to earn her rank." Yveun started for the door and Leona followed.

"That is most generous of you, Yveun Dono." It *was* generous. Sybil had no doubt been given the chance because of Leona's track record. If she squandered it, that was entirely on her, and she'd find no sympathy from Leona on the matter.

"I am quite generous, aren't I?" He was amused.

"Without a doubt. It is why we are so joyful to bend completely before you." They walked through a long hall. Glass arched over top like sailcloth ballooned with wind. Wood and metal made a ribcage at irregular intervals to support it. The Rok estate in Lysip spared no expense in its crafting. The unnatural borrowed from the natural world as stones morphed from uncut to elegant sculptures supporting metalwork that could only be completed by a master craftsman. There were many who fought to rise high enough in society to spend a night on the magnificent grounds. And this was the place Leona called home.

"No half measures." The King recited the motto of House Rok. He paused, making a show of inspecting a carving he had seen hundreds of times.

"Something House Xin would be best to learn," Leona muttered.

"The Xin'Oji is our guest today," the King cautioned against her transparent insult.

"Of course, Dono." Leona bowed and held the position.

A hand floated under her chin. Leona lifted her face at the unspoken command, his fingertips hovering just over her skin—never touching. She should be thankful he avoided making contact. His hallowed flesh was above hers.

And yet, by every God in the pantheon, she yearned for it. He owned her mind with his decree. He owned her soul with his very presence. She had nothing more to give him if he gave her his touch as well.

He looked down at her, and she up at him. Leona reveled in the silence, in the feeling of his attention on her. It was that feeling that pushed her to victory in every duel she'd ever fought as the King watched on. She lived for him and silently affirmed it every time she thought he might be asking without words.

The King dropped his hand and departed. She waited a few steps before following behind. They were never seen walking side by side before anyone of importance. That spot was reserved for his life-mate, the Rok'Ryu. But Coletta'Ryu was rarely seen outside of her quarters.

The red room was aptly named. Wood stained in various shades of the color alternated in a pattern on the floor and up the walls, even on the ceiling. It was sparse compared to the other adornments in the Rok manner, and made the single, golden chair look all the more important.

A child turned away from inspecting the Dono's throne a little too closely. Petra Xin'Oji To was younger than fifty, and already the Oji of a Dragon house. No, Leona knew better than to underestimate the *woman* before them. She had challenged her eldest brother to a duel at twenty and won. Her mother fell before her when Petra turned twenty-three. The woman had challenged her own father at thirty and consumed his heart in its entirety to gain his rank and title. They said she didn't even flinch as she imbibed her sire's still-beating strength.

Petra may look a child. But her gold eyes shared the same qualities as the Yveun Dono's. This was a woman on a mission. And those eyes looked right through their King to the chair upon which he sat. Everyone knew Petra's lust for the throne, and it was that desire that had turned House Xin from the annoyance it had been under Petra's father, to a threat.

"Petra'Oji," the King said after he had settled in his throne.

The woman with midnight blue skin crossed over and knelt before her King. "Yveun Dono, you honor me by this invitation."

"Do I?" The King rested his chin on the back of his hand. Leona remained poised at his side.

"I suppose only you can confirm that." Petra stood before she was given leave to do so. It made the muscles around Leona's claws strain against the skin, pushing out the razor sharp talons as far as they would go. "It isn't every day I am summoned to House Rok's most noble of estates."

"Indeed it is not." The King wasn't handing Petra anything.

"Stunning, really. I can't imagine how long its construction took." Petra folded her hands before her. The woman clearly had no interest in the construction of the estate and its trimmings. The two House leaders were digging in their claws and waiting for someone to push hard enough to tear flesh.

"With a House as noble and established as House Rok, we can afford to take our time on things." Yveun Dono's lips curled into a snarling smile. "And how is your estate faring, Petra'Oji?"

"The latest revisions are coming along nicely, thank you." She smiled widely, showing her teeth.

The edges of Leona's lips parted, just enough to flash her elongated canines. She did not *want* to tolerate this eager upstart's encroachment on her King's honor. But she *did* tolerate it, only as long as Yveun Dono did.

"That is most excellent to hear." Silence filled the room following the King's statement. Leona watched it settle over Petra. It crept under the other woman's skin, multiplying and manifesting until she had to speak.

"But that is not why you invited me here today."

"It isn't?" Yveun Dono rested his elbow on the armrest of the throne, looking bored.

"A letter, or a whisper, would have sufficed if you wanted to talk about remodeling." Petra squinted her eyes, barely.

"Speaking of whispers, have you heard from your brother?" The King finally began to circle around his point like a carrion bird.

"You likely have more recently than I. Is he not your counsel on matters of treasury?"

*Petulant child.* Leona kept the thought to herself, barely.

"That is not the brother I am asking for." The King sat straighter in his chair.

It was a fraction of movement, but it betrayed his increasing impatience with Petra's obstinacy.

"I didn't even realize you knew I had a younger brother, Dono. You honor House Xin with this interest you have taken in us." Petra lied through her teeth —teeth Leona fantasized about smashing with a variety of instruments.

"Where is Cvareh?"

"I believe he is still at the Temple of Lord Xin, praying to the Death-giver for wisdom of the ends."

Yveun Dono was no more convinced by Petra's lie than Leona was. "Does he pray often?"

"Only when he thinks he needs our House Patron's wisdoms."

"And how often does Cvareh need the guidance of the Death-giver?" Yveun Dono tilted his head to the side, just barely. "He isn't renowned as being particularly ambitious."

"Yveun Dono, do take care; that is my brother of whom you speak."

"'Take care', Petra?" The King dropped all formality from her title. It was a pointed and successful jab on the King's part, judging from the expression on the Oji's face. "What exactly must I 'take care' of? I already care for our people, for Nova, for the misplaced masses in the land below the clouds. I take care of an astronomically large yet finite amount of resources to ensure there is more than enough to go around for both us and the Fen. I am mindful of the tax their irresponsibility has put on a world we now know we share. I oversee their guilds to ensure proper teachings. Am I not taking care of enough?"

Petra was silent, the most sense the girl had shown since the encounter began.

"Or must I also take care of your family's fragile sensibilities as well?"

"I will look after House Xin." There was almost a growl to Petra's words.

"Will you, Petra? Or will your willing lack of ideals lead them to ruin?" The woman's lesser experience compared to Yveun Dono's was telling. A few words twisted around her House's motto—*ends before ideals*—and she wound up so tightly that Leona could almost smell the quiver in her muscles. House Xin was too proud, too bold. "This is not about House Xin, Petra. This is about the good of our people, the longevity of our traditions, the eternity of our ways, the future of our world. A future we must pursue with no half measures."

"No half measures," Petra repeated the motto of House Rok. "It must be easy to say from where you sit when any half measure does not come off Rok's measuring stick."

The fruity taste of blood laced Leona's mouth as she bit her tongue to keep from speaking. The King could defend himself; he didn't need her to step forward and give Petra a verbal or physical lashing. But she still hoped he would ask.

"Careful, Petra." The King would give no more caution than that. No matter how badly Leona suspected he wanted to be off with Petra as well, they couldn't just kill another House's Oji. There were rules to be followed when it came to duels. If they cast aside the foundation of their society's hierarchy, they'd be left with the anarchy Loom experienced before Yveun Dono had begun to restructure it. "Now, I will ask you again. Where is Cvareh?"

"Then I will tell you again, he is high in the mountains at the Temple of Lord Xin."

The problem was, even though they all knew it to be a lie, there was no *proof*. So Petra and the whole underbelly of Dragon society called House Xin would continue to unfurl whatever plot they were playing at. At least until Yveun Dono had enough evidence of treason to bring down even an Oji.

"Then it should be no problem for him to attend my summons."

"Actually, it is." Petra's triumphant smile returned. She knew she had the upper hand. If they'd had anything they would've been out with it, and she was going to stick to her idiotic story until they did, it seemed. "He is in solitary meditation, and will not leave until he has heard the guiding words of our Lord. I'm sure you understand the importance of seeking the will of our House Patron, Dono."

"Quite."

"Why the sudden interest in Cvareh? Would you like to employ him as well?" Petra asked.

"I believe him to be involved in a crime." One would expect such a claim from their supreme leader to silence Petra and wipe the smug grin off her face, but she just kept smiling.

"How ghastly. But I'm sure my dearest Cvareh has not had any part in it."

The King leaned back in his throne. "We will see, won't we? If you are lying, there will be grave consequences on your whole House."

"Your glory is all ends House Xin seeks." Petra's words were poetic, pretty, and utterly insincere.

"I'm sure." The King waved a long-fingered hand.

Petra bowed, heeding the dismissal with grace. She spun like a dancer and strode out the room with long, measured steps. Leona watched the young Oji go, boring holes in the door with her eyes long after she left.

"Ease, Leona," the King reminded her again as he stood.

"She's lying to you, Dono."

"I am aware." He started for the door himself, trusting Leona to fall into step.

"Cvareh stayed with his brother here. He could've easily uncovered what we had. It had to have been him; only a Xin would take the schematics," Leona insisted, trying to persuade someone who was already of her mind.

"And he is no doubt carrying them to Loom to find someone who can finish the engineering of the Philosopher's Box."

"Should we increase our efforts in watching the Rivet's Guild? Even the best watchmen close their eyes to sleep." It would make sense for Cvareh to head there. The engineers of Loom would be the ones to finish what the last resistance had started.

"I trust you to it," the King agreed, starting for a different set of council rooms.

"I bend to your will." Leona bowed.

"However, even more so, I want your sister to bring me back what is rightfully mine." The King paused, giving Leona a long stare.

"I will see that she does," Leona vowed. "Personally, if I must."

"Very good." He nodded and continued on his way.

Leona didn't know what was holding up Sybil beneath the clouds. But frankly, she didn't care. In Leona's world, there was only success or failure. There was no 'almost', or 'close enough'. Leona had given Yveun Dono her word now. If she had to, she would raze Loom to the ground to avoid failing him.

# 8

## ARIANNA

underneath the train and casting halos around the dim lighting of the Old Dortam station. It was the last train of the day to embark along the winding trail that curved through the mountain range to the south of Dortam and out toward the coast.

Florence's inability to spend the dunca from Ari's mission proved a favorable happenstance. It was handier to have the money in notes to exchange for three tickets on a sleeper car. Ari had initially been thinking of stowing away, but she wanted to eliminate the number of things that could go wrong. They were already traveling with a Dragon; the last thing they wanted to do was engage in any activity that could raise suspicion.

Ari stood with Cvareh as Florence approached the ticket counter. Iron gates extended on either side, and train staff waited at each of the small entrances. It was the only thing that stood between them and finally getting out of Dortam, and Ari was holding her breath at the thought.

Their disguises were simple but effective. The three of them would be medical travelers, seeking out the colder air of Keel—conveniently where the Alchemists' Guild was located—to help with their highly contagious, skin-rotting affliction. Florence had thought of it from something she'd read in a book, and Arianna was content to not question. Flor was playing the nurse—the only one among them who could show her face.

Arianna and Cvareh each covered their faces with cloth medical masks and large goggles that hid their eyes. Ari kept her hood down to avoid too much suspicion, but Cvareh's was raised. Luckily, his skin was a shade of steely blue that could almost pass for gray in the right light. It was the best they could hope for when the bloody Dragon couldn't even make an illusion.

Then again, he *could* stop time.

His face became the sole object of her focus. Her hand tingled from where it had raked against his teeth. The ghost of his tongue ran along her skin. She wondered how her power stood up to his. He would know now, since he knew how much magic he expended to stop time and how much hers replenished. Were they well matched? Or could he indeed overpower her? Ari had never imbibed from a living host, and the notion suddenly fascinated her.

"I have our tickets." Florence's cheer was almost believable. Arianna stepped first, Cvareh half a step after as she'd instructed. They both fell into place behind the youngest among them as they approached the gate. "For the three of us."

The ticket-taker tore all three tickets in half at once, passing one part back to Florence.

"Step widely, you two," she instructed, waving them around the man and onto the platform. The train staff didn't look twice. Between the mask, the goggles, the hood, the haze, and the darkness—Cvareh was passing as a Fenthri. A large Fenthri. But Arianna suspected that her standing next to him helped. "Don't get anywhere near this nice gentleman. You don't want him to catch your sick."

Others on the platform took heed of Florence's loud cautioning to the ticket man and gave them a wide radius. Ari smiled proudly under her mask. She'd helped raise quite the cunning little sneak these past two years.

"Let's see. . . Our car is. . ." Florence led them down the long platform, continually checking the tickets. "Right here."

Arianna had traveled by train a couple times in her life, but she was quick to forget how little traveling Florence had done. The young woman stared in wonder at the plush red carpet and patterned metals, embellished with fabric, of the sleeper car. Cabins lined one side of the hall, windows on the other.

Florence was so taken by it all that she momentarily forgot where they were going—a distraction quickly remedied with a small cough from Ari. Their cabin was small, as most were in second class. It would be tight, but manageable for the few days they would be on the train. This was a trip for business, not pleasure, and Ari was certainly *not* going to spend more than she had to on the Dragon.

One long sofa was on the right, a low bar for basic effects on the left. Over the sofa was a second bed that could be folded down from the wall. It was cramped with the three of them and Ari was stuck awkwardly shuffling around Florence and the Dragon to pull the curtains over their window and lock the door behind them.

"Flor, you did a great job."

"I was so nervous, I thought I'd be ill!" The girl fell onto the sofa with a dramatic sigh and began rummaging through her bag for a foil-wrapped chocolate.

"It didn't show." Arianna pulled the mask down from her face and rested her goggles atop her head. Her eyes fell on the Dragon as he carefully inspected the metalwork with one of his bandaged hands. "Well, Lord Dragon, fashionable enough for you?"

"And how long have you been waiting to use that quip?"

Arianna was dangerously close to appreciating the Dragon's adaptability in managing her sarcasm.

"But yes, it is quite fashionable. We would use wood on Nova for something like this. I'd never thought metal could look so... soft."

The compliment caught her off-guard. Her immediate reaction was to probe for falsehood. But she could see none in the way he delicately traced the star-like shapes the intersecting diamonds of raised metal made. That sent her mentally pin-wheeling in the opposite direction. If this Dragon thought he could win her over with a more delicate approach to her world and people, he was certainly wrong. Ari sat heavily on the sofa, stretching her legs as long as they could go in the narrow compartment.

"Look, Flor, he admits the whole of Loom shouldn't be burnt to the ground." Arianna closed her eyes, satisfied at having the last word.

"I don't think he ever said he thought it should be."

Arianna cracked one eye open. Florence had the audacity to grin at her. *Traitor*.

Cvareh lowered his hood, his blood orange hair spilling around his head like a halo in all directions. In about thirty seconds he went from being a narrowly passable Fenthri to looking entirely Dragon. It soured Arianna's stomach with the sobering reminder of why they were on the train.

"Don't take too much off," she cautioned him. "Never know when a stray conductor could decide to poke a head in."

"That happens?"

"Sure, looking for stowaways or people who have overshot their tickets." Florence gave Arianna a pointed look at the end of the statement, which Arianna held knowingly. It was their second time traveling by train together. The first time, they had been those stowaways in hiding from the conductors and train workers.

Yet another reason for Ari to be silently glad they'd had the money in cash to buy the tickets—she had the opportunity to take the girl on a train properly.

With a sharp whistle and some calls from the platform, the train ground to life. Florence pressed herself up to the window, pulling back the curtains just enough to peer out. Arianna watched the hazy lights illuminate the fabric in increasing frequency until they zoomed by in a race to meet the impending blackness that awaited them at the city's edge.

Arianna stood. The gentle sway of the train was making her tired, and she wasn't ready to be lulled to sleep just yet. She wouldn't feel comfortable until more space was placed between them and Dortam. They'd never found out what happened with the Dragon Riders. They'd overheard whispers and hushed conversations on their way to the station, but no one spoke too loudly and no one knew if the Riders had truly left Dortam to return to Nova, or just left the area. The farther they got from the city without incident, the more relaxed she'd let herself feel.

"I'm going to go to the dining car. It's late, but they may still be serving something since the train didn't get moving until just now. Flor, do you have a preference?" Arianna made it a point not to ask Cvareh.

"No, anything is fine." She was entranced by the outside world blurring by as the train steadily gained speed. "Actually, should I go?"

Arianna's mask was halfway on when her student recalled the illusion they were working to uphold. She considered this, weighing the options. "We can both go."

"Why are you unmarked?" Cvareh's attention hadn't wavered from the cheek she had just covered with her mask.

"Because I was in the guilds before *your kind*." Her skin prickled at the retort —at the memory of the time before the Dragons.

"Florence said you're a Rivet." Arianna glared at her student for imparting such information to the Dragon. He continued, "Why not just get the mark? Then you wouldn't have to hide your face. Wouldn't it be easier?"

"Because I do not want the mark." There would be no way a Dragon could ever understand. It was like asking a Revolver to fix an engine, or a Harvester to use just enough medicine to save rather than kill. Even if she believed he wanted to understand—which Arianna *didn't* believe—he still couldn't.

"But you wear it anyway."

The iron of her pin was cool under her fingertips. "I can remove this." The man was infuriating, and she wasn't going to defend herself to him. "Tattoos should be choices, not brands."

Cvareh was silenced and seemed to heed to her words. The tattoos Arianna did bear burned underneath her clothing. They reaffirmed her position.

"Now, we are going to find food. Stay here, and don't get into trouble. If you do I'll—"

"I know, you'll cut me. Or kill me. Or have me kill myself." He flopped into the corner by the window and pulled back the curtain a sliver, just enough to watch the gray world slip further into darkness.

Arianna concealed a smirk under her mask. He was fun to toy with, more fun than she'd had in a long time. Sure, her jobs kept her satisfied enough knowing she was bringing a measure of harm to the Dragons' system. But seeing an actual Dragon caused any measure of pain by her actions? It was an unparalleled joy.

"Are we going to make it to Keel in one piece?" Florence asked as the door closed behind her.

"That's mostly up to him." Arianna lowered her voice as they walked through the corridor. It was dim now that they no longer had the light from Old Dortam's platform. Small sconces filled with bioluminescent bacteria in water rocked with the sway of the train, bathing the passage in a weak glow.

"Why did you take the boon?" Florence was still mastering the skill of intimidation. Her penetrating stare was nothing more than a harmless reflection of Ari's own insistent looks.

"Because I want the wish." She rewarded her apprentice's efforts with a real response. The easy way out would've been to hide behind her hate for the Dragons. But Ari would give Florence more than that. She'd earned it with her boldness, and with the risk she was willing to take.

"*Why* though?"

Ari had carefully built her walls over the years. She'd made them thick and tall around her most guarded truths, and were constructed along the lines she'd drawn when she'd first met Flor. The lines kept the other woman just far enough away that Arianna could sleep at night with some small assurance that her student would be safe, from even her. They were the same lines that showed Arianna where the edge to oblivion was. It was the only thing that kept her plunging into the madness revenge begot.

These walls, her guards, were oddly shaped, however, and they let Florence see a picture that Arianna knew didn't quite make sense. Ari had told Florence of her hatred for the Dragons and everything that the wretched creatures wrought. Flor was smart enough to also know that Ari was a woman on a mission. She'd likely figured that much out from their first meeting.

Not a single day had gone by in the two years she'd been around Florence that Arianna wasn't silently haunted by the ghost of her failed mission. The banner had fallen upon her shoulders, weighted by guilt amid the winds of change that swept across Loom. It was the only thing that still truly mattered in her world—or would have been, if she hadn't met Flor. It was an unfinished portrait that would now be the masterpiece of her revenge. And it was missing one brush stroke—a stroke a Dragon could give.

They had stopped walking and by the way Florence was staring at her, it had been Arianna who had halted their forward progress. Arianna reached out and laced her fingers with the girl's. She looked at her apprentice in the way she reserved to signal the imminent announcement of the final word on a matter.

"I need this boon, Flor, because there is something he can give me. I will never be free until I finish what I made myself for. And, as much as I abhor the fact, it's something he can provide."

# 9
## CVAREH

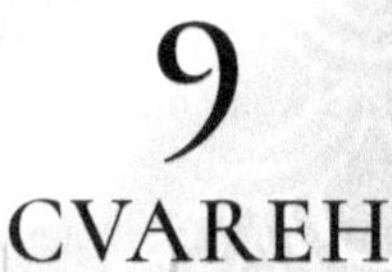

Cvareh had never had much of an opinion on the mechanical boxes that whizzed around Loom like hornets on unknown missions, but he was quickly finding one. He was about to go mad—or maybe he already had. For on the third morning, he found himself debating the fact with his favorite diamond shape in the corner of the ceiling.

There had been no magic whatsoever on the trip. That was a strong and fast rule from the great and always correct Arianna. Sarcasm and eye rolling aside, Cvareh didn't actually disagree with the mandate. They seemed to have managed to give the Riders the slip by some miracle, and using any magic would only increase their chances of discovery.

He glanced over at the woman known as the White Wraith and wondered if the magic he'd imbibed from her helped mask his own. Or perhaps she had treated the inside of that bunker with some unknown substance and the Riders lost the trail. Cvareh was learning that his traveling companion had a knack for being two steps ahead and one calculation over-planned.

She also had a knack for being more annoying than a no-title upstart determined to gain rank through a back-alley duel. There wasn't a thing Cvareh could say that wasn't countered in some way. Honest questions were responded to with bitter retorts. It had him seriously wondering if he had somehow hurt this woman in a past life.

He rested his temple back on the wood by the window. He hadn't changed his clothes in days—days! And he hadn't left the room for more than the call of nature, and even that was with an escort. He felt like a prisoner on the run.

Which, when he considered it, was almost exactly what he was. Though if he was caught, he'd be killed on sight rather than imprisoned.

The world outside the window had changed dramatically. Dortam was land-locked, nestled in a valley in the center of mountains. For a day and a half, they'd wound around narrow tracks high above sheer cliff faces. Overnight, however, the land had flattened and the train picked up speed as it shot out of tall hills and toward the flattening coast.

They passed towns and small villages that crept up out of nowhere and went running away toward the horizon as soon as the train passed. One or two times, they stopped at a small platform and a few people got off—fewer got on. But everything went as smoothly as butter gliding across a hot pan.

In his moments of frustration, Cvareh bemoaned Ari's existence. But the farther he got from Dortam, the more he realized his spur of the moment decision to ask her to take him to the Alchemists was a wise one. He knew nothing of this world or its people. He didn't know why the thin grasses grew so feebly, a pale yellow gray color rather than the vibrant viridescent to which he was accustomed. He didn't know why men and women buttoned and bundled themselves like swaddled babes, barely showing any skin—often times not even their hands.

He couldn't tell the highborn from the low. And it was difficult to discern who had wealth and power from those who didn't. Everything looked much the same as everything else. Ornamentation on rooftops and windows was fine, but not outdone. Nothing stood out, nothing fell apart. New Dortam had been a world away from Nova, and even that was more similar to the cities he was accustomed to than these rural towns.

It was small wonder the Dragon King demanded all Fenthri be marked with their guild rank. Without it, there would be no way to tell them all apart or make sense of their backward society. He kept such thoughts to himself, of course, as they were certain to upset his present company.

"Four hours to Ter.5.2," a conductor called from the thin hall outside their cabin. "Four hours to terminal."

Arianna stood and reached above them for one of the bags. She stacked paper money in perpendicular bundles, counting to herself. Cvareh watched her hands as they flipped through the bills, sequestering out batches before repeating the process. Her fingers didn't joint exactly the same as his. Cvareh flexed his fingers, unsheathing his claws momentarily.

"What happens if it rips?" He should have known better than to ask the question by now, but silence and boredom had him in their hold.

"Then the bill is void," Arianna answered as though the fact was obvious.

"So why make the money paper?" It seemed ill advised.

"What else would it be made of?"

"Metal?" *Like on Nova.*

Arianna paused her counting and looked at him like he was stupid. Cvareh was many things, but he was not stupid and the look made him bristle. "We have more important things to use our metals for than money."

He stared as she returned to counting, wondering if he had actually said the comparison to Nova rather than thought it.

"Flor, we'll barely have enough to buy passage on the airship, I think." Arianna went back to ignoring Cvareh.

"*Barely*." Florence picked up on the key word in Ari's statement.

"I may need to do some work while we're waiting to get on." Arianna began laying out the belt and harness he had only seen her remove yesterday.

Cvareh had taken it as a good sign when the woman felt comfortable enough with him being in her presence to remove her weaponry. Though it could've just begun to chafe. He shifted to scratch an itch. Gods knew he had reached that point as well.

"Not as the White Wraith, I take it?"

"No," Arianna affirmed. "I don't want people to know I've left Dortam. Plus, I won't have time for a job of that scale."

"People will find out you've left Dortam if you do *any* work." Florence leaned back into the sofa with a small grin. "Subtlety isn't your strong suit."

Arianna glared in the girl's direction. But unlike the ones she regularly cast Cvareh's way, this look was light and playful. He'd begun to wonder as the nights slipped on what the real relationship between the two women was. They shared the narrow sofa while he took the upper bunk at night. Florence was too old to be Arianna's daughter. Sisters, perhaps?

"I'm going to heed my needs before I get all strapped in," Arianna announced, donning her mask and slipping out the room—careful to not let the door open wide enough that Cvareh would be visible.

"What will she do?" Cvareh asked. Florence looked at him, confused. He'd found a friend in the girl—that was undeniable. She listened to his questions and did her best to answer them. As a result, Cvareh picking her brain had become a quickly adopted ritual whenever Arianna left the room. "For work."

Florence made a noise of comprehension. "If we're lucky, just some pick-pocketing. But I don't think Ari has limited her skills to just that in ages, if ever. I'm sure there will be whispers of the White Wraith expanding her hunting grounds before we board for Keel."

Cvareh waited a long moment for Florence to expand in more detail, but she didn't. For once, he decided against probing further on the topic. There was a worried cloud hanging over the girl's head as she engaged in a staring battle with the tools of Arianna's trade. It was as though she silently accused them for the habits of their master. While Cvareh found the woman abrasive, rude, and hideous, Florence saw beauty. He wondered where he'd have to stand to make sense of the White Wraith the way the young Fenthri did.

"You two are close." His observation wasn't a question, so Florence didn't answer more than nod. "How did you two meet?"

"I was running." Florence didn't pull her eyes away from where they had fallen on Arianna's gear, but she was no longer seeing anything in the small compartment. "There was a group of us...we all decided we would leave the Ravens together. We would strike out for freedom. But we were caught. Most were killed, some imprisoned." The girl's knuckles turned white from where they gripped the seat. Cvareh could hear her heartbeat quickening, the tension in her breath. She was nervous saying just that much. "I happened along Ari on the way and I begged her to take me with her. She agreed."

Florence pulled herself from her thoughts and looked at him with a forcefully brave smile. The crawling unease he felt at the sight of flat Fenthri teeth was beginning to subside. He stared at Florence's rounded cheeks and delicate nose, her small ears and dark gray skin. She wasn't pretty by any stretch of Dragon logic. But a little kindness was helping him no longer find her repulsive.

"I guess she has a habit of helping people who need to get places."

Cvareh snorted at the girl and flopped back into his prior spot, knowing the woman in question would return shortly. "She's helping me because she wants her boon."

Ari returned before another word could be said on the matter. Cvareh watched her work as she began to don her harness once more. He was beginning to have more questions than answers when it came to his boon holder. And, while Cvareh usually found unknowns challenging and thrilling, he looked at Arianna and only saw danger. Judging by the woman's glares, she didn't want him looking at her at all.

Ter.5.2 had surprising splendor despite its uninspired moniker. Trains created a patchwork of raised rails across the condensed city. Smaller city tracks bumbled along, weaving in and out with open-style boxes filled to the brim with people. Busy streets hummed below them, their occupants unconcerned with the new travelers the vessel was going to impart upon them.

Women wore corsets, tight around their torsos, which accentuated billowing blouses. Fitted jackets adorned with intricate embroidery and rope embellishments matched plumed hats and wide skirts. Overall, it was a sea of muted colors and industrial practicality. But Cvareh caught glimpses of brightness here and there. A crimson feather, a sky-blue lapel, a bright mint under-sleeve ruffle. Against the demure palette, these snatches of color seemed to shine like jewels in a mine.

"You should begin wrapping up," Florence reminded him.

Under the weight of Arianna's disapproving stare, Cvareh obliged.

The train steadily lost speed and the station engulfed them. Metal ribs stretched glass between them, supported by stone columns on each platform. Men and women bustled along the stretches of concrete between trains, heading to and from their destinations.

Cvareh stared in wonder. It felt like the apex of a world he had never so much as considered in all his years of life above the clouds. Six trains were lined up, two more platforms vacant. Conductors shouted and soot-covered workers hastily moved all the necessities required to maintain and fuel the metallic creatures. These were the vessels carrying the lifeblood of the Fenthri to and fro.

"Stay with us." A hand closed around his forearm.

Cvareh followed the gray fingers up to Arianna's covered face, cast in a plum shade as a result of the goggles he wore.

"And keep your head down," she commanded.

He obliged, letting her lead him in tow. Cvareh swallowed his pride, reminding himself that this was not the time to worry about his rank and dominance compared to hers. There weren't any Dragons to witness him deferring to a Fenthri, at least.

Or so he thought.

"Bloody cogs," Arianna hissed. "Florence, stop."

Cvareh looked ahead, where the crowd thinned enough between them and the station's exit to see what gave Arianna such cause for concern. Four Riders lined up along the exit. Each of them had a long strand of hair falling over their ears, every bead signifying a victory in a duel for their position. The shortest was ten beads long, which was nine beads more than Cvareh could boast had he decided to become a Rider at that moment.

They were all shades of red—elite of House Rok, he had no doubt. He snarled instinctively under the tightly bound mask over his face. It was nepotism at its finest and a statement of where House Rok stood. *No half measures*, they said; Dragons were either for the House or against it. Those against didn't last long.

"Get yourself under control." Arianna tightened her grip on his forearm, startling him back to reality.

Cvareh relaxed his face and his magic with it. He would give them away with his hatred for the Dragon King's House and it would no doubt play into Yveun Dono's ploy with sending all his own.

"Florence!" Arianna had taken her eyes off the girl only for a moment, but it was too late. Florence had approached the customs line with them a few steps behind.

"Tickets," one of the Riders demanded of her. Florence produced them— Cvareh watched as they quivered in her outstretched hand before the Rider snatched them away. "From Dortam? Your traveling companions?"

"Are here." Florence motioned to Cvareh and Arianna. "Though, I wouldn't get too close. They have the onset of Necrotizing Fasciitis. I wouldn't want you to catch it."

"Do they?" The Rider seemed unconvinced. Cvareh's heart pounded. "Where are you headed?"

"To Keel."

"Home of the Alchemists?" The Rider's scowl deepened. He seemed to look only at Cvareh.

Other travelers continued to go through the line of Riders without problem, a couple questions and they were off. The rider before them was suspicious. Cvareh could practically smell it on him.

"If anyone can help the condition, it will be an Alchemist." Florence took a step forward and the Rider blocked her path.

"You smell like Dragon blood." He looked straight over Florence at Cvareh.

"Likely my fault." Arianna lifted her goggles without missing a beat, showing her magenta eyes.

"Chimera." The Rider spat. "Filthy thief."

The Rider had no idea how right he was. Chimeras had a poor reputation on Nova, especially since half of them got the required organs through illicit trade. Trade that Arianna engaged in and clearly took pride in, as her smile was nearly visible from under her mask.

"Get out of my sight." The rider waved them on in disgust and Florence took an eager step away.

One of the other Riders called over to the man who had been interrogating them, asking what the holdup had been. The words were likely lost on his companions, but Cvareh understood the Royuk clearly.

"Invalids and Chimera," the Rider answered. "That's what reeks of foul blood."

"How can you be sure it isn't Cvareh, then?" the other Rider jested back in Royuk.

Cvareh ground his teeth together at the use of his name without any titles. He could learn to live with the slight from Arianna, who hated everything, and Florence, who meant well but didn't know anything. But these were Dragons. This was intentional. *It was personal.*

"Inept and dirty blooded, sounds like House Xin all right." The first Rider roared with laughter.

Cvareh twisted and Arianna grabbed for him. But he was too far gone mentally and physically. No one would slight his House like that to his face, not while he drew breath.

The satisfaction of ripping out the Rider's throat was deep and true, but short-lived. Golden blood poured between Cvareh's fingers, his magic preventing the rider from healing. The heart would die shortly, from lack of air and blood-loss, but by then the other three Riders would have Cvareh on the ground and vivisected.

He could see Petra's face, he could hear her words scolding him as though she already knew what he'd done and was magically whispering across worlds to him. His pride had blinded him and he'd lost sight of the long game. In defending House Xin's honor now, he'd thrown away the possibility for his family's glorious future.

A dull *thunk* reverberated up through the Rider's body and into Cvareh's hand as a dagger plunged into the man's heart. Cvareh felt Ari's magic pulse through the Rider; the dagger twisted, pulverizing the heart before it retracted into her waiting palm. It was the first time he had ever been relieved to see one of those blades.

"You idiot," Arianna muttered, before she started on one of the other Riders.

# 10

## ARIANNA

*Dragons could not be trusted.*

She'd known this much to be true all her life. When the first Fenthri broke through the clouds of Loom and uncovered the Dragon homeland, it began a chain of events that proved Dragons were opportunists and liars. From the Dragon King promising equality between Loom and Nova, then enslaving her people, to the Guilds being overthrown and turned into a mockery of their former glory, to what happened the last time a resistance stood against them. At every opportunity, Dragons acted in their own self-interest, pursuing their own goals at the expense of others.

*Dragons could not be trusted.*

Arianna's magic pulsed through her fingertips as she commanded the dagger at the end of her line like a barbed whip. It cut through the air with a sharp whizzing sound that rang louder and more true to her ears than the cries of the other Fenthri at the fight that had broken out among them. She managed it like a cat and a tail. It was part of her, but moved seemingly with its own mind.

Her other dagger in hand, she launched at one of the remaining three Riders. Three Riders, and two of them—Florence wouldn't be much help. Arianna loved numbers, but she hated those odds.

Cvareh moved for the third Rider. His claws flashed in the sunlight that flowed unfiltered through the glass ceiling above. Her ears picked up the sound as they locked against the Rider's, bone grating on bone.

They had been through the line when he attacked. It made absolutely no sense. They were free and clear and there had been no reason for it. He had willingly endangered them all for nothing. If they made it out of this scrap alive he would have some serious explaining to do—assuming Arianna didn't just get on the next train back to Dortam and leave him to fend for himself.

That was an appealing thought, the idea of taking Florence and running from the fight. But Arianna didn't give it too much heed. There was no time to think that plan through and besides, she was already committed to the struggle. At the very least, she'd get to slay some Dragons, and it was always a good day when that happened.

The Rider before Arianna spun, kicking through the air. He moved with deft precision and a speed that spoke of no movement wasted. Arianna turned and ducked, the kick passing over her head. With an outstretched leg she tried to hook the heel that still supported the majority of the Dragon's weight.

The Rider hopped, shifting weight to the foot he was previously kicking with and—in one motion—bringing up his other foot into Arianna's face. Her nose sounded like celery snapping; Arianna thanked every stroke of luck she'd ever had for the thick cotton covering her face, hiding the blood that no doubt exploded from it. She tumbled back and ignored the pain, twisting the dagger in her hand to a saber grip, then lunged forward again, targeting the Dragon's chest.

A swipe of her dagger, a parry from the Dragon's claws or a twist for Arianna's blade to hit a shoulder, a forearm, a hand. The Rider took all forms of punishment in order to protect his heart—the one organ whose destruction would prove a fatal injury. The Rider caught one of the jabs of her blade and with a swift motion, snapped Arianna's wrist with ease.

Arianna cried out and retreated. She switched the dagger from one hand to the other, giving the bones in her right wrist time to knit. The Dragon didn't want to relinquish the hard-earned upper hand and continued to strike. A blow to the chest knocked the wind from Arianna, almost rendering her twist to avoid the talons closing in for her throat useless.

The hits racked up. Arianna struggled to avoid any significant blows. Punches she could take, but there were too many people around to take a hit that broke skin. As loath as she was to admit it, Arianna was outclassed. Her eyes wildly scanned the room, looking for alternative solutions, trying to formulate a plan.

A familiar explosion burst out from behind her shoulder. It was the worst thing she had ever felt. It meant Florence had joined the fight.

With a cry of rage, Arianna ducked under the Rider's open-palmed jab. A claw caught on her shoulder, tearing through the white fabric and nicking Arianna's skin. The Rider's eyes widened, looking at the superficial wound that was already quickly healing itself. Arianna took the distraction as an opportunity and plunged her dagger into his heart.

Two rose-colored hands closed around hers and the Dragon's stormy blue eyes stared into Arianna's goggles. They were open, unfiltered. The moment before death could only beget clarity.

"What *are* you?" the Rider rasped.

"The White Wraith." Arianna twisted her dagger and felt the last of the Dragon's heartbeat fade against the blade.

She pivoted. Her golden line wrapped itself around the neck of the Dragon approaching Florence in a rage, no doubt from the shot she'd just landed and which his skin was still knitting to repair. Arianna pulled her hands back, yanking on the line. Her magic did the majority of the work, but the physical movement was instinctual, like a mother wolf defending its pup. She wanted to feel the tension in the line, the closing of the loop around the Dragon's neck.

The refined steel cabling was nearly unbreakable, and though the Rider clawed at his skin, seeking purchase on the slowly tightening tether, it was futile. She felt his magic pulse against the line; it shuddered, the tempered gold refusing his command. Arianna pushed her magic a little further, dredging it up from her toes and drawing it out through her hands. The loop closed, decapitating the Rider cleanly.

With a flick of her wrist, the dagger at the end of her cable twisted and reared back, stabbing into the Dragon's heart for good measure. Severing the head from the body was good enough to merit a kill, but anyone who attacked Florence earned death twice over.

Florence missed no opportunity. Arianna wanted to be proud, but the girl was worrying her half to death with this sudden bout of recklessness. It reminded Arianna of herself in the worst of ways. Flor popped open the hinge of her revolver and decided on a new canister with expert ease. She was a Rivet through and through, no matter what was tattooed on her cheek.

Arianna had found the best teachers for her, and it showed. Despite having never been in a fight, Florence moved with the precision of a trained Revo. She kept only one revolver chamber loaded at all times so she could hand select each canister based on the changing needs of the conflict.

Tracking the muzzle of the gun over the Rider that was still engaged with Cvareh, Florence planted her feet and pulled the trigger. It was a smaller version of the canister she'd given Arianna on her mission at the refinery—small enough that it required no extra magic besides what Arianna had stored in the gun with a flare of Alchemical runes. A beam of pure magic shot straight and true, punching a hole through the shoulder of the Rider that loomed over a bloody Cvareh.

She stumbled, dazed. Arianna knew that look: glazed, dull eyes sent reeling from a sudden surge of foreign magic. She'd inflicted it on enough people to know it well and had seen it in Cvareh's eyes when he'd imbibed from her.

This was their chance.

Arianna sprinted over to Cvareh, pulled him off the floor and wrapped his arm around her shoulders. The man was built like a bag of bricks and even Arianna's muscular legs strained against gravity, pulling him to his feet. If she could run against the slowing of time, she could run and support him—or so she told herself repeatedly. With a magical command, her line retracted, the gears in her winch box whirring.

"Time to go!" she called to Florence.

Her apprentice nodded. With a jerk of her hand, she snapped her revolver closed, another canister loaded in the chamber. Florence looked at the Rider, nearly recovered from her last shot.

"Filthy Fen," she sneered.

Florence lowered her gun slightly, her aim changing from the Rider's heart to her feet. Arianna gave an approving nod and Florence pulled the trigger. They had no canisters on them that could sufficiently destroy a Dragon's heart. Their chest cavities were practically made of diamond. And even if they did, it would need to be Arianna shooting it in order to give the canister enough magic to be lethal.

The explosion was small by Florence's standards. Enough to stun, but not enough to hinder. Its real purpose was obvious as the reaction of the chemicals plumed thick purple smoke into the room. Remaining Fenthri coughed, trying to blink through the smog. Florence pulled up the goggles that sat around her neck and settled a mask around her nose and mouth.

Arianna gave her an appreciative once-over as they sprinted out into the sun. Florence panted softly, but returned the gesture in kind. The girl was brilliant for thinking of practical, multi-functional disguises. Flor's planning and foresight had bought the three a few precious seconds. Now, it was up to Arianna to figure out how not to waste them.

# 11

## FLORENCE

It felt like the side of her face had been pistol-whipped. Florence's cheek had swollen to twice its size, pressing her eye half-shut uncomfortably. It was true what they said about Dragons, that their bones were twice as dense as the average Fenthri's. No wonder the lone resistance on Loom had been squelched effectively the moment it had sprung up. The Dragons were superior in nearly every way.

Her eyes drifted over to Cvareh. The Dragon stumbled along with Arianna's help. If the Rider had messed him up that badly, Florence couldn't even fathom how strong she'd really been. The Dragon hadn't even fallen after being shot through with a magic canister.

"Where are we headed?" Florence dared ask the question. Arianna had that faraway look that always overcame her when she was thinking.

Arianna snapped back to reality. "The port."

"There's no way we can board an airship now. If they had a customs line in the train terminal, they'll certainly have one on any airships—especially those headed for Keel."

"We'll see when we get there. I'm just hoping to use all the people to mask our trail." Arianna glanced at Cvareh. His wounds had nearly healed, but it was taking a magical toll on him and he bumbled along, exhausted. He looked like Ari did after a particularly rough mission. Healing might be in Dragon blood, but it certainly wasn't without cost. "Flor, you did well."

The statement came like a rogue beam of sunlight breaking through the clouds. Florence had never seen such a thing happen, of course, but she'd heard it was possible and if it did happen, she imagined the encouraging smile Arianna was giving her would feel the same. She'd been terrified. Rushing in headfirst with reckless abandon was more Arianna's mode of operation. But she'd take the praise in duplicates if Arianna was the one giving it.

Arianna stopped suddenly, pulling into a sidewall. Florence didn't question and followed suit. They crouched next to a rubbish bin that reeked of spoiled fish and sour milk. Florence was grateful that Dragons didn't seek out blood trails entirely with their noses; otherwise they might have had to bathe in such a foul concoction.

The cause for Arianna's wariness became clear as the unique cry of a Dragon's glider echoed across the clouds. Both women turned their eyes skyward, seeking out the ominous rainbow trail—but neither saw it. With a dull thud, like a metal spoon hitting the bottom of a pot filled with water, the Dragon crossed through the clouds that separated Nova from Loom.

"I've never seen a Rider retreat before." Cvareh frowned, massaging his shoulder. It had hung at an odd angle previously, but was now almost right again.

"Maybe it's a good sign?" Florence was hopeful.

"Never." The Dragon squelched her optimism on the spot. "She's going back for reinforcements. She has our scent now."

"Dragon—" Arianna started tensely.

"Am I back to Dragon now? I thought I had been upgraded to 'Cvareh' on the train."

If Florence had been in his odd, supposedly fashionable shoes, she wouldn't have been trying Arianna's patience at that exact moment.

"If I call you mongrel you'll answer, after that stunt you pulled," Arianna snarled.

Florence expected Cvareh to rise in kind, as he usually did. But the man tilted his head back, exposing his neck and chest. Florence was oddly reminded of a dog exposing its stomach to the leader of the pack.

"You're right. It was stupid of me."

Arianna clearly didn't know how to handle this sudden subservience, and Cvareh's out-of-character actions seemed to annoy her all the more. Florence leaned against the rubbish bin, too tired to care about the smell and already getting used to it. Ari grabbed the Dragon's face, pulling it toward hers.

"Can Dragons track blood or magic across water? How well?"

Cvareh considered this for a long moment. "We don't have large bodies of water on Nova like on Loom—and nothing salty. If we could scrub the trail of our scent before getting on the water and kept the magic to a minimum, it could cover the smell enough—better than the open air would."

"Do you think you can keep the magic 'to a minimum'?"

"Yes." Annoyance at Arianna's tone and manhandling was beginning to creep into Cvareh's words. Florence shifted, preparing to put herself between them like she had back in the bunker.

"You're sure? No more running off and attacking Riders for no good reason?"

Cvareh finally jerked his head from her grasp. He swatted her hand away with a glare and the two locked eyes. They were like counter-weights on either side of the scale. Different, but painfully similar—more so than they wanted to admit.

Florence could see them from a step away, and that step was a half a world of perspective. He was the sugared art on a cake and Ari was the plate and utensils. They saw an enemy in each other, mortal opposites, form versus function. Florence saw two things that were undeniably different, but surprisingly complementary.

"If you knew what they'd said you wouldn't—"

Ari rattled off a string of guttural sounds that echoed up from the back of her throat. Florence knew that Ari could understand Royuk, but she'd never actually heard her teacher speak it. The sounds were perfect, nearly identical to the accents the Riders used.

It was perhaps too similar; Cvareh's talons were unsheathed in a second. He lunged for her and Ari released him to grasp for her dagger. The sharp points of each of their weapons pressed into the other's throat, their noses almost touching.

"I don't give a damn about your House," Arianna growled. "When you are traveling with me you put it aside, and you do as I command."

"You ground-born, soot colored *Fen*," Cvareh snarled in kind, his lips curling back to expose his elongated canines.

Florence placed a hand on both their shoulders, trying to ease tensions. She had worked so hard to make her hands conjure explosions that it was odd to use them to diffuse. "Both of you, stop. What's done is done. This isn't helping." Eventually, Florence had no doubt that appealing to their mutual sense of reason would fail. But for now it seemed she had yet to reach that point. "Ari, you are clearly working on a new plan."

"I am." The taller woman stood. Florence noticed a small slash in her coat, but miraculously, no black blood stained the white. Now that Florence thought about it, she'd never seen Arianna bleeding at all. . . But perhaps that was a given since the woman healed as fast as a Dragon. Arianna distracted Florence from her thoughts as she continued, "But you're not going to like it."

"Why?" Creeping dread crawled up Florence's spine at Arianna's tone. If the woman said Florence wouldn't like it then Florence had no doubt whatever it was, she'd absolutely hate it.

"I'll tell you when I decide it must be done." Arianna glared back at Cvareh, still heaping mountains of blame on his shoulders for what had happened with just her eyes.

Florence looked hopelessly at the Dragon and stood as well. He was clearly no more pleased with himself than Ari was. Dragon or Fenthri, the look of guilt seemed to be the same. Still, he pulled himself to his feet with them and stood on his own. He didn't do the one thing Arianna would find even more intolerable: give up.

Ter.5.2 was the primary port for the Revolvers' territory. It served both air and sea, a relatively short distance from the land terminal the three of them had entered in on. High above, at the tops of skeleton frameworks and spiraling iron staircases, were the airship platforms.

Large cruising vessels boasted over-sized balloons strapped atop tiny but luxurious passenger cars. Men and women dressed in bright jewel tones that matched the few Dragons they walked alongside. There were smaller, more practical airships parked alongside the opulent dirigibles. They had wings shaped like fish, finned rudders and arcing bodies. Gold glinted on them, magic enabling journeys by air.

The Dragons had brought the sky to Loom.

Below were seafaring vessels. Giant freight cruisers stacked with crates fought against their roped tethers. Ore overflowed from cartons as men and women bearing Rivet tattoos argued with those bearing symbols of the Revolvers. Once in a while, Florence caught sight of a circled master, but the majority were journeymen with filled marks.

But the most common mark was what set Florence's blood to churning beneath her granite colored skin. *Ravens*. For every one Dragon there were three Fenthri in the port, and for every one Fenthri with any other mark there were three Ravens. Florence blended in perfectly; no one looked at her mark twice, and no one questioned the trio. She looked like she belonged. And that was the worst part of it all.

"Flor," Arianna spoke gently but Florence still spooked, pulled from her thoughts. "In here."

Arianna had quite the taste in lodging. The bar stunk of stale vomit and sea scum. There wasn't a single patron and Florence had no doubt it had as much to do with the overall atmosphere as it did the fact that they had just opened.

"You have rooms?" Arianna asked the barman.

"For a price." The man targeted his eyes right on Florence's mark. "Traveling?"

"I'm their escort." She felt as awkward as she sounded trying to play the part.

"Right." The man believed her as much as if she had said she was a Dragon. "Forty dunca, one room, eight hours starting now?"

"Why eight?" Florence couldn't help herself.

"I'm not used to people wanting to stay around for all that long." The man grinned. Half his teeth had rotted out.

"Eight will be plenty." Arianna fished through her bag. Thankfully, the satchel was designed for being turned up-side-down in all of Arianna's various scuffles and the dunca hadn't been lost in the station. "Eighty dunca."

"Two rooms, or sixteen hours?" the man asked, running the bills through his fingers.

"One room, eight hours, and forty dunca for you to forget we were ever here," Arianna clarified.

"Mum's the word." The man snickered and waved them toward a back hall.

Arianna picked a room, seemingly at random from the doors that were slightly ajar. She locked it behind them with a begrudging pause. Florence knew her teacher was mentally taking apart the lock several times over, scowling at its simplicity.

"You know he'll sell us out to the highest bidder." Cvareh pulled off his goggles as if he needed unhindered sight to stare disapprovingly at the room.

"I know." Arianna leaned against the door like a guard, leaving Florence to take the small stool. None of them was brave enough to try the pallet intended to be a bed. The floor was likely cleaner. "But it'll spare him from running his mouth at the very first opportunity that there was a Dragon traveling with two Fenthri staying in his back room."

"How would he know I was—"

Arianna stopped Cvareh by pointing to his hands. The bandages had ripped off when he'd used his talons in the fight. At best he could pass for gray, but there was no denying the shape of his nails, even retracted.

The Dragon spat a word in the heavy tones of Royuk. "So what do we do now?" He sighed heavily and slid along the wall to the floor.

"We wait for nightfall and stow away in one of the cargo ships."

"Cargo ship for where?" Florence still remembered Arianna's promise that she wouldn't like her plan. For emphasis, the woman's stare was openly apologetic. It only made Florence more worried.

"Why a *ship*? Wouldn't an airship be faster?" Cvareh asked.

"It would." Arianna ignored Florence's question completely. "But that's also what they expect—us to take the most direct route."

"They're going to be canvassing everywhere we go, every major city, every major transportation line," Cvareh said. "Even if they weren't, there's the matter of their ability to track my magic."

"And I'm still very curious as to the exact *why* surrounding their motives in tracking you down." Arianna gave Cvareh a penetrating stare. The Dragon set his chin and met it. He was the only person Florence had ever seen challenge Arianna. Then again, Florence didn't exactly see Arianna with very many people.

"I've told you all you need to know."

"Yes, yes, that you're working to overthrow the Dragon King." Arianna snorted, showing how much she believed that particular bit of information.

Florence wasn't as convinced of Cvareh's lie. The Dragon was certainly going to great risk to get to the Alchemists. It was the guild that stood the furthest from being under Dragon control, hiding behind their insistence on secrecy for their experiments. It had been the home of Loom's original resistance.

But even the Council of Five—those foolish few who had attempted to fan spark to flame and free Loom from under the Dragon King in those early days— had perished to the might of the Dragons. The Fenthri stood no chance, outclassed as they were in strength and magic. Florence had grown up hearing the tales of the Council of Five, but as a child's cautionary tale against being too bold. The Council was not spoken of lightly, and never with praise.

"But I don't disagree with you, Dragon." Arianna sighed, continuing, "The Riders will be canvassing every major hub, and an airship is very noticeable if it is not traveling between those hubs. Not to mention your scent is notable."

"So then how will we move?"

"We'll take the Underground." Arianna turned to Florence, and it was suddenly clear.

"No," Florence breathed. "I won't go back there again."

"Flor—"

"You promised me!"

"Then stay here." The words were said gently, but they hurt more than Arianna intended.

Florence fidgeted on the stool, shifting her feet, trying to catch her breath and her balance at the same time. *Tunnels*, endless tunnels that turned the underbelly of Ter.4 into a rat maze. It was known as "the Ravens' playground" by bold new initiates, and "the Ravens' folly" by the far more sensible masters.

When she had escaped those tunnels, she vowed to never enter them again. She had gone in one of ten and come out one of three. The unending blackness had taken its toll on them. They had paid their dues for her freedom many times over.

"I can't lead you through them." Florence shook her head violently. "I wasn't leading last time and I don't remember."

"I know, Flor, I know." Arianna's hands smoothed over Florence's shoulders. The motion did little to soothe her racing heart or calm her nerves. "But we must use them. They're the only straight shot from Ter.4.2 to Ter.4.3 that assures no chance of anyone sensing Cvareh's magic or picking up his scent. From there we can cross to Ter.0."

*She wants to cross the wasteland.* Florence shook her head. It was clear this was a Rivet making a traveling plan, because no Raven in their right mind would suggest such a dangerous and backward journey to Keel.

"That still doesn't solve your problem of navigation." Florence was grasping at straws, anything to make Ari reconsider.

"I'll have help." Arianna's eyes told Florence she had yet to reach the worst of it. Those wretched, expressive Dragon's eyes suddenly looked so foreign. This woman, this woman who had pulled Florence from the shadow of death, would now plunge them willingly back under that shade.

"Who?" Florence asked, though she already knew the answer.

"Your friends."

Florence's mouth dropped open. Arianna was reckless—that much Florence had always known. But never once had she thought the woman was stupid enough to break out two inmates from the floating prison of Ter.4.2.

# 12

## LEONA

 diminish, turning the sky the color of summer cherries. The world was awash in a pale red haze, sparking the accents on the Rok estate as though everything was graced by tendrils of flame.

Leona basked in the warm glow, the last fading heat before the chill of night tainted the world. Too fitting that House Xin would be done in blues that mirrored her least favorite hours. She opened her eyes, staring at the archways curving over the balcony's entrance.

*House Xin.* The name alone put a foul taste in her mouth. There had not been a whisper from Sybil in four days since she descended to Loom. What was taking her so long to find the boy?

Yveun Dono grew more impatient by the hour, and Leona couldn't really blame him. She turned her head and looked into the room beyond—his drawing room. The King sat atop a raised dais. Behind him was an identical circle embellished with a gold band and even more circles ringed in gold. He looked as though he sat atop the earth, and the moons and suns rose at his back. Her King could pass for part divine.

"You seem cheerful," his voice rumbled from across the room out to the wide railing Leona had made her perch.

"Dono?" She sat straighter, draping her legs on the inside of the balcony.

"You're not one often caught smiling to herself."

Leona pressed her fingertips into her cheeks, catching the offending emotion spread across her lips. Thankfully, it was just the two of them present, and she had no secrets from her sovereign. "I was thinking that it is a lovely evening."

The King paused, looking out over the veranda where Leona sat. He considered the sunset as though he hadn't even noticed the passage of time over the past few hours. His face relaxed, just a fraction. There were only a handful of people Leona suspected would notice the subtle shift in his brow that occurred when the King transitioned from their supreme leader to just a man.

"I suppose it is a nice evening."

Leona averted her eyes, focusing on the horizon once more. Her magic flowed hot through her veins at the King's agreement; it churned in delight, sparking against his as he suddenly appeared at her side. He moved as effortlessly as the wind, as soft footed as starlight.

Her eyelids felt heavy as he ran a claw up the line of her spine. They were so close she could feel the air shifting from the movement, a hair's width from her flesh. He still withheld his touch from her. *They* were nothing. But he was her everything—and what made them dangerous was that he knew it. His breath was warm on her cheek, the only thing he let touch her skin as his face hovered over her shoulder.

She waited for him to say something more. The silence held ciphers of truths that lingered between them, written in a script that neither knew yet how to decipher. This would not be the moment they were given sound.

Yveun Dono pulled away and returned to his desk. Leona continued to stare at the horizon. Neither said anything further until night had begun to overtake the sky.

"I think it's time to dress for dinner," he announced.

Leona rose to her feet a moment after her King stood, then crossed the balcony and fell into step just behind him. They left the room and she saw him to his chambers. His manservant took over and Leona was dismissed from her post.

She started for the dining room, taking back halls to avoid any other House Rok nobility. Coletta'Ryu would be about to dress as well, and Leona's feet purposefully avoided the walkways the queen was known to haunt. It wasn't hard. Yveun Dono's sickly mate didn't wander far from her bed or gardens.

She was halfway to the dining room when she heard the crack of a glider breaking through the clouds below. Leona rushed to the window and scanned the darkening sky. There was the telltale glitter of magic fading on the wind...

A single ribbon where there should be several.

Cursing, she made her way to the landing platform. All the while, Leona was waiting for the sound of more gliders, but none came. A total of five Riders had descended to Loom and only one had returned? Something was off—and Leona, as head of the Riders, would find out.

The platform was a wide, open expanse of cement. Ironwork weaved against tall grasses and wild flowers on the perimeter. The manor opened like the mouth of a fish gasping for water and Leona was equally hungry for information.

The Rider eased their glider onto the platform. It looked lonely as the sole vessel returning, its wide, golden wings dwarfed by the potential capacity of the landing pad. Leona raised a hand to her forehead, pulling away stray bits of garnet colored hair. A familiar woman released the pulleys on the back of the glider and hopped off with an exhausted sway. Bruises from the exertion of flying the glider quickly faded from her skin.

Leona crossed over to her. The Fen slaves stayed behind, waiting to service the flying contraption. They knew their place well and wouldn't interrupt.

"Sybil." Leona dragged her thumb across her palm. Her sister copied her, cutting a golden line into her flesh. The two clasped hands, gold smearing against gold before it could dissipate on the air.

"Leona To." Her sister never forgot Leona's proper title.

"You are...alone?"

"There has been trouble."

Sybil—sweet, nervous, uncertain, aspiring Sybil. The girl nearly stuttered over her words. That was the moment Leona knew there would be no helping her from what awaited. Leona didn't have to know what 'trouble' her sister was speaking of. This was supposed to have been a straightforward mission, simple enough that even a novice should have been able to complete it.

"Say no more. It is not me you will need to answer to this night."

Sybil's face paled at her sister's severity; Leona could practically smell the fear radiating off her. She turned and started for the red room. It was the room Yveun Dono preferred for meetings he wasn't looking forward to.

The King was waiting for them, dressed in the rich velvets and heavy fabrics of his evening garb. His chest was bare from the opening in the middle of his sleeveless robes. They spilled over the edge of the chair and pooled around his feet. A wrapped belt held up wide-legged pants that swayed slightly as he shifted his feet.

"Sybil, you have returned to me." The King smiled wide, displaying his canines.

Leona stopped at the door. She couldn't help her sister now. Sybil walked to the center of the room alone. Whatever awaited her, she had brought upon her own head. There was no helping it.

"Yveun Dono." Sybil sunk to a knee. "No half measures in my love for your rule."

Leona rolled her eyes. Yveun Dono's attention shifted slightly, his mouth twitching in genuine amusement. Sybil never learned, no matter how many times Leona explained. Yveun Dono didn't have time for needless praise and pomp from his loyal lowers. There was only one thing he wanted from them: results. Everything else was just a cheap excuse that disgraced the true meaning of their House.

"Yes. . ." the King drawled. "Sybil, why are you alone? I sent you with Riders and then granted two more at your sister's suggestion to seek you out after you had not returned in two whole days. Now, you stand before me alone."

Leona could smell her sister's rising panic.

"Tell me, are my other Riders waiting on Loom in dramatic suspense, holding Cvareh in chains until you summon them up here?"

"Not quite, Dono.. . ." Sybil faltered.

No one spoke. The silence grated on Leona's ears. Sybil was failing test after test. She had crossed the threshold of incompetence and was now flirting with suicidal foolhardiness.

"Sybil, you were asked a question," Leona pressured.

"He landed in New Dortam, but eluded us. We found him among the scum in Old Dortam, but then he escaped—"

"How does Cvareh *Xin*, a man not known for his prowess in duels or particular cunning, escape *five* of my Riders?" Yveun Dono flexed his hands, his claws extending just barely from his fingertips.

"He has help."

"Help? From who? Only one glider was stolen from the Rok estate and no other Houses are permitted the technology."

"A Chimera," Sybil clarified. "And another Fen."

"A black-blooded monstrosity, and a Fen." Yveun Dono ran his fingertips over his lips. "You're telling me *that* is what has made fools of my Riders?"

"They killed the rest."

Leona wanted to throttle her sister. The details were obvious; saying them did nothing to help her case. But blended with her annoyance was intrigue. As impossible as Sybil's claims seemed, the fact remained that four Riders were dead. Even with incompetent leadership, that shouldn't happen.

"Where is Cvareh now?" Yveun Dono asked.

"He escaped us in the port city of. . . Territory 5?"

*Ter.5.2*, Leona thought to herself. It had taken months for her to memorize the various cities of Loom. Numbers on numbers. Ridiculous. Someone had explained the logic of it to her, but it was all dull and gray and forgettable, just like the Fen themselves.

"Cvareh Xin escaped you? A lowly Xin, a Fen, and a dirty Chimera not only evaded but killed my Riders, *twice*?"

Sybil lowered her head, and her silence was sharper than any executioner's axe. Leona shifted, blocking the room's only exit. Yveun Dono stood.

"Sybil, look at me." Magic lapped against the King's lips as he spoke. It radiated off his tongue, slithering into Sybil's ears. "Tell me, what hand do you favor the most?"

Her sister was frozen on the outside, unmoving, barely breathing. But Leona knew that inside, she was waging a futile mental war. The King's magic was strong and undeniable. His influence couldn't be ignored, not when he threw that much power behind it.

"Tell me, Sybil." The tone Yveun Dono took as he softly beseeched Sybil would've been enough to make Leona do his bidding, no magic required.

"M-my right." The magic won out. The second her head snapped up to meet his, Yveun Dono shifted his magic.

His eyes seemed to glow in the dimly lit room as they met Sybil's. The faint taste of blackberries filled Leona's mouth, flowing in from her nose. The King's magic had a sweet palate, but almost too much so. Like something that had been left on the vine for too long and was one day from rotting.

"Right it is then," Yveun Dono whispered. "Give me your hand."

His magic reduced Sybil to a puppet with invisible strings. As long as the King's stare was unbroken, she was his.

Her right hand rose up from where it rested on her knee and extended to the King. Yveun Dono took it with grace, all the while his eyes locked with Sybil's, holding his magical control of her mind.

The moment his magic shifted and Sybil regained command of herself, it was too late. The King's onyx claws were out, magic and pure rage woven between them. He brought them down on Sybil's right hand, where they punctured through tendon and bone, ripping meat and flesh and stringy ligament as he shredded the offending appendage.

Her sister cried out in pain as the King twisted his wrist. He rendered Sybil's fingers to nothing more than pulp, her palm in shreds, before cutting her hand off at the wrist. Leona stared darkly at her younger sister as she nursed the stub at the end of her arm. She could feel Sybil's magic trying to regrow the appendage, but to no avail. Dragons could regrow almost anything if their hearts and heads were intact—and if a stronger Dragon wasn't committing himself to blocking the magical healing process.

"Dono, Dono," Sybil wailed. "Forgive me. Spare my life."

Yveun Dono looked down at the bloodied mass of what he had hailed as one of his Riders in disgust. His magic was still locked with Sybil's, stopping hers from healing the wound. He started back for his throne.

"Very well. *I* will spare your life." The King sat. "And I will defer to your commander, my Master Rider, for administering any remaining discipline."

Leona met her King's red eyes, still glowing with magic in the near darkness of the room. He radiated effortless authority. She dissected his decree, looking for the scrap of his true will in it. If there was one, he was hiding it. The King appeared to be giving her a genuine choice.

Her sister was still huddled, wounded. Pathetic tears streamed over her cheeks and soiled the floor upon which their King walked. *No half measures.* Sybil had given the King her word and failed time and again. Now her eyes had the audacity to seek forgiveness in light of her shame. Her sister clung to the desperation to live more than she sought the glory of their house.

*Shameful.*

Leona wouldn't explain her actions. If her sister had any sense left in her, any pride remaining as an Anh of House Rok, she would know. They were one body, and they worked to serve one mind—Yveun Dono's. Any who didn't were a cancer ravaging the system, leeching resources for their own selfish gain. There was only one course of action when a tumor had grown.

Sybil's eyes went wide in shock the second Leona's hand plunged into her chest. The sharp edges of ribs raked against her fingers and wrist. Her blood mingled with her sister's for what would be the last time. Leona held Sybil's frantically beating heart in her palm. Golden blood dribbled from the younger Dragon's mouth.

She stood over her sister's corpse, the heart still twitching in her fingers with the dying pulses of Sybil's magic. She offered the organ to the King.

Yveun Dono turned his head in a slow, deliberate side-to-side. "It was your kill."

Leona raised the heart to her mouth, tearing into it with her teeth. Her canines rendered the tissue into thin strips that were palatable on her tongue and easy to swallow. Power surged through her; Leona's head swam. She gorged herself on magic and meat until her vision blurred and her stomach felt fat.

"Imbibe her strength. Take her magic." Somehow Yveun Dono was right before her. She hadn't even heard him move. "Take your trusted two—Andre and Camile."

His hand was lacing around hers. He was touching her. The King was touching her. Leona's whole body flushed on a high she had never felt before. Magic mingled with hers, filled her, overwhelmed her.

Golden blood slicked between their fingers, the sticky liquid fading in the air. Leona looked up at her sovereign and breathed the taste of blackberries. If she was ever to die, she would want it to be by his hand; she would want him to be the one to feast on her heart and engorge himself with her essence. She would want her magic to cloud his head and make him feel heavy. She would want him to be drunk on her as she was drunk on Sybil.

"Take your fastest glider and make your way to Loom." He lowered his chin and met her eyes.

"I will take back what is rightfully yours," Leona uttered.

The King's other hand snaked in her hair, under her braid. It tensed, claws scratching against her scalp, hair tangled and pinched between his fingers. The mostly-eaten heart fell to the floor with a dull, wet *splat*. Leona locked eyes with Yveun Dono, giving him the ability to take over her mind if he so desired. He could take whatever he wanted from her. There was nothing she wouldn't give.

"Not quite," he rasped. His voice consumed her, his magic thrilling her to the bone. Leona's chest swelled to press against his, as if she was offering him her own heart—everything she ever was and would be. "You will act as my hand. For I am the only one to *take* what is *mine*."

Yveun Dono yanked her head back. Leona hissed, more in delight than pain. His canines raked against her bottom lip. The kiss exploded violently, smearing across their mouths with the bright sharpness of heavy summer berries, as the King used Leona's body for vindication of every heated truth he breathed into her exposed skin.

# 13
## CVAREH

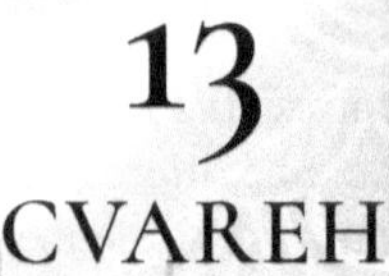

for a short five minutes, then slumped against the wall on her stool, staring at nothing. Cvareh might only have known the girl for about four days, but it had been a long four days mostly spent in close quarters. He could read her, if only just.

Cvareh had studied the people of Loom all his life. He'd learned of the Five Guilds and the specialization of each of them. He'd studied Fenish, the language of the people. But being on the ground itself was a surreal experience. It was like he knew the notes, but he couldn't hear the melody that was being sung. He could say "Rivet," but he didn't understand what that really meant—and every look from Arianna over the past few days had confirmed as much. But nothing made it clearer than Florence's expression.

The girl was in distress. A line marred the space between her brows, her young face twisted in a scowl. Cvareh understood the plan Arianna had laid out —more or less. He knew of Ter.4.2, and the Underground seemed like a logical enough choice to move quickly without being discovered. He understood the word "prison" in the sense that his mind could come up with a definition, the equivalent word in Royuk, but somehow he wasn't speaking their language yet. The gravity he felt at the idea of a prison break was a weightless cloud compared to the lead in Arianna's eyes and, so plainly, Florence's heart.

He wanted to help. Petra had made him smile thousands of times when he was sad. His sister knew exactly what to say to encourage him. But he only had four days of knowledge to draw from when it came to the young Fenthri.

"Florence?" Arianna gave him a cautionary look the moment her pupil's name crossed his lips. The girl was oblivious to her teacher's protective urges, but her eyes came into focus slowly at the sound of her name. Cvareh put his pride aside and sought an absolution from his ignorance from someone who was twenty years his junior. "Can you explain to me how your revolver works?"

"What?"

"Your revolver. I watched you oil it on the train, and then you used it in the scuffle. I know you're not a Chimera and don't have magic. . . So how did you manage a shot like that?"

"You want to know about guns?" she asked timidly.

"If you'll teach me." Cvareh prayed he hadn't misread the hopeful note in her voice incorrectly.

Florence was moving again. Spurred back to life, she rummaged through her bag on the floor, pulling from it a small red tin that Cvareh recognized instantly as her gun care set, another medium-sized box where she kept her powders, and her weapon. She moved off her stool to sit in front of him on the floor.

Cvareh lusted after the empty stool that would insulate him from the grime and dirt, but he made no motion. His clothes were ugly and dirty, and the stool was really no cleaner. It certainly wouldn't be comfortable. Plus, Florence had already set up shop in front of him, and this was for her.

"Well, it's not *that* complicated." She put the revolver between them, pointing to different parts. "You have the hammer, the cylinder, the trigger, the barrel and the muzzle. The hammer cocks back, engaging the trigger when you're ready to fire. It strikes against a canister in the chamber and that exchange of force causes a chemical or magical reaction—a small explosion." Her voice lifted on the last word. "That explosion is sent through the barrel and out the muzzle, propelling a bullet. Or whatever else is in the canister."

She held up a small chunk of metal. It was pointed on one end and flat on the other. Cvareh accepted it from her to inspect, pleased the action delighted her.

"The bullet sits on this end of the canister, near the primer—that's what the hammer hits." She produced a long hollow tube that, sure enough, the bullet could be fitted into. "What I fill the canister with, and how much, determines the type of shot."

"But how does magic come into play?" Cvareh passed back the canister and bullet to Florence and picked up the gun. The hammer and muzzle were gold. Poured into the side of the barrel were golden shapes he vaguely recognized, but couldn't place. He peered down the barrel and noted the inside was gold as well.

Florence's fingers wrapped around the barrel, pulling it away from him. "Never point the muzzle of a gun at something unless you're ready to shoot it."

"But it's not loaded." Cvareh didn't appreciate being treated like a child.

"It isn't now. But it could've been. It's just good practice. Every young Revolver learns that."

"Ah, Flor, if he wants to point guns at his face, why don't we let him? It's not like the shot would kill him. Maybe he should learn the hard way and have to sit around a few weeks like a blob while he grows back part of his brain," Arianna quipped unhelpfully.

"If he wants to learn, he should learn the right way." Florence turned to look at her master and Cvareh followed the girl's stare.

He opened his mouth to retort with equal sarcasm, but the look on Arianna's face stilled him. She looked past Florence, who continued on about something, and stared straight at him. Her rounded face was relaxed, her lips forming a thin line that he would almost dare call an appreciative smile. Cvareh gave her a small nod, swallowing down the bitterness her verbal jab had filled his mouth with. Arianna shifted her eyes to Florence, and made him question entirely if he'd read the expression wrong.

"In any case," Florence continued, turning back to him, "the magic lies in the runes. It's something the Alchemists developed, similar to tempering metal. A Chimera, or Dragon I suppose, charges the metal with magic. Different shapes hold different types of magic."

She cocked the hammer back, showing him the striking point. Sure enough, there was a rune there that mirrored a similar one etched onto the flat end of the canister. Cvareh turned the canister over once more, staring in wonder. *Magic that could be used to manipulate the physical world.* For half of his life, for centuries on Nova, it was something that couldn't be done. Magic existed only in the mind, the realm of the ephemeral. It couldn't be used to make explosions, lift gliders, turn wheels or do half the other things the Fenthri had been able to devise. For as strong as the Dragons were and had always been, there were things that eluded them—things the Fenthri could do and they could not.

He passed the canister back to Florence and his hand fell to the folio around his waist. That was why he was on Loom. It was that power he sought, to change the natural order and challenge the laws of the world. The power Cvareh hoped could build an army and lead his family to victory.

"But," Florence continued, "as time goes on the runes can lose their magic, or get worn down."

"They need to be recharged," Cvareh reasoned.

"Which is where Arianna comes in." Florence directed the tiniest of smiles at the gun, rather than her teacher.

Arianna looked weary as she echoed a similar expression, unbeknownst to the girl. "I think I'll go and work a bit. And figure out what ship is headed for Ter.4.2, and how we're getting on it."

Florence didn't acknowledge Arianna for the first time. She didn't even turn. The older woman stood, waiting, crumbling under the weight of the silence from her pupil.

*Here it is, then.* The one thing that could break the White Wraith.

Catching his eyes, Arianna's face transformed. She shot him a nasty look and stormed out the room. It was a glancing blow, a warning. They both knew the longer they stayed around each other, the more familiar they would become. No matter how hard she tried, he would learn her secrets, at least some.

But that would come in the days leading to the Alchemists' Guild. For now, Cvareh focused on one task at a time. And there was still unfinished business sitting before him.

"Flor." He tried out Arianna's familiar name for the girl. She looked up in surprise, but didn't scold him for using it. "Why don't you want to go to Ter.4.2?"

Her fingers ran over her gun kit, as though she couldn't decide what tool she needed to solve the problem presented to her. When that proved futile, she moved onto her powder box, shifting through the various tins. But Cvareh knew her answers weren't in there either. He was patient, and waited for her to come to that conclusion on her own.

"I was born a Raven." Her fingers finally stopped moving when they rested on her cheek. "But I wasn't any good at it—useless, really. . ."

"You got a mark," Cvareh pointed out.

"And I *barely* passed that test." She shook her head. "I shouldn't have. I had help."

"Your friends?"

"My friends." Florence dropped her hand with a heavy sigh. "I wish I could've been like Arianna and escaped the mark entirely."

"Why?" Cvareh didn't understand. At every opportunity, he donned the symbol of House Xin. It was as much a part of him as his skin color. It signified who he was, where he belonged. No matter how far he went in the world, being Xin would always be etched upon his identity. Who wouldn't want that?

"Because then I could've been truly free." She sighed wistfully. "People wouldn't look at me and see a Raven, they'd see *me*."

"You mean you could be a Revolver."

"I could be anything I desired," she corrected.

Loom had a backward system before the Dragons. People going wherever they wanted, doing what they wanted. For a society that Cvareh had been always taught favored logic, it didn't seem based on reason.

"When it came time for the second test, I knew I wouldn't pass. Half of us wouldn't. But we knew more then. We knew there were days before the Dragons when people studied as they wished. When you could be more than where you were born and what you were born into. So we escaped."

"Anyone caught running from the guild can be put to death." The laws the Dragons put into place suddenly seemed less sensible when he stared in the face of someone perfectly capable who would be lost from the world were they strictly upheld.

"Anyone who fails the first or second guild test is put to death with certainty. If you run, they may just jail you in an effort to persuade you to come back before killing talent... That's what happened to my friends."

"But you're not dead or imprisoned."

"I'm not."

"How?"

Florence was silent for a long time. She focused on selecting canisters from the ones she had made, and made one or two new ones. From time to time, she'd look at him from the corner of her eyes, expectant. Cvareh rested the back of his head against the wall and waited. He wouldn't repeat himself, and didn't need to. He just needed to be patient enough that she'd be out with it on her own.

"My friends and I escaped through the Underground," Florence said briskly. "Seven died, three of us made it out. Two were caught in Ter.4.2."

"How did you—" Cvareh already knew the answer to his question. He knew who got Florence the rest of the way into obscurity: the only woman in the world who seemed to evade all capture, all pursuit.

"She saved me." Florence smiled, seeing him put it together. "I wouldn't be alive if Arianna hadn't smuggled me with her onto that freighter."

Dots connected, one after the next, forming a time line that spanned across blanks in history. Arianna met Florence, took her to Ter.5. They made their way to Dortam and she set up a name for herself as the White Wraith, enemy of all Dragons. But why? Everything before her meeting Florence was still wrapped in the enigma of chaos.

"Was she living in Ter.4.2?" he ventured.

Florence shook her head. "I don't really know. And before you ask, I don't know where she may have came from. I don't really know much more than you do. She's a Master Rivet—"

That was news. He hadn't known she was a master.

"—and she hates Dragons more than anything. Her first rule in taking me with her was that I would never ask anything else."

"And you never did," he observed.

"And I never did. It doesn't matter who she was. It matters who she can become. . ." Florence's hands paused on one of her boxes, pausing mid-close. She spoke only for herself, barely more than a whisper. "If only I could make her see that."

# 14
## ARIANNA

Arianna was a stone gargoyle atop one of the spires surrounding the port of Ter.5.2. Magic pulsed through her fingertips, wrapping around the cabling and clips, making its grip on the ironwork surrounding her sure and strong. She watched men and women go about their business.

Dragons walked with guild masters on and off airships. The sight alone made her want to retch in disgust. Fenthri—no, not just Fenthri, *guild masters*—fraternizing willingly and openly with Dragons. She remembered a time when guild masters embodied everything pure and true in the academic world, when they were the pillars of guilds. Now, they spilled their secrets for their oppressors like dogs returning a fetched ball.

The world had changed in the nearly three years she had sequestered herself in Dortam. Every day, it slipped further and further from the land Arianna had been born into. Now, it seemed to race toward a future that cared little for the past.

The line nearly cut into her flesh, she held it so tightly. She was no better than those she judged. She worked with a Dragon, harbored a Dragon; she'd let a Dragon imbibe from her. The line finally bit into the same hand Cvareh had, drawing blood. Her mind betrayed her, filling her with thoughts of the way he looked at her while he consumed her.

Arianna snarled at the memory, scaring it into the recesses of her awareness. She uncurled her fingers and watched the wound on her hand heal slowly. She was part Dragon, too, more than she would ever admit to anyone.

"Eva. . ." She touched her wrist and the tension faded from Arianna's shoulders. "I'm headed back. I'm going back, finally. I will finish what we started."

*That* was what separated her from those she watched fraternize with the Dragons below, from the Chimera who prided in being part Dragon. Arianna did not act for herself. She hadn't taken on Dragon organs for pleasure or self-centered power. She didn't help Cvareh for his own sake, or to use his boon for personal gains. She'd done it for her mission, for Loom, but most of all for her vengeance.

Arianna waited for darkness before moving. Three freighters remained docked after the sun set and she already had her eyes and suspicions on one being their best chance for getting to Ter.4.2. But there was one place that would have all the information. Before leaving, and just after docking, Arianna had watched the captains of each of the vessels make their way into a building across from where she perched. She saw them through the third floor windows as they talked with a portly man. This same stout man locked up his business only after the port had gone quiet and the last of the light had diminished from the sky.

She leapt off her ledge, the cord pulling taught and spool whirring as she dropped in free-fall. Kicking her legs in front of her to swing, Arianna set her second line flying toward a crane that loomed high above the docks. The cable clipped to itself, locking with magic. As soon as the new line was fastened, the first unwound and retreated back to its spool.

Changing lines and cabling with her winch box was mindlessly simple. Her hands knew how to move, her magic operating on instinct. She soared through the night unhindered. No barrier, no watchmen, could keep her out.

The wind howled in her ears and her nose singed with the smell of the sea. She was weightless as she soared high above the port. She was well out of the glow of the lamplight below, and the creaking and clanging of vessels against their tethers with the shifting tides masked the sounds of her lines and winch box.

Arianna kept her knees loose, bending and curling her body inward to help absorb shock and sound as she landed against the building's exterior. She cast a cautionary eye across the docks. A few sailors and pilots milled about, attracted to the glow of smoking parlors and bars.

Letting out the line, she lowered herself to the third floor windows of the port authority. Her goggles enhanced her Dragon sight, rendering the darkness a mere annoyance rather than a hindrance. The windows opened at the halfway point, no doubt to let in cool sea breezes during warmer months. Simple locks, nothing that would pose a real problem. . .

She fished through one of the smaller bags on her belt. She could just break the glass and be done with it. But Ari didn't want to do anything that could raise suspicion before the ship they were on was well out of port. Her tool looked almost like a ribbon of gold, flat and hard, it didn't bend as she shoved it halfway through the window jamb.

Arianna shifted her weight on the line, allowing tension and physics to hold her in place more than magic. With her mental capacities freed, she applied them to the strip of gold. It wiggled to life, working its way into the room. At her command, it wrapped itself around the lever of the lock and pulled. The window clicked open, and Arianna slipped effortlessly inside.

The office was well lived in. The leather wing-backed chair was cracking in places of heavy use. The desk had dimples from where forearms had rested for years.

You could learn a lot about a person from their home, and offices were nothing if not second homes. The man was a creature of habit. He paced when he was nervous—judging by the threadbare tracks in the carpet—and he never missed a day. His records had been methodically checked every morning and night for the past year.

Arianna flipped through the port manifest, the record of every vessel, its contents, and its crew. The cargo ship she'd selected for them was named *Holx III*. She suspected that a ship named after the capital city of Ter.4 would be headed in that direction. She slowly flipped through the papers, careful to do so in such a way that she could return them exactly as she found them.

"*Holx III*, cargo. . . Textiles, safe enough," she mused aloud. "Arrives and departs at night." There wasn't much time; she flipped the papers back in place.

By ship, it would take just under twelve days to travel to Ter.4.2. The *Holx III* was a simple freighter and would likely cruise around 27,800 peca an hour—or 27.8 veca an hour. Arianna breathed a sigh of relief when she saw it ran with a refined engine. Most of the regular runners were outfitted with engines that could run on magic or steam to help save on coal. There would always be room for another Chimera on board a magically-propelled vessel.

Her fingers paused over the ledgers she had been returning in order. Her eyes narrowed and Arianna skimmed the records, trying to put her finger on what her mind was telling her wasn't quite right. She flipped the page, then the one after, and the one after that. That's when she found it—or rather, didn't find it. Not one vessel had headed for Ter.2.3, the main port of the Alchemists' territory, in nearly a year.

Arianna hunted like a Dragon on a blood scent through the port authority's records for evidence of even one vessel headed for Ter.2.3. Sure, it was a far voyage and likely to only be made once every few weeks, even months. But to have *none*, in or out? That made no sense.

It had been the Alchemists who developed the first Chimera. The Rivets were the ones who'd soused out the refining process in their steel mills and all the applications for gold. The Revolvers were close behind, eagerly finding further uses in their guns and explosives. It was the Harvesters who supplied them all with their base materials and the Ravens who moved the entire world—people and goods. Yes, the Five Guilds of Loom were a connected system, a chain in which every Guild formed a link.

So why was one being cut off?

Arianna's hands rested on the file drawer as she closed her eyes in thought.

The Revolvers needed Alchemical runes for their weaponry and refining. The Alchemists' Guild hall was in the city of Keel, nestled in the center of The Skeleton Forest, where they needed weapons to fend off all manner of beast. Stopping all trade from the Revolvers would basically be a death sentence for a city that lived in constant fear of wolves, bears, and the endwig.

Cries of reverie from the street brought Arianna's attention back to her purpose: get them out of Ter.5. She'd let the anomaly surrounding the trade routes remain just that, simmering in the back of her mind until she had some explanation for it.

The port authority safe provided a sufficient distraction, pulling her mind fully back into the present. It was complex enough to be a challenge, but not enough to annoy—ideal, really. She lifted some of the tariff and taxes funds. Not so much that it would be immediately noticed or prove detrimental to the running of the port, but a tidy amount sufficient to grease a captain's gears enough that he'd take on three extra crew.

Locking the safe behind her, Arianna scanned the room, comparing it to her mental image of its appearance when she entered. One or two things showed small signs of having been moved, but only to eyes that were looking for inconsistencies. People only saw what they wanted, and there should be no cause for suspicion until their vessel was well out to sea.

She closed and locked the window, slipping back into the night through the front door. Come morning, the port authority would be none the wiser of their late night guest.

When she returned to the inn, there was talking on the other side of the door; Florence's laughter gave her pause. Arianna had felt guilty the moment she'd proposed the notion of navigating through Ter.4 with Flor's old comrades. The young woman's mental collapse had been poison more potent than any Arianna had ever drank. So to hear laughter now... it fit a gear in the mechanics of her heart back into place.

Her expression fell at the resonance of Cvareh's voice. "I can tell you that Dragons wear much less than even that on Nova."

"What about modesty?" Florence asked.

"What about it?"

"Having everything so… on display all the time. Wouldn't that make people nervous?" she ventured timidly.

"Why would it? If anything it displays our physical prowess and discourages duels."

Arianna opened the door with a disapproving glare in Cvareh's direction. He looked up at her, barely stopping short a dramatic roll of his eyes. Arianna's fingers twitched for her daggers but remained at her side.

"You're corrupting my pupil with your tales of Nova," she seethed. Florence had a clever mind, too curious for her own good, and she always saw the best in people. Arianna knew that just a taste of Nova was likely to leave the girl wanting more, no matter how many times Arianna told her that Dragons were not to be mingled with.

"I think it's fascinating." Flor smiled.

And that was what kept her from sewing Cvareh's mouth shut. He had begun to endear himself to Florence. No matter how much Arianna hated him, she wanted Florence to smile even more. So she would do as she'd always done with Florence. She'd linger in the shadows, hovering in a place not even the girl could see her. She'd give her pupil the freedom to spread her wings, fly, be curious and inquire, experience the thrill of feeling on her own. Florence would work with the fear of falling because Arianna believed that fear was necessary to grow, but she'd always be hovering nearby, ready to pick up the girl if necessary.

"If architecture and fashion are corruption, perhaps Loom could use a bit more corrupting." Cvareh's mouth curled upward and his lips spread.

The expression was strange. He wasn't baring his teeth at her. Their points remained hidden behind his bottom lip. It was...a smile. A *Dragon* smile. It unnerved her endlessly.

"We need to move," Arianna announced. "First, Flor, I need the grease pencil."

"You're going to do it?" Florence blinked.

"I'm out of options. Our prior disguises aren't going to work where we're going."

Florence was clearly curious, but she produced the grease pencil kit from her bag. Arianna sat at the stool, passing the tin to Flor to hold like a mirror. Florence stood patiently while her mentor collected herself. The mark would wash off; it was not a tattoo. But every time she put it on her cheek, it felt like forfeit.

Arianna shifted her feet, her coat draping over her thighs. She swallowed the lump in her throat, pulling her cheek taut with her left hand and steadying her right. Her hand was skilled from thousands of hours of schematic creation, and it moved smoothly over her ashen colored skin as she penciled in the symbol of the Rivets.

Coat and harness resumed, she was again the White Wraith: more than Fenthri, more than Chimera, more than Dragon. She cast aside ethical whims and personal grudges. She was the extension of her benefactors' will, and she would work for them even after they were long dead.

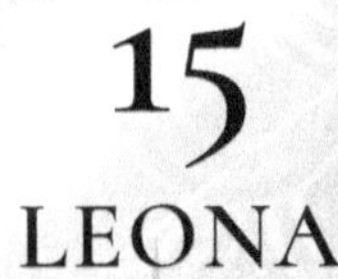

# 15
## LEONA

LEONA LET OUT A RALLYING CRY AS HER MAGIC SURGED THROUGH HER PALMS, into the golden handles of the glider, and across the golden accented wings to propel the contraption upward.

The wind bit her cheeks and whipped her braid behind her. The brisk morning air tasted like freedom, a new dawn heralding a new day—*her* day. She had no choice but to scream and cry and shout and snarl, because she was the Master Rider. She was a dog let off its chain. She was the untamed storm. And she had been unleashed upon Loom below.

Bending her knees and leaning forward, Leona banked her glider, casting a glittering rainbow across the Rok Estate. She wanted to give Yveun Dono one more taste of her magic. To write it across the sky like a promise that she would not fail him.

Her cries were echoed by the two Riders just behind her on either side. Their screaming vessels tore through the air in formation as they banked heavily down off the side of one of the floating islands of Nova. The Rok Estate dominated the top of Lysip, its main hall and gardens expanding out in all directions as far as the eye could see. At its edge stood smaller buildings of state, chambers provided for Rok'Kin and Rok'Da. Further still were accommodations for To and Veh in society. They all basked together in the sunlight like jeweled turtles on river rocks.

Beneath, the island extended downward. Society's lower rungs lived in the shade of their uppers. Leona had been born in one of those suspended towers, reaching for the clouds rather than the heavens. She'd played in the honeycombed parks between them and worked her way up to the sunlight above.

With Sybil dead, the only time Leona would see this shade now was when she descended to Loom.

*Sybil*. Her sister's magic had been strong and Leona could still feel it in her veins, burning through her. It was fading quickly, but she'd relish in the ghostly resentment that tried to turn her stomach sour. But nothing could spoil this day, for it was the first day that dawned after she had known Yveun Dono.

The King had not explained himself—not last night, not with the dawn. She suspected he never would. He didn't have to. He had made it apparent that he would take what was his. And Leona was nothing if not that.

She adjusted her grip on the handles, the clouds nearing. Throwing a look over her shoulder, she checked that Andre and Camile were still with her. Camile had the face of a cat; her curious amusement at Leona's mood was apparent. Andre wore a grin that was half snarl. This man and woman were more her blood than Sybil had ever been.

Lysip was shrinking further and further behind them. When she returned victorious, she would seek Yveun Dono's blessing to duel Coletta'Ryu. The woman was sickly, and would prove an easy kill. But to challenge a Ryu required the Oji's blessing. After last night, and after she brought home Cvareh's head, she suspected she may have that unprecedented blessing.

Before the first Fenthri broke through the clouds, the Dragons had called the seemingly impenetrable barrier the Gods' Line, as it separated their world from the next. Boco, the bird-like creatures they used to fly between the islands of Nova, lost control of their wings as they neared the speeding winds that always wove through the clouds. Every Dragon who tried to descend on the back of a Boco fell violently through the line and was never seen again.

Certain death by falling into the afterlife had made attempts to descend unappealing. And for hundreds of years, no Dragons tried. When the Fenthri barely broke through the clouds, only to be shortly torn asunder by the winds themselves, Nova learned that it was not the afterlife on the other side of the line but another world entirely. Curious Dragons—fools—attempted to cross once more at the site of the first breach, but fell to their deaths. It was their corpses that provided the organs that led to the first Chimera being pieced together by the Alchemists.

Once the Fen had magic, the God's Line was nearly obsolete. They still struggled, scraping together enough power to cross. But the technology they developed was finally in Nova's grasp—a technology Dragons had been meant to have in their talons all along.

Leona re-centered herself on her glider, the bottom of her boots connected to the platform with magic and sheer will. She had descended a few times, though it never gave her much cause to be fond of the process. The wind was deafening, the clouds blinding. She pointed her glider nose down and plummeted forward.

Gravity was her friend. It fought vertigo and, in free-fall, she didn't need to exhaust magic on keeping herself airborne. That magic was better spent holding a thin corona around her and the vessel to protect herself from the winds. Her fingers froze; her braid felt like it would rip from her scalp.

Magic cracked, reaching a crescendo as she pushed through, parting the clouds and opening Loom to her like an abysmal present.

The echoes of two more descents reverberated through the mountaintops that surrounded Dortam. Leona trusted Andre and Camile to be where they were supposed to be. If she couldn't count on them to make a descent, she had brought the wrong Dragons as her left and right.

The blackened, pointed rooftops of Dortam reminded Leona of a porcupine's spears. It was a sad, stinted world beneath the clouds. The people were smaller, the plants brittle and hard compared to the lush greenery of Nova. Fen were made of the rocks they cherished so much. Whereas Dragons… they were made of life itself.

"There!" Camile called over the wind.

Leona followed her finger to a broken rooftop. The second they got close, Leona could smell it. She could practically see gold on the ground.

"Xin are built like porcelain dolls. Little Cvareh bleeds from falling off his glider," Camile jabbed.

Leona let her subordinates put down the annoying Dragon House. She even partook from on occasion, delighting in the verbal jabs. But this time, she stayed silent. The smell of blood was faint. It had long since disappeared on the wind. The trace that was left was little more than enough to make a mark.

She hated Cvareh. She hated House Xin. And she still fantasized about all the ways she could pull out Petra's lying teeth one by one. But Leona wasn't going to let it blind her. Sybil had underestimated her foe. Petra was nothing less than a monster, and if Cvareh was cut from the same cloth, he shouldn't be written off lightly. All his appearances at the Crimson Court could be just that— appearances. Who knew what truly lay beneath.

"The trail goes cold," Leona noted. Tracking Cvareh wasn't going to be that easy, or even someone as incompetent as Sybil wouldn't have failed. "We head for Mercury Town."

"Oh, gross," Andre balked. "It smells rancid there."

"And where else do you think we'll find talk of Cvareh?" Leona grinned. It was intended to be playful, but her smile was wide enough to show her teeth. She was the leader and it never hurt to reinforce that fact.

"Lead on. If we are to dredge up the worst, we must go to the worst." Andre motioned a cherry colored hand for her to continue and Leona spurred forward.

If there was a Dragon in Dortam, talk of it would get to Mercury Town. Leona didn't think for a second that Cvareh would get very far before a harvester set eyes on him. It seemed her sister had the same idea.

"I think it's an improvement." Andre tilted his head to the side, assessing the rubble and carnage that was left to rot.

Leona sighed, lowering her glider to the ground, crushing dead Fen underneath. Sybil had no tact, no reason. She reaped chaos, but it was too easy for things to be lost in chaos.

"Anything would be an improvement." Camile toed one of the fallen Fen's heads, rolling it from side to side. "They're at least quieter when they're dead."

"That's part of the problem. Dead Fen don't talk." Leona looked through the silent streets. The usually busy Mercury Town had been reduced to death and stillness. She tried to think like her sister, wild. If she landed in Mercury Town with Sybil's disposition… She'd reap destruction wantonly. "Camile, with me. Andre, that way."

"Follow the trails of destruction?" The man preempted her expectations.

"See what you find," Leona affirmed. "Whisper to Camile if there's anything."

Andre and Camile faced each other, cheek to cheek. They each spoke a series of sounds, nonsense with no meaning, into the other's ear. Leona felt the whisper link establish between them. Now, the moment one of them said their activation word, they could speak with the other across any distance—as though one was whispering in the other's ear.

"So I set the whisper link, *hmm*?" Camile hummed as they began to follow the trail of destruction that wound in the direction opposite Andre.

"I have a whisper link back to Lysip to report." Leona barely contained a smirk. Yveun Dono's activation word had been a flesh chilling, guttural growl that she would gladly scream to have echo through her again.

"I wonder with who? You're quite cheerful for someone who just killed her sister."

"Don't play me for a soft fool. I am not Tam." She brushed off Camile's not-so-subtle inquiry. Whoever the woman suspected, she was wrong.

"That you are not." Camile grinned gleefully. "Tell me, how did her heart taste?"

"Like a cherry, and it exploded much the same in my mouth." Her triumphs were never something she would hide.

"Sybil would—"

Leona held up a hand and Camile was instantly silenced and on alert. The wind had picked up for just a moment. On it she had caught the hint of a familiar scent.

"This way."

Camile kept up easily with her bounding strides. The farther they got from the epicenter of Sybil and the prior Riders' destruction, the more Fen were about. They scattered like rats, not one putting up a fight before the Dragons once more in their midst.

The smell nearly overwhelmed her as Leona rounded an alleyway. To the eye, there was no sign of the fight that had taken place, but it had surely been bloody. Camile's talons unsheathed slowly.

A Rider had died here. They both recognized the scent. Layered atop it, almost triumphantly, was the brisk smell of wood smoke, a distinctly Xin smell. *Cvareh.*

Leona walked through the empty dead end. Magic burned under her feet and hung in the air. A silent memorial for months to come to the Dragon who had lost his life in the spot. She knew the essence of the Rider, Cvareh was easy enough to take note of. . . But there was one more.

"The third, what is it?" Leona asked Camile.

"It's...floral? House Tam?"

"Not quite. . ." There *was* a heavy floral note, almost like honeysuckle on a hot summer night. But mingled with it was a sharper smell of cedar, like one of House Xin.

Sybil had mentioned Cvareh had help, but she said nothing of another Dragon from House Tam or Xin. That would make this a very different hunt. Leona continued to try to dissect the smell, fighting to peel back its layers. But there was only a trace amount, and the heavy rose smell of the House Tam rider who had perished overpowered the rest of them.

Her sister said there'd been a Fen and Chimera helping him. Leona had smelled Chimera blood thousands of times from the slaves at the Rok estate. Their blood was black for a reason—it was dirty, muddled, rotten. This was clean and sharp, but unlike anything she'd ever inhaled before.

"Leona, this way." Camile interrupted her thoughts.

Leona followed, giving up the strange third scent for now. Camile was on the trail of the fallen Rider, no doubt picked up by Fen vultures that were already picking the carcass clean. It led them through winding, narrow back passages into the depths of Mercury Town—into the beating heart of the muddled, rotten blood Leona had just been comparing against.

The Fen man who waited at the door didn't seem surprised to see them. They made him uneasy; she could hear his heart racing in his chest. But he didn't run from his post, didn't avert his eyes. Instead, he greeted them.

"We are expecting you." He opened the door.

Leona strode in fearlessly, claws out and gleaming. Some Chimera and Fenthri guns posed no threat to two Dragon Riders. The only thing that could bring down a Dragon in Dortam was another Dragon.

"Welcome, ladies!" A tiny man clapped his hands. His white skin stretched over his bones, giving him a disturbing similarity to a walking skeleton. Beady eyes appraised them as though they were meat. "When I heard the glider, I just know you would come and investigate your fallen friend. I just know." He waggled his finger in the air. "You see, the most terrible thing happened. I caught two men dragging the corpse of our King's noble Rider off for harvesting. Now, I tried to get the corpse from them, but they overpowered my men and used this room to—"

Leona hovered over the weak little man, moving with Dragon speed to clamp her hand atop his mouth. Blood beaded around where her claws dug into his cheeks. She could kill him in seven different ways right now and each seemed more delightful than the last. But that would be the course Sybil would've taken: kill first and ask questions later. As tempting as that approach was, it had yet to yield results.

"I am not interested in your lies," she growled. The alabaster-colored wretch's men seemed to be caught in limbo, unsure if they should engage or leave their master to fend for himself. Leona peeled away one finger at a time before removing her hand. She sheathed her claws and dragged her fingers across the man's bloody cheek, drawing lines of crimson across the nearly glowing white of his flesh. "You seem like a smart man."

She was lying.

"Tell me what you know, and I'll let you keep every last organ you illegally harvested, and all your lives. A fair deal, no?"

"Quite fair." His voice trembled slightly as she dragged her knuckles up and down his neck.

"How did the Dragon die?" Leona asked.

"His heart was ripped out."

*Cvareh then, without doubt.* "Who did it?"

"I hear talk of a Dragon running through Mercury Town, blue."

Cvareh again. This wasn't new information. Leona's fingers walked around his tiny neck, ready to throttle. "Where was he headed?"

"No one could find him." Leona's hand tensed, causing the man to wheeze. "But I have a theory."

"Is it a theory you'd stake your life on?" She curled her lips as she spoke, showing her teeth. Her patience was about to run out.

"I hear word of a fight against Dragons at the Ter.5.2 station, three days after your friend died."

"*And?*"

The man spoke faster at Leona's urging. "It takes three days to reach Ter.5.2 by train from here."

"I already knew he was seen in Ter.5.2. Tell me something I don't know."

"What do you know about the White Wraith?" The man smiled at Leona's immediate reaction.

Now *this* was certainly new information. The infamous White Wraith of New Dortam had been an annoyance for over a year. They had tried to send Riders down, but one ended up dead, and the rest were made fools of. Yveun Dono eventually deemed it a waste of time to fight an enemy that would not stand up for a duel and only fought from the shadows.

She pulled her hand away for him to continue.

"People say your Dragon ran with the White Wraith through the streets here." The man adjusted his velvet vest.

Something didn't add up. "Why would the Wraith help a Dragon?"

"That, I cannot tell you." The man held out his hands hopelessly. "Have I earned my harvest?"

"Keep your pilfered magic," Leona sneered, starting for the door. Camile was silently in step, her claws still extended.

"Oh, I almost forgot." Leona paused. "You see, I happen to be the main contractor of the White Wraith. So I know a few things you may want to hear about how he conducts his business."

Leona squinted at the hustler. She would be impressed if he wasn't a Fen. "Name your price."

"I want a living Dragon."

"Too steep," Leona scoffed. She knew what men like him would do. They would chain up the Dragon and pick them apart slowly, slow enough that the Dragon would re-grow flesh and organs to be harvested again indefinitely.

"Then another corpse—a strong one."

"If your information is worthwhile." Leona could think of a few members of House Xin she'd like to throw down to Loom for this scavenger to lick clean. And there were always those with no rank—they were practically born to be organ fodder.

The man sat in his chair, a tiny throne for the pitiful king of a worthless scrap of dirt. "The first thing you must remember is the name Florence."

# 16
## CVAREH

He had always been taught that Fenthri didn't have magic. Dragons turned up their noses at the plain creatures of Loom, the hardened, stony residents of the rock below who lacked raw power surging through their veins.

It was the Dragons that had been the fools.

Cvareh had never seen a Fenthri work. The few Chimera that had been brought up to Nova to maintain imported golden machines were kept almost exclusively at the Rok estate; he who held the gold held the power in the sky world above. The Chimera slaves were kept out of sight, trusted to do what they must to keep the devices that had become so integral to Nova running.

On the third day into their voyage, the *Holx III* had suffered engine troubles. Problems with the pistons set the crew to scrambling, and Arianna stepped in. The woman hoisted wrenches as large as his calf, sweat rolling lines through the soot and oil caked on her flesh. She worked tirelessly through the night, changing out lines, welding, creating tools from scratch.

Cvareh was only below decks to support with his magic as needed. Arianna had been reluctant to ask him, but Florence was insistent after the fifth hour. Cvareh knew why the second he arrived.

Arianna's strong shoulders were beginning to sag and her posture was slacker than the normal board-straight height she usually carried herself with. Running back and forth between drafting tables in the small cabin attached to the engine room and maintaining her patches while she rambled off numbers in search of a permanent solution had taken its toll. Arianna didn't have energy to expend on magical pursuits. So when something golden needed to be lifted, or turned just so, Cvareh was there.

Arianna stepped away from the iron, brass, and gold monster she'd been wrestling with all night. The ship's Rivet handed her a soiled cloth, which she uselessly wiped her hands with. The woman was absolutely filthy.

"Cvareh," she summoned him without turning. "Strike the flywheel."

Cvareh stared at the tube of gold attached to the shaft of the mechanism. With a mental command he drove down its weight. It pushed against the shaft, turning the flywheel to life.

"All right, Pops, try the combustion pistons now!" Arianna had to practically scream to be heard over the sounds of the engine groaning to life.

The ship's Rivet—Pops, as everyone called him—raised his thumb in the air as some symbol of affirmation. With the help of another crewmate he engaged a different set of machines. Somehow, despite all the noise, Cvareh heard Arianna's sharp intake of breath. She held it, waiting with as much tension as a harp string.

After a few minutes, the woman put her hands on her hips triumphantly. She curled her lips in a flat-lined smile of admiration at the engine. Cvareh didn't find it beautiful, not compared to the breathtaking aesthetics of Nova. But there *was* something...lovely, in her admiration of the thing she had created.

The flywheel spun, pistons fired, and the noise increased until Arianna finally turned. She rested an oily palm on his shoulder. *Another shirt ruined.*

Her lips moved, but he couldn't make out the sound over the cacophony of the engine.

"What?" Cvareh tilted his head, shouting in her ear. His eyes focused on the patch of skin at the corner of her jaw, usually hidden by her thick hair. The white strands were clumped with sweat and clinging to her neck. A faint scar ran around the base of an ear that had been capped with steel to prevent it from regrowing pointed—an ear that was a dusty sky color. *A House Xin shade of blue.*

"I said let's get above decks." She slapped his shoulder, unaware of his revelation, and led the way.

Cvareh was a step behind, not wanting to make his sudden discomfort obvious. It was only logical that, as a Chimera, she could have some parts from a Dragon that belonged to some rung of his House. He knew she engaged in organ trafficking. So why would it suddenly bother him?

Pops met them topside. "I don't know what we would've done without you."

"You would've figured it out, I'm sure." Arianna rubbed sweat from her face with the back of her hand.

"I'm not certain about that." The weathered sailor's dark leathery skin folded around his smile. "I've been on this ship for twenty years now, making these runs. We've only had people ask to work aboard in exchange for passage thirty or so times. . . But not one has been a master."

Arianna stilled. Cvareh felt her muscles tense. She fought the instinct in her wrists to seek out her daggers. The longer he spent with the woman, the easier she was to read.

"Your mark is washing off, miss," Pops clarified.

Arianna brought her hand to her cheek, recognizing that not all the grease on her hands was from the engine. "What will the captain do?"

"Cap is a fair man. He won't throw an illegal on a dingy to row back to Ter.5 after she just saved us from being trapped behind schedule." The old man buried his hands in his pockets, more amused than anything. "You're young for a master. Who was your teacher?"

"Master Oliver."

Cvareh hadn't heard the name before. He wondered if she still realized he hovered. And then put a quick stop to the wondering; Arianna was a keen woman, constantly aware. He wouldn't discredit her by thinking she could have somehow forgotten her surroundings like that.

"Master Oliver." Pops shook his head, humming quietly over the name. "One of the best."

"He was the best," Arianna corrected adamantly.

"What ever became of him?" the older Rivet inquired.

"He died."

"I assumed..." Pops's words faded into the silence, inviting Arianna to continue. She didn't. "Well, he passed on his learning to hundreds, and his mastery. Those are the marks of a good life."

Arianna nodded her head a fraction. Pops walked in one direction, she in the other. The woman started up a narrow metal stair for the walk above the engine room, around the smokestack.

Cvareh followed.

"What do you want?" Arianna placed her elbows on the metal of the deck rail, rested the small of her back against it, and looked up toward the sky.

"You must be exhausted. Why not go to bed?"

Arianna snorted in amusement, arching a curious eyebrow at him. It clearly conveyed the weight she placed on his supposed concern for her wellbeing. Cvareh rolled his eyes, leaning on the railing as well, and looked out to sea instead.

"I'm watching the smokestack." Her voice was void of any bite. It was almost the same tone she reserved for Florence. "I want to make sure we're up and running again before I go collapse."

"Good of you to do for people who could turn you in for being unmarked the moment we dock."

"*Ooh*, cynical. You've been around me too long." There was an almost Dragon-like wildness to her grin. Cvareh chuckled and shook his head. "But they won't turn us in."

"How can you be so certain?"

"They're honest men and women." She shrugged. "I believe what Pops said about the captain."

"A thief concerned about honor." He laughed.

"Honor is what I fight for—honor, justice, freedom, and above all, Loom."

"I didn't take you for such an idealist." Cvareh shifted to face her, resting his hip against the railing. Arianna's eyes fell from the sky, where they'd been following the trail of billowing smoke, to meet his. Neither said anything for a long moment.

"You never asked."

He contemplated it. Somewhere, in the week they had spent together, he was certain he had. But he would give her this. For the first time, Cvareh yielded to her. Because she was fundamentally right. If he had asked it had certainly been defensive or insulting. He hadn't asked to know. He hadn't asked in such a way that implied he would listen.

"Why did you take my offer of a boon?" Cvareh dared appealing to her logic. "You're clearly well learned, and you use it to your advantage to get what you want. You're a Chimera, so you can use magic. What does a boon give that you don't already have?"

"The one thing I truly want," she whispered, not looking at him.

"Arianna, what is that?" He shifted closer, to hear her over the sea wind, to not miss a word that fell from her lips. His fingers brushed against her elbow.

Arianna's head snapped down, looking at the offending contact. She pulled away with an expression of horror, laced with confusion. Cvareh tried to make sense of how that touch had elicited such a reaction.

"I want Nova to burn." Arianna looked him right in the eye and Cvareh couldn't find a trace of lie. "And I will use your boon to help me do it."

Cvareh didn't back down. He curled his fingers into fists to keep his talons from unsheathing out of instinct when she threatened his home. "Why?"

"For what you have done to Loom."

"What *we* have done?" he balked. "We have given you magic, we have gifted you with progress. We have imposed logical systems of government, a hierarchy in which everyone knows their place and how they fit."

She began to laugh, though he failed to see how what he said was funny. Arianna grasped her stomach and her shoulders trembled with barely containable, malicious mirth.

"You—*you* gifted *us*, with progress?" She shook her head. "Dragon, check your history. Your people fell from the sky. We were the ones to give you wings, to make your magic useful."

"It was quite useful to begin with."

"And we knew how we fit together before. We were a chain, every Guild forming a link that supplied the next, which made Loom work." She prodded a finger in his chest. "Then you came, and put gates on the system. You tried to turn links in a chain into rungs of a ladder, one atop the next. Our trade has yet to recover, our output is only half of what it was, without the Vicar council the Guilds do not communicate, and that's not even touching on problems with educating our youth now that they are trapped within your asinine notion of 'families,' condemned to their guild only to be killed off if they don't make the cut."

Cvareh didn't know where to start, didn't know if he should engage physically as she encroached on his space. He didn't know if he should try to correct her. Or if there was something to be understood in everything she was telling him.

"Dragon." He had been demoted again. "I do not presume to know your ways. I have studied them, but I do not *know* them. Frankly, I don't care. Keep your Nova logic up in your sky world and leave us alone."

Arianna eased away slowly. If looks could kill, Cvareh would be dead a hundred times over. She panted softly from her tirade. When she took another step, Cvareh's hand closed around her wrist before he could think to arrest it.

He stopped her.

*Why did he stop her?*

Frustration knitted his brow. This woman was going to drive him mad long before they ever saw the Alchemists' Guild. She had her prejudices and Cvareh knew that she would keep them no matter what he said, but that didn't stop him from speaking. "You're right, Arianna. You don't know anything."

"Unhand me," she snarled.

"I listened to you." He released her. "Now listen to me."

Miraculously, she stayed. Perhaps it would've been better if she'd left.

"The Dragon King kills your people, just as he kills mine. The hierarchy he is imposing upon your world, service and servitude at the cost of well-being, is the same as he imposes on ours. I want to see him dead. That's why I'm here."

The blood rushed into his ears, deafening all sound other than the echo of his confession. He'd never said such treasonous words aloud before. That had always been Petra's role. She was the brave one, and he was just her right hand.

"I want Yveun Dono dead," Cvareh said again, just to prove to himself he could. "And I want a new world order too. For Nova *and* Loom. The Alchemists hold the key to making it happen. Once we're there—"

"—we will find the power to change the world?" she finished, her flat tone deflating him to match. "Everyone on Loom knows of the Council of Five. But that resistance died long ago, and their hopes for the future with them."

"I will build a new hope. My family will, Loom will, and you can too."

"I gave up building hope long ago." She sighed and looked out to sea. Her face was soft, still a mess of soot from her earlier work. It looked more right on her than any powdered makeup Cvareh had ever seen coloring the cheeks of the women on Nova. "It relies too much on trust that is too easily broken."

Arianna did turn then. Cvareh watched her go, a strange ache growing with every step. He hadn't expected to lighten the load of his heart upon her. Even less had he thought doing so would begin to bridge the harrowing gap of the past she lived in, and the future he wanted to build with her help.

# 17
## FLORENCE

*Territory 4, home of the Ravens.* It was an ugly blemish on the horizon until it grew large enough to consume the sea whole. Just the sight of it turned her stomach sour and her palms clammy. She had sworn she would never return. She had been happy in Dortam with Arianna. There shouldn't have been a reason to come back.

Florence's focus shifted from her teacher to the man standing at her right. Things had been changing between those two. Arianna seemed more relaxed around Cvareh, just when Florence's resentment was beginning to peak. If it weren't for him they would be back in Dortam. She would be sleeping late with Arianna in their giant bed, scolding the woman for taking unnecessary chances, and keeping the house tidy between private lessons in back rooms of Mercury Town with some of the best teachers in the Revolvers.

To think, she had even been excited by the notion of the journey when Arianna had first suggested it. Now Florence would give anything to rewind the clocks and beg for a different decision to be made. Or at least beg to be left at home.

The buildings were similar, almost identical to those in Dortam, just as the structures in Ter.5.2 had been. No matter what city she went to in the world, the same, gray, towering spires would meet her with their black shingled roofs, stone awnings, and exposed clockwork. The Rivets were Loom's primary architects, and once they had perfected designs that worked in nearly every climate with most available building supplies, they were copied and repeated across the map whenever a new city needed to be constructed.

It wasn't at the cost of foolhardiness. They'd made use of the natural quarries and mountains when building Dortam. Ter.5.2 had seen more windows on coastal facing walls to let in sea breezes. And here, in Ter.4.2, buildings were wound up with the bridges and tracks running at three different levels of the city. They spanned canals and roadways with graceful arches. The buildings themselves moved to meet the Ravens' innate and insatiable need to spread their wings.

"Flor, it'll be okay." Arianna's hand clasped around hers.

Florence turned away from the city and looked into the lilac eyes of her teacher. Was the woman ever afraid of something? Was there nothing that could turn her insides into a squirming pile of grub-worms?

Even Dragons—who Arianna hated—she did not fear. She challenged them with open eyes and broad shoulders. Florence never wanted to meet the thing that brought Arianna to the quaking precipice of terror.

"We will move fast." Arianna's encouragement meant nothing other than good intentions. Even if they moved as quickly as possible, Ter.4 was wide. It would take them at least a couple weeks to cross, and Arianna planned on traveling the majority underground to prevent Cvareh's magic from being sensed by the Riders.

"When will you head to—" Florence glanced over her shoulders at the crewmembers preparing to dock. "—to see my *friends*." She almost choked on the word.

Ari turned, and Florence followed her attention out to a distant point on the horizon. Standing against the choppy waters and undercurrents of the inner sea was a rocky outcropping—a desolate, barren island dominated by a single large structure. Sheer walls towered upward, unmarred by windows or doors. Iron spikes lined the ground, as much for intimidation as function. At the building's center, a tall tower rose up like a single guard looking over the highest security prison in the world.

"By tomorrow night," Arianna announced.

"So soon?" Florence looked back sharply at her teacher. Arianna usually took days, weeks even, to prepare for bigger jobs. But she wanted to tackle the floating prison in one day.

"Yes, soon." Arianna had the audacity to smile, as though they were commenting on a mere train delay, or Florence forgetting to buy the necessary powders for a canister. "I promised you we would move as quickly as possible."

That made Florence feel the tiniest bit more at ease.

"Plus, the sooner we get to the Underground, the better."

And that returned Florence's mood to rock bottom.

The ship turned in a wide arc, gliding into its place at the end of a long pier. Sailors and dockhands were there to tie off ropes and secure lines as the gangplank was lowered. Florence gripped her bag tightly, staring at the line where the gangplank met the dock. That was it: her last chance to run. If she crossed that line she would be committed to the rest of the journey. Time was running out to return home. Once Arianna freed her friends and went underground, there would be no going back.

Florence looked at the crew. They'd been lovely people, half Ravens, but none had recognized her. The youngest was Arianna's age and Florence didn't think it likely that she had any real overlap in the guild with them. If she asked, she knew they would let her stay for the ride back. She could work for her passage and head back to Dortam. *Someone needed to look after the flat. . .*

"Flor?" Arianna noticed she hadn't fallen into step with her and Cvareh. "Are you coming?"

Florence took a deep breath. It expanded her lungs, making more room for the crippling fear that locked her knees in place. Then she exhaled it, and moved forward.

"Yes, sorry."

Luck had brought her and Ari together, and the past two years had been the best of Florence's short life. She'd learned more than she ever thought possible. She'd seen new sights. She'd even met a Dragon and run from Riders. Compared to all that, facing Ter.4 should be nothing.

Gripping her bag tightly, Florence descended the gangplank onto the hard poured concrete and stone of the dock. She didn't look back at *Holx III* once, their business concluded. Instead, Florence looked at the black skyline that zigzagged against a gray sky. The sounds of engines whirring filled her ears with an uncomfortable din, reminding her of futile hours spent in workshops trying her hardest to connect gearshifts, cranks, and Rivet-designed pistons to axles.

Those milling about the pier paid them no mind. The trio didn't carry much, only one bag for each of them that was now lighter in the absence of what they had consumed already on their journey. Cvareh was back to wearing his mask, goggles, and hood, bundled up tightly. Arianna covered her face as well, rather than drawing on a mark with a grease pen.

Cvareh had argued about the necessity of it the night before, given how open they had been with the crew, but Arianna was insistent. The crew had been likely to find out the truths of their identities on such a long voyage in confined quarters; appealing to their honesty outright had earned them some endearment even. But people on the street needn't be the wiser. Furthermore, while the occasional Dragon could be seen in major cities across Loom, it was incredibly uncommon and would attract immediate attention.

The streets of Ter.4.2 were set up in a grid pattern. Much like the naming system of cities across Loom, they were numbered based in the order they were built. It was simple, straightforward, and easier than remembering unnecessary names. The only named streets or cities were the very first, and that was always after the founder of the city or, in the case of Guild cities, the first Vicar of the Guild.

The smell of burning oil was so thick in the air it was heavy on the tongue and the revving of engines echoed off buildings as three-wheeled trikes tore through the streets at breakneck speeds. Ravens shouted and hollered to each other, trading jests and challenges as they wove through the narrow alleyways and slid around turns. Florence was older now than the first time she'd seen the gangs that dominated Ter.4. As a child, she'd been fascinated with the pitted bronze bodies and curving handlebars that wrapped around the leather seats of the trikes. That fascination still existed, alongside her apprehension.

The motor-trikes moved without rails, at speeds regulated by single riders. It was a rite of passage in the Ravens to build your first bike, win your first race, and join one of the gangs that prowled the streets. It had seemed foolish then, the idea of riding such a tiny machine at speeds so fast it could wipe tears from your eyes. She'd seen what accidents had done to riders.

But, *then again*, now that she was a bit older she could see it was no less reckless than deciding to play with explosives for a living. Adulthood just meant finding the variety of crazy that resonated the most with you and doing it until you died or it killed you—whichever came first.

"Where are we headed?" Florence asked as they wound up an iron spiral stair to the narrow pedestrian catwalks suspended between the ground and the bridged rail above.

"To my place."

Ari's words froze Florence mid-step. To *her* place? Wasn't their flat in Dortam her place?

"Keep moving, Flor." Arianna glanced over her shoulder and Florence took the steps two at a time until she was right behind Cvareh again.

"What do you think?" she whispered to the Dragon.

"Me?" He seemed surprised she engaged him.

"Who else?" Florence put on a brave grin, trying to imagine how the city might look to someone who didn't have the same history with it that she did.

"It's quite unlike Nov—anything I've ever seen before." He caught himself mid-sentence, giving a quick glance to the crowded walk around them. "Why is it so different from Dortam? Or Ter.5.2?"

"Every territory has evolved to fit the needs of its guild. Dortam and Ter.5 have much more condensed cities, usually protected by mountains, to make use of flatter land for explosive testing." Talking about Ter.5 and the Revolvers, even for a moment, made her feel worlds better. "Whereas Ter.4 is the home of the Ravens. The ground is reserved for experimental vehicles. Trains run above. Airship platforms are up top. There are also the walkways we're on now that kind of weave between all of them."

"And the Underground?"

"*Shh*," Florence hissed. She glanced at the group of vested men who had walked by. Only one glanced back at them. "You don't speak about it."

"Why?" Cvareh obliged, but seemed honestly confused.

"Because of what happens there." Florence gave him a small grin. "Because it's difficult to regulate and that means that we don't want Dragons to know about it."

Cvareh snorted in amusement.

Arianna led them to a quieter section of town. The closest station was far enough away that the train whistle had to echo to get to them. The alleyways below were too narrow for even a trike. It was purely residential, which meant that most people weren't milling about during normal working hours.

Florence knew they'd arrived the moment she saw the lock on the door. It was handedly Arianna's craft, though it was less sophisticated than the turning locks she was used to from her teacher. This had a series of dials in which Ari entered a four-digit pass code.

She couldn't help but notice that Ari entered the code with them both watching. The woman didn't rest herself against the wall between them, or quickly turn the tumblers to prevent her or Cvareh from seeing. 1-0-7-4. Florence remembered the number. Ari either placed little value in the abode, or she wanted Florence and Cvareh to feel as though they had the ability to come and go easily. It was a notable shift from the Arianna Florence had first met, who had made her earn the ability to know the key into their flat in Dortam.

The flat was small—one room with a heavy layer of dust atop everything. The air was stale and the curtains had been shot through by time, small holes in the threadbare fabric letting in winks of light from the outside.

There was one large daybed, pushed against the far wall. A drafting table was squeezed in at its foot. Schematics done in Arianna's hand had been pinned up all around. To the right, by the small galley kitchen and only separated room— the bathroom—was a long workbench. Empty shelves lined the wall above it. The wood grain showed remnants of chemical burns and stains.

Ari's eyes went there first, and time seemed to stop for the woman. Cvareh poked his nose around, curiously drawn to the faded schematics and blueprints. Florence remained by her teacher.

"You never told me you had a place in Ter.4.2." She closed the door gently behind her.

"There wasn't a need. I never thought I'd be returning to it." Arianna shrugged half-heartedly.

Florence took in the one-room flat again. It wasn't much, certainly. But owning property—any property—in the major cities of Loom wasn't easy. You had to be a graduate of a guild, at least, and usually preference was given to masters. Of which Ari was one, Florence reminded herself. But the woman was young, unmarked, and had to have achieved her mastery after the Five Guilds fell to the Dragons—meaning there hadn't been much time for her to secure her own living arrangements on the merits of her guild rank.

"We'll only be here briefly." Florence didn't know who Arianna was struggling so hard to convince. "By tomorrow nightfall, we'll be moving again. By the dawn we'll be gone."

the door. "And don't act like you've never cleaned up a mess before. I know how many invisible beads you both wear."

They all flashed their teeth madly. The Riders were the King's men and women, the Dono's most loyal warriors. If they were to be thieves, nothing would keep them out. If they were to be advisers, none would give better counsel. And if they were to be assassins. . .

Then let the scent of blood put a gnawing hunger in their stomachs.

# 19
## ARIANNA

"BECAUSE TIME WILL BE ON MY SIDE." ARI LOOKED TO CVAREH FOR confirmation that he understood her meaning. A dark shadow passed over the man's face. *Good. He understands perfectly.*

"You cannot possibly be serious." He shifted as he spoke the words and Ari did the same. Barely perceptible movements braced them both for the storm that was on their horizon.

"But I am." She welcomed the lightning that sparked in his eyes.

He moved on the crack of thunder that heralded the tempest that had been looming between them. His long fingers scooped up the neckline of her coat, tensing. His claws shot out, ripping holes through the otherwise well kept garb of the White Wraith.

"Are you mad?"

"Maybe." Arianna gave a quick look to Florence for the girl to ease away, she could handle herself. She also didn't know what Cvareh was about to do. If Flor got wrapped into the scrap, she'd never forgive herself for it.

"You know how well that went last time. It set the Riders right on our tail," he snarled, his nose nearly touching hers.

"And if I recall correctly, you were fine. We killed one Rider and evaded the others." Her hands were at her side, ready to grab for her daggers if need be. "And we would've lost them entirely if you hadn't gone rogue at Ter.5.2."

"Don't make this out to be that I owe you." Cvareh's tongue was heavy with the sudden spike in his magic. "If anything, you owe me for giving you the opportunity of a boon."

Ari laughed off the influence he was trying to synthetically apply on her. She threw her own magic behind her words, just to make a point that they seemed to guards. The idea of being watched proved a stronger deterrent against unwanted behavior than the actual, physical presence of someone watching.

From Arianna's limited time to research, she had come to the conclusion that there were between five and fifteen guards on staff at any time. But they were all heavily armed and well trained—trained to kill before asking questions.

She pulled the oars a short way out from the rocky island, allowing them to coast toward the shore. When they were within a stone's throw, she stood, easing herself out of the boat and into the water. Arianna held onto the skiff, inspecting the walls, waiting.

She extended her hand and he took it. It was like a dance, and she was leading. Everything Cvareh had been taught screamed against letting another be in control. It was opposed to the dominance structure of Dragon society. But with Petra, obedience spun from loyalty was a familiar feeling for Cvareh—a feeling that Arianna was slowly stealing for herself as well.

Arianna pulled him from the boat with the crash of a wave. He tried to nimbly exit the skiff and was met with mixed success. Luckily, his flailing was kept to a minimum this time, and Arianna didn't feel the need to have another heart to heart.

She unclipped a small disk from her harness, settled it into the boat, then waded into the water far enough that she could free the vessel from the tug of the waves. They walked together up the shoreline with cautious stares trained at the dark guard towers. Four towers, and only two were ever manned at once. His eyes darted between the three corners he could see, fighting for some sign of where the guards might be. It was his first taste of the harrowing feeling of possibly being watched without knowing by who or from where.

They slunk between spikes of all sizes, erected to ward off ships that would ram the prison for a mass breakout, to the base of one of the towering walls. Without hesitation, Arianna's hands adjusted the cabling through her harness and freed her clip. She spared one glance for him. That was all the confirmation Cvareh knew he would receive.

She closed the gap between them, her hips flush against his, her abdomen pushing into his body as she bent backward, seeking space to navigate the cabling around them. Cvareh swallowed, wondering if she could hear his heartbeat when she leaned into him like that to tether them together. Life and power surged through her, a blend unlike any he had ever known. Knowing that he'd soon have it again made him crave it all the more. It made him want to cling to her until he had bled her dry.

His arms snaked around her back, holding her to him. He was slowly going mad, and she couldn't be calmer; he couldn't even hear a whisper of her heart. Arianna gave a small nod and Cvareh braced himself against the howling winds of time.

He breathed it into him, letting his lungs become a cocoon for the sands of the hourglass. It burned instantly, all the way down his throat. Like a flock of birds, they fought and scratched against his insides, seeking freedom from their unnatural cage. The world slowed as he gained dominance over the minutes of the clock and in seconds that felt like eons, he won control over time itself.

Arianna was moving. He felt her magic clearly through the vacuum of space he had created. As his magic encased her, her magic ensnared him. They were their own world and Cvareh was barely aware of movement. He focused only on keeping control as time fought for freedom from his lungs.

It shredded his insides, filling him with blood. His lungs began to decay, becoming necrotic in mere moments due to magical exhaustion. The world shuddered. He wouldn't be able to hold his breath for another second.

She slammed him against the wall. A scream tried to escape his throat, but all that was there was blood. It poured down her shoulder in the darkness. Arianna pushed herself against him. She clutched his waist, her feet planted.

"Do it."

He was too happy to oblige.

Cvareh yanked on the back of her hood, catching hair with it. Her head twisted backward and pulled her face into a grimace, exposing the one part of her body that wasn't covered in layers of fabric. Magic faltered within him, struggling and failing to heal his ailing lungs.

He sunk his teeth into her eagerly. He fought to keep himself from tearing out strips of her neck in his zeal for her power. Cedar and honeysuckle flooded his mouth, mixing with the smoky musk of his blood spewed on her shoulder.

It was pure power. It was the essence of life. More than anything, it was *her*.

He invaded her through her magic, pillaging and rummaging through every dark corner. He could smell the tang of regret harrowing her behind every shadowed awning of her memories. He could hear the echoes of longing crying out through the lonely hallways of her daily consciousness. He could feel the heat from the flames that consumed her waking moments whole, a pyre in the lighthouse of her wayward morality that burned for one thing alone: vengeance.

She was an enigma, a strange creature of contrasts. And, for the briefest moments when he imbibed off her living flesh and blood, *she was his*.

Arianna pulled herself from him, and he barely relinquished. Drunk off her power, his mind swam, clouded. Her hand flew up to her shoulder, smearing the blood from where his lungs had failed and come up golden, covering her wound until it healed. Their eyes met and he felt the same urge as he had last time—the want to drown in her.

She lowered her hand, her stare wavering but not breaking. Her eyes challenged him to say something, to move for her again, to do anything. She threatened the same in kind. He could read every twitch of her muscles. She wanted to level the score, to put him in as vulnerable a position as he had just had her.

What was equally terrifying and thrilling was in that moment, he would have let her.

# 21
## ARIANNA

There was nothing like this feeling. She had experienced much in her twenty-two years of life. But the sensation of someone stripping her down to an essence that even she couldn't describe was incomparable to any other situation she had found herself in.

Arianna had devoted herself to person and cause. She had wholly and completely loved as a friend, as a lover. But this was something entirely different.

And utterly terrifying.

Once more she was caught bare before him and she hadn't even scratched his surface. Her hands twisted in his clothing, ill-fitting and basic as it was. She wanted to rip it off and push him down. She wanted to sink her teeth into him and show him that their world moved on her terms.

It had only been seconds since they ascended through the empty window of the guard tower. But time falling back into place had made it seem like an eternity. The nagging sensation of things moving once more brought her attention back to the present. The sound of footsteps nearing reminded her of where and who she was, what she was doing.

She was Arianna. She was the White Wraith. And she had a job to do.

Her fingers relinquished him, quickly working to unstrap his body from hers. The cabling retreated into its spool with a thought. She kept her eyes from his until the effects of the imbibing wore off both of them. She had no interest in making herself vulnerable again before him. He had already made her feel that way without even knowing it.

*The only way arrogance and confidence are similar is that both can get you killed, Arianna.* The words echoed back through her mind from a woman long dead. This man, this Dragon—he was nothing like her Eva. Arianna refused to accept it.

Arianna pulled out a token. On it was an alchemical rune. Florence said the range wouldn't be terribly far, but exactly how far "terribly" was, she couldn't quite say. Ari pressed her thumb into the rune and pushed her magic through it, willing heat. It shattered under her fingertips and, at exactly the same moment, an explosion cut chaos into the quiet night.

The bomb on their skiff drew the attention of the exterior guards and Arianna bounded through the interior door of the tower. A long tunnel connected the outer wall with the guard tower, one of four. Through the window slits on either side, Arianna got her first glimpse of the floating prison. Concrete and steel fitted together to construct a grim image of desolation. Every cell had an open barred wall facing a narrow walk that spiraled around the entirety of the prison —the only way up or down.

On the edge of the walk, facing the inner tower, were painted the numbers of each cell. Arianna quickly made a note of the highest and lowest. Once she knew that, she could calculate approximately where any cell was using basic estimations of height and spacing. The largest variable remained finding what numbers she needed.

The door at the end of the suspended, tunneled bridge opened. A circled Revo leveled a gun with a golden barrel at them, his vermilion eyes nearly glowing in the darkness. She didn't even miss a step. She kept charging down the stretch head on.

His wrist tensed and Ari slammed herself against the right wall. Cvareh moved in lockstep, pressing himself on the opposite wall as she had hounded him to do—when in doubt, she went right, he left. The gunshot was louder than an engine's piston firing and she was certain her ears were bleeding, though her magic worked immediately to repair the damage.

Cvareh winced, covering his ears. But Arianna had a different kind of instinct. Her gun was already drawn. The trigger was pulled before the Revo had time to lower his.

But he was well trained, and he predicted her shot, falling to the ground at a diagonal. Arianna dropped her gun, reaching for her daggers. The man stood, bringing a fist covered in brass knuckles into her gut. Her stomach collapsed, expending the air in her. She curved forward and used the momentum to bring the dagger into his throat, tearing through his windpipe.

"Grab my gun!" she shouted to Cvareh, pushing through the door to engage with the other guard at the top of the Tower.

The woman knocked the knife from Ari with the side of her revolver, then grabbed for Ari's wrist, holding it away as she tried to lock the muzzle of the gun onto her face. Ari spun, slamming her opponent into the wall, the other dagger in her hand. The woman twisted her grip.

Gunfire echoed through the small, barren room, a pockmark steaming in the ceiling from an incendiary round that narrowly missed Arianna's head. The woman slammed her foot into Arianna's heel, trying to trip her. Ari held fast with a grimace.

A steely blue hand jutted over her shoulder, grabbing the woman's neck. Ari felt the heat from her Dragon at close proximity. She watched the muscles in his forearm tense as they pushed his claws through the woman's throat, killing her instantly. He withdrew, shaking the red blood off his hand with a grimace and then held out her gun.

"Thank you." Arianna accepted her weapon from the man and trusted he'd hear the words in more ways than one.

"Lead. I'll have your back." He glanced back toward the hall. Both their sets of Dragon ears were picking up fast-running footsteps, men and women alerted to their presence by the commotion.

"I'll trust you with it, then." The words were cumbersome. Her lips didn't want to form them, but Arianna discovered that something could be right and uncomfortable at the same time. Her footsteps stalled as she rounded the staircase leading down the central watchtower.

He looked at her in confusion. That same emotion was reflected in her every thought. She had left someone behind before. She had done so knowing they would die for her sake, for the sake of their mission.

Arianna held up an accusatory finger. "Dragon, don't you dare die on me."

Cvareh was visibly taken aback at the proclamation.

"I want my boon," she added hastily, and disappeared further down the Tower.

There were five guards, of this she was now certain. Two sets of footsteps from watchers in the Towers. The two they'd killed in the central guard tower. And one below her still.

But time was still of the essence. The explosion from their skiff was likely to draw attention on the shore, assuming none of the guards had fired some kind of signal flare she and Cvareh missed from being indoors since time stopped. Logically, reinforcements were coming, and Arianna gave them six minutes across the stretch of water between the floating prison and the mainland, and perhaps another ten to get themselves and a boat in order—she'd round down to fifteen.

It meant she had ten minutes left to kill the remaining guards, find the cell she needed, break out Florence's friends, steal a boat, and evade any pursuers on the water. Ari grinned wildly, flashing her teeth as a volley of gunfire rang out between her and the guard before her, echoed by shots above. *Plenty of time.*

The man ahead used a single round shotgun, powerful but slow. He knew it too as he reached for the saber strapped to his hip. Swords. Now there was something she didn't mess with. Swords were archaic and only two types of people used them as a result: arrogant newbie Revos who wanted to show off, and masters. Since the man bore a black circle, she wasn't betting on the former.

The slightly curving blade echoed against its scabbard, its single edge gleaming wickedly in the lamplight. Arianna grabbed for her cabling, quickly clipping her dagger to it. Her weapons wouldn't stand up; she knew when she was bested. So it was time to throw a skill of her own into play. Magic.

Her dagger fluttered around him like an annoying fly. He batted it away with his sword, dodging and half-stepping closer. Arianna tuned out the sounds of the battle above her and targeted the Revo. Malice burned through her, ignited by frustration. She didn't want to kill this man or his allies, she had no delight in it. Their deaths were a means to her end, more bodies sacrificed upon the altar of the lost future she had been striving to build alone in the years following the collapse of the last resistance.

He didn't stand a chance against the beam of pure energy that fired right through his chest.

Ari holstered her gun and leaned against the wall, catching her breath. She was killing Fenthri for a Dragon. It was a truth so insane she had no other option but to believe it was real. Yet she couldn't muster the same hatred for Cvareh. There was a desperate sort of survival in him too.

She shook her head with a breathless laugh at herself. *I actually believe he's fighting against the Dragon King.* What was the world coming to?

The commotion above quieted as Arianna reached the central office of the prison. A shelf of large ledgers directed her to exactly what she needed to know. There were only a few things to monitor in a prison, after all: the scheduling of the guards, general maintenance, food, and who was where.

"Glad to see you could manage two Revos," she remarked as a familiar set of footsteps treaded down the stairs.

"Did you have any doubt?" He wasn't even winded.

"When it comes to you, I have nothing but doubt." Ari glanced over her shoulder. He had a few cuts that were already healing and half his sleeve seemed to have been blown off, exposing cut muscle beneath. "Did you shoulder a shot straight on?"

"They weren't expecting it." Cvareh stood at her side, looking at the ledger she was assessing. She was impressed, but he saved her from saying so when he pointed at the list of names. "Shouldn't we just call out and ask for them by name?"

She rolled her eyes dramatically. "Yes, because no other prisoner would claim to be someone they're not at the prospect of escape."

"Point taken." He turned, leaning against the table and closing his eyes. "Sounds like we're alone."

"For now," she agreed. "Though more will be here soon." Her eyes fell on the names she had been searching for. Arianna dragged her finger across the page, checking the dates they were imprisoned against when she met Florence. It matched. "But we have who we need."

The floors of the tower that were eye-level with the cells had only slats for windows. The wider ones were at the top, where a guard could survey both prison and sea without being visible. Arianna looked out over the compound. Shouts and calls were starting to rise from inmates who realized something was amiss.

"There." She pointed at an enclosed tunnel on the ground. Bloody *everything* was enclosed so the guards were never visible to the prisoners. "Run down the Tower and get halfway through that tunnel. Use this."

"How?" Despite his confusion, Cvareh accepted the disk she passed him.

Arianna ran his fingers over the alchemical rune Florence had etched onto the surface of the bomb. "Here, focus your magic here. Imagine it heating, melting."

"Right." He bolted for the stairs.

"And make sure you're a good distance away when you do!" Arianna called after him.

"Count on me!" he shouted back.

Arianna gripped her golden line tightly. That was the dangerous thing. The longer they spent together, the more she thought she could.

Hopping up on the windowsill, Arianna glanced down, finding numbers 127 and 138. Unfortunately, the prison was too well run to put partners in crime next to each other. But they were at least close. She set her sights on the higher of the two, her line shooting out and latching to the bars of a cell just above.

The shouts of the offended prisoner whose cell she used as an anchor point were drowned out by the rush of wind in her ears as she leapt into the open air. Her winch box whirred, pulling her up as she arced across the length of the gap between the inner tower and the cells. Kicking out her feet, Ari tumbled onto the narrow spiraling walkway, her cord unhooking and retracting into its spool.

"Falling airships, woman!" the girl behind the bars exclaimed. "The Vicar Raven know you got that setup? Because I'm thinking she may want a schematic."

"Do I look like someone who'd work with the Vicar Raven?" Arianna turned her cheeks.

"Unmarked? Be careful or they'll lock you in here too. You've too much talent for them to just kill. They'll try to break you first." The girl grinned madly. She folded her hands behind her back, swaying from toe to heel.

"Dead men don't lock doors, Helen."

"Guard killer *and* you know my name? Aren't you just the epitome of mystery?" The girl laughed and shook her head. Hair that Arianna presumed was once the color of snow hung in dingy, matted chunks around her face. No one ever praised the floating prison for its treatment of inmates.

"Add, 'the woman who broke you out' to that list." Arianna unrolled a strip of tools attached to her hip, setting on the lock. She whistled to herself. "Now, what Rivet built *this*?"

"A master, I think." Helen watched in amusement. "Some of the other Rivets here have tried. You have tools, but I don't know if. . ."

Arianna tuned her out. The lock had a closed front, no keyhole. All screws and connectors were concealed within, making disassembly difficult. The key slot was thin and flat, which Ari presumed to mean the keys were like cards embedded with a series of notches that depressed tumblers at the opposite end of the lock box.

She had two more explosives on her, but she really didn't want to waste them. It was likely that she wouldn't have another opportunity for Florence to restock before they fled into the Underground. And using a bomb assumed it would damage the lock enough to crack it without injuring the prisoner within.

First things first, she had to get into the lock to disengage it. Fortunately for her, this wasn't a job that required discretion. She ran the pads of her fingers along the seams, searching for a weak point in the welding. The prison's inners had been exposed to the sea and salt air since its construction in the early days of Ter.4, and if there was one thing metal didn't like, it was the combination of time, moisture, and salt.

Her nails fell into a hairline groove on the side—a fatigue failure. She went for her thinnest golden tool, driving it into the crack and twisting the flat head, widening the gap. Keeping one pin in place, she reached for a second, repeating the process hastily until the front was halfway off. Unfortunately, the top part of the weld proved to be much stronger.

She needed more leverage.

There was enough space now for her slimmer, sharper dagger to fit. Arianna inwardly winced at the idea of sacrificing the edge of her blade like this and made a mental note to sharpen it later. She twisted it, grunting with the strain. The cover bent just enough for her to get a look under.

It was as she suspected: several pins at different intervals, waiting to be lined up. That was the design flaw. Unlike a normal lock that required pressure on the pins throughout a turn to disengage, this only required the pins to be engaged correctly at the same time for the bolt to be pulled back. Ari could see why it was effective given the circumstances—mostly enclosed design, unique key to discourage people from trying to pick it, unconventionally shaped access to the pins. But once it was cracked, it put up no fight.

"What in the Five Guilds *are* you, lady?" Helen asked as Arianna pulled open the door.

"Someone who's looking for a favor from you."

"Get me out of here, I'll do anything you want." The girl grinned, taking Ari's invitation and strolling out of the cell onto the landing. She took an instinctual breath of air. Though it was chemically no different than what she had been breathing through the bars for two years, Arianna could only suspect that it was a little bit sweeter in that moment.

"I need you to take me through the Underground."

"Tall order," the girl hummed.

Ari smirked, admiring her cheekiness. She was negotiating with the woman who had freed her as though it were nothing. "Florence is waiting for you now at its entrance."

Helen froze. "Flor? She made it?"

Ari nodded. "Now, run down. Head for the tunnel out."

The girl stared skeptically for one long moment, but she didn't have many options—linger and be jailed again, or flee and trust Arianna at face value. Ari greatly appreciated that she was the sensible type. As Helen ran, Ari hooked herself into the bars and jumped over the ledge down to the landing below.

She ignored the calls of inmates pleading for their freedom. There were real criminals mixed among those who had been jailed for failing to follow the Dragon King's mandates, and she had no record of who was who. For all she loathed the Dragons, Ari wouldn't spite them at the risk of putting someone actually dangerous back on the streets of Loom.

Helen was slow, and by the time she had made it around the large loop of the walkway Ari had finished unlocking the door of Will's cell, explaining the same overview of the situation in the process. They were just starting down when the explosion she'd been waiting for rattled the enclosed hall below, blowing out chunks of stone and cement. Dust plumed skyward and Ari looked for a certain blue shadow to emerge from its curtain.

Coughing, Cvareh didn't disappoint her.

"Took you long enough!" she called over the increasing volume of shouts from the other prisoners.

"It's not like you were waiting," he noted as they reached the cement floor at the ground level.

"I can still judge you for taking that long to figure out a simple bomb." The corner of her mouth twitched upward in what could dangerously be called a grin.

"Bent axles, what in the five is a Dragon doing here?" Will blubbered.

"He's a friend," she answered without a thought, stepping into the hall.

Cvareh's golden eyes squinted at her. Arianna didn't even need to turn her head to know his expression. She was just as shocked as he was. The word slipped out before she'd had time to think it through. *He is nothing more than the Dragon who offered you a boon*, Ari insisted privately.

A well-kept speedboat was docked in one of two open slots protected either side by rocky outcroppings. Arianna looked to her companions. "I trust one of you can captain this thing."

Will and Helen's heads snapped to face each other.

"Helm?" Will asked.

"You get engine." Helen grinned in reply.

The two sprinted up the gangplank, assessing the ship as quickly as Ari did a clockwork machine. She had no doubt they already knew the top speed, drag, handling—everything about the vessel. Florence might not have been a born

Raven, but from what she'd said of her friends, they were. And these were things that, once trained, were never forgotten.

"You sure it's safe?" Cvareh followed her aboard. He took a step closer, adding softly, "To let them drive?"

"Safer than my doing it." If there was one thing no one wanted, it was Arianna behind the wheel of any vessel that was more than a rowboat or paddle trike.

"If you insist, I'll trust you." He shrugged and situated himself against the railing.

The words turned over in her head. But before Arianna had a chance to dive into the depths of their implications, a distinct rainbow streak blazed a trail through the darkness over Ter.4.2.

# 22

## LEONA

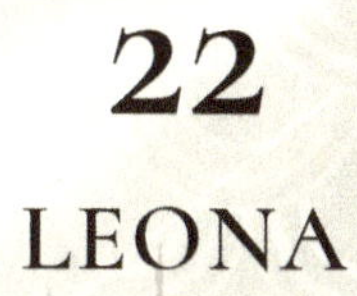

It was faint and distant, but even a tiny spark of magic in this desolate industrial wasteland felt earth-shaking. This was more than a spark, though. This was magic she didn't even know Cvareh had. This was as powerful as a Rider's would be.

She bared her teeth in malicious glee, knowing she had him, and would soon kill him for Yveun Dono.

Leona sprinted to where she and her riders had landed their gliders on one of the flat rooftops of the port three days ago upon arriving to Ter.4.2. It had been three horrible days of waiting and debating that now came to a satisfying conclusion. They would take to the skies once more and she would hunt down Cvareh like the Xin dog he was.

Magic wrapped around her feet, holding them to the platform of her glider. She pushed power under the wings, drawing it upward, overflow glittering off like fireworks in the night sky. Andre and Camile were close behind, moving without need of instruction.

It didn't matter if they were there or not; the Xin fool was hers anyway. Leona wanted to bathe herself in his blood. She wanted to return to Nova and have there be no doubt as to whose flesh had torn under her fingers.

Loom was darker than Nova. It lacked both starlight and moonlight due to the God's Line that always obscured the sky. She pushed magic into her sight—not enough to blind her, but enough to pierce through the blackness, looking for the source of the magic.

A signal flare drew a line into the sky as if to point an arrow in the right direction. *The prison?* Leona didn't waste thought on why Cvareh would head to such a place. She didn't need to know the method to his madness. She only had to put a stop to it.

She was closing in and fast, close enough to hear the echo of an explosion over the water. Leona gripped the handles of her glider more tightly. It was an island, which meant there would be only one way off of it. Arcing around the prison, she scanned for a port of some kind. It wasn't until her second loop that she saw it.

"There!" she screeched to Andre and Camile, directing their attention to her discovery. "You two kill any Fen and Chimera. Cvareh is *mine*."

Her comrades bared their teeth in understanding, pitching their gliders forward. They shot down toward the boat as it raced out of the harbor. Leona laid her eyes on him for the first time.

His blood orange-colored hair tousled around pale Xin flesh, whipped by the wind off the sea and the speeding vessel. He was short for a Dragon, Leona noted, a pitiful looking thing that didn't radiate half the power of his sister. The Fen in white standing next to him was nearly the same height.

A Fen in *white*.

No, no that wasn't a Fen. That was a Chimera of a different variety. That was the source of the odd blood smell Leona had been tracking across two territories. The woman had a strange and cataclysmic sort of power about her. The madness and blood lust that surged through Leona's veins seemed to cry out in recognition of an equal. An instinct that, even despite being faced with a Chimera, Leona heeded.

The White Wraith—*a woman was the White Wraith*—calmly loaded a small tube into the pistol at her hip. Andre sped toward her, claws out, ready to make a killing blow. The woman reached out her spare hand in a confident gesture and Cvareh took it. Chimera and Dragon, the strangest unified front she'd ever seen.

Magic surged over Leona, splitting her skull from ear to ear. The world blurred and she lost focus and seconds. She blinked rapidly, trying to ground herself once more by pushing aside the strange sensation of lost time. Her eyes scanned the boat in an attempt to pin down what had just occurred.

Andre was no longer on his glider, no longer boasting the upper hand. He was on the deck of the ship, a hole shot through his chest. Cvareh was doubled over, coughing blood as he stumbled toward the corpse of the felled Rider. The ship lurched as the empty glider crashed into the sea next to it.

*That was how he'd gotten so far*. Leona banked once more through the sky, circling like a bird of prey. The bastard could stop time. Only one in a hundred Dragons were born with that ability and Cvareh Xin was one of them. There was truly no justice in the world. She looked in disgust as he consumed Andre's body. Talent worthlessly fed to the lowest House in Nova.

"Push, don't stop," the Wraith screamed to the helm of the boat.

They were halfway between the prison and the mainland. Leona scanned the horizon. *Where were they headed?*

The vessel was cutting a diagonal path through the water, away from the main port and the second boat of Fen attackers coming at them. The stretch of land at the end of their trajectory was dim and black, little waiting for them. Leona growled. Too much thinking, not enough doing.

"Camile, fly ahead, cut off the boat. When it dodges, I'll flank."

Her remaining Rider nodded affirmation. Camile's focus remained steadfast in the wake of Andre's death. They were the King's Riders and that meant that, if they were lucky, they would die serving their sovereign. Andre had merely reached the logical conclusion of his duty.

The rush of the chase was beginning to get to Leona's head. She wanted to run down her prey. There was no darker glee that lit up her heart than the notion of a well-earned kill. And now she had two, Wraith and Dragon.

Camile did exactly as Leona had instructed, charging the ship head on. The Wraith sprinted to the bow to meet her, gun drawn. She had a steady draw and sure aim, but with the moving of the waves and Camile's evasive bobbing, her shot missed. Without time stopped, they were a lot more difficult to hit. Leona seized the opportunity, heading toward the rear side of the vessel where it banked, the deck tipping toward her as the driver turned wildly.

She found herself face-to-face with the second unexpected discovery of the evening. Cvareh was holding a gun. The born and bred Dragon noble was holding a crude Fenthri weapon. It looked awkward in his hands, but he tracked it on her anyway.

Glyphs on the exterior of the gun flared bright enough that it lit up the entire deck and surrounding sea. It fired at twice the size, speed, and power as any Chimera's would, forcing Leona away. The weapon cracked and crumbled under the strain, falling to pieces in the Dragon's hand.

So, Petra had been hiding this unpolished gem all along. Cvareh was rough, untrained, and generally timid. Underneath it all was true power. The closer they neared land, the more she realized her grave error in underestimating him. He was the younger brother of Petra'Oji and Houyui To, *of course he had strength*.

Camile rejoined her in the sky as Leona let out a cry of frustration. She was done toying with them. "We head to land," she declared. "Cut them off there."

Pushing her magic under her, Leona sped ahead of the boat, keeping in line with its course. She was done fighting over the salted sea and its dangerous depths. On land, she would have the upper hand. She wouldn't underestimate them a third time.

The secondary boat was close enough to open fire, but Cvareh's crew seemed uninterested in engaging. They pushed onward, ignoring all other distractions and opponents. Like a beam of sunlight, they penetrated the inky blackness with speed and certainty. But nothing was ahead of them. A wall of tall bars connecting the sea with the Underground canals and sewers blocked their path.

They were going in hot and fast on a straight collision course for the giant grate, suicidally determined to outrun their pursuers to their deaths. Leona pulled back, unwilling to follow to that watery grave. If Cvareh wanted to kill himself, she'd let him.

The White Wraith turned, watching Leona as she fell away. Leona could feel the woman's eyes on her from underneath the gleam of her magically enhanced goggles. She raised an empty hand and gave a wave, as though bidding farewell to the world.

An explosion ripped the sea apart. The boat turned and zigged, fighting against the currents and waves that pushed against its bow—keeping on course in a display of driving mastery. The rusted iron bars of the grate shattered into pieces, hot molten metal glowing like the jagged teeth of a giant beast in the darkness.

The ship allowed itself to be swallowed whole by it.

"Where are they going?" Camile called. "What do they hope to find under the city?"

And then it hit her. Leona screamed as she realized she'd been thwarted again. This Chimera was making a fool of her. The woman was two steps ahead, preempting Leona's every movement. Leona thought House Xin exhausted the depths of her hatred. But no, this was a rage unlike anything she'd ever felt. It was bitter and rough and raw, and coursed through her like swallowed rocks.

"The Underground," she snarled, panting, worked into a frenzy. "We pursue!"

The moment they crossed into the back thresholds of the Underground, they would be lost. Leona knew better than to follow into that tumultuous blackness, a place where the sun had never shone and true wretches made their home. Even as a Rider, there were some things she had to admit bested her.

The tunnel was narrow and getting smaller by the second. The boat was forced to dock inelegantly, as half its side was smashed in against a narrow walk. Leona skidded her glider against the surface of the water, evading a shot from the Wraith.

"Go!" the Chimera called to her companions.

Leona's eyes fell on a Fen girl with long black hair. She was just as the tiny man in Ter.5 had described. Tiny enough for Leona to pick her up and snap her in two as though she were a wooden doll.

She jumped onto the walk, letting her glider sink into the water. She'd recover it with magic later. Stable ground had never felt so good, and Leona wasted no time in launching herself for a deadly attack. The Wraith thought she'd be aiming for her, but Leona's claws sought a different foe.

The woman in white was fast. She changed from bracing herself to charging forward in a mere instant. But she wasn't fast enough. Leona's claws sunk into the tiny Fen's shoulder, ripping through muscle and sinew. They missed the lethal mark, but the message was clear as the Wraith threw her away with a cry of rage.

"Flor!"

*Yes*, yes that sound of anguish was what Leona lived for. It sent the previously calm Chimera into a frenzy. The woman charged Leona in a blind rage.

"Arianna!" Cvareh called after her, as he locked claws with Camile.

Leona dodged as the woman threw a golden dagger at her, then ducked when the Wraith pulled it back, hearing it whistle by the side of her head. This "Arianna" was a force unto her own. Like a thorny whip, a second dagger shot out from her hand, tethered to a golden line. Fearless, with complete disregard for her own well being, she launched at Leona headfirst.

"We have to go!" A man's voice—not Cvareh—called from farther down the hall. "We can lose them in the Underground!"

The flurry of attacks didn't stop.

"Arianna!" Cvareh kicked Camile in the chest, sending the other woman scrambling to avoid landing in the water.

Arianna ignored the Dragon. She continued, relentless. Leona grinned at her, and grabbed the dagger rather than dodging. Golden blood streamed down her wrist and elbow.

"If you don't kill me now, I'll hunt down your little pet. I'll kill *Florence*," Leona swore, wriggling as far as she could under the woman's skin.

The Wraith inhaled sharply the instant she heard the name. The Chimera's attacks were becoming sloppy, worked into a fever pitch. It was only a matter of time before—

Leona saw her opening. Her fingers tensed, and she jabbed her hand forward for the Chimera's chest.

And they sunk into the side of Dragon flesh. Cvareh's arms wrapped around the Fenthri woman as he grimaced aloud in pain. Arianna screamed at him in frustration and the sound was cut short as another piercing flare of magic assaulted her mind.

When the haze from magically stopped time cleared, Leona was left with nothing more than Cvareh's blood on her hand, the echo of a collapsed wall, and the rage of an unfinished fight.

# 23
## FLORENCE

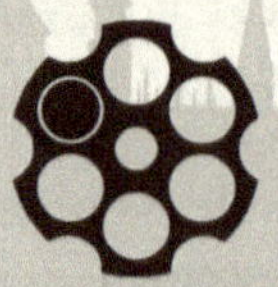

The only thing that made Florence ignore the pain in her shoulder was losing sight of Arianna with the Dragon Rider still attacking. Will planted the charges as Ari had no doubt instructed, as Florence had been told was the plan from the start. She sagged against Helen, trying to hold in the crimson waterfall that poured relentlessly between her fingers on a march to drag her down the river of death.

"We can't—Ari—we have to go back for her." The panic of seeing her friends again was replaced by a greater, more pressing fear of her teacher, her friend, being trapped on the other side of the wall. It pushed aside all reason and logic surrounding Ari's competence.

"The Riders are distracted with them," Will shot back. "We can lose them here."

"I'm not leaving them behind!"

"Yes you will." Helen's words were cold. Helen, her *first* friend, the *first* person Florence had left behind for her own sake.

"No, I won't," Florence insisted. She wasn't the girl she'd been then. She was sixteen now, nearly middle-aged. She was a woman who would stay with the people she loved even if it meant death.

The debate ended in a blink. Cvareh appeared seemingly out of nowhere, collapsing to the ground, and Arianna with him. Blood poured from his mouth and from the wound on his side, but Ari seemed blissfully unharmed.

"Flor!" Her teacher scooped her up in her arms. "Flor, we need to stint the bleeding, now."

"Cvareh—" Florence swayed from blood loss.

"We need to keep going!" Helen interjected frantically.

"Heard." Will ran back to join them, firing at the planted charges.

The explosion sent them all flying, rolling head over heels. Florence cried out in pain as the wound on her shoulder tore further from the force with a violent *rip*. The wall collapsed between them and the Riders, heralding a silent aftermath and pitch blackness.

She blinked into the darkness, creeping panic raising every hair on the back of her neck. She was back in the Underground. One extreme emotion after another was the only glue holding her together, but even that had its limits. Pain was beginning to dot stars against the void and Florence blinked frantically, her senses ringing.

Arianna pulled the cap off a torch, bathing the passage in a faint reddish glow. Helen and Will were finding their breath again, coughing through the dust, rolling to their feet. Cvareh wasn't moving.

"Flor, let me see it." Her teacher moved for her.

"Will can help me." Florence continued to apply pressure on her shoulder. It hurt, but she'd been trained by Ari for years in "what if" scenarios.

"Me?" Will balked.

"Ari, he's not moving," Florence insisted at her hesitation. "What's the point of all this if you lose your boon?"

"Boon?" Helen repeated in a sudden moment of clarity.

Ari scowled at her. It was a face Florence didn't get to indulge in often because it was one she only made when someone else was right and had bested her with the fact. Florence smiled tiredly.

"Pack this into the wound, and then stitch it up with this." Ari shoved some supplies into Will's hands.

"Do I look like an Alchemist?" He regarded the medical tools with skepticism.

"If you haven't learned this yet, learn it quickly: I do not like to be crossed or questioned," Ari growled. "I'm leading this trip and you would still be rotting in that cell if it wasn't for me. I will put you back there personally if you don't help Flor."

Will laughed with a shake of his head, moving over to her. He set down the supplies in the flickering light of the torch that burned harmlessly on the ground between the five of them. "You made a scary friend, Flor."

"I did. . ." Florence watched Ari as Will began to pack her wound. Her teacher flipped over the prone Dragon, regarding him thoughtfully. There was a softness to Ari's brow that Florence hadn't seen her adopt around the Dragon before. She had been Ari's first priority, but there was genuine concern for Cvareh alighting the woman's violet eyes.

Ari ran her hand over the oozing wound on his side, bringing her fingertips to his face. Florence watched as she pried the Dragon's mouth open. Her teacher opened her mouth a fraction and bit down with a grimace.

*Blood*, Florence realized. Ari was a Chimera and that meant her blood had magic in it, and the magic that lived in blood had the power to heal. She was giving the man her strength, literally forcing life down his throat.

Arianna knelt at the Dragon's side, bringing her face down to his. Her body blocked the act, but Florence didn't need to see the details to know what was happening. Ari pulled away, waiting a moment before leaning forward again and repeating the process, slowly dribbling blood into the Dragon's mouth from her own.

Helen sat opposite Florence. "So, who's your new friend?"

"She's not really a 'new' friend."

"I was being relative." Helen knew just how to twist the knife. She and Will were her first friends; everyone would be new compared to them.

"Arianna, she's my teacher. She found me when I emerged from the Underground and took me to Ter.5 to learn from the Revos." Ari glanced over her shoulder at the mention of her name, but continued to focus on a slowly stabilizing Cvareh.

"So you made it to Ter.5 then?" Will had almost finished his sloppy attempt at stitches. Turning to look at him was a mistake. It hurt her shoulder the second she moved her head and it made her catch sight of her ravaged flesh.

"Only with her help." She would've never made it anywhere without the help of others.

"I'm glad one of us made it." Helen leaned back on her arms. She was scrawny, thin—all leathery flesh beyond her years stretched across brittle looking bones. Will had clearly passed his days keeping active, but Helen had never spent much time on physical pursuits to begin with. She'd shrunk drastically in the time she'd spent in the floating prison.

"I should've stayed with you. I panicked, and I ran when the constabulary came. I didn't raise the signal and—"

"We know what happened," Helen interrupted.

"We were there." Will wore a tired but coy grin.

"I'm trying to apologize," she floundered.

"We know you are." Helen didn't miss a beat.

"We're not cross with you." Will ruffled her hair.

"Well we *were*," Helen corrected. "I ranted at length about you to him through the cracks in my floor… But we'd be pretty awful friends if we held a grudge for two years over an honest mistake. Even if it was one that landed us in jail."

Tears had boldly ventured down her cheeks from pain and fear, but now they fell in earnest. She'd been so afraid of seeing her friends again. Florence had relived the moment of their capture countless times over the past two years. Will and Helen had been exploring a safe route up to Ter.4.2. The moment Flor had seen the men and women of the law rounding the corners with their torches, she panicked. She knew if she'd been caught she would've been killed or worse. She wasn't like Will and Helen; both had been candidates for a circle. She was a

Arianna didn't know how to react. The woman who always had something to say was at a loss for words. For the first time, he'd gained mental ground against her and pushed onward.

"Why did you save me?"

"I didn't." She tore her eyes from his, looking down the hall as though the beast of offense lurked in its depths.

"You did." His hand curled around his side, touching the site of his most foolish act since he'd been on Loom. He'd risked the schematics being torn at the least, and death at the worst. Cvareh debated which would have actually been more terrible. He could be selfish and say his own death. But if he did say that, even to himself, the words would be hollow and lack conviction. In the scheme of Nova, Loom, and House Xin, the highest purpose he had was to see the schematics for the Philosopher's Box to the rebels building a new resistance in the Alchemists' Guild. That would be a catalyst for far greater and lasting change than him haunting the halls of Xin manor. "Leona's claws pierced my heart."

Arianna was visibly surprised by the news. She mulled it over for a long second. "So the red bitch is named Leona?"

Cvareh couldn't stop himself from laughing. "You pick up fast. Though we call her the 'King's Bitch' in House Xin. My sister invented the short name."

"I can get behind it." Ari grinned, and her flat teeth didn't bother him in the slightest.

"I'm not surprised. I could imagine you both getting along. You're similar," he confessed.

Ari huffed in amusement at the notion. "I doubt there could be more than one woman like me. Otherwise I'd fear for the future of the world."

"Luckily for us all, then, she's not of *this* world."

Arianna actually laughed. It was soft and breathy so as not to wake those sleeping. It wasn't a pretty sound by any stretch. But it was genuine, and that added a sort of spark to it that reminded Cvareh of the Arianna he saw when he imbibed from her. Potent and heady and sparking with life at the corner of every movement.

"I like the attempt at wit, Cvareh. Don't abandon it."

*I've been upgraded from just "Dragon" again.*

"You still haven't answered my question." He braved exhausting her good will toward him.

"I haven't," she agreed softly. "I was more worried about Flor than I was for you. She was the one who insisted I focus on healing you rather than giving my attention to her."

He shouldn't have expected any different. Their relationship had been set in stone from the start. He would orbit wildly around her hatred for Dragons, her emotions preventing him from crossing her inner threshold. His path would be set by the perfect tension her moods, her eyes, her face, her mouth, *her very existence* held him in.

"But I'm glad she did."

The statement was so faint that he almost asked her to repeat it. As delicate and pure as the lake waters of Shina, it was something he never imagined could come from her. He wanted to hear it again. He instantly desired to know what would make her speak like that in perpetuity. So enamored by it was he, that Cvareh didn't even question why.

"Now, take watch, and wake me if you hear anything." Arianna rested the back of her head on the wall, closing her eyes.

"You can trust me."

"So it seems."

The words should've made him elated. But there was a heavy note of skepticism that weighed them down from having the same effervescence as her prior declaration. It echoed in the heart she'd saved, and cast a shadow of doubt on everything that was building between them.

# 25
## LEONA

"SO, WHAT'S THE PLAN?" CAMILE KICKED HER FEET OFF THE EDGE OF THE rooftop where they had decided to land their gliders. She picked her teeth with one of the tiny finger bones from the Fen they'd taken their frustrations out on.

"I'm still working that out," Leona confessed, much to her displeasure. The whole night had been one catastrophic failure after the next. Leona was proud enough to feel an insatiable desire to rectify the events with the sweet solution of a vengeful rage. But she wasn't foolish enough to run in headfirst at the next possible opportunity.

This was the White Wraith's home. She had every advantage of skill and allies. Leona had researched Loom in depth, as had been her duty. But practical application of knowledge was always harder than attaining the knowledge itself.

"Why is she helping Cvareh?" she mused aloud.

"Who?" Camile reminded Leona that she couldn't read her mind.

"The White Wraith." Leona began to think aloud. "She's the self-proclaimed enemy of all Dragons. The pale man in Dortam said she'd take any job if it hurt a Dragon or Dragon interests in some way."

Camile hummed in agreement, rubbing her bloated stomach. The Fen flesh wasn't sitting well with Leona either. Though the killing had been satisfying; at the very least the gray people were good for that much.

"So why help Cvareh? He's certainly a Dragon—"

"Undeniably so."

"—and he's acting only in the interest of his Dragon House."

"Could that interest overlap with her interests?" Camile mused. The woman was smart. The details of their mission were on a need-to-know basis, and Camile didn't need to know every fact that Leona was privy to. But she could work well enough around the blanks. "What does Xin want more than anything else?"

"Power, their 'ends before ideals,' the throne."

"But to do that they'd need to overthrow Yveun Dono. And that's certainly not happening as long as House Tam keeps 'all things equal'," Camile said with an arrogant huff.

House Rok had been in power for hundreds of years. It would take an army to stand up against a House with the amount of manpower and resources Rok had amassed in that time. Xin may be able to take them to task if they had the support of House Tam. But Tam and Rok made cozy bedmates, leaving Xin short of the manpower they'd need for a civil war.

*And if they couldn't find an army on Nova. . .* Leona bolted upright.

"I've an idea," Leona said. "But it's still hazy at the edges."

"Going to disappear for a chat?" Camile turned her attention back up to the sky. Boring and gray every hour of the day, just like the rest of Loom.

"I'll be back." Leona waved the other woman's inquiry off. She wasn't in the mood to field any comment on who she was talking to.

She rounded down the quiet stairs into the living quarters—or maybe they were working chambers? Seriously, the Fen had no sense of originality; every room looked the same. Crimson blood still stained the floor from where her and Camile had violently redecorated.

Leona raised a hand to her ear and whispered, *"Tarukun."*

The word had no meaning. It was a series of sounds she'd strung together when she'd first learned how to whisper and stuck with ever since. But that was the way it should be to avoid random conversation as a result of saying a common word.

Magic tingled between her fingers and her ear. There was a faint pulse along a thin, invisible tether, a line that connected her all the way back to Nova.

She waited, knowing that it was possible she was waking her King. But as loath as she was to do it, Yveun Dono would want an update. Though waiting for him to activate his end of the whisper nearly killed her.

"Leona," he very nearly purred her name. "Tell me good news."

"Regretfully not." Leona made no excuses. As much as she despised having to admit her shortcomings, hiding them would be far worse. Yveun Dono was silent as she recounted the events of the night prior, and that silence stretched toward infinity after she finished her retelling.

"I know you did not wake me merely to report failure. You are far too savvy to my will to do such a thing."

Leona's heart soared. Even in the wake of shame, he put faith in her. Rather than lashing out, he gave her another opportunity for redemption—one she would not squander.

"Yveun Dono, I know what Cvareh—all of House Xin—is after."

"Do you?"

"They want to make an army of perfect Chimera to stand against you," she declared boldly, praying her logic was sound. "If they managed to create a working Philosopher's Box and solve the issue of forsaken Chimera, they would be able to make Fen as strong as Dragons."

His silence told her everything.

"Dono, my sovereign, I have put this much together on my own. . . But I cannot decide upon a heading. Would they travel to the Rivets to find an engineer who could solve the riddle of their box? Or would they head to the Alchemists, to put it in the hands of those responsible for splicing Chimera into existence? Has there been word from those loyal to us in the Rivets' Guild since I left?"

Yveun Dono rightfully preferred his inferiors to be able to reach their own conclusions; he didn't have time for nor interest in holding their hands through every decision. But this was a risk Leona deemed worth taking. At worst, she would upset him marginally now by asking for guidance, rather than enrage him later with another failure.

"The watchers you appointed in the Rivet guild have been silent. And they would report immediately should Cvareh appear. If he goes there, let him be lulled into a false sense of security until you arrive for his heart." Yveun Dono's voice shifted into the cold and calculating tones of a commander— the true and cunning nature he masked under the charm he applied for his Crimson Court. "However, the Alchemists prove. . . resistant, even still. It has been merely two years since their last petty uprising was squelched, but they remain obstinate in their tiny corner of the world. They hide much behind their veils of secrecy, so much so that even my eyes are blurred. I would not find it surprising if they felt inclined to harbor a Dragon like Cvareh, given his desired ends."

"All else aside, perhaps my presence may remind them that no guild operates in half measures when it comes to loyalty to their King." Leona grinned faintly to herself, savoring the idea of having an entire guild under her boot and hanging on her every beck and call.

"Indeed."

"Then I make my heading for Ter.2," Leona declared. "And this time, I will not fail you."

"See that you don't."

Magic popped and the link between them fizzled. Leona lowered her hand from her ear. They would move a lot faster with their gliders than Cvareh would be able to travel in the Underground, even with two renegade Ravens. She had time before he would emerge again—if he emerged again. Though, Leona knew if he were lost to the creatures of the depths of Loom, she would be disappointed at fate for stealing her kill.

*Yes*, she started up the stairs, *Cvareh and the Wraith will be mine*. But she wasn't going to be made a fool a second time, and she was no longer going in blind. Leona now knew what type of forces she was up against.

"You look surprisingly chipper," Camile assessed as Leona returned to her prior place.

"We're heading back to Ter.5."

"Oh?"

"We need to pay the Revos a visit." Leona flexed her fingers, sheathing and unsheathing her claws. They were trusty, reliable weapons. She hadn't been like her sister, adopting every new killing tool that came into existence; she'd favored the tried and true methods of slaughtering her enemies for years. But that was up on Nova, and here on Loom the fights were different. "Cvareh had a pistol."

"A fragile one," Camile scoffed.

"So let's get some better ones." Leona bared her teeth, showing that the matter wasn't up for discussion. The Revos would give her something the world had never seen before, something so powerful that it would slay even Wraiths, and Dragons who could manipulate time.

# 26

## ARIANNA

It wasn't until Arianna was grasping onto the side of a strange mine cart-like transportation machine, with two Ravens laughing gleefully at every pitch-black corner they took at break-neck speed, that she grasped the concept of the Underground also being described as the "Ravens' Playground."

"Is this it?" Helen called back to Will. "This is the best she has?"

"Rusty!" Will replied with a shout, pulling another lever on the contraption housed in a back compartment of the vessel. Arianna focused on it—trying to figure out how it worked—rather than the mind-numbing feeling of being hurled through the unknown while trusting the most annoying girl she'd ever met at the wheel and the clinically insane at the engine. "Flor, you have any grease?"

"When have I *ever* carried grease on me?" Florence couldn't plaster herself any tighter against the side of the cart if she tried.

Ari hated seeing her distressed. But there was something about the girl's fear she found the slightest bit endearing. Despite Flor's Raven tattoo, she was a wrench in a toolbox of screwdrivers here. Ari had only ever known her pupil as a

Revo in training. But now she saw clearly why Florence had felt the need to flee the Ravens. There would be no way the girl could pass the mandatory Dragon tests imposed on Guild initiates to cull out those who lacked talent and manage the population they'd sent into a spiral when they'd removed Loom's breeding policies.

"You *had* to pick this cart. Didn't like the other rider," Will huffed.

"We'd need two riders and only one of these," Helen answered. "Stop complaining and just manage my speed!"

It wasn't long before Cvareh was emptying the contents of his mostly empty stomach over the railing. Ari laughed with the rest of them at his expense and he alternated the rest of the day between fuming and panting softly, muttering prayers under his breath to Nova's endless pantheon. At least, Ari assumed it to be the rest of the day.

Hours were lost to the darkness of the Underground. She'd originally tried to keep up with her timepiece, but quickly abandoned the idea. They pushed every hour they were awake at her behest, moving as fast and as far as they could beneath Ter.4 before exhaustion took over.

Cvareh and she alternated watches. They needed less sleep. Having magic in the blood that constantly healed their bodies and kept them in shape increased their ease of survival tenfold. It also made the fading conditions of the Fenthri in their party all the more obvious. Living creatures weren't meant to make these halls home for extended periods of time. The strange sleeping schedule and hours upon hours of darkness took a toll on the body as much as the mind. Laughter faded from the group first, talking second, and soon the only sound that filled the air was the screeching of brakes and the clacking of metal wheels on veca after veca of track.

They were four days into their journey and somewhere around Holx, according to Helen, when the last of their rations ran out. The empty bag stared back at Arianna, more vacant than every tunnel she had faced during the hours of their travel. They weren't going to make it to Ter.4.3 without additional supplies.

"What are you going to do?" Cvareh watched her thoughtfully as she retreated away from the last of the diminished supply bags. The other two mostly empty sacks were in the cart with the sleeping trio.

"I don't know yet." Her mind had yet to work out the best solution. It was strange to admit it, however.

She never confessed to Florence when she needed time to work through a plan, or operated with less than one hundred percent certainty. The girl was someone Arianna wanted to look after, care for—someone whose well being Arianna wanted to ensure into eternity. And, while Arianna could see the woman she had become in the past two years, part of her still clung to the idea of protecting the shaking, scared little crow who had run lost through the streets of Ter.4.2.

"They're not going to last long."

"No, they won't, not at this pace anyway."

"Is there something down here you could hunt?" He was making an effort, she'd grant him that much. But the effort was ill placed; he just didn't know enough about Loom.

"Not down here." Rather than taking the easy insult, Ari explained: "The softest things are glovis grubs. But they feed off rocks, so they're filled with corrosive acids. The people who do eat them. . . don't last long."

But those people didn't die. The chemicals in the glovis ate away at their bodies and corroded their minds until what was once Fenthri became something between man and monster. The Wretched were worse than forsaken Chimera. At least the forsaken had a timer on their lives. If the Fenthri body managed to adapt to consuming the glovis' flesh, they could survive indefinitely, haunting the tunnels.

"Up then?" he reasoned.

"I seem to have no other choice." She adjusted the strapping on her harness. As much as she didn't mind wearing it, she was ready for a reprieve that would let her take it off.

"When are we going?"

She laughed with a shake of her head. "There is no *we* on this trip. Alone I can navigate whatever streets or plains wait above us effortlessly. If I'm looking out for everyone, it'll slow me down."

"I can look out for myself, and you know I'll help look after them," he insisted defensively.

"I know," she confessed. A similar sensation to the one she'd felt a few days ago washed over her, and Arianna assessed the Dragon in the darkness. Without light, he looked the same as any Fenthri would—save for the black slits of his eyes and his physical size. Perhaps that was why she was beginning to feel easier around the man. But that didn't quite make sense, as Arianna didn't find relief, but rather a small disappointment, in not being able to see the colors she knew him to be. "And I will trust you to do it."

"What?"

"I'm going alone. I'll only be gone an hour, and I'm certain they'll sleep the entire time and then some . . . But I'm trusting you to look after them." The words still made her uneasy because it meant that she really was daring to put her faith in another Dragon. But they came more smoothly than she expected.

"Be careful, Ari. First you trust me, then you may actually like me." He leaned against the wall with a smug grin.

Her emotions ran wild. Arianna tried to get them back under control but didn't know where to begin. Correcting him on his use of Flor's shortened name? The ease by which he assumed her trust? The implication that she might actually enjoy him and his company?

Or perhaps it was the fact that, yet again, he reminded her of a woman who was long dead.

"Don't push your luck." It was a weak return, and she knew it. But she wouldn't be too hard on the man, she insisted to herself; she told him she'd liked his newfound sass and it would be contradictory to squelch it.

His eyes followed her as she woke Helen softly, helping the girl out of the cart without waking Will or Florence. She could feel his attention prickling at her magic until she disappeared around a winding tunnel, Helen leading the way. And yet, she still felt his presence long after. It was a shadow connected to her heels, waiting on her as her footsteps echoed through the caves, no doubt audible to his Dragon ears.

That sensation faded away as a hazy dawn faded into view. Helen blinked blearily at the light, the small amount nearly blinding after spending five days trekking with nothing more than torches and the faint glow of glovis eyes lining the tunnel walls. Fresh air kicked the dust around, making no effort to pierce the depths of the Underground. Nature heeded the lines between above and below; it was the boldness inspired by steam and guns and magic that inspired Fenthri to blur it.

"You're going to make it back?" Helen yawned. "Do you need me to wait here?"

Arianna made a show of pocketing her grease pen. "I can follow the line." She tapped the mark she'd drawn while walking.

"You're sure? If we get separated, there's no hope of finding each other down there," the cartographer cautioned.

"So go back and sleep, and don't move for a while—if you can manage that."

"Sleep, yes, understood." Helen's dramatic salute quickly deteriorated into another wide-mouthed inhale of air. She passed the hardened eye of a glovis from hand to hand. It still emitted a faint glow even after the creature's death, and Ari watched the speck of light as Helen traveled back into the depths.

The fog embraced her as Ari emerged, breathing fresh air for the first time in what felt like forever. Standing *alone* for the first time in what felt like forever. She wasn't accustomed to traveling in a pack.

She looked over the dusty plains of Ter.4, a steam engine rolling across the ocean of tall grasses in the distance. Master Oliver had taken her under his wing when she was still so young. They had traveled the world together, just the two of them. And then the Dragons had come to ruin it all. To confine guilds to their territories and initiates to textbooks rather than true learning.

Still, when she watched the sky lighten over the plains, the quiet dawn on a mostly barren land, it looked as it had then—smelled as it had then. Arianna stepped forward, putting Wraiths and Dragons and boons and misplaced Ravens behind her. For a brief hour, she navigated the world as nothing more than a Fenthri woman.

Three hare and a bag full of edible plants later, she returned to the world below. Escapes were wonderful, but impermanent and shallow. She was made of stronger mettle than those that fled into the warm bosom of nostalgia.

The fingers of her left hand trailed through the grease line, following it down and through the winding passages. Silence flooded her, and it wasn't until Arianna was nearly to their resting place that she realized the source of her unease.

It was *too* quiet. She heard no breathing, no discussion, no clanking of the cart over the rails as its occupants shifted in their sleep. Her pace quickened and Arianna sped to meet the last corner, already knowing what would greet her.

Nothing.

Her line ended where it had begun in a spot she knew she could not be confusing for any other. Panic swelled to a crescendo and Ari forced it down with a hand on her dagger, as though she could ward off her emotions with golden blades and lock them away behind spools of wire. She stretched her hearing, but stillness greeted her in all directions.

Wherever they had gone, it was far and fast—enough that even her Dragon ears couldn't pick up the faintest squeal of wheels on rails. Her breathing quickened as the options unfurled before her, and Arianna picked up a faint scent.

It was one she'd come to know on their travels—the crisp, fresh smell of burning wood. *Cvareh.* Her eyes drifted over to the wall, led by her nose, and Arianna ran her fingers along the fresh scratches in the rock. He had bled here.

Balling her hand into a fist, Arianna screamed, punching the rock so hard blood exploded and her bones snapped. Her anguish echoed through the caves uselessly, the ears she wanted to hear were too far away. But there were more things to hear her than a Dragon and a few misplaced Ravens in the Underground.

She drew her daggers, her bones already knitting, the pain sharpening her mind. A primal hiss echoed up to her, followed by the clicking of pincers. Ari placed the tip of her dagger in the wall, slowly walking backward.

"That's it. . ." The sound of metal on stone grated through the tunnel like an alarm for any in the vicinity. "Follow me."

Helen's words were still fresh in her mind: *no hope of finding each other once separated.* Arianna watched as the darkness melted around the shape of a Wretched, lean ropes of muscle suspended over bones and wrapped in the thinnest of pale gray skin. Useless eyes—white and beady—were placed behind the gaping orifice that was once a Fenthri mouth. Acidic saliva glowed faintly, oozing between pincers that clicked in excitement, tracking her movements.

A second emerged in her field of vision, followed by a third. Arianna slowly pulled her dagger away from the wall. At the least she'd draw them off Flor, or try.

"Right, then." She flipped her grip on her dagger, clipping in the second. "Who's first?"

The beasts hissed the moment she started to speak. Their long claws scraped against the stone, charging for her with gurgling madness. Arianna let out an animalistic roar in reply.

Wretched and Chimera lunged for the kill.

# 27
## FLORENCE

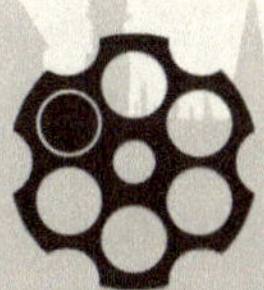

The Wretches chased them on all fours down the tunnel. They hissed and clicked, moving unnaturally fast through the darkness, dotting a trail of glowing saliva that steamed pock marks into the stones behind them.

Florence's shoulder ached and burned as she struggled to keep her balance in the jostling cart. Will strained against the levers in the back. Helen was rigid at the wheel, trying to keep them on a course she could track in her mind.

"Ari. What about Ari?" She grabbed for Cvareh. He was the only person she could distract with her panic, the only one of the three she could lose her head around. Helen and Will had their hands full enough trying to keep them from dying in a swift and terrible crash.

"We can't go back that way." He bared his teeth in a fearsome snarl at the creatures in hot pursuit.

Florence's hand shrunk away from him on instinct at the terrible look that overcame his face, wild and savage. It was the face of the Dragons Ari had filled her head with over the past two years and one she hadn't witnessed with her own eyes until that moment.

"Those things are exactly what I'm worried about! Ari's alone with them!"

Ari, her teacher, her friend, a woman who was a shining and steady light in Florence's otherwise gray world. She had left someone precious behind in the Underground. Again.

"At this exact second, I think you should be more worried about *us* being alone with them!" Cvareh shouted.

A Wretch dove from a side tunnel. Cvareh instinctively placed his body between its sharp pincers and Florence. He grunted in pain as he slashed into the creature and acidic blood poured over his hand. With an aggravated roar he threw the body away, and it bounced limply down the cart path.

"Can you not get acid on our only means of transportation?" Will scolded, motioning to where erosion was already weakening the side of the cart, boring holes in the rusted metal. "We're pretty far from the Holx yard and I don't think we'll stumble on another this deep."

"Why don't you ask the monsters? I'm sure they'll be happy to oblige. Or should I just let it into our cart next time?" Cvareh growled in reply, rubbing his knitting flesh.

"Can you all not talk so much? It's taking a lot of focus to keep us on track!" Helen's words had both a literal and figurative meaning.

Wretches on their tails, Arianna nowhere to be found, and the only thing separating them from being lost in the Undergound forever was the map that spun madly inside Helen's head. They were falling apart at the seams, cracking under the pressure. Florence swallowed.

*Fight or flight.*

The instinct rose up in her, hot and searing under every nerve. She dropped her bag, falling to the floor of the cart with it. Flight after flight, she'd run through life. From avoiding responsibility in the guild, to running out on Will and Helen, to letting them leave Ari now.

"What are you doing?" Cvareh asked as she frantically tried to make sense of the state of their current supplies. It wasn't much. She couldn't restock with everything she'd needed in Ter.4.2—there was no substitute for Mercury Town.

"I'm trying to get us out of this mess." She passed Cvareh her revolver, loading it with three canisters. "Hold this."

He took the gun skeptically and turned back to the Wretches.

"No, you're not shooting them. Don't fire a shot." Florence dumped one canister over the side of the cart, the precious gunpowder lost to the air whipping around them. It hurt her very soul to see it wasted, but she didn't have anywhere else for it to go and she needed a blank vessel of some kind.

While she was up, she tried to assess how fast they could be going, but the numbers all blurred in her head. *Ari would know what to do*, a voice in the back of her mind nagged. But Ari wasn't here. She was, and someone had to think of a solution, however wild and reckless.

"Helen, when's the next downhill?"

"Uh. . ."

"Helen."

The other woman spun the wheel frantically.

"Helen! Log it aloud, recount later to figure out where we are, and take the next downhill," Florence demanded.

"Understood." Helen began muttering to herself, a method Florence knew the girl used to help commit things to memory.

Florence's hands shook as her brain replayed chemical after powder, reaction after reaction. She shuffled the deck of everything she'd been taught from Ari, from her Revo tutors, from books. She threw out every ounce of conventional wisdom on explosives and bombs; she needed the most unstable reactions. The world was upside down, and the only way it was getting righted was with an explosion that would shake the foundation of the earth itself.

She cradled the canister in her hand, trying to counter the sudden movements of the cart so nothing would be set off prematurely. Helen was finally able to fulfill her request and the cart tipped forward. Will frantically twisted and pulled, trying to temper their fall.

"Let it go, Will!" Florence demanded. "Let it all go."

"But if we gather that much sp—"

"Just do it!" Her order didn't vibrate with the same resonance as Ari's would have, but it carried equal weight.

He flipped a few levers, and the cart became a bullet barreling down the darkness. The sound of the Wretches grew distant and Florence exchanged the pistol for the canister in Cvareh's hands. The faint glow of the glovis eyes they'd harvested rattled around the bottom of the cart, illuminating his confusion.

"I'm going to shoot three times. On the second, you throw that and wait for the third shot before you push every ounce of magic you have into that gold pin." She manually placed his thumb over the pin at the end of the canister, the spot where the golden hammer of a gun would strike.

"You got it."

"Flor. . ." Helen had stopped muttering.

"Ready?" Florence raised the revolver.

"What do you think you're doing?" Will shouted.

Florence spared him a brief glance before curling her finger around the trigger. "What Revos do best."

She fired. The first shot exploded against the ceiling. On the second shot Cvareh threw, and rock began to collapse in place. On the third shot he did exactly as she had instructed, and the three, their cart, and everything in it were sent flying forward by the shock wave.

The earth groaned and Florence groaned with it. She instantly panicked, thinking she'd gone blind somehow, only to remember that she was working with nearly no light. The tunnels rumbled with shock waves. Large chunks of rock began to fall and Florence heard the first satisfying hiss of a Wretch crushed beneath one.

Another set of spider web fractures cracked across the ceiling above them. Florence pushed herself to her feet, running on pure adrenaline as the world spun. "We have to move."

She wrapped her arms around Will, hoisting him to his feet with all the strength she possessed. Her left arm couldn't get a good grip on him, and just as she nearly lost her ability to support his weight, he found his balance.

"Helen?" Florence called further up the tunnel, scattered glovis eyes gave them barely enough light to see by.

"I have her," Cvareh called. Helen was cradled in his arms; Florence suppressed her panic at the sight. If their navigator died, they would be stuck forever. "Hurry!"

They sprinted forward through the dark tunnels. Florence and Will led with a glovis eye each. It wasn't until the last echo of the cave-in that they all collapsed at once, chests heaving, exhaustion crushing their shoulders.

Florence and Will crumpled to the floor. Cvareh gingerly laid a moaning Helen next to them. He squinted into the blackness beyond their tiny fragments of light.

"Hold your breaths, for just a moment." He motioned, and they obliged. "I don't hear anything. . ."

"We either scared them all off, cut them all off, or told them exactly where we were with that." Will rubbed his ears. "Next time you feel like going explosive crazy, warn us?"

"I did. You just—" she interrupted herself with a hiss of pain as she shifted.

Florence looked down at her arm. Will's clumsy stitches had been ripped wide open. Blood poured from the wound, merging with blood from a secondary location where the bone in her forearm protruded from her body. She felt faint almost instantly.

"Flor, Florence." Cvareh was at her side, propping her up, supporting her as Ari would. "Hang in there."

*Hang in there for what?* she thought grimly. They had no food, were down to two canisters and one pistol, their medical supplies were depleted, and they'd lost their transportation. No one was coming for them. Even if Arianna tried— and Florence found herself hoping her teacher wouldn't do something so foolish —she'd never find them. Even if she somehow knew the right path, she'd never make it to them now with the cave-in.

Florence tilted her head back and rested it on the rock, panting softly, unsure how much of the darkness at the corners of her vision was due to blood loss and how much was just lack of light.

"It's like then," Helen whispered.

"We'd pushed the cart too fast, we'd made too much noise." Will's eyes glossed over, looking at the past they were all reliving.

"Drew them right to us." Helen turned her head, staring at Cvareh. "I thought with a Dragon, we were nearly invincible."

The expression that briefly overtook his eyes was heartbreaking. He felt guilty for their situation, despite having no real obligation to. They had thought him near invincible, a god among them, as if by virtue of his blood alone he could be their savior.

And that was the thought that sparked an explosion of possibility in Florence's mind

"Helen, how long to Ter.4.3?"

The other woman sighed heavily, looking up at the nothingness that coated the rocks above them. She muttered under her breath, and every second she took doing so oozed another bit of life from Florence's veins. "We'll have to loop back toward Holx, maybe not. Depends on how fast we can find another vehicle. Accounting for us going *all* the way back to the higher levels right beneath Holx...maybe four or five more days?"

Longer than she wanted, shorter than she'd thought. Helen and Will were beaten up, but their wounds looked superficial enough. Food would be an issue, but if they had to go that close to Holx anyway, they may find someone they could trade with or one of them could brave sneaking up. Then again, there were always the glovis. . . Ralph made it through three of them the last time they were all in the Underground before he died.

So there were options for all of them; they could make it to Ter.4.3 safely underground and keep Cvareh's magic hidden from the Riders. Florence knew Arianna would head there eventually.

That left the matter of Florence.

She would not make it, and they had no supplies to mend the amount of blood she was losing, even if they somehow managed to set the break. Florence pressed her eyes closed, turning to Cvareh. By the time she opened them, she had made up her mind.

"Cvareh, have you ever made a Chimera before?"

# 28

## CVAREH

underneath Ter.4 had been one harrowing moment after the next that he was sure did nothing for the luster of his skin or wrinkles around his brow. They surfaced from the quagmire bloody, beaten, thinning, and blinking against the faint twilight of sunset in Ter.4.3. But emerge they did, in one miraculous piece, and thanks in no small part to the dark-haired girl at his side.

Cvareh had a whole new appreciation for the girl—no, woman. She was sixteen, barely more than a *toddler* by the lifespans on Nova. But, for a Fenthri, it made her almost middle aged. This was a woman who was coming into her prime and knew what she wanted.

At least, that's what he had to believe. Because he'd been feeding her his blood for five days now. The magic had a strange affect on the not-yet-Chimera Fenthri. Without a proper transfusion of blood she couldn't be made into a full Chimera, so his magic didn't take hold like a proper imbibing would. It also began to work away at her stomach and mouth, creating bloody sores that would be aggravated with every feeding, heal as a result of the magic, and then be made worse again as the magic faded.

Imbibing like this would eventually kill her. But she maintained both their spirits by reminding him that they were already headed to the home of the Chimera—the Alchemists' Guild. Once she had been given the blood properly, gold mingled with red to make black, she would rebound stronger than before. Such was the way of Chimeras; Florence should need no more living proof than the woman she had made her teacher.

*That* particular woman was elusive for two days after they emerged from the Underground. They holed up in squalor, but it was far safer than the depths they had endured and even scraps were better sustenance than what they'd had available previously. Cvareh began to fear that perhaps Arianna had not escaped. That she had gone back and was met with an ill fate of pincers and the Wretches they had left behind.

If she died, would he know? Was there something about the magic of the boon contract that would alert him to its dissolution? He had no idea. She'd been an enigma from the start and the woman was content to remain such even when she wasn't around to give him a hard time.

For two days, Florence went and sat at the port of Ter.4.3. She had an unending belief that Arianna would somehow know to find her there. Where it stemmed from, Cvareh wasn't quite certain. But she was resolute enough to kill herself for it.

On the third day, he walked with her, bundled and hidden. It was taking longer and longer for her to traverse the area from their hideout to her waiting spot and, after fearing she wouldn't return yesterday, Cvareh had made up his mind to go with her from then on. He could do little more than give her blood, but that he would do... even if the idea of piercing his flesh above ground settled restlessly across his consciousness. But if he didn't, eventually, the girl would die. And he'd promised Arianna he would keep her safe. More than that, he wanted to see her safe for himself.

A pop sounded in his ear, echoing from a great distance away with the closeness of someone clicking their tongue by the side of his face. He looked out over the port, feeling the tether form between him and his sister, tugging at his ear. Cvareh rose slowly, giving Florence a reassuring squeeze.

"I'm going to take a short walk."

"I'll wait here." The girl gripped the bench seat for support. He would have to let her imbibe tonight or else she would certainly be beyond help.

"I'll be right back," he promised.

Cvareh strolled away, at least until he was out of eyesight. His pace quickened and he ducked into a side alley, wedging himself between some shipping crates. With a quick glance, he rose his hand to his ear, magic crackling into his skin and across the void that separated him and Nova.

"Petra," he whispered.

"I was beginning to wonder, little one." Genuine relief flooded her voice and Cvareh felt instant guilt at the idea of making her worry.

"I haven't been in a position to talk."

"Yveun Dono sent Riders after you. But I heard no word of capture or kill and I know he would boast of it had his red bitch been successful." She was utterly triumphant at the sound of Cvareh's voice, knowing they had so far thwarted the best efforts of House Rok. "Still, with your silence—"

"I move slower than expected, but safer than we predicted." It was irony to say given all he had faced, but with Arianna he had been far safer than he would've been venturing out on his own. Though his luck might be thinning on that front.

"You have made an ally?" Nothing escaped his sister.

"I have."

"Who?"

"She is—"

"*She?*" Petra's expression was readable through the word. She'd heard the shift in his tones, the note placed under the pronoun at the mere thought of Arianna.

"—the White Wraith," he finished determined.

"My brother has befriended the infamous White Wraith?" The echo of Petra's chuckle whispered back to him. "You're certain she's on our side?"

"I am," he affirmed.

"She has quite the reputation. I don't know if I would trust her."

"Then trust me. There's nothing she would do that would hurt me." Why was he so confident? She'd spent days illustrating how little she thought of him. She'd spent hours annoying him for the sake of it.

"What have you done to tame this beast?"

"Just trust me that I have this under control."

"Do you?" a voice spoke from above him.

Cvareh's head snapped up to the top of the pile of crates he'd been hiding between. There, perched at their top as though she had materialized out of thin air itself—like a wraith—was the woman in question. The connection with his sister fizzled from lack of focus and his hand fell from his ear.

"Tell me what control you're exercising." With the grace and nimbleness of a cat, she dropped before him, rising slowly. "You know what hangs on your response."

"Florence is safe." It was mostly true, at least.

Arianna visibly relaxed, leaning against the crates with her arms lazily folded over her chest.

"How did you find me?"

"I've been waiting for you to mess up and use enough magic to leave a trace in the air." She reached forward and he expected her to grab him, to smack him, to grab her dagger and hold it to his face in an instant. But her hand wrapped around his shoulder in an almost reassuring manner. "I'm glad you're all right as well."

"You just want your boon." He laughed nervously, not even knowing why he was nervous, not knowing why he was so eager to write her off.

"Oh I do." She didn't waste breath on denying it. "But I'm still glad to see you in one piece." Arianna stepped away and, for the very first time, he wished she hadn't. "Now, take me to her."

Cvareh led the way, though his relief at seeing the white-clad woman faded quickly. Florence's shoulders sagged as she continued to clutch at the bench, waiting diligently for her master's return. Waiting even if it meant her death. It was a loyalty that could not be bought and in that brief moment, he wondered if it was a loyalty Arianna had actually earned.

Arianna stopped in her tracks a few steps away from the young woman. She spun on Cvareh and he was surprised she didn't burn her cheeks for all the fire that sparked from her eyes underneath her goggles. *She knew.* He could sense it with every move she made.

"What did you do to her?"

# 29
## ARIANNA

 she wasn't about to give him.

"What did you do to her?" she repeated, her voice rising. She didn't care if the world heard her, if they all watched as she tore the man limb from limb.

"I didn't—"

"He didn't do anything I didn't expressly ask for." Florence was on her feet. Arianna watched her fingertips track along the bench, keeping her steady. The girl looked frail. Her steps were small, her ankles threatening to revoke their support at any moment.

"Flor. . . You. . ." She didn't have words. The world had fallen away, crumbling into a vortex of emotions. The anger, confusion, rage, and panic she'd felt for days not knowing if she'd ever find her Florence again vanished. Pure relief flooded the vacant hollow in the center of her chest. Ari scooped her up, holding her, stabilizing her. "I'm so relieved."

"I am too." Flor's arms snaked around her waist, holding her in kind. Arianna sighed softly into her hair, content to know the most precious person in her world was safe once more. Both their hands pressed into the other's left shoulders for a long moment.

But there was a *smell* that interrupted her bliss, that tainted and changed it. Ari finally pulled away, bracing herself to handle the truth that was already apparent. "You reek of him."

"Arianna," Florence spoke firmly and evenly. "There was no other way. If we hadn't made the effort, I would've died. There was an accident after the Wretches—we're lucky to be alive at all."

Ari chewed over her tongue to keep it from spitting venom. She had never wanted Florence to endure the pain and danger of becoming a Chimera. She had never wanted the girl to feel the draw of magic, the lust of possibility for one more organ, one more scrap of stolen power.

"I had been thinking about it for the past year." Florence squeezed her forearms. "As a Chimera I can do more; I can make my own weapons better than with your help. Not that your help isn't marvelous, but it's that—"

"I know, Flor." Arianna smiled tiredly and squeezed the girl's arms in reply. She wasn't sure if Florence was trying to convince her, or herself. But what was done was done.

If she could smell Cvareh on her, the girl had already ingested quite a bit of his blood. Florence's body would go into full rejection if they didn't complete the transfusion sooner rather than later. There was no going back.

"But this does change things." Arianna thought aloud, looking between Florence and Cvareh. "I've been here for five days now, no sign of the Riders, so I'll trust we lost them in the Underground. Cvareh, did they know where you were headed?"

He shook his head. "Most would reason I'm headed to the Rivets, I would think." He patted the folio strapped around his waist.

The Rivets? *What exactly does he have?* Ari regarded him skeptically for a long moment.

"Then I think we should risk an airship, instead of traveling on foot across Ter.0," she decided aloud.

"Are you sure that's wise? We'll be easier to find in the air."

"We will be." There was no point denying or disagreeing. "But if the Riders have headed down to the Rivets in Ter.3, they won't be anywhere close enough to smell you."

"Still. . ."

"You're *sure* they don't know where you're headed?" she pushed at his indecision.

"They shouldn't know."

It wasn't the answer she was looking for, but it would have to be enough. Florence wouldn't—couldn't—make the trip on foot. She needed a transfusion within the week, and an airship would guarantee their arrival well before then.

"Don't do this on my behalf," Florence interjected quickly. The girl was too smart. Of course she put together the reason for their change in plans. "After all we've been through to get this far, if we're caught now because we take a risk just for me, I would never forgive myself."

"And if we let you die what was the point of making the effort to save you at all?" The Dragon clad in grubby Fenthri clothing crossed over to Florence. Ari watched as he patted her pupil on the shoulder in admiration.

Despite his face being almost entirely covered, Ari knew clearly what his expression was. She could almost feel it. She didn't want to allow the fractures shaped like his face upon her heart. She didn't want this Dragon to cut down the measuring stick she used to keep the world at length with his tenderness toward Florence.

"You made your decision, and it seems we have as well." She never thought there was a space for her and the Dragon between the two letters of the word "we". "We'll get on an airship tonight. Most of the vessels here seem to be headed for Faroe, but we should be able to find at least one to Keel."

"Ari, most of our supplies. . ." Florence shifted uneasily from foot to foot. "I lost them in the accident in the caves."

"We didn't have that much anyway." She brushed off the girl's concerns, focusing on what was important—the fact that she was all right. "Plus, I've had five days here waiting for you. What do you think I've been doing?"

"I should've never doubted you." Florence laughed, but it was a hollow sound that served only to hide a wince.

"No, never," Ari teased. The world was right with Florence at her side again. She'd spent most of her life without the girl. But now she couldn't imagine a world that didn't have her in it, and she would fight tooth and nail to keep her there.

Cvareh led them back to the place they had made their home. It was a small stretch of fabric suspended between some crates that offered little protection from the elements. Curled underneath it were her two filthy prison birds—thin, worse for wear, but in one piece. Helen's eyes rose and grew wide as she realized who she was looking at.

"Oh, you made it," she said dryly.

"You should've never had any doubt," Ari proclaimed, heaping on an equal portion of her own brand of arrogance. Doing so made her guilt potable. Florence had been forced to stay in this squalor for days while she had been sleeping in relative comfort in the abandoned store she'd broken into.

"Well, now that our little family is finally back together, what's the plan?" Will looked at Arianna.

"You did your part." She wasn't going to bury the lede. "As far as we're concerned, your freedom has been earned and you owe me nothing further." Boon aside, she didn't actually enjoy the feeling of people owing debts to her. She didn't want anything from anyone.

"We're leaving for Keel on the next airship we can find," Florence explained.

Her two friends shared a look.

"You are," Helen agreed. "But we've been talking, and since your teacher will not be hunting us down, we're going to head back into the Underground."

"What? Why?" Florence looked frantically between her friends.

"We're not bad at this whole 'moving people' business," Will started.

"And we think it *can* be a business," Helen interjected.

"Minus dealing with the Wretched." Arianna couldn't stop herself.

"Yes, well. . . When we're moving things—people—we'll do so on our own terms. We've learned every time we've maneuvered down there."

"You're not joining us?" Florence couldn't seem to process it.

Will shook his head. "Flor, we've always ridden in separate trikes. Sometimes we can ride side by side, but our destinations are different."

"Unless you want to join us, instead?" Helen asked hopefully. "We need a Revo for protection, just in case. You really are brilliant with gunpowder."

Florence fought to hide a smile at the well-deserved flattery.

"Plus, you could help ferry more people out of the Guilds, just like you, to live a free life doing whatever they choose."

It would be a noble cause, Arianna admitted. One that would resonate strongly with Florence as someone who had used that method herself to avoid the fatal outcomes of failing the Dragon tests. Florence had every reason to say yes.

And yet, Arianna desperately wished she wouldn't. If Florence disappeared with these two, she would likely never see her again. Florence would become her own White Wraith, operating outside the law and in the greatest secrecy possible. She would be at constant risk.

Arianna wanted to be happy for the girl. She wanted to support blindly. But the panic the very thought put in her made her tongue act differently.

"You could stay," she said softly. Florence looked at her in shock—shock Ari hoped wasn't stemming from excitement and relief. "But you should come with us to the Alchemists first. You won't last long without being transitioned to a full Chimera, even less without Dragon blood."

*If the girl leaves these two, the chances of her ever rejoining them decreases greatly*, a nagging voice in the back of Arianna's mind assured her. She only wanted what was best for Florence. She hadn't lied.

Florence looked between Ari and the two Ravens. She desperately wished she knew what was going through the girl's head.

"I can't." Florence shook her head. "Will, Helen, I can't go with you."

"You're sure? Will you meet us after you become a Chimera?" Helen squinted at Ari skeptically while the Wraith fought to keep a triumphant smile off her lips.

"I don't know. . . But Arianna is right. I need to go for that, at the very least." There was no room for hesitation in Florence's words and Arianna was pleased to note that her student clearly thought of the whole matter as her idea. "I've come this far. I need to see Cvareh through to the Alchemists. And even after that, who will make Ari's canisters for her?"

"She can always buy them." Arianna was going to sew Helen's mouth shut. She did not want to lose Florence to these people. She felt like the girl had only just entered her life and now they were trying to take her away.

"The canisters they sell in Mercury Town are wretched." Florence shook her head firmly. "I'd never let her have those."

"I'm lucky to have a Revo like you looking out for me." Arianna nudged Florence's shoulder with her own, satisfied it seemed she had no intention of leaving her side anytime soon. It wasn't every day you had the opportunity to meet another gear that fit so well against your own.

She mused on the fact as she led them all to where she had been holing up, promising Will and Helen some supplies to get them on their way. Meeting the two Ravens had proved to Ari how special Florence was, how unique it was that she had slotted nicely into Ari's world. But it equally illuminated something else she never expected. Everyone she'd met in her life could be organized into two categories: those who fit in seamlessly, and those who didn't.

She never expected Cvareh to fall in with the former, rather than the latter.

# 30
## CVAREH

Of all the ways to travel, the airship was the one Cvareh liked the best. *Anything* was better than the Underground—he'd consider diving head first into the Gods' Line before venturing down into those forsaken depths again— but it wasn't the most recent harrowing experiences that colored his opinion on the matter. They had traveled decently well on the train, and he had traversed skies and land alike on the backs of boco on Nova. But this, *this*, was something completely different.

The ship was hoisted on magic and mechanics. A giant balloon, filled and strapped into the top of the airship, supplied the majority of the lift. The rest was seen in the faint trail of magic that glittered off from the propellers on each of the golden-tipped wings, fanning out widely. The front of the airship was pointed and drawn up like the bill of a fish-eating water bird. But the back was open. Multiple tiers of viewing decks connected in to the dining room, the gaming parlor, and at the end of the residences that filled the top deck entirely.

Everything was done in pale woods and iron, accented with other dark and light stones like marble. As pretty as it was comfortable, it was the closest to home he'd felt the entire time. And that was no small wonder, as Dragons seemed to be regular patrons on airships. There were aesthetic elements the Fenthri regarded as fascinating marvels—like the curling vine-like banisters, or the wave embellishments around the cabin windows—but for a Dragon, they were nothing more than calls to the aesthetic that surrounded them on Nova.

Even now, as he stared down at the lower observation balconies, he could see the inspiration of some Dragon designer at work in the way the tile was laid and the arcs were off-set slightly. Cvareh rested his elbows on the wooden railing and watched the faint trails of magic spiraling in the wind before disappearing. It had been such a wonder, the first time he'd seen magic manifest itself in the physical world. Now it was commonplace, so much so that he didn't even think about it. And, if he *did* think about it, it was associated with Yveun Dono's Riders and their gliders. It was something that brought grief, not wonder. *Yet another thing the Dragon King has taken from us all.*

"What's so fascinating out there?" Arianna rested her elbows next to his. For a whole day, she had worn proper clothing. The coat of the White Wraith had been safely tucked away and forgotten about.

Now, her coat was of a military-inspired sort, intricate roping braided down her chest, knotted on either side and tied over clasps in the middle. The design was mirrored on the sleeves and collar. He particularly appreciated the designer's choice to add a similar embellishment right at the small of the back, though he said nothing about it.

He didn't want to admit that he had studied the taper of her trousers or the shine of her shoes. He would never confess to admiring the elegance with which she could tie her cravat to emphasize her Rivet pin. And he didn't even dwell too long on how aware he was that the roping on her jacket brought out the purple of her eyes.

"Nothing." He answered her question before his silence brought her eyes to his. "And there's actually something rather blissful about that fact." It was nice not to worry about Riders, or the Wretched, or anything else Loom had on it.

"I'm glad you find it blissful." Her tone had become bitter in an instant when her initial question had seemed so light and harmless.

"What have I done to upset you *this* time?" he asked with a sigh. She gave him a look. The more he acted like he didn't care about her moods, the more bothered she became. Cvareh savored it guiltily.

"Do you know why there's nothing out there?" Her voice had gone soft again. It was an odd contrast that Ari pulled off easily as the woman who could wear men's clothing and look wonderfully feminine while doing so.

"Because we're flying?"

She looked at him like he had just made the most idiotic statement she'd ever heard. "I mean why there's nothing on the ground beneath us. No lights, no ports, black above and black below."

"We're over Ter.0, aren't we?" It clicked for him.

She nodded, turning her attentions to the darkness once more—both within and outside.

"You were born in Ter.0, weren't you?" If she remembered the time of the Guilds before the Dragons, then she was born before Loom knew what families were. Back in the primitive days when they rounded up men and women of breeding age to reproduce on the island of Ter.0—a place owned by none of and all of the guilds.

"And I spent my first ten years studying there," she elaborated willingly.

"Then you were initiated into the Rivets after formative education?" he probed gently. It was the most personal information she had ever disclosed at once and he didn't want to say or do something that would bring it to an end.

"'Formative education.'" She repeated with a grin. It was coy and arrogant on the surface, but it had the same undercurrent that tugged down her shoulders. "*Oh-ho*, you have read about the history of Loom."

"I have." Cvareh shifted closer to her, keeping their conversation just to themselves and not speaking loudly enough that the few others milling about the deck could hear. "At least what's been written on Nova about it."

"Which I'm sure is mostly slander and propaganda."

He couldn't argue. "And the other third is just incorrect, I'm coming to find."

"Are you?" Arianna turned to look at him. She'd grease-penned in the symbol of the Rivets on her face again to avoid questions. Cvareh found the mark clashed with the curve of her jaw and the cut of her cheek. It was somewhere it didn't belong, and he suppressed the urge to take her face in his palms and rub it off with his thumb. "What else were you taught about Loom?"

"That its people are weak," he answered easily. "All my life, I've been told the Fenthri are pitiable creatures. That they were simply roaming around in a barren world, barely surviving by trying to establish an order they couldn't maintain—hence no king or supreme ruler—and that the Dragons were their saviors."

She snorted in amusement.

"The Dragons have done nothing for Loom but cause disruption in a system they shouldn't have touched because they didn't understand it."

"Help me understand it?" He wanted to know more. Cvareh mentally insisted it was a result of spending time on Loom, and that was certainly a part of it. But he wanted to know about her. What had made Arianna into the woman she was. A woman who outclassed Dragon and Fenthri and Chimera alike.

She said nothing—barely moved, barely breathed. Her silence made him hang on her every action all the more. He waited for what was percolating in the back of her mind to bubble forward.

"What will you do, Cvareh, after you make it to the Alchemists' Guild and deliver what it is you've carried so far, so diligently?" Arianna stared him down, pinning his toes to the floor with the weight of her interrogation. In her mind, she drew honesty from him like moisture from a cool stone on a hot day.

"I don't know," he confessed. "I may return to Nova to help my sister. She's lied for me, I believe, making up some story about where I am to prevent my arrest."

"What do you call the King's Riders then?"

"Think of them more as assassins than knights while they're here." He shrugged. "I'm not supposed to be on Loom, so they're not technically hunting me. Being here is all one big gray area."

She snickered. "I'm not sure if you intended that as a pun, but it was rather funny."

Her joke was so foreign from her usual seriousness that Cvareh had to stare and process it for a long moment before he realized it had been sincere. Arianna had found humor in what he said. Not only had she not immediately assumed the worst possible implication for his words, but she had found *humor* in them. It was a far cry from the woman who'd held blades against his tongue, threatening to cut it out if he bothered her.

"I hadn't." He laughed lightly. "But it is amusing in hindsight."

"You seem close with your sister," Arianna mused after a long moment. "I'm not surprised you have a whisper link with her."

He almost asked her how she knew about the link. But for someone who never seemed to miss a thing, it was simple to see how Arianna had arrived at the conclusion. He'd mentioned Petra fondly before, and he'd told Ari he had magic in his ears. She'd seen him reporting in.

"It would make sense that you would want to go back to her," Ari whispered so faintly that he almost thought the wind was playing tricks on him. But his hearing was too good for that. He knew exactly what she'd said, and the quickening of his heartbeat knew it too.

"I could stay." They were the only words he could say that would offer a brief respite from the pressure that had been building in his chest.

"What?" She straightened, her arms sliding off the railing. One hand rested on it as Arianna turned to face him.

The look she gave him almost made the feeling worse. Did she realize how her eyes pleaded? Was she aware of the softness in the slope of her shoulders, or the way her hand had crept closer to his on the railing? Cvareh instinctively responded in kind, his body language unfurling to meet hers, to face her chest to chest as they had so many times.

"For a little, I'm sure I could stay, or I could leave and come back quickly." His words were making no sense. His mind was making no sense. Nothing about them had ever made any sense and yet...he thrived off her. Her blood, the way she pushed those around her, her sharp mind and sharper blades.

"Why would you do that?" Fear penetrated her stare. She was nervous of his answer, which made it all the clearer that she was becoming aware of what was happening—what had been happening—at the same time he was.

This woman had become something more to him. He didn't know what quite yet. But he wanted to find out.

"Because I have work I can do with the rebels at the Alchemists' Guild. I can help them," he lied, mostly. Her lips pressed into a small frown; she knew it, too. Before she could press him on it, however, he changed the direction of the wind that blew between them. "What will you do after you have your boon? What do you even want your boon to be?"

Arianna fought a war against his words. She struggled to such a degree that the pain from the battle made it onto her face. Why did she fight so hard to keep him out?

"All my life, well, almost. . . I wanted the Dragon King dead," Arianna breathed. "But I know your boon won't be strong enough for that. I know asking for that would solve nothing. Overthrowing one tyrant only makes room for another. So, if I am selfish, I would ask for something simple: the death of a Dragon."

"Who?"

She shook her head.

"*Why*, then?" He didn't want to let go of the connection they had found between them. Not when he was finally seeing the true colors of the gray woman who had enchanted him.

"Because the Dragon betrayed us all. He was responsible for the death of the last rebellion. The deaths of my teacher, my friends, and the woman I loved."

*The woman she loved.* He knew Fenthri didn't share the Dragons' concept of family. He knew they had structured breeding before the Dragon King took over and reorganized their guilds and society. He knew that, despite the fact they could not reproduce and therefore the union could bear no true meaning, the Fenthri would couple with the same sex if it suited them to do so.

He knew that. But now it stood before him and he suddenly had to pass an opinion on it. And the only emotion he found was disappointment. Heartbreaking disappointment.

He scolded himself internally. Even if she had been the slightest bit sweet on him, what did he think could come of any type of relationship with a Fenthri—a Chimera? There was almost no point in exploring it.

"I have told you of my heart." Arianna leaned against the railing, folding her arms over her chest as if to guard the remaining details she hadn't shared. "Tell me of yours. What makes you so convicted to reach the Alchemists?"

Cvareh sighed softly, other matters still clouding his mind. It wouldn't hurt to share the schematics with her. She might know what it was, but that could only prove his sincerity for her cause at this point.

Unfastening the folio on his hip, Cvareh pulled back the top flap and selected one of the smaller pieces of schematic. He didn't know what it detailed, some inner working likely. He passed it over to her and she stilled instantly, taking it.

"They're schematics for the Philosopher's Box. With this—"

"Where did you get this?" she uttered, deathly quiet. Arianna remained focused on the paper in her hands. Her fingers tensed, crumpling the edges. "Where did you get this?"

"I was told that—"

"You were told?" Her jaw thrust forward as her eyes rose to scrutinize him. He could practically hear the grit of her teeth. "Told what? Told by who?"

"I was told this was what the rebellion had been working on after the One Year War. That the Dragon King thwarted the possibility of creating a perfect Chimera army. We knew if I had it, I could earn the trust of the Rebels and we could continue work."

"You could earn their trust," she repeated mockingly. "No, now I see what this really is." Arianna crumpled the paper in her fist.

"You can't do that!"

She prodded him in the chest. "I will never take you to the Alchemists. I will never let you close. If you get off this airship and even think about heading to the Guild, I will cut you down where you stand. Crawl back to Nova, Dragon scum."

Arianna stormed past him, the paper still in hand.

Cvareh was left to catch his balance as her shoulder clipped his. He was left wondering what he had done, how his branch of peace had been turned into the first shot fired in a new war between them. He turned to call after her and, as if sensing his intention, she spun in place.

"And don't you think about coming near Flor or me ever again," she snarled, then continued in toward the cabins.

The other patrons of the ship whispered to each other, tittering as though they had just witnessed a scandalous lovers' quarrel. Cvareh didn't know what they had seen. Because this wasn't the Arianna he knew. At every turn the woman seemed like she was someone different. Every bit of clarity he'd gained into her true nature only served to confound him further.

# 31
## FLORENCE

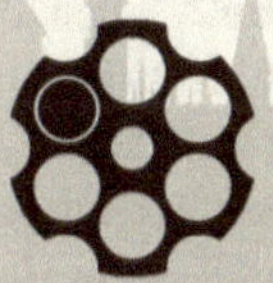

ARI SLAMMED THE DOOR BEHIND HER SO HARD THE DESK THAT WAS BOLTED TO the wall next to it shook, a small tool rolling off its surface. Both Arianna and Florence paid the out-of-place screwdriver no mind. Ari looked at anything else but the paper she'd left on the table with a shout. She set to pacing the narrow cavern, her feet quickly forging ruts in the plush carpet.

"What's going on?" Florence finally asked, when it was clear the woman had no intention of doing or saying anything more than fevered mutterings.

"I knew it. I should've known all along," Ari seethed. "He was never our friend, Flor. He's a Dragon and a King's man in his own way. He works for the King himself."

"What?" The machine in Ari's mind had jumped three gears and Florence couldn't figure out how she'd gotten from one spot to the next.

"This whole time, he's been working for the King. It's been a ploy to get us to trust him. It's just like last time. He came down and he's convinced us that he can be trusted, never mind what his real motives are."

"Ari, stop." Florence grabbed her friend by both shoulders, which trembled slightly under her fingers—a feeling Florence had never felt from Ari before. Fear and rage mixed potently, bleeding into her veins.

She kept herself calm. It would do no good if Florence blindly agreed to what Ari was claiming. One of them had to keep her head and sort through this as logically as possible. Florence tightened her grip. "Arianna, take a deep breath and get a grip on yourself."

"Flor, you have no idea—you, you bled so much for this man, you put yourself in a position of being forced to become a Chimera—" The word still brought ample shame to Arianna's face. "And he was playing you all along."

"I don't believe you," Florence declared. Her head was getting fuzzy from standing so long. She was practically bedridden all the time now from the effects of Dragon blood without being a proper Chimera. It had only taken one day on the airship for Florence to realize that Arianna had made the right decision in taking the risk, at least when it came to her own wellbeing. She would've never made it in a trek across Ter.0.

"You have no idea what he's done. What he intends to do."

"Then tell me." Florence sat, finally. Her hands fell from Ari's shoulders to her hands. She pulled the other woman down toward her. Arianna reluctantly obliged, falling onto the narrow bed they'd been sharing for the journey. "What happened that has you in such a state? You and he were fine over dinner."

*Better than fine, actually.* It had been slow coming, but in the weeks they'd spent together, Arianna and the Dragon seemed to have found a kind of mutual peace. After the floating prison and the Underground, that peace blossomed into appreciation. Florence had watched it grow all along, two people determined to hate each other realizing just how much they could complement each other.

Florence knew why she liked Cvareh: He reminded her of Ari. Certainly, they weren't identical. But they were both driven, both determined; they both set course for something only they could see on a distant shore. She suspected Ari saw much the same in the man, that he sparked memories within her. But now, those memories seemed to be rife with pain.

"He wants to see Loom forever under the thumb of the Dragon King. He wants to keep us under the Dragon's control for eternity," Arianna repeated her earlier words, unhelpfully.

"If you want me to believe you on this, Ari, you'll have to give me some better proof," Florence encouraged gently.

"My word isn't good enough?"

Florence gave her an encouraging smile, and shook her head. "Not this time, I'm afraid. I know Cvareh. I've already formulated my own thoughts and opinions on him. This is not a story of times long gone that you recount for me and I must take at face value. This is a situation in which I have my own empirical evidence to support what I believe to be true. If you want me to change my mind, you must present new evidence."

Arianna stared at her for a long moment. Something in Florence's words had penetrated through the mindless aggravation and hurt. Ari shook her head, laughing bitterly.

"Since when did you become the scientist?"

"I have a good teacher," she replied easily, nudging Ari with her shoulder. "Now, tell me what's happened."

The other woman sighed heavily, running her hands through her cotton-colored hair. Indecision didn't fit Arianna well, and she struggled every second she spent thinking about Florence's request. But finally, Ari stood, walking over to the slip of paper she'd discarded with such passion earlier.

Just looking at it brought a scowl back to Ari's face. Florence had to brace herself once more for the torrent of emotions that ripped through Ari and broke over her shoulders.

"This. *This* is what he's been struggling to deliver."

Florence examined the paper closely, leaning forward to get a better look. Parts were done in pencil, and those had been smudged by Ari's treatment. The darker lines done in ink over top persevered, however. It looked like some kind of pumping mechanism? Or perhaps an engine? It wasn't something designed to explode, of that much she could be certain.

"What is it?" She failed to see how this tiny bit of a Rivet's sketch had upset Ari so much—even if Ari, as a Rivet, could decipher its intention. It was next to useless in its current state. She knew schematics required dozens of drawings, often of the same thing, to make assembly and creation expressly clear.

"It's a sketch detailing a part of the Philosopher's Box."

"What?" Florence had only heard of such a thing existing in theory.

It was regarded as a clever exercise for students of all ages. What if a perfect Chimera were possible? One who could possess all the powers of a Dragon and not become forsaken from the stress of the magic on their body? How would that change Loom? How would it make things different?

Most knew the answer: It would make everything different. With access to that much magic on Loom, they could create larger, more intricate machines without the need of backup mechanics to run them. They could successfully fly their own gliders up as high as Nova without losing control. They would need less food, so the Harvesters could spend more effort on deeper mining of rarer minerals. And they could stand a fighting chance against Dragons.

The Philosopher's Box would change everything, and that was why no one believed it could ever be real.

"This is meant to be a Philosopher's Box," Ari insisted again. "You can see it in the casing, the way it open and closes in place of heart valves here, right here."

"In place of heart valves?" Florence repeated, confused. She'd always imagined the Philosopher's Box to be a sort of Chimera-making contraption—like a golden coffin.

"Yes, it's obvious by the tension in the springs and the way this is drawn to have a circle stopper."

Florence would have to take her word for it.

"Let's say for a minute that I believed you on all this." Ari looked instantly hurt that she would imply any differently. Florence continued, determined. "That this is a part of a schematic for an actual Philosopher's Box. Why would Cvareh bring it to Loom, to the resistance? Doesn't that seem like he's trying to help us?"

Arianna didn't miss a beat. "He's doing it to earn their trust. He wants them to think they can trust him."

"And what if he wants them to think that because they actually can?" Florence shook her head. "If he just wanted to try conning them into belief, couldn't he have brought anything and said it was a piece of an unfinished Philosopher's Box? By the time they finished investigating, he could have what he wanted."

"It's more realistic if he brings them the real thing." Ari set the paper back down on the table with a sigh.

"You don't quite believe yourself. . ." She stood, taking a step toward her teacher. Florence wrapped her arms around the woman's waist, resting her cheek in the center of Ari's back. "You want to, you're trying to, but you don't believe the words you're saying, either."

"I do."

"You don't."

"How can you say that with such certainty?" Arianna grumbled.

Florence laughed softly. Her teacher, the brash and beautiful. "Tell me this: Does Cvareh still have his head and heart intact?"

"He does." Though Ari's tone implied it was a fact she might regret. An error she might be inclined to remedy sooner over later.

"Since when have you spared a Dragon's life when you thought he was guilty of crimes against Loom? Or even the sincere possibility of committing crimes against Loom?" Florence waited a long second, giving Arianna a chance to grab for straws at an answer she knew she didn't have. "That's right, you don't. So somewhere in you, you must be questioning this. You must be wondering if what he's saying is true. His actions must have spoken to your heart clearly enough that you know he is not the evil you're painting him to be."

"You don't know him," Arianna whispered.

"After all we've been through? I think I have a pretty good idea. And I think you do too." Florence rounded Arianna, leaning against the small table for support. The older woman looked down at her tiredly. "Ari, I don't know what demons you face. I know they're there, but I promised you I would never ask. Don't let the shadows of the past smother the possibility for a bright future."

It looked as though she was going to triumph. Arianna's face relaxed, but the older woman's eyes pressed closed, and she took a deep breath through her nose as though bracing herself.

Arianna opened her mouth to speak, when the airship lurched violently. Florence stumbled, off-balance and too hopelessly weak to correct herself. Arianna grabbed her, supporting her as a primal cry rose from outside. They heard the sound at the same time and it washed the gray from both their faces— the magical *zip* of a Dragon Rider's glider.

"Bloody cogs." Arianna was tearing off her clothing, throwing it about the room in a sprint for her harness and coat. "They weren't supposed to have any idea where we were headed. Do you see now, Flor? The man lies! He's in cahoots with them."

"Then why are they hunting him?"

"It's all a ruse!"

The ship jostled again. Florence gripped the table for support. "This is a pretty deathly ruse."

"You just stay here." Ari tightened her harness, feeling for her daggers, running some line through her winch box. "Stay here for now, and don't be anywhere I can't find you. I have a feeling we'll be needing to make an exit before we reach port."

Florence nodded, looking about the room, already making a list of what she needed to pack. "But find Cvareh too."

"Oh, I will." Arianna left with murder in her eyes.

She sighed heavily, leaning against the table. If she could go her entire life without ever seeing another King's Rider, that would be ideal. Florence leaned back, wondering for a brief moment how she would make that come to pass. Her hand rested on the paper and Florence brought it up for inspection with a sigh.

Such a tiny thing had caused so much drama in what had been going so smoothly.

It was then that she noticed a small area that Arianna's fingers had covered the first time she'd shown the page to Florence. Her eyes looked over it once, twice, three times. A few notes were scribbled on the paper, ripped off in the corner where the drawing had been taken from a larger schematic.

Florence didn't even read what they said. She was too obsessed with the way the 'h' curved in the script, the weight of the 'a', the overall slant and clarity of the letters. The penmanship was unmistakable.

It answered the question of why Arianna had been so upset—how she had known so much about the paper—at least enough that Florence could now make educated guesses. But those only created deeper questions. Questions she had sworn never to ask. Questions about Arianna's history.

Why was the woman's handwriting on a schematic she claimed Cvareh had acquired with malicious intent? Why was her penmanship on *anything* that could even closely resemble the Philosopher's Box?

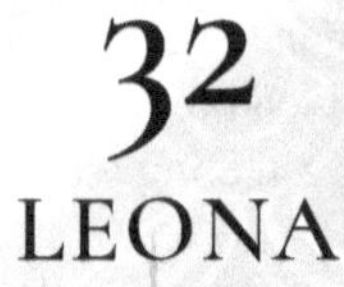

# 32
## LEONA

Leona should be exhausted. But the moment the airship had emerged from the starless sky, like a shining beacon heralding her triumph, there was nothing but power under the wings of her glider. There was nowhere for them to run. No sea to mask their scent, no Underground to crawl into like rats.

She had been expecting to face them in Keel. After all the Wraith's precision and care in their travels, Leona expected them to think of some other way to cross the last of the distance to the Alchemists' Guild. Some way that wouldn't trail their scent through the air in all directions.

She didn't rule out the possibility that it was some kind of trap or attack. After all, the Wraith could make seemingly any situation work to her advantage. If she could turn a prison break into a victory against three of the King's Riders, she could somehow turn an airship into a floating fortress.

So Leona wasn't taking any chances. She wasn't interested in being elegant or tactful in her approach. She wasn't going to imagine herself above the Wraith. She was going to fight in the most underhanded ways she knew how. And she was going to finally bring victory for Yveun Dono.

Strapped over her back was a large weapon. It was cumbersome to wield and awkward to feel, but the Revolvers had assured her it was capable of an explosion like no other. Leona stabilized her glider and planted her feet. She looked over to Camile who did the same without needing to be told.

"Let's clip its wings." Leona reached for the weapon.

"Leona'Kin, there *are* members of House Rok on that vessel." Leona smelled them, too. Not many, but a few mixed among the bland stench of Fenthri and haze of other Dragons.

"No half measures, Camile." She tracked her weapon over the wing. "If they are strong enough, they will survive."

It wasn't too tall of an expectation. Dragons were hearty and House Rok was the strongest of them all. If any emerged, Leona would see them to whatever business they had on Loom personally.

Camile did the same with her gun. Leona had to hold in laughter at the sight. Her companion looked ridiculous with a weapon in hand. Though the same could be said of her. It had been Sybil and her pack that ran with guns. Leona and her acolytes always preferred the Dragons' traditional means of destruction: claws.

Still, when on Loom she would fight as the Fenthri did if it served her means. The thinking was a very Xin approach. But to kill a Xin, she conceded, one needed to think like a Xin. Terrifying as that might be.

Leona leveled her weapon and gripped the trigger. The Revos had given them only one canister each, insisting they wouldn't need more. When Leona pushed back, delicately and not so delicately, they still did not come up with more canisters, saying that the chemicals and powders required simply weren't kept in stock.

Leona forced her magic into the long gun. The second she did, runes lit up along the handle and barrel. Once activated, she had no choice but to keep feeding it. They leeched magic from her hungrily, siphoning it out through both hands. The runes glowed in the darkness so brightly they drew their shapes with beams of light in the hazy night air around her. The last rune on the barrel sparked, joining the rest.

Leona wasted no time and pulled the trigger.

A bolt of magic shot forward in a straight line and missed the wing by a small margin. Leona screamed in annoyance. She was sure it was her sister's heart that lingered somewhere in the depths of her magic that cackled hellishly, scolding her for all the times she'd skipped shooting practice.

The magic ray continued forward, striking the ground far below. In a reverse chain reaction, the beam exploded backward, fanning out in all directions. The edge of the magic clipped the wing she had been aiming for, which had already moved well ahead, and disintegrated the edge of it on contact. At least she'd taken out some of the gold helping keep the airship aloft.

Leona threw away the weapon and grabbed the levers of her craft with a heavy sigh. The Revos hadn't been lying to her. Despite all her boasting and arrogance, it had taken a lot out of her to make such a shot. Bruises dotted her skin where blood vessels had broken. She focused on nothing more than keeping her glider aloft, letting her magic slowly replenish through the fatigue.

Her attention was pulled left as another shot exploded from across the airship. Camile's magic burned a slightly different color from Leona's, but it was just as large. Even better, it hit its mark. Leona howled with bloodthirsty joy at the sight of the beam of magic cutting through the wing of the airship.

Magic glittered across its surface, hungry for sustenance. It consumed the wing whole, and the side of the airship when the beam expanded. Even better, the shockwave clipped the delicate balloon helping hold the ship aloft. It expelled air with a mighty wheeze and the vessel lurched through the air, swaying and dropping precipitously with only one wing to support its flight.

Leona looked at the triumphant smile Camile wore and rolled her eyes. "Don't you start bragging."

"The one thing Sybil was good for!" Camile called back.

"You practiced shooting with Sybil?"

"Someone under you needed to know a little about Loom's weaponry. I thought it would pay off eventually." Camile winked.

Pay off it did. Leona vowed that when they returned to Nova, she would see Camile rewarded handsomely by the Dono. She would figure out later what that reward would look like. For now, she would remain focused on what would get her back to Nova: killing Cvareh.

Men and women ran around the airship, shouting and screaming. Just a tiny little act and their peaceful night was thrown into delicious madness. Leona rounded the airship, watching them sprint to the back balconies in confusion. She caught glimpses of crowded hallways and utter chaos within.

But she didn't see Cvareh or the Wraith.

She would remain on her glider until she had visual confirmation of them. And, if she must, she would hand-pick them from the airship's rubble. On the lowest balcony in the back, a crowd was beginning to amass. They tripped and stumbled over the pitching of the airship as it continued to fall through the sky. Small gliders were being loaded frantically. Dragons stepped forward to man each of them, their magic more certain to provide sustainable lift or flight than any Chimera's.

Leona made an involuntary gagging motion at the sight of it. Dragons helping Fenthri. It was disgusting. She wanted her kin aboard those tiny fliers, certainly. But Fenthri? Let them all die; there were far too many of them anyway.

Still, she hung back. She waited. She would not charge in hastily. She would let her plan unfurl like a banner of victory on the winds she had called up beneath her wings.

Leona was taking another loop toward the front of the airship when she felt the characteristic snap of magic across her mind. Time resumed itself normally —there had been only a second of stillness. The Fenthri moved as normal, completely unaware of what had happened. But the Dragons all looked at each other blearily.

She frantically searched the decks for the source of the time-stop. A commotion summoned her attention, men and women shouting in panic at a group of three that had pushed their way onto a tiny emergency glider. The young Fenthri—Florence—shouted at her master, who was fending off others from getting on their emergency escape. In the back was Cvareh, looking like the complete idiot he was behind the relatively simple handles.

This was what she'd been waiting for. Leona dove, landing her small vessel hard atop the heads of Fenthri, crushing them into a bloody smear on the deck beneath her. The other Fen scattered and pushed on all the edges of the deck in panic. More rescue gliders launched. The Wraith's girl pulled a few others onto the platform where she and Cvareh stood.

Leona charged.

"Cvareh—go!" the Wraith screamed.

"Ari!" Florence cried.

"Go, go now if anything you ever said to me was true." There was a bitter pain in the Wraith's voice that hadn't been there before.

"I'm not letting you go anywhere!" Leona lunged.

The Wraith spun and met her, blade to talon. Leona bared her teeth and the woman did the same. She was truly hideous, flat teeth and gray skin clashing with bright Dragon eyes. But she moved with the speed of a Dragon, and responded with the strength of a Dragon, and she had no hesitation in any of it.

The small glider carrying Cvareh and the Wraith's girl dropped away. Leona turned her head skyward. She didn't see Camile, but she trusted the other Rider to respond. "Camile! On Cvareh!"

"Oh, she won't be," the Wraith announced triumphantly. "Canisters that can take down Dragons in one shot are rare. I'd been holding onto that one. . . But I was hoping for you."

Leona roared, pushing off the Wraith. The woman slid as the deck tilted, the captain struggling to keep the airship as level as possible. She spun in the crimson blood of her fellow Fen that oozed from under Leona's glider.

She was expecting the Wraith's barbed whip. And rather than dodging it like a fool, she snatched it from mid air, her hand on the hilt of the golden dagger. It struggled against her fingers, like a bird trying to break free. Leona held it all the tighter. She yanked, trying to catch the Wraith off-balance.

But the Wraith jumped, and the winch box on her hip propelled her to Leona. She stepped off the ground on her toes, twisting in the air over the line to bring her heel across Leona's face. Leona reeled, releasing the dagger to free her hand. She slashed and the Wraith dropped backward, rolling away as Leona tried to shatter her bones with a mighty step.

They matched blow to blow, dodge for dodge as the failing airship plummeted through the sky. Leona knew they were nearing the ground when the Fen began to take their chances jumping for trees rather than meeting the earth with the airship. She growled and threw the Wraith off her, leaping for her own glider.

"I'm not letting you go!" The knife on the end of the Wraith's line looped around her neck, forcing Leona to fall backward or be choked into submission.

Free of the cable, Leona gasped for air, the bruising in her neck quickly healing.

"If I'm going down, you're coming with me," the Wraith declared.

"You'll die, and I'll be unscathed, ready to skin your little pet and Dragon alive." Leona snarled, still sliding her feet back to her glider. Even if there was a chance for her to survive the carnage, she didn't want to risk a stray beam or spear of wood carving her through the heart. Not when her glider rested right next to her.

"I don't think so," the woman grinned madly. The wind howled through her words, across the deck littered with bodies and carnage from their fight and the chaos that had erupted from the falling airship. "I have a boon to collect. And I'm not going to die before I get it."

"We'll see about that." Leona began sprinting for the woman and this time. The Chimera didn't even flinch, boldly standing her ground. There wasn't another second to be wasted as the airship reached its terminal destination. The Wraith waited for her charge.

They both half sidestepped in weak attempts at dodges. Claws cut through gray Fenthri skin. Daggers tore through Dragon bone and muscle.

And *gold* exploded on both sides.

Where Leona had expected a heart, her fingers landed on something metallic. All training faded in utter confusion as she ran the pads of her fingers over its square shape. She gasped, blood bubbling up her throat from the dagger in her chest.

"What are you?" She whispered, staring at the place where her fingers protruded from the other woman's chest.

Gold blood streamed down the Wraith's garb, identical to Leona's. She tried to look over the woman's face time and again. Was she somehow a Dragon in disguise? No, an illusion would've faltered by now.

"*What are you?*" Leona repeated. Her ears howled as she tried to piece together what she had been fighting the whole time she'd been hunting Cvareh on Loom.

"I'm *perfect*."

The woman twisted her dagger, once, twice. She spun it in place, pulverizing Leona's chest cavity. She felt bone shatter under the blade, sinew stretch and snap against its edge. The Wraith stepped away, reaching for Leona's chest.

*She was going to eat her heart.*

Leona wheezed. She clung to life, clung to her duty. It was the best death a Rider could hope for, a death while serving their King. She clung uselessly and weakly to the woman's forearm as the White Wraith ripped the remnants of her heart from her chest, bit into it, and ended the life of the King's Master Rider.

# 33
## CVAREH

He had flown a sum total of one other glider in his life. That time it had been in a rush as well, stolen. He'd barreled down toward the Gods' Line in utter terror, gripping the handles with all his might, pushing as much magic as he could into his feet and around the body of the glider.

It had been how he'd started his journey. And now it seemed it would end much the same. He had no idea what was below him. The faint glow of lights dotted the fast-approaching horizon, winking in and out from the trees that swayed, blocking their path.

"Ari's still up there!" Florence's eyes were glued to the smoking remains of the airship, plummeting down to earth like a swan at the end of its song, taking one last dive.

He gripped the handles tightly. After what she'd said to him, he shouldn't care. She'd stolen his schematic, she'd cast him aside, she'd shown him exactly how little he meant to her. And now...now he should shrug her off like she was nothing. He should focus on the final sprint of his journey. If she wanted to deal with the Riders for him, he should take the gift without a second thought.

But he strained his neck, looking over his shoulder. She was still up there, headed toward death on his behalf. It tied knots in his stomach. It flipped his heart up-side down. It broke his resolve.

Pantheon above save him, he might care for the woman more than he'd ever bargained for. That brash and unfashionable Wraith had lived up to her word from New Dortam. She had stolen his heart after all.

Cvareh looked forward again, grimacing inward. Yes, let the first woman he'd developed any kind of confusing but substantial feelings for be a Fenthri. Not just any Fenthri, but *that* Fenthri.

"We have to go back for her." Florence grabbed his arm, pleading.

"Flor, I'm trying to prevent us from dying right now. It's what she wanted. It's what Arianna wanted," he repeated uselessly, as if that would absolve him of his frantic worry for the woman. "She's stronger than any Chimera I've ever met. She's stronger than most Dragons I've known. If anyone will survive, it's her."

"She's as mortal as you or I! She only dons that illusion because it suits her."

"You think I'm not aware of that!" he snarled. Florence looked at him in surprise. "You think I am not aware that she is just a woman underneath that white coat? I assure you, I am painfully, frustratingly, confusingly aware."

The girl stilled. Her hands fell from his person to grip the railing of the oddly shaped glider for stability. She was still weak, he noted. She would continue to decay until she had her transfusion and made the transition to the halfway state of existence known as being a Chimera.

"When did it happen?" Florence whispered.

Cvareh looked at her, cursing her for being so astute. But if anyone were to notice, it would have been Florence. After all the time she'd spent with him and Arianna, she would sense the subtle changes with even the most cursory observations.

"I'm figuring that out myself." He didn't mince words. "But now isn't quite the time."

Three Fenthri huddled in the front of his glider, clinging to the railing for dear life. Florence had insisted the three join them. The girl refused to take a whole glider to herself despite Arianna's goals and worries. Her good nature even in the face of danger and death shined through.

"Brace yourselves," he shouted as the first tree scraped the bottom of the glider.

Controlled falling he could barely manage. But the amount of magic required to keep the wings aloft, descend evenly—they were skills he'd never learned or even thought to work on. The added difficulty of dodging the silent sentinels of the dark forest made the idea of a smooth landing impossible. He just hoped he wouldn't kill everyone before they touched the ground.

Branches scraped at them as they broke through the tree line. Cvareh's right eye was gouged out by a rogue wooden hook and he cried out in pain, fighting to keep his focus on the task at hand while his eye slowly regrew. He swung right and left, pulling on the handles, his magic straining to keep them aloft and avoid the thick trunks of the trees.

They came in hot and fast, crashing against the ground and sending a tidal wave of brush, leaves, and dirt scattering away in all directions. Two people up front were thrown off, and Florence nearly was as well. Cvareh grabbed for the young woman, pinning her against his chest as he grabbed the railing with his other hand. The glider finally slammed into a fallen tree, tipping forward and purging the last of its contents.

Cvareh twisted in the air, placing himself between Florence and the ground. He had all the wind knocked out of him and his back was shredded from a twig or ten as they skidded to a stop. He panted for air, not moving for a long moment.

Florence did the same before rolling off him with a groan. They both let the world spin and slowly settle into place. The high canopy of the forest was thick, not allowing any of the ambient light from the moon above the clouds that coated Loom through. It wasn't much better than the Underground.

Loom was a dark world of gray people and horrors. It was full of struggle and nine-hundred and ninety-nine reasons to die. The Fenthri were the people who found the one reason to live, time and again.

As if to prove the point, Florence sat with a groan. The girl, for all her bruises and exhaustion, moved before he did. He watched her blink, trying to process in the darkness.

She jumped when a large rumble shook the earth, followed by the boom of an explosion through the trees. The airship had finally joined them. Florence grabbed her shirt over her heart, struggling to her feet, pushing herself forward, stumbling, getting up again, striving to get to her teacher.

Cvareh wouldn't let her struggle alone. He stood as well, crossing to her front and kneeling with his back to her.

"We'll move faster if you let me carry you."

Understanding, Florence wrapped her arms around his shoulders, letting him grab her thighs. She weighed next to nothing. He suspected her long raven colored hair was half of her overall mass. He knew where they were headed, and started in that direction.

"Where are you going?" one of the other Fenthri called to them. "We should stay with the glider. They'll send search parties from Keel."

"You can wait. We had someone on the airship we're going to find," Florence replied.

"No one survived that. And going wandering in the Skeleton Forest alone is just inviting the endwig to attack," the man cautioned.

"You don't know the woman we're looking for. There's no way she'd let a little airship crash kill her."

"Suit yourselves." The man shrugged. He pulled a signal flare from the compartment of the glider and shot it up into the air.

Cvareh and Florence walked in the opposite direction. He set a sustainable pace, quick but not fast enough to exhaust him before they reached their destination. Florence's small head rested on his shoulder, her breathing consistent in his ear.

"Thank you for going back for her," she whispered.

"You never had any doubt I would." He smiled tiredly at himself.

"It's in the opposite direction of where you want to go."

"No." He shook his head. "This is the exact direction I want to go."

The three of them had set out for the Alchemists' Guild together. They would make it together, he resolved. He wasn't leaving Arianna behind. He still had a lot to learn about the woman. He wanted to understand every flavor he'd ever tasted of her. He wanted to know what made shadows cloud her eyes in broad daylight. He wanted to know what made her different from anyone he'd ever met.

They arrived at the crash site without incident. Panting, Cvareh eased Florence to the ground. He took gulps of air, trying to split through the scents.

"Ari!" Florence called. "Arianna!"

Smoke, oil, coal, grease, steel, iron, wood, bronze, pine. They filled his nose, lit up like a giant candle and the twisted airship was the wick. He walked in a circle, inviting every scent.

Then he got a waft of strawberry. Cvareh looked around him in panic for the light, out-of-place scent. *Leona.* Where was she?

His talons shot out from his fingers. A growl rose in his throat. If the King's Bitch survived at Arianna's expense, he would switch them personally in the chambers of Lord Xin. He would steal his Fenthri's soul back from the gods themselves.

The scent led him to a sight he wasn't expecting. He should've known what it meant when it didn't move. Leona's body had been thrown from the airship and lay face-first in the pine needles not far off, her ruby-colored skin illuminated by the orange flames. Cvareh knew she was dead before he flipped her over and saw the hole in her chest.

*Arianna had done it.* She'd killed the King's Master Rider. Cvareh wanted to cheer, but a sort of quiet fear underscored the thought. This was Leona, a woman with more beads than any other Rider. She was known for being equal parts ruthlessness and loyalty. And she'd been felled by a Chimera.

The wind shifted, and his nose was no longer cluttered with the smoke and flame.

"Who is that?" Florence called nervously, seeing the body he was crouched over.

"We're safe, for now. She's dead." Cvareh stood, sniffing the air. It was clear and fresh, just the heady scent of pine riding the wind. *Had he imagined it?*

Another gust, and the rogue scent of cedar cut through the trees, accented by honeysuckle. It brightened the night and restored his every sense. His feet found strength, his heart beat harder, his mouth watered. Even his magic pulsed outward, an automatic reaction to the magic he had imbibed.

It was like smelling his favorite meal when he hadn't eaten for months. It was like finding the accent to a fine coat. He didn't need her, but gods he wanted her.

Arianna lay prone a short distance from Leona's glider. She'd been trying to fly it away, he realized. Magic that most Dragons struggled to muster, she'd tackled when presented with no other choice.

"Ari! Is it Ari?" Florence was slow behind him. He heard her curse under her breath as she collapsed against a tree to regain her strength before continuing forward again.

"It is." He fell to his knees beside the woman.

"Is she alive? Is she breathing? Will she be all right?"

"She's alive." He didn't know the answers to the rest of her frantic questions.

The woman's magic was weak and struggling to repair the internal bleeding that was drowning her. Her left arm was twisted and her foot was snapped. Cvareh popped them back into place so they'd heal right.

Even unconscious, the pain of it brought a moan from Arianna's lips.

"Can you give her your magic? Like she gave you?" Florence asked.

It would certainly help. But he'd never let anyone imbibe off him before. It raised warning flags, despite the fact that she'd let him consume her magic.

Scowling at himself, Cvareh bit his tongue. Blood filled his mouth from where his canine had pierced the muscle. His hands grabbed her cheeks gently, situating her face upward. He couldn't stop his thumb from smearing away the remnants of the drawn Guild Mark. It was nothing but a blemish on her beautiful face.

Gently prying open her lips, Cvareh leaned forward. He felt her breath on his cheek as his face neared. His own lips parted slightly, letting the blood drip into her mouth. He waited, mouth on hers, for her reflex to swallow.

For a woman who looked like she was made of stone and steel, she was soft and warm. She was strong, and yet in that moment seemed so fragile under his hands. He opened his mouth again, letting more blood—more magic—seep into her.

He didn't like this delicate Arianna. He wanted the woman he knew back. He wanted the woman who would challenge him at every turn. Drive him crazy. Push him to the edge that made him want to cling harder and beg for more. He wanted it all. He wanted her to always be at his side, threatening to cut him if he was stupid.

His magic began to grow in her. He felt the connection of warmth it sparked from his body to hers. Like an ember fanned to a flame by both of their lives. They were entwined, slowly, surely, certainly. As long as he lived, she would. He would see to that much.

He opened his mouth again and her tongue pressed against his, her mouth moving to fit his hungrily. Her teeth raked against his lip and blood smeared between them.

Cvareh's fingers pressed around the back of her neck, and he almost held his breath. He wanted to stop time for her, with her, so that he could savor her shamelessly for another long moment. But he pulled away, meeting her open eyes—they glowed the color of lavender in the night, heightened by the flood of his magic.

She didn't push him away, she didn't scold him, she didn't reach for her daggers—if she even still had them. Arianna stared up at him, and he stared down at her, holding her face, holding her in the small corner of the world in which they existed. And if he were to exist nowhere else, ever, he would be content.

"I finally know what you taste like," she whispered.

If she had asked, he would've let her have a second chance at the flavor.

# 34
## ARIANNA

A cool gust rushed through her veins. It was crisp and fresh, like winter air across a frozen lake. Shocking to her system, but not in a way that slowed her down. Rather, in a way that reminded her what the reason was for her very existence.

Hovering within the sensation, encased in the taste of cold, was the earthy smell and flavor of wood smoke. Comforting in the most basic way possible, Arianna imbibed it hungrily. Her mouth was eager to consume the sensation, to consume *him* before her mind caught up with the conscious awareness of who *he* was.

She fished gently with her tongue, then not so gently with her teeth. The technical term for the act would, without doubt, be imbibing. But all Arianna could think of was how long it had been since she had last been kissed. She didn't *need* sensual pursuits. If she did there had been ample opportunity throughout the past two lonely years to find some at various parlors in Mercury Town.

But needing, wanting, and enjoying when presented with such, were all different. And in that moment she enjoyed the weight of his mouth on hers. She savored the slickness of his blood, the icy rush of his magic, the crisp, heady flavors of wood smoke. She enjoyed it all shamelessly until he pulled away.

Until she was faced with reality once more.

Fire lit up the side of his face, the smell of actual smoke flooding her nose. Her mind began working instantly, figuring out the who, what, where, and why of her situation. She was alive, which must mean she'd managed to fly the glider long enough to ease her landing.

But underneath her mind, a different sort of machine purred. It was the one in her chest that occupied the place of her heart, and it hummed in a way she'd never heard before. Well, it didn't *actually* hum differently. She knew better than to think emotions could change clockwork gears and screws. In fact, she was glad emotions couldn't. But she heard it differently. She heard the world a little differently. She'd had her first glimpse into the truth of the man that was encased under his pale azure skin and it resonated deeply with the memory of another woman she once loved. It was no wonder she'd been able to grow any fondness for the Dragon. She just hadn't been willing to see it until that exact second.

"I finally know what you taste like," she breathed in relief. It was like finally cracking into a safe that had been driving her mad with its contents for weeks.

"Ari. . ." Florence whispered weakly.

Arianna was pulled upright at the sound, nearly hitting Cvareh in the face with her forehead. She looked frantically for her student. The glow that had surrounded her from the imbibing slowly faded into the harsh detail of reality.

"Flor!" She held out her arms and the girl came crashing into them. Arianna held her tightly with all her might. "You're all right. Grease every gear, you're all right."

"I should be saying that to you." The girl hiccupped and tears came.

She pressed her eyes closed, pressing her nose into Florence's hair. Her darling Florence was in one piece. Arianna could sense the growing decay in her, but that was no better or worse for the fall. She opened her eyes, looking at Cvareh.

Without the haze of the imbibing, she remembered the tension from the last time they had spoken and it seemed he had as well. He regarded her cautiously, his expression searching. Arianna wished she could give him what he searched for. She *wished* she could—that was a scary thought. But she couldn't. No matter his nature to strive for a better tomorrow, his perseverance in the face of no natural aptitude, or his ability to see right through her reminded her of Eva. . .

He was not Eva.

He was a Dragon. A Dragon who had her schematics for the Philosopher's Box from years ago. Schematics that, the last time she had seen them, were in the hands of a Dragon who had betrayed them all.

"Thank you," Arianna forced out through her confusion. "For keeping Florence safe."

"You don't need to thank me for that." He shook his head. "I wanted to. She's my friend too, after all."

Florence pulled away to smile at Cvareh. No matter what Arianna said, she would believe until the end he was sincere in his desire to help them overthrow the Dragon King. The girl was young, and she could afford the indulgence of hope.

"Well, I don't see the point of wasting further time. . ." Arianna stood. "Even though it's not in Keel proper, the Guild will still be a long trek on foot."

"At least we won't have any more Riders after us," Cvareh pointed out optimistically.

"How do you know?" Arianna was skeptical. The notion seemed too good to be true.

"I'm fairly certain the Dono doesn't have many more Riders on retainer. And he may not risk them after how many he's lost."

"I remember the last time you were fairly certain about a Rider," she snapped bitterly.

"Ari, don't be mean," Florence scolded.

Arianna squinted at the girl. Florence had taken his side a few times over the past weeks, and it was becoming a trend she didn't enjoy.

"Cvareh has only been helpful."

"Yes, well. . ." Arianna had no interest in arguing with Florence. Not when they had somehow made it all the way across the world in one piece despite Riders, prison breaks, and Wretched. "We should get this helpful one to the Alchemists. It's not far now."

In the dim light of dawn they set out through the forest. She and Cvareh took turns carrying Florence on their backs. Florence would insist she could walk on her own and they'd let her, but she tired quickly and began to lag behind within minutes.

Words were scarce between them. They each nursed their thoughts and still-healing wounds before conversation. Arianna would glance at Cvareh from time to time out of the corners of her eyes, but she never caught his.

He still carried the folio on his hip, a hand covering it protectively. It was worn and weathered now from their journey, the leather scratched and curling from wear. When he took his hand away there was an outline of where he usually placed it from fretting so much about its presence.

She could kill him now. She could strike him down before they ever made it to the Alchemists' Guild. Or she could spare him, and merely rip up the schematics.

But that was a painful idea. Arianna had only ever torched her work once, and it was like cutting off her own arm. Progress was never meant to be stinted, and even failures weren't to be destroyed. That was how she'd been raised; that was what her teacher had instilled in her. So even then, in the final hours of the last resistance, it took the dying wish of her late master to force her hand in doing what must be done.

Even then, some of her research escaped.

She navigated the Skeleton Forest on memory. She had run through its trees as a girl. She had spent years of her life in this territory. Now, she walked with the ghosts of her memories. She had returned, but there wasn't any more closure waiting for her here than there had been in Dortam. There was no balm to the wound that ached in her chest. It would bleed eternal, unhealed by any magic or medicine.

The heart of Keel was still a good two days off on foot, but Arianna knew when their journey was nearing an end. The Alchemists were reclusive, protective of their research. The Guild itself was offset outside the outer walls of the city to discourage any from entering its grounds by accident.

Magic sparked from golden stakes driven into the trees. They glowed faintly in warning. Arianna continued, unbothered.

"What was that?" Cvareh rubbed the back of his neck in the same spot Arianna had felt the pressure. Even Florence seemed more alert, despite not yet being a true Chimera.

"The door bell of the Alchemists' Guild," Arianna replied grimly.

She could leave him now, leave him here. She could give up on her boon, or cash it in much later when she hunted him down again. The Alchemists were on their way through the forest to see what magical creatures had crossed through their line. Arianna knew how they worked and she knew it would be less than an hour before their trikes came humming through the trees, billowing steam and sparking with magic.

But Arianna continued forward. She insisted that Cvareh had nothing to do with her decision; it was entirely based on Florence. The girl needed the attention of an Alchemist and Arianna would never leave her alone or settle for less than the best care.

It took a little bit longer than expected for the hum of the engines to be heard through the trees, but Arianna knew the sound. Florence and Cvareh looked on with curiosity and almost excitement at the prospect of finally being at the end of their journey.

The trikes were a larger version of the ones the Raven gangs rode around on. They could sit three people apiece, five if they had a platform suspended between their two gigantic back wheels. Guns were mounted on their fronts, flanked by spikes. The Alchemists took the endwig and the other rare—but deadly—creatures that lived in their forest seriously.

Their eyes were a rainbow of colors. And if they didn't have Dragon eyes, the Alchemists sported Dragon ears or hands. Every one of them was a Chimera, a requisite at a certain level of the Guild.

"You're survivors of the crash?" one of them asked.

Arianna didn't miss how most of them kept their hands by their weapons. But if what she had learned in Ter.5.2 was true, they didn't have enough ammunition to shoot first and ask questions later.

"More or less," she replied. "We seek the Guild."

"The Guild does not take visitors," another replied.

"I have a delivery," Cvareh spoke. Arianna resisted the urge to throttle him. She didn't know what was more annoying, the fact that he was about to say something stupid, or the fact that she could sense he was about to say something stupid. "I come bearing help for the rebels against the Dragon King."

The Alchemists exchanged a look and burst out laughing.

"No rebels here, Dragon." The lead rider leaned back in his seat, folding his arms. "We're all happy to follow our King's decrees."

Arianna snorted softly in amusement. But as much as she enjoyed seeing Cvareh put in his place, it wouldn't solve their predicament of getting to the guild. "He speaks true. Bring us to the Vicar. If there is no new resistance brewing, harvest him for wasting your time."

"Ari!" Cvareh hissed.

"What?" She arched her eyebrows at him. "You're certain there is a resistance, and you're certain that what you carry will help it. Right?" He said nothing, silently fuming. "If you are, there's no real risk to you."

The Alchemists looked at each other, silently debating it. The leader gave a nod to one on the wings and the girl touched a hand to her ear, covering her mouth with her hand, muttering under her breath. They were used to being around people with Dragon hearing, because she spoke so softly that not even Arianna could make out the words.

After several long minutes, she straightened, giving a nod of affirmation to her leader.

"Very well, then." He shrugged. "Onto the trike at the end with the three of you."

They obliged, and the vehicles were speeding through the forest at speeds befitting a Raven. Still, Arianna sat calmly. She knew these drivers had ridden through here countless times to fend off the endwig attracted to the scent of blood and carrion that always lingered around the Alchemists' Guild hall as a result of their studies.

Her eyes drifted over to a far point, invisible through the dense forest. She wondered if the place that had been their laboratory was still black and gray, a dark spot on the living forest of magic gone wrong. Or if the Alchemists had rebuilt, and were working there anew.

She wondered, but she prayed she would never find out.

# 35
## FLORENCE

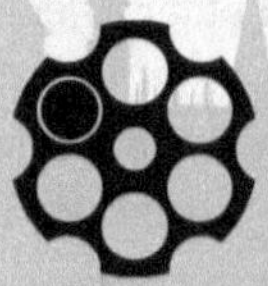

The wind whipped through her hair, knotting it even further than the airship crash had. It licked moisture from her eyes as she blinked into the reckless speed that would've made Will and Helen proud. *Perhaps they should've come along after all.*

One of the trikes to their right pulled ahead. Magic flashed around the man's fingers, sparking flares on the ground in reply. *Traps*, Florence realized. Their curving and illogical route was suddenly making more sense. The ground leading up to the guild hall was riddled with traps, discouraging man and monster from wandering too close.

They crossed through a tree line into a scorched and salted section of earth. Nothing grew and dust drifted across the ground. High above, on a lower wall, men and women watched them from behind the barrels of guns.

Florence found it ironic. The guild that made the guns allowed anyone to walk through one of its six main arches that connected its sprawling campus with the city of Dortam. But the guild that merely bought the guns put the weapons to more use.

A hulking portcullis with bars four times her height rose slowly. They rode under, and through a set of metal doors that were nearly a peca thick. Dust swirled up from under the tires of the trikes as they rolled to a stop in a small inner yard. What Florence had thought was merely an outer wall proved to be a solid structure connecting to the inner tower. It rose upward and then tapered off again with the final thin column stretching high above the tallest trees in the Skeleton Forest. It reminded her of a many-tiered cake; the thought instantly made her mouth water for something sweet.

They were led through a second set of metal doors, gold lining their edges.

The core of the guild was hollow. Florence couldn't suppress a gasp as they entered the central atrium that stretched all the way to the rooftop.

Golden lifts lined the circumference, whizzing silently on the magic of their riders. It was well illuminated with the ghostly pale glow of electric lighting. With an endless supply of magic to run generators, Florence suspected that outfitting the guild for electric hadn't been hard. But it had been recent, judging by the wires that were tacked up along the walls like copper ribbons.

"We'll need you to leave your weapons here," the man who had been leading them instructed.

Arianna and Cvareh exchanged a look.

"Suit yourselves." Surprisingly, Ari didn't put up a fight.

Florence watched as she and Cvareh passed over their pistols. Ari was out of canisters, so the weapon was useless to her. Cvareh maybe had one left, but his claws were ten times as deadly as his shot. She was surprised when Ari passed over her blades. But no one made any motion for the winch box on her hip or the spools of cabling.

Arianna's motion gear was unorthodox even for a Raven. Rivets had a hard time deciphering it at a glance without a background of who she was and what she did. None of the Alchemists seemed to even consider the fact that she walked with a noose that could move on its own.

"If you could sharpen my blades while you have them, that'd be great." Ari smiled cheerfully, patting the Alchemist on the shoulder. The girl who was taking their weapons rolled her eyes.

"Hurry up, then." The leader was impatient, ushering them toward one of the lifts.

The gears under the platform churned to life against the pitted tracks that ran up the wall. The Alchemist was silent, focus clouding his eyes. Arianna folded her arms over her chest. She gave the appearance of being nonchalant, but Florence could feel the tension radiating off her. Then there was Cvareh. He didn't even bother with appearances, fumbling relentlessly with the clips of his folio.

For Florence, despite all her exhaustion and her slowly waning strength, she stared in wonder at the world around her. She was getting a glimpse of the most secretive Guild in the world. These were the hallways in which Loom had been changed, the place that had cultivated the scientists who uncovered the ability to refine metal into gold, the doctors to make the first Chimera; some of the greatest thinkers of the ages had lived in these rooms.

Within them, she felt for the first time what Arianna had been telling her all along: the Loom she knew was the shadow of something grander. Every Guild was told by the Dragons what they would be. The students were told what to learn. The people were told where to study. They were kept sequestered like livestock and expected to produce, yet a mind imprisoned was not a mind that could think great thoughts.

The other Guilds regarded the Alchemists with skepticism and jokes. They were either perceived as being hermits, hiding in their corner of the world. Or as mad scientists, muttering over their vials and experiments. They might be a bit of both, she decided.

But if they were mad, they were mad because they kept dreaming when the rest of Loom merely slept in stasis. They pushed out others to preserve their way of life. And it was here that a rebellion could be born.

The elevator stopped at the very top of the tower. Florence stared down at the atrium. On the floor was the symbol of the Alchemists: two triangles, one pointing up and one pointing down, connected by a line—symbolizing earth and sky.

The landing led to a set of wooden doors emblazoned with the same symbol. Their guide knocked, but let himself in after only a second. Florence's heart raced as they entered the office. The room was littered with workbenches made out of metal. Vials and beakers cluttered their surfaces. Tubes connected them, transporting bubbling liquid throughout the cluttered lab. The concrete floor was stained in some places, rough in others from various chemical spills.

"Just a second," a woman's voice called from somewhere in the back corner. "I'll be with you in just one second!"

Arianna stiffened. Florence watched her hand twitch for a dagger that wasn't there. After being nonchalant through the entire encounter, she was panicking *now*?

"Sorry about that, I had just gotten it to the right temperature. . ." A woman with coal-colored skin and ashen hair rounded the tables, weaving her way toward them through the lab. She wiped her hands on a stained apron, lifting goggles onto her forehead. They left a ring on her cheeks from having been there for an extended period of time.

The Vicar Alchemist said nothing as she locked eyes with Arianna. Arianna remained tense as well, a scowl fighting at the corners of her mouth.

"It's you," the woman breathed in shock. "You're alive?"

# 36
## ARIANNA

She thought she recognized the voice from the first second, but being face to face with the woman was far worse than she'd ever imagined. Arianna wished she were literally anywhere else in the world.

"It's been some time, Sophie." What did one say to the self-centered best friend of the dead woman she'd loved?

"It is you, then?" Sophie repeated in shock, leaning against one of her tables, almost knocking over a pipette stand in the process. "You died, two years ago...You died with the rest of them."

"I have been called a wraith."

"Why are you here? Did you come back to help us? Arianna, this is excellent, together we can—"

She held up her hand, stopping Sophie before she ran away with her thoughts. "I'm not here for you." She pointed to Cvareh. "I'm just delivering him."

"What?" Sophie looked between them in confusion. "Who's he?"

"He's the one we told you about," the Alchemist who had led them there reported. "The one who claims to have a message for some sort of rebellion."

"Drop the pretenses, Derek. These people are friends."

Sophie was getting ahead of herself on that fact, but Arianna held her tongue on the matter. Perhaps the woman had changed with time. Believing in Sophie's good nature and ability to change would be the ultimate proof of Florence's influence.

But she didn't want to think on it. Now that she knew the Vicar Alchemist was someone from the last rebellion, all she wanted to do now was get out of the Guild as fast as possible.

She glanced at Florence from the corners of her eyes. There was still that loose end to tie up. She may have to use whatever good feelings Sophie held for her to get Florence the treatment she needed. Ari would swallow the thought of staying a night or three under the Alchemists' roof for that. But no longer.

"It's not a message." Cvareh stepped forward. "I have something I stole from the Dragon King. I brought it as a measure of good faith from House Xin. We want to align with you. We want to help you overthrow him."

"Large words from a Dragon." Arianna was relieved to see that Sophie could manage some measure of skepticism. "What do you have that you think could sway us in such a manner?"

Cvareh opened his folio and finally produced the stack of papers that had started everything long before they'd even brought him to her. The very sight of them filled Arianna with anger. It was a frustrating contrast, that a man who had come to fill her with an odd sort of curiosity and infatuation could also bear something that turned him into a vision of pure loathing.

He presented Sophie schematics with both hands; Arianna felt sick. She knew all she had done, everything she had put Florence through, was to allow history to repeat itself.

But a different feeling sparked as the documents changed hands. Cvareh looked at her with wide eyes. He'd felt the spark too. The scales had tipped, and the subconscious drive that had pushed Arianna to get him to the Alchemists' Guild now was transferred to him. *He was hers.* The boon contract had been fulfilled.

"Sophie, foremost," Arianna interrupted before the woman could get a good look. "I have a favor to ask."

"For you?"

Arianna nodded. "For old times' sake." She wanted to vomit in disgust at playing that card.

"Of course, anything. What do you need?" Sophie smiled sweetly, but Arianna could practically see her mixing the elements of their conversation to form an imagined debt that Arianna would now owe her.

"Florence was injured en route here. She had to imbibe as a Fenthri." Sophie didn't seem surprised. She could likely sense it in the girl from the moment they walked in the room.

"You want her to be a Chimera?" Sophie clarified.

"She must be, or she'll die. There isn't much time left before her organs are beyond repair. This has been going on for weeks now."

"I see." Sophie grimaced. "Derek, prepare a transfusion room, begin as soon as it and the young woman here are prepared."

"Thank you, Sophie." Arianna didn't need to lie about her gratitude. "If you'll excuse us, we've had a long journey. . ."

She had to get out of the room. She'd do *anything* to get out of the room.

"You can rest in a vacant Master's chambers. I trust you still remember where they are?"

"I could never forget."

"Help yourselves to whatever you need. I'll find you later and we can discuss further what you can do to help our cause." Sophie smiled and Arianna grated her teeth, trying to smile in kind.

Taking Florence by the hand, she practically dragged the girl from the room. She had to get on the lift before Sophie had a chance to really look at what Cvareh had brought her. But Arianna knew there would only be so long she could avoid *that* conversation.

# 37
## CVAREH

electricity. The desire to not let her out of his sight no longer stemmed only from his growing fondness for the woman, but now from his desire to fulfill her every wish—any wish. All she had to do was ask it of him. He feared the longer she went without demanding the boon of him, the further her very presence would drive him to insanity.

Still, he struggled for focus on the matter at hand instead of the Chimera who had just left the room. The woman was staring wide-eyed at the papers, slowly thumbing through them. He suspected from her expression alone that she already knew what they contained.

"They're for the Philosopher's Box," he announced proudly. "I uncovered that the King had acquired them from a Rivet here on Loom during the last rebellion. I'm afraid I don't know all the details of what or how, but I thought it could be of use."

The woman placed them aside on the table, looking at him skeptically. It was not the reaction he'd been expecting, to say the least.

"I've traveled quite far to bring them to you. House Xin hopes the schematics can be finished and once they are, we will supply the necessary Dragon organs to see perfect Chimeras made," he fumbled over his words. The more he talked, the less she seemed inclined to him. "I know they're unfinished but—"

"You have no idea what you've brought me, do you?" The Vicar placed her hands on her hips.

"I know exactly what they are," he insisted. This was not how it was supposed to go, not in the slightest. At the least he'd hoped for some gratitude for his assistance. All he was getting instead was skepticism and a small dose of amusement.

"How, exactly, did you find out they were there?" The Vicar folded her fingers before her.

"I overheard a conversation in the villa of the Dragon King."

"And why were you there?"

"I'm the Ryu—the second in command of House Xin," he clarified. "It's not uncommon for noblemen and women to be invited as guests of the King." It was a sort-of lie. Noblemen and women from across Nova were invited on various occasions to visit with the Dono or attend his Crimson Court. Members of House Xin, less so, certainly. But that hadn't been why he'd been there that day. Cvareh kept his mouth shut over the true nature of his then-purpose. He didn't want to add to her skepticism by confessing he'd been visiting his brother.

"You're either a well-trained liar, intentionally kept in the dark, or are the most oblivious creature I have ever met." She shook her head, fanning out the papers in the limited space on the table.

"Why?" Horror at the idea that the documents weren't what he'd been led to believe crept over him as if Lord Xin himself had come from the afterworld for Cvareh's immortal soul. "Are they not for the Philosopher's Box?"

"They most certainly are," she affirmed to his relief.

"Then they should be invaluable to the resistance," he insisted. "And the fact that House Xin would risk both our station and the life of their Ryu to deliver them to you should speak volumes of our loyalty. The King's Riders pursued me in a failed attempt at assassination for these. Just confirm with Ari or Florence." He prayed Arianna wouldn't fabricate something else to knowingly spite him.

"Ari? She lets you call her by that name?"

"Well. . ." He hesitated. He hadn't ever been given express permission.

Vicar Sophie laughed, shaking her head again. "You are oblivious on all fronts, then."

He opened his mouth to speak, but she continued, finally ending their game of cat and mouse.

"You come to Loom seeking our trust for your House. But you don't seem to grasp why we would distrust you in the first place."

"I know what the Dragons have done to Loom. I know you wouldn't have reason to trust me." Being treated like a child was grating.

"You know why any Fenthri might harbor dislike for the Dragons. But you don't grasp why *we* would," she emphasized. "It may be as you say, that you risk your life in trying to bring these to us. But you don't know what you've brought with you of far greater value."

"Stop talking in riddles."

"You thought I would find value in these schematics, when you have brought me the woman who created them?" Sophie smiled as the realization hit Cvareh.

"The-the woman who created them?" he repeated dumbly, at a loss for all other words.

"You call her Ari, like you're close. But you have no idea who she really is, do you?"

No denial could parry the sword of truth the woman brandished. It cut a bleeding line into his heart atop the space where Arianna's name had been etched, and left the wound to fester with the faint smell of betrayal.

# 38
## FLORENCE

DEREK LED HER INTO A SMALL ROOM. A CHAIR WAS IN THE CENTER OF IT, restraints hanging ominously off its edges. Florence eyed them with trepidation. But anything would be better than the way she felt now. She was exhausted all the time, unsteady on her feet, and over the past few days had felt strange pains beginning to creep up on her that were becoming worse and worse, and took longer and longer to go away.

"It hurts," Derek explained, seeing her staring at the restraints. "But we can't have you thrashing about when it happens or you may rip out one of the transfusion lines. If you did, that's the end of it."

"I see." Florence was happy to have an explanation, even if it was a miserable one.

"Unfortunately, we can't give you anything for the pain." He motioned for the chair. "Since the blood is being purged and cycled through your body, anything we could give would be out in minutes."

"I understand." She sat down, willing herself to be still as he began working on the restraints.

Derek paused at her wrist. His steam colored eyes drifted up to her. "It's okay to be scared."

"I'm not scared."

"You're trembling." He shook his head, tightening the leather around her wrists. "What made you want to be a Chimera? To propel engines?"

He was taking note of her Ravens' Guild Mark. "I'm actually a Revo."

"Oh? I bet you fool a lot of people then." He accepted her declaration. It was something that Florence wasn't used to.

"I do," she agreed hesitantly.

"If it gets too much, we'll give you something to clamp down on so you don't bite your tongue off." His hands tightened the strap around her forehead.

"Is that a legitimate concern?" If she was only trembling before, she was shaking now. Every muscle in her body was tense. "I don't understand this—what's about to happen?"

Derek paused what he was doing with the brass mechanism at the chair's side. "We slowly begin to take out your blood. I'll monitor your vitals; the more blood we can take out without completely killing you, the better."

"What's the difference between 'completely' and 'incompletely' killing someone?"

He chuckled. "Right, sorry, Revo. . . 'Completely' meaning that your body has gone far enough into failure that magic alone will not be able to revive you."

She made a noise of comprehension.

"At which point, we begin introducing Dragon blood, slowly. It mixes with what's left of your blood and your body acclimates to the magic."

"That's why Chimera blood is black and not gold or red?"

"Exactly." Derek smiled reassuringly. After the vote of confidence from the Vicar he had warmed up significantly, and Florence was never more grateful than she was in that second of sitting in the chair waiting.

"So, why does it hurt?" Nothing sounded particularly terrible. Even if he cut her to make her bleed, she'd endured worse pains.

"Fenthri bodies aren't made for housing magic. I'm sure you're familiar with forsaken Chimera?" She nodded and he continued. "When the Dragon blood is first introduced and hits your system, it's...well, for lack of better words, killing you. But it begins to heal you almost at the same time. Since we do it slowly, it doesn't actually result in death." His voice trailed off and Florence's mind treacherously filled in "normally" for him at the end.

"So I'm dying and being revived a bunch, in a row." Florence looked at the ceiling, bracing herself. "Well, I've never died before, so at least I get to cross that off my list."

Derek laughed. "You're an odd one, aren't you?"

"That's what you get for planning to run away from your guild at thirteen, doing so at fourteen, meeting the White Wraith, and becoming her explosives resource in the span of two years."

"Yes, that would do it." He processed her words for a long moment. "The White Wraith, the spurn of Dortam?"

"The same," Florence affirmed.

"Never imagined I'd see a legendary fighter of Dragons keeping the company of one."

"Cvareh isn't like most Dragons." Florence was instantly defensive. She was exhausted on his behalf of everyone assuming the worst of him.

"Oh, I know."

"You do?"

He nodded.

"How?"

"Because not most Dragons willingly offer their blood to make a Chimera."

"What?"

"What do you think we've been waiting on?"

Within the next minute, the door opened and Cvareh appeared. Sure enough, he sat down on a small stool next to her. Florence looked on in shock.

"You're giving me your blood?" She wished she could find more eloquent words, but all else failed her.

"Technically, I've been doing that for some time already."

"But that was necessary."

"As is this." He leaned against the wall. "I'm the one who brought you here, who took you from your home. I feel responsible for the fact that you're in that chair."

"You shouldn't."

"I do."

"Well you shouldn't—" Her reason was interrupted by the needle that pierced the flesh of her forearm. A second punctured her bicep a little further up and the machine at her side began to whir.

"You're going to start feeling sleepy," Derek informed her. "But I need you to stay awake as long as possible."

Florence watched in fascination as a tank of blood began to fill in the machine. The Alchemist walked around the room, puncturing Cvareh's offered arm. Sure enough, her eyelids grew heavy, her head thick.

"Florence, stay with us," Derek demanded.

"Right, right. . ." she mumbled. Compliance was becoming awfully difficult. Her vision blurred and her thoughts became sluggish. She wanted to talk, but she had reached a point at which she was no longer certain she could say anything at all.

That's when the pain hit her.

A different set of gears was now whirring on the machine. It was pumping blood from Cvareh's veins into hers. Just as Derek said, the sensation was excruciating. Florence tried to avoid screaming, but eventually failed.

"Hang in there, Flor." A large hand closed around hers. "I'm here. . . It'll be over soon."

"Well, actually—" Derek started unhelpfully but was stopped short.

"It'll be over soon," Cvareh insisted.

She tried to pry open her eyes. She tried to make sense of what was happening. But it felt like knives were being stabbed into her muscles straight to her bones, only to shear the meat from her skeleton.

Florence breathed heavily. She tried to think of anything else, but the pain was blinding and *everywhere*. It flowed from her arm but soon it was behind her eyes, under her heels, in her chest; there wasn't a place it didn't touch.

"Florence." A stern voice cut through the noises of her agony. "Florence, look at me."

She pried open her eyes and her attention drifted from Cvareh to the new voice that had joined them. Arianna's mouth was set in a grim, determined line. The woman's hand was curled around Florence's fingers alongside Cvareh's.

"I made it through this, and you are stronger than me," Arianna declared.

Florence mentally disagreed, but the thought escaped only as a whimper, as if her body wanted to prove her point for her.

"Hang in there, Flor, a little longer."

They both spoke words of encouragement—more like sweet lies—as she suffered for what seemed like a whole week. But, sure enough, it slowly began to pass and the light at the end of her tunnel vision began to sharpen and grow. Her chest heaved. She couldn't get enough air.

Her body transitioned from utter pain to feeling stronger than it ever had. She could *feel* the fatigue leaving her muscles. The strain of tensing constantly while she'd been in agony was smoothed away magically. Despite the excruciating suffering, Florence wondered why she hadn't made the transition sooner. *It felt that good.*

"Looks like she's out of it," Derek noted. "We'll run this for a bit longer, until her blood runs nearly gold."

"I thought my blood would be black?" she rasped. Her vocal chords had yet to knit from all the screaming.

"It will be," the Alchemist affirmed. "But we want as much Dragon blood in you as we can get. And since we have a willing donor, well, let's be a little selfish, no?"

"I don't want to hurt Cvareh," she breathed, her voice slowly coming back. The magic seemed to place priority on what was vital, followed by functions she put demands on—like her sight or voice.

"You're not going to hurt me," he insisted.

"The Dragon is right. His body produces blood much faster than yours does, even as a new Chimera," Derek said. "Your blood will run black when his fades and your body begins producing new Chimera blood on its own. We just reprogrammed your liver, in essence."

Florence nodded and Derek began removing the restraints. He left only the ones on her right arm until he finally turned off the machine and plucked the needles from her skin nonchalantly. Florence watched as she bled a dark gold that was quickly stopped by her flesh knitting.

"Just rest here for a bit. Don't try to get up yet." He started for the door. "I'm going to get some medicine, just to be safe, and some food."

"Then it's to bed with you," Arianna finished as he left the room.

Florence smiled tiredly at her. Ari always had looked out for her, ever since they first met. It wasn't until this trip that Florence really noticed the fact. And her opinion of it shifted colors alongside her blood.

"Did you ever think I would be a Chimera?" She flexed her hand, imagining herself as much stronger than she likely was.

"No, and I wish you didn't have to endure that," Arianna muttered.

"But I'm rather glad I did." She spoke softly, hoping her words didn't upset Arianna too terribly.

"Flor—"

"Ari," for the first time, Florence interrupted her teacher with purpose. "I can be someone now. It didn't hit me until I was here, until we made this journey. But I can do more than just make guns and bombs. I can *use* them. Everyone here is fighting, and I can help them."

"What are you saying?" Quiet panic tinted her voice.

"I want to help the rebellion."

"They haven't confirmed there is one," Arianna pointed out.

Florence gave her a look that she hoped communicated how much she appreciated being treated like she was stupid. "Well, if there is, I want to help."

"Why?" Arianna's arms dropped to her side. Her shoulders fell. Even Cvareh took note of the uncharacteristic change in the woman.

"Ari, you taught me to believe in possibility. I escaped the Ravens not because I truly wanted to find my calling, but because I just didn't want to be killed when I couldn't pass the aptitude test." Florence sat straighter, her back coming off the recline of the chair. "You were the one who taught me to see Loom as it could be. You wanted me to strive to dream, and I thought you were crazy but I did it anyway because you were the person who saved me and because I wanted to appease you. I never saw it.

"But I see it now, Arianna. I see it now, your vision. I want to fight for it with these people. I can make a difference here. I can fight for real, positive change." Florence swallowed, Arianna's stare a black hole that was consuming her optimism and emotions. "Y-you can too. You can do what you always wanted to do. You can really fight against the Dragons. Can we stay?"

"No," Arianna dismissed her outright.

Florence stared in shock. "Why? *Why?* Isn't this everything you ever said you wanted?"

"Flor, we were fine in Dortam, you and I. We can go back, we can live our lives."

"You taught me to see past what Loom is to what it could be, and now that I can, now that I do, you want me to stand to the side?" Florence balked. "What did we do this for? What did you do this for? Wasn't it for a boon to help you change this world?"

Arianna didn't answer, and her silence stung to a degree that was nearly as great as the transition had been. Florence fell back into her chair.

"Do you really want what's best for Loom?" she whispered. "Or do you only want what's best for yourself?"

"Watch your tongue."

"Watch yours, Arianna." Florence was on her feet.

"Should you be standing?" Cvareh had been entirely forgotten.

"Don't lie to me—tell me straight. Did you ever have any intention of really fighting to win back the Loom you claim to love? Or have you only ever fought for the past under the guise of being a champion for the future?"

Arianna scowled down at her and Florence looked up without hesitation or remorse. Maybe it was the new blood in her veins that made her bold. Maybe it was the struggles she'd overcome on the journey. But she was no longer the girl Arianna had found on the streets of Ter.4.2. She no longer needed saving, which meant Arianna could no longer fill the role of savior. Florence was becoming something more, and she needed Arianna to rise to the task and do the same.

The silence stretched on for too long and Arianna stepped away. Betrayal hit her hard in the chest. Her teacher, her friend, the woman who had been her everything, was walking away when the bombs were dropping.

"I hope you decide to grow into your words," Florence said softly. Arianna didn't even turn. "I hope you decide to stay with me, as my friend. I hope you decide you can live up to who you say you are. That you can support me in what I want even if it's not what you wanted for me."

The door clicked closed as her only reply.

It had been three days since Florence had last spoken to her. Three days of wading through din of the Alchemists Guild hall, lacking direction and purpose. Three days of watching Florence recover, stronger than ever.

The girl threw herself into acclimating to the Guild. At some point, she spoke with Sophie and the Vicar had agreed to let her join whatever pathetic rebellion was brewing. That, or Florence was even better than Arianna had given her credit for at making new friends—and Arianna had given the charismatic girl a lot of credit.

Cvareh was nowhere to be found, and she insisted to herself that she was glad for that fact. She didn't need the Dragon in her life. In fact, good riddance if he left her. She didn't need him or the Raven-turned-Revo-turned-Chimera. She didn't need anyone.

At least, those were the lies she told herself. But as Arianna sat tinkering, building lock after lock and useless trinket after trinket, the loneliness grew. After she'd lost everything in the last resistance, she'd gained Florence. And now she'd lose Florence to the new resistance. Cvareh would likely betray them all and she'd be left with ghosts and enemies anew.

"So this is what the great and charismatic Arianna has been reduced to."

"Go away." Arianna didn't even turn from her workbench. She remained hunched over the tiny springs and dials of a mechanical bird. Getting its wings to flap had been trying her patience all morning.

Sophie ignored her, crossing over to the table. She picked up the wingless body of the bird. "Well, if I ever need to send messages via clockwork pigeon, I know who to turn to."

"What do you want?" Arianna was already spitting venom. She was in no mood and was utterly unapologetic about the fact.

"You know what I want." Sophie put the trinket down.

"I've been wondering when you'd finally start hounding me."

"I'm not going to be a rusty gear about this."

She didn't believe it for a second.

"I'm going to ask you for your help."

"Oh, is that all? That's a relief. No, then." Arianna returned to fumbling with the wing.

"Arianna—"

She made loud squeaking noises, imitating the rusty gear that Sophie had claimed she wouldn't be.

"Stop." Sophie covered Arianna's hands with hers and the watch she'd been using as a distraction. "You're not a child."

"I was never a child."

Sophie laughed. "Well, there we can disagree."

"I already told you no," Arianna reminded her. "I think we're done here."

"Arianna." Sophie sighed.

"Sophie." She sighed dramatically in reply.

"Weren't we friends?" Sophie had the audacity to look hurt.

"No," Arianna was out for blood. "You and Eva were friends."

"You can't be jealous of her and me. Your presence was the thing that reduced us to nothing. If anything I should be the one cross with you. The woman is dead, let—"

"Don't talk about her!" Arianna slammed her fist on the table, suddenly on her feet. She never wanted anyone to make assumptions about the woman she had loved. Least of all Sophie.

"Let her go." Sophie covered Arianna's hand gently with hers. "It's what she would've wanted."

Arianna pulled her hand away.

"I don't even want you to finish the Philosopher's Box. I just want you to help because I thought it could offer you closure."

*When did everyone become so obsessed with my "closure"?* Arianna thought bitterly. Then the whole statement seeped into her mind.

"You *don't* want me to finish the box?" The words were hard to say, they made so little sense.

"No, we already had a Rivet do it," Sophie announced triumphantly.

This was the competitive, self-centered Sophie that Arianna knew. "Lovely. It won't work."

"As arrogant as ever, I see." Sophie picked up one of the assorted lockboxes, inspecting it more closely. "You do good work—excellent even. But it's wasted if you don't use it for anything."

No one understood. By not using her talents in certain ways, Arianna was trying to protect them all. If the Philosopher's Box went into mass production it was likely to create an endless roulette of power struggles as one army fought against the next, and the next. She'd seen the destruction it reaped first-hand when men tried to get their hands on it.

"I use it for my own purposes." Arianna pulled the lockbox from Sophie's hand.

The Vicar shrugged and started for the door. "We're going to make a perfect Chimera now, if you want to see the fruit of your labor in action."

Arianna stood in limbo as the other woman left. She really didn't want to be involved. She knew there was no way another Rivet had finished her work, not based on the limited notes that had been stolen from her workshop.

But she found herself hastily following Sophie in two more breaths anyway. If nothing else, she wanted to know if the tensions between Nova and Loom were about to get even worse. Because if they were, she'd take Florence by force if she had to in order to keep the girl safe.

The Vicar and Arianna were escorted into a viewing room that overlooked a surgical lab. Within, a Chimera lay unconscious on a table. Alchemists surrounded him, preparing instruments and measuring chemicals. The Chimera had Dragon hands and ears, and that was only what was visible. It was a miracle he hadn't become forsaken yet.

On one table were the new reagents they were going to stitch in: a tongue and stomach were suspended in stasis liquid, condensing in the air and steaming from the temperature difference. Arianna's eyes fell on a new machine. It wasn't much different from the one that had transitioned Florence days earlier. *That* was what they thought the Philosopher's Box looked like.

"Call off the operation, Sophie," Arianna said softly. She wasn't going to openly embarrass the Rivet standing next to her, the man who was likely responsible for the monstrosity that would take another's life.

"You think I'll let you stand in the way of this?" Sophie smiled.

"It's not going to work."

"Oh, Arianna, you can't stand it when someone else does the work you think only you are fit to do."

"This is not personal." Arianna's voice slowly rose. "You are going to kill this man."

She'd gained the attention of those around her.

"Vicar Alchemist?" one of the surgeons called up, uncertain at Arianna's declaration.

"Continue."

"That isn't going to work. He's going to go forsaken the second you disconnect." Arianna spoke over the Vicar.

"I don't know who you think you are, but I built that from sketches drawn by a Master Rivet." The Rivet at her side took offense.

*Well, the line's been crossed. Might as well throw etiquette out the window.*

"And I can tell why you don't have your circle yet, boy. Because that Master Rivet who drew them was *me*."

The Rivet looked between her and Sophie for confirmation. When Sophie didn't object, he suddenly considered his work a second time. "Maybe we should—"

"Start the operation!" Sophie demanded.

"You are condemning him to death."

"Silence, Arianna. You may be a dear friend of mine but this is my Guild, and I will not tolerate such rudeness."

Arianna held her tongue. They were a lot of things, but they weren't *dear friends*. Time and age couldn't change that fact, it seemed.

The operation commenced, and the Rivet at her side paled as they began removing the tongue and stomach of the man on the operating table. Another Alchemist manned the fake Philosopher's Box. Blood spiraled in tubes, filtering out the Fenthri blood, turning it gold. The fact that the machine had that much working terrified her. The boy at her side was smart to have deciphered the filtration system. It wouldn't be a stretch to think he could achieve real success through enough trial and error.

The problem wouldn't come until they sewed the man up, let him heal, and unhooked their cumbersome box. Arianna waited for it, watching for thirty minutes as the Alchemists finished. Emotions drained from her heart.

It was what had made Eva different. She had been an accomplished Alchemist and still held regard for life. She didn't see creatures as her playthings like these people did—as though the world were a large cage that merely housed their test subjects.

The man's eyes opened with a groan. He sat, and the Alchemists all held their breaths. He made it to his feet before he began to howl in pain. His eyes went bloodshot; his mouth began to foam.

"Put him down, Sophie, he's forsaken," Arianna demanded.

"Don't do anything." The Vicar held out her hand to the woman beside her who had reached for a gun.

"Put him down." The man was growling, beginning to lose his mind. Magic was spiking wildly around him. The golden tools that littered the room shook, shuddering to life at his distorted and unfocused commands. "Your Alchemists are about to start dying, Sophie."

The forsaken Chimera roared and lunged for one of the Alchemists who had been operating on him minutes earlier. The fall to forsaken was fast when that much magic was pumped in at once. Arianna's reflexes kicked in, but the gunfire echoed before she could steal the weapon. The Alchemist lowered her revolver. The forsaken Chimera was dead in one shot.

"Well, this was fun." Arianna turned, anger rising in her. Anger at her greatest work being pilfered and treated as though it was simple enough to be figured out in days. Anger at Sophie's disregard for the life of her fellow Fenthri.

At the Alchemists' ever-apparent fault—progress without consideration for what that progress might reap for the world.

"Arianna, help us." Sophie stopped her. "You can turn the tides. You can change our world."

"Change it how?" She spun to face Sophie once again. "Do you even know? Have you even thought what a Philosopher's Box might do?" She already knew Sophie had no good answer so she didn't even give her time to offer one. "No, I didn't think so."

"Do you know what Eva told me she loved in you?" Sophie called down the hall after a long moment. "Your vision. Your pursuit of progress."

Arianna stopped, clenching her fists. She took a deep breath and let it go, unwilling to rise to Sophie's goading. Even if what she said was true, the woman Eva the Alchemist had loved died at her side two years ago. That Arianna had not survived her final act: slitting Eva's throat.

# 40
## CVAREH

Word of the incident with the forsaken Chimera reached Cvareh's ears within the day. He found it odd how no one seemed to mourn the poor soul. Surely, the man had been *someone's* friend or family? But the world continued as normal, so he did as well. There was much work to be done in establishing a rapport between House Xin and the fledgling rebel group. But every time he thought he opened a door or had some stroke of luck, it closed back in his face.

Cvareh sat across the table from the Vicar Alchemist. Sophie was allegedly reviewing the latest schematics from her team of Rivets. But Cvareh sincerely wondered if she could grasp their contents.

"My sister asks me for updates."

"Updates on what, exactly?" Sophie hummed, flipping the pages.

"She wants to know if the rebels will stand with her bid for Nova's throne." He hastily added, "Of course, in exchange, she'll gladly support Loom's interests in her new regime."

"We aren't fit to stand against—or behind—any regime." Sophie finally deemed the conversation worthy of her full attention. "Our 'rebel army' is full of initiates with no experience on just about every front.

"Our supplies are being throttled by the Dragon King. We have to rely on other loyalists of the old ways, and black markets, to get the ammunition we need to merely defend ourselves, let alone stage a rebellion."

"But you have the schematics of a Philosopher's Box. . ." he offered weakly.

"I have part of the schematics, and the woman who can finish them won't help me. And, even if she did, it would take me years to acquire enough reagents to stitch up that many Chimera."

The ghastly electric lighting cast long shadows on the woman's skin. He wondered how old she was. She couldn't have been more than Arianna's age, which made her less than half of his age. But she handled herself as though she was eighty. The Fenthri lived half as long as Dragons, and aged twice as fast.

She leaned forward, folding her hands before her. "We keep having these meetings, Cvareh, yet they do not yield results. I am left with no Philosopher's Box, no reagents, no supplies. You want us to work with you? Give me results."

"And if I get these results, will you support my sister?" He remained focused on his mission, focused on the one thing Petra had demanded of him: leave Loom with the promise of the army they needed.

"If you get me even half of these results, I will support you or whoever else you want me to," Sophie swore.

"Then consider it a deal." Cvareh stood.

"Really?" She chuckled. "I'll believe it when I see it."

He must be acclimated to Loom, because the rude dismissal only made him bristle so much. The slights against him he could forgive, and he had the feeling he'd need to forgive much more to achieve what he wanted. With that in mind, he headed straight from one room occupied by a sharp-tempered Fenthri to another.

Arianna had made a virtual sundries shop of clockwork items in the workroom she'd stolen. Even as he arrived some Alchemists were leaving, turning over mechanical locks in their hands with fascination, and cackling over the ideas of all the trouble they could use them for. Things were going to be interesting for a bit in the Alchemists' Guild with Arianna's work in house.

Her head jerked up at the sound of him, as though she'd known it was his eyes on her with the feeling of his attention alone. Perhaps she had. He could find her in a crowd by just her footsteps now. Why would it be far fetched to think she would know him by his stare?

Arianna's mouth pressed into a line, and Cvareh was equally talkative. They hadn't said a word to each other since arriving at the Guild a week ago, despite crossing paths. The last time she'd really said anything to him was when he'd let her imbibe from him.

His obsession with the woman was nothing more than an infatuation, he'd begun telling himself. But one look from her had him questioning everything. To say he loved her would be a stretch. To say he wanted her, wanted to understand her? That was much closer to the mark.

"I want to talk to you." He finally broke the silence.

"I figured that's why you were here," she drawled, returning to the little box before her.

He'd spent so much time around her as the White Wraith that he'd forgotten she was a Master Rivet. Her skills with machinery, locks, buildings—they all contributed so seamlessly to her success as a thief and organ runner that he didn't look at them as separate from that chosen profession. There was something almost soothing in the way she tinkered.

Soothing, and restless.

If he shifted his thinking, it wasn't far-fetched to see the reason for her attempts at finding peace in gears and coils. Cvareh sighed to himself, crossed to the worktable and sat in the chair opposite her. She pretended he didn't even exist.

"I came here to ask for your help."

Arianna continued to ignore him, and for the first time he preferred it that way.

"I came to Loom to bring the schematics for the Philosopher's Box to the rebellion here because my sister wanted to use it as a bargaining chip for their alliance. On Nova, our House has been the lowest on the social ladder for centuries. I understand that may not mean much to you. But to us, it's everything. And Petra is the first chance we have at taking the throne. She's young, and strong, opinionated as anyone, and she fights for who and what she believes in."

Ari reached for another tool, working as though he wasn't there.

"I think that's what I see of her, in you." His soft words finally drew her attention and now that Cvareh had it, he wouldn't let it go. He would lay it all out on the table. He would do what he should've done from the start and let her know exactly who he was and what he wanted. "I don't know how the King got the schematics. I know, now, you were the one to make them. So I can't imagine how they fell into the hands of the Dragon King and I can only assume it has *something* to do with your general hatred for my people and the failure of the last rebellion."

Her challenging stare told him he was right.

"But if I had known they were yours. . . I would've returned them to you, rather than bring them here."

"Liar." Arianna whipped out the word as though she'd been waiting all along for an opportunity to use it. "Why would you sacrifice the bargaining chip that you said yourself means so much to your family, and your sister?"

"Because of the predicament I'm in now," he answered easily. "Partial sketches are almost useless. But the help of the woman who made them? That's worth something far greater."

"Did Sophie send you?" Arianna scowled at the mention of the Vicar's name.

"Not directly," he confessed. "But she has put a high price on the alliance of the rebellion."

Arianna sighed and turned back to her box. She struggled with a tiny gear, trying to force it onto a peg and into place. It just wouldn't go.

"I may have done all this out of order. But I want to earn your trust."

"For your family."

"For my family," Cvareh confirmed. "And because I want to know why I can't seem to stop thinking about you at every turn. Why I find the shade of your skin and flatness of your teeth charming, when a few months ago I found it repulsive."

"What are you saying?" All emotion dropped from her voice. It was virtually unreadable to his ears.

"I don't know what I'm saying." Cvareh stood. "But I want to find out. And I intend to do so."

"A Dragon earning my trust?" she scoffed, back to the Ari he knew. "That could take years."

"Good thing I'm a Dragon. Years are something I have." Cvareh chuckled and grinned. "If I have to, I'll stop time."

That *almost* earned him a smile, and he'd take almost. Cvareh was nearly out of the room, his mission accomplished for now, when something else struck him. He stopped and turned to find Arianna looking up at him in confusion. He would capitalize on whatever good mood he'd earned.

"One more thing. Whatever you think about me... don't believe me, think I'm a total liar, take no heed of my truth." The thought stung him a bit—the idea that after all they'd been through she could still not trust him. "But if you listen, not just hear, but *listen* to one thing I say, let it be this: patch things up with Florence. You will regret it, Ari, if you let her vanish because of your own stubbornness."

THE BED WAS COLD AND THE ROOM, THOUGH NICELY SIZED, FELT A MILLION VECA wide. There was no rumbling of Cvareh's deep breaths while he slept. Florence's heat wasn't warming her sheets. Arianna was left alone—as she had been for a week now—with her thoughts.

She had almost worked up the resolve to leave the Alchemists' Guild without Florence, when Cvareh had visited her that afternoon. He'd come baring himself to her in ways she hadn't expected, and didn't want to believe were true.

Because believing would mean trusting a Dragon again.

And then there were all the claims Florence had made against her. Arianna stared listlessly at the ceiling. The girl had seen vision in her, when there had only ever been vengeance. Both drove, both were pursued with all the passion of the soul.

But a soul driven by vengeance was a selfish soul. A soul driven by vision was a generous one—one that bore itself before others and put the needs of the many before the needs of the few.

There was a time that she had actually possessed those traits. A time when they weren't just vacant, labeled pegs on the walls of her personality. She had written them off when the rebellion died. Eva, Master Oliver, and the Arianna they had known died alongside them.

She was nothing now, and that had enabled her to be an extension of her benefactors' will as the White Wraith. What Florence had seen in her was nothing more than a mirror of the potential that lived in the girl herself. Potential Ari eagerly reflected and wanted to grow—as if its vines and roots could curl around the fragments of her heart and pull them back together.

Arianna sat up, rubbing her eyes tiredly. Even Sophie's words about Eva had stuck with her. What would Eva think if they met now? Was Arianna still someone she'd want to love?

Chasing ghosts down empty halls, she stood, padding on silent feet through the Master's passages of the Alchemists' Guild. Eva was dead. Whatever she would or wouldn't love no longer mattered. Now, Arianna had to live for the living—for herself.

Arianna turned the knob of Cvareh's door, letting herself quietly into his room.

Even amid her virtual silence, the Dragon woke. Talons jutted from his hands, ready to ward off a shadowed attacker. She leaned against the door, waiting for him to calm himself, to realize who was there. It only took a moment.

"What are you doing here?" he whispered.

She could hear his quickening heartbeat, feel his magic responding to hers. Arianna crossed over to his bed with purpose. He sat straighter as she made herself at home without his permission, drawing up her legs to sit atop his sheets.

His words about her played relentlessly in harmony with everything else she'd been coming to terms with. Arianna had heard them clearly, but they were so difficult for her to process. This Dragon and she had embarked on an odd journey with each other. It was a winding path that had taken them across Loom, and what she thought was to be their final destination had turned out to be a resting point before the next, greater trek.

"I want proof," she announced.

"Proof of what?" Cvareh asked skeptically.

"Proof that your sister is who she says she is. That *if* I help this resistance— and her—get their footing, I will not just be replacing one tyrant with another."

The fact was that Loom was headed toward another war no matter what she did. If it was in one year, or twenty, eventually the rebels here would grow enough, become reckless enough, that they would attack. Loom wasn't meant to sustain itself as it was. That Ari believed above all else. Tensions would be omnipresent until things with the Dragons were settled in a far better manner than their current arrangement.

"Whatever proof you want, I'll get," Cvareh said hastily.

"I don't want it from you."

"What then?"

"I want it from *her*."

"Her?" It took him a second to put it together. "Petra? My sister will never come to Loom. She can't. There are too many eyes on her."

"I never said anything about her coming here."

"You want to go to Nova?" Cvareh couldn't process what he was hearing. The idea of Arianna on Nova was preposterous—she could agree with him on that.

"*Want* may be a strong word, yet. . ." Arianna sighed softly. "I've been standing still for far too long, hiding behind excuses and poor attempts at belief in something, anything."

"Is this because of Florence?"

"Among other things." He may have been ready to bare his soul to her, but Arianna wasn't there yet. They were still too much of nothing and not enough of everything for her to expose herself emotionally.

"So you patched things up with her?" he asked.

"I'm on the way to doing so." Arianna was pointedly ambiguous, and he fell down the rabbit hole of drawing his own conclusions. The Dragon no doubt presumed she'd spoken to Florence about her plans. But Arianna would face Florence again when she could be the woman the girl had seen in her all along. She would apologize with her actions before her words.

"I'm glad." The Dragon genuinely sounded it. *Sincerity, from a Dragon.* The idea was far-fetched in her mind, but Cvareh continued to make a strong case. "I'll speak to my sister, and figure out a way back to Nova for both of us."

Arianna shook her head. "We should go now. The more time you take, the more opportunity I have to back out of this."

"But we have no way of breaking through the Gods' Line. . ."

"The what?"

"The clouds," he corrected hastily.

"Yes we do," she declared triumphantly. "You didn't think the Alchemists would let a Rider's glider sit in the forest to be picked apart or rusted to dust, did you?"

"Leona's glider is here?" He'd heard nothing of it.

"I found it when I was nipping through storerooms for parts." She stood.

"The nipping around bit I believe. The rest seems suspect."

Arianna grinned and extended her hand to the Dragon. "I like this newfound sass of yours, Cvareh. Don't give up on it."

"As you ask." He took her right hand with his left. It was awkward, but it suited them. She went right, he went left: two halves of the same whole.

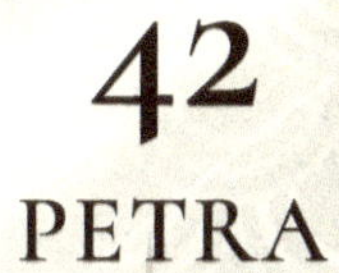

# 42
## PETRA

IT WAS THE SECOND TIME SHE'D BEEN SUMMONED TO THE ROK ESTATE IN A FEW month's time. It wasn't that Petra didn't enjoy inspiring frustration and anger in the man who was supposed to be revered as her supreme ruler, because she did —she enjoyed it a lot. Shameful amount, really. But she just had other things to do.

Running a House, managing nobles, and overseeing the wellbeing her family was enough to fill anyone's plate. Throw on regicide and treason while trying to broker deals with—apparently—the most temperamental Fenthri there were? She barely had time to sharpen her claws these days.

She clicked her tongue off her teeth, pulling lightly at the boco's feathers, guiding it with her knees to bank toward the landing area for nobility. Other giant birds milled about, some saddled, some not. Their iridescent feathers shone in the midday sun.

With the buffeting of large wings, her cerulean mount landed with a dignified caw. At least Petra found it dignified. She didn't speak boco, and some of the other birds ruffled their feathers at whatever it was her Raku had said.

Petra patted him lovingly on the bill. "You annoy the feathers off these gaudy chickens."

She might not speak boco, but she suspected Raku understood her language as he cooed gleefully in reply. Spinning, she adjusted the thick beaded necklace that ran down front and back, sauntering into the Rok estate as though she already owned the place.

"I haven't met you before." She gave a wide smile to the Rider who was escorting her to Yveun Dono's infamous red room. The thought of it made her yawn. He did it to be intimidating, but it made him predictable and dull.

The real way to intimidate people was to capture their imagination. The imagination was far more wicked than anything someone else could think up because it knew every insecurity to play off. Yveun Dono was too overt. House Rok sharpened their blades, but not their minds.

"We have not had the pleasure, Petra'Oji." Nothing about the Rider's tone made Petra think that meeting her was a pleasure. She raked her fingers through her golden curls, drawn back and pinned away from her face.

"You have two whole beads I see." She made a scene of fussing over them. "What an accomplishment."

The man almost swatted her hand away. He might be new, but he was trained enough to avoid making that mistake. If he struck her, she would kill him. Not even Yveun Dono would bother denying her that duel.

"Dono, I have brought Petra'Oji," the Rider announced as they crossed into the threshold of the red room. The man strode ahead of her, assuming the place at the side of the King.

Petra tilted her head. *Now this was too delicious not to comment on.* "Yveun Dono, did you change staff? Or is our dear Leona sick?"

The King's claws dug into the throne. He was on edge. No, not on it—past it. Further than she'd ever seen him before.

Petra drew her magic within her, bracing herself subconsciously against the King's aggression. If he wanted to fight her here and now, that would be fine. In fact, it'd save her a lot of time and effort if he just challenged her to a duel. But she wanted it to be a *fair* duel, one that didn't involve outside interference. And the Riders seemed to have their own definition of fairness when they claimed they were all one to begin with.

"You know what happened to her," Yveun Dono snarled.

He looked like an old man guarding a stupid bone. Petra didn't tell him so. She just continued to play dumb. "Me? My lord, if I knew I would gladly tell you as your most humble servant. . . But I'm afraid I've been overseeing the smiths lately, working on establishing our own gold tempering mills here on Nova as you yourself requested."

And for every one she set up for the King, she set up one for House Xin.

"You are on your last line, Petra," the King barked. "Leona is dead, and I demand Cvareh's head for it."

He led them down the exact path Petra had been expecting.

"Cvareh had nothing to do with it. He's been praying at the Temple of Lord Xin, as I told you months ago." Petra watered the seed she'd sewn and watched it flower.

"If you're lying to me Petra—"

"See for yourself, Dono," she interjected. "If you are so concerned, venture to the temple. While he is in private mediation, I imagine even the gods would forgive the intrusion of our supreme ruler."

"Perhaps I will." He grinned madly.

*Oh, Yveun Dono, you make this too easy.* He thought he was calling her bluff while she watched him play right into her palms. House Rok certainly hadn't stayed in power for so long because they possessed the most wit of all the Dragon houses.

"Very well. I will gladly go with you. I haven't seen my brother in far too long." She smiled easily, flashing her canines.

The King stood, furious. "If you are lying, I will kill you."

"I'm not lying."

"Then lead on, Petra'Oji, and we will see where we stand when the sun falls."

She led without hesitation or concern. She'd stalled the King's demands for an audience long enough that Lord Agnedi had turned his lucky eye on her. Cvareh had arrived just that morning. And a few hours was plenty of time to hide a glider, position her brother where he needed to be, and mask the curious scent of the Chimera who traveled with him.

Petra smiled as she mounted her boco, running her fingers through his feathers. She rose to the sky like a proverbial curtain. The stage was set and the actors she'd so carefully selected were in their place. It hadn't all gone according to script, but *oh*, if the climax hadn't proved interesting. She'd sent Cvareh down with schematics of a Philosopher's Box, and he'd returned with the inventor herself.

She would focus on that fact later. For now, she had a King to make her fool.

# 43
## FLORENCE

FLORENCE RAKED HER HANDS THROUGH HER HAIR, TEASING OUT THE TANGLES from sleeping. It was nice to finally have a certain level of cleanliness back in her routine. Her hair had been so knotted upon arriving to the Guild that she'd been afraid she'd have to cut it. Luckily, she saved her dark locks with about an hour of careful brushing.

Her morning routine still took some getting used to. All the clothes were in their proper place. There wasn't a Rivet tearing through closets and coming in at all hours from odd jobs, leaving her soiled clothing lying about. Her room was neat and orderly, as she preferred it and as it had been her whole life before Arianna.

But now it seemed sterile.

She hadn't found the courage to talk to her teacher. *Former teacher? Teacher.* Since the day of her transition. It wasn't that she didn't want to, but that she had no idea how.

Arianna wanted Florence to go back to her and apologize. She wanted the girl she'd known in Dortam. But Florence had changed, and she wasn't going to hold herself back for the sake of someone who claimed to want what was best for her but couldn't live up to those words in practice.

Ari was being the fool, Florence was being stubborn, and she wondered how much longer they could both go before something broke. She just desperately hoped that all that gave was the silence, and not her morals, or Arianna's love for her. She pulled on some of her borrowed clothing and started the day.

The connections Florence had gained in Mercury Town and the convenient knowledge of two transporters in Ter.4's Underground was proving more useful than she ever imagined for helping the resource-starved Alchemists. She'd spent most of her days with Derek, working on how to get them more ammunition so they could actually make a stockpile, rather than just using it regularly to fight off endwig.

In the hours she wasn't there, she was helping the armorers see how they could stretch their supplies further. Sometimes, she ran into something that made her wish she was still on speaking terms with Ari—or something that made her wish for the Revo teachers she'd had in Dortam. But Florence was determined to power through it on her own, even if it meant some late nights of trial and error with her newfound magic.

"Good morning," she greeted Derek. He occupied one corner of a laboratory he split with a girl named Nora. She was a late riser due to her midnight bursts of inspiration, and they usually had the desk to themselves.

He stared at her skeptically.

"What?" Florence wondered if she had only thought she brushed her hair and it was still a tangled mess.

"Did you know?"

"Know what?"

"You know what," he pressured.

"Actually. . . I don't." She hadn't the foggiest what had gotten him so twisted in knots.

"You really don't know?" Derek eased off, sitting across from her.

"I don't know what I don't know?" Florence thought about the self-posed question and struggled to see if she'd said it right. "What am I to know?"

"Your friends stole the Rider's glider we pulled from the wreckage of that airship crash."

"I didn't know you had the glider." *Out of everything to focus on, she picked the fact that the Alchemists had taken one of the gliders?* "Where did they go?"

Florence folded her fingers together, gripping them tightly. They'd left her behind. It was all for what she said. Maybe she'd been right, maybe she'd been justified, maybe she still was, but none of that expunged the pain at the thought of being left alone.

"Well, with a Dragon glider, they could've gone anywhere far and fast." Derek leaned back in his chair, terribly amused by the situation since he lacked all emotional investment. "But the morning watch says they charted a course skyward for Nova."

"Impossible. Arianna would never go to Nova." Florence couldn't believe it.

"Think what you will. . . But that happens in the dawn, and now, the Vicar tells me that we must increase our preparations. We must remain diligent, she says, because one 'never knows when the resources we need could come'."

Florence knew for all the help she'd been, the Vicar wasn't talking about her. It'd take a greater force to sway the tides in the favor of the fledgling rebels. A force that might be mustered by a Wraith, and a Dragon.

"We should get to work then," Florence resolved with a small smile.

"There's much to be done—just in case we have the opportunity to overthrow a King."

"Just in case?" Derek grinned. The man clearly believed she knew more than she did. But all Florence had was her intuition. Then again, when it came to Arianna, her intuition was rarely off.

"Just in case." She gave him a small wink and looked over all there was to be done.

Arianna's, Cvareh's, and Florence's stories continues in book two, The Dragons of Nova.

**Get your copy and read now:** https://elisekova.com/the-dragons-of-nova-loom-saga-2/

# ELISE KOVA

# THE DRAGONS OF NOVA

LOOM SAGA · BOOK TWO

*for Robert*
*and all your colors*

# 1

## ARIANNA

she valued her life a lot more than a superfluous notion like trust.

His hands, the color of the blue-gray sky that stretched above them, clutched the handles of the vessel with less than inspiring certainty. They shook as though they held birds or writhing snakes, not gold. His magic flowed through the metal and into the glider beneath them, filling the air, giving lift and speed, before discharging out behind the glider's bat-like wings as a full prism's worth of color.

Arianna clutched his waist, pushing her own magic under her heels, rooting herself to the glider in a battle against gravity. The contraption was not built for two and she had to manage her magic carefully to avoid interrupting the flow of his—a fate that would send them spiraling back earthward toward a near-certain death from the fall. His magic was fluctuating at best; the man had clearly never been taught how to pilot a glider and didn't even understand the basics of how magic was channeled through the gold to give it lift.

It would be easy for her to assume control. He was powerful, but she would have no reservations and a firm understanding of how the glider functioned.

Arianna grit her teeth and kept her magic wound tightly around her feet. She let him struggle silently. Piloting a glider was something that, as far as Loom was concerned, only a Dragon could do. Even a strong Chimera couldn't sustain the magic required to give it stable lift for very long. Which meant that there was no way Arianna should be able to.

She *could*, however. She could pilot it more gracefully than the Dragon she was pressed against and the fact made her dangerous. It was a secret so great it would make her both revered and hunted should it ever be discovered. So

Arianna kept her mouth shut. She remained the Chimera, the White Wraith, and nothing more.

Her eyes drifted down behind them at the diminishing earth. Loom spread out beneath her, smaller and smaller until the tallest trees in the forest looked like toothpicks, and the coastline was nothing more than the teeth of a cog she could fit in the palm of her hand. Down there, was the Alchemists' guild hall, reduced to nothing more than a speck, and in it was Florence.

Her dearest friend, her ward, her Florence, had set out to change the world. The girl had challenged Ari to do the same and dream again as she once had. But the birth of dreams stained reality. Dreams charted courses beyond the line of possibility that the present drew. They turned that forbidden threshold into an invitation, one that offered no absolution to those who boldly ventured into its alluring unknown.

Arianna knew this all too well.

She had dreamed. She had carved her infamy from the impossible. The dreams had wrapped reality in a sweet illusion that had turned sour with betrayal. If she dreamed again, she would no longer dream for the world. She would not risk leaving another mark on such a scale. She would merely be a player in other's dreams—like Florence's.

When the girl awoke this dawn, Arianna hoped she would understand. There wasn't room for goodbyes between women of action. It would be wasted words. If Florence wanted to assume the post of a visionary, she had to weigh the importance of deeds before the importance of words, not just from Arianna, but from the whole world.

"Brace yourself!" Cvareh shouted over the gusty currents.

The winds howled with greater ferocity the closer they got to the thick clouds that perpetually engulfed Loom. Ari grabbed her elbows at Cvareh's sides, locking muscle against muscle as she pressed into the taller man. The closer they were to each other, the less possibility for drag or for a rogue gust to get between them and knock her off.

His magic washed over her in pulses that increased in frequency until they were a sustained force across the entire glider, including her. Surviving through the clouds required a hefty amount of protection—a corona. This was the second barrier that prevented a Chimera from piloting a glider. Built into the handles Cvareh gripped were golden channels designed to funnel magic into a protective shield. Even if a Chimera could manage lift, it wouldn't be enough to sustain a suitable corona that would protect against the wind.

Light sparked across them, shining like scales, as the wind battered the magical force-field. Ari's refined goggles were whitewashed from the magic and clouds, her ears nearly deaf from the roaring wind that echoed through the magical barrier—a paper-thin separation between them and certain death.

But she never closed her eyes.

She remained alert, poised to take over should Cvareh falter. She would not die this day and certainly not due to someone else's incompetence. Arianna waited, her breaths shallowed with nerves, until they broke through the line that separated the world she knew below, and the world of Dragons in the skies above.

Magic snapped audibly as they crossed the threshold between worlds. Ari blinked into unfiltered sunlight for the very first time.

Her eyes had no trouble adjusting. They had been cut from a Dragon and implanted in her sockets. Her irises closed to thin slits and adapted instantly. But her mind rejected the blinding light. It was a struggle to process, like a ribbon of magnesium exposed to flame.

*How could anything be so bright?*

The sunlight illuminated every nook and cranny of the world that floated before her. It defied all logic, hovering in the empty air in violation of every scientific law that formed the load-bearing walls of the structure of her life. *Nova*, the homeland of the Dragons. She was loath to admit it, but the sketches in books hadn't done it justice.

Diamond-shaped islands drifted like icebergs through tides of wind. Inverted towers and honeycombed living quarters had been carved into the shade of their underbellies. Sunbeams winked through the hollow spaces where gardens thrived and waterfalls fell into the nothingness below, spilling a seemingly infinite amount of liquid into the void as if it were tithing for an unknown god.

Smaller masses floated around the larger ones, like islands to continents. The glider rose higher and higher, giving Arianna her first glimpse of the tops. The land was as colorful as its people: purple mountains offset against emerald trees, gold splattered atop grasses as if the sun itself had been poured out. Every building was painted and adorned on all possible surfaces. Not one had escaped the artist's brush or sculptor's touch. *Every. Single. One.*

"What do you think?" Cvareh shouted over his shoulder.

Arianna wanted to quip back with some scathing remark. It was tacky. It was over the top. It was too much of everything. There was no appreciation for the beauty of simplicity. But her tongue had gone soft and spongy, and her usual wit hadn't caught up with her.

"It's not what I expected." She wouldn't give him the satisfaction of more than that. "Now focus on not getting us killed."

He must've agreed with the sentiment, because Cvareh said nothing further. Ari could feel his magic thinning. Bruises were beginning to form on his skin as his body broke down from the exertion. Arianna had no doubt he had a large mark around his torso where she'd been gripping for her life. But the man had yet to speak a word against her potentially painful proximity or hold on his person.

The glider banked. Carved into the far side of the mountains, she could see the outlines of a grand series of structures that defied all sense of logic and necessity. They were suspended in the air, connected by gusty bridge-ways and narrow spiraling stairs. Cvareh tracked them to a large building above it all at the top of the mountain.

"You need to slow us," Ari cautioned nervously, realizing he intended to land on a flat alcove just on the other side of the structure.

"I'm working on it."

"Work on it more urgently." They were coming in far too fast for such a narrow ledge. Numbers flashed through her head, estimations based on estimations, but in every scenario they were splattered against the back wall of the wide-mouthed cavern.

Cvareh tugged on the handles, his magic straining in spite of his obvious will. "You want to try flying this thing?"

The question was obviously meant to be rhetorical, but Arianna had to bite her tongue from answering a resounding *yes!*

She waited until what she estimated to be the last possible second for Cvareh to pull himself together and get the glider back under his control and on a proper trajectory. He met her expectations of failure. Ari pushed her magic into him, into the glider through her feet. It wasn't possible to assume complete control without gripping the handles, but it had the desired effect. His magic was vastly weakened by the dominant influx of her own, resulting in the almost total arrest of the vessel's momentum—and thus knocking it off the suicide course it had been propelling them along. Arianna mentally accommodated for the falter by adding extra lift beneath the wings.

They skipped like a stone on water, skidding to a stop with a crash that crumpled one wing and sent them both tumbling from the glider. Ari's ears were ringing from the sharp *bang* of metal crushing against stone. She winced at the sight of the technical masterpiece that was a Dragon glider reduced to half a heap of scrap.

"Are you all right?" Cvareh drew himself to a seated position, taking note of her expression.

"Takes a lot more than that to fell me." Ari quickly checked for any rogue cuts or scratches she'd need to hide.

"Isn't that the truth?" He stood. "We need to get moving."

"To where?" Ari was already in step behind him.

"The Temple of Xin."

Arianna had studied Dragon culture enough to know of the culture's pantheon—the twenty needless gods they prayed to for everything from love to peace to luck. She could list off a good fifteen, maybe even all twenty, but Arianna could only align three to what they were said to be the gods of—and Xin was one of them.

Lord Xin, the death-giver and patron of the House of his namesake—Cvareh's family's House.

"Unless you can sprout actual wings on Nova, I doubt we'll be going anywhere anytime soon." Arianna shuffled toward the edge of the cavern, looking up and down. The walls were sheer and frustratingly smooth. Climbing would be a trick. Her mind was already turning around what they could salvage from the wreckage of the glider to help them scale the face when magic popped faintly around her companion.

Cvareh murmured softly to himself in Ryouk, the language of the Dragons. Arianna's ears picked up half of the conversation, but he spoke too softly for her to catch anything substantial. She stepped closer and his hand promptly fell away from his ear.

"Wings are coming."

"What does that mean?" She raised her eyebrows.

He laughed. The infuriating Dragon had the audacity to laugh at her as though she were a child inquiring about how water turned to ice. Arianna narrowed her eyes at him in warning.

"You'll see." He leaned against one of the side walls, folding his arms over his chest.

The Dragon had become bolder around her and Arianna hadn't done enough to discourage the disdainful behavior. His mannerisms were his own, but every now and then she saw the shade of someone else in them. Someone that gave her pause even when she was at her boldest.

"I'd rather you just tell me." She leaned against the wall at his side with a hefty sigh.

"By the time I did, you—"

The air from the flapping of large wings buffeted the side of her face and Arianna turned as a loud screech nearly deafened her. A giant bird-like creature had been saddled with an ornate leather seat like those intended for horseback. Her fingers closed around the hilt of her sharper dagger.

A Dragon the color of pale sea foam sat poised on its back as the bird perched with ease on the ledge. The rider had golden eyes not unlike Cvareh's, but his hair was a darker shade, closer to the color of fired brick or wet clay. He ran a hand through his shoulder-length locks, smoothing them from the ride. His eyes drifted to her instantly.

"You brought a Chimera?" Disapproval radiated from the man's pores.

"The ends, Cain." Cvareh's tone had a cautionary punctuation, the words strung together with a vibrato of authority Arianna had never heard from him before. It made her look sideways at the man she'd traveled across Loom with.

"Looking forward to hearing more of those." Cain shook his head. "Come on then. Petra'Oji wants you in the Temple post haste."

Cvareh made a start for the bird, Arianna at his side. He stopped her with an arm. "You need to wait here."

"Excuse me?"

"The boco can't take more than two riders at a time."

"Then leave this petulant Dragon and take me." Arianna motioned rudely to the man named Cain. Cvareh had earned his name; all others would as well.

"What did you call me?" The man on the boco growled.

"Peace." Cvareh held out his hands between them. But amusement was alight in his eyes—amusement for her.

Bloody cogs, first his boldness and now she was endearing to him? She was losing her edge.

"Wait here. Time is of the essence and I can't explain now. Cain will come back for you," Cvareh said.

"If he doesn't—"

"He will," the Dragon cut off her threat. "Trust me, Ari."

She rolled her eyes and leaned against the side wall again, arms folded across her chest to communicate her general displeasure at the situation. Cvareh shook his head, squeezing awkwardly into the saddle behind Cain. She watched them depart, questioning the choices that had led her here.

Arianna drew her dagger and commenced flipping it in the air, attempting to take her mind off the fact that she had just willingly walked into the Dragon's den.

# 2

## PETRA

Petra walked the tightrope of treason. On either side were the voids of failure, an oblivion from which there was no escape. Dangled at the far end before her was the title of Dono, Queen of the Dragons, glory of House Xin. The sight of it was enough to keep her toeing a line that even the most suicidally ambitious dragon wouldn't dare to walk.

She grinned madly into the wind, baring her canines to an invisible foe.

Islands of Nova flashed beneath her, reduced to green blurs by Raku's speed. She fisted his feathers and altered course slightly. The other three bocos behind her followed suit.

She had the Dono and two riders in tow. Their magic sparked with aggression, but only one held weight. Yveun Dono, King of the Dragons, barely held his emotions in check. She knew when his eyes fell on her back by the ferocity that lit the wind between them.

He knew he'd been played. It had been a plan years in the making, ever since Finnyr had slipped. Petra had cut it from the cloth of knowledge given to her by her elder brother—the King's financial adviser for Loom. That knowledge of the Philosopher's Box would be the pattern for the tapestry of her ultimate victory.

She'd moved carefully, sending Cvareh to acquire the documents and entrusting him to get them to the resistance on Loom. Her younger brother was underestimated by the whole of Nova. She'd kept him in the wings, cultivating his skills when no one watched. When the time came he was overlooked and slipped through the cracks, just as expected.

Her years of patience were now paying dividends. She knew he was stronger than anyone gave him credit for, but even Petra had not expected her brother would be the one to slay the King's Master Rider. Poor Leona; for all her airs and appearances, she was felled by sweet little Cvareh. Not bearing witness to her ultimate demise had already become one of Petra's few regrets.

Now the King sought justice for his slain bitch. He wanted Cvareh's head in recompense, and that was a price Petra wasn't going to pay. When Cvareh arrived hours ago, Petra had lifted the baton on the next movement of her orchestrations. Her brother was seen to the Temple of Xin. The Chimera he'd brought...well, that was an unexpected deviation that she had yet to attain a full explanation for.

Petra shifted in her saddle. *One thing at a time*, she reminded herself. The Chimera was hidden, for now. She'd deal with the creature later when she didn't have a King in tow.

Her shadow zipped across the God's Line far below, jumping on and off smaller islands as she crossed above them. The isle of Ruana, twice the size of House Rok's Lysip, came into view. Mountains curved on the far ridge-line, spilling bountiful plains and fertile farmland in their shade. It was impossible for Petra to keep a smile off her face when her home came into view. No raging Dragon King could damper the way her soul soared alongside Raku as she crossed the threshold of Xin land.

Far on the horizon, at the highest peak, was the Temple of Lord Xin, the Death-bringer. It shot upward, like a sword spearing the land itself, in a single column: a pointed obelisk that both unified and severed earth and sky. Against the morning light, it was awash in ominous shadow.

Petra adjusted her grip on the boco. She feared no mortal man, but the gods were another matter. She would repent to the Death God in triplicate when this was over for using his temple in her fight against Yveun Dono. In the meantime, she could only hope Lord Xin turned his eternal gaze upon her fondly. Petra would believe that she was truly his chosen daughter, so if there were to be death dealt today, it would not be her or Cvareh's.

With a chorus of flapping, the boco quartet landed on a nearly too-small ledge at the base of the temple. A yawning entrance, simple and unadorned, waited before them, cut and smoothed from the gray mountain stone. Petra dismounted alongside the others, silence their fifth companion.

She toed to the threshold of the entrance, the bright daylight cut in a sharp line of shadow. Petra closed her eyes and covered them with both palms, a sign of servitude and respect. One knew not what waited in eternity; the crossing happened only when one's eyes closed for the final time.

Petra stepped into the temple.

Her eyes adjusted quickly to the dim lighting. Not a single candle burned and the world beyond cast long shadows over the twenty sculptures that lined the long hall. Nineteen alternated placement on either side, visages of every other god and goddess in the pantheon. Lord Tam held out scales, Lord To cradled an open manuscript with the delicacy of a babe, Lady Che held her trumpet of truth to her lips—the statues stretched on and on, atop their ornate daises.

There was one variation to the statues found in Lord Xin's temple: they all wore a large veil atop their faces. The shroud of death was settled upon every brow, including the sculpture at the very end of the Lord of Death himself. Lord Xin's visage had been carved with such elegance that his layered robes seemed to move with ethereal grace, even in stone. His veil was stretched taught over unknown features, pulled by an invisible wind. He looked as though he could at any moment become flesh and steal the life from any of his divine brethren.

Some worshipers took note of the unorthodox party as they traversed the hall. They offered bows of their heads to the King, though Petra was certain the gestures were far less than the prostrations he was accustomed to on Lysip. But the King's demeanor was unchanged. Yveun Dono was either humbled into muted silence in the presence of the Death bringer, or he was too upset for his magic to hold any further aggression.

Petra led them back behind the statue of Lord Xin and into a narrow stair. Darkness engulfed them, so thick that even her eyes couldn't penetrate it. She slid her hand along the wall, recognizing every subtle shift of the craftsmen's work. Her feet knew the exact spacing of every step, memorized over years of pilgrimage.

One of the Riders stumbled, the noise breaking silence's purity. Petra withheld a snapping remark, not wanting to shame her Lord further by doing the same herself. Still, she bared her teeth at the blackness behind her.

It would be in her right as the Xin'Oji to kill any who shamed her House's patron without need of a formal duel. Yveun Dono certainly knew this, and his measured steps were barely audible; even his breathing was hushed. Certainly, his magic sparked violently, but he kept his physical manner in close check. He would never make it that easy for her.

The weight of the stone grew suffocating as they continued to spiral upward. Silence stretched into infinity. Darkness tore at the mind, turning seconds into hours.

The Riders' breathing became labored, and not from the strain of the stairs. Petra didn't turn or offer them even a thought of pity. Yveun Dono kept pace and didn't falter.

Slowly, the sound of wind whispered freshness to them. They took one more wide curve and arrived at the apex of the obelisk. A single oculus cut through the darkness like a triumphant banner. It offered the temptation of a world beyond, a lone portal and no more.

Upon the floor was a circular divot, recessed as if the light itself had worn away the stone in time. Cvareh was curled within it like a snake in an egg, taking up nearly all available space. He was as naked as the day he was born. His palms covered his face and his body was still. His barely moving shoulders betrayed that he was alive at all.

Petra crossed over to her brother. His months-long meditation had been pretense, but now that he was swaddled within the embrace of Lord Xin, she would observe convention—and not just for Yveun's sake. She knelt down at the rim of the recessed area, covered her eyes with her palms and brought her forehead to the floor.

"End bringer." Her hushed whisper sounded like a shout. "Your child beseeches you, return Cvareh to us. Return him in both body and soul with your infinite wisdom and eternal truth."

Three breaths, and Cvareh stirred. His breathing quickened to a normal pace, his muscles rippling under his powder-fair skin. With painful slowness he rolled forward, his face still covered by his hands in a position that mirrored Petra's. His back straightened, each vertebra clicking into place. His head tilted back, and he finally pulled away his palms, blinking into the light.

She sat in tandem, opening her eyes as well. The relief that flooded Petra didn't need to be faked. It surged through her at the sight of her brother, powerful and whole. The Lord of Death had not taken his soul yet from her side, not down upon Loom, not now as punishment for using his temple in her maneuvering against Yveun Dono. He rose again, and again, stronger than ever.

Cvareh's blood-colored eyes finally drifted to her. They shone like two golden disks in the sunlight. She had whispered the plan to him as she organized it on her way to the Rok Estate. He had known she would be there, but a tangible joy pulled at his expression, tugging it into the realm of inappropriate given their current venue.

"Forgive me for pulling you from your meditation, brother." She pushed through the moment. There was still work to be done. "Our divine King has demanded to speak with you."

Cvareh played his part just as she'd instructed. Her brother was the perfect soldier. He never questioned and he was always attentive when she spoke.

"Yveun Dono—" Cvareh cleared his throat, as though he had not used it in months and it troubled him to speak. "It is an honor to be sought by you."

"Cvareh Xin." The Dono could not keep a growl from his voice. He stalked across the space with restrained and measured steps. "Where have you been these past months?"

Confusion furrowed Cvareh's brow. "Forgive me, Dono, but I fear I don't understand your question." He lowered his eyes demurely, radiating nothing but subservience to the King looming over him.

Yveun leaned forward and Petra reminded herself to breathe. She'd instructed Cvareh carefully on what he needed to do. A scrub of perfumed salts until he bled, a wash of boiling water; when his skin had knitted he was to cut it again and smear his blood atop himself. And, by all the gods, he was to do it nowhere near the Chimera or anything else of Loom.

The King inhaled deeply. Petra knew she had won from that single sniff. His mouth pressed into a line and he breathed again in quick succession.

"Do not play dumb with me, child," Yveun growled. "I know you have not been in this temple."

"Has it been weeks?" Cvareh's face paled on command. He turned to Petra and then looked back at the Dono in false confusion. "My King, I've been seeking the words of my Lord. Time has escaped me… If you called on me and I did not answer then—"

"Do not lie to me, you thief." Yveun's claws shot out from his fingers. They gleamed in the light, sharpened by grating on bones from years of duels.

Petra stood slowly. Her own claws itched for release. If she could goad Yveun into a mistake now, she could claim the throne.

"Yveun Dono… We are in the Temple of Lord Xin, Patron of my House. As his mortal hand and protector of all Xin, it is my duty to defend my kin." She drew her height. Petra was three fingers shorter than the King but she felt evenly matched as she threw her magic against him without fear of repercussion. Cvareh could handle two fresh Riders if he could slay Leona. The King would be hers. "I have tolerated your affronts against my brother and have violated my Lord's sacred code to bring you here. But if you maintain these slanderous claims before man and god, I will evoke the Deathbringer and demand your atonement for them."

Her claws finally unsheathed to punctuate her words in a sweet release. It was the first time she had bared them before Yveun and doing so was a thrill unto itself.

Yveun's lips curled in a snarl, exposing his canines. But he didn't attack, and he didn't speak further. While preserving all the dominance he could, he stepped away.

His retreating magic left a bittersweet aftertaste, a surge of power that Petra craved. It was delicious to feel it shrink before her and she wanted to feel the sensation again and again. At the same time, she wished it had been the first and only time she'd feel such a thing. For if such were the case, then the title of Dono would be attached to *her* name.

"Caution, Petra." The King dropped her title, slapping her across the face with words. Petra remained mentally fettered. "If you continue down this path you shall evoke the Death-bringer indeed. But it shall not be my atonement he seeks. Do not let your ambition blind you to your ideals."

Yveun Dono stepped away, knowing he'd been beat. With Cvareh in the place she claimed, acting so perfectly, not a scent of Loom on him, the King had no proof—for now. To challenge them would require the King to own up to his shames—Cvareh having bested both him in stealing the schematics from under his nose, and his Riders on Loom. She would see the sun and moon rise together before she expected Yveun to imbibe on his own humility. Petra watched as he departed back down the bleak descent of the Temple of Death, knowing it would not be the last time their tensions would rise to a near boil only to be iced again.

She relaxed her hands, claws retreating *for now*. "You are mistaken, Yveun," she breathed. "Ends before ideals."

# 3
## CVAREH

Cvareh would trade his soul for a well-tailored pair of trousers and tastefully matching shoulder adornments. It was ice cold atop the mountain and he fought shivers as the air nipped at his bare skin. It was still tender from healing after the abuse he'd put it through at Petra's request.

*Petra.*

He followed his elder sister down the long staircase he'd sprinted up only an hour before. He couldn't see her in the darkness, but he could feel her. She was bright and sharp. Her magic smelled crisply of pine. Her steps were measured and even, the lithe, sinewy muscles in her legs betraying strength hidden from the casual eye. Her breathing was even, unlabored, unfaltering. She'd met the Dragon King and walked away as though it was a matter that caused her no more concern than choosing what to wear in the morning.

Meanwhile, Cvareh's knees still trembled. Yveun Dono was an imposing force. He was not to be trifled with and made no hesitation in making it known. Cvareh had enough experience to last a lifetime fighting against his Riders; the last thing he was inclined to do was fight the King himself.

But he kept himself together in Petra's presence. He worked to mimic her stoicism. His sister was far more devout to the Lord Xin than Cvareh was, and he would do nothing to offend her faithful sensibilities to Lord and House.

She didn't so much as look back at him the entire length of the hall. Cvareh noticed the occasional curious glance, and the knowing look from worshippers, but no one commented. He mirrored Petra's movements as she covered her eyes with the heels of her hands and crossed the threshold into sunlight.

His sister took a deep breath, spreading out her arms as if to invite all of Ruana into her embrace. The sunlight danced along her golden curls, striking against the midnight blue skin of her shoulders. Petra was nearly the same height as Cvareh, but her body was cut and primed. She was born to be the Oji he adored—alongside everyone else in House Xin.

"Cvareh!" Without warning, a switch flipped in her demeanor. She spun on her heel and pulled him in for a bone-crushing embrace. "How I have missed you, little brother."

"And I, you." He had missed being enveloped in the scent of pine, the familiar feeling of her muscles beneath his palms, the pleased hum that thrummed across their magic when they were in the other's presence. Petra was born to be Oji, and Cvareh was born to be her Ryu.

"I insist you tell me everything." She pulled back, leaving space for business to come between them.

"I must insist on clothing first." He let himself shiver in the wake of a mountain gust for emphasis.

"Very well." She started for her boco. "Come home. It has been too long since you graced the halls of the Xin manor."

"I see Raku put on weight while I was gone." Cvareh patted the boco's side as he situated himself behind his sister. Riding a saddle without trousers was bound to be a positively miserable experience, and he'd turn his thoughts to anything else.

"Muscle," she insisted.

"Of course." Cvareh grabbed his sister's waist as they took to the air.

Ruana spread out like a lover beneath him once more, inviting and familiar. This time he could appreciate the splendor of his homeland. For now, it appeared as if they'd evaded Yveun Dono, which meant his life was secure for a little longer.

In the distance he saw the towns of Abilla and Venys, sprawling toward the largest city on Ruana, Napole. He imagined the soaring vocals of the last opera he'd seen there drifting to him on the wind, and was instantly set to wondering what was playing now. Cvareh felt like a Dragon seeing the upper half for the first time. Everything was wondrous; everything felt new. The sights and sounds he had taken for granted all his life were now shining in the eyes of a man who had resigned himself to the real possibility that he might never see them again. The eyes of a man who had seen nothing but steel blended with bronze and steam for months.

His sister tilted and Raku banked. Cvareh moved with them as their course altered. They no longer tracked along the sloping valley, but aimed instead for a smaller mountain nestled between the grasslands and the Temple of Xin.

"You've made progress," he observed.

"The winds have been kind to the workers," Petra affirmed.

Cvareh had been born in a smaller estate much closer to the heart of Napole that was now used to house the Kin and Da of House Xin. When Petra killed their father, assuming the Xin'Oji title, she had deemed the older estate unfit for the current House Xin. She'd hand-picked the best architects from across Nova, pulling them in on the most ambitious project to date. Any who deemed her vision impossible met an ill fate.

Petra's methodology had reaped rewards, as it so often did. Now, the Xin manor was the jewel of Ruana. Its spires defied logic as they curved and wound together like mating snakes. Rooms hung as freely as ripe fruit on the vine in the free air. Tunnels burrowed into the mountain itself, opening into cavernous meeting spaces, only to be rolled out like lapping tongues to meet the illogically suspended towers.

A smile thinned his lips. He wondered what Arianna and all her Rivet sensibilities would make of his wondrous home.

"That's a new feeling." Petra glanced over her shoulder, catching him in the act.

"What is?" He tried and failed to play dumb.

"That pleased pulse across your magic. That coy smile."

"Hardly."

Petra laughed like song bells. "Cvareh, your efforts to conceal the truth to me are futile. You whispered to me about a woman—the White Wraith no less. Now, you bring a Chimera home to me whom I can only assume is one and the same."

"I promise I will tell you everything once I have clothes on." He shifted uncomfortably in the saddle, ready for Raku to land on the waiting stretch of stone beneath them. "What's the style of the day?"

"Magenta seems to be quite popular among the tea house socialites," Petra answered over Raku's fluttering wings, easing them back to the earth.

Cvareh made a gagging noise. "Rok's influence no doubt." The color would clash terribly with his skin.

"You'll pull it off fine. Or, there is always the tried and true Xin blue," Petra consoled, seeing straight through him. "For now, indulge me and wear last year's fashions so that we may catch up."

"If I must." Cvareh sighed, already half dressed.

Servants had met them on the platform, preempting their needs. As soon as Cvareh had dismounted, his feet were in the wide legs of lounging trousers. While Petra had been speaking the help had woven a delicately embroidered shawl around his arms and across his shoulders. The final adornments were affixed about his neck, a silver chain with many loops, black stones reminiscent of the Rider's beads weighting their apexes.

Those same servants disappeared back into the shadows and off even the edges of Cvareh's subconscious as he followed his sister into their home. The floor of the main entry hall had been done in glass, save for a stone lip on the outer edge. The mountain beneath it had been carved away and radiant sunlight from the clouds far below filled the room. Petra walked boldly across it, Cvareh following in her steps.

She settled on a raised dais as the doors closed. A throne of stone, simple yet imposing, its angular lines cut into the hazy light projected upward from the floral-patterned glass. Cvareh wondered if Yveun Dono had yet to see his sister's hall. The statement it made was hardly subtle.

"Now, tell me all that has transpired." Petra's tone changed the moment she sat upon the throne. Gone was his adoring little sister, overwhelmed with excitement and relief at the sight of him. In her place was the Xin'Oji, the deadly and fearless leader who had desired nothing more for the entirety of her short life than to be Dono.

Cvareh approached, settling himself cross-legged on one of the wide lower rungs of her dais. He remained poised with his back straight, instinctively answering her unspoken demand by assuming his place. If she was to be the Oji, then he was to be her Ryu.

"Flying the glider proved to be more of a challenge than expected. I didn't get far before crashing in New Dortam, the Riders close on my tail…"

The words spilled from him as he watched the events of the past months replay before his eyes in double time. Things had grown hazy, especially at the onset. Details had faded into the obscurity of unimportance, shrouded by the more pertinent and immediately relevant parts.

One shining element remained in crystalline focus. At every turn and twist, he could see Arianna perfectly. He could recall with ease the expression she wore the first time she'd driven him to stop time. He remembered the contours of her face when her gaze softened as she looked at him on the ship crossing to Ter.4.2, the first moment he had seen beauty in the unique skills she possessed. Cvareh's memories were painted with her, making their mere recollection an unparalleled delight.

His tale wrapped up with the Alchemists' Guild. It was the most somber note of all he said. Despite all the progress he'd recounted, he and Arianna had left Loom at a place of tension and strangeness. But when he spoke his last words, the taste of honeysuckle tinted with cedar filled his mouth, evoked by the mere memory of the imbibing they had shared following the airship crash.

Petra hadn't moved the entire time he spoke. She remained still and contemplative. Her magic was withdrawn tight to her body, betraying nothing.

"How long will she stay?" his sister finally asked.

"I don't know," Cvareh confessed. His summary had hardly been short, but it proved impossible to explain that he found himself in no place to question Arianna. "I presume she'll want to leave as soon as she is confident in your leadership."

His sister shifted, drawing her fingertips to her lips in thought. "This is an amusing little Chimera, isn't it?" The corner of her mouth curled. "She has you quite ensnared and now designs to make me submit before her as well."

"She is not one to be underestimated."

"Oh that much is well apparent. Anyone who could kill the King's bitch shouldn't be." Petra laughed with glee at the mere mention of the former Master

Rider's demise. "Leona, felled by a Chimera. Lord Xin can be delightful at times." His sister straightened, pulling herself from her musings. "You know this woman—"

"Not quite," he corrected, noting his sister's tone.

"Then know her better." Petra smirked. "Tell me, Cvareh, what must I do to earn her trust?"

He was still figuring that out himself. Cvareh stared at the decorative hem of his pants, patterns of leaves woven and cut into the edge. He debated quietly with the fabric until he had a decent answer. There were only two things in the world Cvareh could say with certainty were important to Ari. Two things that would prove someone an ally of the woman who called herself the White Wraith.

"Prove to her you love Loom."

"I hold no love for that dreary rock."

He knew it to be true, and instantly felt foolish for phrasing it as he had. "Prove to her, then, that you are aligned with Loom's interests."

"I know not what those are and furthermore, I don't care."

Cvareh closed his eyes a moment. Petra was a force unto herself, and now he had Ari to grapple with on Nova in addition to her. The idea of praying to Lord Agendi for luck grew more appealing by the minute.

"If you do not care, then assure her Loom will have sovereignty." Cvareh met his sister's eyes. "For all you care about the title of Dono, Arianna cares for Loom."

"If she believes this, she will make the Philosopher's Box for me? She will hand me my army?"

"For Loom, there is nothing she wouldn't do."

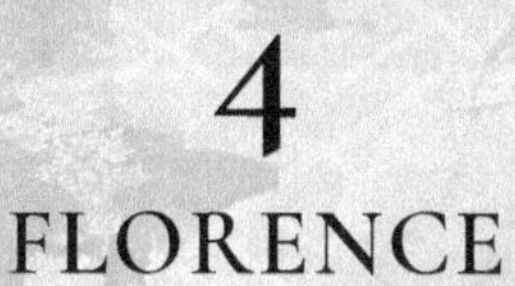

# 4
## FLORENCE

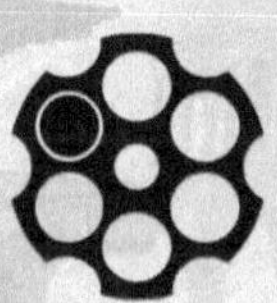

Beads of sweat rolled down Florence's cheek, sliding slowly over her outlined Raven tattoo. She drew breath slowly through her nose, hissing it out between her teeth to keep them from chattering. The room was frigid. Her blood was boiling.

She held a golden canister between her index finger and thumb, blinking at it through the goggles. There was a small mountain of gunpowder at her right, and a half dozen reactive chemicals at her left. She could be blown five ways to eternity with one wrong move.

"Adding mercury..." she breathed, entirely to herself. With deliberate movements she reached for the beaker she knew held the element in question, lifting it precisely to the canister in hand. She watched as the liquid metal flowed into the concoction in the golden tube.

Magic pulsed from under her fingers in uneven bursts. Controlling it was like trying to hold lard with her fingertips. Every time she thought she had a grip, it slithered from her grasp, leaving only remnants. It left her struggling to clasp it again, to find the same weight she'd held it with mere seconds before.

If she messed up now, she'd kill herself and blow out a wing of the Alchemists' guild hall with her. One wrong move, one improperly measured powder or chemical, one second of too much stabilizing magic, was all it would take. A tiny smirk graced her lips as she eased the beaker back down to the table.

This tension was what she lived for. It was one half of a whole, scales that tipped with her every movement. She spent minutes—hours—creating, only to reap destruction tenfold with her products. It was what had drawn her away from the Ravens guild, the transportation experts of the world, to the Revolvers.

A sharp, metallic scent filled her nose. Smelling chemical reactions taking place was a new sensation. Naturally, large-scale or prominent reactions might be discernible to any chemist. But this was different. Her senses had been changing since she had become a Chimera. Her whole body was adapting to the introduction of Dragon blood. In the two weeks since she had changed, she'd grown half a finger taller. She slept less and ate less, but had far more energy.

As loath as Arianna would be to hear Florence say it, she did see the benefits of being a Chimera—of being a Dragon. It had become easier to understand why the Philosopher's Box was so sought-after. A perfect Chimera—one that could have all the Dragon organs at once without the magic corrupting their mind, rotting their body, and turning them forsaken? Such a thing would change the world.

But Florence couldn't make such a box. That skill set rested solely with the woman she had called friend and mentor. And now… now Florence didn't know what she was to that talented inventor.

She set the canister into its slot on a stand. Her hands had moved through her thoughts. The distraction made them steady and certain rather than clouded by too much focus weighted on a single task.

Arianna had left without a word. They'd fought, she'd been aloof for about a week, and then vanished beyond the clouds above. Everyone seemed to expect Florence to have some insight as to Arianna's methods, but she had none. She'd never had any. The trappings of the woman's mind were an enigma Florence had never been fit to unravel.

Florence capped the canister with certainty.

She'd not been entirely honest with the Alchemists. She couldn't quite fit her suspicions about Arianna's departure into words, not in a way they'd understand. It was a feeling more than logic. After their last conversation, if all she knew to be true about the woman held fact, then Arianna had left to do what needed to be done. Florence marveled at the notion that it might have been her words that compelled Arianna to do so, but only at night when she waited for sleep.

By day, there was work to do. Arianna was above the clouds with Cvareh, hopefully not killing every Dragon she saw on sight—*that* would be bad for relations with the rebellion. Florence remained on Loom, helping those same rebels whom she now fancied herself part and parcel of.

She reached for her latest modified revolver. It was heavier than the standard issue due to all the gold she'd used. Along the barrel were etched Alchemical runes. Not more than six months ago, those same runes were nothing more than grooves beneath her fingertips. Now, they tingled across her flesh, begging for magic, whispering back to her of the power she'd stored in them. It was an interesting sort of science that had to be felt as much as it was learned.

Florence grabbed her pea coat and slung it over her shoulders, venturing into the heart of the Alchemists' Guild.

It was quiet in the early hours of the morning. Most still slept and the golden elevators were silent. She no longer needed the assistance of another to make the lifts move. With a thought, she reached out to the metal magically, forcing it downward. The gears beneath the platform groaned to life. Their teeth slotted into grooves on the wall, clicking down the length of the tower that served as the heart of the most secretive guild in the world.

She ventured out into the Skeleton Forest, as hazy as the impenetrable layer of clouds above Loom. Ghostly wisps wove around trees and obscured shrubs. Magic singed across the back of her neck, alerting her to all the traps the Alchemists had placed to ward off the deadly Endwig. Florence was careful to avoid them; if the traps were mighty enough to slay one of the haunting creatures, they would no doubt render her to a pulp in seconds.

Just beyond the edge of the traps' territory was where she'd made her range —a decent winding walk from the guild hall. Florence didn't presume her activities had gone unnoticed. Her detonations weren't exactly subtle. But she hadn't expected to find a trike waiting for her.

A man lay out in the seat of the vehicle, his knees draped over the handlebars. His hands were folded behind his head, their obsidian skin nearly blending in with the iron of his hair in the dim light. He wore a loose shirt, barely decent enough to be counted as a dressing for bed, and loose pants that were nearly the same shade of brown as the bronze of his vehicle.

Florence was accustomed now to Derek venturing about in such a lax state of undress, but it had been the cause for much surprise the first early morning they'd worked together.

"I was wondering when you'd show." He beat her to the first word.

"I might have never. I don't come out here every morning." Florence continued onward, narrowing the distance between her and the trike positioned right at the start of her makeshift shooting range.

"You come out here every morning you get up early to finish a canister." He peered at her with one golden eye. It was a dark color, nearly smoldering red. Against the dark ash of his skin, it looked like an ember that remained in wait for the chance to spark fire again.

"I didn't know you paid that much attention to my work." Florence rounded the large tires of the vehicle. On the other side was a long stretch of bare forest. Holes of upturned earth marked the spaces that Florence had used as testing grounds for bombs. A tree wider than four of her rested perpendicular to her line of sight. Countless pockmarks pitted its surface from rounds long past. Whole chunks had been reduced to sawdust along the stretch of trunk. Today, if Florence's round worked as she hoped, there would be another gaping maw in its bark.

"I've paid attention to your work from the first time I saw it."

That wasn't untrue. Derek had always heeded Florence's input. But only when it came to the things that were important to him. She'd been all too eager to help the rebellion however she could, and with her connections in Ter.4's Underground through Will and Helen, and ties in Mercury Town, that meant assisting with getting the Alchemists the necessary supplies the Dragon King had been trying to throttle.

To date, Florence had only very minor successes on that front, and she could tell that it was beginning to grate on the nerves of the powers in the Alchemists' Guild. Florence opened the hinge on her revolver in frustration. No matter how much she explained otherwise, they saw the tattoo on her cheek—the outline of a raven—before listening to her about where her skills lay. She knew nothing about how long it would take to get supplies across the world. She didn't understand the nuances of seafaring. And train schedules made her eyes blur over. The Alchemists needed a true Raven to accomplish what they wanted; Florence could make the right introductions, but she was useless beyond that.

"You're going to break the gun if you keep loading rounds like that." Derek drew in his feet, sitting upward in the seat of the trike.

"Actually, this is an alpha model. The hinges are more durable than the beta versions, cast in high heat steel." Florence held up the gun, inspecting it in the light. "I've also reinforced the locking mechanism and tightened the springs. It's meant to hold up under the strain of active combat, so it can take a bit of abuse from canister loading."

Derek was silent, but she could feel his eyes on her back. There was a certain type of power that came from knowing she had done something to earn stiff-lipped respect. Eventually, she might even get through to him and the rest of them that her value extended far beyond the marking on her cheek.

*Let him watch,* Florence thought as she pushed small piles of dirt on either side of her feet to assume a wide firing stance. She wanted him to see the fruits of her labor. To respect her ingenuity like she had respected Ari's for years.

Power surged though her arms. It was leeched from her blood like sweat from pores on a hot day. It oozed through her hands and flowed in a perfect channel to the runes along the barrel. It wrapped around the canister like a constricting serpent.

Her finger curled around the trigger. That was always her favorite moment: the half second when her skin first came in contact with the trigger of a gun. It was a surge of power. Judgment encased in metal, welded together with the ability to change the world with the merest twitch of muscle. In that breath, everything else faded away, and Florence felt like the universe hung on her will.

The last rune along the barrel lit up. The charge was too slow, but she could work on that later. Florence took her aim and pulled the trigger.

The gun exploded in her hand with a rain of shrapnel. She tumbled backward, half in surprise and half from force. A clumsy beam of energy shot forward, radiating outward and carving a ditch into the earth underneath the line of its shot.

She hit the ground ungracefully, bringing a hand up to her stinging face. Bits of metal were lodged into her cheek. The pain was ringing in her ears and the exhaustion from her magic working overtime set in, forming bruises along her legs as it tried to heal the cuts on her face.

"You're going to kill yourself," Derek muttered.

Florence hadn't heard him move, but he was now squatted before her. One hand curled around the more intact side of her face. She blinked away the haze as his other hand began to pick out the bits of metal. Even when he wasn't trying to be graceful, his movements held a surgical precision. Her eyes settled on the tattoo on his cheek: two solid black triangles, one pointing up, the other down, connected by a line.

"It wasn't a bad attempt." It was clear his compliment was nothing more than placating. *No, it was a positively miserable attempt.* Embarrassment stung the back of her throat, becoming more potent with the taste of blood.

"Then I never want to see a bad attempt of yours." Derek knew she was lying, his chuckle told her so. But the statement was void of any sting.

Her magic had set her face to knitting at the expense of some burst blood vessels. That was the way of magic. Florence had always known it, but this was the first time she was experiencing it. When magic was overused it turned the organs it lived in—which, in Flor's case, was her blood—brittle and necrotic. If too much magic was used, the body was pushed beyond repair.

She looked with clarity and a heavy sigh on the broken remnants of her revolver. She'd need another, more gold, more chemicals… She wasn't looking forward to another trip to the armory.

"Up with you." Derek took her hands, pulling her to her feet. "Nora wasn't up late last night. She'll be awake soon and wondering where we are."

The man relinquished her fingers and walked back over to the trike. Florence stood in limbo. She felt trapped between the failure of her passions and the weak successes of a duty she'd never wanted.

"Flor?" Derek called from atop the vehicle.

"Coming." She left the remnants of the gun in the dirt. Failure was a missed shot; quitting was never reloading the gun. She was Florence, student of the White Wraith, and she did not quit.

# 5
## ARIANNA

Arianna immediately took issue with Cain's tone. "You think I can't figure that out?"

She settled herself on the back of the giant purple flying chicken, hating the feeling of a living creature under her rather than something mechanical. She'd nearly prefer the busted glider over the bird. At least it didn't have a mind of its own that could rebel when she was in the open air.

"Well?" He drew out a long pause at the end of the word, looking over his shoulder.

"You don't think I'm actually going to touch you, do you?" Arianna gripped the back of the saddle with both hands for show. Her legs pressed tightly on either side, stabilizing herself.

"Technically—" His eyes darted down to where her hips were pressed against his backside by virtue of the shape of the seat.

"I don't want to hear it, Dragon." Arianna narrowed her eyes and reached for her dagger. "Cross me and I will cut—"

"Suit yourself." Cain shrugged and snapped the reins.

With a mighty caw, the bird lurched off the ledge. Arianna's stomach was instantly in her throat. She held on with white knuckles and all the determination that came from being keenly aware of how vulnerable she presently was. Arianna had absolutely no control: not of the bird, not of the man before her, not of where he was taking her.

"Where are we going?" She needed to take something back from him, even if it was just knowledge.

"The Xin Manor." Arianna hadn't actually expected him to answer. "The

Dono will be on Ruana soon, and we need to try to scrub the stink of Loom off you before he arrives."

"Dragon—" she half snarled.

He jerked the reins and the bird banked hard to the right around the mountain. Arianna's grip slipped and she teetered in the seat. Still her hands didn't seek out the stability of his form. She righted herself, collapsing the muscles in her stomach, compressing those in her back, and weighting herself in the seat.

Cain gave her another quick glance. "You're a stubborn one, aren't you?"

Arianna fantasized about all the ways she could peel his green-blue skin off his bones the second they landed.

"My name is not 'Dragon'." He turned forward again with a self-righteous squaring of his shoulders. "It's Cain Xin'Da Bek."

She rolled her eyes dramatically at his back. "Cvareh told me much the same when we first met."

"That's Cvareh Soh to you, Chimera." She'd struck an obvious nerve as his tone shifted.

"So defensive," Arianna mock-praised over the howling wind. "Cva would be so proud."

Cain gave a sharp whistle and the bird dropped into a free fall. Arianna's shoulder muscles strained from the tension she put them under as she worked to hold onto the saddle rather than giving in to the Dragon. She'd show him that Fenthri were not to be underestimated. That *she* was not to be underestimated.

Just when she thought she'd go deaf from the howling wind, he pulled again, leaning into the curve of the mountain. Arianna learned fast and moved with him. The centrifugal force held her in place.

"Cvareh had to earn his name, as do you." Arianna didn't miss a beat when the bird leveled again.

Cain laughed at the sky. It was different than the way people laughed on Loom. This sound was loud, full-bellied, a half-roar of mirth.

"Twenty gods above, what *are* you?"

Arianna leaned forward, finally placing her hands on him. She wanted him to feel her there. To feel the power in her fingertips, to feel her magic. The smell of earth after rain—the scent of his magic—tingled her nose.

"The White Wraith," she whispered.

Three simple words evoked such shock in the Dragon that she thought his neck might snap from turning to look at her. Arianna curled her mouth into a wide smile, baring her teeth. His golden eyes tried to dissect a lie from her proclamation where there was none.

*Good. He'd heard of her.*

Cain turned forward rigidly, his whole body tense under her hands. Arianna relaxed away, resting on the saddle once more. She was more dangerous when her palms were free to grip her daggers at will. Not that he expressly knew that, but she'd relish keeping him guessing. Predictability was the death of fear.

The gray stone of the mountain arched beside them, unfurling like a grand banner. And the gem of that banner was what Arianna could only assume to be the Xin manor. She worked to keep her face passive, just in case Cain turned to face her. She had only a glimpse of the mountainside structure during her harrowing flight in. Now, it grew before her, inviting and impossible.

Stone arched and curved, spinning around towers and lacing between walkways. There were stretches of woven masonry that served no other purpose than aesthetics, as they were clearly too thin and brittle to be supports or walkways. Raw crystal or glass had been cut into it, filtering the sunlight into rainbows upon the walls.

The boco banked again, beginning to descend. Numbers upon numbers whirred in Ari's head as she stared at every arch and tower. The calculations kept coming up as impossible, time and again. This structure shouldn't be standing. It should crumble under its own weight, or be toppled by one of the mighty gusts that ripped around the mountainside.

Arianna lived in a world of calculation on Loom. She understood the laws of nature, what could and couldn't be done. But she was no longer on Loom. She was in a land of endless waterfalls, flying bird mounts, inverted mountains, floating islands, and castles of stone that were held aloft in the sky with the same ease as a paper plane in a breeze.

She dismounted with purpose, her legs steady despite her knees having turned to gelatin. She was Arianna, the White Wraith; the hem of her white coat flapped around her calves, and she would walk like the bloody god she was, come to pass judgment on this backward land. As if sensing her mental declaration, the Dragons who were waiting to greet them in the jeweled courtyard they landed within hovered in the shade of an upper galley. They looked uncertainly from her to Cain, begging silently for some kind of explanation for her presence.

Just for effect, Arianna lifted her goggles onto her forehead, showing off her pilfered Dragon eyes like rare and coveted gemstones.

"Cain'Da." A woman was the bravest among them. *No surprise.* She kept her eyes turned downward as she approached, cloth draped over her arm. Arianna watched as the sapphire-skinned woman peeled his fitted riding jacket from his bare chest, holding a coat void of sleeves as an equally pointless alternative.

Arianna folded her hands over her chest. "Can't even dress yourself?"

"Come, Chimera." Cain looked at her sideways.

"Arianna." She didn't budge.

"If I must earn my name, you must earn yours," he snarled, baring his teeth.

Arianna curled her lips in reply. She may not have the fearsome canines of a Dragon, but she knew how to speak their language. One of the servants balked at the sight. Unfortunately, it didn't have the same effect on Cain.

"Do you think you can intimidate me?" He strolled over nonchalantly. "Do you know how many I've killed?"

"Forced to guess, I would estimate the number to be less than not nearly enough to make me scared." A hand curled around the hilt of her dagger. "You've heard of me, so you must know what I do to Dragons."

"And yet here you are, on Nova." Cain motioned to the air around him. He waited for a retort she was loath not to have. He took a step forward, encroaching on her personal space. "That's what I thought. I don't know why you're here, *White Wraith*." More than one Dragon waiting in the wings visibly tensed. Even in Fennish, her moniker was known to them. "But you're in my home now. And while you are here, you will be an obedient and obliging guest."

He reached for her chin. To do what, Arianna didn't know. But the motion felt sickly condescending following his declaration. She didn't hesitate to draw her dagger. The golden blade was still ringing from its sheath when it sliced into his flesh. Sharp and precise, she cut off the tip of the offending finger before it could touch her.

Every Dragon around them, all five of them, had their claws out in an instant. They lunged from the shadows with snarls and growls, like dogs let off their chains. Cain held up his still bleeding hand, the fingertip already re-growing. The world seemed to hold its breath with his singular command. All except for Arianna's heaving chest.

"I admire the ferocity. But if you turn your blade against me again, I will not stay my talons."

"You can't kill me." She called his bluff. If Cvareh was to be believed, his sister—the head of House Xin—needed Arianna a lot more than she needed them.

At least, that's what she'd let them believe.

The truth was, if Florence's rebellion was to succeed, they needed the Dragons' help as much as the Dragons needed theirs. The rebellion needed Dragon organs, the ability to transport things quickly, fighting power and an established base on Nova. And a certain resource for the Philosopher's Box that Arianna was determined to find in her time on the floating islands.

"I never said anything about *killing* you. You're the White Wraith, aren't you? I'm sure you can use your imagination as to how I would occupy my time instead." He grinned wildly, showing his teeth again. "Now, will you come with me to the baths? Or do I need to drag you there by force?"

Arianna regretted her decision to come to Nova more and more by the second. She was outnumbered tens, hundreds, to one. Individually, the Dragons might fear her, but as a pack they had her trapped like a wounded hare. With all the dignity she could muster, Arianna sheathed her dagger and straightened from a hostile crouch.

"Lead on," she forced through gritted teeth. If she couldn't keep a combative advantage, she'd keep her pride.

They walked into the shade of the gallery and penetrated the castle's innards. Led through back halls and side passages, Arianna did not see another Dragon outside their group. But she could sense them, smell them, feel their magic rippling through the currents of the air. It was loud, like a hundred people speaking all at once. Her senses were constantly flaring with recognition of them, trying to understand and catalog every magical signature. Arianna could only assume that living on Nova brought the Dragons more success at filtering their senses than she was able to muster. She hoped it would prove a learned trait, otherwise the sensation would drive her mad long before she sized up this Petra she had come to meet.

The servants said nothing. They kept their eyes down and their lips pursed. For the most part, they even contained their curious glances. All except for one.

"Why does Cvareh'Ryu bring a Chimera into our home?" the woman from earlier asked Cain in Ryouk.

"The ends justify these means," Cain replied vaguely. He clearly didn't have much more of an explanation himself.

"She smells," the woman whispered, but not quietly enough that Arianna couldn't hear.

"She will be better once she's washed." They continued on as though Arianna was none the wiser to their discourse. She held her tongue, avoiding speaking in the Dragon's language and giving up the game.

"All Chimera reek, rotten blood."

"I know, Dawyn'Anh," Cain conceded, as if heartbroken by the fact that he would have to endure her scent for another moment longer. "But our Ryu has spoken with the support of the Oji."

That silenced the woman, though Arianna could still feel her radiant frustration. The mention of Cvareh put both the likes of Cain and this Dawyn woman into submission. Arianna failed to stifle a chuckle, earning a confused look from her companions that was abandoned when it became apparent she had no intent of elaborating on the source of her sudden amusement.

The idea of Cvareh scaring anyone into submission was laughable. She had put the Dragon in his place too many times to think of him as anything more than… *than*… Arianna paused, struggling to fill in the blank for an all-too-long second… *than Cvareh.*

They finally rounded into an airy room—yet another space constructed upon a foundation of impossibilities. Steam hung thick in the air, clouding around the aromatic scent of the wildflowers floating in the wading pool. An entire wall was made of rippled glass—or some kind of clear quartz, Arianna had yet to decipher which. She hoped it was the latter, because the former made her question what exactly the builders had been thinking using such large panes of glass to stand against such violent gusts.

One side of the pool was made up of the clear wall, giving the illusion that the water stopped mid-air. The tile surrounding it was set in a chevron pattern and glistened with moisture. A small stool sat out by a bucket full of steaming water and an array of tools that were either for washing or stripping off skin— she couldn't tell which.

The entire group remained, two Dragons on either side of the door. Cain leaned against her only escape nonchalantly. The woman—Dawyn—approached her.

Arianna took a step away, avoiding her outstretched hands.

"I will help you." She spoke in a rudimentary attempt at Fennish, a thick guttural accent over top.

"Help me with what?" Arianna knew exactly what she was implying. But she'd stall to underscore her sour opinion of the implication.

"Wash."

"I think I've managed well enough on my own so far in life."

Cain sighed. "Stop being so difficult. If we wanted you dead, you would be."

"As if you could kill me." She kept up her facade. The second she showed weakness would be the second they'd have her. Even if she was outnumbered, she wouldn't act it. "I don't particularly want an audience for my bath."

Confusion marred Cain's face.

*Rusty cogs.* Realization hit her with the grace of a steam engine. Dragons were not known for their modesty. Half of the people staring at her now were in what she considered various states of undress. They truly didn't, and couldn't, understand why she wouldn't want guests during her ablutions.

Arianna had only been naked around two people: Eva and Florence. She had reached a level of comfort with her long-dead lover and still-living student that surpassed propriety and convention.

But this wasn't Loom.

She had ventured above the clouds in pursuit of new opportunities, old truths, and scores still waiting to be settled. Arianna locked eyes with Cain as her hands began unclasping her harness. He didn't even blink as the metal of her winch box and spools hit the tile floor with an echoing clang, chipping one of the ornate tiles. She started on the fastenings of her coat.

He acknowledged the silent challenge, amusement dancing with fascination in the deep gold of his eyes. She would show them all that she could rise to any occasion—on Loom, on Nova, in this world or the next. One by one, the scraps of her clothing fell and the heat of the room dotted her bare ashen skin with beads of moisture.

Cain's eyes never left her face.

# 6

## YVEUN

He felt it seeping out of him, simmering hot, elevating the temperature of the room. He was alone, which was an unfamiliar sensation. Leona had been a figure at his side for decades and now it was as though the woman had never existed.

She'd had her faults, as they all did, but her loyalty was only matched by her ferocity. And, for the most part, she could manage to temper the fire that burned under her skin even when her frustrations struggled to get the better of her. It was a fire he'd stoked in all the right ways, until it burned white-hot and only for him. Nurturing Leona's radical worship of him had been the rare duty that was also a delight.

Now, years of work had been lost in what seemed like a blink on his lifeline.

Yveun sheathed and unsheathed his claws, raking them against the wall of the room he'd been pacing like some lowly caged animal.

It was one of his secret habits. The Dono, the sky ruler, the overseer of the land below, chosen one of the Life-bringer, for all his sweeping palaces and grand rooms, preferred the comfort of a tiny space to think in. A space with only one way out. A space so confined that just the thought of being trapped within it set his heart to racing.

In that heightened awareness of his own mortality, he found clarity. It was as though the stone walls that surrounded him, marred from years of claws scraped against them, were the only thing solid enough to contain the torrents of his thoughts. It was a place where the feeling of lowliness growled for dominance in his stomach once more, and when he ascended, he returned to the world like a merciful god.

Leona and Coletta were the only two who knew of his secret lair. Coletta never came down; she had her spaces, he had his, and they issued the utmost respect to each other in preserving those barriers. They were three times as effective because they maintained that separation, and the world regarded them as a split entity.

Yveun smiled wide, pure delight filling him at the very thought of Coletta. He and his mate, moon and sun. They were two halves that orbited each other and only very rarely touched.

But Leona... She would wait at the top of the narrow stair that led back into his private chambers. She would grant him his privacy, and say nothing of the clawing or howling that no doubt echoed up to her from time to time. She thought herself mightier for it, for knowing the King's secret. Yet another suggestion of Coletta's gone well, only to be wasted by Leona throwing her life away on Loom.

Yveun snarled, his claws straining against his skin as he gouged them into the wall. *Cvareh Xin.* He thought only Petra would be able to elicit a raw, emotional response from him. But it seemed she'd taught her younger brother in much the same fashion. How that meager slip of a man had bested his Leona was a mystery. Seeing the Dragon-child emerge from his supposed meditation only proved the point further.

Cvareh was not a laughable specimen, but he was no exemplar of the Dragon form. Not even the will of the twenty gods should be able to sway the cards in his favor in a duel against Leona. Yveun retracted his claws and folded them over his chest, walking faster.

Sybil, Leona's sister, had said that Cvareh had help upon Loom—a Chimera and Fenthri. Yveun had seen Leona turn Fenthri into ribbons and reduce Chimera to no more than sharpening posts for her talons. Logic told him it was highly improbable for such meager prospects to be a threat to his Master Rider.

But logic had run its course, and here he was—less several Riders, and his Leona gone well before he intended her removal. Cvareh was alive and upon Nova once more. No schematics for the Philosopher's Box returned. An Alchemists' guild gone rogue—or going fast. And no answer for any of it.

When the probable had been exhausted, the only explanation that remained was the impossible.

Yveun launched himself forward with wide steps. He needed more information and there was one way he knew how to get it with any measure of certainty: he needed a Dragon on the inside. Fortunately for him, he had just the blue-skinned worm for the job on retainer.

The world materialized beneath his feet as he left his unorthodox sanctuary. He envisioned that nothing existed while he was in that tiny claw-scratched room, that the gods themselves held their breath and halted everything for the sake of his thoughts. When he emerged, the world shone with their magic, pulled back together in a new shape that carved a path for him to progress.

Yveun pushed against the wall at the top of the stair. It gave and he emerged from the passage that closed to form the back of the large hearth that dominated one wall of his chambers. They were a glittering contrast to the dark, rough-hewn passage he'd just been in. A large platform bed stood adorned with silks. Pillows were tasseled with beads cut from jewels. The desk alone had taken three craftsmen four months of non-stop work to carve.

It was a collection of all his favorite things, arranged only for him and the few he deemed worthy to rest their eyes upon it. Yveun was in no mood for it. He wouldn't soil the essence of his room with his present ferocity. He'd return when he could rest knowing that action was being taken.

Waiting for him in the hall was the man-child he'd been forced to choose as his new Master Rider. Yveun did not even lay eyes upon the boy. He was barely twenty. His age made his three beads more impressive, but all Yveun could see was how scarce they were compared to Leona's.

He needed to call a Crimson Court soon and test the mettle of his Riders. A few would fall, and a few unexpected upstarts would distinguish themselves from the pack. Yveun would pluck them from their humble beginnings for a place on the top of Lysip. He could only hope a woman would emerge from the lot as a potential candidate for Master Rider. He had a much easier time manipulating a creature he could leverage sexuality against.

"Finnyr?" he demanded.

"In his quarters, I believe." The Rider endeared himself to his lord by knowing exactly what Yveun sought in nothing more than a word.

Beads clicked softly around Yveun's neck as he walked, holding a decorative plate that bore the symbol of House Rok over his bare chest. The silver contrasted brilliantly with his wine-colored skin. Around his waist was a simple sash, holding in place a draped cloth in both front and back. Otherwise, his physique was apparent, cut muscle rippling ominously with each aggravated stride.

Even the Rider gave him an extra half-step of space. Nervousness flashed across his magic, assuring Yveun that his choices in how to present himself were well founded. He leveraged his sexuality against his female riders, his physical presence against male riders. In both, sheer dominance prevailed.

In the end, Yveun didn't care if his subjects loved or feared him, so long as the emotion was an all-consuming one.

"Dono," a green-skinned man greeted him and stepped to the side. He was a Kin from House Tam, a ward of the Dono's to assure the other House's loyalty to their sovereign. But, just having him on Lysip wasn't enough.

Around the man's neck was a thin gold chain. The tempering on the metal whispered familiarity to Yveun, assuring him that his magic was the only force by which the metal could be controlled. Keeping the most important family members of the two subservient Houses might have been sufficient for some other, less King, but Yveun preferred adorning his wards with nooses he could tighten with a thought.

Above all else was his dominance over Loom and Nova.

The Rok Estate opened up on the north side, spilling over the hillside in wandering arcades that connected smaller chalets. The Dono smiled, inhaling the potent scent of wildflowers and subservience.

This was where his *most loyal* subjects lived. Chosen Kin of Xin and Tam—immediate family to the Oji and Ryu of the Houses. The Dono invited them to the Rok Estate and gave them some of the most lavish accommodations in all of Nova. They ate like kings and slept like brothel masters. They were given honors of state and management of affairs both on Loom and Nova. It was a life that many could only dream of.

And all he asked for in return was their unyielding and unquestioning loyalty.

He strode past his subservient subjects on a mission towards one of the middle homes. Yveun did not even knock before crossing the threshold of a stately one-roomed chalet. Just the man he was looking for stared, startled, from behind a desk that could nearly rival Yveun's in quality. *Nearly* rival.

"Dono." Finnyr stood only to fold at the waist in a low bow. "I was not expecting you this morning."

"Weren't you?" Yveun folded his arms over his chest, widening his stance.

"My lord?" Confusion shone true from Finnyr's face into his magic. He clearly had not consulted the whisperer for House Xin. Or, more likely, Petra hadn't sent any word of the King's venture this morning.

Yveun let the accusations drop. "Finnyr, where do your loyalties lie?"

"My King, they lie where they have always been, with you and House Rok." His brows, the color of tarnished gold, knitted together, drawing lines in his powder blue flesh.

"I have no room for question in this." Yveun crossed the remaining distance to the desk opposite the other man. "The Guilds on Loom still resist me. Those that do not outright have yet to fully embrace the structure which I am attempting to impose upon them—structure that is the only thing standing in the way of the world below being lost to their own devices as they leech off the earth past the breaking point."

"None have understood the gravity of this more than I."

Finnyr was a smart and resourceful man. What he lacked in physical prowess he made up for in mental fortitude. It was the only thing that had kept him alive for the past decade. He was certainly of no other use to his family. Though Yveun had found creative ways to apply his talents.

"I cannot fight battles on two fronts. I cannot give Loom the attention it needs when I am being picked apart from within."

Finnyr paled to nearly the white of a Fenthri. He'd heard all the layered meanings in Yveun's words. They had not been on entirely good terms since the schematics were stolen.

"How may I serve you, Dono? You are our one true King."

"I hope you believe that," Yveun pushed.

"You are everything."

*That* the Dono believed. Without him, Finnyr would long be dead. And Yveun knew that he held the key to the future Finnyr sought. It was a shameful bargain for a Dragon to make, to seek power and prestige through a means other than sanctioned duels. But Finnyr was a Xin, and the Xin put their ends before the means used to achieve them. They would cut out their own eye and sell it to a Harvester if it benefited their goals, and that was how Yveun had ended up in this predicament to begin with.

"See that I am, Finnyr, and you will have that which you desire someday." The man's eyes were alight at the prospect. Finnyr's very existence rested in Yevun's hands. But the King's future was stacked precariously on the lesser Dragon's shoulders. The brother of Petra'Oji, the man who would inherit House Xin by blood and rank should he somehow best his sister in a duel, or if Petra and Cvareh were suddenly and mysteriously found dead. "For now, I need you to speak with your dear little sister. I need answers."

Finnyr paused. Petra's was one entity that still deflated him with a mention after more than a decade. Shame was a seeping wound and Yveun pressed upon it to get what he wanted.

"What do you want to know?" the Dragon forced through his all-too-dull canines.

"I want to know how Cvareh survived the Riders. I want to know what happened to my schematics." Yveun's claws unsheathed at the mere mention of the drawings that held the most substantial progress made on the Philosopher's box to date. "I want to know what Petra is keeping from me."

"My lord, my sister, she—"

"No excuses and no half measures, Finnyr. You were born in the month of Lord Rok. Show me where your true heart lies." Yveun rested his hands on the desk, his claws raking long lines across its surface as he stepped away. He'd have Finnyr flayed for an hour if he buffed them out of the resin. Yveun wanted them to last as a threat to the man until the whole catastrophe that had been the past three months was behind them. The Dono paused at the door. "Succeed, and I will forgive your prior lapse in judgment in even *mentioning* the schematics to your sister. Fail, and I will not let you live long enough to try again."

Yveun sneered widely, showing off his wicked sharp fangs. He left the man fighting trembles, but felt immensely better himself. There was more to be done, but it was progress for now.

As loathe as he was to see powder blue skin, it had paid off to have the loyalty of Finnyr Xin'Kin To, eldest son of House Xin.

# 7
## ARIANNA

The room she'd been thrown into was uselessly lovely. She circled it a few times, staring out the tall windows to try to get her bearings. It was somewhere in the center of the castle's x-axis, on western side, judging by the increasing brightness that streamed through one wall. She guessed she was somewhere in the middle of the y-axis as well.

Through both windows, she could see the curve of the carved stone, other colored glass portals dotting its surface. Those out the west-most facing window were far and the wall was sheer and smoothed. However, her other window was within an alcove of sorts. Relief carvings of sweeping birds across the face of the castle would make easy hand and foot holds, and it was sheltered from the gusts that regularly rattled the other window.

Why there were carvings on the *outside* of a castle, where only a select few with windows could see, escaped her. But seemingly everything about this place served to confound and enrage her, from the decor choices to the very Dragons living among them.

The bed had no less than ten pillows. *Ten*. As in, the number she would have to use two hands to count to. The fireplace burned cheerfully for a race of people who had skin as strong and thick as leather. Shelves were cluttered with all manner of paintings, bobbles, and strange devices that Arianna could not fathom a purpose for.

Cain had first had the audacity to refuse her winch box and daggers, claiming she was now under the protection of House Xin and such things were no longer needed. Arianna had cut a chunk from Dawyn's throat with a straight razor in an effort to get to her effects before Cvareh's "friend" did.

That had been the man's first mistake. His second was when he threatened to burn her clothes due to the "stench of Loom" on them. Arianna had nearly painted the floor of the bath gold with Dragon blood before she finally submitted. She was outnumbered and it was a battle she'd never had a chance of winning, especially naked and needing to avoid every nick or scratch from the Dragons' sharp talons. But her viciousness had forced them into a compromise— her clothing would be washed and boxed and hidden until it was decided what they were "doing with her."

The satisfaction of backing them into a compromise was short-lived as they, in turn, forced her into the most offensive articles of clothing she'd ever worn. They were trying to make a fool of her with the garb, that much was obvious. Two-thirds of the shirt was literally missing and the skirt was utterly impractical. Arianna was a heinous seamstress, but necessity was the mother of invention and she understood the mechanics and principles behind tailoring.

It'd taken her nearly an hour of muttered curses but she'd finally modified some found garments in the room she'd been locked in into something that suited her a little better. Loose trousers belled around her knees, cinched at the waist. Over top, she wore a long tunic dress, split at the bottom much like her White Wraith coat. Just feeling the hem at her calves brought back reassurances in triplicate.

Dressed and harnessed, Arianna opened the window she'd selected, pushing it against the near-constant wind to be open flush against the outer wall. She placed her palms on the sill, leaning over. Nothing stared back up at her, the hazy clouds fogging over the world of Loom below in shifting degrees of opaque. If she didn't know it was there, she wouldn't imagine there could be anything solid beneath that impenetrable line.

But Loom waited. A resistance brewed. And Florence had cast in her lot with those rebels. Meaning Arianna had no choice but to align herself as well.

She stepped up onto the sill, the wind rising to meet her. Taking a deep breath, she grasped the clip of her golden line firmly, charging it with a jolt of magic. It jumped from her fingertips. The cabling spool on her hip whirred, golden line funneled through the gearbox without resistance, propelled by magic. It shot across the narrow chasm between her room and the stonework by the opposite window. The clip looped around the sculpture at Arianna's silent command, magically fastening to itself.

She gave the line a firm tug, feeling the tension through her harness. There was a moment's hesitation, a second where her throat tightened. Her feet shifted against the sill and then, nothing.

Her stomach shot to her throat and her harness tightened reassuringly as she dropped in free fall. Arianna had used her winch box to perform such a maneuver hundreds—thousands—of times, from heights that would mean her death if she miscalculated distance or the security of her line. But this felt different. The vast nothingness that yawned beneath her rose with alarming speed, threatening to consume her like nothing more than an irrelevant speck of sand in the hourglass of time.

She gripped the line tighter, pushing magic into her winch box with almost violent intent. Her descent slowed as she neared the arc of her jump. Ari felt herself rising upward toward the window and toward the security of established hand and foot holds.

Fear was nothing more than staring into the mirror known as death and seeing the reflection of your own transience, a visage far too intense for many to look upon. But, for Arianna, it was nothing more than an instrument in her toolbox. It had a handle worn from years of grabbing for it time and again. Fear was familiar from taking it into her own hands and using it as deftly as if she were the personification of time's judgment upon all mortal men.

Weighted against the wall, she grabbed for one of the two daggers settled at the small of her back. The blunt, thin tip of one fit nicely into the narrow groove of the window. The locks were simple tension latches; nothing more than a twist of the wrist, and mechanical precision Ari possessed from years of practice, was needed to render it useless.

The window swung open, and she helped herself into the quiet hall before shutting the pane behind her. She hadn't known Cain for very long, but she was already savoring the idea of the arrogant Dragon guarding an empty room. Arianna knew she'd be discovered eventually, or would choose to expose herself. But for now, she'd wander this floating castle on her own terms.

Arianna pulled her own magic in tight, winding it like a ball around her core. She silenced its pulse as much as possible, limiting its ability to radiate from her with each breath. The stillness it created was prone to disturbances from other magic, and Arianna avoided any unwanted encounters with relative ease.

For a castle of stone and glass, it was alive with the scents of earth. Notes of moss blended with fresh dirt and the sharp smells of cedar and sandalwood to create a palette that was slowly becoming definable as distinctly "Xin". Twice, she thought she picked up the scent of woodsmoke, and edged toward corners expecting to see Cvareh on the other side. But it was never him, and she was left to label the emotion that charged through her as relief.

*It would be an immense inconvenience if Cvareh discovered me now*, she insisted. She certainly had no need of the Dragon.

At first, Arianna tried to make notes of the individual Dragon scents, but it quickly became impossible. Every Dragon's aroma seemed unique on Loom purely because there weren't many Dragons. But on Nova, the scents became repetitive and Arianna began to focus, instead, on filtering out all scents but the ones most important to her: woodsmoke and cedar.

No longer concerning herself with logging every Dragon in residence, Arianna shifted her focus to the residence itself. During her schooling in the Rivets guild, she had learned about architecture. It wasn't her forte, but she understood the basic principle as any good Rivet would be able to. With every project, the first thing a designer was taught to look at was the function of the space, followed by allowances for land and materials. The result was a blissful logic across Loom. Everything had a purpose, and the reasoning behind that purpose was simple to see.

She could not see the purpose in half the decisions the architects made here.

Hallways led to nowhere. Rooms materialized in the least logical places she could fathom. Alcoves with what must be months' worth of embellishments on their stonework were tucked away in obscurity. There were switchbacks and odd connections that made it nearly impossible to map the palace in her mind.

After nearly an hour of wandering, Arianna knew the only way she'd be able to find her way back to her room would be to let herself get discovered by one of the wandering occupants. It only made her resentment for the Dragons grow. Of course their way of life would prove as aggravating as their very existence.

She was about to give herself over to the next Dragon she encountered, when the scent of woodsmoke tickled her nose. It sizzled with familiarity she couldn't deny. *Cvareh.* The man was close.

Like a bloodhound, Arianna tracked the essence of magic through narrow corridors and wide thoroughfares alike. Her ears twitched as the scent grew. The familiar tones of his speech, muffled yet from distance, echoed like an invisible whisper tether between them. He had imbibed from her and she from him; there was no place he could hide now where she wouldn't find him, and the fact wasn't nearly as repulsive to her as she thought it should be.

"… She will hand me my army?" an unfamiliar voice echoed from behind the door she'd tracked to.

"For Loom, there is nothing she wouldn't do," Cvareh replied.

Arianna dulled the sharpness of her anger at the idea of Cvareh *correctly* describing the design of her mind to someone else with the curiosity of what else he might say about her. If she knew what he told others about her, she could adjust her actions accordingly when the need to be subversive arose. She stilled her hand over the latch of the wide door, exercising patience.

"Very well," the female voice continued after a long pause. "I will tell this Chimera what she needs to hear."

"Arianna will know if you lie to her."

Laughter erupted at the notion. "Brother, did your time on Loom dull your senses? You think I cannot handle a Chimera?"

*Brother.* That meant the speaker was certainly his sister—the woman Arianna had come to meet.

"She is of Loom, but do not underestimate her for it. Heed my counsel on this, Petra."

"I fear no Dragon, so I hold no more concern for Chimera or Fenthri. I will sing the song she wishes to hear and she will thank me for it. Then I will have my army."

Arianna rolled her eyes and pushed down the door handle. Loathing seared

through her veins and she did little to temper it. She had come up to the
Dragon's world, allowed herself to be bare before strangers and treated like a
simpleton. She had to draw a line somewhere.

"Your song will fall flat, I fear, since I have heard the truth of its melody,"
Arianna seethed by means of greeting.

At one end of the wide room, Cvareh sat in surprise on the second level of a
dais. Above him was a woman who looked as though her skin was made from
the deepest blue ocean waters. Hair the color of Dragon blood spilled from her
head in thick tresses. And, instead of shock or anger, she smiled widely, baring
her canines.

Arianna replied in kind.

"I was told you had been sequestered." Petra's eyes had a nearly identical
color to Cvareh's, but they were similar in no other way. There was a savage
edge to their shape, and they regarded her with a ravenous desire to consume
every scrap of courage Arianna might even attempt to muster.

Arianna would reveal no seams in the iron walls of her resolve. She was the
opposite and equal of this woman. She bent before no man, woman, king, or
queen—and most certainly no Dragon. Folding her arms over her chest, Arianna
leaned against the door, making no effort to cross the room. Foremost, she
wanted to make it clear that she would not approach like some groveling mortal
before an idol.

But not having to cross the floor was also appealing.

What builder would ever think it was a good idea to make the floor of a
suspended castle from glass? Arianna deeply hoped that the multi-colored design
was, in actuality, crystal or stone. Something, anything, stronger than liquefied
and hardened sand. But she had her doubts.

"Were you also told that I cut a chunk from one of your servants' necks? Or
bit the ear off another?"

"Those details were neglected." Instead of anger, there was a twisted sort of
amusement playing between the woman's words.

"Arianna, you should—"

Arianna shot Cvareh a glare.

"Silence, Cvareh," Petra echoed Arianna's sentiment, much to her surprise.
"I am told that you have come to *assess* me for our negotiations with Loom's
rebellion to proceed."

"That's one way to put it." Arianna relaxed her hands, placing them behind
her, ready to grab for her daggers in an instant.

"Cvareh tells me you seek assurances for Loom should I rule. I will gladly
give them."

Arianna snorted. Did the woman really think her words would mean
anything after what Arianna had just heard? "And what do you think your
assurances are worth?"

"The word of an Oji? Very much."

*Well, Petra certainly believes her words*, Arianna thought silently. She was shaping up to be exactly what Arianna had feared. The Dragon would be another ruler that saw herself seated above the world, who paid little attention to the plights of Loom and cared even less.

Which meant Arianna might need to course-correct. If she wouldn't get anywhere with Petra, she would need to secure a way on her own to get the materials needed for the Philosopher's Box. To give Loom a fighting chance in the power struggle to come. Let the Dragons fight among themselves, kill each other off. If they turned their eyes to Loom, Loom would be ready. There were options before her, still, and she would consider them all for Florence's sake.

"We don't have Oji—" Arianna tried to form the word so carefully it bordered on mocking, "—on Loom. So it means nothing to me, Petra."

The claws shot out from the woman's fingers so fast that Arianna was surprised they didn't launch from her hands. Dragons were predictable. If one didn't give in to their excessive system of titles and decorum, they lost all patience. Arianna would push until she exposed the truth of this woman's nature.

Cvareh was an anomaly among Dragons. As was the fact that Arianna found him tolerable. The fact that, in some impossible way, she truly believed he harbored no ill will toward Loom. But it ended with him. All other Dragons thus far had proved just as she'd expected.

"I must remind you that you are not on Loom any longer, Arianna." The woman continued to smile with murderous intent. She stood, unfurling like a sail, her ego ballooning on her magic to a size that was greater than her physical frame. "You are in my House. You are under my protection. Your presence is a liability to the wellbeing of my family, should you be discovered by the Dragon King. You are alive because I permit it. And for all this, you will call me Petra'Oji."

Arianna shrugged. "I'll call you as I please."

The woman stepped forward. Cvareh rose as well, but made no attempt to impede his sister's progress. Certainly, Petra had told him to stay out of their squabble, and Arianna echoed the sentiment. But the fact that he didn't struggle to resist even the slightest urge to rise to her defense told Arianna everything.

He stood behind his sister, at home on Nova. She stood as a foreigner in a strange land on behalf of a Fenthri girl. No matter how close they'd become on their journey, an impenetrable line was still drawn between them. It had been foolish to think the chasm could ever be crossed.

Arianna drew her dagger. Her other hand hovered over the clip dangling from her winch box. Petra stopped in the middle of the room, the glass floor illuminating her from below as though she stood in the sky itself.

"Sheathe your blade. I have no interest in spilling blood here."

"Certainly fooled me." Arianna didn't oblige the command.

"Cvareh told me of your ferocity. He told me you killed the King's Bitch, which tells me two things, Arianna the Rivet." She held up two clawed fingers.

"One, that we are not enemies. Two, that killing you would be a waste. If you are not my enemy and you are a fierce fighter, then it would be a shame to see you die needlessly."

Anger flashed like gunpowder in the priming pan of her emotional arsenal, but it was short lived. For, as frustrating as it was to see, Cvareh's suspicions echoed true. She and Petra seemed to hold something in common, for Arianna had used much the same logic when it came to deeming who was worthy to kill.

"You have yet to prove that you are not my enemy. And you are doing a poor job of endearing yourself to me if you wish an ally." Arianna sheathed her dagger.

Petra smiled. It was an arrogant look, but not sinister. Arianna couldn't shake the condescending feeling of it, however. The Dragon began to walk again, making her way toward a different door.

"My family has been fighting the Dragon King for centuries. A few more days, weeks, months, years, will not hurt me. Time to wait for you to come around is something I have." Petra paused in the open door frame across the room, staring Arianna down for one last long moment. "The real question is, do you?"

Arianna wanted to gouge out the knowing gaze from her eye sockets. The Dragon would live more than six lifetimes of the average Fenthri. Arianna could threaten with the Philosopher's Box all she wanted. But the woman could stall until long after Florence was dead.

Petra hummed softly at Arianna's silence, a purr of victory. "Cvareh, escort our guest back to her chambers before she makes a scene."

Arianna watched the Dragon leave, walking as though she already owned the world.

# 8

## FLORENCE

"I'm telling you I need more." Florence balked at the Revolver who was in charge of the Alchemists' armory.

"I'm telling you, you're not getting any." The man was old; Florence guessed he was nearly thirty-eight. His black hair had begun to twist in weird directions, haloing thinly around the crown of his head. It was salted with gray almost the same color as his skin. The dark symbol of the Revolvers tattooed on his cheek sagged. She'd never met a Revo as old as him before. It wasn't usually a profession that boasted particularly long lifespans. Perhaps being assigned far from the guild hall in Dortam had helped spare him from the Revolver's suicidal groupthink.

"Not a day ago I counted that you had at least two barrels of sulfur. I know charcoal isn't hard to come by, and you don't need much graphite…" He was back to ignoring her as she spoke, counting and checking off quantities behind the gated shelves. "Why are you being so stingy with the gunpowder?"

"Because you're wasting it." He didn't even turn.

"I am not wasting it. I'm trying to help you."

The man shot a look over his shoulder that told Florence exactly what he thought of *that* claim. Florence put her hands on her hips, trying not to deflate. Certainly she'd had some failures… a lot of failures. But she was making progress. It was just difficult to explain that progress to anyone who hadn't seen the implosion beam she was trying to recreate based on what the Riders had used to attack the airship she'd ridden on weeks ago.

"You fashion yourself a Revo." He punctuated the statement with a sigh, finally giving her his attention. "But it shows that you have not had proper training."

"I had ample tr—"

"I looked through your notes."

"Y-you went into my laboratory?" Florence stuttered. There was no more sacred place on Loom than the halls of research. It was more private than a bed and more secret than a bath. She would rather parade naked through the guild than think of someone poking through her research.

"I did." He was utterly unapologetic. "I've been letting you leech off our supplies for weeks. I wanted to see the fruits of your labors… or lack thereof."

"My research wouldn't make sense to someone else. My shorthand isn't common."

"You're right on both accounts. It doesn't make sense to someone else because you are chasing rabbits without knowing the first thing of the hunt. And your shorthand is uncommon for a youth like you, but the style was fairly popular twenty years ago."

Florence pursed her lips, taking issue with his tone.

"The Wraith taught you, didn't she?"

"She did," Florence affirmed proudly. Ari had quickly become infamous among the Alchemists. She'd only been there about two weeks before flying to Nova, but in that time she'd worked the Vicar into a fit, claimed to be the creator of the Philosopher's Box—a *real* Philosopher's Box, and produced so many clockwork locks that half the initiates couldn't get into their rooms after they quickly forgot the complexity of Arianna's designs.

"The woman is half monster and half master. I can't deny it," he continued before Florence could correct him in Ari's defense on the former. "But she is a Master *Rivet*. I've no doubt you benefited from her tutelage. You ask the right questions and you've been trained to think beyond what is there to what could be. You are young but you have the foundation of one truly raised on Ter.0." Sadness lined the man's eyes at the mention of the lost continent, a way of life that had been destroyed by the Dragons. "But she is not a Revolver. She cannot teach you the skills of follow-through on those theories. And, to that end, you are lacking."

"Then you teach me."

The man scoffed, brushing away the notion with a wave of his hand. "If I'd wanted a pupil I would've remained near the guild hall chasing my circle. I've not the time, energy, or interest for a student."

"Then give me the gunpowder so I can continue to learn on my own."

"No."

Florence felt like she was stuck in a loop. "How am I supposed to improve?"

"Go back to the Revolvers, have whomever you claim was teaching you— despite your being a marked Raven—continue to do so."

"Even if I could do that…" Florence didn't actually know if she could. Her teachers likely stopped going to their meeting places when she'd stopped showing up. Arianna had been the one to forge those relationships. "I want to help the resistance."

"Then help us, and don't be a leech on our powder."

"I—"

"Go away, girl. There's nothing more to say." The man turned his back on her again.

Florence couldn't help herself; she shot one nasty face at his ugly salted hair before storming out of the armory. The guild continued on around her. Initiates worked on magic, reagents, pharmaceuticals, and a half dozen other things with all the help and support of a guild behind them. Florence was the only one adrift.

She slunk back to her tiny laboratory with her tail between her legs in the hope of licking her wounds in relative peace. She had only about twenty minutes of quiet before her door opened for two Alchemists. Nora and Derek helped themselves into her space, crowding around her table without invitation.

"You weren't at dinner." Derek dropped a plate before her.

"I'm not hungry."

"Do you know how quickly your body will go into starvation mode if you don't eat?" Nora leaned forward, resting her elbows on the table. "The second it does, it starts breaking down your muscle for energy because it's the densest source in your body. It also destroys your ability to process—"

"I get it. I get it." Florence hooked the plate and pulled it toward her. She *was* hungry, she just didn't want to be around people. But it seemed she had an audience despite her efforts. And, if she was going to be miserable either way, she may as well be miserable and full.

"What has you so upset?" Derek asked after she tucked in.

Florence offered them both a quick summary of her encounter with the armory master.

Derek leaned back and folded his arms, listening thoughtfully. Nora hummed and nodded along, picking off the vegetables that were too bland for Florence's taste. The other girl was the first one to speak when Florence finished her tale.

"He has a point."

"As do I." Florence frowned.

"His is more valid," Nora insisted. "You haven't done much here."

"I'm working on making long-term change."

"At least by blowing up trees in the forest," Derek added dryly, earning him a sharp look. He remained unapologetic.

"You two go through reagents like water. And I've seen how quickly chemicals disappear when you're working on something new."

"But we're Alchemists. This is our home, our guild," Nora reminded her, as though she could've somehow forgotten. "It isn't the place for you to run your... whatever tests you run. You should go home for that."

Florence rolled a canister across the desk as Nora spoke. If she hit it too hard it would blow up the three of them. Though she neglected to mention that fact about the "tests" she ran. "I thought the resistance believed in the old ways of Loom? The notion that men and women should choose to study what they please. That there's more to be learned from working together than apart?"

"We do. But if our resistance falls, it doesn't matter what we believe."

Florence bristled at the implication: the idea that she would do something to contribute to the fall of the resistance, rather than its success. She kept her face emotionless as Ari would have. Or tried to.

"Why don't you just focus on something that will actually help us? Like trying to pin down those friends of yours who can get guns and clockwork through Ter.4?" No matter how many times Florence reminded her, Nora never seemed to fully grasp that she wasn't a Raven at heart despite what was on her cheek. And that getting in touch with Helen and Will was harder than turning steel into gold for someone who didn't understand all the tunnels and transport systems.

"I am trying to actually help you." Florence's plate was empty and she greatly missed the forced breaks in the conversation that came from eating. "But I need more gold and more explosives to do that."

"And I'm telling you that you're not going to be getting any more."

"Have you tried speaking with the Vicar about these matters?" Derek stopped Florence mid-breath. Which was likely for the best, as her patience with Nora was running thin.

"No… Do you think I should?" Florence hadn't properly been in a guild for nearly three years. Additionally, she'd just been an initiate in the Ravens and it had been made clear to her then that appealing to the higher powers simply wasn't done. The Vicar Raven always had the Dragon adviser at his side, and Florence had always heard he was strict about adhering to certain expectations about hierarchy.

But Florence had never seen a Dragon in the Alchemists' Guild, not counting Cvareh or corpses.

"You could try pleading your case." Derek shrugged.

Florence regarded him skeptically, wondering if he was trying to get her into a worse spot by bringing up her losses with the Vicar.

"Or don't." He stood. "It's your choice. But your options seem to be growing thinner."

Derek held out a hand to Nora, which she took. He helped her to her feet, lacing his fingers against hers. The two left Florence alone to her thoughts.

She knew better than to pick up any of her remaining chemicals or powders. When her mind was so wild, she'd only produce greater mistakes. That stress had certainly not been helpful over the past few weeks, when her failures were the only thing keeping her ledgers company.

Florence flipped through her notes, wondering what the Revolver had seen in them. He was a journeyman of the Revos, his tattoo completely filled. He had years of practice ahead of her, and was willing to impart none of it.

She snapped the book shut.

Loom was like a mirror that had been cracked by the Dragons' first descent. Spider-web fractures stretched across its surface, turning a single image into smaller pieces. They were all parts of one whole that fit together, but no longer joined cleanly at the seams. For one dark moment, she wondered if it was a wound that could ever be healed. By what magic could Loom be put back together into a single, flawless piece?

And then Florence made her way to the Vicar Alchemist. She wasn't one to sit in place contentedly. Ari had taught her better than that. Even now, from above the clouds, the woman known as the White Wraith challenged Florence to be better, do more.

She received a few curious stares as she boarded the elevator that went directly to the Vicar's laboratory, but no one stopped her. It seemed to be an accepted practice in the Alchemists that there were times when one needed to speak to the Vicar. At least, that was what Florence hoped. If not, everyone was about to have a good laugh at her expense.

"Enter," a voice called from behind a door emblazoned with the symbol of the Master Alchemist, following Florence's knock.

Florence entered, her heart in her throat. Sophie, the Vicar Alchemist, straightened away from her work table. She pulled the refined goggles off her eyes to get a better look at her visitor.

"I wasn't expecting a little crow."

"Little bullet would be more appropriate," Florence corrected tiredly. Sophie arched her eyebrows in surprise and Florence added, carefully, "Just a suggestion…"

"We'll settle on Florence." Sophie smiled thinly. "Why has Arianna's student come to visit me this day?"

Florence scraped together every rogue bit of boldness before speaking. "I need your backing on some experiments I'm running."

"My backing?"

"Yes, as the Vicar. I'm working on some things to help the rebellion but I need more gold and more gunpowder, at the very least. I've been refused."

"I know." Sophie continued to smile and, in that moment, reminded Florence of King Louie. There was nothing physically similar between the capable looking Vicar and the bony man of Mercury Town. But their eyes, their mannerisms, suddenly overlapped so strongly it set off warning bells between Florence's ears.

"Then you should know exactly why I'm here." If Sophie was like Louie, then Florence would treat her as she would the little king of Mercury Town. The only difference was that she no longer had a White Wraith nearby to keep her safe.

"We're skipping the small talk then? Excellent." Sophie's mannerisms shifted and she returned to managing some bubbling beakers on her table. "Your answer is no."

"Vicar, I need—"

"Whatever you need pales in comparison to the needs of my Guild and this rebellion I'm trying to build."

"I want to help the rebellion."

"Then actually help us." Sophie gave her a challenging stare.

Florence knew that look. It was so similar to the ones Arianna had given her, it was eerie. It reminded Florence, yet again, how little she knew of Arianna's history.

"Let's cut a deal." Part Ari, part Louie, Florence knew how to navigate this personality. "You know better than anyone the needs of guild and rebellion. You know what I need and what I can do. Tell me how I can help you."

"And in return you want access to your resources."

"Naturally."

"Very well." The conversation picked up speed like a locomotive down the tracks. "You want more gold? Go and fetch it yourself."

"Where is the nearest refinery?" Florence didn't know the first thing about stealing, but she'd figure it out if she had to. It's what Arianna would've done.

"Ter.1."

"Ter.5 has no refineries?" Florence balked.

"The Dragon King didn't want us to have such easy access to gold or reagents." They both took a silent moment to curse the King's pragmatism. "We have an allotment that comes along the main tracks through the Skeleton Forest. But it's not enough."

"So you need another shipment."

"One outside of Dragon sanction," Sophie affirmed. "There's another route, but it's never used. It was shut down for winding too deep into the forest and too close to endwig haunts."

"I'm not a Raven." Florence was ready to tattoo the words on her opposite cheek.

"I have secured a Raven to run the engine. I have Alchemists to speak on my behalf. I have a Rivet to ensure things run smoothly along the way."

Florence knew where she was headed before Sophie even finished.

"I do not have a spare Revolver to fight off any who might seek to sabotage the mission. It is not called the Skeleton Forest for nothing. I would not like to see this costly excursion reduced to bones in the woods."

It was neat, tidy, and convenient. Sophie won either way. If Florence succeeded, the Vicar would have more resources and a goal accomplished. Giving Florence a little gold in return was nothing in the wake of that particular victory. If Florence failed, she would be one of those corpses, reduced to nothing more than bones licked clean by the Endwig.

"Do you think I can do it?" Florence was compelled to ask.

"Of course," Sophie praised brightly. "After all, you're the multi-talented Raven, not Raven but Revolver."

Florence took a deep breath and gave Sophie the benefit of the doubt. Florence's failure would mean the death of her Alchemists. It made no sense for her to be hopeful for it or indifferent to it.

"Then I'll do it."

"Wonderful. Plan to leave within the fortnight. I'll spread the word that you're to have everything you need to prepare."

Finally, a gear turned smoothly for Florence. "Thank you."

"Oh, and Florence," Sophie stopped her just as she was about to depart. "I think it goes without saying that this is quite a dangerous mission."

Florence knew that, but she nodded anyway.

"Should you fail, it will mean your death."

There was the whisper of a threat ghosting around Sophie's words, a certainty that couldn't be known unless a promise was being given. Florence kept her suspicion to herself, not wanting to unreasonably accuse the Vicar Alchemist of telling her outright that her options were to die on the mission, or die upon her unsuccessful return. Florence searched Sophie's eyes for something more, something else. But there was nothing beyond careful calculation glittering in their depths.

# 9
## ARIANNA

Arianna wished she had Florence's penchant for explosives. If she did, she would've long since slipped a small disk bomb into Cain's pocket. For one, she liked the man about as much as she enjoyed chewing on rusty nails. But more than that, she couldn't stand the monotony their days had fallen into. It was a very Revolver notion for her, but stripped screws, she'd blow it all halfway to Ter.5 just to see something happen.

Breakfast came promptly with the dawn. Cain hand delivered it, seemingly the only one authorized to interact with her on a personal basis. The first few mornings he nearly scared her into a rage at the sound of someone entering her room. The next few mornings, she began to sleep through his arrival, offering no thank you nor note of his efforts on her behalf. The forced lack of appreciation became more normal with each passing day until sleeping through his coming and going became natural.

Ari still stirred at the sound of someone entering her space. Her hand closed around the hilt of her dagger that she kept under her pillow on instinct. But ritual won out the second the familiar scent of wet earth filled her nose, and she relaxed. Cain never did anything that would warrant her drawing her weapon.

Around lunch, he would come to her and weave a tight illusion over her that shifted her appearance into the colors and more extreme angles of Dragon skin and bone. Arianna would stare at her brightly colored form in the windows and mirrors of the Xin manor as she explored with Cain in tow. It was an unnatural shade layered atop her, a weightless shroud that was nearly suffocating to all that she was.

But it was the only way she could escape her room. Cvareh had made Petra's will clear the last time he'd delivered her back after her second escape;

Arianna's wandering would not be tolerated, given the secret nature of her presence. And, as much as she wanted to delight in putting the Dragons in their places, the truth was she had no ground to stand on for the matter. If Arianna fought, she would only make it so far before being violently subdued.

The foolishness of her impulsive decision to come to Nova weighed on her more with every passing hour, crushing her with each day. She had no route back to Loom. She knew little of the Dragon's society and couldn't even navigate without causing a fuss for no other reason than the shade of her skin. Escape on her own wasn't enough; she wouldn't leave after spending this long on Nova without some kind of success, and if she was to accomplish anything she needed to regain some of her sovereignty.

Arianna vowed to do just that nearly a month into her virtual imprisonment.

"Take me to Cvareh," she demanded of Cain, awake with the dawn to greet him.

The man stared at her for a long moment, then continued his morning rituals as if she hadn't woken at all. Arianna stood. She would not be ignored.

"I wish to speak to Cvareh."

"And if the Ryu wished to speak to you, do you not think he would've come to do so himself?" Cain stared at her from the opposite side of the small table in the center of her room.

Arianna laughed. That Dragon rank and file nonsense wasn't about to work on her. She was born of Loom, and she didn't kneel before any man or woman simply because they wished her to.

"He doesn't know I seek him."

"Then I shall deliver your message."

"I don't trust you," Arianna snapped back. For a retort that required such little thought, it stilled Cain by a satisfying margin.

"I am a Xin'Da, I would never—"

"That means nothing to me." She rolled her eyes with a dramatic sigh, sitting heavily on the bed. "All that matters to me is action."

"Action?" Cain tapped his fingertips on the table, claws sheathed. "And what have my actions done to earn your mistrust? I have gone out of my way for you. I have attended to you daily. Were it not for my magic, you would be trapped within this room in perpetuity."

Arianna scowled viciously, as if to scare away the truth.

"Do you think I do it because I enjoy being around you?" he scoffed. "Quite the opposite, I assure you."

She stared at his hands as they thrummed against the tabletop, her mind made up. "Very well, Cain. If you will not take me to him, bring Cvareh to me."

He snorted, crossing over to her. The Dragon stared down his nose at her with his molten gold eyes. Arianna met them fearlessly. Cain cocked his head to the side.

"Why are you here, White Wraith?"

She rose to her feet, drawing her full height, but the crown of her head only came up to his mouth. Nevertheless, Arianna stood as though she was eye to eye with the Dragon. She would not be made to feel small. She would not be relegated to the space he deemed her worthy of.

"Does it bother you, not knowing why you're ordered to attend to me day after day?" She could only assume he was under orders to oversee her. "The great Cain Xin'Da Bek, reduced to nannying a Chimera. To bringing her food and tending to her needs."

Arianna knew just what places to prod. She knew enough of Dragon society to be offensive when it suited her. Cain narrowed his eyes.

"Now, bring me Cvareh."

Cain moved and Arianna fell backward. His hand grasped for the empty air where her face had just been. She collapsed onto the bed, one hand on the hilt of her dagger. The pillow burst in an explosion of feathers as her dagger tore through it; they floated through the air between them as he landed atop her. One hand supported him above her, the other reached for her face again.

Her dagger rose against his palm, gold dripping onto her shoulder where it bit into his flesh. Arianna scowled. Cain snarled in reply.

"You think you can order me, *Fen*?"

"I do," she sneered in kind at the slur for her people. "Because if you could kill me, you would've already."

He pressed his hand forward, the dagger meeting bone. Arianna's muscles strained against the force, keeping it at bay. Blood fell atop her like raindrops, smelling sharply of the fresh scent of wet earth.

"Why are you here?" he repeated. "Why have you ventured to my home? Why do you insult my Oji and still walk? How do you make demands of my Ryu as though he breathes for you alone?"

*There was the root of it.*

"Bring me Cvareh," she demanded again, quietly. So quiet that his dripping blood against her shoulder was louder with each dull *splat*.

Cain snarled once more, then pushed away. Arianna pushed back, giving him purchase against her dagger and digging it deeper into his flesh. She laced the slash with magic, stinting his healing and slowing the knitting of his skin. The Dragon looked at it curiously.

"You act as though you are truly a Wraith—mighty and untouchable." He clenched his fingers into a fist, blood oozing between them. "But I have seen your flesh." The words stung, reminding her of the impropriety she'd endured before him. "I know under the armor of words and talons of sharpened gold, you are no more immortal than I."

He left quickly, denying her the possibility of a retort. Arianna was set to pacing, her mind racing. It spun like clockwork assembled around every possibility, tooling for every outcome. At the core of the gearbox of her mind, Florence remained.

Arianna crossed over to the window, staring at the clouds below her. Not for the first time, she wondered how her apprentice fared. She'd sought redemption in Florence's eyes, but in doing so had left the girl alone with the one woman whom Arianna had nothing but bitter feelings toward.

Lost in the labyrinth of her mind, Arianna was startled when she heard the door open once more. She half expected to be faced with Cain and some excuse of why she wasn't good enough for his Ryu's time. But the man she sought closed the stately portal behind him.

Cvareh regarded her warily. *As he should*, Arianna seethed quietly. They had not spoken since he last condemned her to the proverbial prison she had been trapped within for the past few weeks. He hadn't so much as sought after her once as far as she knew.

But would she have wanted him to? She owed him nothing, and he owed her nothing but the yet unrequited boon. That was hardly anything significant to pull them together outside of a magical transaction. And yet, she couldn't deny a hurt sort of yearning for it.

"It's good to see you." He startled her by speaking first.

"If that were truly the case, you would've looked in on me sooner." Arianna rolled her eyes, dismissing the sentiment.

"Well, you're not exactly the most approachable woman in the manor." He sat at one of the chairs by her table, glancing at the cooling food. "Is it not to your liking?"

"Nothing is to my liking." She narrowed the distance between them. But the advance felt nothing like it had with Cain. There was a different sort of tension between her and Cvareh, a sort of ebb and flow they both could acknowledge but had been strung along in the current despite. He made her quiver with tension. His presence elicited a physical response as her breath held and muscles tensed. But, unlike her body's response to Cain, it was not her dagger that her hands wanted to reach for. She felt *safe* around this Dragon. It was a welcome sensation that seemed to be magnified by how long it had been since she had last seen him. "I am trapped within these walls, a prisoner of your sister's. But she does not seek me out either. I will not hand the Philosopher's Box to her in a fit of boredom."

"I had never thought otherwise."

"Does she?" Cvareh's silence told Arianna everything. She pulled the chair opposite him around the table to sit before him. Arianna folded her hands, resting her elbows on her knees. "Cvareh, you know that will not work with me."

"I've advised Petra thusly."

"And yet your words haven't worked." Arianna shook her head. This is why she didn't depend on other people to get the job done. "I want to return to Loom."

"What?" Cvareh drew back, his magic fluctuating. "Petra would never allow it."

"I'll find a way out or I'll jump to my death and take the knowledge of the box with me."

"You wouldn't."

"Do you want to test me?" Arianna grinned faintly at the notion. The man clearly thought she placed more value on her own life than she did. She leaned back with a sigh. "Or, perhaps, I'll wish for you to do it."

"That's not what you want the boon for."

"You know nothing about me," she cautioned.

"I know more than you think."

Arianna wanted to refuse him. She wanted to shut him out violently and without remorse. But the door had been opened too wide between them. His mouth on hers ghosted upon her lips, reminding her of the un-crossable lines they'd traversed together. Lines that she might dare walk again if she had the chance. Arianna focused on the curve of his mouth for too long a moment.

She wouldn't let herself give into frivolous distractions. "Here are your options: Tell Petra that I seek passage home without hindrance."

"Or?"

"Or, I demand a pair of hands."

Cvareh's brows knitted in confusion only to untangle with shock when he realized what she was asking. He sputtered, trying to build momentum behind his words. "That's something that isn't done. I can't just—"

"Those are the options, Cvareh. Either would give me my freedom, and therefore her trust in my future actions." Arianna stood and turned her back to him. "If Petra seeks my acquiescence, she must treat me like an equal. Or at the very least, a worthy opponent."

# 10

## PETRA

"There has been another contact from Finnyr'Kin, Oji." A weathered, ancient woman reported from the side of the room where Petra dressed in her riding leathers.

"And does my brother have anything worthwhile for me?"

"He seeks to return home." The whisperer had the sense to pass no judgment on the message she'd received, merely report the facts.

Petra waved the slaves away and busied her hands with buttoning up her knee-length riding trousers with a heavy sigh. Finnyr had gotten it in his mind that he needed to return. She had no doubt it was in some way Yveun's influence; her brother wasn't known for having his own thoughts. Either the Dragon King had made Finnyr's life torturous as a result of Petra's actions against him, or he had ordered Finnyr to seek information on the truth of Cvareh's supposed prayers to Lord Xin.

Either way, it made no sense for Petra to let her brother back into her home. Finnyr would be put in a harder position to feed lies to the Dragon King if he were here. At the Rok estate he could continue to collect information for her on the King's scheming, even if it was an intolerable place for him to be.

"Tell Finnyr he has more to offer House Xin by continuing to express his loyalty to our Dono." The words were sickly false. But the whisperer wouldn't betray that to anyone. It was one of the sacred rites of becoming a House whisperer: no secrets were repeated and all messages were verbatim. All Dragons respected this as much as they respected the other innate laws of their world.

"As you command, Oji." The whisperer gave her a low bow.

"And, Shawin," Petra stopped the woman in the door frame. "Also tell

Finnyr that when I do see him again, I am looking forward to tales of all his time at House Rok."

"Of course." The woman departed.

When it came to matters of House, Petra felt as though she were trapped on a stationary wheel that spun and spun without progress, no matter how hard she pushed ahead. Finnyr was as useless as he'd always been, offering little more to her than his position as a pawn in the Rok estate that freed up Cvareh to remain at her side. Cvareh had returned, but his help was relegated to the shadows as it had always been. He was worth too much to her to risk parading his strengths before any member of the Crimson Court.

And then there was the Chimera.

Cvareh had reminded Petra time and again that threatening the woman would be of little use. But every moment lost due to her stubbornness was another that scraped away at Petra's patience—and she wasn't known for an excess of that to begin with. Petra kept enough of her head to recognize that losing it over the woman's antics would be akin to defeat. She chose to focus on the things she had direct control over, instead, and today those matters were hidden on the far side of Ruana.

She fastened a tight circle of leather around her bosom, draping emerald strips of fabric over her shoulders and fastening them to cuffs at her wrists. The cuffs appeared to be leather on the outside, but their inners were gold, enough to support a corona should she need it. She'd had to leverage the defense four times in her life, and she was not afraid to welcome a fifth if the world so designed.

Men and women stepped aside as she strode through her manor in the waking dawn. Servants, slaves, Anh, and nameless—those for whom Petra didn't even need to spare a sideways glance. On occasion, a Da was about, and Petra would give their bow a small nod of her head. Otherwise, she gave them no heed.

She loved her house like a wolf loved its pups. But she did them no favors by coddling them or tempering her demands. The world would burn under her heels if her designs saw the light of day. Only a strong House would able to rise from its ashes. If she failed to set the example, they were all destined for death.

Raku milled about in a high courtyard. He cooed the moment his giant eyes caught sight of her and Petra smiled in reply to her trusty steed. He was saddled at her request, her favorite oxblood colored seat. Petra wasted no time, mounted, and took to the skies.

Ruana shrunk beneath her, smaller and smaller with each flap of Raku's wide wings. The Temple of Lord Xin rose from the mountainside, shading the farmlands below. The cities and towns speckled the countryside like gemstones in a mine only to cluster together in determination against nature to create cities and centers of art and culture. They were children of earth and sky, birthed from sunlight fractured into a thousand shining colors.

From this vantage, Petra could see all that she fought for. Her home, her father's home, her father's father's home, and all the way back hundreds of years to the great fall of House Xin to House Rok. This was the land where the Dono was meant to sit. And she would see the mantle returned.

Banking across cliff faces and weaving over treetops, Petra made her way around the mountains that curved across the back of the Isle of Ruana. Nearly opposite the Xin estate, tucked behind imposing sheer mountain peaks, was a series of work houses situated atop a slowly blossoming network of mines. From the air, it was easy to mistake as nothing more than a snowy, barren valley. The smokestacks had been carefully tunneled through the mountain itself, hiding the real work of Ruana's first refinery.

Petra tugged on Raku's feathers, clicking a command with her tongue and teeth. The beast curved through the sky, spiraling downward. He landed nimbly on a narrow ledge, well trained to seek the safest footing.

She swung down from the saddle, her long toes curling through the thick snow and seeking purchase against the frozen rock beneath. The wind was icy and bit with savage numbness into her skin. Every pinprick made her feel alive.

She waved her hand at Raku, and the boco took to the skies. He would hunt, or roost, or mate—whatever satisfied his wild nature that morning. Petra allowed the beast to indulge his whims as long as he always responded to the shrill whistle that demanded his presence once more. He was one of the few beasts in the wide world who had yet to fail her.

"Oji," a man greeted her from the shade of a sheltered window. "It is a pleasure to have you in our presence."

"You flatter me, Poiris'Kin." Petra jumped down into the hall where he stood. Despite having no glass or shutters, it was so warm that the snow melted on the windowsill.

"Never flattery, merely truth." The Kin walked forward, knowing why she was there without an explanation. "We are making good progress. Spinning iron to steel is becoming a simpler task by the day."

"The help you demanded?"

"Has been invaluable."

Poiris was a smart man, enough so that Petra had placed him in charge of one of the most important tasks involved in laying the foundation of her new world order. He was leading the charge in assembling the refineries she needed to produce House Xin's own gold. Doing so would free the House from under Rok's thumb. He who controlled the gold, controlled Nova. Once House Xin had their own refineries working, they would no longer need to depend on small allotments or what limited back-winds trading could be done with Loom.

Of course, it wouldn't be enough. Not even close. Petra still needed Loom and the depths of their mines, the extensive capacity of their refineries, the efficiency with which the Fenthri operated. But even small steps were progress. Change did not happen overnight, birthed from plots of wishes. It grew from the grit of sacrifice and blood.

"Have they presented any problem?" Petra asked.

"Quite the opposite." She gave him a look that demanded elaboration. "They tell me we treat them much better than House Rok."

"So even Fen have sense." Wicked satisfaction pulled on Petra's cheeks, drawing her lips taut in a satisfied smirk.

"More than we give them credit for, on the whole," Poiris affirmed.

"Don't go too far." Petra couldn't help but think of the woman Cvareh had brought home. She fashioned herself as clever, but all Petra had seen was a child. She had been too easy to break, sitting quietly in her room, only walking the courses that Petra had designed for her to be led along. She had expected more from New Dortam's infamous White Wraith. "Show me your product."

Poiris led her inward to a great room of whirring mechanisms and molten metal. Petra surveyed it like some fire god. She didn't understand the first thing about how it worked, but she commanded it nonetheless. Chimera stood in the corners, sweat dripping off their faces, as they spoke to Dragons who walked unfazed through the overbearing heat. Giant buckets poured liquid iron into other containers.

"We have the air lance situated to remove impurities in the iron." Poiris pointed overhead to a long tube. "But we are yet working on the reagent lance." He shifted her attention down to the bottom floor far below, where a similar golden tube was being fashioned by a number of laborers.

"You are slowed by gold," Petra observed.

"We believe with what we can attain, we should have it finished within the next six months."

Slower than she wanted, but nothing could be done. A solution was offered and her men were hard at work. She could demand nothing more from them. When a boco was flapping its wings with all its might, it served little to push it harder. That was how riders got thrown from their saddles.

*I have time*, she reminded herself. There were decades of history behind her. She would not sacrifice all her work in haste. At the least, she delighted in the knowledge that she was quietly siphoning off gold and resources for the refineries she claimed to be assisting Rok in building.

"Show me."

Poiris led her back into the hall from the observation deck and they wound down through the refinery's innards. It was simple, rough, and raw compared to the luxury of the Xin manor. But there was no time to fit it with things of beauty. She allowed those living here to bring their own artistic sensibilities to bear, and fashion furniture as they could without raising suspicion, but could do no more for them. It was a pitiable existence, but it had to do. Somehow, the Chimera didn't seem to mind in the slightest.

They had almost reached the ground when a Dragon, unknown to her, came bounding down the stairs behind them. Petra turned with fluid grace, her claws tensing on instinct but not unsheathing.

"Oji, the Ryu has arrived," the man reported.

Petra glanced between the messenger and Poiris.

"You may use my office," the Kin offered.

"See him there," Petra ordered the other Dragon. "Lead on, Poiris'Kin."

They traversed upward on a secondary set of stairs to a homely office. Poiris was notorious for favoring practicality over fashion, but nothing betrayed him more than his working space. It was humble for a Kin and reminded Petra that she had risen him from an Anh. After his work at the refinery was finished, she'd see him situated in a lavish room in the Xin manor. No more rough fur carpets, no more worn desks; Poiris would have the trimmings yielded by the gold he helped create.

"Thank you." Petra gave Poiris a pointed nod as Cvareh was ushered in, and the two were promptly left in peace. Petra placed her hands on her hips expectantly.

"Arianna has some demands." Uncertainty dulled the scent of Cvareh's magic.

Petra did not ease her expectations for Cvareh. Out of everyone, he, as her Ryu, needed to be fearless before her. "Tell me."

"She is restless."

Petra snorted. "I am not made to amuse her."

"She wants to return to Loom."

"Unacceptable." Petra wouldn't even entertain the thought. She had the crafter of the Philosopher's Box. She would do whatever she must to gain the information of its machinations.

"I had a feeling you would say that." Cvareh sighed heavily, running his hand through his blood orange hair. Petra watched it fall over his face time and again as he repeated the motion.

"So you have an alternate solution?" He wouldn't have come to her if he didn't.

"She wants to return to Loom… Or have hands."

Petra considered this for a long moment. "She wants to make her own illusions."

Cvareh nodded.

"Can she sustain the additional magic without becoming forsaken?" Petra knew of the plagues that would set in on Fenthri bodies pushed too far with Dragon magic. She would not be responsible for the woman's death. At least not prematurely.

"I don't think she would've asked if she couldn't." Cvareh was certain in Arianna's self-awareness, Petra noted with amusement. "She wants a shade similar to her skin, light blue, steel blue…"

"A shame you cannot make illusions," Petra stole his thoughts and gave them sound. Another note was made when she realized that Cvareh was truly disappointed. *Her brother would've given the woman his hands.* Cvareh was loyal to their House above all else, of that Petra had no doubt, but no Dragon savored the notion of cutting off their body parts for Fenthri gain. They should loathe it. The fact that Cvareh not only seemed willing, but gleaned some sort of delight at the idea of pleasing her was worthy of note in the slowly evolving dynamic of their relationship.

"No matter, she will have the hands she needs."

"Truly?" Cvareh was shocked.

"Yes, truly. I gain more by appeasing the woman, and a set of hands means little to me." Petra started for the door. Progress churned within her, the feeling of a great wheel beginning to spin forward once more. Yes, this was the White Wraith she'd been expecting. She'd give the woman free reign, she'd give her space to challenge the narrow parameters Petra had put her in—if she dared, and she'd see if the gray Chimera was made of steel or steam. "Fortunately for me, I have two brothers."

Petra grinned to herself. Finnyr had been so eager as of late to help their House. Well, now she really needed him to give a hand… or two.

# 11

## ARIANNA

skin when she spoke. He stared at her as though her illusion had melted away like ice in the sunlight of a summer's day. "You always pause here. Which do you like best?"

"The one on the far left is Lord Xin." He motioned to the painting of a veiled figure wielding a sword.

"That's not what I asked." It didn't matter which one he liked or why. But time had whittled away at her. Time, and silence, and more time. It persisted, encasing her mind insistently and eroding her resolve to hate Cain. She was stuck with him and he with her, for the foreseeable future. They may as well put aside the determination to be at each other's throats.

He seemed to have arrived at much the same conclusion over the past week.

Cvareh had proved himself worthless, and a Dragon to the core. He'd not returned with hands nor a glider to bring her back to Loom. Arianna shouldn't have expected differently. So she waited, and bided her time carefully.

"Isn't it though? I am of House Xin."

"And that dictates your favorite will always be Xin?" Arianna asked incredulously.

"Would it not?"

Arianna laughed and shook her head. "You Dragons accuse Loom of being mechanical, but you are nothing more than automatons competing for the distinction of being most suicidally loyal."

"Gird your tongue." His jabs had been slowly losing their edge with each passing week.

"Cain, we both know we're at a stalemate. You'll do nothing to me because you can't—I'm too precious to your House. I'll do nothing to you because, even if I could take you down, I'd never get out of here alive." She gave him an opening to refute the claim, which he didn't, because he couldn't. "Drop the bravado already. I'm not questioning your loyalty. I'm merely asking for your opinion."

He looked back at the paintings with new consideration.

"The one of Lord Xin is magnificent. It truly is… However, I find the one of Lord Pak calls to me more."

"Lord Pak?" Arianna studied the painting to the right of the veiled god. It was done entirely in grays. If she tilted her head to the side, she could perhaps make out a face, not quite Fenthri, not quite Dragon. It was familiar and unknown, a depth that threatened to embrace but never relinquish.

"The Dark-wielder," Cain clarified. "I was born under his month."

Before the clouds had been breached, Loom had no concept of sun or moon. The idea that a glowing orb of light floated across the sky was still unnerving to Arianna each morning she rose to look upon it. The large moon was no better in its pale and contrasting glow.

Beneath the clouds, the light was muted, diffused. Once in a rare while the clouds thinned enough to betray a potentially circular source of light, but what it was had every Guild guessing for hundreds of years. That said, Loom still knew of the moon's cycles. There were periods of bright nights and periods of dark nights. Arianna remembered the first time she'd looked upon sketches of the moon's phases, thinking about the inexplicable sense it made for some sort of hanging heavenly body to change its shape.

As a result of the "dark nights," the evolution of Loom's calendar had developed a similar pattern to Nova's. Twenty cycles of the moon making up twenty months in a year, the end and beginning punctuated by a full day of light.

On Loom, the months were merely numbered—a simple, logical system of ordered progression. On Nova, the months were named like everything else, difficult to remember and seemingly random.

"What number month is that?" Arianna asked.

Cain regarded her cautiously, as if the question could have some sort of veiled meaning. "The tenth."

She grinned madly.

"What?" Cain frowned, obviously expecting her to make a joke of some aspect of his culture.

"You and I share the same month."

"We have the same Patron?" Cain seemed aghast at the notion.

"That seems to be the case." Arianna delighted in his discomfort about them having anything in common. "What day were you born?"

"The tenth."

She inwardly cursed: couldn't have been lucky enough to have the same day. That would be enough to drive the man mad for months. "The seventh." Perhaps it was a mark of the overall improvement in their relationship that she didn't lie to him. They began walking again and Arianna let the conversation shift. "Why are there only three Dragon Houses, if there are twenty possible patrons?"

"There were more, thousands of years ago. But the others were killed off until only three remained. House Tam proposed a system to keep things equal among the Houses with one overseer and two Houses to keep them in check. A sort of peace treaty," Cain explained. "Once every decade or two, some bold upstart works up the notion to have his own House, supposedly called to task by some Patron."

"But the three in power never let that happen."

He gave her a nod of affirmation, and silence passed between them once more. She began to steer them in a new direction. Each day she'd used the conversation to distract him long enough to let them wander somewhere new. They strayed from what she'd come to suspect was the "approved path," into new areas of the Xin Manor. Arianna had yet to find the glider, but she would eventually. And, once she knew the route, she would not be long for Nova.

"How did you learn Fennish?" They had yet to speak in the Dragon's tongue. It served Arianna better for him to think she couldn't understand his whispered Royuk to servants about her and her care, or the conversations she could pick up as they passed through the halls.

"Petra'Oji wants all Da and higher in the House to be educated in the ways of Loom."

Arianna snorted, earning herself a sour look. "If you are as 'educated' as Cvareh was before he came to Loom, then your understanding of Fenthri ends at a rough attempt at our language."

Cain considered her a long moment. Arianna held his golden gaze, unafraid and challenging. Let him try to dissuade her. Let him speak one word counter to her point.

But he remained silent and—dare she say it?—thoughtful.

Shortly after, Cain realized they'd strayed from the course and promptly returned her to her room. No further words were exchanged on the way, but Arianna had learned enough. Judging from the scent, the halls they'd traversed were near the kitchen, and that was not what she was looking for. She needed to pick up the metallic tang of gears and oil. But perhaps that was looking for something that couldn't be found on Nova. They seemed to have everything but workshops and laboratories.

"Is there something else?"

Cain lingered after he'd released her illusion. Two of the fingers in his hand had broken from holding the magic for so long and they were slowly knitting back into place. "Why have you not yet tried to escape?"

"Escape to where?" If he had a genuine answer to her question, she wanted to hear it. "I can't fly, I have no glider, no boco—"

"You escaped your room the first day."

"Only to be returned here."

"Then you escaped again."

"Only to be returned here *again*," she reiterated.

"I took you for bolder."

Was there genuine disappointment in his tone? "I'm merely biding my time," she threatened with a smile.

He faltered. That was the thing about effective threats: they must possess a grain of truth. In this case, it was completely transparent.

"Whatever you're planning, it will not get past me."

"Like you didn't let me escape either of the other times?" Arianna bared her teeth at the man.

His claws shot out but retracted just as quickly. She'd punched a nice nerve. "You no longer have that machination. You will need to depart through the door —a door I guard."

"You should pray to each of your twenty gods that's not the case. Because if it is, it will only mean that yours will be the first heart I cut out when the time comes."

Cain growled. Arianna's hand was limp at her side, ready to summon her dagger to her palm. If he wanted a fight, she would give him one while there were no others to interfere. His magic flared brightly, assaulting her senses with the smell of wet earth.

But it diminished quickly, fading into nothing more than frustration and a fearsome scowl. The Dragon retreated, slamming the door behind him like a petulant child. Arianna sighed heavily, turning to the window.

She had yet to tire of staring at the sun. For all it hurt her eyes and seared her vision, she was fascinated by its circular presence.

It was also a reminder: Arianna was very far from home, and understood little of the world surrounding her.

# 12

## FLORENCE

The engine that was going to propel them through the dense and dangerous wood known as the Skeleton Forest had seen better days. Better years actually. Long, *long*-ago years. It was an old and rusted thing, paint peeled at every corner and orange lines of oxidation ran down its sides. Florence didn't have to be a Rivet to know that the make and model dated before she was even born.

It should be in a museum, or an artifact graveyard, not the overgrown tracks they were supposed to be traveling on.

Even with her minimal training as a Raven, Florence could see the signs of wear that time had abused into the exposed metal. The cranks between the wheels looked brittle and the pistons were in no better shape. The actual Raven of their group, Anders, had been tearing out his hair over it for the past week trying to get it up to par. Florence wished he looked a little more confident now, running his final checks.

"Where did we even find this thing?" Derek asked no one in particular.

"I feel like some questions are better left unanswered." Nora threw her rucksack into the car that would be their moving home for the next few weeks as they traversed down through Ter.2 into Ter.1. The train was only three parts long —the engine, the tender, the car—and no two parts looked as though they'd come from the same machine yard.

"Flor, come help me with this!" Anders called from the front.

Florence glanced between her chests and the direction the voice had come from.

"We'll load it up," Derek offered.

"Carefully," Florence cautioned. "Or you're going to blow us straight to Nova."

"If there's anything that temperamental in here, we have no chance of making it to Ter.1. I doubt this is going to be a smooth ride." Nora grabbed for one side of the chest.

"Still, be careful," Florence called over her shoulder, making her way up to the engine. "Anders?"

"Flor, pass me a wrench." The man held out a hand from where he was wedged under the engine. "There's a small disconnect here to the cylinder I want to fix and Rotus is up bothering with the whistle. Not that I know why we even need a whistle. If we encounter another train on these tracks we have bigger problems to worry about…"

Florence passed the Raven his tools as he muttered commands. She watched him tinker and toil, remembering all the times she'd seen Will and Helen do the same when they were younger. Florence wondered where her friends were now, what vessel they were currently obsessed with.

"This is almost on tight… Can you check up on the safety valve while I finish up?"

"I don't think you want me doing that…"

"It'll save us time, and I want to get well down the tracks before midday."

"Yes, but I'm not—"

"You were born in the Ravens, no?"

"Yes, but—"

"How long were you there?"

"Fourteen years. But—"

"More than enough time to understand a safety valve," he insisted.

"I left for a reason." Florence chewed the inside of her cheek to keep herself from chewing out Anders and creating tensions before they'd even started on their journey.

Anders paused, sticking his head out enough to inspect her properly. "Do you understand it or not?"

"Not confidently…" The truth was Florence *did* understand it, in principle. But she didn't want anyone depending on her work when it came to anything but guns and explosives. And even when it came to those, she didn't have the best resume for a gunsmith.

"We all understand things a little better when our lives depend on it." Anders passed her a tool and Florence reluctantly accepted it before climbing up to where the safety valve was located at the top of the engine.

Her handiwork appeared to be sufficient, and within the hour they were chugging down the tracks, set along a southerly course. Florence, Nora, Derek, and Rotus took turns helping Anders manage the engine. For the most part, that involved shoveling coal and calling out numbers on gauges.

It was shocking to Florence how ineffective purely steam-based travel was compared to magically augmented vessels. The train was so old that there wasn't a speck of gold on it, and the metal was too rare for the Alchemists to have invested in attaching some before they left. But Anders was an older man, Florence would guess in his late twenties, so he was raised in a time on the fringe of the wide proliferation of magic. Where Florence was unnerved, he was relaxed behind the wheel. Or as relaxed as one could hope to be in a rattling death trap.

Florence was surprised the train held itself together well enough to grind the wheels to life and pull the two cars day after day. It was an imperfect process that changed regularly. Things broke, and repairs had to be creative solutions. She was continually selected as the extra set of hands over Derek or Nora. Anders reasoned it was because of her birth guild. Rotus reasoned it was because she'd studied under a Master Rivet.

After the first week, she stopped all form of protest. She had worked with Arianna enough times on various clockwork gadgets to trust herself when given direction. Each morning she'd get up early with one of the two men and help them with any daily maintenance.

The trees towered around them, encroaching tightly on the untended tracks. Florence watched them whiz by in the fading light. Her eyes lacked focus that reflected her blank mind.

"What is it like in Ter.5?" Derek asked as he plopped down next to her, ungracefully due to the swaying of the train.

"The trees are smaller." They passed the hours doing almost anything to stave off boredom. This was the carbon copy of a conversation they'd had before. But they'd have it again over the endless symphony of chugging metal and grinding wheels. "The land isn't really flat, not unless you're by the coast."

"And Ter.4?"

"More flat land there." Florence tried to dredge up memories of the Territory she was born in, but all that came to mind was the great, moving guild hall of the Ravens. A perpetually changing, ever-moving structure from all the tracks and raceways that curved through its many levels. "Though I haven't ever really explored it."

"Just the Underground?" He already knew the story.

"Just the Underground."

"What's that like?"

"Dark and terrifying." Florence had no good memories of the Underground. She'd almost died both times she'd ventured beneath Ter.4.

"I can't imagine anywhere more terrifying than the depths of the Skeleton Forest." Derek followed her blank stare out the open door of the train car to the whizzing trees. Darkness remained nestled within them, uninviting.

Florence shook her head. "There's light here. There's sky, and up, and down, and headway to be made. In the Underground there is simply blackness. Inky, endless, blackness... and Wretches."

"Perhaps the endwig are nothing more than forest Wretches?"

"You'd know better than I, Alchemist."

"We don't regularly find them in a state we can dissect. Or we would."

Florence inwardly cringed at the idea. Her hands were kept busy with the revolver in her hands, diligently oiling it. Every day it had its turn, following the rifle slung over her back. "What are the endwig like?"

"Nightmare given flesh." Derek's tone was instantly grave.

"Have you seen them before?" Florence studied his face with fascination. It was an expression she knew, one of world-shaking horror—a death shroud pulled taut over one's features, even if they escaped its clutches. She knew the answer before she even asked the question.

"Only once, from a distance. They hunt in the twilight hours; it was my mistake for even being out then."

"What happened?"

"A nightmare."

Florence knew she would get nothing more from him, and she didn't pry. It would be like someone asking her to recreate the sound of the Wretches' pincers, or describe the glow of their mutated saliva as it cut through the darkness like the most ominous beacon one could possibly imagine. She wasn't that cruel.

The conversation faded with the light and the train's steam. They coasted to a stop along the tracks, not risking wearing down their brakes for no good reason. By the time they jumped out of the nearly immobile vehicle, dusk was nearly upon them.

Nora made the fire that they would all sit around. Anders and Rotus were exhausted from managing the train, and did little. Derek kept Florence company as they ventured into the silent woods in search of game, hastily avoiding the impending twilight.

His hearing was better than hers. Pointed and ruby red, he had the ears of a Dragon instead of a Fenthri. Even though Florence found her senses heightened since the introduction of magic—years of ringing from explosions smoothed away due to the healing powers of her new blood—her aural acuity was nothing compared to his. They stalked quietly through the brush in the direction of a water source.

Derek would collect the water while Florence hunted their dinner. She was the best shot of the group and had yet to fail them. Creatures crowded around the streams and brooks that wound through the forest. She'd never hunted before this excursion, but it proved no more difficult than target practice.

Point, aim, shoot.

She adjusted her grip on her rifle, scanning the brush for any signs of life. A fat hare, a small deer, a wild boar—it made no difference. With her gun in hand, they were all made equal.

The rush of water over stones permeated the foliage, blending with the sound of rustling leaves. They broke through the brush and crossed onto a rocky bank. Florence scanned the edge of the small river they had come across.

"I don't see anything." She sighed heavily. "I'm going to track upstream a bit."

"Don't go too far, it's almost twilight."

"Just around the bend." She kept her voice low to avoid scaring off any potential quarry in the distance.

"I'll wait for you." He slung the water bladders off his shoulder and they fell to the ground with a dull splat. Derek began to unscrew them, his skin almost the same shade as the dark leather in the fading light.

"I won't wander," Florence promised. She knew the dangers of wandering. It was what had separated her and Arianna in the Underground. She would only stay along the stream.

Derek vanished behind her as she trekked onward. Time and again, Florence ran her hands over the hinges of her rifle. She felt the tension in the trigger, assuring her that it was cocked and ready. She needed just one creature, and she could return back victorious.

With a grand stroke of luck, a pheasant made its way along the bank with an enticing little coo. Florence dropped to her knees, gun at the ready. The noise of her footfalls was covered by the sound of a nearby waterfall, seemingly the font of the river.

It rushed down around craggy rocks, determined to smooth over the rough hillside in long white strands that seemed to glow in the pale twilight. Florence brought the gun to her shoulder, adjusting her crouch so that one knee was up and the other was planted firmly in the river rock. She lined up the notches down the barrel of the gun, tracking it over the bird.

Florence took a deep breath and fought the urge to close one eye. With the bird securely in her sights, she brought her finger to the trigger and held her breath.

The creature raised its head suddenly, turning in surprise. Florence hadn't heard what spooked the animal, but she didn't hesitate; she took her shot.

With a crack, the bird was dead.

Satisfied, Florence stood, slinging the rifle over her shoulder. It wasn't as much as she'd bagged previously but it would be enough for a night, even split five ways. So relived was she that Florence never bothered to heed to what had nearly scared the bird away from its watering hole.

She didn't realize she wasn't alone until she had the pheasant's clawed feet in her grasp.

The sound of the water rushing over the rocks began to fade. Her head filled with a numbing white noise that set her inner ear to spinning. Florence blinked, turning, looking between the darkness of the trees. She grabbed for her revolver, waiting with heart-pounding dread for something to emerge.

Movement caught the corner of her eye and Florence looked up to the top of the waterfall. Long, clawed, horribly joined and gnarled fingers curled over the edge of the rock. Cresting the edge was a set of horns woven like frozen flame. They were attached to a skeletal face, skinless and pointed in a sharp-toothed snarl.

Eyes like those of a Dragon glowed in spite of the darkness. White on a field of obsidian sockets sunk far into the depths of the creature's head. It was all arms and legs and sinew, a monster that looked as though it had woken from a thousand-year slumber and now sought its first meal.

Its low breathing dulled her senses. There was a wicked sort of magic at play here. Not like the Dragons, not like Chimera. This was a creature born of malice and murder...

And it was not alone.

One by one, horned monsters crested the rocky bluff. Each sang their sense-dulling requiem. Their eyes turned to her with instinctual purpose.

Florence's sweating palm slipped off the handle of her revolver. Her legs had been disconnected from her body. Her hands didn't move as commanded. She could hear nothing other than the mind-numbing, low breaths of the monsters. She could see nothing other than their glowing eyes.

In the fading twilight, she stared at a nightmare made flesh.

# 13
## ARIANNA

THE SUN AND MOON WERE NOT EVEN CLOSE TO THE SAME THING. WHILE THEY both gave off light for nearly equal portions of the day, one was bright and painful to stare at, while the other was muted and ghostly. Arianna had known this before arriving on Nova, but even after nearly two months of her useless tenure in the Xin manor, she remained fascinated by the moon's shifting phases.

The sun was constant. Every day it shone in its perpetual orb-like manner. Bright, blinding, and filtering down through the clouds onto Loom below. But the moon shifted. It went through its phases with no regard for any who might be depending on its light for guidance through the dark night. And once every month, it winked out of existence entirely, as if to remind the world below that they were lucky to have it at all.

Arianna had been forced to be like the sun on Nova: constant, present, dependable. On Loom, her true nature was that of the moon. She could be an evolving creature, growing with every turn of the calendar.

The stagnancy she found herself in was nearly coming to an end.

She'd moved the small table over to the western facing window so she could watch the moon trail through the sky. Arianna enjoyed its ghostly play on her papers, the way it set her firm black lines of ink against the white. She kept diligent records of everywhere Cain showed her, adjusting her map regularly.

There was something in the rock of Nova, Arianna had decided, that made it defy gravity. The islands floated, that much couldn't be argued. Why they were floating she had yet to fathom, and likely never would. Magic was as good an explanation as any. But even magic had rules it must follow, and if *some* of the rock could float, then why couldn't all rock float?

Arianna continued to push the question aside, focusing on what was of most direct importance to her.

The second she'd wrapped her mind around accepting that rock could float, she threw out the parameters she'd been relying on for her mental reconstruction of the manor. If there was no need of support beams, load bearing walls, or secure foundation, the structure could indeed evolve in whatever way the Dragons saw fit. That led her to her next string of logic: What way did they see fit?

Cain had been hard to unravel, but unravel he had. Day by day, Arianna had prodded and worked her way under his thick skull to try to understand what was important to him and the other inhabitants of this world. It was surprisingly simple from there.

Gods. Hierarchy. Beauty before reason.

It was a language Arianna didn't speak, but she was learning. And, in the process, she'd nearly zeroed in on where she suspected the glider was being kept. Her pen paused mid-stroke, the detailed blueprint forgotten.

Her nostrils flared, her mind trying to process the thick scent assaulting her nose. She knew it from all similar aromas like a lock-box that could be fashioned by a thousand Rivets but bore a single maker's mark. It was familiar in the worst of ways. One whiff and a hundred memories assaulted her with vicious purpose.

Arianna stood slowly, reaching for her daggers, sliding them out from under her pillows. She gripped them tightly, her eyes focused on the door as she rounded the bed. The scent grew.

*It couldn't be this easy.* Her lips curled back, baring her teeth in a ferocious snarl. Bloodlust churned through her veins with every mechanical beat of her heart. Her mind screamed for death—for vengeance.

The door lock disengaged and the handle turned. Arianna flipped her dagger into an ice pick grip and reared back. The door opened and the scent clouded every sense. She lunged forward and… stopped short.

Cvareh stared back at her, wide-eyed and caught completely off guard. The edge of her dagger rested between his eyes. Blood beaded around its tip, cutting the smell of cedar with potent woodsmoke. In his hands he cradled a box, one whose contents were so important that he clearly did not risk dropping it even for the sake of defending himself.

Arianna panted, her mind clearing slowly. She blinked and her eyes darted with every close of her eyelids, trying to find the source of the offending scent. They landed on the box.

"What do you have?" she hissed.

"Only what you asked for." Blood ran down his nose in a thin golden line. He had yet to step away from or move aside her dagger. The Dragon placed a foolish amount of trust in her to assume she wouldn't plunge the blade straight into his brain.

"What I asked for?" She was slow on the uptake, slower than she'd ever been previously. But her mind put together the pieces with ritualistic precision in spite of her vertigo. "The hands?"

"Yes." Cvareh rubbed the bead of blood on his forehead the second she pulled away the blade. "Is that how you greet Cain?"

"Only if he's earned my ire." Her jest fell flat. Arianna's mind was entirely on the hands. "I smelled the blood, thought that maybe there was some kind of combatant…"

Her words trailed off as she continued to focus on what he was bringing her. For now, she bit her tongue and kept herself from asking him where he'd acquired them. She would guard that particular question until she was ready to act on its truth. Until the time of her vengeance was right.

Arianna set her daggers down on the table and motioned for Cvareh to place the box before her. As soon as he did, the Dragon took a full two steps away from the vessel in question. The whole idea of what was about to transpire clearly set him on edge. It was enough proof of the box's contents that Arianna didn't feel the need to verify it with her own eyes just yet.

"I trust you know what to do with them?"

"I do. I will need three stand mirrors, thread, needle, and bandages."

Cvareh looked to the door frame and Arianna followed his gaze. She shouldn't have been surprised to see Cain there. She shouldn't have been surprised to see every Dragon in the Xin manor standing there to investigate the potent stink that was now wafting from her room.

The sea-foam blue Dragon looked on in disgust. "You can't possibly—"

"Fetch them for her," Cvareh ordered. There was no space for questioning between the sharp clip of his words.

Cain's nostrils tensed, arching upward in disgust and anger, but he left as commanded. Arianna got a wicked sense of pleasure from his discomfort. The night was shaping up in unpredictable ways. Her plans were changing before her eyes, a new set unfurling like a scroll of truth that had been kept from her until just that moment. Patience was paying off.

"What can I do to help?" Cvareh asked.

"Nothing."

"But—"

"I said nothing." She glared at him, wondering what about a singular word could possibly be confusing.

The Dragon blinked back at her. He didn't understand. He wouldn't understand the source of the rekindled flame of her rage. If anything, his confusion assured her enough to keep him alive, to prevent her slamming him against the nearest wall and skinning him over and over and over until he told her what she wanted to know.

"I know what you are about to do, and you cannot possibly intend to do it alone."

"I do intend, and I will." Arianna was spared further exhausting affirmation by Cain's return. At least someone among them was competent enough to do as she asked and then leave her be. The other Dragon departed with a pointed glare, the supplies deposited haphazardly on the opposite edge of the bed as though he could not be coaxed into entering her room more than necessary under the present circumstances.

Arianna began setting up the supplies on the table. Her hands moved with the certainty of practice. She had done this before with Eva. She had done *worse* before. It was not a delight, but it was not something that was cause for fear. *It was science*, as Eva would say. And science existed beyond right, wrong, and fear.

"Let me help."

"Do you really want to be involved with this?" Her violet eyes met his gold ones as Arianna attempted to burrow under his resolve. It was a plant with shallow roots, easily felled when the earth around it was overturned. She could feel his magic waver before his stare did. "I didn't think so."

Cvareh opened his mouth to speak, but Arianna wouldn't let him.

"I commanded you to harvest one of your own. I am going to cut off my hands, and stitch these on, and use them forevermore as though I was born with them." Arianna tilted her head to the side. "The blood of your kin is already on your palms. Do you want to take that further?"

He was completely disarmed, and that told her everything. Arianna didn't know the depth of the truth yet, but she would find out in time. She would find who the original owner of the hands had been; she'd just confirmed the man she had known simply as "Rafansi" during the last rebellion was someone of House Xin.

"I have been here for weeks, and you could not be bothered with me," she reminded him. The pain was real and bright and angry like a fresh wound. It hurt more than she thought it would, and that only flared her temper further.

"I have acted in no way that was not on your behalf, or in your best interest," he insisted. "But I have had other things to attend to. I couldn't let myself be distracted, and when I am near you… There were matters of my House."

"I understand," she said quietly, letting the clasps of the box falling open ring louder than any single word. "Because you are Cvareh Xin'Ryu Soh, peeled from the blue of the sky itself. I am Arianna the Rivet, steam given the shape of a woman. And our priorities only overlap as much as it behooves your sister to seek my help."

He had the sense not to try to object. Though his face was tormented by enough conflict to make her very briefly question what, exactly, was going through his head.

Arianna put the hesitation aside with a smile, an expression somewhere between an exhausted triumph and a bitter sneer. "So, pretend this is nothing more than what it is: you earning my trust. And get out."

His claws shot from his fingers and an equal measure of hurt and anger was fresh on his magic. It dotted his pores like a midday sweat. She wanted him to fight, she realized. Arianna wanted him to tell her she was wrong and insist that there was some purity beyond simply overlapping desires that strung them together.

Instead Cvareh retreated. He left with wide, hasty steps.

She paid him no further mind. The truth of her words had made them pointed, not the bitterness that had been building in her chest at the weeks of being saddled with Cain. She was here for a purpose, a shifting, changing, elusive purpose, but a purpose all the same.

Arianna walked over to the door, dragging the spare chair behind her. She sat heavily in it, placing some of her makeshift tools in her lap. Running her fingers over the lock like a lover, she made quick work of the panel. She was Arianna, and she would be kept nowhere she didn't wish to be. She'd do nothing she didn't wish to do. She'd let the Dragons think otherwise for weeks, but now it was time to remind them that she was a force of her own.

Within a few minutes, and a few precise movements, she'd dismantled the lock into the engaged position. Arianna stood and swung the chair around, wedging it under the door handle for good measure. She didn't think anyone would have even the slightest bit of interest in coming to her side, especially not after she warned off the one Dragon who could—for some inexplicable reason— have half a mind to do so.

But she could take no chances.

She was about to be in the most vulnerable state imaginable. She was about to spill her secrets upon the table with every drop of blood. And she would risk no witnesses.

Like a ritual, Arianna drew the curtains over the windows, candlelight the room's only glow. It was more than enough light for her Dragon eyes to see with precision. She sat heavily at the table, her reflection a flickering visage in the polished mirrors. Purple eyes stared back at her from every angle.

Arianna remembered when her eyes had been black. She remembered when they had been violently gouged out. She remembered losing all sight, and the moment of stomach-churning terror when she thought she might never see again. She remembered coming to peace with the notion that the face of the woman she loved could well be the last thing she ever saw.

Her eyes had opened again. Sharper, clearer, more precise than she could've ever imagined. Now Arianna inspected her hands. They were the hands that Master Oliver had trained, hands that could dismantle a Rivet lock like it was nothing more than a simple bank vault.

Arianna rested her palm on the table and reached for her sharpest dagger. Her chest tightened. Nature fought against what she was about to do. Her mind flooded with endorphins as it fought against itself. Instinct commanded she jump from the table and drop the knife. It struggled with her hand, trying to force it to shake, wanting her movements to suffer so much that she gave up on them entirely.

But Arianna was stable. She kept her churning stomach quelled. She kept her breathing even.

The knife pierced her ashen flesh. It gouged sharp and true, bit to bone. Arianna bared her teeth, gritting them so hard they ached straight through her jaw and into her neck. Golden blood pooled across the table, mixing with marrow as bone splintered.

Two hands waited for her, the same color as her ears. They held the same scent as the man who had given her organs in a gesture of trust, only to turn and betray all that she loved. Arianna's lips curled back. Her body shook. But she remained focused. She would take his magic once more. She would use it to find him.

She would kill him in blood more frigid than snow.

Arianna repeated it over and over in her head, uttered it like a violent prayer of the darkest variety. She did it again and again to keep the agony at bay as her magic fought to heal her body, to keep her mind right in the wake of shock.

She was Arianna the Rivet. She was the White Wraith. And she would not scream.

# 14

## CVAREH

He could hear every labored breath. He could hear every drop of blood splattering the floor. He could hear each dull thud of flesh that served as a chilling auditory reminder of what was happening behind the door he faced.

Cvareh hadn't moved since being cast out. He had made no motion when he heard her quiet tinkering with the lock. He did not attempt to force entry by breaking the door frame and smashing the chair she'd propped against the latch.

She had not wanted him there. She had chosen to endure the self-surgery on her own. It was as foolish as it was brave. It clouded his emotions with both admiration for her ferocity and aggravation at her persistence that every burden be shouldered alone.

But that was Arianna. That was the torrent that pulled him under every time his eyes rested on her. And it was no wonder why he had purposefully avoided seeing her. Every complex emotion combined with the draw of the boon was too much for him. For weeks he'd wanted to run from it, and now that he was faced with her once more, literally carrying a reason to loathe her, he wanted nothing more than to be by her side. He wanted to tell her that she didn't have to be alone.

Cvareh sighed heavily, closing his eyes. He pressed his forehead to the door. He could smell the bright, unique signature of her magic. It was overwhelming, no doubt from all the blood being spilled from the process of severing her own hands.

He licked his lips.

Clawed fingers curled around the door lever and Cvareh considered how much force he'd have to apply to earn entry. But even if he did, what then? What could he possibly do? He knew nothing of the ways of adding new parts to a Chimera. And somehow, even one- or no-handed, he suspected Arianna would have enough rage to still be a force to be reckoned with.

"Will you wait there all night?"

Cvareh's eyes regained focus, peering through the dimly lit hall at the man who leaned against a far wall. Cain stared back at him, inquisitive. The question hadn't been rhetorical.

"Perhaps." Cvareh didn't really know what he would do. Not when it came to Arianna. Just when he thought he'd figured it out, the woman elicited a different response from him.

"Why?"

Cain wouldn't understand. All Cain saw was the Chimera from Loom, a wretched amalgamation of Dragon and Fenthri that was now stealing magic from one of their House. Cain had not been there on Loom for all the days spent journeying with the brash and beautiful woman.

"Because we need her."

"More that you need her." Cain crossed the hall with measured steps; his walk betrayed both his boldness and willingness to turn at dismissal. It was a delicate dance that only a Dragon could manage. But Cain had earned boldness around Cvareh. The two had grown up together nearly as brothers, and in the dark halls of the Xin Manor with no eyes upon them, Cvareh fashioned them closer to equals.

"Both are true," he confessed.

"Why? What do we need with her?" Cain focused on the House first.

"She can make a Philosopher's Box." Confusion crossed his friend's face, forcing Cvareh to elaborate. "A mechanism that will make perfect Chimera. It will give Loom the ability to stand against the Dono."

"Do we want that?" Cain asked uncertainly.

"It will shift the tides for House Xin."

"And then we will be faced with Fenthri who are emboldened against us."

"We will let the Fenthri govern themselves. Petra has never wanted to be the Dono of Loom. In our great history, House Xin has never governed the world below. Our ends are entirely Nova. We don't need to dirty ourselves with the rock—" Cvareh's appeal to Cain's distaste for Loom was cut short as Arianna let out a sharp gasp. He leaned against the door, listening carefully, holding his own breath while he waited to hear the continued sounds of her labors.

"Petra should be Dono of the world below and above." Cain's loyalty was unwavering.

"She will be the Dono of nothing if we do not gain an advantage over House Rok." Cvareh had sat through too many discussions with his sister to entertain alternatives. They had turned over numbers, hypotheses, plots and plans every which way. Barring the Dono making some grave error—which Yveun was not known for—gaining strength from Loom was their only way to tip the scales and force House Tam's hand.

"I trust you both." Of that, Cvareh had no doubt. "But this does not sit easy with me." Cain motioned toward the door. "You gave her your brother's hands. Of all who would make that sacrifice for the House, she will have the magic of the direct blood of the Oji."

"And it was the Oji's choice." Cvareh neglected to mention that she had already had the direct blood of the Oji from imbibing off him.

Cain sighed.

"I would think this would delight you, as it will mean you no longer need to waste your time illusioning her."

"Am I pleased to be free of that burden? Yes." Cain didn't even bother denying it. "But that means she will walk freely among us. You have given her the ability to pass among our brothers and sisters, to mingle so long as the illusion can be maintained. I don't trust her in my home."

"Then trust in me, and the trust I place in her."

Cain's eyes, nearly a reflection of Cvareh's own, studied him. He kept his height and didn't waver. If he did, weakness would poison the waters of his authority. It was something Cvareh could not afford to have happen. Even though Cain was like a brother, the distance Cvareh held as Ryu needed to be maintained. Petra had worked too hard in crafting it; he could not let his sister down.

"The ends best be great, Cvareh." The other man pushed off the wall he'd leaned against. "Because you are charting a dangerous course." Cain rested a hand on Cvareh's shoulder, a familial motion that showed his sincerity. "Keep both eyes open about this woman. She will gut you alive if it serves her."

"No one knows this more than I." He had seen Arianna's ruthlessness first-hand on multiple occasions. "I'm the only one among us who truly sees her. I am the only one on Nova who knows anything about this woman."

Cvareh looked to Cain with a silent challenge. Would the man think that the time he had spent with Arianna had given him more insight into the woman than he himself possessed? Cain narrowed his eyes slightly, but stepped away with a small bow of his head—deferring to Cvareh's assessment.

Cain disappeared into the darkness, his figure fading in the diminishing light of the oil lanterns that lined the hall. As much as Cvareh wanted to defend Arianna further, he knew he couldn't. Cain's assessment was pointed, as an experienced tactician's should be. But Cvareh still wondered how he'd gathered so much from the seemingly short and tumultuous relationship he'd had with Arianna.

An unusual emotion crept up on him, a jealousy of sorts for Cain's unexpected awareness of Arianna—though it had been Cvareh's decision for him to look after her in the first place. Cain was the only one Cvareh trusted to not be completely overrun by Arianna's mannerisms, which seemed to hold true. Cvareh had thought he needed space from her to clear his head, but now regret for the decision to let anyone else stay at her side was sudden and swift.

The woman had been quiet for some time, but a sharp hiss of pain brought Cvareh's attention back to the door. She continued on. His watch continued alongside her.

He sat, the back of his head resting against the barrier that kept him from her. He closed his eyes and listened to the sounds of her labor. Behind his eyelids, he remembered the first time he'd watched her hands work on the ship they rode to cross the inner sea between Ter.4 and Ter.5. They'd moved deftly, fixing engine problems with fearless precision.

Those hands would be gone, in their place something new. Cvareh had never thought about it quite under the same circumstances, but Fenthri had the capacity to change, to grow. Being a Chimera, adding new organs, they became something more. He had been born into his skin and he would keep it with him until the day he died.

But she was something more now than she was a mere few hours ago.

She was always something more.

His memories played like a soft lullaby in dark harmony with the sounds of her labors. Sounds that, for all their gruesome truths, told him she was still alive. A morbid peace took over him as he waited away the night.

Shifting stirred Cvareh from an unexpected sleep. He blinked his eyes open, wondering how and when he fell asleep. The echoes of Arianna's labors played in his ears and Cvareh tried to make sense of when they'd quieted enough for him to slumber.

The hallway was illuminated with the brightness of dawn, windows cutting beams of light in the quiet corner of the manor. Just as his mind was shrugging off the haze of sleep, the door behind him opened. Cvareh toppled backward, catching himself at the last second with an elbow, nearly colliding with the pair of legs that waited on the inside of the door.

They were a pale blue color, not unlike his own. Leather shorts, similar to what Petra would fashion herself in, hugged mostly bare hips. Strips of crossed fabric bound over her breasts, the dark wine color offsetting the hue of her exposed skin in a way Cvareh would've never himself attempted. And yet, he must commend her for it, as there was something quite striking about the color contrast. Her eyes were the same purple color, but her hair had gained a more golden shade, framing the only thing familiar about the woman staring down at him.

"Since you seem to be suddenly insistent on keeping my company, you can be the one to take me out of this place."

The voice was distinctly Arianna. Nothing could change her tone and cadence. But it was a strange disconnect to see it coming from a Dragon's mouth.

"Up with you." She nudged him with her foot. "I want to see this Isle of Ruana."

# 15
## YVEUN

Yveun tapped his quill mindlessly upon the desk as he looked out over the wide balcony to his left.

The world had been quiet, almost quiet enough to give the illusion that all was right within it. But Yveun knew better. He did not appreciate the silence from his guild advisers down on Loom. He certainly knew better than to think the relative silence from Petra meant the woman had given up on her foolishly grandiose ambitions.

But those were two areas over which he had no control. His advisers on Loom were doing the best they could, considering the current climate within the guilds. The one he'd sent to get a hold on the Alchemists had been put off time and again, enough so that Yveun was nearly at the point of applying force. And Yveun had never boasted a measure of control over Petra, which was part of the problem.

He looked back down at his papers, rubbing his temples. If he looked at the balcony, he saw the ghost of Leona, reminding him of his immense failure in losing one of his greatest assets. If he looked at his work he was reminded of the guilds on Loom and all their troubles.

It all left only one frustration for him to focus on: Fennyr.

The elder brother of his enemy had been given what Yveun considered a simple task. Sniff out some information, *any* information. It couldn't possibly be difficult. But his lack of results reminded Yveun why, despite being older than Petra, Fennyr was not the Oji of House Xin.

Still, Yveun had cause for hope. Fennyr had finally been invited home by Petra. The Dono rarely let his wards return to their respective islands, but he was all too eager to make an exception in this case.

He had been patient, but his patience was finally running out. The man had been gone for three days now, and Yveun wondered what could possibly be taking so long.

He tapped his quill again.

He lamented over the state of Loom.

His mind tortured him with the need to find a suitable replacement for Leona.

He could even smell the stink of the Chimeras House Rok kept deep below from where he sat, wafting up to his wandering mind like a foul potpourri that perfectly complemented his rotten state.

The distractions were unkind and it took Yveun nearly twice his usual time to attend to the resource allocation of both Loom and Nova. It was a delicate balance, one that was getting marginally easier with time, albeit no less tedious. Now that Fenthri were raised and kept in the guild they were born into, there were more exact counts on what each guild needed to sustain itself. Enough years had also passed that it was becoming clearer how many would survive, on average, the guild tests at Initiate and Journeymen to then become part of the general population.

Before, the land below was running through resources like wildfire, uncontrolled and unabashed. Had contact with Nova not been made, Yveun doubted they would have been able to sustain themselves for much longer before reaching their limit. And yet the Fenthri remained ungrateful to the good changes he was trying to implement.

Yveun stood from his desk, gathering his monthly updates. Not much changed with each cycle of the moon, just small shifts in how he wanted to see trade managed. But year after year, progress was made.

Lossom, his current Master Rider, waited outside his room. Yveun had yet to allow the man into his space.

"Tell me of the happenings beneath Lysip," Yveun demanded as they walked. There were precious few hours in the day to waste any. He had yet to grant the young man quarters in the great Rok Estate and, for the time being, it meant he would also serve as Yveun's eyes to the underside of the island.

"There was a dispute between some no-titled and some Bek." Such was par for the course. Two of the lower rungs of society fighting tooth and nail. "A Veh chose to involve himself."

"A Veh?" Yveun was actually interested now. "Why would a Veh bother with no-ranked squalor?"

"Because the no-titled slew all the Bek and proceeded to feast on them before their families."

Yveun considered this. When Lossom had originally said "some no-titled" he had assumed his Rider to be speaking of multiple people—not a single person whose name he merely did not know. That made it all the more interesting.

"And did the Veh put this no-name to rest?"

"The Veh was killed, Dono."

Even after feasting on the hearts of fallen foes, for a no-name to defeat a Veh… This no-name had Yveun's interest. "What does this no-title go by?"

"I do not know." Admitting as much made Lossom nervous. Nothing pleased Yveun more.

"Find out," Yveun commanded. "Or better, bring him to me."

"Her," Lossom corrected.

*Her.*

All the better. In Yveun's experience, women were fiercer fighters than men. He had a list of theories longer than his claws on the why, but it made no difference. All he had to look at was the evidence around him: Coletta, Leona, Petra, Camile, and a handful of other Riders he'd seen come and die. Women approached every battle as though it was their last, and they had nothing left to lose but everything to prove.

"Bring her to me." Yveun would be truly impressed if the man could. It was likely a matter he would pass to Coletta and her quiet flowers, whose unassuming roots ran deep.

"As you wish." Lossom bowed, holding his position as Yveun entered the Hall of Whispers.

It was a long corridor with doors on either side. Emblazoned on every door was a plate that bore two names. The first was the occupant of the room; the second was the person with whom the occupant shared a whisper link. The Hall of Whispers served as the main communication hub for Nova and Loom, and it was entirely under Yveun's control.

Yveun first went to the whisperer who had a link with the Harvesters' guild, explaining the message that was to be delivered down to Loom. He repeated the process for every guild but the Alchemists. Yveun had been hoping that by throttling their resources, he would finally force the guild's hand into accepting his advisement and oversight, but they remained as persistent as ever. They would not relish the alternative methods he would employ if forced.

He was halfway back to his quarters when a slave of House Rok stopped him with all the etiquette that could be mustered for one so lowly.

"Dono, Fennyr Xin'Kin To has returned," the prostrating man reported.

Yveun's triumph spread across his face. Finally, Fennyr had returned and he would have some answers. The slave held his reverence the entire time Yveun was visible. If he hadn't, Yveun may well have killed him in a fit of delight.

The wildflowers of Lysip were in their second bloom. Their potent scent masked all others, effectively clouding magic and blood alike. It was one of the many reasons why the old Donos of House Rok had chosen this spot on which to build the estate. All manner of horror could be hidden behind the lovely petals of dragon snaps, lavender, honeysuckle, and the magical properties of Lord Agandi's Flowers.

He entered Finnyr's home without so much as a knock. The man nearly jumped out of his skin at the sight of the Dono. Finnyr was pale, almost Fen-like in his overall pallor. Even his muted gold hair seemed to lack some of its luster. More disconcerting were the bruises that dotted his skin.

Yveun closed the door slowly behind him, assessing the frightened man-creature. He wasn't concerned for the man's well-being out of any friendly obligation. Finnyr was a tool in a greater game, a useful pawn and a powerful player when deployed properly, which meant Yveun cared about the picture all the signs added up to make. Some kind of trauma had clearly occurred, and Yveun wasn't about to let any more of his chips be taken from him by unknown sources.

"Does Petra know?" Yveun asked foremost. If the rival Oji had ascertained Finnyr's true loyalties, much would change.

"K-know?" Finnyr shook his head, pacing. "No, but her continued belief in my loyalty despite sleeping under your care has come at a new price."

Yveun didn't care what Petra charged her kin for their loyalty. "Did you find out the truth of Cvareh's trip to Loom?"

"Not quite." Finnyr spoke hastily as Yveun began to vivisect him with his eyes. It would be mere minutes before he was doing it with his claws. Given Finnyr's generally depleted state, Yveun wasn't sure how long the other man would survive. "She is suspicious of me, of my loyalty still. She *tests* me still. She doesn't want me to return home often because she says I am more valuable to her here. But she does not give me any information on what is happening in the Xin manor."

"Finnyr, I am not a man who has time for excuses," Yveun snarled.

Finnyr wrung his hands, over and over and over again. "I know one thing."

The fact the Yveun had yet to gnaw on his sinew and bone was encouragement enough for Finnyr to continue.

"She demanded my hands."

"Your hands?" Yveun narrowed his eyes.

"Mine, specifically. She said she needed them, for the glory of the house."

"You mean…?"

"To harvest," Finnyr clarified weakly.

Once more, Petra affirmed what Yveun knew to be a fundamental truth about women: they did not hesitate. They waited for none to spoon them their desires. They took what they deemed theirs gratefully, forcefully, unapologetically, gracefully, or viciously. It didn't matter so long as it rested with them when the day was done.

He admired them for it. Not a dawn rose that he didn't envision how he could be more like his wife in that respect.

"Why?" Yveun asked himself as much as he asked the Dragon before him. Finnyr had magic in his hands, but so did many other Dragons. Many, no doubt, under Petra's direct supervision. She didn't need to call back her brother simply to harvest a pair of hands.

"Because it's Petra and she delights in my displeasure?"

Yveun was loath to admit that he and the Xin'Oji had anything in common, so he let the remark fade. "That's not enough for Petra. She called you from under my care… She wanted *your* hands."

"Cvareh told me nothing else quite matched their specific ends." Finnyr scowled at the mere mention of Cvareh's name.

Yveun had no doubt the careful phrasing was chosen by Petra herself, so he turned it over again and again in his mind, trying to make sense of it. *Matched.* That was the odd word out. "Did you smell a Chimera on him?"

"On Cvareh?" Finnyr clearly couldn't fathom why Yveun would even ask. "I doubt my younger brother knows even the first thing about Chimera."

They were getting nowhere. While Yveun wasted time trying to turn Finnyr into something he wasn't, Petra was clearly unfurling more banners to lay claim upon the edges of Yveun's control. He had stalled enough.

"No more half measures," Yveun muttered to himself.

"Dono?"

"How long has it been since the last Crimson Court?"

Finnyr blinked at the sudden shift in conversation, but recovered quickly. "Perhaps four years? No more than six…"

"I think it is time I summon my nobility together." Yveun grinned with malicious glee, a new plan unfolding before him. There was one way Petra could not keep Finnyr out, or him, or half the noble Dragons upon Nova. "Contact your sister. Be thrilled that you will be the first to tell her that I am holding a Crimson Court."

"When should I tell her this will take place?"

"A fortnight." Yveun wanted to waste no time. He started for the door to return to the Hall of Whispers; there were preparations to be made. "But you did not ask the most important question, Finnyr. It is not when it will take place. It is *where.*"

Finnyr was slow on the uptake, but his eyes widened as he suddenly understood the source of the King's mirth.

"Tell her that she has the delight of hosting the Crimson Court on the Isle of Ruana. And I expect every man, woman, and child under House Xin's care to be in attendance, regardless if they are usual Court members or not."

He would root out the truth himself. He would see the blood of every member of House Xin stain the ground if that was what it took. He was Yveun Rok'Oji Dono, and he did not operate in half measures.

# 16

## FLORENCE

THE ENDWIG CRAWLED OVER THE PRECIPICE. THEY NEARLY FLOATED DOWN around the face of the waterfall like wraiths in the darkness. Florence's eyes were locked on them, their glowing white orbs staring back at her.

They would consume her soul, and her sanity, before they started on her flesh.

The monsters continued their approach, humming in their dark and mind-numbing way. Florence's fingers rested on the hilt of her revolver, though the world around her seemed to be moving under water. The weapon was a steely reminder of the truth: she was about to die. Her brain would be sucked out through her nose and the endwig would fill her mind with its black poison. It would control her. It would use her as a lifeless puppet to draw them back to her friends. To get close enough that their whispering siren song could fatten their stomachs further.

Florence gripped the gun. The noise grew to a crescendo as the creatures fought against her will. They uttered their dirge of self-preservation while Florence's hand shook, struggling to draw the weapon from its holster. The weapon fell to her side like a block of lead, her arm useless.

Sweat dotted her brow despite the chill air. Florence tilted her wrist. The creatures stalked through the water, but all she heard was the incessant humming. She would grin if she could, but it took every ounce of concentration she possessed to squeeze the trigger.

The gunshot was like lightning between her eyelids. Its crack broke the deadly repetition of the endwig, and the searing pain that followed it scared away the thick shadows that had been clouding the edges of her vision. Florence saw the monsters with horrific clarity, her senses her own once more. Twice the size of a Fenthri, hunched over and pale as electric light, they growled at her through dagger-like teeth.

With a roar, the first endwig charged forward. Florence moved to run but skidded to a stop along the river rocks. Her hands moved for her belt, knowing one canister from the next on pure memory. She plucked an explosive round and had it in the revolver in one fluid movement.

By the time the muzzle of her gun was aimed at the endwig still scaling the waterfall, the alchemical runes along the barrel were alight in the darkness. Florence didn't hesitate, taking her shot. Derek said all she had been good for was exploding the forest around the Alchemists' guild; if she survived this, she would make sure he appreciated the irony of the situation as the rocky bluff collapsed, taking the endwig with it.

Florence didn't waste time. Two endwig had already alighted on the ground when she took her shot. They were on her tail and she sincerely doubted that a five-peca fall would kill the rest.

Inky blood dotted the ground behind her as she ran. It diminished with every step, her magic healing the gunshot wound she'd used to break free of the endwig's song. Florence sprinted along the bank, hearing the scraping of stone and the bestial snarl of the creatures behind her. They were gaining, and fast.

She cut into the trees.

"Derek!" Florence screamed into the darkness. His Dragon ears should pick her up clear back to the train. "Derek!"

"Flor?" A familiar male voice echoed back to her.

Relief flooded her chest. He was safe, which was more than could be said for her at the moment.

The swipe of a long, clawed hand whizzed over her head. It sunk into the bark of the tree, narrowly missing its mark. Florence rolled along the forest floor, seeking purchase on the dead brush and leaves.

The second endwig materialized out of nowhere. Its long fingers wrapping around her shoulder, drawing both blood and a scream. Florence dropped two canisters into her weapon and pressed the muzzle of the gun into its neck as it leaned forward to bite off her face in one crunch of its gaping jowls.

Blood exploded the moment she pulled the trigger. Florence didn't know much about the endwig, but she had learned all she needed to from the Revolver at the Alchemists' Guild Hall. She knew the one thing she would care about: how to kill the bastards.

The endwig were tough creatures with bones of near literal steel. Their rib cages protected their hearts by forming an impenetrable barrier not unlike a Dragon's. But at the base of the neck was a soft spot. With the gun angled just the right way, one could fire in through the top of the ribs.

Florence didn't expect she would have the opportunity to make a clean shot that exploited their seemingly one weakness very often.

As she pushed off the creature's corpse with a grunt, the other endwig was on her like a dog lunging for a discarded bone. Florence didn't have a chance to even take aim. The canister singed her flesh as it exploded against the endwig's face in close proximity, stunning it.

Scrambling to her feet, Florence began sprinting once more. Her shoulder oozed lifeblood onto her shirt and vest, her face streaked with flesh-curling burns from the proximity explosion. But the magic that Cvareh had given her by virtue of his blood held true. It healed her wounds and poured energy into her fatiguing muscles. It met the demands she placed on her body and then some.

"Flor!" Another cry rose up through the night, a woman's this time. "Flor, get your Revo ass over here!"

She wished it took something more than an endwig assault to inspire the use of her chosen guild.

The flickering light of Nora's campfire streamed through the trees in shifting beams. Florence's ears picked up the chaotic charge of the other endwig tearing through the forest behind her. Ahead was the small train, already hissing with steam.

"What do you think you're doing?" Nora screamed as Florence broke through the tree line that was almost on top of the tracks themselves. She held out her hand. "That type of explosion is sure to draw out the endwig."

"What do you think I used 'that type of explosion' on?" Florence screamed back. There wasn't any need to speak so loudly or violently; Nora's face was less than half a peca away from hers as the other woman hoisted her into the train car. But it certainly felt good to do.

"Are you all right?" Derek asked.

Florence was relieved to see her split-second judgment call of not heading back to where she'd last seen him along the river proved sound. The man was too smart to wait for her and it blossomed a newfound appreciation for him in a hot flush against her chest. The feeling was equally a product of the near-death situation and her adrenaline, but she knew she'd truly been ruined by Arianna when cold pragmatism was suddenly the sexiest thing in the world to her.

"We're not going fast enough." Florence reached for the leather strap of canisters and explosives wrapped around her body, her mind whirring with all the ways to fend off the endwig. "They'll be on us." She handed them each disk bombs. "Press, throw, push magic in to make heat."

There wasn't time to explain the mechanics of using magic to heat molten gold and start a carefully calculated chemical reaction. She just needed them to do as they were told. Florence had sat back long enough. Life or death: this was the line she was meant to walk.

The first endwig launched itself from between the trees, springing off them and leaving dark grooves in the bark. From the vantage of the train car, Florence had just enough height to stare down the barrel of her gun at the monster's outstretched neck. It was sent tumbling on the ground, all momentum lost, as she killed it with a pull of the trigger.

"Good shot." Nora's praise was lost.

"Derek, bomb!" Florence barked, pointing to where she wanted the explosion. He followed her order as two other endwig lunged from the darkness. The moment his hands were free, she passed him the rifle. "Load it with canisters from the green box."

"Which green box?" he called back.

"The one on the left." Florence fired another shot from her revolver.

"They're coming from the front!" Nora screamed over the crescendo of the engine gaining speed. On cue, the train lurched as an endwig was splattered to a bloody mess on the point of the engine's pilot.

"Bloody cogs," Florence cursed. The Vicar Alchemist had sent her to protect the mission as the Revolver, but one of her wasn't going to be enough. "I'm going to the engine."

"What are we going to do?" The usually self-sure Nora had the face of a cornered hare.

"You're going to fight." Florence passed her a weapon.

"I've never shot a gun before."

"Now is a great time to learn."

"I'm an Alchemist!"

Seriously, Florence was a breath away from shooting the woman herself. "You're dead if you don't adapt! There's three more bombs exactly like the ones you just used, right there. Just fend them off until the train gets up to speed. But don't use any other disks."

Florence had no more time to waste as the train lurched again. They just had to survive until the train reached full speed. For all the endwig were, they certainly couldn't keep up with a locomotive.

She hoped.

The wind whipped her hair around her face as she stuck her head from the train car. Florence reached out for the ladder to the right of the door, scaling up before another endwig could emerge. She swung up just in time as an explosion nearly blew her foot clean off.

"By the five guilds, you two only had three bombs!" she screamed over the wind, not knowing if they could hear. "Ration them a bit!"

Standing, Florence looked in horror at the tracks ahead. Dozens of endwig lined the path, running eagerly to meet the train. She loaded six canisters at once.

Jumping to the tender, Florence lost her footing atop the moving train car. A nail snapped clean off as she sought a grip that would prevent her from being thrown to certain death. If she fell now, she would never get back on the vessel. She'd be torn limb from limb.

Gritting her teeth, Florence rose to her knees, shooting two endwig in the process. She wedged herself between two grooves on the top of the tender. Blood pooled around her shins as she dug them into the metal for a grip where there was none, but she was stable enough to take aim, and that meant she could open fire.

Five shots down, and Florence reloaded her gun. Endwig came relentlessly like a never-ending nightmare. But the train didn't gain any more speed. She repeated the process, waiting for the vessel to be like her bullets, whizzing through the night at deadly speeds.

"Anders, now would be a great time to open her up!" she screamed.

There was no reply.

"Anders, Rotus, we need speed, get us out of here faster!"

Five long claws curled around the door of the engine in answer. Florence watched in horror as the white silhouette of an endwig, dotted in the black blood of a Chimera, pulled itself from the engine room. Florence swallowed hard.

They were without Rivet and Raven, stumbling through the darkness, enemies at all sides. She raised her gun slowly, looking fearlessly at the face of death itself. Her revolver was steady over the rocking of the train.

"You think I'm not used to this?" Her mouth curled into a mad grin. "I've been fighting my way out of the darkness my whole life. And you're not going to stop me now."

Gunshots echoed through the forest.

# 17
## PETRA

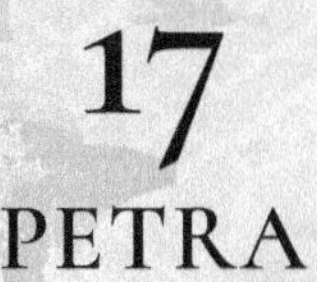

Petra rolled, a tumbleweed of claws and teeth. The man atop her responded with delightful viciousness. Fine-twitch muscle fibers spasmed as she dodged his attack; a claw caught on her neck. Petra raised a leg, propping it against his stomach, and twisted with enough force to send him skidding off to the side.

She found her feet, panting, sweating, stinking of her blood and the blood of a handful of others who had already been subdued beneath her. Yveun Dono did not fight; it was beneath him as the King of all Dragons. Wylder Tam'Oji To did not fight his lessers either, not unless challenged, following Yveun's lead.

Petra was a young Oji with boiling blood that screamed to be set free in a pit. She was met with upstarts on every front, challengers twice her age who continually questioned her merit as Oji. Petra bared her teeth and lunged forward, freeing the man's skin from his bones.

Only the Oji could sanction duels within Houses, save one exception: the Court. Called the Crimson Court due to House Rok's current power, it was the time when all grievances in upper Dragon society were aired. Petra had no doubt that a Court on Ruana proper would hold a countless many challenges for her title as Oji.

Her claws pressed into the man's chest beneath her; fangs raked against the soft flesh of his throat as she mounted him. In one bite she could gouge out his jugular and carve his heart from his ribs.

Petra's claws retracted, her palm resting lightly on his chest. She carefully withdrew her teeth, avoiding puncturing the skin. If she tasted his blood, she would be forced to kill him. There was no other option when one imbibed from the living.

"I need you twice as fast before the Court." Petra stood, her legs on either side of the man's waist in a position of dominance. "If you can't manage that, then dive into the Gods' Line before the first blood."

She stepped away, letting him find his feet. Petra ignored the cerulean man as he scampered off into some hole with his proverbial tail between his legs. Once an order had been given, she didn't engage further; doing otherwise merely invited questioning from her lowers.

"Cain." She caught the eyes of the tall man at the edge of the observation ring, leaning against the wall underneath a sunshade that was nearly the same color as his skin.

"Oji." He bowed and held it, saying nothing more, offering her his complete submission.

Slaves stepped forward from the woodwork, stripping off her soiled clothing. They toweled her with damp, perfumed cloths, wiping away the remnants of combat. A clean robe was draped over her arms and cinched at the waist. She wore it mostly open, the scars that crossed over her chest and stomach from failed attempts on her life on display as a warning to all.

"Walk with me."

He did so in silence, waiting for her to have the first word. Petra led him into the manor, straying past the main thoroughfares and onto the more private halls. Heavy tapestries draped the walls, overbearing and cluttered, one on top of the next. They splashed bright patterns between careful needlework that depicted the famous temples and landscapes across the floating isles of Nova.

It was Petra's favorite form of artwork: carefully built with the patience of thousands of single stitches. Delicate in that all it took was one tear to ruin. And surprisingly functional when it came to muffling conversations.

"You have heard?"

"Of the Crimson Court to be held on Ruana?" She nodded in affirmation. "I have."

"Yveun no doubt plans to use the guise of the Court to cut down our forces, and I have every expectation he will encourage dozens of duels against my person."

"Myself and countless others will step forward for you."

Petra snorted. "It is just us, Cain. You have no need to prove your loyalty to me and I know better than to demand it of you with words. I am a far more competent fighter than you."

He gave no rebuke.

"The more duels I can take, the better for all of Xin. It will send a message to Yveun that my claws are the ones he need fear above all others, while saving most from death in the pit." Petra rolled her shoulders, already beginning to mentally prepare for the beating she knew she would endure in the coming month. She tried to keep herself in shape, but general upkeep and preparation for a Court were two wildly different things. "I need you to gather the most competent fighters and train them well."

"Understood."

"And Cvareh," Petra added. "At night, as you have done before."

"No one will see him fighting."

Petra didn't want her brother to be challenged. The longer he was seen as a useless Ryu, the longer she could move him with relative ease, free of suspicion. But it was foolish to think he would escape public challenge during a Court on Ruana. And if a challenge came to pass, Petra wouldn't step forward for him. As much as she wanted to keep all skills he possessed both in and outside the arena secrets, she needed his position to remain unquestioned.

"I could step forward," Cain spoke, as if reading her mind.

"I will think on it," Petra relented. She didn't have a good answer yet, but had some time to figure one out. "For now, know that when there is a call, I want House Xin to speak first against Rok, always. I don't care how insignificant the grounds for a duel are; it's a Court. Most things pass and Yveun knows it."

"Understood." Cain stopped walking as she did, pausing at one of the intersections.

"Send Cvareh to me," Petra finished dismissively. "I will need to speak with him about all this, and we will need to start assembling the grand pit for the Court."

"I will tell him to seek you out first thing when he returns."

Petra stopped. "When he returns? Where has he gone?"

"He left early in the dawn. With our… guest." Mere mention of the Chimera still made Cain uneasy, despite Petra's endorsement of Cvareh's decision to saddle them together.

*Cvareh went off with the Chimera.* Petra swirled it in her mind like wine in a glass. "Where did they go?"

"I don't know."

"Then it would be rather hard to find him." She shrugged nonchalantly. "The moment he returns, tell him his Oji commands his presence."

"Gladly." Cain gave a low bow, but Petra paid it no heed. She was already turning over the notion in her mind. It seemed her brother was mending some of the tensions born of her first meeting with the Chimera. Perhaps something good could come of the day yet.

# 18

## ARIANNA

 that she had a lot more faith in the man controlling the mount. Her hands rested on Cvareh's hips, her legs tensed alongside his for stability, flush against the taut muscles in his thighs. They moved far more effortlessly together than she and Cain did, a sort of innate understanding between them that she didn't expect to be there but knew better than to question by now.

The two fingers on her left hand had been tied together. It was a bit of a trick to get a grasp on illusions, quite literally. It was a new sort of magic, slithering and amorphous—like trying to form and harden steam into diamonds. The magic was all in the hands, and she found that so long as she held her fingers in a particular position, she could maintain the illusion. Eventually, the bones inside would snap from the strain. Based on what she knew of magic, Arianna suspected that if she forced it long enough, the fingers would begin to rot and die. It would be a fine line to walk, but she'd tight-roped thinner.

So she'd trained the fourth and fifth fingers on her left hand—her less dominant hand—to hold the illusion. Then, once she had it, she fashioned a simple splint to hold them in shape. It was freedom born of binding, and Arianna quickly forgot about the lack of mobility in part of one hand altogether.

Ruana spilled out beneath her as the boco gained height like a bright splotch of paint atop the canvas of clouds below. Arianna tried to use the height of their trajectory to her advantage. There was a possibility that the glider was still in that alcove, unmoved. She suspected a few locations, but it was hard to make out the exact path she and Cain had taken between the mountain peaks when they'd gone to the manor.

"Where does the water come from?" Arianna leaned forward, her chin resting on Cvareh's shoulder to speak over the wind.

"The water?"

"I assumed 'water' to mean the same thing on Nova as it does on Loom." She spoke the word for water in Royuk for emphasis.

"I know what water is." Cvareh pushed back into her in exasperation, their bodies flush for a brief moment. "We drink from the streams and rivers."

It was her turn to nudge him. "I meant, where does it come from to feed the rivers?"

Cvareh was quiet for a long moment. She knew what he was going to say before he said it. "I don't know."

"No one has investigated?" Arianna pointed to a tall waterfall that poured from the side of a far cliff. "If we went in there, where does the water come from?"

"A spring, I presume."

"And what feeds the spring? How does it not run out of water?" She was suddenly reminded of speaking to young initiates in the guild as they struggled to grasp the most obvious of concepts, teaching them to learn through questioning.

"I don't know."

"How do you not know?" she asked incredulously.

"I've never looked." He glanced over his shoulder, seemingly equally confused by her line of inquiry.

"Hasn't anyone?"

"I doubt it."

"Why? Why not? What if it runs out? What if you are a week away from not having any water and you don't know it? There could be a large glacier that has been melting for hundreds of years, trapped in some far mountain valley, and it's soon to be exhausted."

"I doubt it." Cvareh shrugged. "Lady Lei gives the Dragons all we need to survive. She wouldn't have our water run thin before the end of days."

"Lady Lei, the Caregiver."

He looked honestly surprised she knew the Goddess's title, meriting a turn of his head.

"I've been talking with Cain."

"So it would seem." Cvareh tugged on the boco's reins, pulling left. The creature banked away from the mountains and toward the sloping hills that flattened across the island. "Hearing him start to speak of you was a surprise."

"I had to speak to someone or I was liable to go mad." Arianna bit her tongue, holding in the rest of her thought: she was driven to speak to Cain because Cvareh had not come to visit her once. She would not sound so desperate.

"The surprise came more from knowing he was speaking to you in return. He holds no love for Fenthri and even less for Chimera. And, from what I hear—and saw first-hand with a dagger at my forehead—you have done little to endear yourself to him."

"And why would I?" She snorted. "I gathered we weren't going to be friends from the first time he laid eyes on me."

"You seem friendly now."

"Apparently the word 'friends' does have a different meaning on Nova and Loom." She would describe her and Cain more like begrudging allies in their current state.

Cvareh chuckled. "Do you prefer his company, or mine?"

"I haven't had much of a choice in the matter," she reminded him.

"Even still?"

"Yours." There was little thought in the answer, even despite the confusion and annoyance Cvareh had caused her across the past few months.

It sparked a pulse of delight in his magic that set the palms of Arianna's hands to tingling.

Honestly, talking with Cain for the past few weeks had been nearly as thrilling as cutting off her own hands the night before. Arianna flexed her fingers, instantly regretting the analogy. They still felt strange, like phantom limbs given substance.

She had yet to confront Cvareh about their origin, but she let the matter stew. There was time yet. Now that she had freedom on Nova, she had more time for everything. Not much—Florence still needed her—but time enough. The fact that he produced hands that matched her ears connected a few dots for her all on her own, however. She was closing in the lines that explained how he'd even known of, not to mention acquired, her schematics. It meant the man who took them was somewhere close.

Arianna bared her teeth at the notion. The Dragon known as Rafansi was so very near, and she would find him.

Cvareh hissed loudly, jolting forward. "You have claws now."

She retracted them, not even realizing she'd unsheathed them at the mere thought of the man who had betrayed her and the last resistance. "That comes with the territory of having Dragon hands."

"Yes, well…" She saw Cvareh's profile as he considered her hand on his waist. There was a note of recognition, a familiarity in the way he regarded it. He continued before the questions about its origins could spill from her lips. "I suppose it also comes with the territory to know how to pull your claws. You will attract unwanted conflict if you go waving them about, or digging them into people's sides."

"Are you going to *duel* me, Cvareh'Ryu?" she teased. Cain had told her in various brisk snippets—as most of their conversations went—about the importance of Dragon duels.

Cvareh laughed. It was loud and seemed to echo off the hills below and swirl like raw color in the wind. It was a different sound than he'd had down on Loom. Arianna regarded the man thoughtfully. She certainly hadn't acted the same on Nova as she would on Loom. She was out of her element and outnumbered—an unwanted person in a foreign land. It would make sense he would've acted strangely on Loom in the same circumstances.

Which begot a new curiosity. What was he like here on Nova? What was the real Cvareh, and which did she favor?

"Cvareh'*Ryu*?" His mirth was uncontrollable.

"That is your name."

"It is, but twenty gods, I never thought I'd hear you address me with any formality."

"I was hardly being formal." She'd used the title for ironic emphasis.

"That much was obvious. Still, a strange treat to hear it from your lips." A smile was in his words, one Arianna didn't quite understand.

"Where are we headed?" She changed the topic as the landscape beneath her began to give way to smaller towns that only grew against the far horizon.

"That down there is Abilla. They're known for their millineries and cobblers. Some of Nova's finest textiles come from their looms."

The rooftops were shingled with wood, the houses made in all shapes and sizes. Arianna saw large windows and small. Bridges stretched between some; over others, ivy crept across to create a leafy walkway. The streets were cobblestone, or gravel, or packed dirt, winding like gnarled roots around the homes.

They were each coated in plaster and washed in some kind of ink, or paint, or clay. Yellow houses stood against purple ones, trimmed in vermilion or edged in ruby. The gears of her mind created smoke that clouded her head as they tried to find a pattern or logic in it. But if there was some rhyme or reason, it eluded her. It looked as though a child had spilled an architect's models across a mossy surface, then proceeded to draw tall, thin, trees between the shorter balls of foliage connected by spindly trunks.

"See, look there." Cvareh pointed to a river on the edge of town that had flowed down mightily from the mountains they'd started in. "They're washing the inks from the fabrics."

"I know what it looks like to wash ink from cloth." Arianna rolled her eyes dramatically.

"Really?" He sounded genuinely surprised.

"There's a science, you know, to getting the right color and getting it to stick to the fibers. I learned it during my basic schooling on Ter.0."

Cvareh was silent an acceptably somber second following the mention of the demolished Territory on Loom. "I wouldn't have thought you studied something like dyeing fabric."

"Why? There's a practical methodology to it. Furthermore, sometimes you need different colors to mark things like ships or cautionary areas."

"Practical methodology," he repeated thoughtfully. "It would be something like that."

"Let me guess: you do it for these impractical, gaudy rags you call clothes." Arianna picked at his love of fashion and his clothing in the same breath.

He snorted. "For once, I can't disagree with you. These are gaudy rags, nearly a full year old."

She was utterly lost as to why his clothing would have some sort of expiry.

"That's why we're headed to Napole!" Cvareh turned forward with elation. The wind swelled beneath them, carrying them higher.

If Arianna hadn't understood the logic behind the builder's plans of Abilla, she was utterly hopeless when they arrived in Napole. The hills continued to slope downward to the island's eventual end, and houses piled atop them precariously in such a way that reminded her of the castle and its ignorance to all form of logic. The structures leaned against each other for support like jolly drunkards, spires drew long shadows across rooftops, and archways reached down to bustling roadways.

As they descended, Dragons paused, shading their eyes with long fingers to peer at the boco headed earthward. A few raised their hands and even more dipped into low bows, the motion barely visible from their height. Arianna glanced at her forearm, worried her illusion had somehow slipped and garnered the attention. It hadn't.

"Are you that well known?" she asked when Cvareh took note of a genuflecting group.

"I am the Xin'Ryu," he said it as though it should have been obvious. "The Isle of Ruana is Xin's. Everyone here is a Xin."

That was startling. Ariana had been struggling to grasp the notion of family since it had first been introduced on Loom by the Dragons. Two parents rearing a child seemed vastly more ineffective than the communal arrangement of Ter.0 that she had been brought up in. But the size of a single Dragon family now seemed impossibly excessive. *How did they even keep track of it all?*

"There are red and green Dragons here," she observed, the colors blurring together as their shadow cut across rooftops.

"There are. A Dragon's skin color is determined by the island they're born on, their native House."

"So two red Dragons can give birth to a blue Dragon?"

"Technically, though I have no idea why two of House Rok would ever move to Ruana."

"That makes… absolutely no sense." Arianna's head hurt already from the lack of reason surrounding her. If she were an Alchemist and possessed more than rudimentary knowledge of biology, she'd likely be having a conniption. "Why?"

"Because children take after their parents. It's why strong, healthy Fenthri were selected to breed on Ter.0, before the Dragon King mucked up the system and forced this ridiculous notion of families."

She thought he stiffened at the mere mention of "breeding," but perhaps it was her imagination reading overmuch into the shift of his body as he navigated the boco onto a wide platform. Other birds milled about, pecking from troughs and cawing at each other in a way only they could understand.

Here, too, there were silent keepers who materialized from the shadows. They were an omnipresent reminder of the hierarchy Nova steeped itself in—a system that inspired a discomfort in Arianna she struggled to shake. They brought trays laden with fruit and heavy glasses filled to the brim with a liquid the color of Fenthri blood. Cvareh took a glass and refused the fruit. Arianna followed suit, operating under the assumption that Dragons would never willingly drink the blood of a Fenthri.

"Cvareh'Ryu!" A woman strode out from an overhang that was bursting with flowering vines. The sunlight didn't hesitate to expose the bareness of her chest. Everything was too bright on Nova. "It has been some time."

"I've been at prayer to our Lord in the mountains," Cvareh kept his lie.

"So the rumors say." The lie was clearly well known and as flimsy as it sounded, judging by her tone.

Arianna averted her eyes from the exchange, bringing the glass to her lips. She had yet to fully acclimate to the Dragons' way of dressing—or lack thereof. Even as Arianna had donned the fashion, she felt consolation that the illusion would be placed over top her bare skin. Every breeze was a chilling reminder for all the fabric she didn't wear. But donning the guise of a Dragon made her feel oddly less exposed.

She sniffed the contents of the goblet. It had a strange aroma, like grape and sulfur, heady, with a sharp edge unlike anything she'd encountered before. Arianna took a sip, and was overcome by an instantaneous coughing fit the moment it burned her throat.

"Dear me, is your companion all right?" the woman asked.

"Fine," Arianna replied for herself before Cvareh could speak. Royuk was heavy on her tongue, as Arianna was more accustomed to listening than speaking, but her mouth still formed the sounds with the confidence of years of tutelage.

Her accent must have been passable, as the woman didn't comment. "Is the wine not to your liking?"

"It's fine." Arianna had no idea what else to say. She glanced at Cvareh, hoping he'd explain somehow what "wine" was and how she was supposed to respond.

The bastard broke out laughing. "Forgive her." He took a step closer to Arianna. An arm slipped around her waist, long fingers palming the bare skin of her side. "This is Ari Xin'Anh, and recently, Bek."

"So you are new to the upper side of the isle." The woman smiled, flashing her teeth.

Arianna was new to Nova. She was still attaching textbook learning to practical meaning. But she knew when someone was trying to intimidate her. She smiled wide in return and wondered if she'd made her canines long enough in the illusion she'd crafted.

Apparently she had, as the woman broke eye contact first and turned back to Cvareh. "A personal Anh, I take it?"

"Indeed." Cvareh had yet to remove his hand from her person and Arianna was ready to remove it herself. The only thing that prevented her from doing so was the determined grip he had, the swell of his magic at her side that felt as if it were trying to engulf her.

"You are so lucky, Ari'Anh." Arianna instantly didn't like the way her name sounded in the woman's mouth. "To have been noticed by the Xin'Ryu."

Arianna said nothing. She just kept smiling. And drinking her wine.

"How long will you be in Napole?" the woman asked.

"The night." Cvareh guided Arianna inside, earning himself a questioning glare. He didn't change his demeanor. "I trust you have lodging?"

"For you? Always." The woman smiled, thinner, subservient to Cvareh.

They were led down a long hall. A swirling ribbon carved into the wood on either side of them created a dizzying pattern from one end to the next, breaking away from the wall to become the banister for a wide stairway. Arianna stretched her fingers against their binding. Her fifth finger had gone completely unresponsive, the bone likely shattered to dust from magical exhaustion.

"Will this be suitable?" The innkeeper opened a wide door that had the motif of a bird painted across its surface.

The room itself shone like freshly oiled clockwork. Wooden floors were polished to a mirror shine, reflecting light off the many portals that had been bored into the far wall. Silver lined them, curling like tiny serpents that seemed to wriggle in the sunlight, connecting every window to a grand mirror on the ceiling—of all places. A perfectly square bed jutted against the unnecessary curves of the room, its linens softening the hard lines of its wooden base. Arianna narrowed her eyes at the furniture.

"It will do." Cvareh hardly seemed impressed.

"Do let me know if you need anything." The woman bowed, her breasts hanging erotically.

Arianna kept her eyes anywhere else. The woman had a nice figure, certainly. But such a sight should be earned. If given to everyone, it held no excitement and therefore lacked interest.

"I will, Xillia." Cvareh dismissed the woman, shutting the door in haste. He turned to Arianna, and they shared a long look. "I thought you might need to relax your illusion and rest a moment."

Her whole body tensed instantly at the notion. He had preempted her status.

Arianna placed her wine down on a nearby table, grabbed for the splint, pulled it off, and let the illusion fall away with the same gritty feeling as a rain of sand. "Could you smell it in my magic?"

"Smell what?" He seemed confused.

"The illusion beginning to turn." Arianna held up her hand. Her fifth finger was completely limp, almost like gelatin encased in flesh; bruising turned the blue of the hand dark. Her fourth finger hung at a painful angle. She snapped it back into place with a small grimace.

"No, your magic didn't smell any different than it normally does."

"Then how did you know?" Arianna needed to dissect the weaknesses in her illusion. While she was confident in her ability to take on most Dragons, especially now with claws at her disposal, she didn't want to be put in a position where she had to.

"Call it intuition." He shrugged.

Arianna scowled at him.

"And what have I done to offend you now?" Cvareh chuckled lightly.

That only served to sour her mood more. "'Intuition' makes no sense. Intuition is merely a collection of past evidence compiled in your subconscious. There's a reason you thought that. Just like there's a reason for, for this." She motioned to the windows.

"For what?"

"For why they're spaced oddly, and circular—do you have any idea how much effort it is to make a circle that perfect architecturally?"

He appeared to be really considering it, as if for the first time. "They're prettier that way."

She was going to literally tear out her hair. Arianna spun on her heel and stalked toward the bed. Her magic was exhausted and recovering slowly while her fingers finished knitting. She grabbed a fist full of pillow and threw it over her shoulder.

"Now what?" Cvareh leaned against the door, an amused pull at the corner of his lips. She was going to carve that look off his face if he kept it up.

"I'm told there's a bed under here." She continued to cast aside the offending cushions. "I intend to make use of it so my magic recovers faster."

"It's more comfortable if you actually sleep *on* the pillows, you know."

Arianna paused with a dramatic sigh. "Cvareh, no Dragon, Fenthri, Chimera, or creature on Loom or Nova or anywhere else needs this many plush objects to sleep upon. A glass doll would call it excessive."

"However you like it." He held his hands out in a motion of forfeit, but his magic still sparked with amusement.

She turned her eyes away from him, not wanting to see the shine that seemed to almost visibly spark around him. Magic held no light, unless channeled through gold. She really was losing her mind in this backwards land if she began to believe otherwise.

"Yes, remember that." She fell on the bed with purpose. "For I am going to sleep just long enough to recover my magic, and then you shall show me this Napole in earnest."

"If it pleases you, Ari." His voice was nearer. The mattress, in all its softness, betrayed his weight as he sat on the edge of the bed.

Arianna wanted to tell the Dragon that his encroaching presence was unwelcome. That despite whatever kindness he showed her, whatever familiarity his magic held, whatever warmth she could find in the tones of his voice, she simply did not want him there. She had not given him express permission to share her bed. But she couldn't see to bring herself to deny him either.

She *wanted* to lash out at him ferociously. But her magic was more exhausted than she gave it credit for. Her eyelids felt heavy and the bed—even the remaining pillows—were more comfortable than she'd anticipated. She heard Cvareh settle among his cloud of cushions, the plush articles creating a barrier between their bodies. Arianna closed her eyes and did nothing to remove his familiar presence from her side.

# 19
## CVAREH

Nova was different when Arianna was upon it. Familiar societal norms were suddenly cause for concern as potential interactions that could expose her for what she was. *For what she was*.

The thought turned over in his head again and again as he remained poised in such a way that he could watch her sleep. He didn't move out of fear of disturbing her, his arm prickling and then going numb from the strange position. It wasn't the first time he'd seen her sleep, but something felt different without Florence snuggled against the woman's chest.

She was still dressed in Dragon clothing, and her body was on display to him for the first time. The Arianna on Loom had always been buttoned up tightly, reserved and withdrawn. Here his eyes could draw lines up her thighs, trace the hard muscles that cut across her abdomen, the swell of her biceps draped across her covered breasts. They rested on dark marks etched into her skin. Tattoos, but not like the one that should be emblazoned on her cheek. Script-like numbers scrolled across her right wrist, just off to the side of her modest cleavage, upon her left shoulder.

He wanted nothing more than to delicately trace his claw over them. To learn their locations with his eyes, his hand, his mouth…

This woman should be his mortal enemy, and here he was admiring her. Cvareh finally eased onto his back, staring at his reflection in the ceiling. He certainly looked the same, but something had changed on Loom.

The reflection blurred a moment, clouded by the memory of Finnyr's face when Cvareh had told him he needed to remove his hands. He had harvested his brother. Conflict clouded his chest. Sure, Petra had blessed it, even ordered it expressly as the Oji—and there was no questioning nor going back when such an outright decree had been made. Furthermore, him and Finnyr had never been particularly close. After Finnyr had lost to Petra for the Ryu position and was shipped off to Lysip, it was hard to foster a particularly deep bond with his brother. Cvareh had tried, but when Petra had chosen him as her Ryu, rather than Finnyr, it had only exacerbated the problem.

*Still*, Finnyr was his brother. He was the direct blood of House Xin. And Cvareh felt more conflict over his lack of feeling conflict than he did actual turmoil over harvesting him.

Cvareh smiled to himself. Petra would be proud.

The moment Arianna stirred, she donned the contraption she'd designed for her fingers. It was brilliant, really. And with that alone her illusion settled atop her, weaving like a thousand strands of light to form a perfect facade. It was all a testament to her ingenuity and strength, and Cvareh discredited her with his internal disappointment at seeing her as a Dragon rather than in her natural state.

When they left, he made it a point to put his hand on her hip once more. The proximity marked her as his. It affirmed to all Dragons that she was claimed by the Xin'Ryu himself. However small the measure of protection was, he would give it to her gladly.

"How long do you intend to touch me?" she muttered, clearly not sharing his sentiments about the contact.

"Would you trust me if I say it's for your best interest?"

"Hardly." Her head turned as her eyes remained glued on a stall selling wind chimes. Cvareh briefly debated if the word meant she thought he was doing so because it delighted him. "What are those?"

"They make sound as the wind blows."

"I can see that." She peeled her attention away long enough to roll her eyes at him. "Is it for wind storms of some variety? A warning?"

"No, just because they sound nice."

All her questions were in the same vein. Arianna asked why some walkways were suspended and why some were on the ground. He remembered the Raven city, and how each level served a separate purpose. But there were no such motives on Nova. Things were as they were because someone was compelled to make them that way.

Her displeasure mounted throughout the day. Cvareh tried to take her everywhere that made him happy. He took her to his favorite sundries shop, his tailor, to see the best performers in all of Ruana. But Arianna merely continued to withdraw.

He was exhausted, and he wasn't even cultivating an illusion.

They ducked into one of his favorite tea parlors in a quieter area of town. Usually he haunted more fashionable places to see and be seen. But Cvareh avoided them today. He didn't think he or Arianna could handle the expectations of a highly public appearance. And besides, his tailor had yet to cut him anything befitting of the current season. He would certainly not be seen wearing clothes from a year ago—though the fact had likely already reached the ears of the gossips.

The parlor's patrons bowed their heads as he entered. Herbs hung from thick beams that drew lines across a plaster ceiling. They perfumed the air and clouded the nose with promises of brews that would be even more delightful than their aromas. The tea master from behind the bar gave a nod of recognition as Cvareh led Arianna back to an iron gate that served as the parlor's back door.

It opened into the shop's private garden. A delightful nook of Napole with wafting lavender, sunny chamomile, leafy tea plants, and—Cvareh stilled. His favorite scent hovered above them all in a carved arbor that framed the lone table nestled among the greenery. Vining honeysuckle was heavy in the air, the sweet floral notes at once an invitation and a comfort.

He looked suddenly at the woman next to him.

"What?" Arianna was expectedly oblivious.

"Nothing…" The taste of her blood was across his tongue at the mere thought. Had he known all along? Had he sensed it from the first moment he'd met her, the faint aromas that always lingered upon the woman by the very essence of her magic? The smell he so loved was within her veins.

It didn't matter what he knew before. He needed her *now*, more than ever. He wanted to sink his canines into her flesh. He wanted to smear her blood across their flesh, mingling with his. He wanted to drown in her magic. He wanted—

"What may I get started for you?" The tea master was a welcome interruption.

"Whatever is in season," Cvareh mumbled by means of reply. His eyes were on the woman who was easing herself into one of the three seats around the table. Cvareh closed the distance between them once more, pulling his chair slightly closer in the process of sitting. "Do you understand tea?"

"Brewed herbal remedies for colds and other such things are found on Loom."

He couldn't help his laughter, even though he knew it was going to draw out her ire. "This is purely for pleasure, not for medicinal purposes."

"Everything the Dragons do seems to be for pleasure." She stared at the garden and while he would've hoped for a spark of interest or inspiration, the mounting confusion that'd been lining her brow remained. "You build for beauty before function. You spend countless hours on adornments. You make noises with your mouth and tools, calling it song, moving to it and calling it dance, but it serves no greater design." She shook her head in frustration. "You don't even know where your water comes from."

He'd nearly forgotten about that anecdote from the morning. "You're not wrong about those things."

"But what do you *do*?" she pressed. "Loom has given the Dragons Gold, gliders, science, mathematics, a true way of understanding the world. We—"

"That is untrue," he interrupted. "Nova understands the world in a way Loom does not. We understand it through the Twenty Gods above. We understand it through magic." She pursed her lips together as he continued. "You're right, we do not craft engines of steam or write arithmetic that can lift people to the skies. But we understand life, a richer meaning for it than on Loom, and we create joy."

"Xin'Ryu." A young girl with Tam skin delivered steaming mugs of amber colored liquid. Arianna stared so intensely at her that the child was nearly startled.

"Thank you." Cvareh dismissed her, sparing her from whatever had Arianna's vicious interest.

The girl bowed and turned, happy to flee.

"I see where the notion came from," Arianna whispered.

He couldn't fathom what she was on about until the woman raised a hand to her cheek. Cvareh hadn't even noticed the mark. He'd not paid it any credit as he hadn't his whole life. It was a part of his world, as inconsequential as the icy peaks of the mountains or the never-ending waterfalls. He hadn't had cause to look at it differently until a Chimera forced him to see it through her eyes. "The tattoos are how we know when someone has left their native House," he explained.

"Tattoos should be choices, not brands." She tried to pin him down with a deathly glare.

"These are choices. They *choose* to leave their house and join a new one. It's how I and everyone else here knows they are friendly, that they are kin. It is their decision." He reached out and grabbed her wrist, speaking before she could pull away, "Just as these are."

Arianna stared at his hand a long moment where it fell over her own tattoos. If her eyes were actual daggers he'd be cut from thumb to cheek. "Unhand me."

"Explain them."

"Unhand me," she repeated, a little louder.

He acquiesced, but only because he did not want to make a scene. His hand was cold in the wake of her warmth. "I had never seen them before. I want to understand."

She looked away sharply, as if he would vanish because her eyes were no longer on him. He didn't. And so she was left to gather herself to speak. "We call them link marks. They signify a date of importance regarding... a person."

And she had three. For whom? He could guess Florence would be one. Her lost lover another... Was another lover the third, perhaps? Even with a short life span and no notion of family, how a Fenthri could forge such a deeply amorous connection with so many people was lost on him.

"You saw when I dropped my illusion." She massaged her wrist lightly where he had touched it.

"I did. I think they're beautiful." He operated on instinct, offering encouragement when in doubt.

She found amusement in that decision. "They are, because they are significant." Arianna's purple eyes met his and Cvareh felt helpless in their gaze. "They were choices. For nothing touches my body that isn't my choice."

What did that make him?

Cvareh opened his mouth to speak and was interrupted by a velvet-clad man. "Cvareh! I did not expect to find you in the city, my friend."

"Zurut." Cvareh stood, embracing the man in greeting. "It was an impromptu trip."

"Seeing the tailor, no doubt." The man picked a ribbon on Cvareh's shoulder with two fingers as though the color that had gone out of vogue could somehow stain his quite lavish and luxe design. "Are you trying to make a new statement?"

"Hardly. You couldn't be more correct, it was time to visit the seam masters." Cvareh mentally cursed Petra, again, for not ordering clothes to greet him upon his return.

"And what a time it is! I was just there myself ordering a new jerkin to wear to the Court."

"The Court?" Cvareh repeated, certain he'd misheard his friend.

"How have you not heard?" Zurut was in shock. "The Crimson Court will be happening on Ruana within the fortnight. It's been all the talk across the city this afternoon." His friend's eyes drifted toward Arianna. "Though I see your attentions have been elsewhere."

Cvareh had always known that choosing a mate beyond superfluous play would result in quite the talk. It was natural as the Ryu, and sometimes the tea parlors on Ruana were hard up for gossip. But today was not one of those days.

He muttered off an introduction, his mind elsewhere. He couldn't even be certain what name and title he'd given Arianna, if it was the same as the one he'd fabricated before. He couldn't be bothered.

*A Crimson Court on Ruana.*

The Dono intended to wash the streets gold with Xin blood. There would be no harbor, no excuses for why key members of their House could not attend. They were being cornered and led to slaughter. And now he had exposed Arianna as his potential mate, a Xin'Anh, easy fodder for any woman who had sought Cvareh's fondness and the prestige it gave for herself. Cvareh swallowed hard. It was likely to be his first court in the pit.

"Ari." She stood at the tone in his voice alone. "We need to return to the Xin Manor. Now."

He was worried for himself. He was worried for maintaining Arianna's illusion. But his mind remained focused on one thing: his House. He had to return to his sister.

# 20

## YVEUN

Underneath the main continents of Nova, there was the "below". The underbellies of the iceberg-shaped islands had been carved out and hollowed into a reversed anthill of maze-like passages, freezing alleyways, and the seedy abodes where all manner of business was conducted. It was the type of commerce that could only happen in a place where the sun didn't shine.

Below was a place where the threads that bound the structure of Nova together would barely hold knots. Here was where the Anh and lower Da of Houses were sequestered. Further down were the Bek. And further down, still, lived those who barely had a name. Close to the Gods' Line, close to the vulgar world of Loom where only first names were used and all elegant social structure was lost.

It was a place a King should never venture, for it was far, far beneath him.

But it was in these places that he dredged up gold from among the rock and raw metal of his society. Leona had come from these chilled and dank halls. He had been given whispers and guidance regarding the woman he would find down here from Coletta, and Yevun had pulled Leona into the sunlight, molding her into something that truly shone by obliging his whims. Once again, this would be how he would find his next Master Rider.

Hooded and robed, he kept his face downward, focused on the smooth, sinking stairs that wound around a building. Wind whipped against his left side, intent on pulling him from the perch and tipping him into the abyss below. Graffiti stretched against the wall under his palm, glazed with moisture from the perpetual chill. Xin swords and books were painted atop Rok crowns that dwarfed Tam scales.

Blood was thick in the air. He could almost see it alight in the alleyway he turned into. A fruit cocktail of the scents of Dragons who had died from illegal duels.

*How many organs were fed to the Fen below from fights gone awry?* It was a wonder that the race below the clouds hadn't learned of Nova sooner. It was all chance that their world and the world below had been separate for so many years. It had been chance they had connected at all.

He'd been following the blood for hours now. It led him to illegal pits and questionable feeding halls that engaged in the darkest sort of trade one could imagine on Nova—imbibing off the living. It was said that when a Dragon had a taste of a living host, nothing could satiate the hunger that followed other than more blood. It ensured the feeding halls stayed in business with a slew of loyal patrons. It also drove Dragons to madness with the craze that set in when they had gone too long without their last taste.

Still, it would be in one of these places that he knew he would find her. His current Master Rider had about as much tact as a battering ram and, unsurprisingly, turned up nothing when he'd ventured under to ask questions. There were things Yveun knew he would have to do himself if he wanted them done at all. He couldn't send another to do it, for that was no better than a half measure in the worst sort of way. The best foe was one slain with one's own claws.

Revelries and betting flooded his ears as he neared the fighting pit. Yveun entered, unhindered, to take his place among the crowd. The runner of the ring sat at its side before a low table, deciding fighters, calling odds, and taking bets. It reminded him that was a role he still needed filled before the Crimson Court was to happen, lest Petra get the notion that she may suggest one of her own with the Court happening on Ruana. Unsurprisingly, the woman who ran the pit here was a Tam. The balance keepers of Nova were unparalleled in ensuring the best fights by sensing the skill of the fighters involved.

In the pit, two Dragons tumbled. A blue Xin with the symbol of House Rok emblazoned on his cheek and a green Tam with the same. It was a battle of underdogs, and no matter who won, all the red native-born Roks would be pleased with the outcome.

Yveun watched five fights. No one shone. No woman who stepped into the ring fought with the grace and blood lust he assumed his target to possess. Yveun departed in frustration.

He continued on until the clouds below began to turn purple with the first light of dawn. Still, the woman eluded him. Perhaps it had merely been rumor, a grand underdog story those beneath delighted in telling of a no-name, no-rank, rising above and felling those with title and prestige. It wouldn't be the first time, or the last.

Yveun wound upward, climbing questionable ladders and precarious stairways. As he neared the upper side of the island, the conditions steadily improved, but the weight of the world above them only grew heavier. The whole of the rock that supported Lysip was trapped beneath a nearly palpable weight, as if the whole expanse of the island above could suddenly drop its heft into his very lungs. A physical reminder of the world above that was so close and so far at the same time.

All roads funneled into one main tunnel that cut through the island. It was gated and guarded at all times. Yveun made for it with the ease of nearly being home, pulling his hood from his face in preparation to meet the Riders who manned the portal.

A hand shot from the darkness. It wrapped itself around his neck, claws pressing into his throat. Yveun only smiled.

"There you are," he whispered.

"Tell me, Dono," a deep and feminine voice husked into his ear from behind. "What happens if I kill you here? Do I become the Dono of Lysip?"

"Not quite." He made no motion away, assessing the power in the woman's forearm, the tension in her magic, the skill required to hold him in place using her claws while not drawing blood that would alert his Riders with a scent. "Coletta'Ryu would be come Coletta Dono, as this would not be a sanctioned duel."

"So killing you will be for bragging alone." Her fingers tensed.

"How did you know it was me?" he asked.

"Your walk." She inhaled deeply. "Your scent."

"How do you know those things?"

"We know of the sun here below, even if we never see it," she retorted. He'd allow her to keep her secrets, for now. It betrayed her cunning. There were ample plausible explanations: She'd seen him in a past Crimson Court. She'd worked at the estate. She'd been taken as a personal Anh for one of his To. She'd worked with one of Coletta's flowers. It all mattered naught to him.

"Do you wish to see it? The sun?"

She gasped laughter, keeping her mouth by his ear. "You think you can buy your life with pretty things? With shiny baubles and the promise of ruby hallways everyone so lusts after in your grand palace?"

"I hope not. Or you are not the woman I am hoping for." She remained silent, letting him speak. "I hope to buy your life with the promise of the one thing I hope you crave more than all else."

"What do you think I desire?" she purred, her fingers tapping against his throat.

"Blood. More blood than you can gorge yourself on." Dragons didn't become as strong as this woman by remaining pure and not imbibing. She clearly cared naught for taboo and he wouldn't shun her for it. He'd feed this little monster if it made her his pet.

"How will you give me that?"

"Come with me. Come as my new Master Rider, and I will see you have all the blood and carrion your claws and fangs would ever desire."

She let him go. Yveun turned. The woman was cloaked as he was, hooded, and Yveun could only make out a strong chin and hooked nose from the shade of her cowl, but he could not recognize the shade of her skin in the low light. A smirk adorned her mouth, and Yveun was certain he'd won.

"I will think it over." She turned, as if her sole intent was to prove him wrong.

"You would be wise not to disobey your King," he cautioned, claws jutting from his fingers.

She merely glanced at them. "I gave you your life, you tolerate my disobedience. A fair exchange, Dono."

The woman gave a small wave, dropping off the side of the wall and into the depths below. He didn't hear her land, her movements more precise than that of a cat's. Yveun bared his teeth into the darkness, frustrated and delighted at the same time.

He hadn't even learned her name.

# 21

# FLORENCE

 vulgarity with the same reckless abandon as she pulled on the throttle. The train went faster when she cursed at it.

She turned to the pressure gauges, only about three-fourths of which she could actually boast an understanding of their numbers. And of that three fourths, she only had a rudimentary working knowledge. Ari would have been driven up a wall. Helen and Will would laugh at the mere sight of her behind the engine. But none of them were there now.

Florence didn't have an endless supply of numbers that spewed from the depths of her mind, only some vulgar phrases. She was certainly not one of the most gifted Ravens to walk the guild hall in Holx, just a little crow on the run. She had her wits, a basic amount of education in a number of areas, two dead bodies, and a lot of endwig as motivation for some quick thinking.

The train rattled and shook as it gained steam. Embers spit out from the engine gate, singeing her clothes and skin. The vessel lurched violently, sending her scrambling for some variety of hold that wouldn't leave her tumbling out the side of the car. The clamp of teeth echoed by her ear as an endwig nearly missed her shoulder.

With a grunt, she righted herself in the engine room, her hands finding the levers again. Endwig were now splattering against the side of the train. Their attempts at a hypnotic hum were drowned out by the sound of the wheels on rails, the squeal of steel on steel as they rounded a corner in the wood.

It looked like they'd gained enough steam—*finally*—to outrun any real threat from the monsters. Florence still pushed the train hard, like a bullet from the chamber. This wasn't the Underground, where the next move was to proceed with quiet and caution. The endwig slept during the day and fed in the twilight hours. She would take them past the dawn and into the only "safe" time they had now.

They. Florence hoped it was still a case of "they" and not just "her". Nora and Derek only had to fend off the endwig for a short time before she'd gotten the train up to speed. After that it was just a matter of not falling out. Florence began to ease up the steam. If they couldn't handle staying on the train, she really had no hope of helping them all the way to Ter.1.

The train coasted along the track, slowly losing momentum. They'd wasted a lot of coal on their flight, and she'd have to make what was left stretch. That meant using the brakes as minimally as possible and squeezing every last bit of heat out of the steam that it had to give. It was nearly midday by the time they finally ground to a halt.

She collapsed, exhausted, still sweating from the heat of the engine and the stress. Florence leaned against the wall, her head tipped back. She took in long, luxurious breaths of air and savored the silence. The blood of Anders and Rotus was caked on the floor around her. She'd ditched their bodies at some point in the early dawn in the hopes they might draw away the endwig. But their blood remained, and likely would for some time.

The train sighed softly with motion from the back. Florence heard footsteps nearing the engine door. She pulled her revolver, holding it up at arm's length.

Lined up in her sight was a pair of familiar coal colored eyes. Derek slowly raised his hands.

The gun was heavy in Florence's palm. It was like she lifted a cannon made of pure lead, not a revolver. Her finger tensed on the trigger. The hammer struck on the gun.

And nothing happened.

"Bang." Florence had run out of canisters three hours ago. "If you were an endwig, you'd be dead," she lied.

"Good thing I'm not." Derek seemed to have the sense not to point out the falsehood of the weary Revolver's claims, seeing as she'd just saved his life.

"Good thing." She dropped the gun with a loud clang as it met the metal floor and closed her eyes. "Did Nora make it?"

"She did."

"I felt one of your explosions. Damn near knocked me out of the engine," Florence muttered. Exhaustion crashed down on her all at once. She never wanted to open her eyes again.

Derek stepped up into the engine, approaching her without hesitation or question. A hand slipped under her knees, the other rounding her back.

"Don't," she commanded as he tried to lift her.

"Nora is already asleep. I'm taking you back to the car with us."

"No." Florence shook her head. "We're too close to the endwig. I need to sleep in the engine in case we need to make a sudden and unexpected escape."

"Are you our Raven now?"

"And your Rivet. And your Revolver." Florence grinned, opening her eyes halfway. She felt drunk off fatigue and high on the remnants of adrenaline. "It doesn't matter what you want to call me. I promised the Vicar Alchemist I would get you to Ter.1, and you can bet that's what I'm going to do."

Derek rolled on his side, settling next to her. She watched him until her eyelids were spent and her neck was too exhausted to fight gravity a moment longer. Her head tipped onto his shoulder and Derek kept his arm around her.

They both stank of perspiration and blood, but neither cared. He tilted his head, resting it on hers. "Don't be an Alchemist next."

"Why?"

"Then you won't need Nora or me."

She huffed at the notion. "I don't need you now."

He chuckled by way of agreement.

"But I like having you both around," Florence confessed. The two had been annoying for her, but it would be lonely without them on the journey. There was comfort to be found in the warmth of another, and the radiant heat reminded her for a moment longer that she was not alone.

# 22

## CVAREH

THE WIND WAS STILL UNDER HIS HEELS AS CVAREH SPED THROUGH THE HALLS OF the Xin Manor. Arianna was back sequestered to her room, only placated with the promise that he would return later to explain the Crimson Court in full. Ever since Zurut informed him that the Court was coming to Ruana, all he could think about was what he had to do to help Petra and his house.

For all the urges he felt toward Arianna, Cvareh would not let his loyalty to Xin be shaken. She was a new presence in his life, and he was loath to admit that she would likely force herself to be a temporary one. But his House would be his family forever. It was his home, his legacy, the greater picture of which he was only one small part.

He ignored all others, focusing on the one place he expected to find his sister. Up a curving stairway, he ascended to the heart of Xin Manor. The ancients lined the walls. Dragons with mighty bat-like wings and mouths filled with pointed teeth hovered overhead, sculpted with lifelike precision. Candlelight flickered over their faces, slowly diminishing into nothingness.

Cvareh emerged from the smothering blackness into a room of pure light, feeling like he had been born again in the process. His eyes narrowed to thin slits, adjusting to the sudden change in brightness. They found the room's focal point. Not any sort of art, but a woman. Muscles bulged from her skin, fueled by frustrations that Petra had yet to relinquish. Her eyes were locked on the Temple of Lord Xin, visible in the far distance through the glass windows that made up more of the walls than the stone.

"Brother." Petra shifted slightly on the pedestal where she sat.

He accepted her invitation, sitting on the opposite edge. He leaned so their backs and heads would touch. One mind, one body, one unit that existed for House Xin. Cvareh closed his eyes and readied his ears for the words of the Oji.

"Yveun seeks to root out weakness in our House."

"He does."

"I informed Cain that all are to be ready, that we are to be the ones to fight duels. We will open our land to his Court, but I will not give him our blood easily."

Cvareh expected no less. "I will seek out Finnyr for potential challenge opportunities."

"Let it be done."

None could ever say that Petra hesitated. In moments she could assess a situation for an opportunity and decide upon the best course of action. It was more than Cvareh could do in hours some days.

"I cannot keep you from this Court." Her voice shifted slightly at the mere notion of him.

Cvareh gave the world a tired smile. "We knew this day would come."

"I cannot stand for you."

"I understand."

Petra could stand for nearly anyone in House Xin, but not Cvareh. He was her brother and the chosen Ryu. All eyes turned to him to defend the House in her name and carry the title of Oji should she be felled in some form of misfortune other than a sanctioned duel. He would have to defend himself, or he would never be accepted as the Ryu again.

"How many could you kill?"

Cvareh considered it a long moment. The first time he'd really put training to application was on Loom, and that had been a failure overall. Though using any combat against Arianna was entirely unfair... Responsibility suddenly crushed him, the supports that held it over his head breaking the moment he awoke to the real truth of his standing.

"No more than three beads." He put it in the perspective of the King's Riders —a somewhat universal standard for the might of a warrior.

Silence was Petra's way of screaming her displeasure. "You must work with Cain."

"I will."

"Daily."

"I will."

"Cvareh." Her body was so tense he was surprised her muscles had yet to snap her bones from the strain.

"Petra."

"You must not die on me. That is an order from the Oji to her Ryu." The room was so silent he could hear her swallow. "We did not come this far together for you to fall to Rok scum. Go beneath the surface, find duels, gain practice killing."

Unsanctioned duels were something the Oji should discourage at all costs. Yet here she was, doing the exact opposite. The ends would come before the ideals sacrificed to reach them. They were Xin.

"I will."

A different sort of quiet passed between them. A comfortable separation of realities where Nova existed elsewhere and they were the only people in the world of Petra's meditation tower. Cvareh played with Arianna's name in his head, trying to figure out how best to broach the topic.

"Out with it." Petra sensed his turmoil.

"Arianna and I… We went into Napole, and she wore the guise of a Xin."

"Good. I could not handle dealing with the common populous knowing we harbored an odd Chimera."

"I introduced her as an Anh."

Petra didn't move; she hardly seemed to breathe. "You are truly an idiot, brother."

"I did not expect a Crimson Court."

"No, and you wanted to make it known you had found a potential mate." Petra's tone was stretched between amusement, frustration, and exasperation. "She could have been nothing more than a slave, and yet you chose to give her a name of our House."

*Was that what it was?* Cvareh wondered to himself. "I was merely trying to protect her."

Petra broke the room's stillness with unabashed laughter. "From what you tell me of our Chimera, you should be more worried about protecting yourself. I do not think the woman wants nor needs you to fight her battles."

"You know her surprisingly well for someone who has spoken to her once."

"Cain tells me things."

It was Cvareh's turn to tense. It was no secret that Cain delighted in his sister's happiness. They weren't a poor match, either. But Cvareh didn't relish the notion of any man with Petra. Furthermore, the last one who had aspired ended with a few holes in unexpected places and a gouged out throat when he had ultimately displeased Cvareh's sister. And Cvareh actually liked Cain.

"You've introduced her as your own. If she's challenged, you'll stand for her." Duty pulled the command from Petra's lips.

"She won't be challenged," he offered hopefully, not wanting to linger on the fact that Petra had just all but said that Ari's life would ultimately be worth more than his. "Those who know she exists won't care enough to interrupt the flow of the pit with all the duels we will be challenging in Rok. It would be against the spirit of the Court."

Petra hummed in mild agreement, unconvinced. "Just make sure she stands out no more than she already will as the first by your side."

Cvareh straightened away and Petra did the same. As comforting as it was to linger on one another, they both had work to do. Cvareh descended first, winding his way back to Arianna. His thoughts were gray and clouded, not unlike the Gods' Line in the sun's fading light.

He wandered back to the other woman who had given purpose to his days. Cvareh went straight to her room first, before even changing his clothes for proper evening attire.

He gave the door a soft knock, waiting for permission before entering. Arianna was positioned at her table by the Western facing window. He would've thought it would be too bright for anyone to sit in the sun like that, but there she was, day after day. For the first time, Cvareh wondered if she was even happy on Nova.

"Have you attended the Oji?"

"The Oji? You're beginning to sound like a Dragon." He closed the door behind him, crossing over to her desk.

She turned stiffly. He'd heard the sarcastic tone in the way she'd used Petra's title. But Cvareh knew it would irk her more to play into it than make a fuss of it. The assessment seemed to hold true.

"What are you working on?"

"Hypotheticals," she answered vaguely.

The schematics held a weird sort of beauty. Dark wound against light as ink on parchment. Seemingly chaotic conceptions became definite shapes punctuated with calculations that were a language all their own. And, if Arianna wasn't going to decode their meaning for him, he was certainly not going to decipher it by himself. So Cvareh was left to quiet admiration, seeing the form before the function.

"You owe me an explanation," she reminded him.

Cvareh caught her eyes, the demand in them apparent. "I do." He sat back onto the bed and Arianna turned to face him. "The Crimson Court will be held here on Ruana in a fortnight. It is usually held on Lysip, home of House Rok and the current Dono. But Yveun has decided to have it here on Ruana."

"This is significant."

He could see Arianna trying to piece together the parts she'd been handed, but—likely to her annoyance—she had too many knowledge gaps still to truly comprehend the gravity of the situation. "It is. All named members of the hosting House must be in attendance. Usually, Rok is all too happy to have the advantage of their own turf and the inevitable outnumbering—"

"But this time they want to corner you."

Cvareh held his tongue that it could be a literal "you," as he was notorious for avoiding the Court. "Petra and I believe so, yes."

"So what is the real concern? A noble court hardly sounds like cause for too much agony. Worried you won't have the most fashionable garb there?" She snickered, but the smile slowly faded from her mouth at his solemn expression.

"The Court is not some place that we all gather and gossip; we have the tea parlors and wineries for that. The only way for people to advance in Dragon society is by killing the rank above them. To keep things orderly, these duels must usually be sanctioned by the Oji, except during the Court. Then, nearly all duels are heard and seen out… One exception being if the Dono himself decides to intervene."

Arianna stared at him for a long, hard moment. She tapped her nails on the table in quick succession and glanced over her shoulder at the fading light outside. Her magic was as silent as her lips, her thoughts locked away in some place he couldn't reach.

She turned back to him with the look of resolve he associated with overt danger. "You're going to be challenged."

"I have no doubt of it. It's possible you will be too."

"Me?" The idea shouldn't have delighted the woman nearly as much as it did.

"I introduced you as a Xin'Anh today. It's not impossible some woman who had been craving the idea of being my mate could challenge you in an attempt to earn my favor."

As Arianna considered this, she folded her hands behind her head. Her grin only continued to expand. "Someone craving you is almost comical."

Cvareh rolled his eyes, slightly stung from her words. Not overly so, but just a bit more than he'd want to admit. "I am something here on Nova." He would never dismiss the title Petra had given to him, what it meant to his House.

"You are," she agreed easily with a small spring to her feet. Arianna's fingers were like wriggling worms attached to her palms. "And that's why you deserve a real woman, should a woman be your desire."

Arianna advanced on him and Cvareh leaned back, his palms spreading against the heavy duvet that covered her bed. She straddled his knees, looming over him. It was imposing and dominating and it made him want to wrestle her to the ground. It made him want to submit.

"How do you define a 'real woman', Fenthri?" His voice had shifted to something he was barely familiar with. He liked the molasses quality of it as it coated his throat and honeyed his tongue.

"One who doesn't lurk in shadows waiting for opportune challenges because they know you would otherwise never support them at your side." She spoke as though the fact should be obvious, but it was a somewhat foreign notion to Cvareh's Dragon blood. Foreign, but not unwelcome.

Cvareh straightened some, closing a hand's width of distance between them. Arianna was too smart for him to assume she wasn't aware of what she was doing. But what was she doing? Cvareh didn't know, but he wasn't bound by her logical mind. He was a man who could savor beauty and relax in knowing something was because that was how it should be.

When she was near him, like this, everything was how it should be.

"So, when do we begin?"

"Begin?" He swallowed, the word having application to a seemingly infinite number of meanings.

"I may be challenged. You *will* be challenged." Arianna held out her hands.

*No, my brother's hands*, Cvareh reminded himself. The idea sobered him some. This entrancing woman who seemed to hold a universe of possibilities on her tongue—if she deigned to share them—was made of the pieces of his kin.

With far too much focus, claws jutted like magic from her fingers. Arianna's mouth curved into a wild snarl, the somewhat sensual woman from before lost completely to a wild and equally thrilling side. Cvareh's magic heightened as he was aware in a very new way that she had him trapped between her legs, every vital spot within a hand's reach.

"I need to learn to use these." Arianna turned over her hands in utter fascination. "Why don't we help each other?"

"You want to spar with me?"

"I can always twist Cain's arm into it," she said, as lightly as if the proud Dragon had already agreed to the matter.

Cvareh placed his hands on her hips. They were wide with strong bones underneath the muscle and flesh. He pushed her away just enough to stand. Face to face, a breath apart, he kept her in his grip far longer than what was necessary, just to feel her pulse under his fingers.

She didn't step away; she let him hold her there. That fact he was somehow keenly aware of, despite having no reason to know it. He nor anyone else would ever touch her, hold her, keep her, unless she willed it so.

"We begin at sundown every day." Cvareh fought the urge to pull her the rest of the way to him. To press her so tightly against his body that they no longer knew where one of them ended and the other began.

"It's sundown now, Cvareh'Ryu," she observed quietly.

"I suppose it is." Though he had long been admiring the way the sunset lit her white hair afire. "Are you ready?"

"Am I ever not?" She gave him what Cvareh would dare call a coy grin.

It was a question he delighted in not being able to refute.

# 23
## PETRA

Petra ran her claws along the unfinished banister that led down from her personal roost in the Xin Manor. Let it never be said that she didn't make sacrifices on behalf of her House. She had reallocated all hands and tradesmen from finishing different parts of the manor for the sake of building an amphitheater for the Crimson Court.

It had been a couple hundred years since the last Court had been held on Ruana, long ago when House Xin was still in power and the gathering was known as the Cobalt Court. A crumbling reminder of the long-ago glory days of House Xin, the amphitheater had suffered from disuse. No Xin wanted to lay eyes on it, like a shameful scar that would never stop weeping blood.

Petra was determined to see the place resurrected not just to its former glory, but even better than before. The laborers would work non-stop until the Court to complete her grand designs. But they would make the usual venue for the Crimson Court on Lysip look humble in comparison. She wanted retractable sunshades over the stadium seating. Cushions, special just for this Court, made for every seat. Running water, box seats, food and wine service throughout—nothing would be spared.

If Yveun was going to hand them the Court, she would show everyone why they deserved it.

"How does the construction proceed?" Cain waited for her at the bottom of the stairs.

"Slower than I would like." As was usually the case. "But well enough. The foreman assures me that we will have it completed in time." There were only two weeks left before the Court would begin.

"Gathering offenses on House Rok has proved no real difficulty."

She snorted, as if it would have.

"Any word from Finnyr on the matter?"

"He's handed me some good bits of information. I have those who can make the claims already working on ways for them to 'uncover' these offenses on their own." Petra trusted Cain. She trusted him as much as she trusted any other man —the length of her arms and the depth of her claws. But he'd proved a loyal leader within House Xin and a faithful friend to Cvareh. For those two things, she found herself able to appreciate his brisk mannerisms and focused nature.

"Finnyr has proved useful."

"By some miracle," she agreed reluctantly. By far the most helpful information she'd ever worked out of Finnyr was the knowledge of the Philosopher's Box schematics. Petra had heard about the box from the snippets of details she'd managed to attain from the last rebellion. But it wasn't until one night when Finnyr was well in his cups that he boasted he'd seen such plans with his own eyes.

After that, it was simply a matter of more wine, sending Cvareh to visit his brother more often, and patience. Thoughts of Cvareh shifted her attention.

"How do my brother and the Chimera fare?" Petra hadn't been terribly surprised when Cain had informed her Cvareh had elected to work with Arianna over him. The woman had a certain *appeal* for Cvareh that Cain did not. And Petra was inclined to allow Cvareh his desires, so long as he was still ready for the Court when the time came. She'd set Cain to ensuring that much.

"Surprising progress." Cain motioned for a nearby stair, and Petra nodded.

They progressed silently upward, the stairs leveling out upon a high arcade. From the vantage, they could look down upon a private pit she had seen set aside for use of her immediate family. There were few windows that oversaw this pit, and Petra knew who had access to every one of them. She cast her eyes downward.

It was the first time she had seen the Chimera's Dragon illusion. It was skillful, tight upon her and smooth. There wasn't a single kink in it and no bizarre ripple of magic. The pulse that radiated from it was nothing more than what one would expect of a Dragon's magical aura in general. There was nothing about it that would alert even Petra to its presence if she hadn't known it was there.

Arianna spun widely around Cvareh, bringing her fingertips into his neck—a kill. Petra watched as they backed away and lunged for each other once more. The woman tripped up Petra's brother, stumbling him and grabbing for his throat in the process—a kill. They separated again and were soon tumbling, head over heels, until the Chimera had mounted Cvareh like a broken stallion with her fingertips pressing over his heart—a kill.

"She's quite good, isn't she?"

"She is known as the White Wraith," Cain begrudgingly admitted. "At least she seems to have earned her infamy."

Petra watched them round each other, again and again. The longer she watched, the more unsettled she became. It was not just because Cvareh clearly needed to develop considerable polish in the short time before the Court. There was an odd shadow puppetry before her; it ran deeper than the illusion and more mysterious than the woman's apparent skill.

"Why do they not use their claws?" The woman was all teeth and snarls and pure attack power. Yet neither drew blood.

"Cvareh tells me it was her decision. A caveat to their arrangement."

"Did he say why?" The notion seemed far too tender for the woman before Petra. She couldn't imagine Arianna's demand stemmed from mere sentimentality.

Cain shook his head.

Petra continued to stare, trying to make sense of what she was seeing. There was something amiss. She could almost, almost… smell it.

"There is something… *off* about her." Cain gave Petra's thoughts sound. "I thought it the first day she came. I'd mistakenly attributed it to merely being a Chimera, but it's deeper than that."

"Explain." Petra would not rake her brain against something Cain had already begun to make sense of.

"She moves like a Dragon, she acts like a Dragon."

"She's clearly well educated." The woman had designed the Philosopher's Box, after all. Or so Cvareh claimed.

"She's taller than the usual Fen. Her body is stronger. She has true weight to her." Petra held her refute, allowing Cain to continue, hoping he would tell her something more meaningful than mannerisms and muscles. "She doesn't smell of rot."

Petra inhaled deeply, as though she could smell the woman in the pit far below from their obscure vantage. *That's what it is*, she realized. All the Chimera she had ever encountered smelled fiercely of rot, of muddled blood and stolen organs. Arianna had no such scent about her.

"Even when she attached Finnyr's hands… There were no rags of blood in her quarters. She burnt them along with her severed parts. The stink from the procedure should have been enough to set half the manor fleeing to avoid the smell."

"Was there no mark of Chimera blood in her room?" Only Dragon blood disappeared tidily in the air. Chimera and Fenthri blood stained, much like their very existence.

Cain shook his head. Petra considered heading there herself just for the sake of checking. "There was a blood trace, but it was unlike anything I've known— Dragon or Chimera. It smelled of both Xin cedar, like Finnyr, and Tam honeysuckle."

"The room would smell of Finnyr," Petra reasoned, thinking of her elder brother's severed hands. But that didn't explain the crispness, the purity. "What do you think is the cause?"

"I don't know…" Cain struggled with the evidence set before him. If looks could kill, the Chimera who was still besting Cvareh far below them would be struck down and begging for release. "But I do know she has at least four Dragon organs."

"Four?"

"Eyes and ears were visible from the start, even if she's capped her ears with metal so they do not grow into points."

Petra couldn't stop herself from touching her own ear, horrified at the thought of such mutilation of one of the most striking features of a Dragon.

"Hands, now, thanks to Finnyr," Cain continued. "And her stomach."

"Her stomach?" Petra repeated expectantly. That wasn't information that could be encountered casually.

"I saw the addition of holly peas into her food."

Red and unassuming, the holly pea looked similar to any other brilliant berry. But it caused severe indigestion in both Dragon and Fenthri alike. Consumption of just a small amount was usually followed with a day of vomiting and diarrhea. Non-lethal, but severely uncomfortable if one did not possess magic in their stomach. "How very underhanded of you, Cain."

"Forgive me." He avoided her narrowed eyes.

Subversion was something Petra didn't tolerate; it was an affront to their ways. But the matter was done, and the woman in question wasn't a Dragon anyway. "Do not make a habit of such deceptions. You are above it."

"I would not." He looked horrified.

"Good." Petra let the conversation continue, satisfied. "She was unaffected?"

"No sign of troubles."

"There was no way she could have removed them?"

"If she even knows what they are? No. They were added to a strawberry jam."

"You are truly ruthless." She bared her teeth in an appreciative smile. This was what she needed from Cain. She needed someone who was so loyal to their House that he would risk her ire for the sake of its defense.

He gave a small bow of his head. All delight faded when Cain turned back to the pit. Arianna had just bested Cvareh again. "Petra'Oji…"

She wasn't familiar with hesitation from Cain. It made her give him all the more attention. "Be careful with this one."

Petra narrowed her eyes to slits. "You think I cannot fell her?"

"I do not doubt you." The *but* was felt before it was spoken. "But she is something different. She has that many organs and has not fallen. Think of what she might be like with more. More magic? More power? She—"

"You have been heard, Cain," Petra dismissed him abruptly. She would not tolerate dissent or questioning in her ranks. Cain had earned himself good will for investigating the woman, an odd mix given his unconventional methods of doing so. She wouldn't want to see him squander it.

Cain gave a short bow and descended the stairs gracefully. Petra's eyes remained locked on the woman far below. Cain didn't know it, but what he feared was a Perfect Chimera. A creature that was so mighty it could even challenge a Dragon.

Petra grinned madly.

One man's fear was another's salvation.

# 24
## YVEUN

The skies were filled with boco as Dragons of all colors flooded Easwin, the easternmost town of the Isle of Ruana. It was impossible to look in any direction and not see scarlet, cerulean, or viridian. Yveun surveyed the generally unassuming town from his current perch. It was unorthodox to be anywhere but Lysip for a Crimson Court, but it was too late now to question his play.

"How many people worked on getting the amphitheater up to par?" he asked over his shoulder. Slaves silently dotted and lined his exposed chest with a thick paste that would temporarily tattoo his flesh.

"Petra told me she had over five hundred workers at all hours." Finnyr was seated awkwardly in the center of the room behind Yveun. He was appropriately ignored by the slaves, their focus on their master—as it should be. Yet the fact that Yveun had not dismissed him was its own form of honor. Yveun kept Finnyr trapped in the "between", a place few Dragons ever found themselves in thanks to their society's strict hierarchy.

"How did she find the craftsmen?" It annoyed Yveun to no end that Petra had managed to scrape together the sort of display that towered against the distant horizon. The girl was an annoying little gnat, impossible to squish and always flying around where she didn't belong. A gnat that aspired to be a wasp and already fashioned itself thusly.

"She told me she took all hands from progression on the Xin manor. Some others were in Napole still after the initial construction. The rest? Nameless from below, I believe."

"So desperate is she to display her strength that she leans on the shadowed nameless." His insult was for no one but himself. Finnyr was already his obedient servant. The slaves who attended him had no names themselves and therefore no souls and no purpose. Nevertheless, letting out his displeasure into the very air on Ruana sated him some. "I will let you return to her tonight when the day's duels have ended."

"You will?" Finnyr's voice started shrill before he managed to control his emotions.

"Is that a problem, Finnyr?" Yveun held up a hand, stalling the servants' work. He turned to look at the Xin's face. It was harder for a man to lie when you were actively trying to spoon out the truth through his eyes.

"N-no, Dono…" He went pale. "After last time, my sister was adamant that I stay with you."

Yveun keenly remembered the man's bruises from having his hands harvested. He wanted to slice Finnyr up himself and force him to watch his organs being fed and connected to Fenthri as punishment for his cowardice. His voice was a low growl that rumbled over the jagged stones of his aggravation. "I held this Court on Ruana so I might finally learn the truth of what happened on Loom, and the extent of how far Petra's power reaches into the land below— how it may even be increasing here on Nova. You will play your role and return to her as a relieved prodigal child, blessed to be home. You will prove your worth and give me the information I seek."

Finnyr lowered his eyes submissively. "Of course, Dono. I live to serve you in no half measures."

Satisfied, Yveun turned forward again. "I want you to find whatever information you can on Cvareh—of his trip to Loom, of the schematics he stole. Speak to slaves, servants. Offer them a better life on Lysip with the favor of the Dono if you must."

He would never actually allow Xin hands who had served Petra directly to attend him. But they didn't need to know he would see them dead the second they set foot on his home. Their surprise would be delicious.

He locked eyes on the grand, stone amphitheater in the distance. The streets were already filled with music and cheers. Laughter harmonized with song as men and women danced together. The Court was a celebration of life, and death, and everything that hung in the balance between those conflicting yet beautiful forces.

He rode in a litter to the Court. It was a wide platform with low railings and a pointed roof covered in red clay tiles and edged in silver. The wooden base and poles were a fine mahogany, stained to a deep wine color. Textiles the colors of fire shone, silks glinting with sunlight. Sixteen men carried its bulk through the streets.

It stood in stark contrast to the lake blue pennons and people of House Xin that parted like waves around his metaphorical boat. Yveun kept his eyes forward, or on the woman who lounged next to him.

Coletta Rok'Ryu To was thin for a Dragon. She had never quite grown out of her girlish years, her face remaining soft and her cheeks rounded. Her ears pointed more outward than upward and her nose was thin and narrow, cutting between two eyes that looked all the larger for it.

She was his cherry woman. She smelled of the fruit and perfumed herself with it for added effect. Her flesh was creamy-orange, hardly red at all, but it reminded him of the sweet cherries that could be cultivated in the spring. Her hair was the bright red of a candied fruit of the same variety. But her eyes were truly striking, dark orbs that shone with the depth of a rich wine. The kind that could absorb a man whole.

Those same eyes looked listlessly at the world around them, as if it were all more trouble than what it was worth. For Coletta, it may well have been.

"Ruana has not changed much since the last time I was here," she said softly. She was a humble and unassuming counterpart to the loud and dominating presence that was Yveun.

"And how often do you come to Ruana?"

"Too often, in that I come at all." She lay back. Gossip-mongers would continue to perpetuate her weak and sickly state. But all Yveun saw was the visage of a woman who was nothing more than fiercely bored.

"I appreciate your indulgence, Rok'Ryu." He spoke sincerely. Coletta wasn't one for leaving her gardens or… diversions. But she had packed and mounted her boco without question upon hearing that the Court was to be held on Ruana.

"You should never have any doubt." The words were almost threatening, on the off chance he sincerely had.

"In you? Never." Truer words had yet to be spoken that day.

"Besides, you need me." Her mouth pressed into a thin and knowing smile that Yveun could never deny. "So, what role am I playing by day while we are here?"

He was the sun, and she was his moon. Forever in orbit, perpetually watching the sky while the other slumbered. Thus, by day, she operated by his wants and rules. By night, he by hers. "The same role you usually do. No one will challenge you if they think it will be a poor, shameful duel with a sickly Ryu."

Coletta laughed softly. When she smiled he could see the gray of her gums, turned to ash with her secretive and underhanded business.

"Let them challenge me, Yveun, and see how long they live."

Yveun smiled back at his mate, baring his teeth. If anyone did ever challenge the Rok'Ryu, they would answer to him. Yveun would never let another touch his queen. They should *hope* to answer to him. For, if Coletta had her way, the death would be infinitely more painful and drawn out than anything Yveun could devise.

The amphitheater was even more impressive up close. Every fifth column was the sculpture of a Dragon—ones he did not recognize but could only assume were important to House Xin. Wide, bat-like wings extended behind them, supporting the second tier of seating and arcade windows that let in the breezes from above. Sapphires as big as his head made their eyes, shining keenly at all who entered through the archways below.

They were met by a tall man with skin the color of sea foam. His name faded away from Yveun's immediate memory into the realm of unimportance, but Finnyr seemed to recognize him. The two exchanged a tense look before the man led them up a quiet stair.

"The Xin'Oji has prepared this viewing platform especially for you, Dono." He bowed, motioning for Yveun and his party to continue.

The balcony was high, the highest in the amphitheater, laden with fineries and draped in chiffon that danced upon the wind. It was a box befitting of a king positioned among the nameless and slaves.

In all other instances, he would insist on being the highest in a room, the better to loom over all that was his. But at the Court he wanted to be in the thick of it. He wanted to be so close to the pit that blood could splatter his cheeks. He wanted to be—

Yveun walked over to the edge of the balcony.

—where Petra was sitting.

The woman raised her glass of Xin wine with a thin smile. It was a restrained motion, but a quiet jab all the same. Yveun waged an internal war. He could demand her position, but then he would look like the insecure ruler who needed a place to solidify his prowess. Tam would certainly trade him; their platform was in the middle of the arena. But the spot was fitting for those who kept the balance. Furthermore, he was the Rok'Oji Dono, and he *would not* rely on a Tam.

"Wine," Yveun growled, holding out his hand. He didn't even see who supplied it.

He raised his own glass to Petra, staring down the woman for a long moment. She sipped, and he did the same. Yveun turned and stalked to his seat, virtually out of sight for the masses below. No, he asked no man or woman for pity. If he was to be seated above them all, he would appear like a god to rule over life and death and the Dragon Court. He made concessions to no man or woman.

The man who had escorted them to the box departed. Finnyr, Coletta, Lossom, and two of his most trusted Kin remained. Coletta stepped forward, dropping her voice to a hush meant only for his ears.

"She seeks to make a fool of you, Yveun."

"Doesn't she always?" He took another healthy drink from his wineglass.

"You have walked into her home to let her do it." Coletta rarely guarded her tongue to anyone, Yveun included.

"She will be the fool before the day is done," Yveun swore.

"See that she is, Dono." Coletta gave him a cautionary stare. "I grow tired of this game I've let you play."

A growl rose from his throat as his mate walked to one of the plush seats. It escaped as a roar that echoed throughout the amphitheater. A third of the seats were still empty, as the upper echelons of Dragon society slowly flowed in from the revelries outside. But Yveun was done waiting, and they all functioned at his behest.

He threw down his glass. Wine arced through the air like crimson rain before splattering between shards of glass in the pit far below. The very wind itself seemed to hold its breath for his decree.

"I did not travel from Lysip for wine." His voice boomed, echoing off every pillar and person. "I traveled for blood. I traveled to thin my fattening Court. I traveled to see which of you are deserving of your names and which of you have yet to grow into the titles you were born for."

No one spoke. No one breathed.

"Let the Crimson Court commence!" he shouted so loudly the very heavens rumbled. "Who will be the first challenger?"

A man stood, eager for the honor of being the first in the pit, to be the one whose feet would touch that hallowed and unsoiled ground. Yveun bared his teeth in utter delight that the man was one of House Rok. Unsurprisingly, he called against one of House Xin for an offense of cheating committed in his card room.

The two leapt over people and empty stands, descending into the pit as claws and teeth and rage. With no objection from Yveun, they collided. Gold splattered the walls, the smell of freshly cut grasses filling the air from the Xin. It mingled and soured against the smell of huckleberry from the Rok. The two scraped and scrambled for a long few minutes, shredding each other to pulp.

But, as Yveun expected in all things, the man of House Rok eventually won the upper hand.

He tore the Xin man's heart still beating from his chest. He held it up with a primal cry, golden blood running down his arm and dripping onto his face before slowly evaporating into the air. The Rok man brought the heart to his mouth and took a glutinous bite.

Rok and Xin battled into the afternoon. For every one Rok challenge, there were two Xin. Tam may as well have not even shown up. It was clear who was fighting for dominance in this Court. Yveun missed half the fights, his seat positioned too far back and too high for a good view. But every time he graced the edge of the balcony, the Rok fighters below battled twice as hard and went for increasingly vicious kills.

As a result of this poor positioning, it was afternoon by the time he finally realized the House Xin box had been filled. Yveun's blood ran hot at the mere sight of Cvareh, the lying bastard brother of the bitch who pursued his demise as though she had nothing else in the world to worry over.

"Lossom," he summoned his current Master Rider. The man was at his side in an instant. "Challenge Cvareh'Ryu."

"Dono, I have no cause for a challenge against the Xin'Ryu..." Lossom's hesitation was almost enough for Yveun to kick him face-first into the pit below and let whoever desired tear him limb from limb and lick his bones clean.

They had cause a hundred times over. The death of each one of his Riders on Loom would be more than enough for Yveun to order any Rok to challenge Cvareh. But that would first require admitting that the Riders were on Loom to begin with. Yveun growled, caught in a snare of his own shadowy invention.

"Invent one."

"But—"

"I am the Dono, Lossom. Comprehend what that means. If I support your demand for a duel, none will permit him to back out." Yveun walked away from the edge, and toward his beacon of sanity lounging in the shape of a woman.

Cheers erupted from the duel ending. The runner of the ring, one of House Tam for all their love of balance, called for the next challenger. Yveun waited expectantly.

"I, Lossom Rok'Anh To, Master Rider to Yveun Dono, challenge Cvareh Xin'Ryu Soh as a liar, and for disgraces against the Dono's name in the presence of a Rok." Lossom didn't flinch, completing the fatuous challenge with bold confidence. "Let he whose merit runs deepest through his veins live for the night's revelries. Let he whose merit is a facade be reduced to blood upon the ground and shame upon his House."

The arena had fallen silent. Every ear hung on Cvareh's response. Yveun waited with a smirk. Cvareh could not back down. If he questioned the legitimacy he'd look like a coward, for they all knew Yveun was going to allow the duel. It was time for the Xin'Ryu to finally enter the ring and be put to rest, out of Yveun's concerns once and for all.

"I stand for Cvareh'Ryu." An unfamiliar woman's voice rang out loud and clear.

Yveun stood slowly, walking to the edge. He had not expected anyone to stand for Cvareh against his Master Rider. To do so was the most foolish display of suicidal loyalty the Court had ever seen. Because if the one who stood for the accused fell, the accused was also put to death.

Far below, a pale blue woman stood with eyes like late sunset and hair the color of morning's first light. She cut her place in the world with foolhardy arrogance, standing as though she were the personified herald of the Death Lord himself.

# 25
## ARIANNA

"I, Lossom Rok'Anh To, Master Rider to Yveun Dono, challenge Cvareh Xin'Ryu Soh as a liar, and for disgraces against the Dono's name in the presence of a Rok."

Cvareh tensed next to her. His eyes were locked in a grim sort of determination against the crimson man who stood at the edge of the King's box. Arianna could practically hear the echo of the words repeating themselves in his head as the challenger still spoke them.

"Let he whose merit runs deepest through his veins live for the night's revelries. Let he whose merit is a facade be reduced to blood upon the ground and shame upon his House."

Cvareh didn't move. It was as if the man who called himself Lossom had woven a netted spell that trapped him to the spot. Arianna made quick work of sizing up Lossom. Judging from her angle, the height of the amphitheater, and his perspective size, she knew he was larger than Cvareh both in muscle and height.

Her eyes fell on the beads that dangled by his ear. He had called himself the Master Rider. It seemed Yveun had been forced to go with a less experienced combatant after his other Riders had never returned from Loom.

She knew what was about to happen; she'd seen it enough throughout the day. Cvareh would stand, accept the challenge, and they would descend into the ring. No others of House Xin stood. It was a matter for the Ryu to defend his title, and judging from their practice sessions leading up to the Court, Ari had minimal confidence in his ability to do so.

"I stand for Cvareh'Ryu." Arianna jumped to her feet.

"What are you doing?" Cvareh hissed.

"Saving your life."

"This isn't done." He grabbed her arm, trying to pull her back down. "Dragons don't stand for their Ryu or Oji."

Arianna leaned forward, meeting him halfway. Her mouth found his ear as she spoke "Good thing I'm not a Dragon, then."

"Who are you?" The King's voice echoed across the silence.

She turned to address the man who gave face to all her nightmares, the formless evil who stood atop Loom like it was a tailless scorpion beneath his boot. She had watched him all day, studied him in every way she knew how. All evidence pointed to a singular truth: The Dragon King was nothing more than a man.

And men could be killed.

Men could be pinned down and ripped apart and tortured until they begged for release—release that would *never* be given to them.

"Ari Xin'Anh Bek," she recited.

His head turned, looking to Petra. Arianna followed his stare as well, catching Cain's eyes. They were as round as saucers and sparking with anger. She gave him a toothy grin. The man still thought she couldn't speak Royuk. *Well, now he knew.*

Petra glanced at her from the corners of her eyes but said nothing. Ari's play had worked. Petra couldn't speak against her without calling their whole facade into question. She couldn't give Ari any more care than she would any other Dragon. She had to ignore the fact that Arianna was the Fenthri who held the design of the Philosopher's Box in her mind. Cvareh could not stand when someone had stood for him. And that meant she was about to head into the pit.

"Very well, Ari Xin'Anh Bek. You fight with both your life and title as well as that of Cvareh Xin'Ryu." The Dono gave his blessing with amusement, already writing off the duel, and the Rider launched himself onto the stands nearby.

When Lossom was halfway down, Arianna set herself into motion as well. She'd seen enough of his mannerisms to gain an overall understanding of how fast he could move. She'd meet him in the pit.

The scent of blood and magic assaulted her the second her feet touched the packed ground. With no air or wind, it sat trapped on the surface, smothering her senses with the remnants of gore.

Arianna tightened the splint on her fingers one clip. They would be cut off before her illusion would fall.

She sprinted forward, determined to pounce on the Rider the moment he landed. But he sprung off the wall, spinning through the air and landing nimbly behind her. With the advantage she'd sought lost, Arianna was instantly on defensive.

He swung wide and she ducked, jabbing for his side. The edge of her claw caught against his lined and dotted skin, spilling first blood.

Lossom snarled, reaching for her with a clawed hand. Arianna fell backward, rolling away. He squinted in confusion.

Dragons were strong creatures, that much Arianna could not—and never had—denied. Their magic made them formidable. But it also made them predictable. When nearly any wound could be healed in moments, making very few cuts lethal, it meant their fighting styles favored close range and tight jabs. They shouldered wounds gladly that Arianna avoided desperately, and that made her erratic dodges unpredictable to them. It made her method of fighting as sensible to them as their fashion was to her.

She would win this fight without him drawing blood.

She had to.

Arianna lunged forward again. She leaned and spun, his claws whizzing over her back in a near miss. She would give nearly anything for her lines and daggers, but all that was permitted in the pit were claws and prowess. Weapons, coronas, gold, and magic—beyond healing—were all against the rules. Cvareh had taught her that much, to Arianna's dismay.

She sidestepped in and brought her hand up to the man's chin. Startled, it caught, stabbing right through to his tongue. Blood ran down her forearm and cheers erupted from above.

Arianna had never fought with an audience before. All her work had been done at night and in the shadows with the least number of eyes possible on her. She had never felt the thrill of screams and cries of encouragement. She had never fought for sport.

There was something about it, something...*thrilling*. Her heart raced faster and her feet moved with more confidence. She wanted to give the people a show. It was illogical, utterly illogical. Everything lacked meaning, and in that, there was joy. Joy in death, in life, in doing just to do.

Lossom's claws swung closer and closer. Every near miss pushed her forward. Blood still evaporated off his chest from where she had wounded him, from the new cuts she gave him.

She was faster, stronger, more skilled, and far more fearless than this Dragon would ever be. He could not kill those he loved for the sake of the survival of an ideal. He could not cut open his own chest and turn himself into a living machine for the sake of science.

But she could. She could because she was not Fenthri, or Dragon, or Chimera. She could because she had, and would again if fate re-dealt her a cruel hand.

Arianna kicked the Rider squarely in the chest. He stumbled, and she caught his ankle with the top of her foot, pulling it right out from under him. Off-balance, his attacks were thrown wildly. Arianna lunged into them. She pushed him downward and buried her hand in his chest. He struggled against her, his claws digging into her wrist viciously. Her blood mingled with his as it bubbled from the wound she was inflicting.

His heart beat frantically against her palm. For a brief second, she held his life and future in her hand. And then she ripped it from him.

Arianna stood with the man's heart. The arena's momentary shock was only half as deafening as the cheers that followed it in a rush. Her eyes found the Dragon King's high above, but not so far that he was untouchable. Not as far as he should want to be from her.

She stared at him as she buried her teeth into the Rider's heart, and envisioned it was his.

# 26

## FLORENCE

The land had changed.

The Skeleton Forest had thinned and the dominant pines that oppressed their senses at every waking hour of the day had become scrawnier. As the train barreled down the winding pathway, they swerved out to the coast, giving Florence her first glimpse of the tall, rocky bluffs that made the Western side of Ter.2 impenetrable by boat.

The majority of Ter.2 was an imposing place—tall and shadowed, full of harsh rocky outcrops and the forest that boasted some of the most dangerous monsters in the world. But they had eluded the endwig, and lived to see the land change from the cold north to the more temperate, flatter south.

Tall grasses grew like in Ter.4, but the terrain was mostly flat, not hilly. It lacked significant features to the point that Florence wondered how the oceans had not just swallowed it whole. She watched it blur by as they continued on their tiny, overgrown track.

Nora and Derek alternated helping her. She had forced them to learn. She would shoulder as much of the burden as she had to, as they needed, but she could not do it alone. Will only went so far; skill was always required to make up the remainder.

They were begrudging at first, but not as much as Florence expected. She was too tired to question why, and thankfully the reason became apparent soon enough. She had earned an unexpected amount of respect from her companions after the night of the endwig. Her unconventional upbringing had served a purpose.

"How do you know how much coal to add, again?" Nora asked from where she was manning the grate and shovel.

Florence tapped the gauge next to her. "This meter. You want this to stay out of the high and low levels here and here. Ideally, it should sit around fifteen."

"Why?"

"For an engine this size, that amount of power seems to clip us along without wasting power. There's only so fast we can push her, or should…" Florence thought back to the sloppy repairs she'd made across the train following their frantic flight, and especially those she had less faith in holding. At least she'd had some training in the Ravens, but all her knowledge as a Rivet came from watching and helping Arianna.

*Arianna.* The name sat within Florence's heart, still encased in love. The months apart had shown Florence that much. She loved Arianna as the teacher and guardian she had been. The recognition of the fact made the distance, surprisingly, more bearable. It dulled the harsh words they'd spoken to one another and quietly assured Florence of Arianna's intentions. She knew the woman, and she knew that her venture to Nova was for the right reasons. And she knew that when Arianna returned, they would embrace once more and Florence would again be crafting canisters to help both the revolution and the White Wraith.

"What is most important to a Raven?"

Florence used the rattling of the train to mask a heavy sigh. She was always going to be seen as a Raven before anything else. She'd delighted in it when it had served her, when it had made people unassuming of her canisters in Mercury Town or her skill with the revolver. Or when it had helped her blend in at the port of Ter.5.2. But she was quickly learning she would give such things up for the sake of choice.

"Speed, mostly." The echoes of trikes whizzing through the streets of Holx echoed in Florence's ears. "Suicidal speed."

"And for a Revolver?"

Florence paused in surprise. She glanced over at Nora, who stopped her inspection of the gages long enough to search Florence's face.

"You'd know that too, right?"

"Explosions." Florence gave the woman a small smile.

"And Rivets?"

Florence had to think about that for a moment. While Ari was a Master Rivet, she was also not the most conventional of her guild. "Mathematics, perhaps?"

"That sounds terribly dull." Nora scrunched her coal dust-coated nose.

Florence grinned. "I think so too."

They slept together, all three of them, in the back car during the day while they were in the Skeleton Forest, and transitioned to sleeping at night in Ter.1. The air itself in the southern territory was thick; it made the hair on her neck stick without any effort. Florence much preferred working through the day when she would be uncomfortable in the engine anyway, than struggling to sleep in the moist daylight hours.

The nights were cooler, and it made huddling together all the more pleasant. There was a different sort of comfort among them than she'd found with Arianna. When Florence had lain in bed with Arianna, even snuggled together, there was a relaxed ease about it. But with Derek and Nora the pressure sat in her stomach, closer to her abdomen. It was the first time she'd felt such tension. She was smart enough to understand lust, but she wasn't fully aware for whom it stirred.

In all, the trip was mostly peaceful. There was still the stress of maintaining the train and managing the coal, but the old track they rode on was in good enough condition that Florence was confident it'd been used to smuggle things more recently than anyone let on. It was an overall straight shot with only two dead-end switch-offs until they reached Ter.1.2.

The train's terminal was an abandoned yard and they subsequently left it behind. Florence, Nora, and Derek continued on foot. Despite their brands, they were far enough from the Alchemists' Guild hall and past the territory border that they could move without any major concern. Derek carried two large trunks, Nora one, and Florence managed hers and a small case of their remaining powders onto the final train that would take them the rest of the way to Faroe.

They paid into a simple car, huddled with other patrons in bench seats. It was quite unlike her last train ride with Arianna when they had their own cabin; this trip lacked all sort of privacy or grace. Harvesters and others piled into the car, taking all available space, and they found themselves sharing their benches with three others.

Florence was pressed against the window for the two-day ride, and she watched as the land continued to change. The fertile middle ground between the end of the Skeleton Forest and the far end of Ter.1 became rocky and barren, void of life.

"What's that?" Florence squinted at a hole in the earth far in the distance. It looked as if someone had taken a spoon and carved out the land, removing it for some unknown reason.

"A strip mine," one of the Harvesters—Powell—replied.

"That's a mine?" Florence tried to reconcile what was before her. "Aren't mines in mountains? Tunnels?"

"They can be," Powell whispered, trying hard not to wake their sleeping companions squashed into the bench together. "It depends on the mineral we're mining for. If it occurs naturally in large pockets, we strip mine it. If it's in veins, tunnels may be more effective. Some can only be found in mountains."

The Harvester was quiet for a long moment.

"You lived far from home."

"What?" Florence asked, startled. They'd barely spoken more than courtesies, yet he had somehow known that about her.

"There are no mountains in Ter.4, little crow." The man gave a knowing smile. "Which leads me to believe you've spent some time in Ter.5."

Florence pursed her lips.

"Well, wherever you come from, you're far from home." He looked out the window.

"I don't know where home is." She didn't, not anymore. Florence longed for the flat she'd shared with Ari in Old Dortam. But it no longer fit them. Too much had changed. And, if the smaller flat in Ter.4.2 was any indication, Ari had no problem abandoning homes to move on when life demanded it.

"You're young enough that home should be Holx."

"It should be."

"But people are rarely what they should be." The man was older than her, perhaps nearing twenty-five. Older than Arianna, at least, and that meant old enough to know of the time before the Dragons. "Why do you head to Faroe?"

"I'm taking my friends." Florence nodded at Nora and Derek, slumbering the hours away across from her.

"It's your first time in Ter.1?"

Florence nodded. The man leaned back in his chair, his gaze still focused on the mine in the distance as they slowly plodded along past it. Even packed in close as they were, they swayed slightly, shoulders brushing and sides flush.

"The land has changed much, in my years." Florence tried to decipher the somewhat somber note in the man's voice. "The Guild Initiates and Journeymen your age know it only as it is…"

"What's wrong with it?" Florence asked, still hearing the haze of regret that floated through the man's words.

"How long will you be in Faroe?"

If Florence wasn't so accustomed to Arianna, the questions answered with questions might have been grating. But there was a tranquil similarity in the obscured truths and hidden meanings. "I'm not sure."

"Then it will be long enough for you to arrive at your own opinions on these matters."

Florence heard the finality in the statement and rested her head on the glass of the window. The strip mine was now out of view, but she kept her eyes forward as the train swayed in determined progression to the home of the Harvesters. More and more mines dotted the surface of the land as they neared Faroe. Deeper and wider they ran, until the train traversed suspended bridge-ways that spanned a mine directly below them.

She stared over the ominous edge, keenly aware of the thin pieces of steel that separated the train from the seemingly infinite oblivion stretched deep into the earth below. Men and women worked on spiraling walkways on the outer edges of the mine, so far below her that they looked like flicks of dust floating in the mine's smoky haze rather than actual people. So, *so* far below that the explosions they set off were nothing more than flashes of light and dull reverberations.

It was as if the Harvesters had peeled back the surface of the earth to find its soul. And its soul was the very lifeblood of Loom: iron, minerals, oil, and coal.

Faroe was perched in the center of these seemingly endless mines, like an island among an empty sea. Its towering buildings and compact construction was unlike anything Florence had ever seen. Buildings made of concrete had spires of brick built atop them, foundations made from the carved stone left from long-ago mining. Like an impenetrable wall, it was all connected. One city, one guild, every peca of space used. She wondered if Arianna had ever been to Faroe, and if so, what the Rivet's take on the architectural choices were.

The train ran into a station underneath the city. Powell, in his kindness, offered to escort them to the guild hall. Florence was thankful they accepted when he led them through a rat maze of tunnels and tiny elevators that served as the city's only means of getting around.

"Faroe built up when it could no longer build out," Powell explained. "The problem with situating itself at the world's richest mineral deposits meant that most of the land needed to be committed to mining. The Rivets tried to make sense of it, but the Harvesters ended up doing what we do best." He knocked on the rough, bare stone wall next to him. Pick marks still pocked its surface. "We tunneled our way through."

Within the city proper, Florence felt an omnipresent weight. Rock and steel, brick and concrete hovered over her. It compressed Florence's lungs, and she was suddenly reminded of the last time she'd felt such a sensation.

"The Underground," Florence said boldly. It was a taboo subject in Ter.4, and, judging by the rise of Powell's eyebrows, it was known as such in Ter.1 as well. "Did Harvesters help with that at all?"

Powell considered it a long moment, encouraging in that he didn't immediately refuse the subject. "At the time the Underground was first being conceived, perhaps. We did grant them some of our explosives long ago, pre-Revolvers even, to help blast deeper after the ground was broken. But the limestone of Ter.4 is prone to pockets and holes, and the Ravens seemed impatient and determined to make the place their own. Moreso after the Dragons' regulations on the guilds."

The man's tone differed from Ari's at the mere mention of the Dragons. There was no bitter bite, no longing for the past. Instead she heard quiet acceptance. His eyes reflected... appreciation?

The weight was lifted as they ascended to the guild proper. A disk shape at the very top of Faroe, the hall's outer walls were all windows, permitting the gray sunlight and a view of the barren earth beyond. Florence set her bag down slowly, her hand numb from carrying it. As if in a trance, she crossed to the nearest pane of glass. Five times her width, three times her height, it felt as if the view could swallow her whole.

With the flatness of the land she could see for veca upon veca. She saw the dusty clouds that plumed off the ground between the mines. She saw the far explosions that broke into the earth farther and deeper. The mines she'd seen from the train had only been a small part of a much, much larger system.

"What do you think?" Powell asked.

Florence jumped, startled. She hadn't heard the man approach. Pulled from her trance, she immediately sought out Derek and Nora, but they were nowhere to be found.

"They had business on behalf of the Vicar Alchemist for the Vicar Harvester. I saw that they spoke with the right people to get them where they were going."

"Thank you," Florence said sincerely. "You've been quite kind to us."

"You are guests in my home." Powell smiled in reply. "Ter.1 may not be what it once was, but it is still home and I will still love it and see it is shown in the best light."

"You said that before," she noted. "That it's not what it was."

He nodded, but offered no more explanation this time than he had the last.

"Do you mean before the Dragons?" she pressed.

"I do."

She followed Powell's stare, looking out at the land. "What was better, then? How has it changed?"

Powell shook his head and chuckled. "The Dragons changed a lot, overseen directly by the King." Again, unlike Ari, there was no bite at the mention of their oppressors. "Not much was better in my lifetime. We've been on this suicidal path for hundreds of years. If they hadn't come when they did, Loom would be in a difficult spot now."

"What do you mean?" Florence couldn't comprehend what the man before her was saying. There was no path of logic that let her get to his point until he spelled it out.

"The Dragons, Florence. They saved Loom."

# 27
## CVAREH

THE BLOOD SHONE LIKE LIQUID METAL, CAKED UPON HER SKIN. IT PICKED UP THE sunlight like some horrible truth that his mind, in all its efforts, could not fathom. Arianna had killed yet another of the Dono's Master Riders. That should be the fact his mind circled around relentlessly.

But it wasn't.

He stared at where her flesh had been punctured by Lossom's claws. Gold streamed from the wound, mingled with the drippings of the heart she held up in victory. But it was clear enough with every pulse of her heart, clear as Lady Lei's springs and rivers. For the first time, it was as if he was seeing the real woman behind the name.

"She actually did it," Cain said in awe from Cvareh's left.

"This court just got interesting." Petra clapped her hands in appreciation from between them. His sister turned to him, summoning Cvareh from his thoughts. "You should go to the new Soh. She did stand for you, after all."

Cvareh's gaze swung to Arianna, but her back was to him. The woman had her eyes locked on Yveun Dono's. If she wasn't careful, she was going to challenge the King himself.

He moved, jumping down the short distance to the pit. Arianna tuned sharply, but relaxed visibly at the sight of him. Men and women shouted and cheered. Challenges flew above their heads, the Court whipping into a blood frenzy at the upset.

Cvareh's eyes rose from her forearm to meet hers. "Come." He held out a hand and she hesitated, the potent dissonance of the emotions in his magic giving her pause. But he had no hope of reining it in, not until he had explanations. "Come, Ari Xin'Anh Soh."

She finally obliged, and took his hand.

Sweat glistened off her, even through the illusion. A perfect crafting, he realized, because she was already so close to a Dragon. She was stockier than most Dragon females, but she had the height and the speed of one of his kind. She had the eyes and the claws. The ears—if she ever removed the metal caps. She was more Dragon than he had ever given her credit for, than maybe she had ever realized.

And that fact was surprisingly disappointing. It was like everything that made her shine was losing its spark. The picture he had painted in his mind of her was losing all its complementary colors at the idea that there was something so important about her that she had knowingly kept from him. He hated his distance from her, and grew weary of the feeling of her keeping him at arm's length.

They walked out of the light and into the dim of a hall, only to be greeted by other victors and the bold applause of servants. Arianna kept her eyes forward, oblivious to it all. The metal of the splint on her fingers pressed against his skin. Even with the surge of power from imbibing, holding the illusion must be tiresome…

"Where is an empty parlor?" he demanded.

"This way, Xin'Ryu." A servant stepped forward, eager to appease. The girl led them down a side hall and into a modest sitting area, a room of rest and recovery for the victors in the pit. It was perfumed with lavender, incense, and the ripe smell of fruit and cheese that had sat out for an hour too long.

Cvareh dismissed the girl with a curt nod, eager to close the door behind her. The world shut out, there were only the four walls that surrounded him and the woman who had become his enigma. There was no one to pass judgment and no one to bear witness beyond themselves. Ari had yet to face him, yet to confront the truth that she undoubtedly knew he'd seen.

He took a breath, readying himself to speak.

"You're welcome," she interrupted.

"Pardon?" he nearly stuttered in surprise.

"I assume you were about to say thank you." Arianna pulled off the splint from her fingers with a glance at the bolt engaged in the door.

The illusion fell. Her color faded to gray and white. Her tattoos were visible, inked back into existence by an invisible hand. The woman who should have been familiar seemed as false as the Dragon who had been in her place moments before. Her forearm betrayed no marks from the wound, yet Cvareh's eyes were still glued to the spot.

"What are you?" he whispered.

She couldn't have hidden her reaction if she tried. All his senses were honed on her. Cvareh practically heard the spark of tension through her muscles at the question.

"You know what I am." She squared against him as if the room had become a new pit, and they were about to do battle.

"Do I?" Cvareh curled his hands into fists so that he would not unsheathe his claws in frustration. If she wanted a sparring partner, he would rise to task. And this time, he would not stay his claws against her.

"Do you?"

"Don't be circular," he growled. "I saw it."

"Saw what?" She drew her height, coming nearly to eye level with him. "Me stand for you? Me fell your enemy? Me further prove that—" Arianna faltered. "That despite all the reasons I have to hate you, I clearly cannot bring myself to do so?"

The confession was virtually lost on him in his pursuit of the truth. She was trying to shift his focus. He wasn't going to let her, even if it teetered on the verge of words he so very dearly wanted to hear.

"I saw your arm. I saw the blood."

"What of it?"

"It was gold."

"Of course it would be, I had just killed a Dragon. Dragon blood is gold." She took the tone of one speaking to a small child.

Cvareh didn't even let the disrespect sway him from the truth he desired. "Dragon blood *is* gold. So why is yours?"

"You are confused."

"I am not." He didn't remember crossing the room. He didn't remember advancing on her. He didn't remember her taking steps backward, allowing him to do so.

But there they were. There he was, holding her in place with a power he didn't think he possessed. It filled the space behind his ribs, blowing out his chest. If he let it unfurl his sails large enough, it may just be enough to touch her.

"It was an illusion." She stood straighter, trying to not to lose her ground. But she'd long lost the advantage in the encounter. Cvareh wasn't going to give it back.

"That might work on others, Arianna—it likely has. But it will not work on me." He grabbed for the arm in question, holding it up. "I know your blood. I know it like my own. I know it because its very scent torments my waking hours almost as much as your mere visage."

"Then you should regain your head," she snarled, baring her teeth. "For you may be drunk on magic if you think my blood was gold, if you cannot tell the difference between an illusion and—"

His claws jutted forward. They dug deep into her flesh for the first time. They tore through her gray skin to expose the meat beneath. Honeysuckle and cedar filled the room, more potent on his nose than the finest wine he'd ever drunk.

And, sure enough, gold flowed between his fingers.

"You bastard." Arianna went to move but he was faster this time. He pushed her against the wall, grabbing for her other wrist.

"What are you?" he repeated, his voice deepening in resonance to an almost-growl. He had her pinned in place, but likely only due to shock. He'd healed too many bruises and seen her fight too many times to think she wasn't about to throw him off and flay him like livestock. "Arianna, tell me: what are you?" Cvareh's voice broke on the plea. He begged her. The scent of her blood was dizzying, and his entire body and mind desired her and her alone. "Close this gap between us. Let me help you as I want to."

"And what do you want?" She curled her lips.

"I don't know, not truly." He used her breath as fuel for his words, tasting her. "All I know is that I want you."

The snarl fell from her mouth and Arianna searched his face with her brilliantly lilac eyes. He had never held his breath with such anticipation of a woman's judgment—of anyone's judgment. But she held all he was in that moment. She formed his future with her tongue and lips and she was going to destroy him if what spilled from them wasn't everything he needed—not wanted, *needed*—to be for her.

"How do you want me?" she raised her chin slightly, the woman was powerful even while prone.

"Ari…" He was losing momentum. He was losing his footing. The tides were shifting under him, pulling him deeper into her, and she had yet to show any inclination to save him from the swirling depths.

He would drown in her, if only she would let him.

"Tell me, Cvareh. Tell me and I will tell you."

It was a deal too good to be true.

Cvareh leaned forward, slowly. Slow enough that she could fight back. That she could resist. That she had ample time to utter a word of protest. His hands didn't restrain her; instead they caressed her ashen skin like he would the finest of silks in Napole. His fingertips sought out the calluses on the pads of her hands. All his lust, all the lust in the world, would be nothing if she didn't burn for him in return.

His nose brushed along her jawline. Slowly. Tracing the strong curve to her ear. She smelled of dust, sweat, the remnants of Rok blood, sun, and his most favorite scent of all: the sultry notes of honeysuckle. It was a perfume sweeter than any he'd ever been exposed to. It was all he wanted to inhale.

"I want you for my lover, for my mate. I want to lay you down and take you to the pinnacles of delight. I want you… even while not knowing if you could ever grant me your favor." Mentions of her former lover echoed in his mind. Cvareh didn't actually know if Arianna even took a liking to men. He acted on hope, and her lack of refusal—physical or verbal.

"Will you want me still after I kill your King?"

He chuckled darkly. "I will want you all the more for it."

"Will you want me if I refuse your sister?"

That demanded consideration. But desire and love and forever were all separate mistresses. And right now, all three were courting him as one combined. "I will want you even then." His teeth graced the soft flesh of her neck as he spoke.

"Will you want me, even knowing I am a Perfect Chimera?"

The heat in his veins cooled by a small enough margin that he could straighten and look her in the eye, attempting to root out any forced boldness in the claim.

There was none.

The gold blood. Bones strong as steel, as strong as a Dragon's. Her height. Her muscular structure. It made too much sense to be a lie. She had developed and grown with the strength of Dragon blood coursing through her veins.

"Nothing, Arianna. Nothing in your world or mine, or the next, would make me want you less."

She grinned, the flat line of her Fenthri teeth showing. "You're a fool, Cvareh."

"I am," he agreed with a grin of his own.

Cvareh closed the gap at last, and found her lips with his. His chest was flush against hers and his thigh pressed between her legs. He held her fingers with white knuckles, as if to hold in place the tension he was struggling to let out only a moment at a time, savored like sips of the most perfect wine, held on the tongue to embolden the flavor.

Her tongue probed his mouth, pressing into his canine. Blood wet his palate. She smothered a groan.

The sound shot straight through him, forcing his hips further into hers. Her magic, her essence, flooded him. The dam holding the tension between them shattered, and Cvareh grasped her hips, pushing her up further against the wall. Claws shredded against the bindings across her thighs and up into the cloth that covered her groin.

Twenty Gods above, restraint be damned. Cvareh would know all there was to know of her before the day was done. And if he was lucky, he would do it again, and again, and again.

# 28

## PETRA

"What has you so pleased?" Cain asked from her left. He'd been silent for hours, clearly mulling over something. Petra wondered if the obvious small talk would be enough to bring it forward, because her patience only stretched so far and he was already beginning to pull at it.

"The sun is warm, more Rok blood has been spilled than Xin, Yveun has remained mostly tucked out of sight, and my brother seems to have escaped the Court." She stretched her fingers, her claws digging into the chair. She'd only had to stand for two people so far, and while that would permit her to excuse herself from the remainder of the Court if she desired, Petra remained. After all the trouble it was to see the Court to daylight, she wasn't about to step away.

"He seems to have escaped for quite a while," Cain muttered.

Petra laughed. "Does his fondness for the woman bother you so?" Cvareh was certainly a gossip with all his visits to Napole's tea parlors, but she'd never taken Cain for such habits.

"Why doesn't it bother you, is the better question?" As if realizing his own boldness after the fact, Cain glanced around quickly, taking note of any who could've overheard. Lucky for him, the only other guests in the box were close Kin who Petra had no cause to worry over.

"Cvareh is loyal above all to House Xin. If someone is fond of him, then they must also be fond of his House. Their relationship is an advantage to us. Ends before ideals."

"Ends before ideals," Cain repeated.

"Have a little more heart in that," Petra cautioned.

"Forgive me, Oji. It is only, the notion of our Ryu with a… thing… like that woman." Conflict was apparent in both Cain's voice and expression. He believed in the motto of House Xin, but the matter bothered him to an immense degree—enough that it seemed to rattle his very core.

*Oh well. It doesn't matter what he thinks.* There were certain benefits to being Oji, and never having to explain herself was one. Cain would come to his senses sooner or later, or Petra would forcefully remove all conflict on the matter for him.

"Petra, her blood…"

"Was as it should be." Cain was too smart for his own good and had been around the woman for too long. Petra needed to stop this speculation where it was. "It is none of your concern."

"You must have seen it, smelled it. There was something *off* about that illusion. I don't think—"

"I do not need you to think," Petra interrupted abruptly. "I need you to do as I say for the good of Xin."

"That is what I am concerned for, Oji."

"Cain, that is what *I* am concerned for. If you wish to be so concerned for it, then you wish to be the Oji." Petra turned to him, baring her teeth. "Would you like to step into the pit?"

"Never." Cain lowered his eyes and face, submissive.

"Good."

The duel before them finished and a long stretch passed before any challengers shouted forward. It had been an aggressive first day, but they were all becoming overwhelmed with bloodsport. Half the stands had already retired and even the Rok versus Rok duels held less joy for her.

"There is someone I need to see," she announced upon arriving at a decision in her head. "Cain, stand for someone if they're of particular import."

"Understood, Oji." His eyes betrayed his curiosity, but his tone and body language were obedient. She hoped he had learned his lesson sufficiently.

Petra descended into the busy halls and walks of the amphitheater. With most of the stands emptying, many a Dragon worked their way to the town below. Petra did not blend in. The masses parted for her with small bows. Members of House Xin delighted in their genuflections. Tam were pleased to keep the balance, respecting the Oji of another House.

House Rok stepped to the back of the lines that formed on either side of her. They gave nothing more than the obligatory bow of their heads, regarding her with shadowed eyes and mouths pressed into thin lines. Their subservience and respect was drawn from them with force.

The Court had only served to make things worse between the Houses, she decided. The bloodshed had singed their nostrils and reminded them that Nova was not one Dragon family. They were factions, divided and vying for the circumstances that would give them the most power. What was "best for Nova" was defined entirely by what was best for any one individual House.

Petra turned, disappearing through a curtained hall and onto a shaded balcony. The sticky scent of fruit that had been baking in the sun all day upon silver platters created a masking perfume to the carnage that happened in the pit. Petra's eyes fell upon two lounging couples—luckily Xin and Tam.

"Out with you," she commanded. "I require this space."

The Dragons exchanged a look. She could sense their displeasure at the prospect of being uprooted. But they obliged her, every last one.

Petra turned to the slave who stood in the corner by the table, a scrawny little Tam with the symbol of Xin emblazoned upon her cheek. Petra had made sure that all the slaves and low servants were wine- or forest-skinned Dragons. She wanted Tam and Rok Dragons to look upon the men and women who had left their Houses and now wore Xin's mark forever. She wanted to test the slaves' loyalty. She wanted all to see Dragons that were previously Rok and Xin now under her claws, and serving her as the picture of obedience.

"Bring me Finnyr Xin'Kin To," Petra ordered. "You will find him with the Dono."

The servant nodded, departing in haste. Petra walked over to the un-railed edge of the balcony. The sun was starting to dip low in the sky. If Court hadn't been formally ended, it would be soon.

The Crimson Court was always between dawn and sunset. The priests taught that Lady Luc, the Light-herald, was born each morning by the hand of Lord Rok. Each night, she was slain by Lord Xin, to make room for his brother, Lord Pak the Dark-wielder, to overtake the sky. Lord Rok fought against Lord Pak until the dawn… when the cycle repeated.

House Rok held the Crimson Court during the hours of their patron's Lady. Long ago, when it was the Cobalt Court, duels were held at night. Petra tensed her claws, relaxed them. Her mind filled with the fantasy of midnight blue Dragons swirling through the pit like wraiths made from shadow and death, illuminated by the moon, and fighting for House and glory.

"You summoned me."

Petra turned, her thoughts pushed back into the far recesses of her most delightful fantasies. Finnyr stood just inside the still-swaying curtain. Petra tried to remember the last time she'd seen her brother as she assessed him.

He was still small; his time at House Rok had put no might on his bones. It was further affirmation that nothing about Rok or Lysip was inherently mighty. Petra had narrower hips and shoulders than her brother, but her muscle held twice the raw power and her magic was overwhelming in comparison.

Finnyr, her pale-skinned brother with his tarnished hair. The child of House Xin that should never have been born.

"Come, Finnyr." She smiled, displaying her canines, and motioned for the spot next to her. "It has been some time since we last spoke face to face."

"It has." He obeyed, standing in the spot she selected for him.

"You appear to be well. Has House Rok treated you properly?"

He snorted. "As well as can be expected from House Rok."

That was an acceptable answer. "And the Dono?"

"He gives me no cause for complaint."

"Unfortunately," Petra lamented. She would always stand with her House first, but there would be something quite convenient about Yveun abusing her brother, giving her enough cause to challenge the Dono outright.

"He has never harvested any of my parts."

Petra folded her hands in front of her abdomen to keep her claws from unsheathing. Finnyr was familiar enough with the motion that he visibly tensed, realizing what he'd done. Petra took a half step away from the ledge, toward Finnyr's back.

"Brother, who is the Xin'Oji?"

"You are."

"And what House do you belong to?"

"House Xin."

"Therefore, what must you never do?"

Finnyr sighed heavily. "Petra, I was not questioning your decision, I was merely stating—"

Petra's arm shot out without even half a thought behind it. Her claws extended beyond her fingertips like magic daggers. They hovered at the edge of his throat.

"Finnyr, your very existence happens at my allowance," she growled. "You are not to think, you are not to hesitate. It was these traits by which you lost your place as the rightful heir to House Xin. Have some shame and work to make yourself useful."

She wanted to love him. She wanted to embrace her brother as a fellow warrior. If he had been strong, the responsibility of Xin would've never fallen to her. Not that she'd minded, of course. But he was an embarrassment of a brother and had been the shame of their mother and father. His weakness continued to be a blemish on the opinion of their House from the rest of Nova. Unlike Cvareh, it was not a calculated play. Finnyr was truly inept.

Fear colored his magic, even if he didn't let it show on his face. Petra kept her claws at his throat.

"Now, tell me of the Dono." Anger singed the edges of her consciousness.

"I know nothing more than I've told you before."

"You didn't know of the new Master Rider?" Petra scowled.

"I did, but—"

"You did not think to inform me?"

"I did not think it was of note." Finnyr held up his hands, showing that his claws were still not out despite Petra's being at his throat. "You must have assumed, with Leona's death, that the Dono would find a new Master Rider. And with all the other Dragons that perished hunting Cvareh on Loom, the Dono didn't have many choices. Lossom was no one of importance, and a Dragon without much experience."

Petra took her time reasoning through this. The logic stood. If she *had* committed a moment's thought to it, she likely could've reached the same conclusion herself. She eased her hand away from Finnyr's throat.

"Now, sister, *you* did not tell *me* you had such a fierce fighter you were training up within House Xin." Finnyr spoke lightly, as though she hadn't just threatened his life. All was forgiven to the Oji of the House when the Oji had only acted in the best interest of the Dragons whom she sought to protect.

"I prefer to keep many surprises." Petra would not give Finnyr the knowledge of Arianna. She, Cvareh and apparently Cain had managed to keep the truth of her to themselves, and she would see it remained so.

"How many others do you train?"

"Enough to see this Crimson Court to its bloated conclusion."

"Enough to fight against House Rok?"

Petra scowled at the horizon. "No."

Far out there was the Isle of Lysip, the largest island on Nova and the most overrun with fighters. Floating between them was the Isle of Gwenri, home of Tam. And another House's worth of Dragons who would fight for the sake of keeping the status quo.

"Such numbers will never be found on Nova."

"On Nova?" Finnyr knew her too well. He knew where the important parts of her phrasing lay.

"Tell me more about the Dono."

"There is not much to say."

*Useless.* "You live in his home. You eat his food. You mingle with his other To and you gossip in Lysip's tea parlors. There must be more to say."

"The Dono is his own Oji as well. He keeps people at claw's length and only tells them of his plans and movements when he deems it essential for them to know."

Petra stared down Finnyr from the corners of her eyes. "You have done well enough making yourself so small that things are said in your presence without concern. Learning of why there was always a Rider stationed at that records room has paid well in dividends."

Finnyr remained silent.

"You must have heard something else of use to our House."

"I did hear that Yveun went beneath Lysip not more than a month before the Court."

"*Beneath?*" she emphasized for clarity. "Why would Yveun lower himself to such measures?"

"I don't know."

Petra cursed. "Find out."

"It would be easier if he trusted me."

"Then go back and earn his trust."

"I am House Xin, I will never earn his trust." Finnyr sighed heavily. "Unless..."

"Unless?"

"You give me something I could use as a bartering chip to do it." Finnyr seemed determined to toe dangerous lines. She ground her teeth together, reminding herself not to rip out his throat. "Give me something small, something that changes nothing. I could spin it into a lie, even, but the best lie has a grain of truth. Tell me how you are training Dragons like this Ari—for he now knows you have the means for warriors such as her. Tell me of your work on the refineries; are you putting gold aside for Xin? You must be; Yveun would assume this anyway, my saying so would pose no extra risk. Or Cvareh's journey to Loom. Yveun seeks our brother's blood already, him knowing how his Riders were killed would not satiate that lust for violence. And he would certainly not share the truth, as the whole affair is a source of shame considering how many Riders he lost."

"No," Petra spoke quietly, stopping him before he could think of any more useless ideas. "Your words are near treason, Finnyr. You will not bargain our truths for his favor. That makes us exactly what he wants House Xin to be: loyal at all costs. If you must tell him anything, fabricate something. Tell him whatever you please."

"He will know if I am lying. He'll see it lacks no substance!"

"Than become a better liar."

"Petra, I cannot help you if you will not let me in!" A familiar hurt colored Finnyr's voice. "I cannot be loyal to House Xin if I do not know what House Xin needs."

"House Xin needs information on Rok. House Xin needs you to relay information pertinent to our success."

"And I—"

"I have spoken." Petra cut him short. She'd had enough of this tantrum. "Go back to the Dono's temporary estate and come back to me tomorrow with something tangible. Have some self-respect as a Xin'Kin and make use of yourself to our House."

"The Dono has told me that I would stay in the Xin Manor during the Court."

"The Dono does not decide who sleeps in my halls, and he would do well to remember it." Furthermore, Petra could not stand to look at Finnyr for a second longer. Not after this slew of disappointments. If he returned to the manor, she might kill him before the night was over, just so the mere knowledge of his ineptitude couldn't shame her further.

"Petra—"

"I have spoken!" Her teeth clicked together as she slammed them shut into a half snarl. "Now leave, Finnyr."

Finnyr looked at her as if considering disobedience. Lucky for them both, he retreated. Petra took a deep breath of the air that was wholly hers the moment he left.

She had somehow managed to avoid killing Finnyr for over three decades, but every time he was around her it was a test of her resolve on the matter. He was the embodiment of all that she loathed: entitlement without effort, weakness, proximity to House Rok. Petra would not kill a member of House Xin without good reason, especially not her elder brother.

But eventually, she knew it could not be helped if he continued as he was.

Petra stared into the setting sun, the gold fading in the wake of Lord Xin's hour growing nigh. Petra invited the strength of the Death-giver into her heart. So, too, would she someday watch the sun set on House Rok.

# 29
## FLORENCE

"How did the Dragons save Loom?" Florence was utterly baffled. All her life, she'd felt the negative effects of the Dragons' presence in her world.

"How old are you?" Powell asked.

"Sixteen. I'll be seventeen later this year."

"And you're still an initiate?" He raised his eyebrows, referring to her outlined mark. "You should have taken the second round of tests for Journeyman by now."

Florence stayed her tongue, choosing to look out the window.

"I see." She had no doubt Powell actually did. "Revolvers, then?"

She neither confirmed nor denied the fact.

Powell merely chuckled at her silence. "Come with me, Flor."

Florence followed the Harvester away from the outer ring of windows and into a narrow hall lit by biophosphorous. She took note of the same lanterns she had seen in the tunnels below. "Does Faroe have no generators?"

The man glanced at the lanterns. "There isn't much room for anything unnecessary here. Generators take up precious space that could be otherwise dedicated to the essentials."

"I see," she mumbled as they pressed onward and upward.

The stairs wound straight up into an open second floor. Large tables made a ring by each of the windows. Men and women, all bearing a sickle on their cheeks, walked between them, stopping at smaller tables to check things and make notes along the way. Chimera sat in an innermost ring of chairs, their brightly colored ears betraying their black blood.

"This is where we plan new mines," Powell explained. "We have a bird's eye view of the immediate area. Each of the other cities in Ter.1 has towers of their own that function for the same or similar purposes. To the north, it's mostly plotting farmland. On the coastlines, they serve as lighthouses for the sailors as well."

He led her over to one of the tables that sat flush against a window, strategically picking one with the least amount of activity.

"On the maps we mark the depth and location of existing mines, as well as what they're producing."

The map was covered with marks, crossed out and marked again and again. Lines in different colored chalk wound around and between them. Dust from past coloring hazed the paper.

"The chalk is for veins and pockets of minerals, which we then—" He directed Florence to the inner table that sat opposite. "Mark and note how much is harvested. These numbers are compared against historic numbers and reports from the guilds to estimate how much needs to be pulled from the earth."

He motioned toward the Chimera sitting in the middle, engaged in conversations seemingly with their palms, fingertips touching their ears, or with the other Harvesters who walked around the room.

"Then the reports go out to the mines, as well as to another group of Chimera upstairs who then communicate with the Ravens to see the resources are ultimately moved to where they need to go."

"How did the communication happen before magic?" Florence couldn't help but wonder.

"Much more slowly," Powell admitted. "Letters delivered by couriers. Though our overall perception on mining was different then."

"It's fascinating," she admitted. "But I fail to see how this relates to the Dragons saving Loom?" Saying the words singed her tongue; her body physically rejected the notion.

"Look here again." He tapped the papers he'd carefully spread out on the table. "This is one mine and this column is the overall output for all minerals over time."

Her eyes skimmed the years and the numbers. It went back over six decades, a virtual eternity. The figures became more reliable with time, but it wasn't until the year the Dragon King became Loom's sovereign that all the rows were consistently filled in. Despite this, Florence could see the trend clearly.

"It was a lot more before the Dragons."

"It was," Powell agreed, as if she'd suddenly understood. Florence gave him a look that said she didn't. "For generations, the mines sprawled as if the earth went on forever and the minerals we found would never run out of resources. When we found new pockets, we'd pursue. When we ran out, we dug deeper, and deeper, and deeper."

Florence was reminded of the cavernous chasms they'd crossed to reach Faroe.

"The Harvesters had produced the most addicting drug Loom had ever known: progress. We never questioned if we should, only if we could, and the idea spawned the rest of the guilds. We asked and asked, what would we find if we pushed just one peca further into the earth?"

"But because Loom had those resources, the Alchemists made medicine, the Rivets created engines, the Ravens laid track, the Revolvers built guns." She had yet to see the flaw in it.

"And all of these things enabled us to dig further and further. It was a self-feeding system, a chain linked by the need to produce."

"What's wrong with that?"

"What happens when it runs out?"

Florence looked back to the window, to the endless sprawl of mines. She tried to imagine what the land might have looked like before the Harvesters carved into it. "Can it run out?"

"Some mines have already been abandoned as barren."

"Then what?"

"Then we blast and dig until we find a new place to blast and dig farther."

"So the problem is solved."

Powell chuckled. "What happens when there are no more places to blast and dig?"

"There will always be…"

"This world is *finite*, Florence." He motioned to the records and tables. "What you see before you is all we have. The Dragons saved us from ourselves. Magic vastly reduced the consumption of resources. The Ravens now make trains that run purely on it."

"Magic travel, magic moving anything, still requires gold," she pointed out.

"Yes, but the steel only needs to be tempered into gold once. Then it can be used for an eternity," he countered. "The Dragons' existence helped, but the King's oversight of our resources was what pushed the Harvesters' Guild to not just take from the world, but truly try to understand it. We began to pay attention to mines drying up. How fast we'd run out of this or that and how much deeper or farther we'd have to dig to find more. How these scars we've made upon our earth will never heal."

"The Dragon King made new scars." Florence scowled.

"You're bitter about the tests."

"Are you sure you're not a Master?" She checked his cheek for a circle. His mannerisms reminded her far too much of a certain Rivet Master she knew.

"Not yet. My name sits with the Vicar Harvester right now on recommendation, however. It's why I returned to the guild from Ter.4.5."

"Oh…" Florence was immediately humbled. That was one thing the Dragon King had not changed. Mastership could not be tested; it was earned in the eyes of peers. Only a Master could award another Master's circle, and the approval to do so came directly from the Vicar.

"In any event," he said, "when the Dragons introduced the idea of families..." The concept made Powell as uncomfortable as every other Fenthri she'd ever met. "Which, I grant you, is an odd one. Free and unlimited access to reproduction and fertility chemicals widened our talent pools. But we could not sustain that demand on our resources."

"So the pools needed to be culled." She was one such person who was not talented enough to earn her life.

"They do." There was an appropriately sympathetic note to his tone. "The first culling happens before the children grow enough to be any real drain. The second ensures a known population. We know exactly how many people we need to supply at all the guilds. Exactly how much food to produce, how many resources to dig up."

Florence was silent. She was trying to see if she could reconcile herself to a system that would have her killed for not being a good enough Raven—despite being a damn good Revolver. But under the same logic, the Revolvers had their own quota. She didn't have a place there either.

It made her want to scream.

She settled on a scowl instead.

"I understand, I believe, your turmoil on the matter." Powell motioned to the windows and room. "But I want you to comprehend the logic woven behind the madness."

"People should still be able to choose their guild. A finite pool, perhaps, but… The Ter.0 system of learning was better. Divide the finite pools from there. Let all test for all and then separate. It should—"

He rested his palm on her shoulder, squeezing it lightly. "I don't disagree with you." The words were a balm to the fervor that had been brewing in her gut. "There are better ways to execute this system. There are alternatives that would have been more in line with our culture, our way of life. Something the Dragons have yet to fully understand."

At least he admitted that much.

"But we were a runaway train, headed for a half-finished bridge. In such a situation, you do not worry foremost about what wrong turn you took to get there. You reach for the brake and pull with all your might. *Then* you find the right way. But if we didn't reach for that brake, Florence, and make the sacrifices we made, we would have run ourselves off that proverbial ledge and into extinction."

She wanted to point out that she didn't appreciate a very Raven analogy, because he was no doubt assuming it would resonate with her for the mark on her cheek. But Florence held her tongue. She felt bitter and suddenly very, deeply tired.

"This is a lot," she confessed with a mumble.

"We may talk on it more, if you're interested in learning."

Florence considered it for a long moment. She'd learned from the Ravens, the Revolvers, and a Rivet. She'd always been so focused on completely transforming herself from one thing into another, it wasn't until the endwig attack and the weeks that followed on the train that she'd discovered the true strength of combining all parts. Why not see what a Harvester could teach her? Who knew when it would come in handy?

"I am."

"Very well." Powell motioned for the stairs where they'd entered. "Let me show you to a guest room, for now. I am tired from the train and ready to wash and rest."

"Thank you." She hoped he interpreted her gratitude on the multiple levels it was intended.

"You are quite welcome." He seemed to. "Rest up. Tomorrow, I will take you to the organ harvesting rooms."

# 30

## ARIANNA

THE SMELL OF WOODSMOKE WAS ETCHED UPON HER SKIN WITH HIS TONGUE AND teeth. He drew long, delightfully painful lines with his canines. He followed with his mouth, his tongue, his tender kisses and delicate ministrations upon them while they healed.

Again and again, he repeated. They were a room on fire, cedar on smoke. Pain and pleasure made comfortable bedmates, etching his caress upon the steel of her memory with an endless amount of determination.

She wanted him. They had crossed every line and traversed every seemingly impenetrable barrier to arrive with him between her legs. But she yearned for every moment. She yearned for his firm grip on her hipbone, his mouth on her shoulder, his attentions bordering on the meticulous.

There was a broken-ness to their passion, a ritual sacrifice of everything they were for something they could be. Let them dive into the acidic fatalism that would forever be splashed upon their memories. They were going to dissolve into each other until there was nothing left.

She arched off the bed, his hand smoothing across her ribs and onto her back, holding her in place, his mouth upon her breast. She had forgotten the feeling of being vulnerable. Control had fought against its tether, cutting into her palms, and now she let the beast go free.

Arianna's claws trailed up his arms and shoulders, into his blood-orange hair. She watched how it splayed across her chest when she held him upon her.

"You have magic here," he mumbled into her bare stomach. His breaths ran ragged laps around her navel.

"I do." She was already stripped bare before him. There was little else to hide now.

"Where else?" He propped himself over her.

Arianna had seen his bare chest dozens of times; the Dragons weren't exactly fond of clothing. But it looked different now. Hovering just far enough for her nipples to brush his skin, it seemed to take on a different shade, a more appealing curve.

"You know the other places." Arianna slid her palms to the chest she had just been admiring. "Though, I wouldn't mind lungs…"

"You wouldn't." He pressed his mouth upon her.

Arianna sucked his tongue between her teeth, biting hard. Blood poured into her throat and she sucked hungrily, magic exploding once more. She was well and truly drunk off the man—the taste, the feeling. It was better every time and worse each passing second after it faded. She wondered what it would be like to give into every desire and lie here with him until the end of days.

Arianna smiled faintly into his mouth. *What an idealistic notion.* The things the man had done to her…

A growl rose from the back of his throat, which she also eagerly consumed. Arianna flipped them on the small cot, mounting him like one of their flying birds. His erection pressed against her and she, shamelessly, ground herself upon it.

"You witch," he groaned when she finally returned his lips to him.

"Wraith, actually." Arianna pressed forward, kissing up along his ear to the point. "And don't doubt me. There is very little I wouldn't do—especially to you."

He pressed his thumbs into her thighs, holding her in place, pushing her down. Arianna met his demands willingly. It was a war for dominance that was punctuated by winning and losing battles of submission. They took turns allowing the other to be the victor and alternated the joys and struggles of relinquishing control.

She felt the waver in his magic, the fear taking over again. He was thinking too much. The man who seemed to care for nothing but beauty and ease was giving in to the dangers of contemplating all they were and what they were doing. She appreciated the irony of wanting to tell him to let go, to let them have the moment they'd encased themselves in.

Arianna kissed him lightly, absorbing the emotion. She forfeited words for action. She slid onto him and felt that stretching, pressing, pushing, filling sensation once more.

It was for the best. He should be afraid of her—of them. The idea of him and her becoming a "they" would be the worst thing that could happen to either of them. She would consume him. She would use him for her own delight. But if it ever suited her, she would break him. She would cast him from the pinnacles of pleasure upon the cold and lonely world below.

It made her afraid of herself.

Arianna had never let herself go so far. Even with Eva, an understanding and logic had pulsed between them. They had begun as partners, scientific equals, and evolved into something more. Arianna had yearned for the woman. She had embraced the throes of passion with her now-dead love.

She had admired the woman's tenacity and determination. Similar things attracted her to Cvareh, but they stemmed from different sources. There was no logic to Cvareh. Man, woman—Dragon or Fenthri—he was not someone she should find herself with. Arianna snarled, driving her hips harder, faster, as if she could force out the conflict. She hated him. She wanted him. Shades of gray, rainbows of color—they blurred and smeared into gold.

Cvareh pulled her down and she acquiesced. She let him have her mouth, her tit, her shoulder. She heaved her moans into the pillows like curses, or prayers.

Nothing made sense, and she would have him until it did.

They peeled apart an hour, or a minute, later. Time no longer mattered. She would burn it on the passion pyre they'd been immolated upon all afternoon. With it burned her principles and her self-respect. She had coupled with a Dragon as if her life depended on it. But luckily, she had exhausted her ability to care alongside every other muscle in her body.

The ceiling came into focus; it had never been more fascinating. It was the only thing safe to look at. The room was a mess from their tumbling. Things had been broken, furniture had been moved and scratched. Blankets made mountains on the floor, the warmth of their body heat more than enough.

Cvareh didn't move either. Arianna closed her eyes. Already the feeling was returning, the want to place her mouth on his again. It had been *so long* since she had last touched and been touched—since she had even wanted to be touched by anyone. She had clearly yet to find satiation.

"Why?" Cvareh's voice was still deep and thick. It had a purr to it like a well-oiled engine that set her hand to moving, her knuckles brushing against where they'd fallen on his thigh.

"Why what?"

"Why me?"

Arianna laughed. Her voice was hoarse and raspy. "Really? *That's* your question?"

"I have more."

"As do I."

The pillow shifted next to her and Arianna turned toward the sound, meeting his eyes. The understanding that had always been there had deepened. It shone brighter, as if she could see his very magic in the air around him.

"So, why?"

"I don't know," she confessed to both of them.

"You don't know? Something the infallible Arianna doesn't know?"

"I will bite off your tongue. Don't think this changes anything."

"This changes everything." Cvareh sat. "What we are was not what we were."

She watched the muscles in his back stretch. His skin had a certain pallor in the dim candlelight. Flickering shadows danced in lines and muscular curves. Lean and strong. Strong enough to hold her up. Strong enough to support her if she chose to let him shoulder some of her burdens.

"Nothing has changed," her mouth insisted. She spoke lies, to herself, to him, to everything they were. Her body may have been ready, long overdue even, for a lover… but her heart. Her heart was another matter entirely. "We are two people merely filling needs."

He placed a hand between her arm and side, leaning toward her. His fingers brushed the line of her jaw but the touch was different than before, without haste. And yet it still possessed fire. They had not been a flash in the pan. Something burned deeper, more determined. A small flame, but a white hot and relentless one.

"You don't believe that."

"I do."

Cvareh smiled knowingly. She rose upward and kissed the expression. He'd given her no choice. There was only one way to expunge that look from between his cheeks. Still, it persisted when she pulled away.

She kissed him again. She kissed him harder. He tasted suddenly of longing and salt tears her eyes had stopped spilling years ago.

"I know you, now," he muttered upon her. "I know you, Arianna."

Resistance was futile. The man could think what he would; the more she objected, the more he persisted, the more she slid down into him like quicksand. She could hardly breathe if the air wasn't sweetened with the tang of his scent.

"I want to show you something."

"What?" She let his hands tangle in her hair, a mess from the fight and their sex.

"It's not on Ruana, so we'll have to travel."

"Where?" The idea of venturing into the unknown with him was not as frightening as it should've been.

His fingers coaxed out the knots he'd made. "Do you trust me enough to let me not tell you?"

She hated him for the question. She hated him more for the answer that already leaped from her tongue. "Yes." Arianna pressed her eyes closed. How had she arrived at that answer? It was like adding two and two together and getting yellow. "And I will kill you for it."

"I will not give you a reason to." Cvareh stepped away, hunting for his clothes. He made no effort to smooth them, only enough to patch them back together from where she'd torn at them. His shoulder pieces were hopelessly lost. Fortunately, Dragons wouldn't think twice about him walking around in next to nothing.

Arianna followed without instruction, picking through what was salvageable. She was still too Fenthri to stomach the notion of walking in nothing, even with her illusion. Still, the most important piece was the splint that helped her hold her illusion in place.

"Head upward, and tell me if you have trouble finding the departure platform. I'll saddle the boco." His palm fell on her hip, and his magic surged at the touch. It wrapped her up in a familiar embrace, already intertwined before his lips fell on her ear.

"Arhoncedov," he breathed.

It was a sound just for her and it sparked off his tongue with sheer power. He'd cast forth a tether, and now it fell on her to take it.

Arianna took a half step closer, her own arm wrapping around him. Cheek to cheek, she leaned for his ear. It had been a long time since she'd last established a whisper link. The silence that had filled her mind upon Eva's death should have been enough discouragement to ever do it again. She'd vowed not to.

"Ranhoftantu," she replied.

Magic pulled taught with a twang. Another line holding them together under tension. A step closer, when she should've taken a step further away. A yes that should've been a no. And a want indulged before a thought could be applied.

They were drunk on each other still. Their magic was still fresh, and new, and desired. But eventually, they would sober. They would wash away the sweat of sex and the heat of each other's skin. When the time came, what would they find?

# 31
# FLORENCE

Nora and Derek were set up across the hall from her. Florence heard them entering in a haze, but sleep's hold was too strong on her to even cast off her covers. She would ask them in the morning how their meeting with the Vicar had gone.

But when morning came, a knock awoke her, and she found neither was waiting.

Powell stood on the other side of the door in the same, simple, pocketed worker's pants he'd worn the whole journey. Well, judging from the lack of smell and stain they weren't the *exact* same trousers. They were belted, and a loose cotton shirt was tucked into them, sleeves rolled up to the elbows.

"I woke you." His observation seemed mildly apologetic.

"I might have slept for the next two days if you hadn't." She rubbed her eyes with a yawn. He had been right, there was no substitute for sleeping in a proper bed.

"Then I'm glad I woke you, seeing as I don't know when you're leaving and there's much I'd like to show you before then."

"Well, I don't seem to have much else to do." It was nice to feel welcomed by someone, to have them engaged in her wellbeing. Nora, Derek, and the rest of the Alchemists' Guild were poor substitutes in that regard. Since Ari left, Florence had no one to look after her other than herself. "Are you sure you have the time?"

"I will until I won't. I'm at the leisure of the guild's Masters and Vicar. Whenever they reach their decision, I'll find out if I have something to do, or if I'm returning home with my mark as it is," he explained. "Here."

Florence accepted the bundle of clothes he offered. She'd brought her own, but they were still soiled from travel and the prospect of something clean was incredibly appealing. She wondered if he had paid that much attention to her needs or if this was standard hospitality for the Harvesters.

"You can wear what you want, but I thought after the organ halls we may head into the mines, so you might want to wear something you don't mind potentially getting soiled or ripped."

"These days, all my clothes can potentially get soiled." Powell didn't know the half of what she'd been through. The days of her pristine vests, matching top hats, and perfect stitching were gone. Her vests were wrinkled, her top hats lost or left behind while she was on the run, and the seaming at the elbows of every one of her shirts had been torn. "But, thank you. It's nice to have something clean."

Washed and dressed, Florence followed her new friend once more into the Harvesters' Guild hall. Powell was indeed known, as she waited once or twice for him to have short conversations with Journeymen and Initiates. There was an easy comfort about him as he spoke and answered questions. That was what had made him easy to speak to on the train and what, effectively, had forged their unconventional relationship.

Florence had always set Ari on a pedestal in terms of what it meant to be a Master. Her breadth of wisdom. Her intense respect of knowledge. Her reverence for the halls of education that elevated guilds and classrooms from mere institutions to temples of learning.

Powell embodied these things, but there was a different sort of openness to his mannerisms. He worked to include Florence in all the conversations, despite her lack of experience in these areas. He treated knowledge as a delight, rather than a sacred right.

"Sorry for the delays." He leaned toward her so the people they had just bid farewell wouldn't hear.

"It's no problem. It's nice to be included in such a positive atmosphere."

"You were not before?" He posed the question delicately.

A tired smile curled her lips. "The Alchemists' Guild is... a very different place. It suits them. But there isn't much room for a Revolver there."

He made no comment on her reference to herself as something other than her marked guild. And Florence didn't feel the slightest bit of concern at the fact that she'd openly declared it. Powell was smart enough to figure it out—had already figured it out—and she didn't see the point in insulting their mutual intelligence by masquerading otherwise.

"I am forced to take your word for it. I've never been to the Alchemists, and I cannot imagine a place where there would not be room enough for someone as eager to learn as you." His smile was infectious. "Here we are."

Florence wished she could bottle his words and save them for the next time she was struggling in the Alchemists' Guild. Or with the Revolvers... Or in general.

"We worked closely with the Alchemists to develop our harvesting processes for Dragon organs." They walked through a series of narrow halls, washing their hands along the way and passing through antechambers. "We may not know how to heal a wound, or convert a Fenthri to Chimera… But when it comes to removing the organs themselves, we're just as skilled as any Alchemist you'll find."

Florence gave him an encouraging smile at the pride he so clearly felt in his guild. It was heartwarming to see. Powell led them through a door and onto a narrow, raised walk.

Florence's smile melted off her lips.

"This is one of the viewing areas we use to see how they're progressing. There's only so fast you can harvest organs. They re-grow, but you have to make sure they're healthy and strong before you remove them, or they won't work to make Chimera and they'll be weak reagents."

She walked over to one of the glass windows that tilted away from the catwalk, separating her from the honeycomb of rooms below. Florence stared, barely making sense of what she was seeing, let alone Powell's words. A chill swept through her.

Somehow she had let herself believe the organ harvesting pits would have mimicked her experience with Cvareh when she became a Chimera. She remembered the Dragon, willingly at her side, dutiful and pleased to give her his blood.

This was nothing like that.

Dragons, mostly shades of blue and green, some red, were strapped to tables, bound with steel and leather and held prone. Some screamed and thrashed. Others stared listlessly, as though their very souls had been harvested.

Gold blood seeped from open wounds, left to face the air without so much as a bandage. A man's stomach had been carved apart, the skin still peeled back and pinned carefully to keep his innards exposed as the organ slowly grew back. *They don't even want to have to cut back into him again*, Florence realized. The Harvesters couldn't be bothered to repeat their incisions, so they let him heal while vivisected, only to have the process repeated again, and again, and again.

Her palm fell on her own abdomen.

"How did they get here?" She realized she interrupted something that Powell was saying. But she hadn't even heard him over the ringing in her ears. The hall was silent, yet somehow the screams of the countless Dragons before her were so, so very loud.

"The Dragon King supplies them."

Florence took note of a mark on each of the Dragon's cheeks, all the ones that weren't red. A crown supported by a triangle like design. Was it the mark of an animal led to slaughter? What did that make them? What were the Fenthri to this Dragon King, who was willing to condemn his own to such a fate? Just so much livestock awaiting slaughter?

"How are they chosen?" she asked.

"I don't know."

"How do you not know?" Florence tore her eyes away and in the process swayed slightly. Her head spun. "How do you not know what these men and women have done to deserve this… this level of cruelty?"

"Florence, do not think of them as creatures with emotions or will." He placed his hands on her shoulders, trying to both stabilize and soothe her to no avail. "They are magic farms. Think of them as organs and parts. Their bodies just help keep them fresh."

"No." She stepped away, shaking her head. Her mind went to Cvareh, the sometimes comically clueless Dragon whom she had given her life as a Fenthri for to see across the world. The good man who had answered the call willingly to make the blood in her veins black and give her life anew. "They are not. They are just as you or me!"

Powell arched his eyebrows. "I would not expect Dragon sympathy from someone such as you."

"What?"

"A self-proclaimed Revolver, dedicated to tools of death and destruction. One who clearly fights against Dragon systems. Coming from the Alchemists' Guild… it's not a stretch to imagine why you and your friends are here. We've heard the rumors."

Florence glared at him. She hated the truth that was bleeding beneath her and she hated the truth that flew from his mouth. There was nothing but contrasts now in her heart and they were all being brought to a head.

"I don't have all the answers," she admitted, as much to herself as to him. "But this—" Florence motioned to the rooms below her, and the carvers who continued their work upon the helpless Dragons. "This is not right. This is no better than the mining practices you told me about yesterday."

"No, the mines when depleted will not replenish. So long as the Dragons are forced nutrition and not over-harvested, they can remain for decades—a century, even."

That only served to spark further outrage. "Four generations' worth of carnage forced on a single person to endure." Florence shook her head violently, as if she could rattle the images and truths out of her ears. "No, no. This isn't right." She pushed past Powell for the halls behind him.

"Florence—"

"This isn't right!" She wanted to hear no more, see no more. There was no justification. All reason and logic betrayed what sense of morals and heart she had clung to. She wanted to believe in the good in people, but what good was there in this?

Loom survived because of the Dragons, if Powell was to be believed. They curbed Loom's wasteful practices and lessened the tax on the earth. But a new tax emerged: blood. To make the gold that powered the world while the environment recovered, Dragons paid what Florence now saw was a terrible price.

The Dragon King may have been the catalyst for the Harvesters to uncover the problem of Loom's rampant over-production. But the solutions had damaged Loom's culture and ways of life, and required that he give his own people over to darkness and pain.

Florence may not have a neat solution, but she knew she had settled on one thing: She didn't see eye to eye with Ari. That much had become apparent. Ari wanted the past without question, the days of deregulation and progress burdened only by the gates of the mind. Florence knew now that she didn't want that, not after speaking with Powell. But her teacher remained her friend and ally in both heart and principle.

The door to Derek and Nora's room slammed as Florence stormed in without apology. The two were still slumbering, wrapped in bed. Startled awake, Florence sat herself at the foot of their bed, comfortable in both their presence and various states of undress. Her eyes only saw the Dragons, still bleeding.

"I have decided something," she announced before either could speak. "At all costs, we must see the Dragon King dead."

# 3²
## CVAREH

THE BOCOS WERE KEPT IN STABLES BELOW, WHERE SLAVES TACKED THEM AND brought them up on command. But he didn't want anyone but himself touching the seat in which Arianna would sit. He was doting upon a passion most tender and new. But love felt good, especially reciprocated love. Arianna had yet to say as much, but he'd felt it.

He had been with women before, never so intimately, just enough to cross exploratory lines. But that—*that* was what it felt like to mate. They sung the sweet chorus of passion in perfect harmony, a performance that could never be denied. He'd known hands on flesh before, but it was so vastly different when one had truly found the person he was to be with for the rest of his life.

Until she was ready, Cvareh would treat the blossom of their affections with delicacy. He would see it nurtured. He'd move forward, and wait until she removed one of his toes to let him know he'd crossed a line.

So long as she didn't, he would relish every new and crisp feeling. He would do all she allowed for her, to her. He would memorize every crease and curve of her body and do it again should he ever find his memory lacking—which would be often.

He knew the feeling would eventually dull. But for now it was as sharp as a freshly forged blade and, for the first time, it was a weapon he was willing to allow Arianna to use to carve out his heart.

"Cvareh'Ryu, you stink."

He stopped, his hands on the slightly longer saddle he'd been selecting. Cvareh's fingers tensed, but he kept his claws sheathed. He would not draw them on a friend. But that tone would only be forgiven for so long, and the timer was counting down.

"Cain'Da." Cvareh squared his hips and shoulders, the tacking of the boco forgotten. "Mind your tongue."

"You coupled with her." Cain scrunched his nose, marring the line of his scowl. "You reek of sex."

"Who I choose to lie with is none of your concern." Cvareh added a cautionary note to his words. "Watch your words, Cain. We may be friends, but I am still the Xin'Ryu."

"Then act like it." Cvareh had never seen this sort of boldness from Cain. "You are endangering not just our House and future, but all of Nova with this tryst."

"Cain—"

"Cvareh, I am coming to you as your friend."

It should have enraged Cvareh more, but he did give Cain some allowance. They had grown up together and Cain had always been a good man. He had good will to cash in as he saw fit. If this was how he wanted to do it, Cvareh would allow it.

"Speak your piece." Cvareh folded his arms with a small sigh. "But know permissions like this will not be given regularly."

"You know I love House Xin. You know I love Petra'Oji. You know you shall find no one more loyal than I."

Cvareh couldn't refute it so he didn't.

"Cvareh, there is something dangerous about that woman."

"I am aware of that much." A smirk lined his mouth. "I think most of Nova is aware after her display in the pit today."

"That is precisely why I am worried." Cain's scowl only deepened. "Her blood, Cvareh."

Dread was a sobering potion that took effect instantly, dulling the lust and delight that had been filling his mouth and veins all afternoon.

"She has too many organs for a Chimera. She doesn't smell of rot. She's strong, like us. And she—her blood, I don't think that was an illusion—"

"You speculate too much." Cvareh tried to dismiss Cain from hunting Arianna's scent. "She is strong, but that is all."

"It is more than that." Cain stepped forward and his voice dropped. Even though they were the only ones in the immediate vicinity, he looked as though the very walls and leather saddles would take offense to the whispered topic. "I have heard rumors from those who live on Lysip, rumors that the Riders were seeking you for something about a Perfect Chimera. Yveun has tried to keep them hush, but the quietest of whispers are often times the most true."

"You would believe Rok bastards over your own House?" Even if the rumors were true—and damn that they were—Cvareh was still taken aback by the idea.

"Are they lying?" Cain knew him too well. When Cvareh didn't immediately answer, he continued. "Cvareh, the Dono himself fears these monsters, these perfected killing machines. They would be mightier than us. We are born with our magic; they *steal* it. One creature who could possess all forms of magic, who would imbibe without shame as you know they do."

Just the word exploded the flavor of honeysuckle in Cvareh's mouth.

"If something scares Yveun'Dono, why would we not use that to our advantage?"

"Yveun is a monster, you will find no objection from me on the fact. And I wish to see him dead as much as any other Xin, perhaps more for my love of you and Petra. But I do not know if it is best to slay a monster using an even more fearsome beast. A beast we are welcoming into House Xin with little consideration for what doing so could truly mean." Cain cautioned, "What makes you think this new terror could be contained and controlled?"

Cvareh kept his answer to himself, but not well enough.

"Her fondness for you?" Cain snorted, outright laughter churning up through his stomach. "Cvareh, thinking something like *love* can contain a woman like that is akin to thinking you can funnel the winds in a particular direction with a cup of your hands."

"I know her." Cvareh felt an ugly emotion brew like storm clouds in his chest. He did not want to hate Cain. But he also did not want a woman, a Fenthri, to make him hate Cain on her behalf.

"As do I."

"You do not." Cvareh wouldn't hear it.

"How much time did I spend with her because 'you cannot trust yourself to be in her presence'?" Cain threw Cvareh's past words from when he arrived on Nova back at him. "You never said why, but clearly it's because you can't handle her for longer than a few days before you would force yourself on her."

Cvareh lunged. Cain side-stepped and Cvareh twisted to meet him. He kept his fists balled, claws contained. He wanted to pummel Cain, but he wouldn't make his fellow Xin bleed. Not yet at least.

His fist connected with Cain's face. The other man reeled. Claws jutted from sea foam hands. Cvareh pushed forward and slammed Cain against the tack wall, pressing him into the shelves and leathers, one hand on his wrist.

"Do not challenge me, Cain," Cvareh snarled, his mouth wide and teeth bared.

"If I do, will you fight me in the pit, Xin'Ryu?" Cain gnashed his teeth back at Cvareh as he spoke. "Or will you send your Chimera? Will you have a woman from the land below do your fighting?"

He wanted to peel Cain's skin off one strip at a time. He wanted to throw the man on the floor and cut down through muscle and sinew to bone. He would gnaw on his innards and feast on his heart. Cvareh had never bested Cain before in a fight, practice or otherwise. But he knew in that moment he could. Fighting for Arianna somehow made him more vicious than he'd ever been. It gave him a reason to be more dangerous than he'd ever thought possible. Dangerous enough to kill even a Xin. *For her.*

Cvareh threw Cain away. The man stumbled but spun, ready for a continued attack. None came.

"You have made a fool of yourself with this, Cain'Da. Abandon this folly, and return to the obliging man this House needs." Cvareh straightened.

"You know the depth of my loyalty to our House." Cain waited for Cvareh to challenge. He didn't. "Do you think I would question you or Petra if I didn't think it was in our best interest?"

His heart sang the truth of Cain's words. Despite his means, the man worked toward an end he truly believed was best for their House. Cvareh sighed heavily. The fact would keep him alive. "I will keep this from Petra for now, for our friendship. For she would flay you for your disobedience."

Cain had no objection. The man might think he could handle Cvareh in a row, but Petra was another force altogether. The only Dragon foolish enough to challenge the Xin'Oji was the Dono himself. They were titans among men and women.

*And they both fear Arianna.* Cvareh's mind betrayed him. He snarled at the echo of Cain's words twisting in his mind. Petra feared nothing. Petra only needed an ally.

"Return to the Xin Manor, and pray to Lord To for wisdom in this." Cvareh threw a saddle on the boco at random, tightening it for punctuation. "And pray to every Lord and Lady you have breath for that I do not reconsider letting Petra know of your misgivings."

A darkness lurked over Cain's features that Cvareh had never seen before, least of all directed at him. The man had been his friend, his brother, and he was determined to dig a chasm between them so wide that Cvareh could not jump across. Cain saw one possible future, a bleak place where Cvareh would be forced to choose between his House and the woman he had come to love. He gripped the boco's reins, leading it from the stable with a flutter of wings.

"Cvareh'Ryu," Cain called. Cvareh should have never stopped. He should have not allowed any more of Cain's poison words through his ears and into his mind. "That woman will be your undoing. If you wish to damn yourself with her, fine. But for the love of Xin, do not damn the rest of us by taking her into the House's bed, too."

Cvareh did not dignify the statement with a response.

# 33
## YVEUN

"She means to make a fool of you." Coletta nursed a glass of wine, reclining in a chaise.

"That much is apparent to anyone with eyes." Yveun continued to pace the room. It was large and open, with a gaping maw of a balcony and tall ceilings. It was more elegant than he wanted to admit and befitting of his station—which fed his anger further. Petra insulted him with one hand, while lauding him with the other. She toed the line finely enough that he could not challenge without seeming in the wrong to the masses.

"What is also apparent is that you are letting her." Coletta regarded him with eyes the same color as the drink she consumed. Eyes that stripped him bare. Eyes that judged him even more harshly than he judged himself.

"I have not—"

"You are the Dono." When Coletta wished to be heard, none would interrupt her. None would sway her. She was not a flashy weapon like most Dragons, and was all the more deadly for it. "You only do what you wish."

"You would not have had me sit in the place Petra prepared at the Court."

"I would not have had Petra organize the Court at all."

He loved and hated his mate all the more when she was right.

"You did not consult me before this whole affair and you took a half measure on the matter, Yveun," Coletta admonished. "You wanted to make a statement by holding the Court on Ruana. But you merely gave Petra the opportunity to show Nova what a Cobalt Court would look like. The only thing *Dono* about you today was the title servants called you as they fattened you on Xin food and drink while you sat out of sight and out of mind of the people."

His claws strained against his fingers from the tension he put them under. Still Coletta sat, and sipped, and spoke.

"You sent a half-trained 'Master Rider' into the fray, who was made into an even larger fool than you by an Anh." She straightened slightly. "I gave you Leona. I instructed you to nurse her in every way a man can. You had one of the greatest tools of our past forty years of work, and you wasted her."

"There is something deeper here." Yveun knew there must be. He would not let so much power slip through his hands otherwise. There was a variable he was still missing. "The Chimera on Loom—"

"You would blame your shortcomings on a Chimera." Coletta stood, walking to the balcony. "That is the only thing I could imagine to be worse than blaming them on Petra."

Yveun watched as the small-framed Dragon ventured out into the night. She possessed all the grace of a Dono. But Coletta had never desired the title. She couldn't win it by normal measures, so it had suited her better to attach herself to him. They needed each other in different ways.

"It is only through half measures that these things are allowed to happen." She raised her wine to her lips again, savoring the taste. "And if they continue, you will lose everything, Yveun."

She didn't say "we" or "House Rok". The statement was so pointed, it was nearly a threat. She wanted him to be made aware that the House would live without him. *She* would live without him.

He stood to lose the most.

Yveun felt like a man before a god as he approached Coletta. She stood, washed in night, like the Divine Patron under which she was born—Lady Soph, the Destroyer. He hated admitting he had erred. But if he was to swallow his pride, he would do it before Coletta and no one else. He would drink the bitter poison of her words, to save himself from anything else she might concoct.

"Did you know that the most deadly flowers are oftentimes the most delicate?" Her tone had shifted. It had taken a softer note. There was danger in the quiet.

"I would believe it."

"They are beautiful, Soph Pearls, the most delicate of all. When the tiny white flowers finally lose all their petals, the smallest fruit forms. And in this is a toxin that can slay even a Dragon with some magic in their gut."

She smiled, revealing her gray, abused gums. Worn from years of her work, from years of experimenting with flavors. From working up tolerances and immunities. From breaking down her body out of reverence for her Lady. From the belief that to create, one must first destroy.

Coletta held out the glass she had been holding. The wine sloshed, airing with the very darkness itself. The stem of the glass dripped between her fingertips like a moonbeam.

Yveun met her eyes. Coletta changed nothing in her stance. She was as still as silence personified. As ever-present as death itself.

He reached for the glass, showing no fear. He took it from her fingers and he drank. The alcohol burned lightly, cutting the sweetness of the wine. It was a jam profile, sweetened with fruit and aged in light wood. He savored the flavors, holding them on his palette, searching for anything he might have missed, before swallowing.

"Do you like it?" Coletta asked.

"It is the same wine we drank today," he observed.

"It is," she affirmed. Yveun waited patiently for her to impart the importance of having him try something he'd consumed all day. He waited for the spark of magic of his stomach churning against poison. "This is a specialty for this side of Ruana, a favorite among House Xin. So loved that it does not even make shipments out of this corner of Nova."

"I was not aware."

"I know you were not." Coletta shot him a glare from the corners of her eyes, conveying her lack of appreciation for his interruption. If such a look had come from anyone else, Yveun would have killed them on the spot. "Because you have become drunk on power, and are operating under half measures."

Something indeed churned in his gut, but it wasn't poison. No, anger at the truth his life-mate was lying before him tore at his insides. He had become drunk on power, on the idea that he was an invincible force and his rule was as inevitable as the sun rising. And tonight, that would change. There was something already brewing in the air.

Yveun took another long sip. "But you knew."

"I knew." She smiled into the blackness. "I knew, and I knew where the wineries are. I learned of each of the storerooms where the vintage is kept."

"It would be a shame if someone tampered with the brew."

Far on the streets below, the first cry cut through the night.

"Such a shame." Coletta took back the wine, helping herself to another long sip. "For the flavor is right."

More screams as Dragons fell, convulsing on the stone streets that sprawled out beneath them. A symphony of agony his Coletta had produced sang to them with all the beauty of a full orchestra.

Yveun wrapped a hand around her hip and smiled into the night alongside her. It was going to be a much shorter Court than he was accustomed to.

"There has been word from the whisperers to Loom."

"What did they say?" Yveun asked over a particularly high-pitched cry.

"Two messengers arrived to the Harvesters' Guild. They came to sow seeds of dissent from the Alchemists. They are seeking to rise against you. A rebellion has formed."

Yveun cursed under his breath. It was hardly a surprise. An annoyance, the persistence of Fenthri. At least, that was how he'd always viewed it. And that had been the problem. He had treated the men and women in the gray world below like children, poor helpless creatures in squalor, in need of his guiding light.

After all he'd done, they still stood against him.

"What did the Guild do?"

"The Vicar Harvester took their meeting. It was one of their Masters who alerted the guild's Dragon whisperer to Nova of it."

"Without order from the Vicar?" Yveun clarified.

Coletta affirmed it with a small nod.

There was only one reason for the Vicar Harvester not to immediately come to him, not to immediately take the rebels' treasonous heads: they were entertaining the notion. Or they were trying to hide it. It didn't matter which to Yveun; both were equally unforgivable.

The Harvesters had been a loyal guild. From the beginning, they had followed his laws when he had shown them the error of their ways. They had remained in communication. But the Fenthri were fickle creatures. They tried to fit multiple lifetimes in what was not even one-fourth of his.

"I have taken enough half measures upon Loom." This was what happened when one tried to leave room for the foolishness known as kindness. He had tried to be kind to Loom, and this was how the Fenthri repaid him.

Delight rose in his mate. Coletta's magic shifted to a pleased pulse that hummed against his palm. It was a wonderful physical sensation to the auditory wonders of the world falling apart around him. It encouraged him to be one step more vicious, to be wholly committed.

"The guilds on Loom are bold anew. Squashing their last rebellion was not enough, because from its ashes the Fenthri rose again. Attempting peace by allowing them their guild cultures, to allow them to teach, was far too generous. They forget too quickly, and for that, they need a firm hand."

There would be no more exceptions. No more half measures. The tree had rotted; he would no longer pick through the fruit. He would cut it down at the base, burn out the roots. He would till the soil and plant again.

"The world below is broken beyond repair. It must be destroyed and rebuilt."

"Lady Soph and Lord Rok," Coletta referred to both of their Divine patrons with a toast, continuing to pass the glass back and forth between them.

"Tell the whisperer that all Dragons loyal to me are to be pulled from the guilds. They will be moved to New Dortam, where my Riders will shuttle them back to Nova. Then, the Riders will remain on Loom and take over the Revolvers—and their weapons." The plan took shape with vicious precision. "The Harvesters are to be made an example. It will show all of Loom that I am their King, that they thrive by my will and that they will die by it too. If even the most willing and loyal guild could not resist entertaining treasons against me, they and the rest will know none are safe, from the tallest of their mountains to the deepest of oceans. The land below is mine, and they will know it in every unbroken scream."

"Merely the Harvesters?" Coletta pushed.

Yveun's magic surged, his bones hot with power that boiled over into the atmosphere. He wanted to rain magic and blood down upon Loom from the chaos he would unleash on Nova.

"No. Destroy the Harvesters without warning. Lay waste to the Alchemists before their pathetic rebellion can retaliate. Shatter the Rivets' tallest clockwork towers so that nothing may be rebuilt. Stop every one of the Ravens' trains and snuff out trade and communications. Then, when the four are destroyed in absolute, bring the torch to the Revolvers' gunpowder. Explode all those who know how to make the tools of war to disrupt this world's divine hierarchy.

"Let them cry for order from the chaos. Let them beg for a savior to deliver them from the suffering they will know."

"And you will be that savior?" Coletta asked after a long stretch.

"When I return their lives to them, I will be Lord Rok Himself. I will be their red God."

"No half measures," Coletta said with singsong delight.

"No half measures," Yveun repeated, and savored the tuning sounds of discord in the air as he stepped behind the conductor's podium for the greatest symphony of destruction ever composed.

# 34
# ARIANNA

AT NIGHT, THE CLOUDS BELOW NOVA LOOKED LIKE A SEA OF SILVER. THE GARISH
and brightly colored world was washed clean by the pale glow of the moon,
which softened the harsh tones to something Arianna's eyes were more familiar
with. The stars spread out above her infinitely. On one of her first nights she had
attempted to count the glowing celestial bodies, but lost track around three
hundred.

They sparkled and winked, dancing in tiny streaks of light, hiding behind the
glow of the great, bright moon. Certainly the sun fascinated her, but it was the
celestial elegance of the night that had begun to enchant her. There was
something, dare she even think it, *romantic* about it. The night sky, the changing
landscapes, the sparking magic... It had all begun to fit together in her mind to
show her a picture she hadn't even been able to comprehend before coming to
Nova: a world defined by beauty and a people that embraced it above all else.

One such person was under her palms now. Cvareh had been cryptic about
where they were going. All he had said was "off Ruana," but to where and why
he had not revealed. Arianna hadn't questioned, nor forced it from him.

The man had been changing her, against her will and beyond her
expectations. And, today, she had given in to it. Arianna had loved Eva; the
woman had been a mental equal who pulled Arianna's mind into delightful
shapes and caressed her intellect in the right way.

Cvareh was a similar force, but different. His very being was a mystery
wrapped in an enigma. He needed to pose no scientific riddle or postulation. Just
trying to rationalize who he was and why he acted how he did was more than
enough. Arianna wanted him all the same for it.

Ruana shrunk in the distance. Smaller, floating islands drifted through the pale ocean below them. Arianna had been trying to get her hands on a map of Nova for some time, but apparently no one had bothered to make one in recent years. Over time, the islands drifted and their arrangement changed. Dragons navigated by these smaller, unimportant rocks like skipping stones or breadcrumbs that rode on the invisible current of magic that tethered Nova together.

It was as illogical as anything else was in the sky world, and she accepted it now with a grace she hadn't possessed months ago.

"We're headed there." Cvareh pointed to an island at the end of a long line.

"What's there?" She squinted at the barely visible outline of rock in the distance.

"I know you're at least somewhat familiar with the pantheon, thanks to Cain."

Arianna huffed in objection. "I studied well before Cain."

"So you know of the Twenty Gods?"

"Each of the Twenty is Patron of a month on the calendar, and each has an aspect of your world to oversee, such as Lady Luc supplying your water." Arianna grinned faintly at the asinine nature of the idea. But the expression faded. She was riding a giant flying bird across the heavens above floating islands in a world of rainbow-colored people and magic. At this point, it was almost irresponsible to entirely rule out the possibility of some even greater magic overseeing the Dragon's every need.

"Just so." Cvareh missed her expression, guiding the boco as he was. "Every Dragon possesses two patrons, that of their house and that of the month they are born in." He paused, interrupting himself. "What month were you born?"

"The tenth." Even knowing why and seeing the brightness of the sun for herself, it still amazed Arianna that Dragons and Fenthri kept the same twenty-month calendar.

Harvesters had observed the patterns in the light of the moon long before the discovery of Nova—how every thirty days came a night of complete darkness, and every twenty months a day of total light. The Dragons had told Loom it was Lord Rok and Lady Luc heralding the new year with a flaming chariot that lit the night sky. She had always been skeptical but never had a better explanation. Even now that she'd lived on Nova, she still had no better reasoning to offer.

"The tenth month, Lord Pak, the Dark-wielder." Cvareh laughed into the open air. "That would suit you."

"What month are you?" Arianna hardly believed in legends having any bearing on her day-to-day life.

"Eleven. Lord Agendi, the Lucky." Cvareh nodded his head forward. "And tonight, his temple is where I am taking you."

"A temple sounds like serious business." She'd had enough Dragon customs today for a lifetime.

"I will be surprised if anyone is even there." Cvareh soothed her concerns.

"The supreme gods—those who are house Patrons—and elder gods To, Veh, Soh, and Bek, have oft-frequented temples. But Lord Agendi is too far down the pantheon and too far out of the way for anyone to make the journey regularly."

She certainly wouldn't have called the trip convenient. But Arianna was in a good mood. Her body still felt afire from the fight, her imbibing, and their lovemaking. The night air was crisp on her mostly naked form, charging her skin with a pleasant icy sensation.

Cvareh tugged on the boco's reigns, leading it to a wide landing platform connected via a stone walk to a small temple with a pointed roof and lined with columns at the opposite end. He dismounted, reaching a hand to her. Arianna ignored it, helping herself off the boco. Some things were never going to change, no matter what came to pass between them.

"It'll start soon." Cvareh looked up at the sky. "We'll only be waiting a short while."

"For what?" she asked.

"You'll see." Whatever it was, he was so excited about it that she forgave his cryptic nature and didn't press. "Come, let's wait in the shade of the temple."

Around the pathway, and the entire island, were long stalks with some sort of egg-shaped growth on the end. They swayed in the breeze, leaves whispering quietly between each other. It seemed no other plants would survive on this particular rock.

Cvareh reclined on a wide step at the entrance to the temple. Arianna poured magic into her eyes to cut through the darkness and peer within, but was generally disappointed in what she saw. There was a statue of a Dragon man holding a box of silver, a crown of flowers atop his head. Coins and other offerings were piled into his little treasure chest, but not much else adorned the space.

Satisfied, Arianna sat next to Cvareh.

"Might I ask you something?"

"You just did," Arianna pointed out, as though he were a child making such an error for the first time in his life.

"Will you answer it if I ask?" he rephrased.

"That depends entirely on the question. Maybe I will, maybe I'll rip off your tongue." She wasn't used to her threats earning laughter. She wasn't used to being called out when her words were bark with only a tiny possibility of bite.

"Very well, I shall take my chances." Cvareh paused, sobering once more. "The woman you loved…"

Arianna stiffened and Cvareh hesitated. She wondered if he was waiting to see if she lashed out for him even mentioning Eva. She wondered why she hadn't yet.

"Eva."

"Eva," Cvareh proceeded delicately. "You and she… you two…"

Arianna sighed heavily. She didn't want to talk about Eva. But somehow, she felt as if she owed it to the man sitting next to her. The man in whose pleasures she'd delighted in for hours had perhaps earned that much truth. If she was going to talk about Eva, she was only going to do it once. She would tell him everything he wanted to know.

She pulled off the splint, releasing her illusion. The island pulsed with the quiet sort of vibration that all of Nova had. But, like Cvareh had suspected, she didn't sense the presence of another magical being anywhere.

Seeing her skin exposed in the night was instant discomfort. It was her flesh, not the illusion. But it was also flesh Cvareh had seen, that his mouth had worshipped.

"She kissed me, for the first time, here." Arianna held out her wrist. Upon it was inscribed: *20.9.1078*. So much had happened in a mere three years. "She was vivacious, full of life and challenge and heart. She loved like a dream and she fought like a sea monster."

"What happened to her?"

"I killed her." Arianna stared out into the vast sky as if the truths she'd been searching for would be there written in the stars. Stars she never could have seen if she'd never met Cvareh. More likely, the truth would be found in the man sitting next to her. Arianna stared down at the hands she'd recently acquired.

"Arianna, I don't think you should blame—"

"I slit her throat, Cvareh." It wasn't some misplaced blame. It was fact. "We met in the last rebellion. She worked with me on the Philosopher's Box. A gifted Alchemist and one of Loom's experts on Chimera research. She was the best of all worlds and somehow loved me."

Ari leaned back onto her elbows, tipping her head back and drinking in the darkness like sharp liquor. It would fuel her words and make her brave. It already had for years, if Cvareh's gods were to be believed. "She favored Sophie at first. But we were far more well-matched in mind...and in heart."

"Do all Fenthri favor their same sex?" Cvareh asked with as much delicacy as he could muster.

Arianna laughed as a Dragon would, tipping her head back and pouring forth her amusement without reservation. "We prefer what we prefer."

"But loving one you cannot have a child with is futile. You can't continue the family..."

His words trailed off as he saw the look she gave him. She wanted him to figure it out. She would wait as long as he needed, but she would judge him past a certain point if he couldn't come to the right conclusion.

"... and that's not a concern of the Fenthri."

Arianna tapped the stone next to her like it was a bell. "Ding-ding." Her sarcasm was too weak to stand against the weight of their conversation. "The Dragons, this notion of family... For over a thousand years we would head to the grounds of Ter.0 and induce fertility, breed as we needed, the best of the best, raise the children in the guilds."

"It sounds cold and sterile."

"Families sound limiting and suffocating."

He huffed in a tired amusement. "Fair enough." Cvareh looked back to the stars, as though they would give him strength to ask the question he'd been awkwardly shifting around. "Why did you kill her?"

Arianna wished she hadn't resolved to tell him everything. She pressed her mouth into a thin line, as if she could smother the words, extinguish them like a flame. But the truth remained.

"I didn't just kill her. I killed them all." She let out the bleakness of her heart's truth. "Your people should thank me. I was the hand that crushed the last rebellion against your King."

"I don't understand."

"When we discovered we'd been betrayed, that the Dragon we'd trusted was not a double-agent for us, was not an ally against the King, but a man under the King's own thumb, we destroyed it all—or tried to." The smell of burning flesh and reagents gone sour singed her nose anew. Her hands were caked in invisible blood that would never wash away, black and red alike. "I was the only one who could do it. The rest of them had been poisoned. My stomach saved me."

"So the schematics I carried..." Realization was beginning to take over.

"Shouldn't have even existed. They were stolen at the onset of our betrayal."

"Why didn't you kill yourself?" It was a fair question, based on what he knew of her, what she was.

"You know how hard it is for a Dragon to kill themselves. It's no easier for me."

"You really are, then?"

"I'm a Perfect Chimera." Arianna finally brought her eyes to meet his. She wanted him to feel the weight of the truth. She wanted him to cower in fear or see her purely as a tool. But he did something far more dangerous: He didn't change the way he looked at her at all. "More important than overcoming the logistical challenge of killing myself, Eva and Master Oliver asked me to live. She died knowing all our research, everything we'd worked for, was being destroyed. I don't expect you to understand, but for a Fenthri, there is nothing more horrible."

"You fled, detaching from everything, and became the White Wraith. You worked against Dragons," he finished, painfully simple.

"In the hopes that I would someday find my way to the man who betrayed all I loved. In the hopes that it would bring me vengeance." She felt a sudden wave of guilt. He now knew everything, and she had never even told Florence the beginning of her story. When she returned to Loom, the girl would know the truth, Arianna vowed. The girl—no, woman—had more than earned it.

"The boon?"

"Was an opportunity to find that man."

"Why haven't you demanded it of me yet?" Cvareh's confusion mirrored her own.

She stared at her hands. The moment she'd inhaled their scent—a scent etched on her memory by pure hatred—she knew she was close to finding the Dragon who'd called himself Rafansi. But she had yet to speak on it. She had yet to utter those words, "*Take me to the man whose hands these are.*" If she did, she would kill Rafansi on sight. Only she now knew he was a Xin, and an ally of Cvareh. It tore at her gut on so many levels.

"I can only ask once," she whispered. "I want to make sure what I am asking for is what I really want."

"Boon or not." Cvareh sat and took her hand. "I will give you whatever you ask, Arianna."

"Don't offer me that."

"Why?"

"Because you know who I am."

"And that is precisely why I offered."

For the first time, she was at a loss for words. She didn't know if she should capitalize on all the closeness they'd shared over the day to have him bring her to the Dragon who had betrayed all she'd loved. She didn't know if she should cross the remaining distance between them and kiss him. Rusted rivets, the mechanisms that spun her world whirred and Arianna was stuck in place, no longer grasping their logic.

"His name was Rafansi," she whispered, bracing herself.

Cvareh blinked, and burst out into laughter. Arianna withdrew her hand. She didn't know what reaction she expected, but his amusement had not been it.

"That couldn't possibly be his name."

"I would never forget it," she insisted.

"Then he lied."

It was certainly a possibility, one she hadn't ever ruled out. Yet to affirm that she didn't even know the man's name yielded a certain sort of disappointment. "How can you be sure?"

"Because no Dragon parents would ever name their child that willingly."

"Why?"

"That was the name of Lord Rok's failed first—and only—attempt at the creation of life. The lore says Rafansi was a deformed and useless wretch of a creature who only earned his existence from Lord Rok's pity." Cvareh shook his head. "A life earned by pity would be the ultimate disgrace… What an awful name to even be called in secret."

"But fitting," she snapped in annoyance, at both Cvareh's sympathy for the traitor and the fact it left her without a name for the man.

"Perhaps we could find him another way?" he offered, frustratingly helpful. "Do you know his House? Was he marked? What color—"

"He was Xin."

Cvareh straightened instantly, putting distance between them.

She read him like an open book. She felt the pulse in his magic, withdrawing on instinct, reminding him that this was not a woman he should be involved with. He fought against the pull of his upbringing, though, and took her hands with renewed passion. He held her fingers tightly, his eyes pleading as if she could explain why he was doing what he was. As if she had a neat solution for everything that drove them apart.

"Be careful what you offer me, Cvareh," she cautioned grimly, with all the sorrow of an ugly reality. "Your house looks to me to be the herald of victory. But I may well still decide to watch it burn."

"No," he whispered. "I won't let you have a reason to."

Her instant rage at him arguing with her about what she would and wouldn't do was stilled.

"We will find this man, and then I will see you kill him."

"You would let me kill a Xin?" She was rightly skeptical.

"A Xin who takes the name Rafansi and works for the Dragon King against our interests should not be alive." Cvareh smiled the smallest smile of hopeful— foolishly hopeful— encouragement. "I may not be as good of a fighter as you, Arianna. But I have other uses. I can be quite good at finding information. People just say things around me they shouldn't, like they forget I'm there entirely. I will help you find this man, and I will give him to you for judgment of his crimes."

Her brows furrowed and her lips parted just enough to let out her speechless shock. The hands he held so fiercely were the very thing that would allow him to fulfill his promise. He was ready to give her everything she'd wanted since her world ended.

But if he did, would she be asking him to sacrifice one of his own ideals? Would their relationship survive her asking him to deliver one of his own for slaughter? She was afraid it wouldn't, despite his earnest insistence. Arianna stared into Cvareh's eyes, shining bright and gold against the darkness, and saw something that might just be worth more to her than her vengeance.

Those eyes were oblivious to her struggle, and easily swung away, looking to the field. "It's starting."

"What is?" Arianna looked as well, but her answer didn't come from Cvareh.

As the moon reached its apex, the whispering reeds they'd walked through to the temple slowly straightened. Their egg-shaped ends peeled away, unfurling long pedals of red, lined in gold, from within. Their wavy edges tapered to points that curved opposite their center.

A fine mist, like the afterglow of neon, clouded the air above them as the plants' superfine pollen was released into the wind. The rock before her was awash in light and magic. It soothed her weariness from the day; it gave her strength. She felt as though she could live forever if she laid among them.

Arianna stood.

"What are they?" she breathed, stepping toward the blooms. There was no mistaking it.

"The flowers of Agendi." Cvareh was at her side, but he may as well have been back on Ruana. Arianna's mind was moving a thousand veca a second, whirring with new possibilities. "They're particular about where they can grow… So they're found only here and on Lysip. They're said to bring good luck. Do you like them?"

Arianna stepped into the cosmos that floated before her, a dance of magic turned into a fog of the whole spectrum of light. They were unmistakable. Their power even more potent than the last time she'd seen them.

"*Like* isn't the right word…" Arianna trailed off into her own thoughts.

He would take her mannerisms as awe or wonder, and Arianna would let him. It was a safer assumption than the truth that now confronted her. Did she ask Cvareh for the heart of the man who had betrayed her past, at the risk of it damaging all they were, and especially when she now knew he could get her the resources she needed for the box?

Or did she give in once more and let herself dream, and perhaps even look to the possibilities of the future?

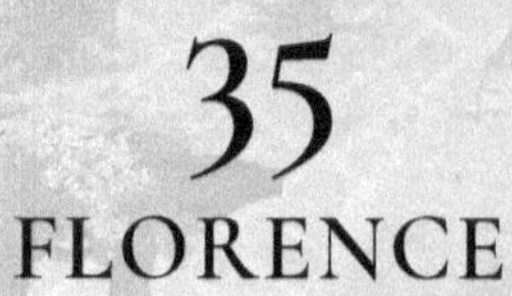

# 35
# FLORENCE

The door to her room slammed open, waking Florence with a start. Powell stood in the frame, his dust-colored hair seeming to fray at the ends with stress. Panting, a mess, he crossed to the bed in a long stride.

"Florence, we have to leave."

"What? Why?" She shied away from his grip, uneasy in the man's presence. She'd avoided and outright ignored him for two days since he had shown her the Dragon harvesting rooms. She didn't know how she could feel about someone who seemed to revere Dragons for saving the world and endorse treating them worse than livestock in the same breath.

"There aren't many trains left and they're filling." He reached for her upper arm, yanking her from the bed.

"Trains?" Florence ripped herself from his grip. "I don't know what you're thinking, but you must be seriously confused." She stood her ground, pointing at the still gaping door from where he had entered. "Now leave my room."

"They're going to blow the guild."

"What?" It was as if she had half the powders needed for a canister and he was expecting her to produce a complete shot.

"We have to get out before they do. There's not much time." Powell reached for her again and she sidestepped away. He cursed loudly. "Pitchforks and sickles, woman, if you want to stay, then *fine*. I didn't have to come for you anyway."

He started for the door. Florence stared at his back in a daze. Even if she didn't fully understand what was happening, she knew desperation when she saw it. She knew what fight or flight looked like in someone who was struggling to fall into their training rather than chaos and cowardice.

Whatever Powell thought was going on—right or not—he really believed they were all in danger.

"Powell, wait." Florence grabbed the back of his shirt. She regarded him with a glare, hoping to make it clear that she was still very aware of the uneasy terms they were on despite their situation. "When you say they're going to blow the Guild…" she tried to speak slowly and evenly, coaxing him into some sense of calm that could bring order from what seemed to be a tempest of thoughts raging in his mind.

"The Dragon King has ordered every guild hall destroyed. We're the first."

Florence's hand went limp, dropping to her side. She laughed. "What?"

"Florence." He grabbed her by the shoulders, shaking her roughly. "This isn't a joke, and we must leave."

It made no sense. The Dragon King was going to destroy the guilds? Why? He needed them. Nova needed their technology and their production and, at the very least, their gold.

"We have to get Derek and Nora." She was already at her friends' door, banging loudly before entering. "Derek, Nora, we have to go."

"Flor?" Nora rolled at her lover's side, groggy.

"What's going on?" Derek was far more alert.

"I don't know," she confessed, hoping they had enough stock in her decision making ability to trust her blindly. "But I believe we need to leave."

"And quickly!" Powell urged.

Derek and Nora, to her surprise, did exactly as Florence asked. They left the bed without further question, not even bothering to tug on more than their sleeping clothes. Together with Powell, the three hastily started down the winding halls of the Harvesters' Guild.

At first, it seemed they were the only people to know what was happening. The halls were quiet and empty; only random scampering as a person sprinted ahead of them, or someone darted from a side room with a bag in tow. But the open doors on either side of them told a different story.

They weren't the first to know. They were the last.

As they wound down, the halls began to crowd with people. They were pushing by each other, forcing their fellow initiates and journeymen out of the way. None seemed to regard Powell as anything more than anyone else, despite his nearly being at Master status.

Everyone was running. Shouting. Pushing and shoving. They funneled into narrow walks that wound tightly beneath the Harvesters' Guild in Faroe, compacting in on each other in tunnels that were not meant for the current capacity.

Elbows pushed against her, pressing her forward as the masses reached a point at which it seemed they could go no further. Florence looked to turn back, but it was already too late. More people had run up behind them, slamming into their backs as she had slammed into the backs of the people in front of her.

They were part of a mass of people attempting to claw their way forward at all costs.

She felt very small, and compressed even smaller. Florence gasped for breath. Her footing was slipping out from under her. She was being carried along by the Fenthri tide. Nora and Derek were nowhere to be found, and Powell had somehow drifted out of her line of sight. She was going to die here, drowned in an ocean of panic.

Her heart raced into her throat, preventing her from even calling out. All there was to see were shades of shifting gray, illuminated by the tunnel's dim lighting. Her ears filled with the groans and grunts and cries, dizzying her mind.

A hand, sure and strong, calloused from years of work, wrapped around her forearm and yanked. Her shoulder popped and her skin bruised instantly from the force. She was threaded through the line of people—barely—to reach her friends on the wall.

Powell held her tightly, preventing the masses from ripping her away from the group again. Derek and he shared a linked arm as Derek held onto Nora with the same might. Florence gasped for breath in the small space Powell created between his chest and the wall for her.

"We have to go along the outside. There's a door ahead, a worker's tunnel, and I have the key," Powell shouted. "When I open it, you have to run. You have to run as fast as you can. Don't look back, don't think, just trust me and run. If you fall, you will be trampled."

Derek and Nora gave fearful nods. Florence looked up at Powell as he sheltered her from the writhing masses at his back.

"Run, and I'll run with you."

He gave a nod, and they pressed forward.

They squeezed in a chain, hands wrapped along elbows, along the outer wall. Derek's nose exploded with black blood as a man behind him pushed his face directly into the wall. Florence was nearly smothered once as someone tried to turn her into a ladder to see above the masses.

"Why aren't they letting us through?"

"Let us through!"

"Why isn't the door open?"

"There are still people here!"

The chorus of shouts was deafening, a cacophony of fear and pleading agony.

Powell reached the door and pulled out the key. Florence positioned herself near his side, Derek and Nora pressed behind. As soon as he saw they were all there, he disengaged the lock, and let loose the floodgates.

They sprinted. Florence didn't look back. Her lungs and legs burned, but her magic kept up. It made her faster—nearly faster than Powell, who was half a head taller.

"This way!" Powell veered left.

They followed.

"Down!" He gripped an iron ladder handle, vaulting over the edge into the darkness below as though it was nothing more dangerous than measuring gunpowder. His hands flipped their grip, his booted feet met the ladder, and he slid into the darkness.

Derek and Nora followed, Florence skidded to a stop. She couldn't see the bottom of that yawning blackness. She couldn't see where the iron ended.

But she could hear the screams behind her. The front of the pack was mere steps away. She had to make the leap of faith.

Florence jumped onto the ladder, her feet landing on a rung. She shifted her hands onto the outside, releasing her feet as well. Her stomach shot into her mouth as she free-fell and Florence had to expend every conscious thought on arching her feet around the outside of the ladder, pressing in with as much strength as she could muster to slow.

The iron burned against her bare flesh, catching and ripping. Her arches shot daggers of pain up into her calves. But she didn't stop.

She fell for a seeming eternity before she finally let out a scream. She was falling into those endless pits she'd seen on the train. The infinite strip mines that spiraled down further and further into the earth, stopping only when they had been exhausted, when the Harvesters had taken everything they could. She was going to fall to her death, and die in the darkness fate seemed determined to condemn her to at every turn.

Two hands grabbed her waist, pulling her from the ladder. They fell together in a heap of momentum. Florence opened her eyes, but was only met with more darkness, darkness so black that she couldn't even see with her improved Dragon sight.

"You're all right," Derek soothed, standing her.

"We have to keep moving," Powell stressed. "We're losing time."

They linked hands once more and marched forward into that endless blackness. The sounds of the other fleeing people began to fade as they were filtered into the worker's tunnels, splitting at forks and dividing into smaller, equally hopeless packs. Men and women were behind them, but their lead was growing. Florence chose to focus on the sound of Powell's hand sliding against the rough-hewn walls, instead of the screams behind them, begging for deliverance from the endless black.

Florence had to put faith in the Harvester before her. This man approached these tunnels with years of knowledge and all the fearlessness of a Raven jumping into the Underground. His mind was likely spinning a mental map not unlike Arianna's would be. The latter thought gave her more hope. If Florence thought of him like Arianna, she could find the faith she needed.

She held Powell's free hand tighter.

They reached another door, this time unlocked. Light flooded the tunnel the second Powell heaved his shoulder into it. Any relief Florence could feel was abruptly cut short by the squealing hinges and the screams that rose like heat off a pyre.

The four of them ran along a narrow catwalk suspended over Faroe's under-city terminal station. Three platforms were vacant; the fourth already had a train departing. Men and women flooded over the platform, trying to press themselves against the vessel in some odd hope that they might stick. That left the fifth train, already billowing steam and clouding their vision high above as the engine began to gather heat.

"We have to make that train!" Powell shouted.

Florence's legs burned, her feet felt like rocks, but she kept pushing forward. She worked through the numbness to the point that sliding down another, long ladder to the chaos on the platform below didn't even hurt her bare feet. Powell continued to forge a path for them, Derek at his side. Florence kept her shoulder against Nora's, elbows linked.

"Powell!" a man from within one of the open cars called. "Powell, here!"

"Max," Powell shouted in reply. Harvesters flooded around them, everyone desperate for the same opening.

"Let us on! Let us on!" the people chanted and cried. They begged and bartered. But those on the car had no solution for them. To make room for those on the platform below required those on the train above to give up their spots.

Powell jumped onto the car, helping up Derek by the elbow. Florence reached for the offered hand when Nora was ripped from her side.

"This train is for Harvesters," a man screeched.

"Nora!" Florence and Derek called in unison. Their friend became nothing more than a lump on the floor, hidden under the stampede of feet.

"Let me on!"

"Nora!" Florence tried to push back to her friend. The man stepped in front of her.

His hands reached out. He was going to grab for her shoulders just as he had Nora's. He was going to take her and throw her to the ground, too. She was going to be nothing more than a lump of flesh on the floor, disregarded in the chaos as nothing more than a life less valuable than those of the people stepping upon her.

Florence reached for the holster that now never left her shoulders. One revolver, six canisters. She drew her gun and tracked the barrel right between the man's eyes.

"Touch me and I will shoot."

*Fight or flight.* Florence breathed heavily. *Fight or flight.* The man grabbed her shoulders. *Fight or flight, fight or flight, fight or—*

*Fight!*

Florence pulled the trigger, blowing off half the man's face at point-blank range. His skin exploded, curling back and away from the epicenter of the blast.

The contact shot vaporized his skull and pulverized his brain. It sent blood and gore flying.

Those around were stunned into a brief moment of silence. The world stilled as everyone realized at once what they should've known all along. Every choice, every decision now, was a judgment call of whose life was more valuable. And every man, woman, and child, would always put their own life before any others, by virtue of instinct if nothing else.

"Nora." Florence took advantage of the moment, pushing people aside, stepping through the gore, grabbing for her friend. Black blood smeared Nora's body, but she remained breathing—dazed, but intact.

The people closed in again, as Florence pulled her friend toward the car. "Don't touch us," she screamed again, cocking the weapon. "Don't touch us or I will shoot to kill."

She waved her gun through the air, keeping the people at bay. She had five more shots; they could overpower her in a moment. But people seemed to favor the chance of potentially getting on the train somewhere else rather than certain death from the wrong end of her firearm.

Derek pulled Nora onto the train, then turned to help on Florence. She found her spot pressed between Powell and Derek. The Harvester's side she was flush against was too hot. It was kindling to the spark of her swift and sudden guilt.

Florence swallowed, looking at the body on the platform. She had never killed a Fenthri before. Not like that.

The train lurched to life, bringing on more screams as the people on the platform were faced with the realization that there simply wasn't enough room for all of them. They chased the train. They jumped for the vessel. Some missed, tumbling under the train's wheels with unsettling thuds. Others managed to find a hold, only to be splattered the second the train entered the narrow tunnel leading out of Faroe.

It seemed like an ocean of black and red blood was going to drown them all.

"Powell…" Florence finally began to catch her breath. "That man…"

"It was you or him." The Harvester at her side verbally recognized the fact, but he didn't look at her. He remained focused ahead, looking into the wind that carried only the darkness of the tunnel. "You had no choice."

"He was of your guild…"

"The rest were as well." Powell shook his head. "I chose to get the three of you on board."

"Why?" Florence asked.

"For Loom. I did it for Loom. The Alchemists and Ravens and Revos and Rivets—rusted sickles, they may not have gotten warning. You may be the last ones. As a Mast—As a Fenthri, knowing at least some of my guild escaped, I had an obligation to preserve the widest reach of knowledge. It was my duty…" For now, Florence willingly chose to ignore the idea that she may be the last Raven, or Revolver, alive.

The train shot from the tracks in the dim light of morning. The world was awash in sepia tones of clay and rock. The morning seemed almost peaceful, until Florence looked back at the guild hall they were fleeing at bone-rattling speeds. High above, rainbow trails curved and spiraled. Concentrated magic glimmered down as light.

"Dragon Riders?" Florence remembered what Powell had said, but it made no sense.

Florence watched as a Dragon leapt from a high rooftop, caught by another mid-air. They began to arc and spiral away, uncaring of the trains and people fleeing. They made no effort to pursue.

*No, why would they?*

Florence realized the truth of it as the very evil in the air iced down the column of her spine. They wanted an audience. They wanted people to see.

She knew what was coming the moment she saw the wide canister lofted above a Rider's head. But Florence still screamed. She screamed before anyone else, because she had seen those canisters before. Hidden away one of the dark nights that she studied in the Revolvers' Guild proper, she had laid eyes on them as every Revolver should at a certain point in their studies. They were a testament to the truth of the Revolvers—that just because they could, did not mean they should.

The bomb fell like a dark omen against a silver sky.

Seconds stretched on as she watched it plummet toward the guild. It was so tiny from her vantage that it was almost as if she could reach out and pluck it from the air. But she couldn't. She could only watch, and hold her breath.

A flash of blinding light, brighter than any day. A wave of heat and air that jostled the train itself. An explosion of magic and chemicals so loud that it silenced all else in the moments to come, both demanding and earning a committed audience.

The top of the guild shuddered and groaned, toppling like the building toys of a toddler Rivet. It began to fall in large pieces as they tumbled away from what had been the epicenter of all supplies for Loom. The room she had learned about with Powell—gone. How many records of their resources, the very lifeblood of Loom, had been lost? The true shock waves of the day were going to reverberate long into the future, long after her cheeks dried and her ears stopped ringing.

But the Dragons spared no kindness. Secondary explosions rang out from deep within the guild. The walls exploded outward, tumbling the very foundation upon which the oldest city in Loom was built.

Faroe was tumbling and with it went all those who weren't safely on a train, whizzing away. Florence's mind returned to those who had entered the worker's tunnels with them, the souls who had sprinted into the darkness and would never find a way out.

The riders watched as the walls shuddered and shook. They stayed long enough to see the spiderweb fractures pop and split into existence. And then they left, as behind them the guild crumbled and burned and violently exploded, reduced to nothing more than rubble and smoke.

Florence watched with the rest of them, with every other Fenthri who screamed and sobbed and then stared silently in horror, at a complete loss for all emotions. They watched as the Dragons razed the first guild of Loom. The Dragons, who had always claimed to be their saviors, their guiding hands, demolished one of the five fundamental pillars upon which their world stood.

Florence burned the image into her mind with the heat of rage. She watched as the city of Faroe crumbled and fell into the hungry abyss that surrounded it.

# 36
## ARIANNA

It had been a long time since Arianna had covered her concerns with the warmth and flesh of another. She'd never make a habit of it, but there was something to be said for it. To want and be wanted. To need, to desire, to delight in another and feel that same delight. They moved well together, for a copious number of reasons, and Arianna turned off her mind and let herself simply be.

The flowers bloomed for only a short period of time, but they didn't need light for the acts they performed. When the time came to mount the boco again, she found herself lamenting the end of the short quiet in the storm that was her life. She dared to say she enjoyed the peace she'd come to find with Cvareh.

But that was precisely the problem. They were at peace only when they didn't think about what their unconventional relationship really meant. The moment she dedicated thought to it was the moment she realized its true folly. They had pulled the trigger and the bullet could not be caught. It was shot to kill, and they would both be right in its path. The question was, did she push him out of the way, and shoulder the pain on her own? Or did she pull him before her?

Arianna rested her cheek in the middle of Cvareh's back, watching the clouds swirl effortlessly beneath them. She wished she could see Loom, however small and insignificant it was from Nova's vantage. She missed her home and its industrial sensibilities.

There had been no word or rumor from Loom. The fact didn't surprise her, given the logistics of communication between the two realms, but she worried for Florence. The girl was no doubt involved in the rebellion and the very fact put her in danger. Arianna hoped she was merely oiling guns in the Alchemists' Guild hall. But knowing Florence, the likelihood of that was slim.

The world would only ever be safe when the Dragons no longer attempted to rule Loom. For as long as they did, Loom would bend and break, rebellions would creep up, the dream of bygone days would flower into bloody conflict. She knew she had reached her decision when they landed in the manor.

"It's quiet," Cvareh observed as they headed for her chambers.

"Perhaps they are still in Easwin?" Arianna proposed, quickly changing the topic to what weighed on her. "Cvareh, I have decided that I will help your sister."

He stopped in his tracks, leaving her to pause as well, a hand on the doorknob.

"Ari?" The Dragon was uncertain, searching. It was as if she'd given him a truth he deemed far too good to be true. But all Arianna could see was that she was giving him certain war.

"It's not for her."

"Who then?" he asked tentatively.

"Florence." He visibly deflated at the name. "Helping your sister will be the best chance of this rebellion she's put so much stock in seeing success, as long as Petra doesn't betray us and try to rule Loom when she has the throne she so wants."

"Logical. I'd expect no less."

Arianna sighed softly. "It's for you as well, idiot."

He brought his eyes back to hers, hopeful.

"You don't think I actually *trust* Petra, do you?" Arianna took a deep breath and braced herself. What she was about to say would no doubt rattle them both. "I trust you, Cvareh. If nothing else I trust that you will do what must be done."

"I will, I promise you. But Petra won't betray you, either." He eagerly followed her into her quarters as she made her way to her desk.

"Good, because I will need some supplies." She grabbed for the journal that was mostly still blank inside, the others scribbled across with random notes, maps of the manor, and other postulations.

Her pen paused as she thought a long moment. What did Sophie say she needed? What would help the rebellion the most? Arianna wasn't born to be a leader and she didn't want to be. She was born to create tools and was content to let others figure out their use.

"Yes, anything. You know I will give you anything," he repeated his dangerous offer.

Arianna withheld scolding him. She would save her boon for as long as she could. She would use it when she had no other option. When it was something he wouldn't give her willingly, or tried to be subversive about.

"Those flowers, I will need them." Merely thinking about crafting the Philosopher's Box again set the hairs on her neck on end. With every pen stroke and mental note made, she felt like she was writing the world's future.

"The Flowers of Agandi? Why?"

"The traitor. He brought them once… I thought he was a simpleton, bringing back something for the sheer beauty of it, a memento of home. But it was a stroke of luck." She laughed at the irony of her word choice. "We discovered that they have a special property in their pollen that can be used as a type of tempering on gold. It helps keeps magic fresh and rejuvenated."

Cvareh's eyes widened. The man was smarter than she gave him credit for, sometimes. He was beginning to piece together why she needed what she claimed. "But it wears off when the flower closes, or dies."

"It does, but if the pollen is tempered properly, the properties stay," Arianna explained. "It keeps the blood from turning black. It removes the strain of the magic."

"This is genius," Cvareh whispered by her shoulder.

"This was Eva's genius." Arianna would never miss a chance to laud her dead lover. Eva deserved that much, and so, so much more. "She was the one to notice her reagents hadn't gone sour in the flower's presence."

"How many do you need?"

"Not too many... well, depending on how many boxes we make. But since they don't grow on Loom and you said they're particular about where they grow even here… We'll need your help getting them. They must be transported quickly and securely so they arrive living and undamaged."

"Petra and I will see that this is done." There was an awe about Cvareh's excitement.

"We will also need more gold." Arianna tried to think back to the things Sophie said were in short supply. "For the boxes, and in general. I think you could perhaps intercept some shipments here to Nova from Loom."

"Far simpler than that." Cvareh placed a hand on her shoulder with a broad smile. "My sister has refineries here, nearly in working order."

"Refineries, here on Nova?" Arianna tried to grasp what this meant for Loom. If the Dragons could refine their own steel into gold, that meant Loom was one step closer to becoming irrelevant. She stared at her supply list. Loom needed the Philosopher's Box. They needed to secure their place in the world's future.

"Not as large as on Loom. But there are even Rivets and Harvesters Petra has brought up to help."

Arianna snorted, trying to imagine the thought. But the emotion was quickly lost. After all, here she was.

"Very well, then. The Alchemists could still use more guns. And any help with transport on Loom. We'll need to leverage the Rivets to put things in mass production."

"We will help how we can." She understood Cvareh's hesitation. Their power was significantly less once they stepped off the floating islands that drifted across the stars. "I will go pass all this information along to Petra."

"I'll finish the list while you do." Arianna drew another line, thinking of any other demands she could make on behalf of her home. Even if Petra ultimately betrayed them. If she could give Loom enough of an advantage to tip the scales, it might be worth it.

*Wrenches and bolts*, Arianna mentally cursed herself. She sounded like the same idealistic girl who had let herself be swept up in the rhetoric of the last rebellion.

"One more thing, Cvareh." She didn't look up from her paper. "Tell Petra to ready the glider for me to return to Loom."

There was an agonizingly long pause. "Pardon?"

"I'll need to return to Loom. I'll need to return to the Rivets personally. I will still have sway there—the Masters will remember me as Oliver's student. I can teach them how to make the box. I—"

"We have everything you need here." Cvareh said hastily. "The flowers, the gold, tools…"

Arianna looked out the window. This shouldn't be so difficult. But here she was, struggling against the truth, fighting for words. "I need factories. I need other Rivets and Alchemists. I need to go home."

"Can you return?"

"Why would I?" Arianna turned to see him trapped in limbo in the doorway. She wanted to stand and walk over and comfort him. She wanted to pull him into the bed and build blockades out of blankets to keep the world at bay.

"Because Petra needs me here." The truth was more deadly than a paring knife between her eyes, though the pain may have been equal. "She won't let me go again. I can't afford the suspicion."

"Understandable. Your place is here, mine is on Loom."

"Arianna, that cold and detached persona will no longer work on me." Cvareh stood his ground, literally and proverbially. "I know you, and I know that you…"

"That I what?" she pressed, seeing if he would really say the words her mind filled in. Cvareh faltered. "You barely know me, Cvareh."

"After tonight, I think I do."

"One day of sex and a small conversation does not give you my mind, all my history, my truths. You will never understand what drives me."

"I don't have to." He smiled soothingly. "I merely have to love it."

"You're being a fool." The man was going to paint color on her gray and dreary dreams, and somehow, she wanted to let him.

"No." He stepped toward her, rather than hastening away to his sister to report that he had finally secured all that House Xin needed. "I think this is one of the few times where I'm not."

That smile, sharp canines and all, was more dangerous than it had ever been. She hooked a hand on his neck and brought her mouth to it. Arianna wanted to taste the flavor of hope again.

"I love you, Arianna. And I will not stand in your way, but I will also not let you flee from this. Reject me if you must, and that will be that. Until you do, I will see my future built with space for you in it."

She searched his face as if she could read the words he wanted her to say off it with ease. But she was tired. There was only so much change that could be expected of a single person in one day.

Cvareh eased away, but there wasn't disappointment in his motions, merely patience. "I should go to my sister."

She watched him go, still caught in the same limbo. He loved her. *Loved.* Arianna placed a hand on her chest, feeling nothing. She remembered what it felt like to have a beating heart, though she hadn't in years. Eva had cut out the heart Ari had given her, and Arianna had built a new clockwork machine to take its place.

She didn't remember anything in her designs that would allow her to love again.

# 37
## PETRA

By the time word arrived to Petra of the mysterious circumstances under which they were suffering, it was far too late to even attempt to save the majority of them. The organs from a slave squished under her feet as she paced the room. Killing the messenger solved nothing, but the scent of blood made her mind sharp and her senses keen. Killing directed her rage at someone worthless, so it didn't escape through her at the people she needed to depend on.

The doors at the far end of the hall opened. Claws out, fangs bared, Petra wheeled in place to look at who had traversed into her space at such a time. There were only about five people she wouldn't kill on sight, and lucky for Cain, he was one of them.

"Cain, tell me news. Tell me something worthwhile." She felt utterly useless, and it was a feeling Petra both loathed and feared. She was the Xin'Oji, the young warrior, the champion of blue. She knew how to fight her way out of any corner.

"Petra'Oji." Cain's bare chest heaved as he fought to catch his breath. "I just arrived from overseeing healers from Napole to Easwin. They began to try to help the living, but their medicines are failing, so they looked to the dead. They suspect poison."

"Poison?" Petra repeated out of pure shock. A shameful death, poison was only reserved for killing animals without marring their pelt or flesh, or for the ill whose hearts could not be safely consumed seeking relief. Petra tried to think of even one poison, but could not name any. "It was not a rash of sour elk? Or an unhealthy growth upon the yeast?"

Cain shook his head grimly. "When they opened the cores of the fallen, half their innards had been completely dissolved."

"Are any surviving?" Petra walked over to one of the tall windows in the hall that faced east. All that was before her were the spires of her manor.

"Only those with strong magic in their stomachs."

Petra hung her head. Her claws dug so far into the stone that they nearly snapped. This was an enemy in the shadows. It was not one she could hunt down. It was not someone she could summon into the pits and make an example of several times over.

She had dealt with a coward. She had dealt with someone who was willing to sacrifice all their ideals for the ends they wanted to achieve. Petra snarled despite herself; the irony was not lost on her. Whoever had done this knew it was a very dark way to twist the Xin motto.

"Cain, I have an important task for you." Petra thought through her next move as carefully as she could manage. But blood clouded her mind and engulfed her nose. She wanted to roar the song of vengeance.

"Oji." Cain brought his heels together, standing taller.

"Find Finnyr, and bring him to me." Petra straightened, looking at Cain's reflection in the blackness of the windowpane. "I only need him alive and able to speak, Cain. His condition otherwise matters not."

"Do you think Finnyr'Kin has anything to do with this?"

Petra was smart enough to tell the difference between true insubordination and inquiry; this was by far the latter. Cain's face was overcome with horror at the very thought. It was heartening, but Petra did not have time for it.

"No…" Petra tapped her fingers along the windowsill. "Finnyr is a Xin, even if he lives under a Rok roof. Furthermore, even if he wanted to betray us, this is beyond him. At worst, he's a worthless little slime, not cunning or devious.

"However, the man whose roof he sleeps under is both." Petra growled the Dono's name. "Yveun has much to gain from Xin fighters mysteriously dying in the night, especially after our showing today."

"I will find Finnyr'Kin."

"See you do so with discretion," Petra cautioned. "We must act carefully until we know what picture is being painted." Accusing a Dragon of engaging in dishonest battles was a high offense if it proved to be unfounded. Even if Finnyr confirmed it was Yveun, Petra still wasn't certain she would be able to outright accuse the Dono of treason.

Dawn had barely kissed the sky when Petra knew Cain had returned. She smelled the man's magic and the sharp tang of her brother's. She had done nothing but pace the room for hours and bark orders at any who entered.

The doors opened and Cain shoved Finnyr through them. Her brother tripped, nearly falling on his face. He was like a skittish field mouse trying to squeak a mountain lion into submission.

"I am a Kin of this House. I will not tolerate this treatment!"

Cain looked to her. It was a delicious feeling—another person deferring to her above Finnyr, the first born, the fallen child of Xin. Petra's claws felt ten times sharper.

"We shall see what you are soon enough," Petra said silkily.

Finnyr turned slowly to look at her. All boldness he had tried to throw around with Cain washed away beneath the shower of her judgment. She poured her suspicions silently atop him and watched as they eroded his resolve.

"Petra, what is the meaning of this?" Finnyr demanded.

"Cain, I wish to be alone with my brother." Petra didn't want an audience for what she was about to do to Finnyr. She didn't want anyone in the manor to know what she could do with her claws. The speculation over what prompted each delightful scream would be a far stronger message to warn others against disappointing her.

"As you wish, Oji." He closed the doors behind him. Petra's ears twitched as she listened for footsteps. There were none, meaning Cain had assumed responsibility as guard.

They would not be disturbed.

"Petra, there—"

"Petra'Oji," she corrected venomously. "You will refer to me by my title, Finnyr."

"There are things I must tell you."

"Oh, I imagine so." She began to advance on him. "Our House, your family, are dying, Finnyr…"

"You can't possibly think I had anything to do with it." Finnyr retreated, shuffle step after shuffle step.

"No, I know better. You're far too inept for that," she chastised. "You're weak. You think small. You require a guiding hand." Claws shot from her fingers at every flaw she named. "You likely aren't even aware of what happened."

"No, I am aware."

"Oh?" She wanted to hear him say it. She wanted him to be so worked up and afraid that he would do anything to prove himself to her. And, in doing so, he would show her his true colors.

"I hadn't come home because I was searching for answers on my end, just like you commanded." Finnyr stood straighter, like a performer in the spotlight. "I overheard a conversation that I think will be of use to you."

He couldn't overhear anything when she needed him to, but suddenly managed without a problem when it was far too late. His inconsistency was beginning to rub Petra wrong. "For your sake, you'd best hope it is."

"It was in the wine," Finnyr said hastily. "The poison was in the wine."

Petra stopped just within arms reach. She stared at her brother for a long moment before raising her hand in a quick motion, bringing its back across his face. Her claws dug long, golden lines in his cheek.

Finnyr reeled. "What, why?"

"Tell me true. Where was the poison put?"

"I told you—"

She grabbed the chain that sat around his neck, the collar the Dono made all his beasts wear, and yanked him by it. Petra placed a hand on his shoulder, tensing her fingers and dragging her claws down his bicep. Finnyr howled in pain.

"Tell me how my people were poisoned!"

"I am telling you!" he snarled. "It was in the wine."

Petra slapped him again, this time with her palm. She ripped a chunk from his ear in the process. "Where did they put it?"

"In the wine!" Finnyr hissed in pain. "Petra, the poison was in the wine."

"Where?" She hit him again.

"The wine!"

"Where was it?" Petra threw him backward. Finnyr stumbled, giving her an easy opening to straddle his feet and hold him against the wall by his neck. Rivulets of gold pooled in his collarbones as her claws dug into the soft muscle of his throat.

"The wine!" Finnyr was nearly at the point of tears. The shameful, pathetic man came undone under her fingers, the truth pouring from him like the blood from his neck. Petra could confidently ascertain that he was not trying to deceive her in any fashion.

She dropped him into a heap on the floor in disgust.

In a display of how low she regarded him, she stalked away, her back to him. *Let him lunge*, Petra seethed mentally. If he dared attack her when her back was turned, she really would kill him. Right now, his death was merely a high probability.

"Cain." Petra pulled open the door. The man was at attention. Cain was not perfect, but Petra was truly grateful to have him in that moment. "Go and have the word spread that all wine on the isle of Ruana is to be cast into the God's Line. Every last bottle, cask, and vat."

"As you command, Oji." Cain made haste away.

Petra slammed the door shut and turned with a sigh. It wasn't even sport to tear her brother into pieces. He had already healed, but he remained on the floor in a puddle of pale blue flesh. She should be done with it and send him to the refinery to function as Ruana's personal reagent farm.

She squatted before him, assessing her broken prey. Petra reached out a hand and he flinched. She slowly began to stroke his hair, as if she were soothing a skittish animal.

"Now, Finnyr, tell me whose poison it was, and don't lie to me."

"Coletta'Ryu's." Finnyr swallowed, trying to wash away his weakness. It didn't work. "It was Coletta'Ryu's poison."

"What?" Petra tried to make sense of this. The Rok'Ryu? Coletta was nothing, worthless, weak and small.

And that would be just the sort of person who would resort to such devious and underhanded means. The person who could not stand in the pit. The person who would attach herself to one of the fiercest Dragon fighters while still offering something of her own to match the bloodthirstiness of her mate.

"I know it was her," Finnyr insisted. "She is known for staying in her gardens, but allows no one else in there. Most assume it's for her privacy, to hide her frailty. But I began to suspect something else when a servant went in and wound up dead."

Petra glanced at the servant she had killed hours ago, the body now cold. She could entirely understand killing someone for being in the wrong space at the wrong time. Especially when that someone was worthless.

"The man was killed without any kind of wound. His chest, head, all intact," Finnyr clarified.

It made too much sense.

"How have you neglected to tell me this?" Petra raged.

"I did not think it important." Finnyr tried to move away but Petra's hand tightened into a fist, yanking him into place with force.

"You did not think it important for me to know that the Ryu of Rok is a shadow-master, a potion-mongering coward?" Their noses nearly touched as she verbally assaulted him. "That she is far more despicable than even her mate?"

"I did not connect the facts! I did not see what was there! Nameless die all the time."

"That is because you are an idiot." Petra slammed Finnyr against the wall. "A useless idiot."

"Petra—"

She gouged out his throat with a hand, blood pouring, bubbling as his words escaped through the open holes as gasping wheezes. Flesh strung from between her fingers like taffy, stretching until it snapped.

"You are useless." Petra let the one wound heal, pinning him down with her knees on his arms and sitting on his chest. She leaned forward, dragging a claw around his eye, watching the liquid ooze out alongside the blood, as she whispered in his ear, "Useless."

She scolded herself as much as him. They had both failed House Xin. He had failed them with his incompetence. She had failed them for depending on it. His punishment would be her claws. Her punishment would be the shame of flaying her brother in a back room, hidden from the world.

"Useless."

She reared back and struck him.

"Useless. Useless. Useless!"

She would slice him, once for every Dragon that had died this night, and then another hundred times for every Oji of House Xin he had shamed. His magic began to falter in its ability to keep up healing between her relentless blows. It reduced his flesh into little more than liquefied meat. He tried to struggle against her but Petra pressed herself upon him until she began to hear bones snap. If he died tonight, he would not die with a face any would recognize. She would see that she never had to look upon the shame of Xin ever again.

Her claws stopped, mid swing. Petra tugged, blinking from her blood-frenzied trance. A hand was wrapped around her wrist.

"Sister, enough!"

# 38
## CVAREH

THE WOMAN PULLED HIM IN SO MANY DIRECTIONS AT ONE TIME THAT CVAREH was surprised his limbs were still attached. He had sensed her hesitation, her wish to withdraw, but she hadn't rejected him outright and he didn't know yet how to fully process the matter. Arianna was a woman who always knew what she wanted, what she fought for. A lack of opposition could mean support, or agreement.

Cvareh scowled to himself at the logic, dangerous in more than one way.

Perhaps she merely had yet to find the way she wished to outright reject him. It was confusing and laborious to try to reason through her mannerisms. But it was something he did gladly. The better he understood her, or tried, the better he could give her whatever it was she needed, be it revenge, or gold, or someone to whom she could finally confess the weighty secrets that she carried alone in her heart.

It would be his lot that the first woman he would design to take for his mate, his life-mate if she ever agreed to it, would be the first Perfect Chimera—and impossibly head-strong. Cvareh grinned faintly to himself. All the reasons he should find her tiresome made her all the more endearing. She had accomplished an inspirational amount in her short life. If Arianna could be all she was, then he could be a man she deemed worthy of her love.

She didn't say she loved him.

She didn't outright reject him.

Their magics and minds had been so close for the past day that he wouldn't be surprised if she began to smell of him and he of her. Even if she said otherwise, he knew more of her than she gave him credit for, and what he knew and felt gave him hope. Cvareh paused, looking down the long stretch that would eventually lead back to her room.

The mere thought of her being near brought a smile to his mouth, a smile that quickly fell when he remembered her desire to leave Nova. The pain of being separated from her was like lightning in his mind, hurt its rallying thunderclap. But love would be the rain, soothing both.

There was a solution here, he merely had to find it.

"Cvareh'Ryu!"

Cain was the last person he wanted to see, especially after the increasing closeness he and Arianna had shared. "Cain, you have yet to recover my good favor," Cvareh cautioned.

"We have far more pressing concerns," Cain's tone was grave.

Cvareh put all else aside. If it was enough to unsettle Cain, it was something serious indeed. "What has happened?"

"The wine on Ruana has been poisoned."

Cvareh didn't even have the capability to process the words Cain was saying. It made no sense. "Why would the wine be poisoned?"

"Think of who such a thing would benefit." Cain scowled with murderous intent.

"Rok bastards." Cvareh rolled another several curses off his tongue.

"All wine is to be discarded into the God's Line. I am to spread the word."

"Go with haste." Cvareh would not keep him a moment longer. "Where is my sister?"

"Her sitting parlor."

Cvareh started in that direction. He had to get to Petra. She would know how to make sense of this.

"She is alone with Finnyr'Kin."

The words made Cvareh pause. He turned to look back at the Dragon who stood several steps away now, and whose words held an unspoken caution. Cain would say no more, clearly. He had been put too far in his place of late to do so. Furthermore, it was not a matter of the House's safety. This was now a matter of family.

"Thank you, Cain."

"Walk in the protection of Lord Xin."

They went separate ways.

If Petra had called Finnyr, she suspected him to be involved, or to know something of the crime. She was dumping all wine on Ruana, which led him to believe the damage was widespread. Dread grew with his every step.

It wasn't until the sharp smell of cedar drifted through the halls of the Xin Manor that Cvareh broke out into a run. He pushed slaves out of the way, focused only on his destination. The scent of blood grew to an overwhelming, pungent stench as he neared Petra's parlor.

Cvareh broke through the door, skidding to a stop at the sight of the scene before him.

Petra was straddled atop what could only be described as the pulp of their older brother. Her claws dripped blood with every swing, spattering around her in wide arcs. She rocked atop his chest like death's lover, a dark and primal savagery overcoming her.

"Useless. Useless. Useless!" she screamed the word over and over.

Finnyr cried and gasped through lips that were sheared back to bone. If he could make noise, then he was alive. That meant Cvareh wasn't too late to save Petra from her own madness.

Cvareh ran to their side. He gripped Petra's wrist, stopping her mid-swing. Petra snarled at his tether.

"Sister, enough!"

"Unhand me," she growled.

"Petra." Cvareh slackened his grip, but he still held her. He needed his sister to feel his magic, their magic, the magic that their brother also shared. "You will kill him if you continue."

"It is because of him that Xin have died this night." She spat the words. "Save him and you are no better than the cowards and butchers he works for."

"Kill him, and neither are you." Cvareh knew his sister. He knew when she needed to be pushed. He knew he was the one person in the whole world who could get away with it. "Did you intend to murder him without witnesses? Without calling his crimes? Without a proper duel? Will you stoop to the level of House Rok?"

Petra panted. Finnyr groaned. Cvareh was left to speak sense into the madness.

"You are the Xin'Oji. Your House needs your example." Cvareh knelt. He focused only on his sister. "No one doubts your ferocity, Petra."

"Move." She pushed him away. Cvareh thought she was merely making space to strike at Finnyr again, but she stood with a small sway. The death of House Xin's fighters and innocent alike had taken something from her. "You're right, Cvareh."

Cvareh remained silent, letting Petra speak. Just as he knew when to push, he knew when to back away. And this was a Petra who would skin anyone or anything alive that prevented her from being heard.

"He doesn't deserve to die a death hidden away." Petra bared her teeth. "Finnyr, I will challenge you at Court this day the moment it convenes. And if you run, I will still challenge you. I will leave it standing for all Dragons to hear." Petra spit on their brother as he groaned, his flesh knitting sluggishly from the tax on his magic. "So that I may hunt you down and kill you at my leisure. There will be nowhere you can run from a duel called in Court."

Cvareh did nothing to help Finnyr up as he tried to pull himself off the floor. Their brother locked eyes with Petra—one eye, the other was still a slow-healing, bloody socket—as if somehow he still thought he could fight her. The majority of his face had been scraped away down to the bone.

"I have powerful people who will stand for me, Petra," Finnyr uttered darkly.

"Who? Yveun'Dono?" Petra scoffed. "Let him challenge me. I invite him! Let us settle this like Dragons rather than the coward he is, poisoning my men and women his only means of securing an advantage."

"Do not cast me aside," their brother cautioned. "I will be your undoing."

"You undo nothing but my honor with your existence."

"You never valued what I could offer this House!"

She snorted. "There was nothing to value."

"House Xin does not need you or any information you can give us." Cvareh interjected himself into the shouting match before it got out of hand again. Both sets of eyes were on him, but he looked only at Petra. "She will produce it."

"Cvareh…" Petra gave a cautionary look to Finnyr. That was already saying too much in front of their brother. Not when they had just effectively disowned him and marked him for death. An animal in a corner could still be dangerous, even one as small as Finnyr. Especially when that corner was backed by Yveun'Dono. "You mean…"

"Yes." There was no doubt they spoke of the same thing.

"Then the night was not a total waste." His sister clapped her hands together as though she cheered for the arrival of the Lord of Death himself. "Cvareh, remove him from my sight. Keep him, tucked away where I can't see him until the Court begins. Yveun wanted him to stay in the manor? Very well, he will stay, long enough for me to kill him."

Cvareh stood over his elder brother. Finnyr glared up at him with the same coldness he'd always shown after Petra had named Cvareh Ryu over him. Cvareh wished it could have been different. He wished he need not look upon his brother with contempt. But he knew nothing else.

This was the conclusion they had all been marching toward from the beginning. This was the breaking point of the three Xin siblings. Their House only had room for two.

Finnyr stood without his help, limping away. Blood trailed behind him as he walked and Cvareh stayed at his side all the way out of the room, then closed the doors tightly behind them with a heavy sigh.

He looked at his elder brother with a weight in his chest, a vacuum left behind by the joy Arianna had placed there earlier. Petra wanted to see Finnyr locked away and then led to slaughter. It was a shameful death.

"So where will I be kept before my slaughter?" Finnyr rasped through his yet-healing wounds, blood dribbling from his chin. "Will I even have time to wash before Court? Or line my skin with the blessings of the gods?"

Cvareh swallowed hard, feeling oddly brave and very stupid. Petra would no doubt want Finnyr locked away in the sparsest, deepest room in the manor. "You will."

He led Finnyr down the halls and away from his sister to the guest rooms usually reserved for noteworthy occupants. Finnyr was his brother, and a Xin; he would present himself well before court. Even if today was the day he would die, he would die a proper death befitting a child of the House.

Finnyr, to his credit, made no effort to struggle or escape. Even if he could overpower Cvareh, Petra wouldn't hesitate to reduce him once more to a golden smear if Finnyr turned now. His brother kept his head bowed and his mouth shut, defeated.

"I'll return in a few hours, right before the Court begins." Cvareh assumed responsibility for the task. Even if Petra hadn't designed it to fall to him, it should be one of them, and she wasn't going to be in the right mindset to escort Finnyr anywhere.

"Little Cvareh, so good to his big sister," Finnyr spoke with his back turned, making a show of dedicating more effort to looking around the room than his pointed comments. "Take a good look at me, Cvareh. This is the fate that awaits you. She'll cast you aside the moment you're no longer of use. She'll destroy everything Xin for her ambition, if that's what she must. The end Petra had designed for herself will stand before all her ideals, forever. It stands before me. It will stand before you. If you don't stop her, she will lead everything you love to ruin and you will be left with nothing more than the feeling of Yveun's claws ripping out your beating heart."

Cvareh clenched his fists tightly and still his claws tried to escape. Blood pooled in his hands from his own palms, but he didn't open them. If he did, he would strike Finnyr down where he stood.

"Everything Petra does is for Xin." Cvareh shook his head sadly, reaching to close the door. "It's you who destroyed everything, Finnyr."

Cvareh shut the door and summoned a servant from down the hall to fetch the key. He waited, guarding the room, until it could be sufficiently locked. Even then, he stalled, listening, holding his breath, waiting.

There were no outbursts of anger. No sobs. No screams of anguish. Finnyr was quiet, going about his business as though his impending expiration didn't bother him in the slightest.

Cvareh gave a long sigh and stepped away. This was normal for Finnyr, being a prisoner among luxury, disposable nobility. And he was going to die as he lived—as nothing more than a captive.

# 39
## ARIANNA

The list of her supplies was almost finished.

It was an extensive process to calculate out the amount of various elements she would need to get a satisfactory initial production on the boxes. For the first time in maybe her entire life, she wished she could talk to Sophie. The woman would know how many boxes were a reasonable number to produce. She was far better at planning tactically for things like that than Ari was.

But that was currently impossible, and Arianna needed to give something to the Dragons before she left. She wanted a sort of contract in hand, a written understanding of expectations. The comfort it'd give her would be literally paper thin, but it was something.

She operated under the thought that an initial run of a hundred boxes would be enough to begin to shift the tides in House Xin's favor. Then they'd move into second-stage production, where all the tooling would be perfected and the workers on the line would know the full assembly process with ease. They could make more, faster.

She hoped it would be enough.

The waft of a scent hit her nose, distracting her. Arianna paused her pen on the page. It was the smell of Dragon blood, a sharper, fresher aroma than just trace magic. It wasn't extremely close, but it was near enough.

She stared at her hands. She had decided to look to the future, not the past. She was going to craft a new world for Loom, for Florence. Arianna pressed her eyes closed. She was going to let herself hope and dream again for a future that she might design herself to be a part of.

But the smell of blood was stronger than hope, and more real than any dream. It lured her back to the old addiction known as revenge. Arianna gripped the pen tightly, as if it was a lifeline in the rip current she was about to be pulled into.

The scent grew and Arianna stood. The Dragon named Rafansi was nearby. He was bleeding. Arianna didn't know why, but she felt the immediate tug in her gut that meant if she was not the one to kill him, she would harbor nothing but resentment for the rest of her years. This man had taken her life; she would not also let him take his death on his terms.

*It is better this way*, she tried to convince herself as her body moved on auto-pilot. She would seek him out and have her revenge. There would be no need to involve Cvareh and, in fact, she could still have a boon from him to spend on anything he didn't give her freely out of adoration. *Yes*, she was doing this for him, as much as herself. It would be better for everyone this way.

Arianna walked to the door, poking her nose into the hall, looking around. The smell was stronger, though it seemed to be trailing away. She looked back to the desk, caught between what she had vowed to fight for all her life—a rebellion, a future for Loom—and a quiet whisper that this was the one thing she truly wanted.

The Dragon she needed dead was here. He was here, and vulnerable. She could kill him and then build a future without the shadow of the past lurking somewhere in Cvareh's home. Rafansi was close enough that she could do it and be back in her room before the sun crested the horizon, before any were the wiser.

Arianna tore at her Dragon clothes in a sprint of movement. Yanking open the top drawer of her dresser, she pulled out her industrial trousers. They fit as perfectly as they had before. No matter how much time she spent on Nova, this was the cloth she was cut from.

She was meant to walk in boots designed for function before fashion. She was meant to tighten belts and harnesses about her fully-covered torso, wrapping herself in her own clockwork designs. She was born of stronger things than colors and fanfare. She was born of steam and steel. It had never felt so right to don the coat of the White Wraith.

As she started down the hall, her hands running over her winch box, the bottom of her coat flapped about her calves and she felt like a bloody god. She would not take her revenge in the clothes of a Dragon. She would do it with every advantage she had stitched into herself during every hardship she had survived over the years.

Arianna was not seen if she didn't want to be. She'd spent days, months, slowly mapping out the Xin Manor with the same care as she would a high-paying heist. The halls were surprisingly empty of occupants, which made it all the easier.

She tracked the scent, running in parallel halls upward until she was right upon it. Arianna looked up and down the stretch, seeing and sensing no one. In the distance, she could pick up the edge of magic, but it was weak. Likely a servant, nothing she couldn't handle if she was forced to.

She stopped before the door and took a deep breath to slow her racing heart. Her eyes shot open, blood boiled. He was here. Rafansi was right in this room.

Arianna forced herself to take measured breaths. She forced her head to cooperate. But all she could hear in her ears were the dying words of Eva, of Oliver, of everyone she held dear. She could feel the tug of bloodlust pulling her under its powerful wave, and fought all the harder to breach the surface with clear thinking and logic.

She looked down the hall once more and briefly considered walking away. If she let this man go, she would reclaim control over the one force that had driven her to the brink of insanity for years. She would reclaim her future by snapping the tether of the past.

*Killing him would also snap that tether.*

Arianna dropped into a crouch, peering into the keyhole. Just from the bit of tension the door handle gave when her hand rested on it, she knew the lock was engaged. She reached for the small tools concealed in the belt holding her winch box.

The lock was as simple as the one on her door. She approached it with ease and familiarity. Still, sweat dripped down her neck and her fingers nearly trembled. *Nearly.* She reaffirmed her grip on the pin now slick with sweat in her hand, and held steady.

She was close. She was so close.

The lock disengaged and the sound was louder than a gunshot to Arianna's ears. She slammed down the handle, swinging open the door. Her hand was on her knife, drawing it. The door snapped shut behind her, her blade wedged into the groove to prevent anyone else from entering. She turned, her other blade already in hand.

A Dragon stared at her in shock from the center of the room. His face had paled to nearly a Fenthri gray, his jaw slack. His magic seemed to nearly vibrate with pulses of frantic terror.

Arianna stared at him. Their eyes locked and it was a spell, one she couldn't fight. Here he was, here was the man who had betrayed her. No one to get in her way, nowhere for him to escape, he was hers. Her lips curled in a guttural growl of bloodlust.

"A-A-Arianna?"

"I'm glad you didn't forget my name." Her voice was gravel and broken glass and the sum of countless hours spent screaming alone into the darkness. "I never once forgot yours, Rafansi."

He shuffled backward as she advanced.

"And now, it will be the last thing you ever say."

Arianna pushed off, unloading the tension of her knees into the floor. She grabbed for the golden chain around his neck. The tempering resisted her magic—*no matter*. She twisted, swinging him like a rag-doll down onto the floor.

He fell hard. Arianna went down with him. She panted, her knife rearing back like an adder. She had him right where she wanted him and the idiot was too stunned to do anything. She could do anything she wanted, kill him however delighted her, though nothing would satisfy her hunger for his suffering.

Did she want to scoop out his eyeballs with the point of her blade? Did she want to carve out every organ he ever gave her? Did she want to take his heart and be done with it?

Arianna wanted to scream.

None of it was enough. None of it would be enough to quench her thirst for revenge. None of it would bring back the woman she'd loved, the teacher she'd revered, the friends she'd made in the only true home she'd ever had. She could kill him a thousand times over, and it wouldn't be satisfying to her. Because what she truly wanted, no boon, no vengeance, no vision, could give her. She brought down her dagger.

His hand shot up, catching her wrist. The other swiped for her throat. Arianna caught it. They were in deadlock. Eyes on eyes, blade point and claw point at throats. She shifted her feet, ready to overpower him. She could feel it in his trembling grip—he wasn't nearly strong enough to hold her.

"Wait, don't kill me," he spoke quickly, before she could laugh or scream or even give a growl at the coward's attempt to barter for his life. "Don't kill me, Arianna. I can give you something better."

"Once a traitor, always a traitor," she snarled. Arianna swung backward, pulling on his wrist, feeling the bones pop. She curled herself and brought her feet forward, kicking out his other wrist.

"Yes!"

Her blade stopped a second time, now of her own accord.

The man's face moved oddly as he spoke. His visage was horribly scarred with markings that hadn't been there the last time she'd seen him. Arianna watched his bones knitting before her eyes. Envy bubbled up at whoever had maimed him so effectively; jealousy was quick to follow that somehow she found herself lacking in doing the same.

"Yes, I am a traitor. But it is not you I am betraying now. I can give you something better, more satisfying than my death."

"You have no idea how badly I want this." Her hand had finally given to shaking.

"I betrayed you, Arianna, but I was nothing more than a puppet. If not me, it would've been someone else. What do you get from my death? Nothing. There will be more like me who creep up from the shadows. Kill the man who pulls the strings."

"You'd betray your own King?"

"Once a traitor, always a traitor." He grinned darkly.

A shiver of malice raced down her spine. She wanted to kill him. She had wanted to kill him for years. But he was now a low-hanging fruit. She had him and she could slay him any time. She knew she could overpower him and best him in any fight—that much had already been proven in their short encounter thus far.

Yes, killing him would serve her personal vendetta. But it would mean little for any beyond her. If she killed Yveun… She would cut off the head of the snake.

"I can take you to him, right to him. I can get you in his room before the sun even wakes. No one else can give that to you, no other Dragon will." Rafansi panted softly, continuing to eye her dagger. "It's a fair exchange, my life for the life of the Dragon King. Don't you think?"

Arianna stood, glancing to the window. If she killed him in the manor, she'd have to contend with the other Xin. She could let him take her to the King, kill Yveun, then take Rafansi's life in turn. Arianna flipped her dagger in her palm, once, twice, before sheathing it.

The mere idea, even if it was a farce, of working with him again made her feel soiled. *Eva, forgive me.* But she was going to cast the die and gamble for it all, or nothing.

"Take me to the Dragon King."

# FLORENCE

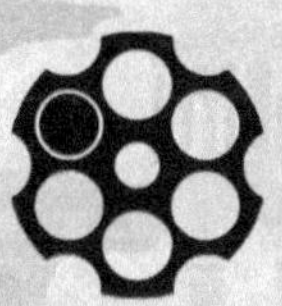

Why?

The word seemed to linger on the tongue of every survivor. *Why?*

They were adrift in the world, separated by the distance of train lines and the bleeding wounds that had been carved deep into their hearts. So the train continued in the only direction it could, on to Ter 1.2. No one objected. No one suggested otherwise. There was nowhere else to go.

An entire guild, an entire people, homeless and adrift.

Florence had wanted to live to see a world where people weren't tethered to their guilds, but she hadn't wanted it like this. She'd never wanted this. She would sit and listen to the wailing tears that were only smothered, not soothed, by time. She rocked silently with the train.

Powell looked equally shell-shocked, numb. The truth of what he had been saying since he had woken her two days ago echoed in her mind, underscoring the parted lips and drifting eyes that now made up his face. She waited for it to wear off, but she could only wait so long before her burning questions threatened to immolate her fragile sanity.

"Powell," she whispered, hoping to get his attention without disturbing any who dozed around them.

"Florence?"

"You said the Dragon King ordered the attack." His silence was affirmation enough. "How did you know?" She didn't ask him why. If the man knew why, his state over the past two days would've been different. He would've been angry, frustrated, regretful. But he seemed as confused as her in that respect.

"There was a whisper." His voice mirrored the word. "From the Revolvers'

Guild. It was a warning that the King's Riders had taken over. That they demanded explosives en mass. That the Harvesters were to be the first example."

"'The first example'?" Florence repeated. "You don't think the King means to attack the other guilds, do you?"

"I don't know." Powell's shoulder rubbed against hers with the swaying of the car. "And we have no way of finding out now."

All the Chimera with whisper links in the Harvesters' Guild had been killed. It had been an impressive hub of communication, one that could rival even the Ravens'. Florence's stomach turned sour. A guild had been destroyed, possibly the first of many, and the world didn't even know. Injustice and pain that went unknown hurt all the more, she had discovered.

Nora and Derek tried to ease her into sleep, but Florence refused. She sat on the edge of the train car, watching the world go by and the distant mines appear and vanish along the dawn-colored horizon, none the wiser to the fact that their world was burning. She envied that distant point, a place beyond the edge of the world where she now lived.

They were the fourth train to arrive in Ter.1.2. That was a relief to all. The people who greeted them on the platform were already equipped with knowledge, and prepared to manage the survivors. They were shuffled along, unburdened by the need for thought, into various inns and temporary encampments that had been set up throughout the too-quiet city.

"I think this is where we part."

Florence was startled to attention by the sound of Powell's rough, solemn voice. She grabbed Derek's arm, preventing him and Nora from disappearing ahead in the flow of people. Florence turned her face up to Powell's, demanding an explanation.

He sighed heavily. "The Vicar did not survive. So there must be a vote for who will assume the mantle. Only four Masters seem to have made it out, however." Pain flashed hot on Powell's features. "The Master Harvesters were all called in on my behalf, to vote."

"This was not your fault." Florence gripped the man's forearm. She tried to push magic into him, despite the fact that he was a Fenthri. She tried to push in her truth—that she, too, stared survivor's guilt in the face regularly. "Powell, look at me: This wasn't your fault."

"No…" He sounded unconvinced. "Anyway, seeing how four isn't enough for a quorum, they voted to grant me my circle and make me a Master for the vote."

"You would have been awarded it anyway." Florence couldn't imagine being awarded Mastery under the current circumstances. It made her heart ache for the Harvester before her.

Her effort brought a small smile to his mouth. "I like to believe that's true." She knew he would always wonder.

"Powell." The other Master Florence had met on the train, Max, called from

a short distance away. The circle emblazoned on his cheek around the
Harvester's sickle seemed almost like an omen of sorrow now.

"I'm coming." Powell turned to leave.

Florence held fast to his forearm. "I'm coming with you."

"What?" It came from Powell and Nora at the same time.

"This was what we came here for," she explained to the Alchemists. "To
speak with the Vicar Harvester about the rebellion."

"The Vicar Harvester was undecided," Nora reminded her.

"That Vicar Harvester is dead. And in light of recent events, I think we have
a better case to make." Florence squeezed Powell's forearm. She wanted him to
feel her strength and certainty. She wanted to be as strong as Arianna was when
the woman had pulled her from the depths of the Underground and told her
everything would be all right. "Powell, we would like to request this of the
Masters."

He looked back to Max who was halfway to them, no doubt having heard the
better portion of the conversation. He was tall for a Fenthri or Chimera, nearly
Arianna's height. His sharp blue eyes assessed her.

"The vote won't be a place for a Raven."

"I'm not a Raven," Florence replied on instinct.

"What are you, then?"

She stopped short of her usual response of "Revolver." Instead: "I'm
Florence."

The man raised his eyebrows. But his response was interrupted by a solemn
bell toll from a nearby assembly hall. He pulled out his pocket watch, inspecting
the time.

"Very well, come along. But they sit in the back," he cautioned Powell, as if
the man was now solely responsible for the three of them. Judging from the
train, it wasn't an unfair assessment.

Usually, a filled hall would seem like a joyous occasion. The rising of a
Master, the appointment of a new Vicar. Every seat was packed with journeymen
and handfuls of initiates.

But nothing had ever looked sadder than the three men and two women who
were seated in the center of the floor. No one spoke for a long minute. The room
was as still as a tomb.

Max stood. "Today, on the thirteenth day of the eleventh month, in the year
one thousand eighty-one, we, the Masters of the Harvesters' Guild, have been
called together to elect a new Vicar Harvester from among us."

Florence shifted her weight from foot to foot. She was short enough that she
had elected to stand in the back of the room on a small box to be able to see.
Plus, even if she didn't fully agree with them, Max's words stayed with her.
While she believed that any Fenthri from any guild should be able to witness the
changing of a Vicar, this did not impact her in the same way it did the
journeymen and initiates who lined the room. They deserved to be closer.

"Do any have a nominee from among us?"

The first journeyman stood. "I nominate Maxwell."

"I second." Another stood as well.

"I nominate Theodosia."

"I third Maxwell."

"Second Theodosia."

"I nominate Powell."

Florence watched with more interest the moment Powell's name was added to the ring. Whoever the other two Masters were, they didn't seem to have the same type of fervor wrapped around them. Eventually, the only names that mattered were Powell and Theodosia.

When it was clear that the room was split, the two stepped forward, away from the Masters, to face their peers. Chosen from a select group, supported by the guild on the whole, now the most experienced men and women would cast their votes for who would lead.

"I vote for Powell." Max was the first to cast his ballot.

"I vote for Theodosia," the second woman decided.

The final man thought it over a long moment. Florence wished she could ask him what ran through his head. What did one think while they were deciding the future of a guild? How did someone even approach a situation like that? It was a skill Florence wanted to imitate and learn.

He took a deep breath and made his choice. "I vote Powell."

Max stood again, as the woman at Powell's side stepped away. "Powell, Vicar Harvester, so voted on the thirteenth day of the eleventh month of the year one thousand eighty-one. Lead with wisdom."

"Lead with wisdom," the room repeated, Florence included. Even though she had never seen a Vicar voting ceremony, she had read about them. And, while this was certainly an unorthodox situation, falling to convention felt right. It harkened back to the old days of the guilds and the traditions they kept—the things the Dragons could only take from Loom if the guilds let them.

"Sow and reap." Maxwell placed his hand on Powell's shoulder.

"Sow and reap." Theodosia did the same.

"Sow and reap." The other Masters spoke the words and joined as well. Soon, the room was one large, spoked wheel with Powell at its center. "Sow and reap" filled the air and connected the Harvesters as much as their physical contact.

"Sow and reap, Powell," Florence whispered, apart from the group. To her surprise, Derek and Nora echoed the same.

It was a dark stroke of luck, but a stroke of luck all the same. Florence leaned against the wall, content to let Powell have his moment and to let the Harvesters find comfort in it. For she was no longer worried about finding time or sympathy from the Vicar Harvester.

# 41
## YVEUN

Yveun was awoken with a sharp knock on the door. He gave a low growl from the back of his throat, expressing his discontent at whatever fool would dare disturb him this early in the morning. He chose to ignore the offender. Instead of flaying them, he curled toward his queen.

Let no one claim he wasn't a benevolent ruler.

There was another knock. Another low growl. And a voice that changed the pace of the early hours of dawn.

"Dono, Dono, I have returned from the Xin Manor." *Finnyr*.

Yveun narrowed his eyes in the dim light. Finnyr of all people would not be so bold before him. Which meant whatever he had learned at the manor was worth risking Yveun's ire. He bared his teeth in the twilight dawn, as if the scent of wine and poison could still waft through his open balcony.

Coletta stood without a word. She drew a sheer vermillion robe around her that floated like an aura of freshly broken sunlight as she excused herself without word into a small side room. They rarely let themselves be seen together, especially fondly. It suited their image better when the perception was the fearsome King and his unwanted Ryu.

Yveun stood, walking to the door. He paused briefly. There was a different magic in the air. Muffled by the door, it was hard to make out. But, judging from its ferocity alone, it was certainly not Finnyr's.

He eased open the door. His posture was relaxed, but every muscle in his body was taught and primed, ready to explode. The claws of the hand behind the door were already unsheathed.

"Who is your guest?" Yveun asked directly, narrowing his eyes at the unfamiliar Dragon at Finnyr's side.

There was no time for Finnyr to formulate a response.

The illusion over the woman rippled the second she moved, too complex to maintain over the bulky clothes she wore. Yveun crisply heard the sound of bone breaking and the slicing of flesh. The scent of cedar assaulted his nose as Finnyr coughed blood.

With a spray of gold, Yveun watched as the careful play he had been orchestrating for years was cut down before him. Finnyr, his toy, his opportunity to slice Xin down and seat a loyal shadow in the Oji's seat, could not be killed here and now. They were too close, Petra too weakened, to stray from the course.

Rather than reaching for the woman, Yveun reached for Finnyr. He gripped the man and pulled forward, un-impaling him from the woman's blade. She twisted her knife through the empty air with a snarl, its mark gone. Yveun threw Finnyr behind him, hoping the wordless Dragon would muster enough sense to crawl from the fighting. All the worthless Xin had to do was keep himself alive, yet Yveun was unconvinced if he'd manage that much.

The woman lunged for him, all teeth and growls and golden blades. Yveun dodged, letting her momentum carry her into his den. He slammed shut the door as she turned.

Two bright lilac eyes stared at him, nearly glowing in the first sunlight of morning. She was gray, bland, swaddled like a babe in industrial garb. A Fenthri turned Chimera. Unmarked. Addressing him like she was a champion.

Yveun wanted to laugh, but he recognized something in her eyes beyond their oddly familiar shade. It was the same look Petra had when she stared at him. It was the same look he saw in the mirror.

A broken lust for something that you would drown the world in its own blood for twice over.

He didn't announce his attack. He didn't throw a threat. He didn't give her the opportunity to know he was about to claim her life. It didn't matter how or why she was here; she was an agent working against his goals and that was all he needed to know. Fools threatened. Killers moved.

But his claws didn't meet flesh. They met a golden dagger that sprung to life seemingly with its own consciousness, like some kind of barbed tail tethered to a line. His hand pushed against the weapon in surprise, cutting to bone on the edge of the blade.

The blade twisted, deepening its bite onto him. One hand closed around his wrist, pulling him in one direction. She landed the first hit square onto his face with claws.

The dullness of shock wore off quickly. Yveun dipped down, pushing the blade and her hand back. He reached with his teeth, sinking through all the mess of fabric and leather to her shoulder.

Most Dragons never attacked with their fangs out of the taboo associated with imbibing. But that made such attacks the perfect opportunity because they were unexpected. The woman gave a grunt, biting in a yell of pain. She let go of his hand, reaching for his neck. His claws gouged into her side and they both drew blood.

But the slit across his throat was enough to make his jaw relax. She leapt away, her dagger lashing out. Yveun parried it with his claws effortlessly.

It was then that he noticed the blood pouring from the wound on her shoulder. The taste it left lingering in his mouth. As gold as his, she did not bleed the rot of a normal Chimera. On his tongue was the taste of honeysuckle, the faint essence of Finnyr, and the recognition that didn't require the other man's obvious interjection.

"Arianna! It's the Master Rivet, the engineer. The one from the rebellion!"

The woman turned to Finnyr, momentarily distracted by who she wanted to kill more. Yveun sprung for her when she was caught in her own loathing, barreling into her like a bull. Arms around her waist, he dug into her. He felt her knife stab into his shoulder.

Golden blood poured over his hands like an omen of all his worst fears.

"The Rivet who claimed to make the Philosopher's Box." The scent of blood made him feel alive, woke his senses and gave him power. Yveun gave an extra push and she tumbled under his weight. "I'm sure you've confused many a Dragon with your trick of bleeding gold."

Arianna rolled away from his violent slashes, her blood leaving a trail on the balcony. The spool on her hip spun and the line whipped forward, keeping him at bay. Yveun ducked, narrowly missing it wrapping around his neck. She panted, reclaimed her feet and kicked, spinning midair, seeking purchase against him with feet or claw or wire.

But Yveun dodged her.

The woman was good, that much he'd admit. Yveun began to laugh, which only seemed to whip her into more of a frenzy. He could see how this creature had killed his Leona. It made so much more sense than the unambitious and untrained Cvareh. He had seen these movements in the pit, another explanation settled just by watching her attacks.

Cvareh was not mighty. Xin was not mighty. It was this girl, this prodigy of two worlds, who threatened him time and again.

As he dodged an attack, Yveun felt the line of a wire wrap around his ankle, pulling. The world fell from under him as he slipped back. She lunged forward, her knee digging into his side. Her blades above him, he didn't even struggle, he merely kept laughing.

It was delightful.

"I expected more of a fight from the Dragon King," she snarled.

"I've no further interest in fighting you, my pet." Yveun relaxed, noting movement from the corner of his eye. "You are more valuable alive, at least for now."

"You've lost." She raised the dagger in triumph.

"And you wasted the chance to kill me like the child you are."

Coletta loomed behind the Chimera who thought she had him pinned. In her hand was the smallest of daggers, little more than a letter opener. Without a single expression crossing her features, she dug the tiny blade into Arianna's neck.

Arianna's spare hand rose to the wound as she turned in shock. But her eyes were already losing focus, the artery quickly carrying Coletta's poison to her brain. The Chimera twisted her blade in her hand and swung backwards.

Coletta stepped back in an effortless dodge.

Off balance and sluggish, the Rivet tipped sideways, landing in an undignified heap at Yveun's side. Her eyes held awareness still. The only thing capable of attacking him. But looks couldn't kill, and Yveun stood.

"She had you on a few attacks," Coletta both teased and chastised.

"I merely didn't want to kill her," Yveun explained.

"I reasoned." Coletta leaned forward, drawing the dagger from the woman's neck. "The poison will wear off within the hour. Move her before then."

Yveun watched with both fascination and chilling horror the gold blood that dribbled from the hole. This was what Fenthri could be capable of, if they were left to their own devices. The ability to become mighty enough to slay Dragon Riders and challenge even the Dono himself. All from the might of stolen organs.

"Your insight is unparalleled." Coletta began to collect her things after nothing more than a cautionary glance that showed she had heard him. Yveun looked to Finnyr, knowing the source of his mate's discomfort. It was very rare for them to have a guest in their chambers. "You have many words to tell me," he spoke to the pasty blue Dragon.

"I will tell you all of them." Finnyr thrust his face against the ground at Yveun's feet. "But we have more pressing matters. Petra has sworn to challenge me today in court."

And Petra would win.

Yveun sighed. The blue sack of flesh before him sometimes seemed more trouble than it was worth. As easy as it would be to off Finnyr once and for all, doing so would be a half measure, the easy route. He had cultivated Finnyr for too long to throw away the effort.

"After yesterday, there need not be another day of Court," Yveun announced. "She will not have a chance to challenge you, as we will be on Lysip within the hour. I will announce the Court ended."

Yveun stared at the unconscious engineer, the woman who had single-handedly caused him so much trouble. There was information he needed from her. But for once, he was going to have the time to extract it. And Yveun would do so with deliciously slow, full measures.

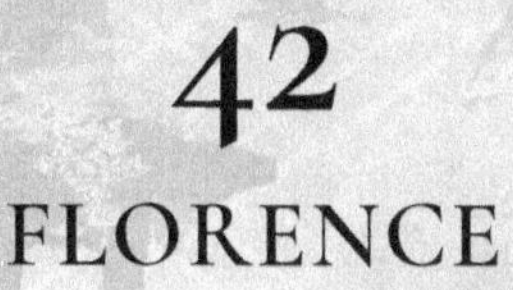

# 42
## FLORENCE

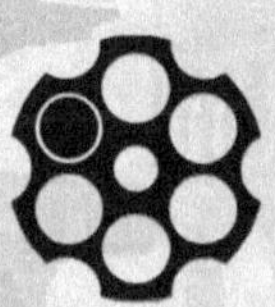

THE ROOM BEGAN TO CLEAR AND FLORENCE BIDED HER TIME. SHE WOULD NOT endear herself to Powell by taking this moment from him. Plus, it was the silent observation that freed her mind time enough to think.

She had come here on behalf of the Vicar Alchemist to secure the loyalty of the Harvesters. Florence glanced at Nora and Derek. Well, she had come here as an escort to those appointed to secure the Ter.1 guild's loyalty.

But a rift was slowly growing between her and her Alchemist friends. Not one of the heart—in that respect they were as close as ever. The rift was one of purpose. Nora and Derek were still being pulled along by the mechanisms of fate and chance. Florence had seen those gears spin too many times. There were two types of people in the world: those who loaded the gun, and those who pulled the trigger.

Florence wanted to be the latter.

She didn't want to live another moment in a world of the Dragons' making. Certainly, there were some Dragons, like Cvareh, who were genuine and peaceful and kind. But the more interaction Florence had with the race, the more she saw that Arianna had been right all along. The Dragons were vicious, destructive creatures that had no true regard for the world. No matter what Powell said, Florence couldn't believe their intentions matched their actions. They were compassionate only so long as it suited them, and even then, it was the Harvesters who found the solutions to the problems Loom faced.

Florence pushed away from the wall, starting for the ever-thinning center of the room. There were only a few journeymen with fully inked sickles on their cheeks, and the Masters. It would be as good a time as any.

"Congratulations, Vicar Harvester," Florence commended sincerely.

Powell's coal colored eyes met hers, offset by the mess of long hair that was perpetually determined to hide his right eye. He looked haggard, they all were. But the man had aged nearly to double his life in an hour. His cheek had yet to be tattooed with a Master's circle and he was already the Vicar.

"Tell me of the rebellion." Powell wasted no time. He knew what they were there for.

"The Alchemists are working toward a Philosopher's Box." Derek stepped forward. "If we have the appropriate amount of gold and organs—"

"A Philosopher's Box?" Max snorted in amusement. "We need solutions, and the Alchemists give us dreams."

"It is quite real, I assure you," Derek responded faster than Florence could.

"Your guild has been claiming such since before you were born." Theodosia stepped forward. "But we have yet to see the product. Stitching together a Chimera with that much magic without falling is impossible."

"We have a solid lead." Nora joined the fray, as if to prevent Derek from being outnumbered by the Harvesters.

"Leads and lies." Max turned to the new Vicar. "Powell, we have other more pressing matters to concern ourselves with. We have to reorganize the guild. We have to rebuild Faroe. We are responsible for what remains of the Harvesters."

Powell's eyes never left hers. The room buzzed around them, yet Powell remained focused, searching, silently calling out to something in Florence's soul that he may have felt all along. What within him had made him speak to her on that train? What connected them with such faith?

"I know where you can go." The idea came to her in that moment, thinking of the fundamental essence that joined every Fenthri at the core. It was the essence that Loom so desperately needed to recover. "I know where you all can go."

"Where?" the elder asked.

"Ter.0."

"From the fisher's hook onto his spear!" Theodosia threw her hands into the air in exasperation. "We have our own wasteland here. We don't need to go to another."

"This is our home," Max agreed. "We won't abandon it."

"I'm not saying abandon it." They didn't understand yet. "I'm saying go to Ter.0, and meet with the other guilds."

"You want to hold a Vicar Tribunal." Powell was the first to realize.

"A Vicar Tribunal? There hasn't been one in over a decade," one of the journeymen interjected.

"Exactly." Florence remained focused on Powell. His decision was the only one that mattered now. He was the Vicar. "The Dragons split us apart, forced us to be silent. They bred animosity between the guilds where there was none. They separated us as children, forced us to learn apart, to compete. They fostered silence with magic. Whisperers may make it faster to converse, but there is no magic that can compare to seeing another's face, truly hearing their plight with your own ears. Anything less is separating, impersonal, dividing. It makes us think the only way we are strong is with their help.

"But Loom was strong long before the Dragons." She addressed the elder of the group, the man who should remember best the bygone days of another time when Loom was free. "We stood together. Links in a chain. One strong, unified, force.

"We gave the Dragons technology. We gave them gold. And, yes, they have given us some insight," she begrudgingly admitted, thinking about Harvesting practices. "But that does not make them our saviors. They did not find the solution; they merely identified the problem. We are our own saviors and we must—"

Powell held up his hand, cutting her short.

"Enough, Florence." He sighed softly, pressing his eyes closed a moment. Florence's heart raced, not just from her risky declaration, but from truly not knowing what Powell's reaction to it would be. The tiniest of smiles curled his mouth when he opened his eyes again. "The Harvesters agree to a Vicar Tribunal."

"Really?" Theodosia shifted uncertainly. "The Dragons torched the Tribunal hall and the rest of Ter.0 in the war. They said if we assemble again, they will do worse."

"What could be worse than what we have already witnessed?" Powell asked. All were silent. "We have no more guild for them to destroy. Faroe has burned. Our mines are stalled. Our fields will go unplowed. Our fishers may be moored for who knows how long, while we attempt to recover what was lost. What more can the Dragons take from us?"

"Our pride, if we let them." The question was rhetorical, but Florence wanted to drive the point home. It was an almost Arianna-like quip and she was instantly proud of herself for thinking of it so deftly on the spot.

"And the Alchemists will not let them," Derek said, lending his support.

"The Vicar Alchemist will support the Tribunal?" Powell asked.

"I have no doubt," Derek affirmed. "Vicar Sophie wants to see the rebellion to power. She wants it for Loom. I'm sure she will stand at the Tribunal."

Powell seemed satisfied by the response. "We will get word across the narrow strait then, to the Rivets in Ter.3. They are connected by land to the Ravens, who can then get word to the Revolvers."

"How quickly can we hold the Tribunal?" Strong words aside, the reality of their situation was becoming very apparent to Florence. Communication systems, in all forms, were down. They didn't even know if there were Vicars left to meet with. Perhaps the Harvesters had been the only ones warned with enough time.

The idea was only kindling to the pyre of Florence's rage. The Harvesters had been a fluke, with all the Masters in the guild at the time. The other guilds had their Masters positioned throughout the territories. They would regroup. And if word spread far enough and fast enough, they could do so at the Tribunal.

"Two months, perhaps?" Theodosia begrudgingly suggested at a silent behest from Powell. "That would give messengers enough time to get all the way to Dortam, and for the Vicars to travel."

"Spread the word like wildfire," Florence suggested aloud. "Invite all of Loom."

"What if the Dragons choose to attack again?" Max was still clearly uneasy at the idea of gathering in one place.

"We have the numbers on them. Even with Chimera alone, we have the numbers." The fact had been known since Nova was first discovered. The sky world was a much, much smaller place than Loom. "The only way they will overpower us is with our own weaponry, coronas, and gliders. And how will they get that weaponry when there is no one to build it?"

"We cannot make a real stand against them," Max pressed.

Derek was quick to speak up again. "Not without the Philosopher's Box."

"You keep saying that, boy, but you have no evidence."

"We do." All eyes were on Florence. "We do," she repeated without hesitation. "We have the person who made the very first Philosopher's Box."

"Lies."

"Her name is Arianna, and she is my teacher," Florence spat venom, protective at the mere round-about accusation against Ari. "She will make the box for the rebellion."

"Arianna, Arianna the…"

"Rivet," Florence finished for Max. "A Master Rivet, at that."

"Who appointed her?" Max asked with squinted eyes.

"Master Oliver." Florence had only heard the name a few times before, and prayed she had it right. Judging from Max's reaction, she did.

"That's impossible." The man shook his head. "Master Oliver was part of the Counsel of Five—the fools who died in the last rebellion. His student, Arianna, she perished with him."

"Except she didn't," Florence insisted. She was exhausted the moment the defense crossed her lips. Standing for someone whom everyone seemed to know more about than she did was wearying. The first thing Florence would do the moment Arianna returned would be to demand an explanation of everything. "She is alive and well, and is securing the resources to make the box," Florence lied, perhaps. What Ari was doing was anyone's guess.

"We will expect to see the box, then, at the Tribunal." Powell's tone left no room for question or interpretation—it was now a caveat. "Once the Vicars see the Philosopher's Box working, we will stand behind the Alchemists' Rebellion."

"I don't know…" Derek started uncertainly.

"Done." There wasn't time for hesitation. Derek shot Florence a look from the corners of his eyes. "Can we count on the Harvesters, two months from now, in Ter.0?"

"I will be there to see the Vicar Alchemist and her Philosopher's Box," Powell affirmed. "And I will personally see that the other guilds come with me."

"Thank you, Vicar Powell," Florence said sincerely.

"The best thanks you can give us is holding up your end of the deal," he cautioned.

Florence nodded. "We will return to the Alchemists' Guild with haste, on the fastest train out."

They didn't have anything to pack, so the three of them made their way toward Ter.1.2's main terminal directly from the hall. Florence knew Derek would have something to say about what they had just done, but it took him longer than she expected. When at last he spoke, the words he found were also unforeseeable.

"Florence, Sophie will stand for the Tribunal, but the box…"

"I don't think she'll want to share it with the other guilds," Nora finished.

"That's lunacy." Florence shook her head with a small laugh at the comical notion. "How would she see the box built en masse without the Rivet's tools and factories? Or get the supplies without the Harvesters and Ravens?"

The two exchanged a look. Florence waited for their nonverbal dialogue to end. When it did, Nora linked one arm with Florence's and Derek linked the other. They walked together as one tight-knit group toward the station.

"Whatever happens, Florence, we're with you," Derek spoke for the both of them.

"You may be the worst navigator we've ever seen." Nora gave her a toothy grin. It slipped when their eyes met and Florence desperately wished she could see what Nora saw in that moment. "But so far, you seem to always get the people who stick by your side where they need to be."

It was a compliment that rang fundamentally Raven, but not. Either way, for the first time, Florence looked beyond the guild affiliation associated with the words and really distilled their meaning. For the first time, she didn't try to correct any link between herself and the transportation guild of Loom.

# 43
## CVAREH

hadn't slept a wink in what amounted to nearly a full day. Even as a Dragon, he was beginning to tap into his magic to find energy. And another day at the Court awaited him, a day that was sure to be awash in blood. The only relief he found was in the thought that the Court would not possibly sustain a full three days, as was the average. After all that had happened, he'd be surprised if it ran a full two.

He dragged his feet toward his room. Even if there wasn't time to sleep, there would be time to wash and dress in something clean. Cvareh never underestimated the power of a pair of well-stitched trousers or a fashionable vest. He would feel far more like himself if he wasn't coated in the blood of his sibling.

His room was intentionally far from Petra's. They could reach different sections of the manor faster and could easily meet in the middle in instances of emergency. As such, it also meant that most of the aesthetic had been catered to his tastes. Thousands of gemstones were inlaid in a dark ceiling, shining like the light from Lord Agendi's flowers. How he had loved them and their magic, only to have his sentiment surrounding them forever clouded by the events of the past day.

There was irony in nearly everything that encompassed him. The woman who was sharp as a dagger and more abrasive than pumice was his lady of flowers. She smelled potently of honeysuckle, a scent he had delighted in long before they met. Her skin was the color of Lord Xin's veil, her hair the shade of Lord Agendi's path. She had been the first woman to so consume him that he had taken her before his patron to mate.

And yet, it had been those same well-loved flowers that had changed her life as well. Had the Dragon who betrayed her never brought them to the rebellion, she may have never found the solution to the Philosopher's Box. Her lover may well still be alive, or maybe they would have perished together.

Cvareh certainly would've never met her, and that would have spared them much confusion at the very least.

Yes, it all seemed to come down to that Dragon's singular act, a man she had named as Rafansi. Cvareh knew he should loathe him in a stand of solidarity with Arianna. But, guiltily, he appreciated the man's dark hand in her life. For it had so clearly driven Cvareh and his Fenthri lover together.

He ran his hands through his clothes, trying to carefully select his ensemble for Court. He did not want to run the risk of re-wearing anything too similar, resulting in a fashion crime he would hear about for years to come. It was a therapeutic process that freed his mind, allowing it to wander.

Arianna had claimed this "Rafansi" was a Xin. *Perhaps a nameless from below?* Cvareh mused. He had neglected to ask Arianna how she'd known his House—if it had been the man's skin shade or if he'd had a tattoo on his cheek. The Dragon could've been someone loyal to Rok originally.

Now, *that* would make more sense. By the time Petra had even heard of the rebellion from Finnyr, the Dono had already begun putting an end to it. The traitor must surely be Rok, or someone with ties into that House.

Cvareh crossed into the bathing room attached to his dressing area. The water was hot on his skin and the steam cleared his head. He perfumed it with rose and hickory, trying to overwhelm his senses with heat and scents so foreign that they would inspire no further thoughts on anything. But it was a futile effort.

Arianna was certain that the man who had betrayed her had been Xin, not Rok. The woman wouldn't have said anything if she was unsure, and she knew enough about Dragon culture now to be confident in such a claim. He didn't think the Dragon she had dealt with was marked, not after Arianna's surprised and curious reactions to the House tattoos. Even if she didn't know the meaning years ago, she did now.

He closed his eyes, sinking deeper into the smooth porcelain of the soaking tub.

Her eyes stared back at him. Tam purple amid a stormy sea of ashen skin. They looked through him, seeing right to his core, as though he was nothing more than a child's riddle. But they hid her truths just as deftly.

Cvareh mapped the curves of her face. He tracked the soft line of her jaw, the surprisingly feminine arc of her cheek. Her hair, the color of pure snow. Had she ever worn it long? Had she always kept it cut just below her shoulder as it was? These were questions he may never know the answer to and the fact shouldn't have stung him so.

Yes, he was enamored with her. Her differences. All her contrasting pieces that made up a whole that could be none other than Arianna. Even the pieces that weren't hers: the eyes, the hands, the ears—

Cvareh's eyes snapped open.

*The hands. The ears.* He repeated it again and again in his mind.

He stood from the tub, his heart racing. The ears she had possessed as long as he had known her. They were an older part, from when she had first become a Chimera—a *Perfect* Chimera—more than three years ago. She had never detailed how she had acquired them, and Cvareh had never asked. He'd assumed it to be some horrible harvesting ring that chained his people and turned them into meat factories. He hadn't wanted to think on it.

But what if they were given willingly, by a Dragon who had been seeking to earn her trust? Cvareh remembered Arianna's accusations when they first met. The fragile stitches he had ripped off the gaping wound within her heart at the fact that he carried her schematics.

He hadn't really listened to what she had said then. He thought her anger had stemmed from the fact that they had been stolen, and her general distrust of Dragons. But no, the woman had mentioned he was merely trying *again* to earn her trust. To betray her *again*.

Cvareh barely had time to towel dry before he was moving out the door, still dripping from his hair, still naked.

If her ears were given to her by the Dragon who betrayed her, that meant he may have given her other things, like her stomach or blood. That meant he had been the Dragon she thought was Xin. Her betrayer, her organ provider—the man was from his House.

"No," Cvareh breathed, and began to run.

Arianna had nearly attacked him when he delivered the hands. Hands that matched her ears nearly perfectly, when he actually stopped and considered it. Hands that smelled of cedar, a scent she had enough organs and perhaps blood to also possess, alongside the much more favored and potent sweetness of honeysuckle.

Finnyr smelled of cedar.

Finnyr, a man of House Xin who lived under the Rok'Oji—loyal to House Rok.

Rafansi, a failed creation of life that lived under the pity of Lord Rok. A name Yveun Dono would not doubt delight in using at every turn, at forcing upon a once-Xin'Oji.

He arrived at her door, panting. He wanted to find her in the room. He wanted to tell her that he had put together everything she had been telling him— and not telling him—all along. That he knew who had betrayed her and, even better, that she could be the one to give the man death.

It would've been perfect. Petra wouldn't have to kill their brother. They could make up another claim for Ari to make in the Court. Yveun wouldn't stand for Finnyr, not when Petra could then stand for Ari and they would be forced to face each other in the ring. No one else would dare step forward in a seemingly Xin-on-Xin duel. It would've been a neat solution to all their problems.

But Cvareh knew, the moment he saw her ajar door, there would be no neat solutions.

He entered the room silently, as if by doing so he could sneak up on the truth and tear it apart with his claws to craft a new reality. He looked hopefully to the bed, though it showed no signs of being slept in. Her Dragon clothes were strewn about the floor. Some tears in them had been made by Cvareh's hands earlier, but new ones tore his hopes asunder. Ones that told him they had been discarded in haste. That their wearer didn't care if they could ever be put on again.

His eyes fell on an open drawer. It was empty. Cvareh's heart may well rip through his chest trying to drown out the ringing of horror in his ears. He pulled out the next drawer, throwing clothes onto the floor, clothes Arianna may have never worn.

He darted to the bed. Feathers filled the room as he threw aside the pillows, his claws unsheathed. He was out of control. Anger, heartbreak, denial, frustration, exhaustion—it all had worn him down. He trashed the room, at first in his search, but then just out of anger when he realized he wouldn't find what he was looking for.

Her daggers and coat were gone.

That meant the White Wraith was now on Ruana. Arianna was at work. And he did not think it chance that this disappearance followed the one night Finnyr himself had returned to the manor.

Cvareh collapsed into the chair, the weight of inevitable truth compressing him into a small, weak being. She had never trusted his family. He had barely begun to earn that fragile gift. *And now…* Cvareh groaned, burying his face in his palms.

It had been his brother that had betrayed all she loved.

With a snarl, Cvareh slammed his fist into the desk next to him, spilling a bottle of ink and sending pens rolling. He looked at her soiled inventory. It had been going so well. Petra had been getting all she had ever wanted, and somehow, Cvareh was getting all he ever needed. But Arianna had yet to find either.

Cvareh was back on his feet. He might still be fast enough to stop the momentum spinning the wheel of fate that threatened to crush them. She had no doubt smelled Finnyr's blood; given her last reaction, his brother's room wasn't far enough to protect him. Really, he should be surprised it took the woman so long to put together the pieces. But the same could be said for himself.

Cvareh prayed to the Twenty that he was not too late in realizing what she had been trying to tell him from the moment they first met.

He collapsed to his knees in the open doorframe of Finnyr's room. The wrinkles in the rug and splintered wood of the door latch told the story of what happened as plain as the daylight breaking through the window. He had failed her by not being fast enough, by not being smart enough. She and Finnyr were gone, no scent of blood to betray a kill. Which meant there was a chance they both left alive, and that was a truth far more horrible than having to deal with the body of a Xin'Kin slain in a duel without witness. Where Finnyr went, the Dragon King—the true orchestrator of Arianna's heartache—was sure to follow. And there was no way Arianna would not take the opportunity to challenge Yveun.

She was going to get herself killed.

He practically jumped back onto his feet. He was on the move again through the halls. But rather than heading to his room, he headed for Petra's corner of the estate.

Petra would know what to do, he insisted to himself. Her mind would've cooled enough that she could think logically, and she would force it to for the sake of the woman who had promised her the Philosopher's Box.

She would do it for the woman Cvareh had chosen as his, he wanted to believe.

"Petra!" He banged on the door so hard the hinges rattled.

"Enter," she called in reply.

Petra was halfway dressed for Court, two servants attending her.

"Leave us," Cvareh demanded.

Petra arched an eyebrow, clearly trying to decipher what had worked Cvareh to a frenzy. But when she gave no question to his order, the two slaves left, closing the door behind them. Cvareh crossed to his sister.

"Arianna is gone." If he wasn't just out with it, he may lose all courage.

"Gone?" Petra repeated.

"She found Finnyr, and she, they, he—she's going to make an attempt on Yveun's life."

"Finnyr?" The mere name elicited a snarl on the back end, rising up from the throat. "Why?"

Cvareh launched into his explanation without thought. Arianna may have kept the matter private. She may hate him for speaking her truth. But it was Petra. This was his sister. His flesh and blood, the woman in whom he had nothing but faith.

Petra was seething by the time he finished. "You should have come to me sooner with these truths. I would've never let Finnyr stay under this roof had I known."

"I did not form lines between them until just now, until she told me enough yesterday."

Petra cursed, knowing he was right. His sister gave him a once-over. "Dress, for the sun has nearly risen and we will head to Court. He will no doubt be keeping her and Finnyr close. We will find them during the Court's distraction," Petra vowed.

Cvareh did as his sister commanded. He was thankful he had already set out his clothes and they were waiting, because for the first time in his life, he didn't care about fashion. He wanted to jump on a boco and fly across the island as fast as he could. He wanted to try to find Arianna before she found Yveun. But a torturous pragmatism whispered that he was no doubt already far too late.

He suspected as much, but he didn't know until Petra and he were standing on the platform about to take off. Cain landed to meet them. Angry lines marred the man's face and Cvareh knew what had been the best day of his life was only going to steadily become worse.

"The Dono has left Ruana," Cain cursed. "Out of kindness to the mourning of House Xin, and to protect members of House Tam and Rok from the sudden illness, the Court has been ended early."

Cvareh turned to Petra, only to find his sister staring back at him.

There was only one reason the Dono would cancel the Court: He deemed it no longer worth his time. And why would he? He had already killed most of the Xin fighters. Finnyr was marked for death and would be far less accessible to Petra on Ruana.

And he now had the only Perfect Chimera in Nova or Loom. He had the woman who could make the Philosopher's Box. He had the key to shifting the tides of fate.

He had Arianna.

# 44
## ARIANNA

SHE FOUGHT A LOSING BATTLE WITH CONSCIOUSNESS. ON THE EDGES OF HER awareness were the simplest of sensations: cold, hard, damp. Arianna tried to pull together the scattered shards of her mind. They lingered out of her reach, jagged and crumbling when she tried to put them back in place. The picture would never be what it once was.

Vengeance, in its own way, had been her greatest hope. The belief that there would be some great justice in the world to be dealt by her. Arianna screamed at herself in the recesses of her mind, at the foolish, idealistic girl she'd never stopped being. It escaped as a raspy groan from split lips.

Reality filtered in around her, breaking through the darkness and alighting the edges of her misgivings. She didn't know what she would live for any longer. She didn't know if she would live at all after this.

All she knew was that she'd lost.

That was the first true thought that returned to her. She'd been bested by the Dragon King. She had fought and trained her whole life, and when the time came, it hadn't been enough. Not Arianna, not the White Wraith, not the Perfect Chimera. She hadn't wanted the mantle, but damn if she hadn't tried to live into it once it had been thrust upon her. Not for nobility, not for honor, just for Eva.

Eva shone brightly in her memory in all her effervescent beauty. That picture was still perfect. But perfection was fleeting, a sight that wasn't long for mortal hands or mortal minds. The woman was like one of the falling stars in Nova's sky.

She faded into darkness.

The darkness was what was real. In that blackness, she fought to find light. She fought for the sake of fighting, for everything left undone. She might be broken, but so long as she drew breath she would pick up the splintered pieces of all she was and use them as shanks between the ribs of those who had crossed her. She'd lived for that one desire before, she would cling to that tether again.

Arianna opened her eyes.

She was face-first on a marble floor. The wide, thin-grouted tiles carried up the walls and onto the ceiling. A room of white illuminated by the light of a single window behind her. It was nearly blinding and Arianna's vision blurred, her senses returning sluggishly from the prison of her mind.

A man slowly came into focus, seated against the door across from her. His powder skin was nearly gray in her hazy sight. Almost gray enough to be mistaken for a Fenthri, almost the same shade as Cvareh, and the same color as her ears and hands.

"I see you're finally awake."

Arianna's lips curled back into a snarl. She moved to push off the floor, her hands weighted by shackles. The chains snapped taut as she lunged in spite of them. Arms bent backward, chest pushed forward, she stuck out her neck and snapped her jaw like a dog, snarling and growling for one more inch of slack. She would rip him apart with her teeth if she had to.

"You can't break those chains," a different voice spoke—familiar, but less so. Arianna turned to find another Dragon leaning against the wall behind her, no doubt just out of reach as well. The Dragon was the color of Fenthri blood, as though the lives of all he'd shattered from Loom below had been poured and hardened into a ruthless mold of irreverent destruction.

She looked down at the shackles around her wrists and ankles. Gold and tempered, she could feel the magic within them object to her attempts to force their locks to disengage. Arianna straightened, swaying slightly with the remnants of the poison that still chilled her veins.

"You have tried to shackle me my whole life. You have yet to succeed," she addressed the Dragon King with a growl.

He looked mildly amused. "Finnyr told me much about you. It's a pleasure to see the Rivet genius for myself."

"Finnyr." The mention of the man's name brought Arianna's attention back to him. The traitor. Underling of the King. "Finnyr Xin."

"You've finally learned my real name. No need for Rafansi any longer then." His lips moved oddly as he spoke, long scars marring them straight to his cheek. "Stupid little Fen, never probing deeper, taking from my open palm eagerly, never questioning what was in my other hand. Your idiot rebels never saw the dagger coming."

Arianna merely curled her lips in a snarl. She hated this man with every thread of her being. She loathed him to the point that he didn't even deserve scalding words. This rage transcended them. "I will kill you," she swore.

"Go ahead." He stood.

It was that simple to goad her into lunging forward. Closer, close enough that she could smell him. That his shirt was ruffled by her breath. But he was still too far for her snapping teeth or tethered claws. Arianna let out a scream of agony.

"Did you really think our great King would let me die? That I would lead you to him if I thought your pathetic attempts to kill him would succeed?"

Arianna questioned everything, all her decisions, and the hubris that had led her to this. She had thought she could take the Dragon King on her own, when so many others had failed. It was arrogance in perfect form, befitting more of a Dragon than a Fenthri.

"I never expected to find you on Nova, not to mention in my family's home." His voice deepened at the mention of the Xin manor. "Did you come with my brother?"

*Cvareh*. The name ripped from her chest and shot straight to her eyes. Arianna blinked, furious with herself. She had let her mind cloud and her eyes go blind to what was before them. This was the price of love; this was her punishment for dreaming.

"How did you survive the poisoned organs all those years ago, the rot from too much magic exposed to your pathetic Fen frame?" Finnyr asked, oblivious to her plight. He raised a clawed hand and dragged it along her cheek, drawing a line in gold. "Is it because of this, because you actually did complete the box? Is that what made you strong? Tell me, Arianna."

Magic laced his tongue. He was trying to use power to influence her. That was an easy trick on Fenthri and weak Chimera. But it was nothing more than a sizzle of annoyance in the back of her mind.

"You will not sway me." She straightened, gathering her height, nearly as tall as he. "My power is far stronger than yours."

"But still falls shy of mine." The Dragon King reminded her of his presence and Arianna turned abruptly, readying some whip of a response.

It was never said.

The moment her eyes met his she felt the icy grip of magic smothering her. She wanted to blink, she wanted to look away, but she was frozen in his stare. It started from her fingertips and swirled into her chest. It trickled up her neck, pressed behind her eyes, whispered through her ears, before it sought entry into her mind.

"Tell me of the Philosopher's Box, Arianna."

He was trying to penetrate her thoughts, to own the recesses of her brain. He wanted to crack it like an egg, scramble its contents, and pour them out to pick the information he needed from the plasma. Though neither moved, she felt him pressing on every part of her. He was smothering her, drowning her. It was like his hands were on her throat and his body weighted her down. The only way out would be to give him what he wanted.

*Let me in*, the magic whispered. *Give it to me.*

"No." Her jaw ached from gritting her teeth. Her lips formed a series of unintelligible sounds that followed, but she did not allow words to come. There was nothing she would say other than "No."

"How many have you made?" He pressed harder, straightening away from the wall.

Arianna wanted to blink. She tried so hard to break that stare, though her body refused all commands. She was trapped and wanted to scream for relief. But she would not give in. She would not stop her struggle. Her magic pushed back harder. She focused on her lips, making them hers. He would violate the rest of her with his presence, but he would not gain her words. "No."

"What do you need to make it?"

She could no longer speak; she no longer trusted herself to. Every ounce of magic in her screamed at once in her mind to give him anything he asked for. His magic poisoned her more than the other Dragon's dagger had. Her stomach turned to sickness. Her forehead grew hot with fever. Her body rebelled against the presence of the foreign power and slowly began to turn septic.

But she would not give in. She would not forfeit to this man. She would die before she did. She would spit up blood from her stomach decaying. She would bruise across her skin from her magic depleting. She would go deaf and blind and have all her fingers snap.

Her hatred was more than all the pain combined. And her desire to sow malice across his land was stronger than his magic would ever be. She would fight against the Dragon King until her last breath because she was Arianna, the White Wraith.

"Tell me how you make the Philosopher's Box!" Golden tears streamed from the man's eyes.

"No!" she screamed in reply.

Yveun shut his eyes, tearing away his magic. Arianna collapsed to her knees. She inhaled long, gasping breaths, gulping for air, for the taste of freedom. Her body shuddered and felt like a room ransacked. Everything was there, but nothing in its place, and all bearing the mark of a stranger's touch. It was merely the pain of bruises from her blood exhausting, but they created phantom impressions in her arms and shoulders and back as if she had just been beaten for hours. As if his hands had actually been upon her.

She was the first to look at him, throwing the gauntlet silently. She gave him her eyes again to try if he so dared. She kept her muscles tense, ready to fight, warding off the trembling that rumbled across her with the aftershocks of being so violated.

The King snarled down at her. "I will gain what I seek."

"You will not."

"I will return and I will try again." He stepped forward.

"You are welcome to." Arianna watched his movements carefully on the edges of her vision.

"You can die peacefully, or screaming like your dear guilds below as they all burned on my command." He squatted down, his knees bending forward. "But either way—"

Arianna pushed off the ground. Her shoulders popped and every last bit of slack the chains had was consumed. One finger on the hand he'd placed on his knee was in range. Just one.

She bit it off in a single bite, spitting it at his feet.

"You Fen trash!" The Dragon King stood with a snarl. He pounced on her, pushing her off-balance.

Arianna tried to bring up her hands or feet to defend herself. But she couldn't find enough movement in the chains in the way he had her pinned. He gouged at her throat with his claws.

She felt as tendon and muscle were shredded. The vibration of the skin ripping was sound in her ears. She coughed, sputtered, and choked on her own blood.

Even still, she smiled. She smiled at the frightened King. She smiled as he retreated. She smiled at his yet-recovering eyes. She smiled as the door slammed shut and her throat began to heal. She smiled until her jaw popped.

Because smiling held in the screams.

# 45
## YVEUN

This was the danger of what the Fenthri sought. This was what he needed to fight against—how their science disrupted the natural order of the worlds the gods themselves designed. The woman was not a Fenthri, not a Chimera, not a Dragon; she was wholly monster and entirely dangerous.

Yveun flexed his still-healing finger, a soft pink from newly mended flesh and still re-growing. The tiniest of claws was begin to form next to the bone, magic strengthening it steadily. He had given the woman half a breath's distance too close and she had taken it.

He wanted to admire her for it, but this was even too much for Yveun. Even he—obsessed with power as he was, and struck by the lack of half measures a Perfect Chimera represented—could not stand for this. If she became even the slightest bit stronger, if she imbibed, if she gained an organ she didn't already have...

There was no way even he would be able to stand up against her.

"Dono, I do not think any more of the boxes have been created." Finnyr scampered along at his side like the worthless rat he was. "She seems to be the only one."

Yveun gritted his teeth. He needed something that could stand against other creatures like that monster. To assume that no more boxes had been made was to welcome the death of everything he stood for. It would be the end of Nova.

"I think we should merely kill her," Finnyr suggested. "If she's only made one box and used it on herself—"

"And who is to say it couldn't be used on others?" Yveun stopped, rounding on Finnyr. "Who is to say that it isn't in the hands of those disgusting Fen rebels as we speak, slowly turning them into something that can challenge even me?"

Yveun held up his hand, showing his finger for emphasis.

"Dono, no one can challenge you," Finnyr sputtered.

The King roared with bitter laughter. Finnyr was still playing a game, a child holding onto an ideal. No matter how many times Yveun drove the point home, it seemed the weak little man never understood. So few could fathom his shame from the mistakes he'd made. He'd only revealed his regrets to Coletta, Leona, and men like Finnyr, who were close enough to his movements that they needed to understand the full gravity of all his risks. For the risks Yveun took rarely ever held consequences only for him.

"Finnyr, I assure you, I am very much a mortal man. While it suits me for the masses both on Loom and Nova to think otherwise, it does not change the fact." Yveun stepped forward, impressing on Finnyr's personal space, trying to make him feel as insignificant as he actually was. "And if I die, Finnyr, so do you. You live only by my grace. You exist only because I protect you and permit you to. Do you think Xin will ever show you love again without my support at your back? The only way you will ever leave here is as the Xin'Oji, and that cannot happen if I perish. Your life is mine."

The man cowered for a satisfying moment. Yveun watched him struggle to steady his voice, but appreciated the struggle all the same. Finnyr would never be a great Dragon, but Yveun needed something from him more important than greatness: obedience.

"Yes, Dono." The man lowered his eyes. "It is an honor that my life is owned by one such as you."

"See that you do not forget it." Yveun straightened away from the smaller Dragon, starting off in the opposite direction. "Now, if I were you, I would find somewhere to hide for the next while until you are needed again. Your use has been exhausted for now, and you will only risk earning my ire if you linger."

He paused at the end of the hall. "Furthermore, your sister is out for your heart. If you think being on Lysip will keep her from hunting you down, you underestimate her."

Finnyr glowered at the mention of Petra, but he didn't object. Yevun continued away, trusting in Finnyr's cowardice more than anything else about the man. He would continue on for the sake of his self-preservation above all else. Yveun had more important things to worry about.

Dragons would not be enough to stand against the threat of the Perfect Chimera. To fight a beast, Yveun needed a more fearsome creature of his own. He needed Dragons that would have no shame in stooping to any level for power and strength. Even if that meant imbibing.

But something even further than consuming the flesh of other Dragons was working through the back of his mind. Fenthri could have the flesh of Dragons cut into them. They had no taboos and no fear of exploring such things. If he found Dragons who would cast aside those inhibitions as well, could they receive the organs of other Dragons? Could he sew together his own Dragon warriors from the strongest parts there were to pick from?

Yveun licked his lips with a morbid sort of hunger.

"Coletta." The heady scents of earth and foliage assaulted his nose the moment he crossed into her domain.

Coletta's world was enclosed by a tall wall, cleverly designed right into the aesthetic of the estate. Large sun shades allowed in light for her plants, but helped conceal the true nature of her gardens from the casual observer on the back of a boco. For any who looked too close would see the ominous crimson spikes that scaled up some of her flowering plants, or the unsettling aroma that lingered beneath the heavy perfumes of unnatural sweetness.

"Yveun," she stood from amid the plants down the path from him. The woman wore nothing, allowing the poisons to brush directly against her skin. Yveun had thought her a fool for it in the beginning. She was sick constantly, frail, always afflicted with horrible boils and rashes. But with time, her body had developed immunities. Now, he would dare argue that she had become the strongest of them all, and no one but him ever saw it.

"Leona. You knew of her well before she lived in our halls."

"And how to pull her strings to tie her to us as something useful." The woman knelt back down, returning to her plants as though they spoke of little more than their preference of meat for dinner that night.

"Your little flowers budding everywhere, they were the ones who gave you such knowledge, no?"

"They did." She resumed her business, plucking flowers as delicately as a hummingbird drawing nectar.

"I have someone else that I need you to find." Yveun didn't enjoy going to Coletta for help. While he wouldn't begrudge his mate the enjoyment of knowing she was needed in his world, Yveun wanted to provide. He did not want to be seen as lacking or half-measured when the woman did not even know how to breathe without giving the act everything she possessed.

Coletta smiled, lowered her eyes and gave a small dip of her head, an elegant curve that offered him subservience—visually anyway. Her chest remained upright, her body strong, her back straight; she relinquished no real power to him. She was a study in contrasts: strength from weakness, beautiful and hideous, dangerous and so tender at the same time.

"She is an unnamed."

Coletta crossed over to a work table next to him, dropping off her basket among a variety of distilling beakers that would make an Alchemist of Loom envious. "I know of whom you speak."

"You do?"

"I told her to stay away until you had solved the matter of Lossom." Coletta spoke lightly while her hands remained busy. "He was a fine temporary recovery for you after Leona. I didn't want you running into the training of a true replacement for our lost girl until you were ready to do so properly."

"Coletta, I would—"

"Remove the growl and spare me the bravado, Yveun." She narrowed her eyes to a dagger's edge. "You cared too much for the girl. Her death affected you, made your head soft. All you need to do is look at your delicate actions following. The fact that Cvareh Xin is even still alive."

Yveun's lip twitched in a rage that was directed more at himself than his mate. He wished she had spoken this truth sooner. But if she had, he may not have been yet ready to hear it.

"Trust me," Coletta breathed delicately, a spell made from spun glass. She stepped forward, resting her hand on his cheek. "I have always seen to it that the path is clear for you to walk. Trust my designs."

His mate was a shadow master, well versed in the underbelly of Nova. Most never realized how deeply her roots stretched while she enjoyed the sun of the world above, and it seemed Yveun had forgotten as well. The death of his riders had turned him into a reactionary beast. He had to trust the hand that rested itself upon him to pull him back on course and chart a route that would lead to their conquest.

"Go under. Find her. She will come with you now." Coletta's instruction was a borderline command. She abruptly returned to her work, the tenderness gone.

"Now?" Yveun clarified.

"*Now.*"

Yveun paused for only a moment. There was more to this than what Coletta was letting him see. He took her hand and pulled her face toward him. She set her jaw in determination, clearly expressing her opinion on his attempt to draw out any additional truth or facts.

He leaned forward and placed a gentle kiss on his mate's mouth that transformed the ambivalent line into a thin smile.

"I love you, in no half measure," Yveun whispered. When the world was falling apart, it made him appreciate the pillar of her ruthlessness all the more. She brewed death at her fingertips and reaped it with words over claws. Most other Dragons would see cowardice, but he saw a stunning commitment to all she was.

Yveun left his Ryu, his true mate, to start for the world below—and to earn his new Master Rider.

# 46
## FLORENCE

"Something isn't right." It was the fourth time Derek had said so in the past day. The train made due course from Ter.1.2 to Keel along the main tracks.

"Take your pick from the garden of Everything Is Wrong. There's no shortage of bounty in the field." Florence settled in the plush seat of the train cabin they'd been given on Powell's behalf. But even if Powell hadn't asked it of the train, they still could've each taken their own cabin if they wanted. The vessel was at less than half capacity and most of the travelers kept to themselves. A heavy weight kept heads down and mouths quiet.

Nora gave Florence a tired look at the discourse repeating itself.

"There should be more Dragons along the checkpoints. They've been monitoring all trains going in and out of Keel for months, looking for an illegal transport of supplies," Derek clarified. "But we haven't seen a single one so far."

"I suppose they only have enough time to burn Loom and not dance on its ashes." Florence folded her arms.

"I don't know why they're not here..." Derek leaned his forehead against the window, watching one of the aforementioned tunneled checkpoints that kept the endwig at bay through the Skeleton Forest whiz by. It was dark and unmanned, so the train continued on.

"Yes, you do." Florence wouldn't stand to see fear and shock dull Derek's sharp senses. "You know why they left."

"No, they still need to…"

"To what? To guard the transportation of goods? Derek, there has to be a guild for the goods to go to."

"There's no way they would do that to the Alchemists." He couldn't even say what "it" was.

"The Harvesters are more essential to Loom than the Alchemists." Derek and Nora both gave Florence incredulous stares at the notion, but she held fast. "If they'll do it to one guild, they'll do it to any."

*Or all*, Florence thought but didn't say. The more she had time to mull over everything that had happened, the more she realized there really was no other alternative. After what Powell had said, after what the Dragons had done… It was to be total warfare between their worlds.

"The Alchemists have fought off the Dragons for years. We're the only guild to refuse to allow them in."

"They don't need to be 'let in' to reap destruction."

"Enough, both of you." Nora pinched the bridge of her nose with a heavy sigh. "Derek, Florence is right, something must have happened. But until we get there, we won't be able to see exactly what." She shook her head and looked out the window.

Florence let the topic drop. She hadn't had a home for most of her life. She was born five years before Dragon contact was made. Her vague memories of Ter.0 were nothing more than the ghosts of emotions and the hazy remnants of bygone dreams. She had been moved to the Ravens, arbitrarily, as part of the Dragons' restructuring following the end of the brief war. There she learned, and she failed, earning a few friends rather than a sense of belonging to a guild. When she left, she did the bidding of the Wraith of Dortam, and was little more than a transient ghost herself.

Florence leaned against the door on the opposite side of Derek and Nora, watching them. She had always found more family in people than places or things. But they were different from her. Their place was their identity, and they belonged to the Alchemists.

So, while all three felt heartbreak the moment they arrived in Keel and learned the Alchemists' Guild hall had been destroyed mere hours after the Harvesters, Florence's pain was of a different sort than her two companions.

The streets of Keel were full of Alchemists, not unlike how Ter.1.2 was now the de facto hall for the Harvesters. However, unlike Faroe, the Alchemists Guild Hall was far enough from the city that the majority of the capital city of Ter.2 remained unharmed. Physically, at least.

Their train was the first to arrive from Ter.1, so carrying the burden of truth was their responsibility. Men and women alike collapsed on the platform. Screams of sorrow harmonized oddly with cries of relief as people embraced in both pain and joy. Some survived, some didn't; their world had been thrown into a shaker and then spilled back out upon the land. Now, it remained to be seen what was left.

"James?" Derek called from halfway down the platform to an Alchemist directing the flow of people.

The man, James presumably, looked around before finding Derek's eyes and giving a wave. "Derek! Nora!"

They met each other in the middle with a reserved clasping of hands in relief at seeing each other again.

"We thought you for dead."

"We nearly were," Derek confessed. "The new Vicar Harvester got us out in time."

"It really is true then?" James's voice took a deeper, heavier turn. "The Harvesters as well?"

"What happened here?"

"Vicar Sophie suspected something was amiss when the day before all Dragons were pulled from Keel. Mysteriously, the King's men who had been so intent on becoming our official liaisons and staying permanently in the guild decided they had tired of the job.

"The Vicar sent a team of men and women to investigate. While they were here in Keel, they were approached by a Chimera living in the city, a graduated journeyman. He manages a store that sells dried fish from the coast, near Ter.1.3. His supplier contacted him, informing him of delays as a result of the attack on the Harvesters' Guild."

"Did the Vicar Alchemist not try to fight the Dragons?" Derek asked hopelessly as they traversed the platform.

"With what weaponry?" James sighed. "You know how it was: there was barely enough gunpowder to make a spark."

The image of that giant canister plummeting through the sky toward the Harvesters' Guild came back to Florence. There wasn't much fight to be had. The Dragons had set out to make a statement about the helplessness of Loom and so far, they had succeeded. They had traveled and killed using Loom's technology.

"How much of the guild escaped?" Florence asked.

"About two thirds."

The three words formed a single golden lining to an otherwise terrible situation. It put the Alchemists in a better position to remain the spearhead of the resistance if the other guilds were in a state that was anything like the Harvesters. But James didn't seem to share her reasoning. His mouth formed a scowl at the news.

"Then it should be no trouble for us to see the Vicar?"

"Sophie is quite busy." James's pointed look at Florence's right cheek was missed by no one. No matter what she did, she would be seen as an outsider to them.

"She'll want to see us," Derek insisted.

"Derek, you may want to wait," James cautioned.

"It's urgent."

He had the right credentials, and James begrudgingly led them out of the station and into Keel proper.

It was Florence's first time in the capital city of the Alchemists. Much like

Faroe was different from Dortam, which was different from Holx, this was another city where the Rivets had put to use the natural resources and terrain to optimize structures. Pine buildings, no doubt constructed from the trees that were cut down to make room for the city itself, were stacked on top of each other around what trees remained.

Metal pipes funneled steam and wires among them, winding across bridges and trailing down walls like eager, industrial roots. It glittered in the early evening light as biofluorescent lanterns sparked to life, swirling like Dragon magic caught in jars. The heavy tree canopy, the narrow windows sparkling with seeming magic... it felt the way Florence expected the secretive city of the Alchemists to feel—dark, but full of promise.

James led them down a wide street to one of the towering trees that was nearly smothered by all the structures built against it and on top of each other. Plumes of steam mingled with an odd trail of red smoke that curled in the air around its upper levels, piped out from what Florence could only assume to be a laboratory within. James stopped just shy of the door.

"Vicar's inside."

He pointedly turned on his heel, starting for the station again. The three of them watched him go with a mindful note. There was no denying the haste with which he had wanted to get away from the place. Combined with his earlier hesitation…

*Was he avoiding Sophie?* Florence kept the question to herself.

"What now?" an incredibly disgruntled Vicar snapped the moment they walked in. Sophie tore her eyes away from her paper, dropping it onto the desk. They gained a different sort of clarity, however, when Sophie saw exactly who sought an audience. "Derek? Nora?" There was a long pause. "Florence."

"We've returned from the Harvesters' Guild, and have spoken with the Vicar there." She got it out of the way first. Florence didn't want any question as to what they had accomplished, especially given the terms she'd left on. It had only been a few months, but it felt like years.

"You actually made it?" Sophie narrowed her eyes in apparent skepticism. "The Vicar Harvester is dead."

"We were there when they elected a new one in Ter.1.2," Derek explained. This seemed to satisfy Sophie for the time being.

Florence was getting rather tired of needing Derek to step in to validate her claims to Alchemists.

"How did you survive?" Sophie's tone shifted to genuine curiosity rather than outright interrogation.

"Florence made friends with the man who is now the newly-elected Vicar on the way to the guild. Because of that, he worked to get us out when the Harvesters received word of the attack."

"Did you?" Sophie's eyes were on Florence again.

"Yes." Calling Powell her friend seemed rather forward. Their relationship had been up and down, odd, and short, but he had gone out of his way to save her life. If that didn't make him her friend, she didn't know what did. It had worked for Ari, at the very least.

"Will he be sending the supplies we need?" Sophie addressed Derek, but Florence couldn't stop herself from answering.

"After what happened to Faroe, I don't think much will be coming out of the Harvesters for some time."

"I didn't ask you," Sophie said casually, not even bothering to look at Florence when she spoke.

Florence clenched her fists in frustration but held her tongue.

"I believe he will help us…" Derek was beginning to look uncertain now. "But circumstances have changed."

"They have not changed in the slightest." Sophie frowned. "Now, more than ever, we must launch an attack against the Dragons. Loom has seen the danger they bring."

"Exactly." Florence saw her opening and took it. "Loom knows of the danger —all of Loom. Every guild is unified once more and will all fight together."

It was like Florence was speaking a different language, there was such a look of confusion on Sophie's face. "We do not need the other guilds to fight."

"What?"

"We need their supplies, certainly, but we do not need their involvement." Sophie scoffed at the very notion.

"How—how can you say that?" It flew counter to everything Florence believed the resistance stood for. Everything Sophie should know. Hadn't this woman been Arianna's friend?

"The Dragons see us as weak."

"And we should show them we are strong."

"No." The word was said so quickly that it punctuated Florence's sentence. "We must let them think we are weak and divided. Wait for them to make a mistake, then strike."

"What if they don't?" Florence shook her head incredulously. It was sheer lunacy. "What if this is merely the beginning?"

"This is a scare tactic, one you seem to be falling for. If we unite, they will merely respond with more force. However, if we show weakness and open doors, they will come down among us to rebuild, just like after the One Year War. *Then* will be our time to strike."

"That could take years. It could never happen! Who knows what they will do to Loom while we wait and do nothing?" Sophie was gambling with Loom's freedom rather than taking it. It made Florence want to scream and stomp. The Dragons had attacked them in cold blood. They had set Loom afire simply because they could. And now? Now Sophie wanted to roll over before them, continuing what had amounted to a pathetic quasi-rebellion in secret.

"And if the rebellion fails, as it did last time, all of Loom will live to fight again if we conduct ourselves quietly. Past failures can still teach valuable lessons, Florence." Sophie remained undeterred.

"Arianna will never go for this. She wants the Dragons dead."

"Do you really know what she wants?" Sophie challenged. "After all, she's been on Nova for some time doing who knows what."

"It has something to do with the Philosopher's Box." Florence prayed that everything she knew about Arianna remained true. She was betting not only everything that she had, but Loom itself, on the fact. "Ari will come back, and she will go to the Vicar Tribunal."

"Vicar Tribunal?" It was Sophie's turn to be incredulous.

"There is a Tribunal happening on Ter.0 in two months. The Vicar Harvester is spreading the word to the other guilds. They expect a demonstration of the box, and the Vicar Alchemist in attendance."

If Florence could pack the look Sophie was giving her into a canister, it would be the most deadly shot she'd ever made. After several long breaths, the Vicar slowly dropped her hands to the desk, standing slowly. She rose to her full height, a head taller than Florence.

"Florence, a word of advice," Sophie spoke as soft as a knife point dragging across flesh. "Be wary of who you speak for. Because you have made promises that you were not permitted to give on behalf of two very, very powerful women."

It was the nicest thing Florence had ever heard Sophie say about Arianna. And it was being used as a pointed threat. She wanted to rebuke the notion. But the fact was, Arianna was just as likely to be angry with Florence for her decision as she was to be obliging.

"It's the only way."

"There are lots of ways." Sophie rounded the desk, running her hand along its edge. "You are young, and you see the only solution as outright warfare."

"What else is there? Your plan to lure the Dragons into some false sense of triumph?"

"That, and many more strategic approaches that wouldn't result in hundreds, thousands, of Fenthri deaths."

"The strategic approach hasn't worked."

"Neither has outright warfare." Sophie referred to the quick failure that was Loom's last war. "Perhaps when you are older, when you have lost more, you will understand this."

"Do not say I have not lost." Florence took a step forward, barely stopping herself from outright attacking the woman. "You know nothing of me."

"I know you are still a girl, quick to ire and stumbling in the pitfalls of pride." Sophie remained poised. "I know you have yet to see the merit of strategic sacrifice to attain one's goals."

"You *must* go to the Tribunal."

"You may not tell me what I must do." The Vicar Alchemist shook her head.

"Derek, you will be on the first train back to Ter.1.2 in the morning. You will tell the Vicar Harvester to call off the Tribunal. You will inform him that the Alchemists will not be working with the rest of Loom, and encourage him to call off this ridiculous notion of a demonstration against the Dragons. Denounce all knowledge of a working Philosopher's Box as the misinformed whims of a child."

Derek looked between Florence and the Vicar of his guild helplessly. But Florence knew what his decision would be. She knew it as clearly as the two interlocking triangles on his cheek.

"Understood, Vicar."

"Good." Sophie returned to her chair, waving them away. "Now, the three of you... get out of my sight."

Nora stepped away and Derek followed, linking arms with her. Florence hesitated one moment. Venom poured from the glands in her mouth instead of saliva, and the brief, challenging look Sophie gave her was almost enough to made her spit it all out on the woman's desk.

But Florence made for the door. She would heed Sophie's words and apply them that very moment. She would make a strategic sacrifice of her pride in the form of a tactical retreat. The Vicar had won the battle, but Florence would not give her victory in the war between them.

# 47
## PETRA

Petra clenched the reins of her boco so tightly that she had to consciously remind herself to ease her fingers so she didn't accidentally snap Raku's neck. In the span of a day, the world had been given and taken from her. She had been ready to kill Finnyr, she had the box, she had the loyalty of Loom. And now, Finnyr was out of reach, the woman—the *only* woman—who held the knowledge of the Philosopher's Box was in Yveun's hands, and that fact threw the loyalty of Loom into question.

Petra bared her teeth into the wind. She was going to get it all back, and then some. She hadn't devoted most her life to a dream the world had told her was futile since she was a child to see it taken from her now. She was born to be the Dono of Nova and there was nothing she wouldn't sacrifice to see that come to pass.

Cvareh rode stiffly at her side. Worry fogged his magic and made the air around him so thick, Petra wondered how he even saw where he was going. He focused ahead, past the late afternoon sun, to Lysip. The islands of Nova floated below them, guiding their track. Eventually, they would deviate and fly around the back of the island, regrouping before launching their plan into action.

The future weighed on Petra's shoulders. They had one shot. Failure meant House Xin would lose everything.

The watercolors of the sky were turning into strong pastel by the time they landed their bocos behind a far hill on the back end of Lysip. Wildflowers and grasses were their only greeting party. Cvareh dismounted, confused when she did the same.

"Aren't you—"

"Yes, yes," she cut him off with a wave. "But I wanted to speak to you first."

"Every moment we waste is another Ari spends with Yveun."

"And he will not kill her." Of that, Petra was certain. "He needs her as much as we do. He needs her knowledge, at the very least, before he could even consider removing her."

The tall foliage brushed against her hips as she reached for her brother. Her hands wrapped around the back of his head and she placed her forehead against his. Petra closed her eyes, imagining their minds as one. Her little brother, full of so much potential, the tool she had kept at her disposal. Sometimes clumsy, but always out for the best of House Xin.

"Your mind is noisy. You must silence it," she cautioned. "I know you are worried for this mate you have chosen. But Arianna is strong. Worry no more for her than you would for me."

"I worry for you plenty."

Petra pulled away with a smile. "All I want you to worry for now is yourself. Focus on what we're here to do. I will make sure to create quite a stir. I'll keep Rok's attention on me for as long as I reasonably can, but you must make haste while I do."

"I will."

"Ends before ideals," Petra reminded him. "Do what you must for our House, Cvareh."

"I will," he repeated.

Satisfied, Petra wrapped her arms around his shoulders, pulled him tight for a brief moment, then mounted her boco once more. They had always been playing a dangerous game, but the stakes never let up. They grew with each passing moment, each passing day. Everything had come to a head so quickly that Petra knew every decision they made from here on would govern the future of their House—and perhaps the future of Nova itself.

Cvareh moved forward on foot, and Petra watched him leave.

She waited long after he disappeared over the hill. She gave him time, stiff in her saddle, impatient but forcing herself to remain. They had landed intentionally far from the Rok Estate. It wasn't a distance he could traverse inconspicuously with any speed.

When the sun hung low in the sky, she took to the air once more. The shifting grasses and swaying, spindly trees below caught the sunlight, shining as if the world itself was aflame. Petra scanned the ground, flying at leisure, satisfied when she finally caught a glimpse of Cvareh. He was near the edge of the estate, entering through the homes where Yveun's political wards lived. It was an area Petra had made sure he was familiar with by having him visit Finnyr often enough.

How he would find Arianna once inside was up to him. She had more important things to concern herself with. Petra landed in the field designated for guests' bocos and summoned a face of pure ire. It wasn't hard given the circumstances.

She stormed for the opening of the Rok Estate, claws out, teeth bared, the very image of an Oji scorned.

"Where is Finnyr Xin?" she barked to the first Rok servant who had the ill fortune of greeting her.

"Xin'Oji, we were not expecting—"

Petra gouged out his throat. It was risky to spill *any* blood on the Rok estate, but the smell of one of their own bleeding would send every Rider running. It would draw all eyes to her.

Sure enough, the soft clicking of the beads of a Rider neared, rounding the corner as an apple-skinned woman stopped at the far end of the hall. She sheathed her claws the moment her eyes fell on Petra. The Court was too fresh in every Dragon's mind for any to be inclined to challenge her, any other than Yveun. Especially not over the death of a no-name slave.

"I demand my brother." She spoke loudly, for all who were gathering. "I demand Finnyr Xin."

"Finnyr is a ward of Yveun Dono." Petra mentally commended the Rider for maintaining a strong and level voice in the face of her rage. "The Dono would need to approve Finnyr's departure."

"The Dono can keep him." Petra snorted. "I merely want to kill him."

"The Dono would need to approve a duel…"

Petra advanced on the Rider. She could smell the fear in the air around the woman. Her dilated eyes, her barely stable hands. The Rider was ready to fight, but they all knew who would win. It would be a life wasted.

"This is not the Court. This is a House matter. Yes, we are on Lysip, but as I, the Xin'Oji, am demanding a duel with a member of my House, it should fall under *my* jurisdiction, not the Dono's." Petra lorded over the slip of a Dragon. For now, she didn't actually care if she was given Finnyr. She would kill him someday, and someday soon. But the longer they stalled, the more of an opportunity she had to raise a fuss over the fact and the more time Cvareh had to find Arianna.

"You are quite right." A new voice stilled the room with its whispering tones.

Petra straightened away from the Rider, looking with curiosity for the source of the sound. A small, frail-looking Dragon had parted the gathering mass of people with her presence alone. Petra had seen the woman before at Courts and a few special functions, but she was as rare as raindrops otherwise. The mere sight of her sent a whole new wave of rage across her skin.

"Coletta'Ryu." Petra had to think quickly or she'd lose all reason to anger. She didn't expect the Ryu to greet her. Yveun wasted no time glowering over her at every chance. What did it mean for this woman to be standing in his stead? He was no doubt somewhere delighting at having the butcher of Petra's people greet her. "Will you see Finnyr fashioned for me?"

"Certainly." The woman gave a thin-lipped smile, submissive and demure. Petra wondered what the Dono saw in her at all. She was nothing more than a coward. "Please, Xin'Oji, come with me. Lysip is a far ride from Ruana and you must be tired after such tragedy has struck your House."

Petra's hands vibrated from the tension her muscles were under as the Rok'Ryu had the boldness to mention her plot against Petra's home. She wanted to rip the woman limb from limb. But that pursuit of revenge would have to wait. She only had Finnyr's word to go on, one Yveun would vehemently deny. As the Rok'Oji, his word was law in approving all duels for the members of his House, and he would not see Petra's claims against Coletta as viable for a duel.

Killing Coletta'Ryu was going to be a much longer game.

"You are too kind." Petra smiled as wide as she could, her lips curling back, her fangs showing.

"House Rok is quite invested in the future of House Xin. We have been for many years," Coletta spoke as she led Petra down a long hall. The Riders and half the staff followed them. Petra knew any would say it was to ensure they were waited on hand and foot. But she knew the truth—it was a visual reminder of Rok's strength. No matter how skilled a fighter Petra was, if she attacked the Rok'Oji, they would show her no quarter. "We would not want to move against your ends."

Petra responded to lies with lies. "And House Xin is nothing but loyal in no half measures to House Rok for their kindness."

Coletta smiled falsely in reply. They were both speaking the same language.

"We can wait in here." Coletta motioned to a lavish parlor that overlooked a private garden. It smelled strongly of the woman and had a lived-in look. Petra bristled at the realization that she'd been led into the asp's den. "Yeaan, please fetch some appropriate refreshments for the Oji and me. Topann, please see to finding the Oji's brother. The rest of you, please return to your duties. There is no need to overwhelm the Xin'Oji."

"Coletta'Ryu, the Riders would like to stand guard," the woman from earlier insisted.

Petra wracked her mind for how to make sure they did indeed stay. The more people who were around, the fewer could run into Cvareh. But she had no reason to demand an audience.

"I don't think it necessary. Let us not insult our guest by even implying that she may do something underhanded." Coletta smiled almost sweetly. "I am perfectly safe with the honorable Xin'Oji."

Petra wanted to tell her she was anything but. However, there was truth to the words. Petra respected the Dragons' ways. She would not lower herself to killing a Ryu outside of a pit; she was better than this woman at least in that respect.

"It is the wish of the Rok'Oji," the Riders insisted.

"Very well, then outside with you so we may relax."

That seemed to satisfy their wishes, and the Riders assumed their places on the other side of the door. Petra listened closely after it closed for footsteps walking away, but heard none. So her presence tied up the Rok'Ryu and the Riders. It was something, at the very least.

"Thank you for your hospitality, Coletta'Ryu."

"It's just us, Petra'Oji, you don't need to pretend any longer." The woman tilted her head to the side in amusement. Something about her demeanor shifted. It was like a cat had grown into a lion in mere moments. Where there had been something unassuming before, now stood a menace.

*This* was the woman who had killed her House in cold-blooded shadows.

"I'm afraid I do not know of what you speak."

One of Coletta's servants, Yeaan, returned with a tray. She crossed silently to the center of the room, laying out a small assortment of fruits and cheese with two wine glasses. One vessel was set out for Coletta, the other placed on Petra's side of the table.

Petra stared at the offending liquid. The woman before her was a monster. Putting in front of her the means she had used to kill her people like a trophy. Petra's nose scrunched at the scent of the wine.

"What is this?" Petra motioned to the glasses, unable to keep the comment to herself.

"Wine from Ruana. I wanted to make you feel at home."

Was this woman so bold that she would really kill an Oji behind closed doors? Petra approached the unassuming vessels as though they could fly off the table and strike at any moment.

"It is quite safe, I assure you. A different vintage than what was consumed at Court."

"A strange happening, that," Petra said quietly. "How all of the wine, from different vineyards, different wineries, was so deadly."

"Truly an inexplicable tragedy."

"One could explain it as poison."

Coletta turned, the fading light of day catching the red of her eyes and making them glow ominously as she assessed Petra. She smiled again. This time, the edge of a canine crept from behind her lips. "You speak of dangerous things, Petra'Oji."

"I believe I stand before a very dangerous woman." It was a dance of words, neither wanting to cross the line into overt threats.

"I *am* the Rok'Ryu." Coletta hummed quietly, walking to the edge of the table. "And Petra, I have been watching you for some time."

Petra bristled at the lack of title attached to her name. That was something, almost enough of something, to challenge the woman on. But still, they had no witnesses to the offense and plenty of people who would lie and object, and stand for the Ryu. As much as she desired it, Petra reminded herself that she would not be killing the Rok'Ryu this night.

"You're a dangerous woman, too. You seek out what you want, you pursue it with a reckless passion. You are relentless." The Ryu took both glasses in her hands, inspecting them carefully. Petra never let them leave her sight. Coletta poured the wine from one glass into the other, filling it to the brim. She repeated this a few times, back and forth. Mixing them completely. "All of Nova knows you seek Yveun's throne. Why haven't you taken it yet?"

Coletta held out one glass. Petra regarded it hesitantly before accepting. But she did not drink. She would not drink before the Ryu did; she knew better.

"I am not in a position to." It was the most honest thing Petra had said to a Rok in a long time.

"No, you're not," Coletta agreed. "At least not honorably, not by Dragon law."

"And I would never be recognized as the Dono, if it was not done through Dragon law." Petra followed Coletta over to the wide window that overlooked an expanse of foliage. It was the only visible window down into the garden.

Petra wondered if this was the place where the poison that killed her House had come from. None of the plants were familiar to her. She couldn't even guess where half of them grew originally.

"I sat quietly, for many years, watching Yveun do as he would," Coletta spoke to no one in particular. "But you changed things, Petra. And left me with no choice but to join the fray."

Petra watched as the Ryu raised the glass to her lips and took a long drink. She waited several breaths, and nothing happened.

"I am beginning to believe that I have more reason to fear you than the Dono."

"Then you are as smart as you seem." Coletta turned to Petra. "I will give you one chance, Petra. Leave now, and remain the Xin'Oji. Give up on your dream to become the Dono, swear true fealty, and I will let House Xin remain as it has always been."

The very notion was ridiculous, and Petra made sure Coletta was aware of the fact with her unrestrained laugher. "You cannot threaten me or my House, Coletta."

The woman's eye twitched at the lack of title.

"And I will never bargain with House Rok. Not when I hold the cards."

Coletta huffed softly in amusement, raising her glass in the light of the orange sunset. "Then, to war."

"To war." Petra clinked her glass against Coletta's, and finally drank alongside the Ryu.

A side door opened and Topann reappeared, Finnyr in tow. Petra snarled, setting down her glass heavily on the table the moment she saw her brother. "I declare now a duel, before the Rok'Ryu, for your life, Finnyr."

"Under what claims?" Coletta asked, per the script.

"Actions against his House." Killing Finnyr was going to be a fringe benefit of the night. Petra's claws shot from her fingers.

"I approve this duel."

Finnyr tried to make for the door the second the Ryu spoke the words. Topann closed and stood before it, preventing him from leaving.

"Y-you, the Dono still needs me," Finnyr pleaded with Coletta. "You can't let me die like this. He would not allow it!"

"Look at you, Finnyr, pleading to a Rok for your life." Petra spat at his feet. "You pathetic little coward."

Petra pulled back her hand. She was done dealing with her brother. She would go right for his heart and end it once and for all.

A chill swept through her, swift and sudden. It shot up her spine and into her stomach, pouring forward as blood from her mouth. Her knees knocked and her lungs burned.

Petra shuddered, and fell.

*No.* The word seared her mind. Coletta entered her blurring field of vision, looming over her like the Lord of Death himself.

"H-how?" Petra stuttered. Nothing made sense. "I-I am an Oji."

"You think a title will protect you, Petra," Coletta spoke down to her. "That has been your greatest flaw. You put so much stock into titles and rank that you forget what gives them power—fear."

The woman squatted next to her, narrowly avoiding the blood Petra was spitting up as she gasped for air.

"You failed your House. You, who should believe in whatever means necessary to achieve your ends, never even thought that I would kill you here."

"You drank from the same glass." Petra tried to defend herself in what she knew were her final moments.

"And you know nothing of poison." Coletta smiled, wide and open-mouthed. Her teeth were dull and small, eaten away beyond her young years. Her gums were worn and gray, curling and tired. Her breath smelled of death. "But I do. I know of poisons well. My body, too; it is strong with them, invulnerable to them. I also know that you do not have magic in your stomach."

"F-F-Finnyr," Petra growled up at her brother. She wished she had the strength to stand, just enough to kill him. If she was going to die, she would take one of them with her to the halls of Lord Xin.

But she didn't have the strength.

Her body was in revolt. Her magic surged but couldn't keep up with everything failing at once. If anything, the effort to heal resulted in her organs wearing out from magic depletion. She could feel herself turning septic, growing rotten with each passing moment.

"You should have taken my deal, Petra." Coletta stroked her hair like a child. "It's a shame to lose a woman on Nova as strong as you." The Rok'Ryu stood with a sigh, as though the matter actually did cause her strife. "Finnyr."

Petra rasped with laughter. Between the blood and death's heavy veil she could still see her brother tripping over his own two feet to get to her. Even when he was handed carved meat on a platter, he couldn't find the knife to spear it. Her mouth curled in an expression that was part snarl, part grimace.

"Y-You will ne-neh-never stand as O-Oji," Petra forced from between chattering teeth.

"It was mine all along." Finnyr knelt beside her. His hand wavered.

"Cvareh w-w-will kill you." Petra bubbled up laughter through the blood in her throat. "You were never meant to stand as the ruler of House Xin. You—"

His hand plunged into her chest. She felt her brother's fingers close around her heart. Petra closed her eyes; death was upon her, and there was no point in fighting it any longer. She would watch her House for the rest of time from the halls of Lord Xin. She would watch, gleefully, as Cvareh finished what she started decades ago with Finnyr.

She would see her younger brother kill the elder, a task she should've done years ago.

Petra Xin'Oji To's last discovery in life was the sensation of what it felt like to have her heart ripped out. The act she had done to many was finally performed upon her. With her final breath, she embraced the veil of the god she so loved.

# 48
## CVAREH

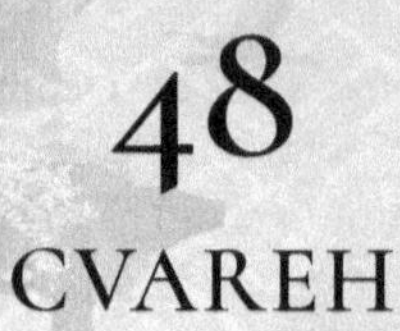

Petra was counting on him. Arianna was counting on him—even if she didn't know it. The future of House Xin was counting on him.

It was the same sort of weight he felt the last time he had crept through the Rok Estate for the schematics. Now he felt it in triplicate, looking for the woman who created those same drawings. There was a twisted and cruel sort of parallel drawn between them that had started long before they'd ever met.

Cvareh knew the moment Petra had arrived, since every man and woman who had been milling about the halls quickly sprinted off with eager whispers. His sister was always cause for attention, and the Xin'Oji calling for the blood of one of her kin was added fuel to that particular fire. Cvareh just hoped she kept her word from back on Ruana that she would not actually kill Finnyr.

He had promised that honor to Arianna and, after all Cvareh had come to know and realize, she well and truly deserved his brother's blood.

In the fading sunlight, the Rok Estate was undeniable in its glamour and overpowering in its lavishness. Rooms of grandiose proportions dwarfed him, glittering with gold and gemstone. He used the scale to his advantage, keeping his head down and the scarf of the drab, humble clothes he wore high around his face. Peeking out just above the fabric was the symbol of House Rok. He'd inked it shortly after sneaking into the estate, using an idea he borrowed from Arianna.

He wasn't known on sight here. Petra had kept him from many a Court and function across the years, making his appearance only vaguely familiar to any not of Ruana. Once more, Petra's foresight served them well when another head-bowed servant crossed paths with him and paid him little more than a glance at his cheek.

Cvareh knew his general headway to the holding pens of the Rok Estate. Most Houses had something of the variety for containing Dragons awaiting a duel—or for when the Oji couldn't decide if a duel was even merited at all. It was where he should've taken Finnyr, rather than putting him anywhere remotely close to Arianna. Usually, the pens remained empty; Cvareh had yet to meet an Oji would couldn't make a split-second decision on such matters.

He heard the shifting of beads from around the corner and stopped his progress, listening carefully to the movement. Without doubt, a Rider was stationed at the door. If he needed any further proof that Arianna was likely being held in one of the rooms in the hall beyond, that was it. They wouldn't exhaust a Rider on something so trivial, otherwise.

Cvareh leaned against the wall, stilling his breathing, trying to slow the very beating of his heart so he had time to figure out a solution to his predicament. Did he try to draw the Rider away and then circle back to the door? If he attacked, the scent of blood would draw others. He pressed his eyes closed and uttered a quick prayer to Lord Agendi and Lord Xin. He asked the first to cast his gaze on this endeavor, and the second to do the opposite.

Cvareh rounded the corner.

The Dragon looked up from inspecting her claws. The woman had only two beads and Cvareh didn't instantly recognize her. If she wasn't at the Court, she might not know his face either. Cvareh adjusted his wide scarf and hoped the mark he drew on his cheek was clear enough and hadn't smudged.

"What do you want?" the woman sneered at the very sight of him. But she didn't attack.

"Your presence is requested upstairs." Cvareh kept his voice level and his eyes lowered. He hated taking his sight off the woman, who could decide to lunge at any second, but he had no choice. The more suspicion he raised by acting out of character, the lower his chances of getting inside. "To deal with the Xin'Oji."

"The Xin'Oji is here?" The woman sighed heavily. "What trouble is the blue devil trying to make now?"

Cvareh kept his mouth shut. It served his image, and if he didn't, he might have spit out a hasty defense of Petra. He'd learned the hard way to keep his mouth shut in a train station on Loom in a confrontation that now seemed an eternity ago. It was a mistake he wouldn't now repeat.

"You sure you don't want to go back to her and beg for your place in House Xin? They may invite you to their tea parties and wine tastings if you do."

"My loyalty is, and always will be, to House Rok." Cvareh forced his mouth to make the words when his heart revolted at their very thought.

"Good boy." She patted his head. "Make sure no one goes in. If you do, I'll rip the muscle from your bones."

"Yes." He assumed his place against the door.

The woman started down the hall. Cvareh's heart raced. As soon as she was out of sight, he was going to find Arianna. He was going to get them out of there. He kept his eyes focused on the Rider's feet.

"Oh, what did you say your name was, Xin traitor?"

Cvareh looked up on instinct, anger flashing hot at the mere mention. Their eyes met and she tilted her head to the side, staring at him with more intent at the spark of resistance. Cvareh quickly lowered his face.

"My name…" he hadn't thought of a name. "Rafansi." Cvareh cringed instantly at the first thing that came to mind.

"Rafansi?" She started back toward him with a snort of disbelief that echoed Cvareh's reaction when he'd first heard the name. "Look at me, Rafansi."

Cvareh had no choice but to oblige. The illusion was melting around him and he'd only add heat to the flame if he resisted. If he was careful, he might be able to save the situation.

The woman stopped. "What kind of a name is that?"

"Any wonder I tried to get away from my parents on Ruana?" he tried to jest.

"Say, *Rafansi*, were you at the Crimson Court?" She leaned forward.

Cvareh shook his head, amazed he could while under the tension of his muscles.

"Shame. You could've watched the pampered prince of Xin cowering behind an Anh to do his fighting for him." The woman stepped away, shrugging. "I wonder if he could even stand up in a fight."

"Better than any Rok could." The words flew from his mouth like caged birds escaping at the first opportunity.

The woman froze. "I thought you looked familiar," she snarled.

*Twenty gods above, I didn't learn anything on Loom.* Cvareh chastised himself as he watched her muscles tense from her knees to her lower back.

Cvareh lunged to the side, expecting the twisting strike. His claws unsheathed, he pressed forward and up into the armpit of the Rider.

"Xin coward," she snarled, pushing him away, raking her claws along his arms in the process.

Blood spilled to the floor, a warning call to any Dragons in the proximity. Cvareh cursed aloud. There was no time, no point in subversion now. He was going to fight his way out alone.

The Rider lunged for him and Cvareh side stepped. He countered; she thrust right for his chest. Cvareh twisted out of the way of her wicked sharp claws. The Rider wasn't half as fast as Arianna, Cvareh realized in delight. He had been training for weeks with a creature far more deadly than some two-bead.

They came together, twisting, snarling, spinning, and splitting apart once more. Cvareh stumbled, falling to his hands, his feet wide in a crouch. He pushed back then lunged forward, wrapping his arms around the woman's waist. She slammed into the door and it swung open, the lock broken.

They tumbled into a narrow hall lined on one side with doors. Cvareh pinned her to the floor and sunk his teeth into the soft flesh of her neck. Blood and magic exploded into him. But it was a sour taste, fuel for what he needed to do and nothing more. There was only one woman whose blood could make him hunger, could make him lust.

His hand sunk into the Rider's heart, ripping it from her ribcage with brute force. Cvareh tossed it aside with a dull splat, uninterested in eating it. His mouth was already filled with the unwelcome tang of the foreign woman.

Motion from one of the rooms sounded like rainbows and fireflies and the brightest of magics against his ears, against his body. It sparked life into the dim corridor. Cvareh sprinted for the last door on the left, swinging it open. The smell of his mate assaulted his senses and Arianna looked up at him like some deadly, caged predator.

"Ari…" he breathed in relief.

Her lip curled in disgust at the mere sight of him. "You will let me out of these chains so I can properly kill you."

"I can explain but—"

"He was your brother!" She lunged. She must have known full well the range of the chains, but she did it anyway. She was jolted to a stop, just short of where he stood inside the door. She chomped and foamed at him in rage, a rabid wolf at the end of its leash. "He was your brother!"

"I know." That only served to make her angrier. "But I didn't know then. I didn't figure it out."

"You idiot, he was your *brother*!" The woman he admired for the equal ferocity of her mind and body was reduced to animalistic rage, functioning only on instinct. And those instincts now told her to tear him apart. Lord Xin give him strength, because if what she needed to be made whole was his heart, he would tear the organ from his body himself and serve it to her on the finest silver platter. "You didn't tell me. He was your brother. You supported him. You—"

"You didn't tell me!" Cvareh snapped back angrily. "Surely you knew when I brought you the hands, but you said *nothing*. Did you not think I would help you? Could you not trust me? I offered you everything!"

"He was your brother!"

"And I want to see you kill him."

Arianna stopped all movement, stunned.

"I want to see him die by your hands, Arianna."

He placed his hands on either side of her face and crossed the line of safety into her reach. He pressed his mouth against hers. She stilled all movement for a long moment. He felt the warmth of her breath on his cheek, the heaving of her chest on him. It was life and everything good in the world. Finnyr would be a worthy sacrifice for this woman's pleasure.

Her head twisted and she tore off his bottom lip with her blunt teeth.

Cvareh reeled backward, holding his bleeding face. Arianna spit his flesh at him. Anger still consumed every inch of her. But she was no longer raging.

Twenty gods above, this woman was the only creature he'd ever met for whom tearing off his flesh was a step in the right direction toward the return of stability and sanity.

"You think *now* is a good time to be kissing me? Bloody cogs, your incompetence is only rivaled by your idiocies." Arianna shook her head at him, standing strong on her feet. "Now, free me so I can kill you properly after we escape."

He should've left her there. Had anyone else spoken to him that way, they would've been promptly killed and forgotten, especially given her prone state. But Cvareh found himself inspecting the locks at her wrists.

"I don't have the key."

"You don't have the key?" She sighed heavily. "You really are useless for this whole rescuing thing."

"I didn't—"

"I know, you didn't think. Hardly a surprise." She was a vicious sort at the moment. But he'd take verbal lashings over physical ones. It was its own kind of progress. "I need gold, untempered gold. They took my harness and tools."

All the ornate trimmings of the Rok Estate came to mind instantly. "A moment."

Cvareh sprinted out to one of the earlier rooms. For now, it seemed the bloodshed was far enough away from other Dragons that it had yet to attract attention, but he was certain their luck would run out. Lord Agendi only had so much good spirit for him, and he kept cashing in prayers daily.

Using his claws, he ripped out a chunk of the ornate gilding, bringing it back down to her. "Will this do?"

"Well enough," she admitted, begrudgingly awarding praise. Arianna focused on the gold and her magic filled the air.

Cvareh watched as it lifted itself from the wood, isolating the strip of metal. She took a deep breath, and the sliver turned hot. Arianna didn't even wince as she burned her fingers to blistering on the molten metal, shaping it into a fine and slightly curved point. Her fingers had healed by the time she tested the pick in the lock, only to be burned as she adjusted the shape a second time, and a third, until there was a soft *click*, and the shackles fell away one by one.

"Now we need to—"

She lunged for him. They fell to the floor and Arianna had him pinned in a mere breath. One hand was at his throat, claws pressing into his neck, drawing blood. The other hand was drawn back, ready to attack his chest.

Cvareh didn't struggle. He submitted beneath her, gave her the control she so clearly craved. If she needed to physically see his heart to know it didn't beat against her, he had already decided to permit it.

"Tell me why I don't kill you."

He stared at her, his tortured lover. Her soul had belonged to another. Eva had broken it into pieces with her death. It was not meant for his hands to fix.

"Tell me!" Arianna screamed. "Give me a reason, Cvareh. Tell me why I don't kill you!" Her hand quivered like a shackle was still attached, holding it back from diving into his chest.

They were running out of time, especially if she kept drawing attention with noise and blood. "Because I love you."

Arianna's face twisted as the invisible soldiers who fought wars in the dark battlefields of her mind plunged their claws into her all at once. "That's not good enough."

"Because I love you, and because you love me in return."

Her eyes shot wide open. "I do not."

"Why didn't you kill me then, on the airship? Why not after? Why not on Nova, when I avoided you because I could no longer stand being in the same room as you without touching your skin? Why not when I brought you my brother's hands? Why not a moment ago? Why not now? *Why?*" He needed to hear it as much as she needed to say it. They'd been dancing around it for so long, a waltz on the deck of a swan-diving airship.

"Because... because I want my boon."

"Then why haven't you spent this precious boon?" he pressed. She was too logical for this.

"Because I don't know what I want."

He sighed softly. "Yes, you do. You want this. You want me."

"I only wanted you for a night." Fallacy colored her magic.

"You wish that were true."

"Damn you, Cvareh." She cursed loudly. "Damn you!"

Arianna pushed away from him, swaying as she stood.

"You want to kill my brother. I want to see you do it. Petra's already marked him for dead! You want to free Loom from Dragon rule, and Petra will give that to you. I will help."

"I—"

"No more objections, Arianna. You know it's true just as you've known all along that the man who betrayed you was closely connected to me. Perhaps, somewhere in that brilliant mind of yours, you'd already deduced the possibility of our familial ties." Cvareh appealed to her sense of logic, her sense of reason. She was too smart not to have put it together. Even if she hadn't consciously admitted it, she knew it was true.

"Everything has changed," Arianna whispered.

"Nothing has changed," he insisted. "There's not much time. Come back with me to Ruana."

"This isn't about you," she said sharply. "The King, he said something, something about destroying the guilds. I have to return to Loom."

"Yveun Dono would never."

"You're clearly delusional if you really believe that he would not resort to whatever extreme he deemed necessary." The very statement made him wonder if she somehow knew of the poisoned wine.

"We'll be stronger together."

"I don't even know if I want to look at you." The raw honesty of the statement cut him low. "I'm going to find a glider, and I'm going home."

Arianna started for the door. Cvareh reached out, grabbing her wrist, stopping her. He couldn't let her leave, not like this. She, the woman who had so claimed his heart, was leaving, and he honestly had no idea if she would ever return to him. If she would ever let him return to her.

She stared down at the offending hand, clearly waiting to see if he was going to willingly remove it or if she needed to cut it off. Cvareh chose the former.

"Ari, I'll wait."

"For what?"

"For when Loom is ready to join my House in this fight." He pointed to his ear, reminding her of the whisper link they established and that either had yet to break.

Arianna stared at him with her violet eyes for one long moment. They scanned his face as if memorizing its every curve and edge. He wondered what she saw in him.

"We don't need you," she whispered. "You'll only betray us again."

"Do not lump me with my brother's sins because it is easier for you to remain angry!"

She started down the hall once more, ignoring the comment. Cvareh watched as the first and only woman he had ever loved marched willingly into the hornet's nest of enemies that was House Rok. He wished desperately to know what she was thinking, just once.

Arianna paused and spoke without turning, "Don't whisper me first, Cvareh. Or I will know that everything was merely for your House, and Loom will never side with you."

Cvareh stared long after she was gone, the image of her back imprinted on his eyes. To most, the statement would seem like the definitive end of all possibilities. But not to Cvareh. He'd come to know something of the White Wraith's logic. And in the smallest corner of his heart, it gave him hope.

For if she cautioned him against an action that would make her not work with him, it meant that despite everything, the woman still considered him her ally. She still regarded *them* as a possibility, perhaps even an inevitability if nothing further was damaged between them. Repeating this fact to himself, Cvareh started back through the estate, making haste through every hallway, killing the two servants who saw him.

Petra was doing an exceptional job of keeping the place busy, for he hardly ran into anyone on his way out.

# 49
## ARIANNA

There was a swirling tempest in her chest. Its winds caught pains old and new, blending them with loves familiar and yet to be fully realized. The longer she spent in his presence, the greater the likelihood it would tear her apart.

She didn't want to love someone at the cost of her ideals. She didn't want to need someone attached to the murderer of the last person she needed. She didn't want to set her heart free in a world that was slowly shifting closer and closer to the end of days.

She had spent too long on Nova. She had let her mind be swept away by music and paintings. She had let her body grow fat with magic, let her mind languish. She needed to return to Loom. There, everything would make sense again. She would remember who she was and what she needed to do.

Arianna gouged out a Dragon's throat with a grunt of frustration. Her claws severed the spine and she cast the body aside, continuing onward.

The truth continued to stare her in the face every time she caught a glimpse of the blue of the nighttime heavens. The hue reminded her of the curtains in her room at the Xin Manor, reminiscent of the color of the sky when she and Cvareh set out for the temple.

She *did* love him. Despite everything, it was true. Of course, if she was going to fall in love again, it'd be a Dragon. And would she pick just any Dragon? No, she had to pick the brother of Rafansi. The traitor. *Finnyr*.

Arianna slammed a Dragon against the wall. It was a tiny thing, and had been trying to avoid being seen at all. The boy let out an almost-squeak at the feeling of her claws pressing into his chest.

"Gliders, where are they?" she snarled.

The child nearly wet himself.

"Gliders." Her claws bit through his flimsy Dragon clothes and into his skin. "Maybe I'll let you live if you tell me where they are."

"Up those stairs." He pointed. "Down the hall, second corridor, and out."

She dropped him and continued upward. There was one thing that seemed to be similar across all races of life: the need for self-preservation.

The gliders were exactly where he told her they would be. Some Dragons attempted to block her passage, but they didn't put up much of a struggle. Arianna saw Chimera looking on from the edges of the platform, golden chains looped around their necks. The gold reeked of the same scent as her chains had, tempered to the King's magic alone. Arianna couldn't break them if she tried. Chimera slaves bound to do the Dragons' bidding.

Yet they moved as one to the sides of a glider, doing nothing to bar her access.

Arianna sprinted over and mounted the vessel. She rested her hands on the handles, feeling magic surge from her fingertips through the interior channeling of the glider and into the wings.

"You won't be able to fly it."

"Yes, I can." Arianna shifted her weight.

"Only Dragons can." The man seemed tired, like he'd had this debate countless times. "Chimera don't have enough magic."

Arianna held up her palm and drew a claw across it, showing them her gold blood. It mattered little now, keeping her secret up on Nova. Let them talk. Let the Dragons know she was real and she would come to kill them with an army of Perfect Chimera just like her.

The Chimera looked on, stunned, like she was one of the Dragons' gods come to life. She wished she could tell them that she was, and that she had the power to save them, but they were lost causes. She couldn't bring them back to Loom with her and she had no doubt that when the Dragon King fell, he would take everything he could with him—assuming they weren't killed for not barring her access now.

"I can't save you." She felt compelled to apologize.

"We know," a woman replied. There was some comfort in hearing the tones of Fennish spoken again. "But we can save you."

"What?" Arianna asked in confusion.

"Go. We'll see to it that you can't be followed." The Chimera closed in on the other gliders with tools in hand.

She pushed her magic into the wings, strong and even. Arianna focused her will and commanded the glider like an extension of herself. *Up,* she demanded mentally, and the glider took to the sky.

Arianna soared on her own for the first time. There was no illusion of another Dragon, no airship captain, no bird-like beast propelling her upward.

Just her and her magic. The sight of the glider caused quite a stir, but by the time she was noticed, she was too far for any of them to reach her.

She leaned forward, shooting across the hills and towns of Lysip to its far edge. The Chimera might be on her side, but she couldn't have absolute faith that they would dismantle every glider before some Dragon got to them. Arianna pushed hard over the edge, spiraling around the underbelly of Lysip.

Finnyr's face seemed carved into the shadows of the clouds beneath her. She was deliberately leaving her opportunity to kill the man behind. Arianna swallowed, and let it go. She'd waited years; she could wait longer. Charging in recklessly had failed, so when she returned for his head it would be with an army at her side. It would be with his brother helping deliver him to her justice.

Ari began to gain speed, and braced herself for the winds that rippled the surface of the clouds below attempting to bar her entry home. Arianna pushed more magic, steadying herself, sparking a magical corona to encase her. She was ready. She would—

"Stop." The shout was laced with magic that sizzled across her mind, penetrating the vulnerability of surprise and fractured focus.

Arianna looked toward the source, following the trail of magic back toward Lysip's underbelly. Her eyes met a pair of fire-red orbs that seemed to glow with raw power in the distance. *Let go*, they urged her. She stared, vapidly confounded by the presence of the King of the Dragons in the underside of the island. But there he stood on a ledge, holding her eyes and mind in his sway.

*Let go*, he mentally urged again. Her hands shook.

Between the shock and magical exertion, Arianna's fingers uncurled. It was only a second—the feeling of air rushing between her digits and over her palms —but she was jolted back into awareness.

A second was all it took.

The magical trail that had been following her the whole time dimmed as the glider lost its fuel. Arianna found herself spiraling in the air, trying to grasp for something that was never where she expected it to be. Her other hand ripped off the remaining handle with the force of the wind.

The clouds were coming fast and she had only one chance to try to get to the glider and form a corona that might be her only shot at survival. She twisted her body in the air, trying to swim through nothing toward the one life raft that would save her from an ocean of death.

Her fingertips touched gold as the clouds engulfed her with their howling winds.

# 50
## FLORENCE

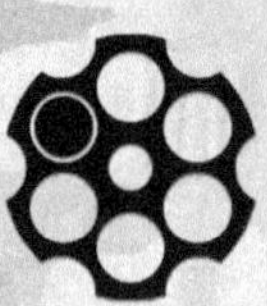

THE FOREST AT NIGHT WAS COOL, DESPITE SUMMER ENCROACHING ON THEM. Faint light from the gray sky above was almost completely smothered by the tree canopy. The leaves rustled in a faint wind, echoing the restlessness of the Fenthri below.

Florence had followed Derek and Nora to a group of their friends. She recognized James from earlier, but the rest were vaguely familiar faces, a tight-knit group of Alchemists that had no interest in allowing a wanderer to penetrate their ranks.

Perhaps that was the problem with Loom. They had all been told to stay in their place, to follow their guild marks, to not question when it had been their nature for so many years to question everything. The older generations resisted, but Florence's age and younger? They knew no better. They had grown up accepting the idea that Loom was as it was for some unknown reason, even if they didn't fully agree with it—even if history didn't agree with it.

That was the danger of Sophie's plan. She spoke of sacrifices, but the sacrifices she was risking encompassed the very future of Loom. The longer they spent accepting the Dragons' rule, the more they would all forget. It was easy for Sophie to say otherwise from where she sat; she was of the last generation. Her heart had been hammered into shape before the Dragons had ever ruled.

The young ones who sat among them now were still taking form. Florence watched silently from her seat at the far end of the table, closest to the open window, as the younger initiates slowly trickled from the room. When they were older, would they even remember a rebellion? What world would they inherit?

"You've been quiet," Nora noted, tearing some bread off the loaf in the center of the table and shoving it into her mouth.

"Just hungry," Florence lied. Well, it wasn't a complete lie. She *was* hungry. But that had nothing to do with her silence.

Nora hummed, clearly unconvinced. "Does it have to do with what the Vicar said?"

"What else?" Florence mumbled, wishing the conversation would change. She had yet to work through the best response to Sophie's decision.

"You spoke with the Vicar Alchemist?" one of the women seated at the other end of the table interjected with surprise.

"When we returned," Derek affirmed.

"What did she have to say for herself?" The woman stabbed at the food on her plate with renewed purpose.

"In regards to…" Florence left the question hanging. She wanted to see how the woman would finish it. Her tone was too similar to the one James had spoken with when they asked about the Vicar earlier that day.

"Killing her own guild."

Everyone at the table suddenly found everything else in the room far more fascinating than the Master speaking, or the three people she addressed.

"Explain yourself." Derek was visibly uncomfortable with the narrative being constructed before him.

The master exchanged a look with another circled man at the table, as if tacitly asking—and being granted—permission. "When we learned of the Dragons' plot, we made to evacuate the guild as fast as possible. But our Vicar didn't want to risk alerting the Dragons to our attempts. She didn't want to see Keel attacked in place of an empty guild hall, or in addition to."

The logic was very real, and instantaneously uncomfortable.

"She wanted to give the illusion that nothing was amiss."

"She left a third of the guild in the hall." It escaped Florence's mouth the moment she thought it.

"She told them we were moving in groups to prevent suspicion. The first group left. Then the second, her with it. It wasn't until we reached Keel proper that any of us realized her intent…"

"… and by then it was too late," Nora whispered.

Florence rested her elbows on the table, her chin sinking into the heel of her hand in thought. The reasoning, however horrible, made sense. No one would ever really know if Sophie's calculation had paid off. Keel wasn't attacked, but who could say if that was for Sophie's decision or merely because the Dragons never had any intention of destroying the city?

"You went to Ter.1 to seek help for the rebellion, didn't you?" One of the Masters asked. If their trip had been a secret, it wasn't any longer. "We must see an end to these Dragons."

The tiniest sliver of light appeared on the floor of Florence's mind as a door of opportunity cracked open.

"We did go to Ter.1 for help with the rebellion," Derek started delicately.

"And? Were you successful?"

"Not quite…"

Florence was going to smash through that door with force if she had to. "We were successful," she said, injecting herself once more into the conversation. "Not only the Harvesters, but the rest of the four guilds of Loom want to align with the Alchemists. This is Loom's fight, and they will stand with us, give us the help we need." It was a bit of an embellishment, but Florence believed it to be nothing but truth. There could be no other way for the future to unfurl. Surely, the other guilds would see this logic.

The two Masters exchanged a look of relief, and a surge of power flowed through Florence. She had always seen tools of destruction as the way to gain control. Hope was a much more dangerous weapon.

"Florence—" Derek urged her for silence, but she ignored him.

"The first Vicar we spoke to was uncertain. But after his untimely death, the current Vicar Harvester was all too happy to agree to a Tribunal at Ter.0."

"A Vicar Tribunal?" The Master sat back in his seat. "I never thought I'd live to see the day."

"Well, you may not…" Florene gave a heavy sigh, picking at her food anew. "The Vicar Alchemist refused to attend, demanded the Tribunal be called off."

"What?" the woman gasped. "Derek, is this true?"

Florence felt mildly guilty for the position Derek was put in as he looked between her and the Master. "Well, yes."

"Why?" the entire table seemed to demand at once.

"Vicar Sophie said that it is best for the rebellion if we submit to the Dragons, for now. Lure them into a false sense of security, strike when they're not expecting."

The Master stood so quickly his chair nearly went tumbling behind him. He slammed his palms on the table in visible rage. "She still has her head in the clouds from the last rebellion. There is no Council of Five to lead us any longer, not unless we make one by banning together. There are no great minds to lead us through this dark night. If we do not ignite the flame of our own lanterns, we will lose the way."

"What do you think should be done?" Florence asked, as if she had never even mentioned the Tribunal.

"The Vicar must go to Ter.0. Sophie must work with the other guilds. The Dragons have asked for war; we must give it to them."

Whispers of agreement turned into murmurs that then gave birth to outright spoken affirmation.

"There is no way Sophie will agree." She tried to muster all the delicacy she had.

"We must make her agree."

"And if she still doesn't?"

The Master sat heavily, suddenly deflated. "If she still doesn't, then we will honor her wishes. For the world will slip into true anarchy if the guilds begin to go against their Vicars."

"Who would have suspected the Harvesters were lucky for their Vicar dying," Nora whispered.

"It was certainly convenient for them," the Master agreed, most of the table echoing the dangerous sentiment.

Florence remained at the table until the lamp glow was dim and the food had long since been finished. She listened to Masters and journeymen alike lament their situation. She listened to how they would want to do things differently.

By the time the last of them finally broke away, her mind was made up.

She knew where gunpowder would be kept. She'd know it by logic and looks alone. All good Revos were trained how to properly store their explosives.

"Florence," Derek called after her, arm in arm with Nora. The two exchanged a look, and Nora gave a small nod, breaking away and starting in the opposite direction. Derek sprinted the distance between them.

She looked into his dark eyes, searching, waiting. She would not say the first word, not this time. He had sought her out, after all.

"You're walking a dangerous path."

"I'm walking the only path." She shifted her weight, still assessing if they were, indeed, talking about the same thing. "Will the rest of them see it that way?" She gave a nod in the direction of the now-empty hall.

"I can't say for certain…" The very idea of it made Derek uncomfortable, but he was not objecting. He had yet to speak a true word against it.

"Say for you." Florence took a long step toward him, their toes almost touching. She ran her hands down Derek's forearms slowly, encircling his fingers with hers. The touch demanded his attention. It was slow, but not quite sensual; demanding, but not quite heated. There was a certain life-changing weight to it that almost negated the need for a link mark. "Here, now, no one is around, Derek… What do you want, as an Alchemist?"

"I want to fight," he whispered, as though the words themselves could damn him in some way.

"Good." Florence squeezed his fingers.

For the first time in her life, she thought about kissing someone. She thought about closing the gap between them and placing her mouth on his, about crossing the line of familiarity into desire. It would be easy to do, almost too easy, and somewhere inside herself, she knew it wouldn't be unwelcome.

"Why do you stand with me?" she asked, holding them in place, letting the world fall away in the gaps between her words.

"Because you see the world differently. You have a connection to the greatness that Loom was, like the elders… But you look with eyes like mine, like Nora's, to how that will change to make a future for all of us. You've seen so much." Derek swallowed. "Because you're as undeniable as a pulse."

"Stay with me, Derek. Stay with me. Tether the rest of them to you, and stay with me."

"Are you sure you want this?"

"This is what I was made to do." She let him go, allowing him to reach his own conclusions. She was satisfied.

The rest of them were chained to something: love of a guild, loyalty to a Vicar, memories of the past. Florence did not live in bondage. She had struggled for so long trying to find a place where she belonged that she had never stopped to see the innate benefits of belonging to nowhere. She could do things no one else could do. She could be things no one else could be.

Florence helped herself into the room where they kept the gun powder. The lock hung open on the door. A quiet invitation, the first "accident" in a series of many to come in the following minutes and hours.

The canister she made was simple and small. It would be a quiet shot, one with the power it needed and no more.

As she continued silently back through the city, across bridges that spanned the trees and through spiraling outer staircases, Florence cemented her resolve. She wondered what Arianna would think. The woman would undoubtedly find out. Would she be angry, or proud?

In the end, it didn't matter. Florence wasn't doing it for Arianna. She was doing it because she believed it was right. Because it was what Loom needed, and in the name of a cause she was willing to die for. She had set the future she thought the world needed in motion; she would accept the responsibility that came with keeping its momentum.

The door to the Vicar's chambers was unlocked. Florence rounded the desk from behind which she had been reprimanded mere hours before. Behind it was another door that led upward to a makeshift laboratory. Magic hummed quietly in the air. The bubbling of beakers over tiny torches masked her footfalls. There was a power in sneaking, in moving unknown to all. It was a predatory rush and she wondered momentarily if Arianna still had the same feeling when she donned the coat of the White Wraith.

Florence opened the door to the uppermost level over the course of several breaths. It sighed softly, but the speed silenced any squeals from the hinges. There, sleeping under the moonlight filtered through the clouds above Loom and the thin curtain, was the Vicar Alchemist.

Florence adjusted the grip on her revolver.

Now was not the time for second guessing. Now was not the time for hesitation. There was one future before them, kill or be killed. Any who didn't see that were a risk to the rest of them.

*Strategic sacrifices* had to be made.

Florence crossed the room in a few wide steps. A floorboard creaked from her unhesitant movement and the Vicar stirred. Florence raised her arm.

Sophie's eyes opened to the barrel of a gun. Florence didn't give her more than a breath. Her pupils barely had time to dilate in shock, to register what was happening, before it happened.

Florence squeezed the trigger.

A single shot echoed through the streets of Keel. It was the first bell to usher in an assembly the following morning, in which the Masters of the Alchemists' Guild appointed a woman named Ethel—a woman who had been seated at the opposite end of Florence's table the night before—as the new Vicar Alchemist. The transition was smooth, simple, and well received by the guild entire.

No one spoke of the mysterious departure of the not-Raven, not-Revolver, who had been in their midst for months. Not one Alchemist searched the airships headed for Ter.4 for a coal-skinned, ink-haired girl. No one even breathed a word about finding the assassin of the former Vicar.

Sophie's death was a mystery, and the culprit was nothing more than a whisper on the wind.

# 51

## YVEUN

It was not long after Yveun descended beneath the surface of Ruana that he was approached. He always knew what Coletta's little shadows looked like, when they chose to show themselves to him. Coletta dried and lacquered flowers for each of them, which they wore as pendants. His mate was too particular to assign the different buds and colors at random, but whatever system she used, he'd yet to decipher it.

It was merely another layer to his Ryu, a mystery cocooned in the delicate webs of her mind. Yveun was content to let her keep her secrets, for doing so both afforded him freedom, and odd benefits like the one that now stood before him.

"You will take me to her?"

The figure nodded.

There was no further exchange. It was one of the many unspoken rules he'd picked up along the way and followed with ease. He never tried to see their faces or otherwise uncover their identities. They would not speak, only gesture yes or no to questions with a nod or shake of the head. He never asked anything unrelated to the task at hand.

The woman led him into the dim, dank depths of the underworld. The condensation on the walls combined with the general filth made it appear as though they were actually oozing, as though he was in the innards of some kind of grotesque beast.

They shimmied through passageways and wandered around storerooms that connected to equally unappealing alleys. They stepped over the remnants of carnage and the destruction left from illegal duels. The stench of blood and rot quickly became so potent that Yveun had to mentally keep his hand at his side, lest he end up walking with his nose covered the entire time like some kind of delicate Fen.

He adjusted his wide hood as they entered the imbibing parlor. The man behind the counter looked up but stopped shy of addressing them. His guide held out her pendant. Just the sight of it silenced the owner and dropped his gaze.

The shadow woman lifted her finger, pointing toward the end of the hall.

"The last door?" Yveun whispered in a higher note than he usually spoke.

The woman nodded.

Yveun left her and the man behind him. He had what he had come here for. The door ended up being not a door at all, but a heavy curtain that was well framed. Still, he didn't knock, and he didn't announce his presence.

His Master Rider was laid out upon a lounging chair. Arms and legs stretched every which way, muscles cutting out from underneath the skin. She was naked, save for the thin coating of blood that seemed to cover most of her body.

But the blood wasn't hers. She had engorged herself to the point of her stomach growing fat and her eyelids heavy at this little illegal parlor. Her body moved slowly to life, her eyes opening just enough to see him.

They were a bright purple, the color of lilacs, and seemed to nearly glow with power. It gave him pause. They were so similar to eyes he had only recently lost a battle of wills and magic against.

A smile crept upon his mouth. It pleased him that his new Rider and the Perfect Chimera known as Arianna would share similar eyes. Let them both be monsters.

"I was told you would be coming again," she purred, a fat cat on its bed.

"You're House Tam." He focused on the expansive and unbroken display of her emerald skin.

"That's what you choose to say?" She laughed at him.

*She* laughed at *him*. This was going to be a very different Master Rider than his Leona had been. He couldn't wait to discuss with Coletta what methods she'd suggest he employ to ensure the woman's loyalty.

"And you're not marked as loyal to Rok."

"I haven't had a reason to be."

"Marked? Or loyal?"

"Now you're asking the right questions." She slowly drew herself to a seated position. Her hair was short and as wild as she, spiking in every direction. "Let's say both."

"And if I give you a reason?"

"It's what I've been waiting for." She stood, as tall as him.

*Yes, this woman will do nicely.*

"I was sold the idea of coming here by one of the flower women. She told me there could be an exciting opportunity for one such as myself, but that I had to wait until the time was right."

"So you made your own excitement in the meantime."

"I did, though I'm getting bored." The Tam woman sauntered over to him. "Tell me, King, is the time right?"

"It is." He let her put her hands on him. He let her slip her palms under his vest, over his chest, and onto his shoulders. She touched him fearlessly and without reverence. She touched him like an experienced lover who knew exactly what she was looking for. "I want to make you strong."

"I am strong." She gave him a coquettish grin.

"I want to make you stronger."

"Will it feel good?" she breathed into his ear.

"The best you will ever feel." Yveun smiled into her neck. She had no idea what he had in store for her. He would find Alchemists and bring them to Nova. They would sew and stitch until she was the Perfect Dragon.

"Will there be blood?"

"So much blood."

She quivered, whimpering softly as if his words had put heat straight to her groin. The woman smelled of fallen Dragons and freshly healed wounds. Coletta had done a good job identifying this one for him. Yveun's palms fell on her narrow hips.

She straightened away. "Now?"

It took him a moment to realize she was talking about imbibing. But when the woman raised a clawed finger to the top of her breast and carved a golden line down to her nipple, blood dripping off its peak and onto the floor, the point was made well and truly clear. She smelled sweetly of dewy honeysuckle. She looked like some kind of dark goddess, bleeding both life and pleasure from her tit.

"Not now," he refused, though the thought was certainly appealing. His hand cupped her breast, thumb flicking over the nipple to smear the offered blood across its surface. It hardened at his touch, a rigid point coated in gold. "For now, I wish to take you to the surface, and find you marked as mine."

"If I must." She raised a hand to her cheek. "I think I'm far more appealing without any tattoos on my face."

She had a sharp chin and a crooked nose. He wasn't inclined to agree that anything could harm the overall aesthetic, or lack thereof, of her face. But Yveun didn't argue. The appeal of this woman was not feminine curves or pleasant features. She was raw strength. She was wild and carnal, danger personified as flesh, and it was rare for Yveun to find anything that set him to throbbing more.

"Come, my Master Rider."

She grabbed for her tattered cape, throwing it over her shoulders.

Yveun paused in the door frame. Looking over his shoulder, he asked, "What is your name?"

"Fay."

*Master Rider Fay.* It would work.

When they left, neither the flower woman nor owner of the establishment was anywhere to be seen. Yveun and Fay helped themselves out, she no doubt skipping on the bill. They didn't speak much up the pathways. It wasn't until they were halfway up that he heard the certain *zip* a glider made when it took to the skies.

Yveun raced down a narrow walk, heading for the glimmer of sunlight he saw at the end. It was a precarious balcony, but a good enough vantage for him to see the rider shooting by. It was not a Dragon of his, but the Rivet. Yveun growled in rage. She had escaped. And not only had she escaped, but she'd stolen one of his gliders and was riding it better than any of his own Riders.

"Stop!" He shouted, his voice echoing with magic, as Arianna gave a wide turn and spiraled down toward the Gods' Line.

The Chimera stilled. His influence reached her. Yveun knew it wouldn't be enough to truly sway her in any way. She was much too strong for that. But all he wanted to do was give the word enough of a jolt to gain her attention.

Once he had it by virtue of her eyes, he wasn't letting go. Yveun poured every ounce of will and asked for something very, very simple. The more complex a command, the easier it was for the person he was commanding to refute it. This was a simple wish. Two words. Just the mere distraction they would cause could be enough.

*Let go.*

When he saw her fingers uncurl, he knew he'd won.

The girl flopped through the air like a fish out of water. She was a rag doll that had been cast aside, headed toward its ultimate demise. If he could not have her knowledge, no one would; he would see her dead. The woman plunged into the clouds a mere hand's width from grabbing the glider.

To have even a hope of surviving, she'd have to find a way to reach it and then summon the magic, mid-air, to muster a corona. She'd either have to sustain that magic, or fly it again to survive landing.

Yveun cursed aloud.

Had it been anyone else, he would've taken them for dead. But not Arianna. He had been trying to kill this woman for years, and yet she persisted.

"Who was that?" Fay asked, caressing his forearm as she pressed her breasts into his triceps.

"The first person you are going to hunt down, kill, and consume."

The woman on his arm shivered in delight and it was enough to bring a small smile back to his lips. He had tried to hunt Arianna before. But it had always been in half measures. He hadn't known the girl, not really, to issue a full command. But now they had both seen each other. Now he had a Master Rider worthy of the name, and he would not stop halfway when molding her into the perfect killing machine.

*Let the Rivet return to her bleeding world,* Yveun thought darkly. Let her know only hopelessness, before her imminent demise.

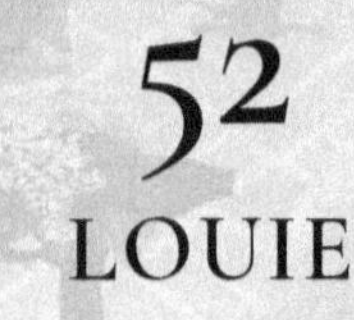

# LOUIE

WHAT A TIME TO BE IN THE ORGAN BUSINESS. DRAGONS BLOWING GUILDS UP. Guilds blowing themselves up. The world had gone crazy and there was only one thing he was certain of: everyone could use a little bit more magic right about now.

"King Louie, we have received reports that a glider has fallen into the remnants of Dortam."

After the destruction of Mercury Town, Louie had decided it was time to invest a bit in the real estate business. Dortam had always been dangerous, but it was taking a new turn with the past year's events. He found a comfortable spot down along the main train line out of the city. Close enough that his men could pop into the Revos' world whenever they needed something, but far enough away that he was well removed. Conveniently, it also positioned him better to run down the line in the opposite direction to Ter.5.2, which opened a whole world of opportunity for exporting.

Business had been going so well that he was considering moving operations permanently in that direction. Or even onto Ter.4 altogether. He'd been contacted by two very interesting Ravens at the behest of a certain girl he once did business with for the infamous White Wraith of Dortam. It almost made him feel bad for selling out young Florence to the Dragons. *Almost*.

But all was well that ended well. The girl clearly survived and was none the wiser to his decision to trade her for a few organs. Organs he never got.

"Would you like us to investigate?" Ralph asked.

Louie took his eyes away from his personal harvesting operation. "Let's continue this upstairs. The smell is overwhelming."

Ralph followed him upward. They switched back in a half dozen flights of stairs up to ground level, and a few more to Louie's new "throne room". The depth helped hide the scent of harvesting, so Louie had purchased the building immediately when he had discovered the depth of its underground portion. Bloody cogs, how he loved the Revolvers and their need to build a bunker into everything.

Not to mention, it had an excellent view of the mountains of Ter.5 that turned into a front-row seat to watch Dortam burn days before.

"Has there been word on if it took off again?" he asked.

"No reports of such."

"Any Dragon activity?"

"None seen."

*Curious*, Louie thought to himself. He had good instincts. It was part of what made him so effective for so long. Good instincts, determination, and the proper amount of ruthlessness to tie it all together. They lived in a cold world, no point in rewarding it with warmth.

"I shall go investigate myself, I think." Louie slipped on a pair of leather gloves, carefully selecting the proper goggles and mask to match. Dortam was a smoking wasteland.

"Do you think that's wise?" Ralph folded his arms.

"My men work harder when they think I could appear at any moment," Louie explained. "Furthermore, there's something odd about this one. A Rider returning alone?"

"Perhaps they were checking to see if the guild was truly destroyed?"

"That explosion rattled the world itself." Louie chuckled and shook his head. "Even if that were true, why has the glider not left yet?"

"Perhaps it has, and was unseen."

"And, if such is the case, I will just be checking to ensure my men are leaving no stone unturned, no valuable untaken, and no organ left to rot."

Ralph knew better than to continue objecting when Louie had made up his mind. He knew who paid his salary, after all.

Trains had long since stopped running along the main tracks into Dortam. The only engines that went in and out were small vehicles fashioned for single-track runs. Fast little things lifted right from the high-speed thoughts of the Ravens themselves. Louie didn't know the first of how it worked, but the two Ravens, Will and Helen, had agreed to supplying schematics for his Rivets to reproduce as a sign of good faith in their business agreement to funnel weaponry to them from the Revos. What two Ravens wanted with the guns, Louie didn't know nor care to find out.

He, Ralph, and two others kept on retainer whose names Louie never bothered to learn, sped toward Dortam in the late night.

The center of Dortam, where the guild used to be, was nothing more than a smoldering crater. Louie had kept his ear to the ground, following the destruction, trying to make sense of the presence of Dragon Riders and sudden silence that seemed to sweep across Loom. He was slowly gaining a picture that explained why the Revolvers would blow their own guild five ways to rubble.

The refinery still burned, keeping other parts of the city aflame with it. Buildings still tumbled. Smoke still darkened the air in all-too-quiet Dortam.

Louie couldn't be bothered for any of it. The days slipped from one to the next, and people struggled. Everyone fought so hard for everything they thought was so important and, in the end, what did it get them? Piles of ash.

"Ralph, tell your men to seek out my other excavators and have them all report here with their current findings for my review," Louie instructed. "You will lead me to where this supposed glider landed."

Ralph did as he was told, sending off the other men and starting through the carnage in the general direction of what was once Mercury Town. Louie was winded within minutes, and questioning his decision to come out at all. It was hard work scaling all the rubble. He had people for this.

But the prospect of a Dragon glider was far too enticing. Technology he didn't get his hands on often, at least not until the first glider crashed in New Dortam months ago. If he had a few more mostly-intact machines, he might be able to finally reverse engineer the mechanics the Rivets kept under such careful lock and key. That would really accelerate his business in new and exciting ways.

It was nearly enough to make him giggle with glee.

"According to the reports, it should be somewhere around here." Ralph helped Louie onto the top of a fallen building, trying to get a better vantage.

It was hard to see through the darkness, even harder with the perpetual haze that clouded the air. "Do you see anything?"

"No, I—" Ralph stopped and pointed. "Over there."

Louie followed his finger, looking through the night. He squinted, trying to see what his right hand man had seen. Just when he was about to regard it as nothing, his eyes caught a flash of gold.

"Yes, yes!" He clapped his hands gleefully. *Oh this was fun.*

They made haste across the remaining distance. Ralph was his strong arm, pushing materials out of the way and clearing a path for them to get to the glider. It was further than he expected from their previous vantage. But the trip would be well worth it, Louie kept reminding himself whenever his clothing snagged on a metal snarl or he had to climb over a particularly steep chunk of concrete.

They approached the glider, and both stopped at the same time. Louie didn't need to ask if Ralph saw what he saw. For there was no denying the spot of white shining in the faint moonlight as if protesting the inky blackness that tried to close in around the figure.

The glider was half atop the woman, a Chimera by all appearances. But there was something different about this one. Louie stepped forward.

"It may not be safe." Ralph stopped him.

"Anything worthwhile rarely is." Louie grinned madly, brushing him away.

Ralph stayed in his place.

Louie approached the semi-crushed figure with interest. For the first time, he saw the creature up close. There was no mistaking it—the unique coat alone was proof enough—each detail met every first-hand account perfectly.

The White Wraith was a woman.

But that was not Louie's most important revelation of the day. No, there was something far, far more curious about her. A spear of iron was stabbed directly through the side of her stomach. Her body was, no doubt, struggling to heal the wound despite the presence of the foreign object. But no magic could remove the iron, so blood continued to ooze around it before slowly fading into the night air.

Louie squatted next to the unconscious woman, touching his fingertips lightly against the wound. Sure enough, the blood was warm. It was truly coming from her. He had encountered many valuable things over the years and dealt in everything from secrets to organs, weapons to schematics. But Louie had never found something so rare, so precious, and so dangerous that it could change the world.

He grinned, already thinking of the possibilities for how he was going to work this discovery to his advantage. Not only did he have what he well suspected to be the infamous White Wraith of Dortam in his clutches, he also had a Chimera the likes of which Loom had never seen. Though he didn't understand exactly how, he knew the creature before him would shake the very foundations upon which their world was built.

He had what guilds wanted and Dragons feared.

*He had a Chimera that bled gold.*

Don't miss the epic conclusion of the Loom Saga, The Rebels of Gold.

**Get your copy now and start reading:** https://elisekova.com/the-dragons-of-nova-loom-saga-2/

USA TODAY BESTSELLING AUTHOR
ELISE KOVA
THE
REBELS
OF
GOLD
LOOM SAGA · BOOK THREE

*for Rebecca*
*the woman who can turn black text gold*

# PART
# ONE

# 1

## ARIANNA

*DRIP.*

Some kind of coupling or welding had come loose.

*Drip.*

Arianna groaned softly. The sound brought her body back to life from what felt like death itself.

*Drip. Drip.*

There was not a section of muscle tissue that didn't protest in fiery agony at her insistence on movement. She was in tatters from head to toe, her mental state no better. Her fingers twitched and the joints popped softly.

*Drip. Drip. Drip.*

"If a Rivet doesn't fix that soon, the wrench will touch their temple before it touches the pipe." Using her voice—what there was of it—was enough to make her head feel as though it was splitting open.

A loud *clang* shot between her ears as metal met cement. The aforementioned tool slid across the ground with all the cacophony of an industrial machine gone awry, and came to a stop at her toes.

Arianna's eyes cracked open.

The room came into focus slowly, very, *very* slowly. Hazy orbs formed into the cold glow of electric lighting, two sconces illuminating the weeping condensation that poured down the wall she faced. A skeleton of piping ran across the ceiling. Arianna's eyes followed the lead lines to the corner where one usually found such imperfections and sure enough . . .

*Drip.*

"Convenient for me. It seems I have a Rivet right here who could perform the fix."

Her lolling eyes stilled. Arianna could only muster the strength to move so much of her body at one time. Refocusing, she tilted her head forward off the cold metal. She drew her shoulders in, only to be arrested by the restraints strapped across her entire body.

A crimson face loomed before her.

Yveun'Dono, the Dragon King.

Arianna snapped her eyes shut and used the darkness to drop a curtain on the memory of the last time she was so confined. The last time someone had held her captive.

"I'll need more than a wrench for that . . ." she mumbled. No matter how broken her body was, the machinations of her mind ground to life around numbers. She had to keep herself moving, couldn't allow herself to freeze. The pipes were lead construction, likely fifty years old based on the jointing techniques. "I'd need a welding tool."

She shifted her vision from the ceiling to look at the speaker. A corpse lounged in a chair pressed flush against the door and stared back at her. He was lanky, all knobby bones and translucent skin. His black hair was pulled back tightly, stretching the skin of his face and turning his beady eyes to near slits.

She had traded being the captive of one king for another.

"King Louie."

"Not so much a king anymore." The man grinned wide enough to show teeth yellowed with age. "Kings need kingdoms."

She put a pin in that statement. It was too early to ask questions. So Arianna said nothing, and let Louie continue in the face of her silence.

"It's well past time we met face-to-face, my dear White Wraith."

A single sentence had never said more. He knew who she was. She knew who he was. "Glad there's no need for pretense." Arianna continued to take stock of her situation. "And I am not 'your dear.'"

"You're not? And here I was hopeful that the White Wraith would be fond of me."

"Not in this lifetime," she muttered, wishing her voice sounded stronger. Her head ached, but Arianna didn't allow the pain to betray as anything more than a narrowing of her eyes. *How did she get here?*

Arianna quickly assessed herself. She was likely underground, judging from the condensation on the walls and the heavy stillness that often came from such locations. Louie was here, a man she'd never interacted with before and certainly wouldn't have gone to for help. And she'd been right to avoid him, evidenced by the restraints holding her against an organ harvesting table—a tilted contraption that propped her at an angle, bound her down so she couldn't escape or struggle as someone, theoretically, cut her flesh from her body.

Yes, she knew where she was as it pertained to this singular room. But none of it indicated how she had arrived here. For that, she needed to go back further.

She'd escaped the Dragon King's prison with Cvareh's help. *Cvareh*. The name brought on a deluge of emotions, none of which she was equipped to handle under the circumstances. Arianna pushed the onslaught from her mind. Just another item to put a pin in, for now. Tackle one problem at a time.

She'd stolen a glider. Yveun's voice rattled through her mind again. *"Let go."* Her memories after that numbered three snapshots: Nova shrinking above her. The glider's metal handles just under her fingertips. Her body slamming against the contraption as she hit the clouds that separated the two worlds.

Then, nothing.

She must have fallen down to somewhere in Dortam, close enough to Mercury Town for Louie to get his grubby little hands on her.

"How did you know who I am?" Arianna willed her voice to sound the slightest bit more stable. Maybe it would, if she weren't diverting so much focus to merely keeping screams of pain and frustration dormant. Her mind was moving too slowly for her to tolerate. "I always sent someone else to meet with you."

"Your coat—among other factors—was a giveaway." Arianna desperately wanted to know what these "other factors" were. "And 'someone else'? Let's call her by name, shall we? *Florence.*"

If she were more in her right mind, she never would have given him the chance to say the name. Nor would she have risked giving away how much that single utterance meant to her with her traitorous face. Horror and heartache swept across her like a burst steam pipe, no doubt altering the landscape before she could patch the rupture. In a matter of moments she mastered herself once more—but Louie watched her closely, and the scalding emotion had left its mark.

"Quite a little upstart, that one." Louie made a display of picking lint off his knee to hide his satisfied grin. "Are you certain she's not a Rivet? Because she seems to be redesigning the world according to her own secret schematics." His eyes returned to her slowly in the wake of her silence.

Arianna struggled to keep her face impassive, to betray nothing, to give up no more weaknesses—for Florence's sake, if no one else's. But her heart screamed for any word of the young woman who had been her ward for years. The less she said before she had full control of her mind, the better.

"You don't know . . . do you?" Louie whispered like a child just discovering where their parents hid the sweets.

"I know enough."

"Where are we?" He called her bluff without so much as blinking.

"Mercury Town," Arianna surmised. The slowly widening grin—almost a snarl—on his face convinced her she had guessed wrong. "Oh? Did you find some new hole to terrorize?"

"Mercury Town is the hole." Louie shifted, bringing his left foot off his right knee and settling it to the floor. Leaning forward, he placed his elbows on his narrow thighs. "I suppose it's going to be hard to strike a deal with you if you don't understand the situation you're in."

"What makes you think I'd strike a deal with you?" She hated the feeling of ignorance. It was like drowning in a sea of ink, the world obscured, clarity lost. Her mind didn't know how to proceed in such a void.

"I have no doubt you'll prefer it to the alternatives."

"And what are those?" *Give me information,* her hungry mind pleaded. *Something, anything.* She needed just enough for a direction. For a strike to her flywheel to get things moving again. Her magic was slow, body aching, mind stunted. Something had to improve, or everything would break.

"Alternative one." Louie held up a skeletal finger. "I keep you here forever, and harvest you as I would any of my other pets."

"Resorting to harvesting and trying to pass off black organs? That's a new low, even for you."

"Black organs? No, no." He let out a wheezing chuckle and lifted another finger. "However, that does bring me to alternative two—I sell you back to your Florence and her rebellion for the heftiest sum I can imagine."

"Florence wouldn't pay for me." Arianna hoped. She didn't want the girl to waste any resources on her. She didn't want Florence to risk anything further by being near Louie and the dangers that seemed to lurk perpetually around him.

"Oh, I think she would. How else will she live up to her promise of producing a Philosopher's Box?"

Arianna barely missed the final point over the ringing in her ears.

"Or three . . . You cut me in on the deal to produce the infamous box. You show me what's been making you so deadly all these years. You show me the schematics that let you bleed gold."

All at once, the pain vanished. The buzzing between her ears stopped. And everything went numb.

# 2

## FLORENCE

WIND BLEW DUST OVER THE RAMPARTS OF TER.0, CURLING AROUND THE GHOSTS that were the only other occupants of the crumbling glory of a world long lost.

It was a wasteland of sand and rock, littered with hollowed skeletons of gnarled iron and cement that rose insistently from their shadowed graves. Florence tilted her head back to gaze at the shifting skies and semi-translucent clouds that swirled between worlds. Her pale companions played a game of hide-and-seek—mostly hide—with the moon.

She was the only creature alive here. She was the beating heart and shallow breaths of a land forgotten. She was the only remnant of life to return to this broken corner of their world.

No, she wasn't the only one. She was merely the *first*. All of Loom would come to converge in this once-hallowed place of knowledge. They would return, and the Vicar Tribunal would be born anew.

It was a beautiful idea—one she'd believed in enough to shoot a dangerously stubborn vicar between the eyes for. But now Florence was forced to admit her hasty plan that led her to this point hadn't been thought through as much as she would've liked.

Somehow, everything would work itself out, as it had her entire life.

The next morning, Florence moved again. She traversed the cracked earth and rubble toward a structure that was once a distant point on her horizon. Like a mighty hand's fingers stretching up from the horizon, five points reached toward the sky as if to grasp the universe.

Florence trudged along. She didn't have much—just the basic necessities she'd collected in Ter.2.3 before chartering a boat. Her pack grew lighter with each fading night.

On her seventh day in Ter.0, she crossed through the gate. The wall housing it had been blown apart on either side, but the gate still stood, a symbolic entrance standing in defiance of time—and Dragons.

Florence stopped to adjust her tattered frock. She combed her fingers through her hair, though she imagined this did little to tame it. Her knuckles brushed the tattoo that marred her cheek. But Florence gave it no thought, choosing instead to adjust the tilt of her top hat.

The hatter in Ter.2.3 had only a few options for her. The current top hat she was sporting offered only one buckle around the base and a *single* feather. It was a style from two years ago, and nothing like the fashions she'd seen in the windows of Dortam practically a lifetime ago.

But it was something.

It was the regalia of the woman she had once been. She'd carry the remnants of her past life into this old world so that both could be rebuilt together. Florence dropped her hands and continued through the gate.

Ter.0 was once the breeding center for all of Loom. Every year, the five vicars converged upon this place to share knowledge, and initiate their reproductive cycles together. A selection of initiates, journeymen, and masters from each guild remained after the tribunal, to teach the children the fundamentals of thought and the basis for the world in which they all lived.

Florence was born here, but she had no recollection of this place. She was one of the thousands of children split among the guilds when the Dragons assumed control of Loom. She was selected for the Ravens and left to die.

And she would have, if she hadn't fought her way out.

The main entry to the Hall of Ter.0, the most important building in the world, was blocked. Its massive doors had splintered off their hinges and tilted against each other drunkenly, leaving Florence to seek another entrance. Windows cut beams of light from the hollow center of the hall through to the shaded ground below. Florence strolled across their beacons until she came upon a rubble-strewn entry she could crawl through.

Inside, an anterior passageway snaked around the perimeter of the hall. Florence pressed forward until she reached the grand atrium—the center for all learning and knowledge. The grandiose glass dome that had once arched above it all was shattered into hundreds of shards that painted rainbows across the marble floor.

With glass grinding beneath her heels, Florence stepped into the sunlight, and onto the stage of destiny.

She strode to the center of the atrium, surrounded by still-standing statues of the five guild symbols. The revolver chambers, the raven, the sickle, inverted triangles, and crossed tools for the Rivets—they were all there, but none seemed to fit her. None defined her. She did a half-turn, taking in the remnants of what was once the foundation of Loom.

"It'll do," she mumbled. It wasn't much by way of fortification or construction. But, for now, it could house the pieces of their ailing world. It could hold the Vicar Tribunal on ceremony alone, if nothing else.

Glass cracked and snapped under footsteps.

Florence turned. Her pistol was drawn and pointed at the source of the sound before she could blink.

A woman emerged from the shadows. Her hair was loose, flowing like moonbeams down her back and around her face. The pristine shade reminded Florence of Ari, but this woman's skin was a deeper hue, a more shadowed slate, not unlike Florence's own flesh. She wore a smart bronze-colored coat with gigot sleeves, offset by a stripe of steel blue tied in a bow around her bicep. The composition brought out the powder blue stitching of her dress.

"I am not your enemy."

Florence uncurled her fingers from the pistol grip, easing off the trigger, and returned it to its holster. "So it would seem. You're not Dragon." Florence looked over the stranger, and the contrast of soft curves and delicate fabrics that seemed to protest against the gritty world in which they existed. "Who are you?"

The woman brought a finger up to the filled tattoo on her cheek. "Shannra, the Revo."

"Florence, the Revo."

"I know who you are." Shannra crossed the distance between them with deliberate steps. "All of Loom knows who you are."

"Do they?" Florence couldn't stop her fingers from twitching toward the gun. The last time she'd been out of hiding as a named entity in the world was the night she killed the Vicar Alchemist. It would make sense if they were hunting her. Though she had heard no word of a manhunt while she was in Ter.2.3, and vicarcide would have prompted both—rumor and hunt.

"Of course. The woman who inspired the first Vicar Tribunal in years, who sparks rebellion like wildfire, would be known across the world."

"The Dragons did the work for me in sparking a rebellion," Florence said warily. It was true. Uprising was an easy sell when the world was kindling to burn at the hands of their oppressors.

"Perhaps, but you directed it." Shannra played with a particularly large shard of glass, sliding it with the toe of her boot. "You organized us."

"I've done nothing yet." There were many more steps for Florence to take, and even if she took them, she could well be marching the world she loved to its death.

Shannra just hummed, giving a wide sweep of her arms and motioning to the room around them. There was a delicate deadliness to her, Florence decided quickly, and secrets sewn between the powder blue stitching of her skirts.

"Why are you here, Shannra?" The girl had a filled Revo tattoo on her cheek. No doubt she was younger than Florence, and already achieved Journeymen.

"I'm here to see the world die, and begin anew."

"Cryptic." Florence put her hands in her pockets in an effort to seem less intimidating. It was a meaningless gesture; even with palms stuffed against her thighs, she could still outdraw almost anyone. Of that she was confident. She had to be, or she would hesitate when the moment mattered most.

Shannra laughed, a sound like the crescendo of a chorus. "Fair, fair . . . Then I'm here to help give you what you need."

"And what is that?"

"The Philosopher's Box."

Her heart stilled. The magic in her blood pushed inward, as if to guard her immediate, instinctive response of hope. Hope was dangerous. And yet, Florence had positioned herself as the harbinger of it, because it made the people around her so much more effective. Hope was indeed a danger—but it was also excellent leverage.

"What do you know of Arianna?" Florence asked finally. Her hands were still conveniently close to her guns and, depending on what this beautiful Revolver said to her, she could easily reach for them.

Shannra twirled a strand of hair around her fingers with a coy smile, knowing exactly where Florence's mind had gone. One look told Florence that she knew too much. More than anyone should.

"King Louie sends his regards."

Florence reached for her pistol without a second thought.

# 3
## ARIANNA

Damn the man for having the foresight to tie her down, because if he hadn't, she would've spent her dying breath savoring the feeling of his skull disintegrating against her fingers as she clawed out his eyes.

"I don't know what you're talking about," she said, wishing she hadn't taken so long to voice her denial. Arianna curled and uncurled her fingers, moving something, anything, trying to get blood pumping to her brain at any cost. Louie made almost the same motion before he spoke.

"Oh, White Wraith, don't you think we have a better rapport than that? Since when have you known me to seek something I cannot easily attain?"

"I don't think *you* ever actually attain anything. As I recall, I did most—all— of the work on every heist." Arianna added a scoff in an attempt to get a rise out of the man. If she could throw him off his emotional center, she could regain some vantage.

"All the more poetic, then. As it seems this time will be no different." Louie shifted stiffly, folding his skeletal hands together, seeming utterly unbothered.

"I can't give you something I don't know how to create." If changing the topic didn't work, she'd try denial next. She'd try everything until something stuck, until her mind was solid enough again to think clearly.

"There was a time when I might have believed you." Louie stood slowly. Arianna narrowed her eyes at his deliberate, yet unsteady, motions. She expected the King of Mercury Town to have a little more . . . grace?

He reached for a holster on his hip and drew a tiny one-shot pistol barely larger than his hand. It was the sort of gun Arianna imagined Florence laughing at, if she ever saw it. The man pointed the weapon at her shoulder.

Arianna narrowed her eyes down at him. "You sure you can handle that? Seems like you're having trouble."

"Point blank shot at a tied-down target? I'll take my chances." Louie tightened his grip on his gun. "Question is, do you want to? I don't have any interest in shooting you, really. We had such a good stretch as business partners, and I'd much rather not poison the waters with a gunshot to prove a point."

Her scowl was so deep it hurt. She knew exactly what he was doing. Proof of her being the Perfect Chimera pumped through her veins. One shot wouldn't kill her. Bloody cogs, against all the other pain, it likely wouldn't even register. But there would be no denying after that.

"How did you find out?" Arianna asked. She instantly loathed the smug look on his face.

"You have your Florence to thank for that." Louie made a show of re-holstering his gun, as if he was doing her some grand favor. "After all, she was the one who let the world know that you, Arianna, the Master Rivet, pupil to the renowned Oliver, and the woman who supposedly perished alongside the Council of Five in the last rebellion, can make the Philosopher's Box."

"You know your history." Her voice had gone soft. But unlike the delicacy forced on her when she first awoke, this was a deadly sort of quiet that she found suited her much better.

"When I found you, bleeding gold, dressed in white . . . it was all too much of a coincidence to write away."

"And I confirmed my identity when I woke."

"Now, don't be too hard on yourself."

"Placate me again, old man, and—"

"No need for name-calling." Louie's chuckle devolved into a wheeze. "It makes things much more efficient like this. You know the situation; no need for us to play coy. So, which option—"

"You said Mercury Town was a hole." Her brain was beginning to work again, and she wasn't going to let him get away with spewing nonsense. The twitch of Louie's lips was the only thing that betrayed his annoyance at her interruption, but it was more than enough to satisfy her.

"The Revolvers saw to that." He settled back into his chair. "How much does Nova really know?"

"Assume I know nothing."

"Seems an easy assumption." It was now her turn to prevent her lips from twitching in annoyance. "The Dragon King ordered the guilds destroyed."

"Destroyed," she repeated involuntarily, as though it would make more sense if she said it again herself, slowly. It didn't.

"Destroyed." He echoed her horror in what was notably the first time they'd agreed on something. "For our insolence. The Harvesters were the first and they were hit the hardest. From what I hear, most of the masters were at the guild for a vote when the King's Riders dropped the bombs. The

Alchemists were next. They lost their hall and at least a third of their members.

"The Revolvers . . ." Louie paused, as if offering a moment of silence to the noble fools of the weaponry guild. "They'd fought it from the start."

"They sought to protect Loom from their own mechanizations," she murmured.

"They quickly realized there weren't many options, and less time," Louie continued.

"They killed themselves."

"In a blaze of glory. It was an explosion befitting a funeral for the Vicar Revolver himself."

"The Ravens? Rivets?" It was terrible news atop terrible news. Still, she wanted to know the fate of her guild.

"Ravens were spared, thanks to the Revolver's efforts. The Rivets were hit, but the Riders didn't have the same firepower to raze them. Bent but not broken, from what I hear."

Ari took a moment just to breathe. The Rivets guild, in all its gorgeous mechanical glory, still ticked along. "And Florence?"

"Ah, yes, Loom's champion."

Arianna tried to keep her face passive—*just the facts*. But judging by Louie's reaction as he spoke, she failed. At last, she acquiesced; her hand had been shown for what it was. "She's alive then?"

"She thrives." He paused, clearly for dramatic effect. "So says my confidant."

"Confidant?" Arianna asked cautiously, though she didn't know why. She already knew what game Louie was playing at. He wanted the box and proximity to power; he wanted her to play along. Putting a loaded gun right next to Florence was the frustratingly perfect move.

"I sent a good friend of mine to her, just to help see things set up properly on Ter.0. After all, Florence is the one who got the Vicar Harvester to call the Tribunal."

"There's to be another Vicar Tribunal?"

"It's been a while, hasn't it?" Louie massaged his knees and Arianna wondered if they ailed the man. She could only speculate about his age . . . but he must be well into his forties, practically ancient for a Fenthri. "Children who have never even stepped foot on Ter.0 will be caucusing there for the first time to determine the fate of the world. Reminds you of the old days, doesn't it?"

"Take me to her, to Florence."

"I don't think you're in much of a position to make demands, Arianna."

"You were willing to make a deal before." She had to speak his language, stick to safe territory, stick to business.

"Give me access to the schematics for the Philosopher's Box and I will take you anywhere in this wide world you want to go. Even back up to Nova."

"Florence," she repeated firmly.

"The box?"

He was relentless. And even though Arianna knew the answer, she asked the question anyway. "Why do you want it?"

"Reasons that I think should be obvious."

And they were.

There was a time when he who owned the gold owned the power. But such a time was ending. Now, Loom and Nova stood on a new precipice, an age where power came from those who could manufacture weapons in the shape of people that bled gold. There was abject disgust at the notion that she would help usher in such an age.

But it was an age Loom had been headed toward since the first Chimera. If it hadn't been her, it would've been someone else.

"If I agree, you'll take me to her?"

"You have my word." Louie put his hand over his vested heart. "It's bad for business if I go back on my deals. Plus, we both have far, far more to gain by being friends."

"If I agree, you'll do as I say?"

"Within reason."

She settled back against the harvesting table, looking at him with narrowed eyes. She had to get something out of this, for the time being. There was no possible way she'd give Louie unrestricted access to the Philosopher's Box. For as long as she could manage, she'd regulate who knew what.

"On Nova, there is a flower for the Lord of Luck. This flower has four petals . . ." Her voice trailed off for a moment and Arianna thought back to her night with Cvareh on the island. She wanted to feel the same anger she felt toward him previously, but it was already weakening into an uncomfortable question: *What are we?* "Be my Lord of Luck here on Loom and grant me four wishes. Four things, whatever I design to help the rebellion, to help Loom, in the coming months. And when we are finished, you will have your schematics."

"I'm not a Dragon." Louie chuckled. "I think what you seek is a boon."

"I actually already have one of those. So I suppose you could call me a collector of sorts . . ." Arianna spread her lips and barred her teeth like a ravenous Dragon. "Plus, a boon is only *one* wish. I want four of you."

"You ask too much." He ran his fingers over his lips. Arianna could practically hear him thinking through the admission of her holding a boon.

"You ask for the power to change the world—to make you richer than ever before, and ten times as formidable. I ask you to honor four favors." She managed to shrug against the tight restraints. "Seems more than fair."

Louie stood, pulling his chair away from the door. "Very well, Arianna, you have your deal." He reached for the door latch, clicking it open. "We shall leave at dawn for Ter.0, and your Florence."

# 4

## CVAREH

Even when his heart was heaviest and his mind in turmoil, the unhindered wind and free cries of the wild boco traversing its currents evoked a sort of calm. There wasn't another flyer anywhere around him, leaving the Xin'Ryu mostly to his thoughts.

Dawn began to seep between the stars—a melancholy hue that marked the end of Lord Xin's hour and the start of Lord Rok's.

*Rok.*

The mere thought had Cvareh looking over his shoulder. Far in the distance, hazy with the wisps of the God's Line, was the ghostly silhouette of the Rok Estate. He squinted against the darkness, pushing magic into his eyes and piercing the shadows, but another boco was nowhere to be seen.

He had split from his sister, Petra, to allow her to make a distraction while he went in search of Arianna. What sort of distraction Petra had in mind, he couldn't fathom, and now he wished he'd had an idea. Cvareh looked forward again.

His sister would be waiting for him back at the Xin Manor.

The isle of Lysip grew before him. It was a familiar shape. Cvareh knew every cut of the mountains and every switchback that wandered through its rolling jade hills, down into the great city of Napole at the far end.

But there were no festivities in Napole, no flame dancers on rooftops or revelers pouring wine until the bottles ran dry. As Cvareh rode his boco, Saran, as their shadows cut across the city below him, he was staggered by the quiet. *This* was a city in mourning, a place where men and women had lost family, loved ones, to the tyrant known upon their wide world as Yveun'Dono.

Cvareh tightened his grip on his boco's reigns. There was no bottom to the depths of Rok depravity, and in that endless pit was where they had found the will to poison the wine and bring an abrupt, dishonorable end to the Xin and the Crimson Court. While none could pin the act on House Rok, it was known. Cvareh could almost feel the truth being whispered behind tightened shutters and on the shuddering rasps of mourning lovers.

Roks may have weakened them, but in the same act, had provided House Xin with all the rationale and motivation ever required to stage a rebellion.

And that rebellion hinged on one person—a Chimera who smelled of honeysuckle and tasted of dreams. There were competing motivations in him. The first was admonishment that he had ever let Arianna return to Loom. He had let go the singular person who could provide Xin an army that could stand against the might of Rok.

But had he not released her, she would've never fought for—alongside— them. The other voice in his mind reassured him of the fact, just as it reassured him that for all her pain and anger, and for all that she put a world between them, her heart still spared a beat for him.

Cvareh swallowed the debate and ignored the aftertaste, focusing on his flight path. The Xin Manor was beginning to peek around the mountains ahead. Before he could even contemplate Arianna's mind and motives and if she would ultimately support House Xin, he had to think first about how to stave off Petra's ire for letting their inventor return to Loom unhindered.

At least, Cvareh hoped she had returned to Loom unhindered. He'd seen a glider rise from the Rok Manor on his way back to his boco. Then a second, not long after. But anything else . . . that was in the hands of the Lord of Luck Cvareh had been born under.

The shroud of silence hung heavy even at the Xin Manor. It was early yet, and no servants arrived at his usual landing balcony to attend to Saran.

"You know your way to the stables, right?" Cvareh patted the beast's feathery neck before dismounting.

It cooed softly, tilting its head in reply.

"If you want to stay here, you're welcome to," Cvareh added. Cvareh had always known that Raku, Petra's trusty mount, was the smartest of their birds.

His chambers had been tidied. He'd left them a sopping mess, only returning to ransack his clothes to find acceptable garb for his excursion. Those articles now smelled of Rok, and Cvareh was prompt to strip them off and cast them over the balcony rail. He paused, watching the trousers and arm adornments be swallowed up by the God's Line, and hoped they didn't fall on some poor unsuspecting Fenthri's head. Knowing his luck, they would, and that Fenthri would be Arianna.

With a sigh, Cvareh went inside. He had only begun to receive his latest tailor orders. No clothing seemed quite appropriate for the situation. So he donned a loose fitting robe, a sort of belled sleeve and wide-sashed ensemble that put the masculine lines of his chest and abdomen on display in a way he was rather fond of. It was most certainly a color from last season, but it brought out the dark umber notes of his blood-orange hair in a way he'd always liked.

He only had to look presentable enough for Petra.

His door clicked closed quietly behind him, and Cvareh descended the window-lined hall that would lead across the manor to Petra's chambers. Footsteps drew his attention; Cvareh's eyes locked with another set of golden irises.

Cain—his childhood friend, his confidant, aspiring mate to his sister—looked at Cvareh with an unfamiliar expression. Cain opened his mouth to speak, then promptly closed it before opening it again.

"What will we do?"

Cvareh couldn't help but grimace. No doubt, Petra had correctly anticipated or deciphered his actions of letting Ari go. "Arianna will continue to support us," he assured. "Even on Loom, she's returning to reunite with the rebellion and—"

Cvareh lost the final word. Cain crossed to him in a tempest. He grabbed Cvareh's robe by the lining of the collar, the man's claws punching holes through the silken fabric.

"Cain—"

"You think I care about your Fen pet right now?" he growled. Cvareh was instantly reminded of one of their last fateful encounters in the stables at the Crimson Court. He'd hoped the tension of that meeting had been washed away by the events of the past day.

"You'd do well not to refer to her in that way."

"Petra is dead and all you can think about is Loom?"

Cvareh froze. He didn't care for the ribbons that Cain was slowly cutting into his fine clothing. He didn't even pay attention to the full depth of rage and pain in the other man's eyes.

*Petra is dead.* These three words echoed so loudly in Cvareh's mind that he went deaf. He saw Cain's mouth moving but no sound accompanied it.

Petra is dead. Petra is dead. *Petra is dead.*

"What?" Cvareh blundered his way back into Cain's speech. "What about Petra?"

"You . . . you don't know." Cain's grip relaxed. His golden eyes changed from a fiery hue, alight with magic, to a smoldering ache. They glistened in a way Cvareh had never seen before. "She was with you, Cvareh. Your Oji was with you. How do you not know?"

Before Cvareh had a chance to explain his and Petra's plan—how they had split up for effectiveness—and before he had time to ask again what Cain meant, he was interrupted again.

"Cain'Da, Cvareh'Ryu." There was a note of genuine surprise on the quiet words of a servant who had appeared in the hall below them. "Your presence is requested back in the main hall."

Throne room. It had been the throne room before. Cvareh wanted to correct the boy. He wanted to be like Petra and inspire fear over something as simple as the use of a proper name. But he couldn't speak.

If he opened his mouth, he would scream. Or vomit. Or beg for answers. Or some combination thereof.

*There must be some mistake*, his mind protested as they descended through the fresh opulence of the Xin Manor. It stood in contrast to the Rok Estate's antiquity, a fact underscored even more by having just sneaked through the latter's halls. But Cvareh saw none of it. His mind barely registered that his robe was reduced to tatters. He moved on instinct and somehow found himself at his sister's most beloved room.

The stained-glass floor was illuminated with the first light of dawn. It splashed colors on the ceiling and walls of the long hall in happy contrast to the heavy melancholy that dominated the air. Most of the staff and servants were lined in rows, looking toward the raised platform where Petra's meticulously fashioned throne stood.

In front of that throne was a ruby-skinned man. Cvareh didn't know him but he recognized the beads of a King's Rider when he saw them.

"Good of you to join us, both of you," the Rider praised brightly. "We heard you had returned, Cvareh'Ryu, from your late-night *adventures*."

Cvareh didn't believe for a moment that the Rider didn't know exactly where he'd been. Cvareh barred his fangs in a wide grin. He was not to be tested right now. The past day was beginning to tug on his shoulders to the point of pain, contorting his muscles under the weight of something he couldn't yet fathom.

"Don't you mean Cvareh'Oji?" Cain corrected darkly from his side. For all their differences, and even when he dripped with anger, Cain still stood for Xin. If that fact ever changed, Cvareh's world would truly have ended.

"Not quite." The Rider turned back to Cvareh, smiling, fangs gleaming. "Cain Bek was gone for a while. I trust he informed you of the death of your sister."

*Petra is dead.*

"I require some clarity." It was all Cvareh could muster. Something had to begin making sense. The sad eyes of his House surrounded him, wary gazes begging for an answer he didn't have. He didn't even know the questions to ask.

"Ah, well, then allow me to inform you that your sister, Petra Xin'Oji To, has perished on this day."

Cvareh could see the ghost of his sister behind the man, sitting proudly on her throne. Her golden curls cascaded over her shoulders and down to the curve of her hip. A woman among women, and warrior who could best them all.

"She was challenged to a duel in the Rok Estate," the Rider continued.

There were whispers now, but all Cvareh could focus on was the ghost of his sister. It was a figure that already threatened to haunt him until the end of his days.

"A duel between whom?" Cain asked. "A Rok, no doubt. For if she was slain by a Rok, the title of Oji falls to Cvareh."

"I know well how titles work," the Rider chided with a condescending smile. "We use the same ones in House Rok. And you would do well, Cain Bek, to remember where House Rok sits." *At the top*, the Rider allowed everyone to mentally fill in the words. "No, she was challenged by a Xin."

They all knew who it was. There was only one man it could've been. For the only other Xin present at the time of Petra's death was Cvareh, and every last man and women assembled knew that Cvareh would have never challenged his sister.

"On the fifteenth day of the month of Soh, eleven years after the annexation of Loom, Petra'Oji was slain by Finnyr'Kin in a duel of her challenging."

Cvareh stared through the Rider. He looked back to the ghost of his sister in all her power and glory. She had a might that should only be thwarted by the Gods themselves, and Finnyr was no God. There was foul play here. Deceit and lies abounded everywhere Rok stood.

"Coletta Rok'Ryu and Yeaan Rok'Soh bore witness to this honorable challenge and kill. It determines before the Divine Twenty and the mortals below that Finnyr Xin'Kin To will henceforth be known as Finnyr Xin'Oji To."

In this moment, the Rider's words were muffled, garbled. The visage of his sister moved her lips, and all he heard was Cain's voice again, ripe with pain and colored in grief—*Petra is dead*—before the ghostly presence vanished, and left the halls of the Xin Manor forever.

# 5

## ARIANNA

SHE WAS RELIEVED TO BE FREE OF HER BONDS. THE FEELING OF ENTRAPMENT IN that dank little room was too similar to what she had endured on Nova at Yveun's hand. Even though the man before her was the antithesis to the hulking Dragon King, and her surroundings looked nothing like the architecture found in the sky world, there was something disturbingly similar to both situations.

"So, where are we?" Movement helped, but thinking helped more.

"Suburb of Ter.5.2." Louie moved at a snail's pace, and Arianna was reduced to a shuffle to avoid striding past him. "It was a warehouse I was using to transfer goods from Dortam to the port of Ter.5.2, and vice versa."

"How far does your reach actually extend?" Arianna didn't know why he was suddenly sharing all this information with her, but if his tongue was well oiled, she'd encourage the words to flow.

"Far enough." Louie paused at one of the switchbacks, giving her a smug smile.

"I suppose you weren't known for your transparency."

"The opposite, actually."

He pushed open a door that was quite light when Arianna caught it, despite the heavy-looking wood-and-bronze framing. They arrived in a homely upstairs room far more domestic than Arianna expected. A long wooden table was lined with pewter stools, one of which was occupied by a red-eared Chimera.

"Adam, go fetch our little crows from their tinkering."

The man named Adam stood and Arianna regarded him warily. She knew Chimeras got the luck of the draw when it came to organs, but seeing red Dragon flesh evoked a completely new response in her. He was oblivious to her apprehension, however, and left the notes he'd been looking over to disappear through a galley door.

"I'm going to need your help." Louie drew her attention from the table as he rounded it in his deliberate manner.

"With what?" Arianna was surprised when he slid the papers toward her. It seemed her needlessly complex planning for how to sneak looks at them was no longer necessary.

He fanned out the papers, an assortment of technological specifications, schematics, unit numbers, and more. "We need to outfit this airship for magic, using this much gold." His finger settled on a quantity.

Arianna scoffed. "Impossible."

"You seem to be someone who makes the impossible, possible."

"I'm an engineer, not a wizard."

"Well—" Louie was cut short by the galley door opening again. Two children strode through. "*Ah*, thank you for joining us."

"A delight to be here, m'Lord!" Helen gave a dramatic bow in Louie's direction.

Arianna tapped her fingers against the table. Magic rippled through the muscle and bone of her forearm, pooling in her fingertips. It was a conscious effort not to unsheathe her claws and throttle the two Ravens.

"If it isn't Helen and Will . . ." Why was she surprised? She really shouldn't be. Arianna had last seen the girl barreling through the underground at breakneck speeds. Anyone who possessed such equal parts stupidity and suicidal tendency would certainly find her way into Louie's employ.

"Been a while, huh?" Helen raised her hand in greeting, nonchalantly strolling over to the table. "What a small world. You work for Louie, I work for Louie…"

"I do not work for Louie," Arianna corrected. "He works for me."

Helen seemed taken aback by this, and her eyes swept to Louie.

"We have an arrangement." It wasn't much in the way of concession on Louie's part. But Arianna was operating under the idea of choosing her battles at present, and this one wasn't worth fighting.

"I knew you stooped low, but working with children, Louie?" Arianna keenly remembered Louie's statement regarding Florence being "observed" by one of his lackeys. Was he keeping Helen and Will here by force, to get back at the girl? "What threats did you have to make?"

"Flor introduced us," Helen announced, as if it was something to be proud of. Well, Ravens were notorious for rushing in headfirst with reckless abandon. "She's been busy while you've been having a vacation on Nova."

"I was *not* on vacation," Arianna snapped.

"Whatever you'll call it then."

"Enough of that, both of you." Louie leaned against the wall, looking as though he could hardly stand for another moment. "We're all on the same side. No need to be at each other's throats."

Arianna could think of quite a few reasons to be at the throats of everyone in the room. But, begrudging as she was to admit it, for now it did suit them all to get along.

"I've already begun to fill in the Wraith on our airship," Louie said to Helen and Will.

"I had some ideas for that." Will approached with caution, and Arianna regarded him in kind. At her side, he leaned over and pointed at a hollow point in the wing of the glider. "I think, right here, we can use it as a main sort of magic artery for lift in both wings."

"Save on gold by piping in the wings instead of on the outside . . ." Arianna's mind folded and unfolded the idea onto the blueprints before her, seeing how they laid atop the glider. "It could be possible." She pointed to the back of the wing. "Discharge through here?"

"Not unless you don't want us to be able to turn." Will shook his head. "Need movements in the flaps."

"How about the end of the wing then?" It was like her mind betrayed her; helping them along was the last thing she wanted to be doing. But it would get her to Florence. And perhaps even more important, it stretched her brain in ways it hadn't been for months on Nova.

It was good to be home.

"That might work. I'll need to check."

Arianna nodded, glancing over the quantity of gold. "I'll need a proper drafting table." She looked up to Louie. "Somewhere I can work."

"Does this count as a wish?" The coy bastard grinned his thin, little smile.

"Hardly." Arianna kept her voice level, scooping the papers and tapping them on the table. "It's a demand, and it's necessary to give you what you asked for."

"Yes, yes, there's somewhere by the hangar that should suffice."

Arianna wondered what constituted a "hangar" in Louie's makeshift world. She wondered what counted as "suitable" too, and was more afraid of the latter than the former.

"Then let's get to work, children."

"I am not a child!" Helen said.

"Let's go." Will grabbed his friend by the elbow, tugging her from the room. Ari was short behind.

"One more thing, Arianna."

"Yes?" She stood with the door half-open, but let it close when he gave it a pointed look. "We will stop in Holx for refueling."

It made sense; Holx was the capital of Ter.4, and even when the world was in disarray it'd still be well stocked. "Helen and Will know you're taking them back to the guild they escaped from?"

"They have faith I'll look after them." Louie waved away the concern. Arianna's only faith in Louie was that he'd look after no one but himself. "While we're there, I need you to acquire something for me."

"Acquire? You mean steal."

Louie hummed his affirmation. "You must think so poorly of me."

"Louie, I have to care about you to think poorly of you. Die in a ditch for all it concerns me."

"You should be more concerned, as I give you great power in this world." Sure, he was well connected, but Arianna had every faith she could be self-sufficient without him if she needed to be. It merely suited her to go along with him, for now, as the path of least resistance.

"So, what is it that you need the White Wraith for?"

"I'll give you the details when we arrive. In the meantime, focus on the airship and fixing your tools. They were badly damaged in your little fall."

Arianna snorted at the word "little." There was a time where not having her daggers would have been cause enough for panic. But now that she could produce claws from her fingertips, they seemed slightly less critical.

Arianna moved for the door but stopped. "One more thing." She looked at the little man. "If you go back on our deal, if you give me one reason to suspect you're out of line—"

"I'm always out of line."

Arianna resisted the urge to roll her eyes, and chose, instead, to hold her gaze level. "I will kill you and everyone you ever loved, horribly."

"Of course." His mouth cracked into a smile, a wild, little grin of pure mirth. Arianna knew where his mind was before he opened his mouth to speak. "That will be easy for you, as I've never loved anyone but myself."

Arianna let him have the last word. She needed time to think over how to threaten someone who fought for nothing but himself.

# 6

## COLETTA

Coletta poured liquid fire into her mouth. She swallowed it down, a blessing that tasted of damnation. Her fingers cupped the stone mortar, one hooking the pestle to keep it from her face. Her elbows trembled from the weight of the vessel, and the pain.

The poison reached her stomach like a throbbing punch that made her abdomen clench so tightly it pushed the air from her chest and collapsed her lungs. It unfurled agony like the wings of death and took flight through her veins, ravaging her insides. Her magic pushed against the poison on instinct, fighting to keep her knees locked, striving for consciousness.

Still, she drank from the mortar like a babe to a tit. There was delight in the hurt that came from allowing her body to be brutalized by a concoction of her own creation. She charged toward the threshold where pain became pleasure, and nimbly leapt over the edge. Death transformed to triumph.

She killed herself time and again to feel her body reborn, to emerge stronger with each draught.

Coletta lowered the bowl, the sticky residue of the poison weeping down its sides in faintly umber-colored rivulets. Another day, another draught, and death yet avoided. There would soon be no poison, no concoction or illness that could fell her.

She pulled a sheer, silken shawl back over her shoulders from where it had slipped down her back. The last of the poison was finishing coursing through her system, and Coletta decided a walk would keep her joints moving through the final shivering aftershocks. She stepped away from her sheltered outdoor laboratory, and into the gardens proper.

Flora and fauna encroached on the narrow, ruby-tiled walking path. Flowers uncurled their petals in a vibrant rainbow of color. There were thorny vines that had the most delicate of buds, long stalks that drooped with too-heavy blossoms, and spindly wide-leafed trees that clung to each other like happy drunks.

Two large, mostly harmless, trees sheltered the garden from prying eyes that might glide past on the back of a boco. Yveun's cautiousness had led her to plant the giants of her little kingdom, his concern that her "hobby" be discovered by someone undesirable was both charming and unnecessary. Dragons never saw plants as anything more than ornamentation.

It was a battle easier conceded to her mate than fought. She would kill any who learned the truth of her garden before they could utter it to another soul. And if she was honest, she liked the shade the trees gave, even if it made the garden a touch cooler in the ever-encroaching winter.

"Coletta'Ryu." A woman emerged from around the bend of the path. Ulia. She kneeled, head bowed.

"He has returned?"

"He has, my queen."

Around the woman's neck was a pendant—a small white flower, lacquered. Her mate had his collars of gold, tempered only to his magic, nooses at his command. Coletta's markers were far subtler, yet known well enough, and just as effective.

"This flower . . ." Coletta shifted her fingers, reaching up to touch the delicate petals of a flower identical to the one Ulia wore. "Do you know what it is?"

"A snow bud."

"Indeed. An unassuming name, isn't it?"

"It is." There were times, brief times, when Coletta wondered if the little buds that did her bidding actually agreed with her *unique* approach to conflict. But the second she exhausted mental capacity on such musings, she remembered that she didn't care. Obedience earned in fear was no different than that engendered through love, honesty, or deceit.

"Do you remember what it does?"

Ulia's eyes fell on the living version of her pendant, still cradled in Coletta's long fingers. She was young for a flower—just thirty-nine—but Ulia had proved her loyalty in a very short time.

"Paralysis," Ulia said finally.

"Yes, but only the stigma." Coletta touched her fingertip to the red knob that extended out from the center of the flower. "The petals actually provide the antidote to this natural immobilizer. Most don't even realize these properties exist, since consuming or brewing the flower neutralizes the negative effect." She dropped her hand and stepped over to the kneeling girl. Coletta reached out the same hand, guiding Ulia's face upward to meet her eyes. "Remember that, Ulia. One thing can both give and take away."

"Should I fall from your favor, it would be an honor too great for a wretch like me to die by a potion crafted by your hand, Coletta'Ryu."

The corners of her mouth twitched upward in the nearest imitation of a smile Coletta would ever give. "Yes, sweet Ulia, you will never betray me."

"Never." Ulia slowly, reverently, and with the slightest scent of fear in her magic, brought Coletta's hand to her mouth, kissing her knuckles once.

"Now." Coletta pulled her hand away, her dominance reaffirmed. "Take me to dress for dinner."

"My queen, Yveun'Dono is . . . occupied."

"I realize." The girl was young enough to underestimate her. It was endearing, to a point. "I would care to look on him before he is finished."

"As you wish." Ulia stood and bowed her head as Coletta strode past. She waited three breaths before falling into step behind.

There were two entrances to Coletta's garden—one to her private quarters and one to Yveun's. She rarely had reason to cross through the latter. Barring dinner, her mate usually came to her.

Her own portion of the Rok Estate was smaller but no less opulent than the rest. Red lacquered beams cut across a pitch-black ceiling, every fourth beam framed by two posts on the whitewashed walls. It was simple, striking, and reminiscent of all her favorite poisonous flora.

At the end of the hallway stood her primary sitting room. Hexagonal in shape, every wall had a door, perfectly centered and mosaicked in ruby. The door directly across from the hall was her bedroom; spiraling right around the room were the portals to her bathing room, second laboratory, library, and dressing room. Of these, the little buds that served as her personal handmaidens were only given permission to enter the last.

"Do you have a preference this evening, Ryu?" Ulia asked as Coletta seated herself on the oxblood leather ottoman at the room's center.

"I do not." All her life, the world had whispered of her shortcomings, *What a terrible Dragon she made*. Coletta cared nothing for fashion and in many cases preferred function over form. She appreciated fineries, but only insofar as they had purpose. But ignoring trivialities uncluttered her mind, allowing her to dedicate all her energy to a singular focus: domination. In this way, she was one of the greatest paragons of her species. If only the rest of Nova knew.

"How about the lavender?" Ulia asked from behind her. "It brings out the shades of wine in your skin."

Coletta smiled, wide and wicked, at the word. Rarely did she reveal her nubby teeth and rotten gums, ravaged by years of poisoning herself for the sake of immunity, for strength. But thoughts of her grand display on the Isle of Ruana —and of Petra shuddering on the floor of the Rok Manor—made it near impossible to contain her pleasure.

By the time Ulia's footsteps neared, Coletta's face was as blank and composed as daylight: emotions drawn inward, face passive, eyes hard—this was the way to greet the world.

Ulia presented a simple, armless sheath that slipped over Coletta's shoulders and split into strips at her hips. They danced and swirled around her legs as she walked. The silken material stitched with gemstones betrayed its finery, but it was otherwise simple. It showed off her thin frame and the soft, squishy skin clinging to her bones.

Demure. Frail. Delicate.

Three things no Dragon wished to be. The world whispered it of her, even as she slipped death into their drinks and food, and between their ribs.

"I do not need you to escort me to the dining room this evening, Ulia," Coletta said as they traversed back through her garden.

"As you wish." The girl gave a small bow. Coletta appreciated her unquestioning obedience, even when she broke form. Actions like that kept Ulia close. If the girl knew it or not, they kept her alive.

"I would, however, ask you to see that wine is set out." She felt the corners of her mouth twitch again in a near-smile. But letting the same person see her smile more than once in a single week—in a single day no less—was far too much. "Go to the cellars. There should be a newer vintage from a winery here on Lysip."

"Yes, my lady."

Coletta gave the girl a nod of dismissal and started in the opposite direction.

Yveun's halls were cluttered compared to hers. Ironwork, reminiscent of the fanned wings of a Rider's glider, arched over her with curling tendrils of metal lacework reaching down in wide, concentric circles. Beyond was what Coletta had termed the sailcloth room, a billowing half-glass roof that looked like the puffed sail of a lake boat. On and on, the walls were adorned and the floor gleamed with a proud, polished finish.

On and on, Coletta ignored it all.

She listened, but there was not another soul to be heard. Even magic hearing would not have revealed a single sound. Yveun had likely sent away every Dragon, high and low.

Nearing his chambers, Coletta pressed on a wall. It looked no different from anything else, the wood paneling near flawless. *Near flawless.* A small groove betrayed the narrow door that swiveled open at her insistent force.

Clicking the door back into place, Coletta found herself in an unlit, narrow hall that ran parallel to the first. There were many secrets in the manor, and she made it a point to know them all.

Coletta walked without light, running her fingertips along the wall as she proceeded with measured steps. She avoided pushing magic into her eyes, for that could be sensed—or worse, smelled. The darkness slowed her steps, prevented the carelessness of haste that might give her away.

It seemed, however, there were some allowances that could be made for noise.

Yveun, for all his strengths, was still a man and a Dragon. A man with desires, and a Dragon bent on domination. When the two forces combined, the results were hardly silent.

Coletta heard them—heavy breathing, gasping, grunting, growling. Ahead, a few beams of gray light broke through the darkness. Coletta walked toward them like a beacon.

Where the main hall sloped downward, her private corridor remained level. She now found herself peering down at a familiar room—Yveun's private sleeping chamber.

Blood dripped from his back where long gashes, already healing, had been dragged across his skin. Beneath him, a woman as green as Coletta's fauna writhed and arched her back as they rutted like dogs and sounded much the same. Yveun's face twisted, his head thrown back in a snarl of pleasure that was nearly drowned out by the smacking of his hips against the woman's backside.

It was the first time she'd laid eyes on the creature her little buds had selected for their Dono. Fae, they had said her name was. Little and less was known about her, but Coletta knew the one thing that mattered more than all others: Yveun had taken a liking to her.

Unlike Leona, he had charged forward with this one. He had mounted the creature like an animal, and like an unbroken boco, she was fighting back. The lovers rolled over, and Fae swiped at Yveun's face, drawing yet more blood. He snarled in kind, digging his own claws down her arm.

Their mouths met before smearing golden blood over each other's skin.

They were drunk on each other. Coletta watched as her life mate, her king, sexed another woman in a way he had never done to her. His face contorted in bliss; Coletta looked away, having both seen and affirmed enough.

Fae might own the Dono, but Coletta owned Fae. Everything was moving according to plan on Nova. Now, before she'd give in to the demands of her quietly grumbling stomach, she would check in with her odd little Fenthri to see how things were progressing down on Loom.

# 7
## ARIANNA

WHEN DUSK SETTLED UPON THE WORLD, ARIANNA WAS NOTHING MORE THAN A white smudge against a gray sky.

She peered down at Holx through her modified goggles from the rooftop of one of the airship yards. She'd been scouting since the afternoon, observing people's comings and goings, studying the flow of machine and man alike.

The home of the Ravens' Guild was unnaturally quiet. Or perhaps the quiet was *too* natural. Arianna heard howling winds and cawing birds, benign sounds at odds with the screeching trikes and revving engines Holx was famous for.

The one guild the Dragons supposedly hadn't touched had, nevertheless, ground to a slow crawl in the wake of the fall of their world. It was unnervingly somber, a quiet testament to the devastation the Dragon King had reaped from his sky city.

Malice sparked within her and was promptly quieted by the thought of Yveun. *Looking down on her, his claws on her flesh . . .*

Arianna rubbed her neck, urging tension and the memory away.

She had a job to do, and there wasn't nearly enough time to properly prepare for it. All she had was some basic information from Louie—oddly specific in some areas, completely blank in others—and whatever she could observe before nightfall.

It wasn't nearly enough time to break into the guild's hall.

As the sun fell behind the clouds that perpetually blanketed Loom's sky, Arianna rose. She held out her hand. Magic pulled against her palm, drawing out a line from her winch box like a serpent from its den. The cord was cast in gold and tempered to her magic alone, the closest thing to a loyal friend she had at the moment. It was time to shake off the dust that had settled on her shoulders in Nova.

Arianna looped the cord around a heavy pipe that ran around the rooftop, clipping the line to itself. She walked to the edge of the building and put everything else behind her. Up here, she didn't need to be Arianna the Master Rivet. She could cast aside the loose ties to Nova as Ari Xin'Anh Bek. She would ignore that her shroud of anonymity as the inventor of the Philosopher's Box, the Perfect Chimera, had been lifted. She certainly wouldn't spare a thought for Arianna, the rebel who had twice failed to slay the Dragon King.

She was merely the White Wraith—nothing more, nothing less. She was a vessel for her benefactors. All the rest, she would leave on the rooftop.

With a wide step and a whir of gears, Arianna tipped herself over the edge.

Golden cabling spun from the spools attached to her belt by the winch box. She ticked off seconds in her mind, calculating how much line she'd used based on the speed of her free fall and the distance covered. She'd know when to stop and swing onto a ledge, to magically unclip her line and cast it toward the next building, swinging from ledge to ledge until she reached her target.

Holx was a city of layers, each stacked on the next to create a labyrinth of tracks and walkways. She followed one track now; it had virtually no lights along its sides and would be almost impossible for Fenthri eyes to pick out in the growing dark. But with her Dragon eyes and refined goggles, she had little issue.

"Follow the red-lined trike path to the guild," Louie had instructed. It was one of his more oddly specific notes, and was followed immediately by one of his decidedly less specific: "Once you get to the end, you'll figure out a way in."

*Thanks, Louie*, Arianna thought grimly as she reached the end of the red-lined path. Arianna waited for headlights and the roar of engines to vanish before easing herself down from the mostly abandoned upper paths she'd been traversing. But where there should have been an egress awaiting her, she found instead the fresh cement of a portal recently sealed.

She looked back up. There hadn't been another ledge on her descent, no other obvious doorway. "Up" wasn't an option, and before her was blocked, which only left . . . down.

The depths of Holx held a darkness that even her goggles and eyes couldn't penetrate. She presumed she was somewhere close to the ground, or already below it. She might even be closer to the land known as the Raven's Folly—the Underground—than she was the airship. She dared progress no farther without some kind of light; begrudgingly, she drew the duller of her two daggers.

She pushed her magic into the hilt and up through the blade—just enough to heat the metal to a faint, reddish glow. She'd fix the dulled point later. For now, the ambient light of semi-molten gold was enough to reflect off her surroundings and give her a rusty picture of where she was.

To her right was another track that dead-ended in a walled-up portion of the guild. Below and to her left was a perpendicular road that intersected with a narrow bridge. Arianna squinted. She moved her blade left and right, watching the shadows dance away in opposite directions.

One shadow didn't budge.

Letting loose more slack in her line, Arianna's winch box clicked her further down the narrow gap between guild and street, leaving no doubt she had crossed the threshold into the Underground. Just above the narrow bridge, she cycled her legs in a running motion along the wall—back and forth, building speed.

One hand on the dagger, the other on her winch box, she prepared for her one chance to successfully make this jump. There wasn't even a ripple of apprehension across her nerves. At the apex of her parabola, she pulled the linchpin on her cable.

Arianna's stomach shot into her chest as she went into a free fall. She clutched the dagger with all her might.

The wooden bridge groaned under her, sagging with her weight. Arianna tumbled and dug her free hand into the grooves, using claws and splinters to gain purchase on the decaying walkway.

Now her nerves raced. Her chest heaved. Her eyes dilated, adrenaline providing a clarity no magic could ever match. Arianna grinned into the blackness, holding her cooling dagger away from both herself and the wood.

It felt good to be back at work.

She rolled onto her stomach and hopped up. Letting the fading heat of the dagger continue to give her just enough light, Ari summoned her gold line back to her spool. When it was wound up tightly, she focused on her next challenge.

The door was old and rusted, and the lock looked equally frail. Arianna sighed. She had so wanted an actual challenge when it came to breaking into the guild—the opportunity to exercise a bit of finesse.

With a smash of her boot, the door nearly fell off its hinges and alerted the ghosts of the Ravens' Guild to her forced entry. This doorway had been long forgotten; not a soul stirred in the dark tunnel it revealed. She moved forward fearlessly, guided by the light of her dagger.

Eventually, she came to a circular room with six connecting archways. Arianna paused in the room's center. Bruising had started to blossom on the fingers that clutched the dagger, working up her wrist with slow purpose. As her magic exhausted, her body began to break down, one burst blood vessel at a time.

She had to find her way up before her light faded.

In the thin layer of dust that coated the floor, a single track led from one hall to the other. *Someone must be using this old intersection.*

The two halls breathed from one to the other as if they were old friends, whispering little secrets. Wind pushed the flaps of her coat against the backs of her calves ever so slightly. Arianna chose her path based on the knowledge that cool air sought out warmer temperatures.

Her suspicion was affirmed as the hallway began to rise. The faint roar of engines guided her upward past two forks.

She was nearly breathless from magical exertion by the time she saw light, and Ari took a moment to compose herself. The faint glow of a doorway three pecas away told her she'd finally found a way out. She didn't know if it would lead her into the guild proper; she wouldn't have been surprised if she'd somehow overshot the hall entirely.

Arianna tilted her head back and closed her eyes, letting her breathing slow and her skin mend. In so many ways, she was her best in moments like this: alone, working for what she needed, taking odd jobs with a clear beginning and end.

But that would mean leaving Florence adrift in a rising sea of chaos. It would mean never seeing Cvareh again. Arianna didn't want to admit why that fact put such a profound ache in her chest. A life of crime and obscurity would have to wait, at least for now.

Arianna opened her eyes and kept moving.

The doorway opened onto a walkway above a large track. As she crossed the threshold, a trike came whizzing around a far corner, speeding underneath her in a blink. She couldn't even make out that a person was driving the machine, and for that reason alone she was confident there was no way the Raven would've seen her as anything more than a rogue guild member wandering the halls.

The Ravens' Guild had a helix of two tracks spiraling around a central core. The only way to get up, according to Louie, was by driving one of those chaotic machines to the desired level. Down the curving track, a large yellow "2/1" was painted on the far wall.

*Well, that's convenient.* She didn't have far to go. The item Louie had asked her to procure could supposedly be found on level two—the main train terminal for the guild.

In the distance, another catwalk loomed above the track. She waited for two more trikes to pass before casing her line and perching on the railing. The drivers may not notice a random person on the catwalk, or a relatively thin golden line, as they no doubt focused more on not dying in a splatter on one of the curving walls . . . but they would likely not be able to miss a woman swinging from walk to walk.

The sound of an engine in the distance announced the impending arrival of another rogue trike. Four more sped by, then there was a brief stint of quiet. Arianna took her chance, jumping off and using her magic winch box to pull her to the far walk.

It only took three more leaps to arrive at the landing for level two. Steam billowed out from a large archway, half-blocked by a heavy steel door that hung partially closed. The tinny screech of train brakes echoed through the halls.

Arianna watched as men and women flowed in and out of the entryway. Louie hadn't warned her of this.

The Ravens' Guild managed the shipping and transport for the world, often using their guild hall itself as a key hub. It made sense there would be only one entrance—an entrance that could be locked down in the case of a nefarious force trying to gain entry.

Arianna did the only thing she could think of: wait and watch. Ravens pulled up in their various vehicles, parked them, and went about their business. There was seemingly no order to their comings and goings.

*If only I'd brought my grease pencil.* Etching the guild's mark on her cheek would have made things easier, but she was hardly dissuaded. It was almost mechanical now, seeing different ways to gain access wherever she wanted to go.

Arianna fastened the toggles on her white coat as high as they went, obscuring most of her face to the nose. She reached under the catwalk and ran her hand along the thick layer of exhaust grime that coated the wood and iron from years of use by all manner of vehicles. As suspected, her gray skin was turned black; Arianna rubbed it on both hands and applied it to her cheeks, then to her coat.

She had three more requests of Louie. If she had one to spare, she'd spend it on demanding the man wash her coat himself, just for the sake of seeing the king get his hands dirty once.

Goggles down, hood up, covered in soot and grease, she might be able to pass as a Raven. Between racing trikes, Arianna descended quickly using her golden cable. She scampered up to the parking area, crouching as one odd-looking four-wheeled vehicle pulled away.

By the time another Raven approached, all they would see was a grime-covered woman hunched with her eyes on the floor, striding with purpose into the most important terminal in the world.

She may not agree with the Raven mindset or methods, but Arianna couldn't deny a cathedral of innovation when she saw one.

Fifteen tracks, neatly lined and almost all occupied, sat underneath a vaulted ceiling high enough to stack half the trains on top of each other with room to spare. There were passenger vessels and cargo transports alike. One engine made Arianna do a double-take.

It was no doubt experimental. Arianna had never considered that placement of gold before to help drive thrust. Half of it made sense, but the other half would likely result in inefficiency. Unless . . .

She pried her eyes away. That was *not* what she was here for. She refocused on the windows that lined the wall opposite the end of all the tracks—the terminal offices.

It reminded her of the last time she'd broken into an office for shipping information. Back then, she'd been ferrying a particular Dragon.

"Watch where you're going!" A Raven threw her a rude gesture as they narrowly avoided a collision.

Arianna put her head down and kept moving forward. She had to get what she came for, and get out. She was allowing Arianna the Rivet and Ari Xin to exist where there should only be the White Wraith.

It was amazing how little mind the guild members paid her. They continued along with their duties, oblivious to the intruder in their midst. There seemed to be fewer than she would've suspected, however. Perhaps they were thinned as a result of the shifting efforts due to the budding rebellion?

Up two flights of stairs, Arianna found herself in another empty hall. This one was lit—a far significant improvement over her earlier wandering.

Every office, save the first she passed, was quiet. Almost unnervingly so. Low numbers of initiates and journeymen, desks without people to man them . . . This was supposedly one of the busiest stations in the world. Why was it so quiet?

Arianna made quick work of the door lock, easing herself into the dimly lit office. A single light for which there was no switch glowed overhead. A beacon perpetually shining, waiting for the trains that never stopped, even long after people stopped tending them.

There was nothing particularly special about the room. But every detail was exactly as Louie had described. The desk—suspiciously wounded with a deep notch in its right corner—faced the doorway. Two bookshelves stood on her right-hand side, three on her left. Arianna went to the shelf in the farthest corner.

*19.32*

The innocuous number was imprinted on the second-highest shelf. Binders of identical size, shape, and color were slotted side by side along its entire length. Each bore a number on its spine in ascending order, the last marked 1081.

This year.

This was where Louie's dictation had ended. All his careful instruction had taken her to this shelf, to the records all the way to the right. This was what he wanted her to steal.

She opened the unmarked folio. A sort of Raven's code was scribbled across from dates. Numbers and symbols, nothing more.

Louie had no doubt assumed she couldn't decipher the meaning. And, without more time, she couldn't. But he was underestimating her, a mistake that many found harmful to their health.

Arianna might not know the Raven's code offhand, but she knew she was in the main terminal for the transport of all goods and peoples across Loom. She knew that 19.32 was a very specific number, identical to a certain density. And she knew one alchemical symbol that continued to appear across the pages: a circle with a ring around it.

The symbol for gold.

"All right, Louie," she whispered. "I got your book." The only linger question was what exactly Louie planned to do with it.

# 8

## CVAREH

"Say it again." Cain's voice was the first to break the silence. "Say it again!" Never before had a Dragon growled with such rage. It would be enough to startle the Goddess of Warriors herself.

"In light of these events," the Rider continued, ignoring Cain, "Yveun'Dono, in all his generosity, has been gracious enough to allow Finnyr'Oji to return to these halls as your House's leader."

"Gracious enough?" Cain snarled. "*Gracious enough?* He likely killed her himself!"

"Cain Bek, I will let this slide without a challenge, seeing as House Xin is currently in a time of transition—" The Rider would not even say *grief*. He wouldn't give them that decency. "—But your Ryu is still present and, in such a case, can authorize a duel."

The mention of Ryu brought Cain's eyes swinging back to Cvareh.

Cvareh wasn't ready for all the emotions and demands wrapped up in his friend's gaze. He could barely handle his own emotions; how would he handle another's? What did Cain think he could do?

Petra had trained him to be her right hand, to function as she needed. He was a vessel for his sister and without her . . .

"Are you really going to let them get away with this?" Cain demanded. It was a verbal slap across the face, a violent tug out of the ocean of his grief and onto the beach of reality. It was what he *needed*. But what he *wanted* was to sink into those forever depths that had the same chilling embrace of Lord Xin. "If Petra is dead, then—"

"Enough, Cain." Cvareh grabbed for the other man's wrist the moment he saw the tension ripple down Cain's bicep. If the man unsheathed his claws now, a duel would be inevitable. Even if Cain won, it would just throw the situation with Rok into further chaos.

All eyes had turned to the altercation between the two men. The brother, and the would-be lover of the woman who had led them fearlessly toward a vision so many generations had never even dared to whisper, let alone desire. Cvareh didn't know what to do with their attention.

*Petra would have known what to do.*

He cleared his throat and spoke words he never thought he'd say. "When will Finnyr'Oji—" his brother's name tasted of bile "—be arriving?"

The Rider's mouth curled back in a triumphant smile. House Xin had always been the lowest in Dragon society, but this was a new feeling.

"He will be sent within the day." The Rider stepped leisurely down from the pedestal. "I hear the duel was fearsome. He's taking time to recover."

Cvareh remembered Finnyr's last altercation with Petra. *That* had been fearsome. He had seen it with his own eyes: his sister atop his brother, knees digging into chest, blood from his shredded face up to her elbows.

"Recover under a Rok roof," Cain mumbled, not quietly enough.

"Well, he does feel quite at home there," the Rider goaded easily. "After all, he's lived under the generous care of the Dono himself for years. I couldn't imagine actually wanting to return to these bleak halls."

"I chall—"

"Cain'Da, silence!" The echoes of Cvareh's voice seemed to resonate from half the open mouths in the room. Even his friend was stunned to silence. "The Rider had quite the trip here, and will have another long journey home. I suggest we let him leave with haste."

It was phrased to Cain as a suggestion, but it was a poorly veiled demand.

The Rider flashed his canines to Cvareh first, then Cain, and then every Xin assembled at the manor on his way out.

"You shouldn't have let him walk out alive." Cain's bloodlust was insatiable. Cvareh expected it would be for some time.

"Dueling him would serve little purpose."

"Petra would not have let him leave after such disrespect." Cain found the spot and pushed hard.

"Petra is not here!"

Silence, again.

The two men squared off, huffing short breaths that could just as easily become tears as they could become screams of anger. Cain's magic ballooned to three times his size. Cvareh's claws itched for extension.

But Cvareh took a breath and stepped away.

"Petra is not here," he repeated, softer. "Fighting that Rider will not bring her back and neither will fighting me."

"So we are to tolerate disrespect now?" Cain motioned as though he was somehow speaking for the whole of House Xin. "We are to let them walk on us?"

"We are to survive." *It's what she would've wanted.* Cvareh didn't have to speak the thought to know the entire room was in agreement.

All eyes were on him. They looked to him for answers he didn't have, for plans he had yet to formulate. He didn't even know what Petra had intended, all the moving parts that only she had kept track of.

"This is what Yveun wants." Cvareh didn't know if it was pain or loathing that made him drop the Dono's title in that moment. But he prayed it wouldn't become a habit, and that the Rider was far enough away not to hear. "He wants us weakened, divided. He is doing to us what he did to Loom."

"Loom?" Cain was at him again. "You bring up Loom *now*? Are you Cvareh Xin, or have you given up your name like a Fen? What next? Will you paint your skin gray?"

"I said silence, Cain." Cvareh's voice had gone quiet. He didn't want to fight Cain, but the majority of the House didn't know where he had spent the past months. They didn't know who Ari Xin really was. "And yes, I bring up Loom . . . because they are the one chance we have to fight our way out from under Yveun's thumb."

Cain eased away.

Without the immediate threat, Cvareh could properly appreciate the confused looks on the faces of the other members of the House. Was now the right time to tell them? When would Petra have said it?

"I will explain, in time." The fewer people who knew right now, the better. Powers were shifting, and the world was changing around him. "For now, I need your faith."

"You have it." A man Cvareh did not recognize spoke up from the crowd. Agreement was slowly voiced from all around him.

Cain continued to glare.

"Then we shall prepare for the arrival of my brother." He couldn't bring himself to say "Finnyr'Oji," not just yet. "See that his quarters are cleaned and properly appointed."

Cvareh waited for someone to move, to execute his order, but all bodies in the room remained eerily still, all eyes trained on him, expectant. Finally, a woman spoke.

"Prepare his chambers?"

"Yes." He didn't see how he'd been unclear on the matter.

"But Cvareh'Ryu . . . Will you not challenge him? Will you not fight to be our Oji?"

Cvareh would have given anything to not have to answer that question.

# 9
## COLETTA

THE ROK ESTATE HOUSED THE MOST WONDERFUL DINING ROOM IN THE ENTIRE world. It had a table made entirely of iron that stretched long enough for forty people to sit underneath a ceiling of frescos, lit by a thousand candles. It was a room of pure magic and power that would make even the finest Dragon blush at its decadence.

That was not the room where she and Yveun dined.

Instead, they sat at a basic wooden table, barely large enough to seat four comfortably. The windows were simple rectangles, the mullions made of pine. There were no adornments here, no paintings or carefully sculpted statues. Carved into the only entrance and exit was the symbol of House Rok. It took up the top half of the doorway: three triangles supporting a crown.

Coletta looked down as the servants delivered their food from the kitchens. Her flowers would take over during the second half of dinner, when discussion actually began. For now, she'd let the average man and woman see her as the weak Ryu they all expected her to be.

When the servants retreated, Yveun raised his glass first to his lips, then toward her. "You picked as stunning a vintage as ever, my Ryu."

"This is a new one I wanted to try." Coletta watched how the crimson liquid coated the inside of the glass, trickling down in tiny lines. "It's grown here on Lysip."

"On Lysip? Where?"

"To the north. The rocky earth and claylike soil give it that mineral taste." Coletta set down her glass. Putting her fingers on either side of its stem, she swirled it around thoughtfully. "It's about time viticulture came to Lysip. While I appreciated the irony of House Xin making a crimson beverage I think it's far more fitting for this to be an area of Rok expertise."

"I never thought of the color." Yveun copied Coletta's motion before setting the glass aside.

Coletta did the same, and the atmosphere shifted.

"Fae is to your liking?" She phrased it as a question, but they both knew better.

"More so than Leona, even."

That was the answer Coletta wanted to hear. "I believe she will be good for us."

"I couldn't agree more." Yveun chewed his food for a long moment. "She will be the ideal asset to finally hunt down the Perfect Chimera. Truly fitting."

Coletta hummed thoughtfully.

"You disagree."

"Let the Chimera be." Like always, the Dono was narrow-minded when it came to things that eluded him, things he felt entitled to. Ah, to have the mind of a man, and have the world rendered as such a simple, linear place. "She has already made a fool of you too many times."

"Which is precisely why—"

"Why we will not allow it to happen again." Coletta did not appreciate being interrupted. She inhaled. Yveun made no motion to speak, so she continued. "The next time you see the Chimera will be when her death is assured. For now, we must keep Fae here to secure order on Nova."

"On Nova?" His pores practically oozed sex at the idea.

"She will go with Finnyr."

Yveun paused mid-drink, then slowly lowered his glass to the table. He ran the pads of his fingers over the rim of the glass. She could almost see him working out how quickly a boco could get to Ruana and back.

"Would it not be better to keep her here? It will be hard for her to earn the respect of the other Riders if she is off in the Xin Manor. How will she win beads?"

"She has enough beads for three strands of hair." Coletta took a small bite of the meal. The flavors were well balanced.

"Underground fighting pits and back alley brawls do not a Rider make. We can't recognize those kills for beads."

"Do you think she cares?" Coletta reached for her wine again.

There was a good reason she always saw wine set out. If Yveun was well mannered, they enjoyed it together. If he was stubborn but tolerable, she enjoyed having something to take the edge off. The few times he was outright unpleasant toward her, Coletta fantasized about how easy it would be to place a lethal dose of poison in his glass.

"So she goes with Finnyr, then." Yveun finally resigned. "For what purpose?

House Xin will not appreciate us sending a bodyguard for a man they no doubt want to kill."

"Since when have we cared what House Xin thinks?"

Yveun laughed. It was a delightful sound, so genuine that even Coletta could admit it made him particularly attractive.

"Petra is dead. They are clawless. Now is the time to press harder, not pull back. No half-measures."

He repeated their House motto, toasting her as he did. "'Break them again when they are already broken, and see they rebuild in a way we find fitting.'"

She raised her glass to her lips with a smile. Yveun had the look of a king, but his mind was always a step behind hers. They made for a formidable pair in that respect. He was every inch what Nova wanted and Loom needed in a Dragon King; she was every scheming thought required to maintain the façade of his qualifications.

"I believe Fae has magic in her ears. Set up a whisper link with her so that we may know what's going on," Coletta suggested.

"But—"

"I will not be going anywhere." She waved the notion away. It was kind, but unnecessary for him to reserve that channel of communication for her alone. Allowing him to establish a link with Fae would not only give them a direct line to the Xin Manor, but would also please her mate, deepen his bond with Fae. "Set up a link with her."

"If you insist." Yveun couldn't conceal his excitement at the notion, though he mastered his face into seriousness. "There's another matter I wish to discuss about the woman."

"You have my attention." And what a rare commodity that was.

"I assume you know of her . . . *tastes*."

"You mean her proclivity for imbibing?" The delicate manner in which Yveun brought it up made it clear they were speaking about more than feasting on the heart of a fallen foe. This was imbibing from the living. "Yes, I am aware."

"An idea has crossed my mind."

"Oh?" Coletta always enjoyed Yveun's ideas. They were either fantastic—an equal match for her own—or they reminded her why she was usually the strategist between them.

"All this nonsense over a 'Perfect Chimera'—a Fenthri that can possess all Dragon organs containing magic without falling. Why not a perfect Dragon?"

Coletta paused, considering the idea. The difficulty of a perfect chimera for the Fenthri came from the fact that their bodies weren't meant for magic; they struggled to combat the rot that resulted from forcing magic on a body not intended to contain it. Dragons did not share this same barrier.

"You want to give Fae organs as a Fen Chimera would receive."

"I want to make her strong."

"The woman is plenty strong as the gods made her." Coletta ran her fingertip across the lip of her wineglass until it hummed softly, stopping the moment the vibrations made sound. "But I agree with you, Yveun. And I do not think she would be opposed to the idea."

"Excellent. Then we shall keep her here until such time as—"

"No, she will leave with Finnyr as planned." It was one of Yveun's better ideas, and Coletta would reward him for it—in time, in her own way. But keeping Fae on Ruana while sending Finnyr to the snake pit unprotected would not be that reward. "That is most important. I will seek out Fen slaves who bear the Alchemist triangles, and we shall experiment first. After all, if Fae is to be sculpted as the perfect Dragon, we must perfect our process foremost."

"Very well." He hummed. "Speaking of that which we will sculpt to perfection . . ."

"Loom?"

"Loom." Yveun rested his elbows on the table, lacing his fingers in front of him. "What word have you from your little flowers on the gray rock?"

"The Fen are, indeed, demoralized. But it seems that one is spurring another rebellion."

"Stubborn, suicidal creatures." Yveun shook his head as a father might, faced with a petulant child.

"They are convening on Ter.0 for a Vicar Tribunal," Coletta continued, reciting her information, not bothering to correct Yveun's incorrect assumption that it came from a Dragon on Loom. Even Fenthri would sell out each other for the right price.

"Vicar Tribunal. How long has it been since I've heard such a notion?"

"Not long enough."

"Indeed." Yveun laced and unlaced his fingers in thought. "I suppose I should be impressed that enough vicars survived to have such a gathering."

"Fenthri lives are fleeting." Coletta sat back in her chair, thinking of the brief periods of time the Fenthri walked the earth. A Dragon could easily live upwards of one hundred twenty years; Fenthri were lucky if they saw forty-five. How did one approach life knowing existence would be nothing more than a wink in time's great eye? "I'm sure they rotated new ones in hastily."

"Too true." Yveun placed his wine glass down. "I shall go to this Tribunal."

Coletta's eyes fluttered closed as she inhaled slowly. "Why would you deliver yourself to them?"

"Did we not raze them as vengeful gods do? Now, I shall descend as a god appeased, merciful and calm. I will show them the beauty of their submission."

"You mistake poetry for practicality." Coletta shifted uncomfortably in her seat. She knew from the look in her mate's eye that the battle was lost.

"I will bring order and offer peace. Even House Xin was offered that."

"And what great dividends that paid."

"The Fenthri know they have been beaten."

"They have not known it ever. How many times must we destroy them before you see that they will never bow willingly?"

"We have never destroyed them so completely before," Yveun countered.

Coletta was ready to strike back by pointing out the fact that they were far from destroyed if they were already organizing a Tribunal. But she knew when his mind was made up. There was little point in fighting the matter now.

"Very well." Coletta gripped and released the arms of her chair. "Go to them when you please. But meet with the leaders only, and do so under the banner of peace. Outnumber them in manpower, but avoid striking."

"It is hard to parlay for peace when claws are drawn."

"If they accept the natural order of things—" Dragons on top, Fenthri groveling far below "—then we shall all rejoice for the peace and prosperity our world will share. However, should they refuse—" and Coletta already knew they would "—then you shall heed me on such matters henceforth until Loom has returned to sense and order."

Yveun was silent for a long moment. Long enough that Coletta was afraid he truly had lost all sense and was going to deny her. "Very well. Your guidance has yet to lead me astray. And in any case, should Loom deny me yet again, I fear my patience will have been exhausted for good."

Coletta was counting on exactly that.

# 10

## ARIANNA

Like a swarm of angry hornets, airships of all shapes and sizes buzzed in the skies above Ter.0. The roar of engines below mirrored the sound, magnifying it, harmonizing with it. It was more life than the barren earth had seen in years.

Arianna stood on the deck of Louie's airship, goggles on, wind whipping her hair across her face. She could barely see land from around the back fin of the vessel and the stretch of the wings, but what was visible filled her with curiosity and dread. Ter.0 had been the foundation on which the order of Loom once stood. What would this new world order look like, built on the ruins of the old?

The airship touched down on a rocky stretch of mostly flat earth. Arianna worked her way through the narrow interior to the hatch that was currently being opened by one of Louie's other lackeys—a man whose name Arianna had never thought learn.

A sliver of light peeked from behind the door as the latches disengaged. Arianna's eyes adjusted quickly as the door swung open wide. Nothing would ever be as bright as the sunlight on Nova.

Raven-tattooed men and women rushed around the makeshift airfield, waving flags and directing passengers off landing strips. Runners sprinted between high points of rock, delivering messages after every new ship landed.

There were massive ballooned ships and tiny glider-like vessels parked side by side. Most were Raven-marked; the next most common guild symbol was for Rivets. After that, Alchemists . . .

Arianna didn't see a single Revolver or Harvester.

"You may find it easier if you disembark." Louie's voice cut through her thoughts.

She offered no explanation or apology for her hesitation and ignored the man trying to work around her to get the departure stairs set up. Impatient, Arianna jumped the short distance from the airship to the ground. She landed in a crouch, then recovered, taking in the sights and smells of the world she was no longer observing from the shadows.

This was the land where the Vicar Tribunal was founded. This was where Loom had thrived, where she had been born. This was where the Council of Five banded together against the Dragons, where her lover died, where her life was forever changed. It seemed a piece of cosmic poetry that this could well be where she would die.

As promptly as the thoughts came, Arianna moved on from the notion of her own mortality. That was something she'd written off as unimportant years ago.

"Where are you going?" Helen called after her.

"To find Florence," Arianna shouted back, half-turning. They had now exchanged a total of seven words in one week.

"Perhaps you may find it faster to come with us." Louie motioned toward the trike lurching to a stop beside them.

A woman with long white hair, hanging loose and becoming a knotted mess, pushed a pair of streamlined, single-lens goggles up onto her forehead. "Sorry I'm late," she said, speaking directly to Louie.

"Hardly so." Louie walked around to the cart attached to the back of the trike, accepting one of his bigger lackey's help in getting into it. "How is our favorite rebel?"

"Fine, fine. It's a bit of a mess here, with everyone."

"A Raven's nightmare." Arianna was close enough to hear Helen mumble.

"Logistically, yes, but it's kind of like the Underground, I've heard some say. They never get to have this much fun driving or piloting in the sunlight. Not a single rule or regulation on vehicles in sight. Speaking of, looks like your ship had some interesting modifications . . . Heard you'd have a rainbow tail, didn't expect it to be so clean."

Arianna couldn't stop herself from rolling her eyes as she began to make her way to the benched cart with everyone else.

"We had a Master Rivet to conceive and implement the modifications." Louie motioned to her, bringing their driver's attention with it.

"You must be Arianna." The slate-skinned woman didn't miss a beat.

"And you are?"

"Shannra," the woman replied. "Florence told me all about you."

Arianna's blood seemed to boil and freeze at once. She wanted to know everything about Florence and didn't want to think of some random stranger knowing more than her. Fear at this idea rose like bile.

So much had happened. Would Florence still look to her for guidance as she once had? Would the girl value her as she once did?

"I look forward to her telling me all about you."

"Typical Arianna." Shannra laughed but had the decency to heed the conversation's conclusion. She turned forward, revving the engine to life.

The lurch of the trike jolted some tension from Arianna's muscles. The airfield passed in a haze of Ter.0 dust, airships, and homeless Fenthri. She was close to Florence now and the only thing that mattered was seeing her again. Everything else in the world could wait.

Off in the distance, the spires of Ter.0 grew in size. Arianna squinted at the diffuse light of Loom, trying to better make out their shape.

"They're stabilizing them," Louie explained without invitation. "Won't look like they did before the Dragons descended—that'd take years."

Arianna didn't miss how Louie did not imply if they did or didn't have years to take. "Assuming the Dragon King doesn't kill us all first."

"I doubt he'll do that."

"Let me guess: you're also now some expert on Nova's politics?" Arianna refrained from commenting that, of the two of them, *she* was the one who had just spent extended time on the floating islands. She was the one who had an all-too-personal encounter with the Dragon King.

"I am the best organ dealer in all of Loom." Louie's chest swelled against his vest—so much that Arianna was afraid he might crack a rib. "It is important I pay attention to inter-world politics."

"'The best' may be a bit of a stretch." Arianna leaned back against the railing behind the bench.

Louie cracked a smile. It wasn't one of his usual thin-lipped, tight expressions. It showed his teeth, yellowed with age, and his black gums that recessed away from them.

*Black gums*. The man was a Chimera. Arianna made careful note of the information, filing and storing it safely away. He had no visible Dragon parts, which meant he only had blood. Or he had something unseen to the naked eye, like a stomach . . . or lungs.

The gears of her mind ground to a halt.

There was an odd disconnect between her body as it moved closer to Florence, and her mind as it thought back to the only Dragon she'd known personally with magic in the lungs—Cvareh. She wanted to be in both places at once. It was a divided soul that Arianna had never known before.

Arianna played off her silence by twisting to get a better look at the once-great towers of Ter.0.

"What did they look like before?" Helen asked.

Louie and Arianna both opened their mouths at the same time.

"After you." He motioned with his bird-boned hand.

"No, I'm curious what you'll say," Arianna admitted. "The last time I was here . . ."

"You couldn't have been older than twelve."

*Ten, actually*. Arianna kept the thought to herself, owing Louie no information on her past. She turned it back on him instead. "How old were you, Louie?"

"Well, I was here a few years before the One Year War ended." He paused. "I would guess around . . . twenty."

Arianna didn't know what surprised her more: the fact that Louie was easily over forty years of age, or that he outright admitted to the fact. She inspected him as he continued speaking to Helen.

His black hair was carefully pulled back, so taut it stretched wrinkles in his forehead and around his eyes. The parchment-whiteness of his mouth was lined with folded shadow around his lips. And his eyes, as sharp and piercing as a hawk's, had a cloudiness to them that one commonly found in advanced age.

Even with his Dragon blood, Louie was a man well into his twilight years. What did someone with such little time left fight for? Arianna looked over to Helen and Will, who were both listening intently to Louie's descriptions. What were any of them fighting for?

Dusk promised dawn to no man.

"All around here—" Louie gave a small wave of his hand "—were schools and dormitories."

"Where breeding happened?" Helen clarified.

"Indeed."

"Where you were born." It was impossible to tell from the upturned slabs and forlorn remnants littering the road that this place had once been anything more than a rubble field. But Arianna still remembered what it used to look like with precision.

"Not quite." Helen gave a sly grin. "I was born in Holx, just after the Dragons instated family law."

Arianna couldn't stop her jaw from dropping. Helen was eleven. Oh, the girl's insufferably childish nature made sense now. She was a Raven, an explorer, a curious soul, one who had seen beyond her years. But she was five years younger than Florence and had yet to reach adulthood.

"I know, I'm clever for my age." Helen beamed proudly.

"Makes sense why the Dragons didn't kill you." Helen's time in the floating prison of Ter.4.2 finally had an explanation. The guild had locked up a child rather than executing her for running, to preserve what would no doubt be one of the greatest Raven minds of their generation—as loathe as Arianna was to admit it.

"I suppose I should be grateful." Helen's face fell as she looked out at the wasteland. Arianna wondered if she saw the iron bars of her cell in the curved rods of steel that protruded from the ground like industrial saplings, growing from the remnants of the old world. "So all this was beautiful?"

"It was . . ." Arianna answered this time. She, too, had finished her schooling early, choosing the Rivets' Guild and meeting Master Oliver when she was younger than even Helen. She remembered the land as it was then. It was a different sort of beauty than she'd seen on Nova. But her memories of Ter.0 glittered more brightly than the floating sky world and all its colors. "It all moved like clockwork. Teachers from every guild took up residence. We learned from the best in all disciplines."

"Sounds boring." Helen yawned. "All I want is maps and speed."

Arianna huffed in amusement. The girl was such a little crow. "Why did you run away from the guild, if you are so akin to it?"

Helen shrugged. "Freedom. Isn't that what all Ravens want? Freedom to explore, go where you want, when and how. Take your life back from the world and hold it in your hands?"

"Who knew it was possible?"

"What?" Helen asked.

"We can agree on something."

Helen looked just as surprised as Ari felt.

At the center of Ter.0 was the old meeting hall of the Vicar Tribunal. Where the dormitories and labs occupied the surrounding area, the five-towered hall stretched up and casted its long shadows like hands on a clock. Louie had been correct: work had begun to stabilize the Towers and reinforce them as residences.

Shannra drove the trike around the main entrance to a flat area on the side that had been allocated for parking.

"This is it!" she announced, quieting the engine and hopping down onto the dusty ground.

"This isn't going to fall on us . . . is it?" Will asked skeptically, stepping out of the cart.

Arianna couldn't fault the boy for his skepticism. The towers above them tilted uneasily and the winds that blew plumes of dust around them created an illusion of a drunken sway. Arianna adjusted her goggles over her eyes, squinting upward against the filtered sunlight from the clouds above Loom.

"They took a beating at the end of the One Year War. But structurally, they're still intact." She saw the straight lines of load-bearing pillars and walls running up like arteries underneath the crumbling cosmetics. "Foundation's holding. Just the aesthetics—" what little aesthetics Loom ever indulged in "—that seem to be falling off."

"Wonderful. So I won't die from the whole thing collapsing, but from a bit of debris dropping on my head." Helen rolled her eyes and folded her hands on top of her head.

"And if you don't die from either of those, I'm certain the Dragons will see to it," Louie noted as he disembarked.

Arianna grimaced at the notion. Ter.0 hadn't survived the last Dragons' attack. What did they hope to accomplish by holing up here for the next one?

What was Florence thinking?

"This way to Florence." Shannra started for an archway, as if reading Arianna's mind. "It's a bit mad if we go through the main hall."

They ascended a steep flight of stairs. Old piping clung to the smooth, industrially plain wall, cracking the stone where it protruded. On the first landing, Arianna heard voices, but it wasn't until the second landing area that she managed to see their source.

Below them, in the center of the five-towered hall, was the central meeting area. She remembered it from her classes as a child. But her most vivid memory was standing with Oliver, masters from each of the four other guilds, and a handful of others who were ready to die for Loom.

Now, where they had stood, where the Council of Five had made their pact to stand against the Dragons, to stand for Loom, wayward and homeless Fenthri roamed in a sort of controlled chaos.

Men and women poured in through the main entrance, funneled from the airfield and no doubt the few water ports still viable for docking. Some carried luggage, some had their hands laden with books. Others had empty palms and tattered clothing.

Barefoot and booted, the masses of Loom were ushered into the one place that had always stood against the Dragons: Ter.0. It was the home of the Vicar Tribunal and testament to the old ways. It had been the Territory people didn't dare speak of, for fear of being accused of inciting rebellion. And now it was where Loom would begin anew.

Arianna no longer had trouble understanding Florence's logic.

When Loom was all but destroyed, one place would always be home to every Fenthri, regardless of one's guild. The wayward Raven Arianna had taken in years ago had the wisdom to bring them back there.

A smile snuck up on her as Arianna looked through the arcade of windows, at the flow of people below. It was a smile that quickly faded at the sound of a lone voice.

"Arianna?"

Arianna turned to meet two dark eyes, black as the outlined Raven on the girl's cheek. The filtered light seemed to shine brighter, and the crumbling world built itself anew, simply because *she* was in one beautiful piece.

"Florence," Arianna whispered.

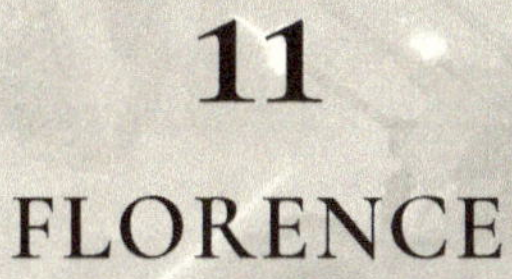

# 11

## FLORENCE

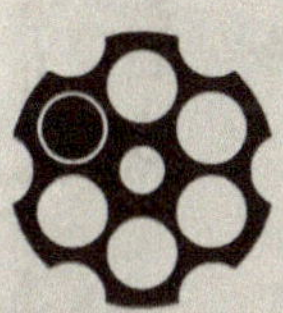

"Arianna . . ." The name flowed from her like a familiar creed. It echoed old sentiments and resonated off the new corners of her personality that had been built in the white-haired woman's absence.

There she was, Florence's teacher and guardian, just as she remembered her. They'd been separated for months, and Florence had traveled half the world, across three territories, since they'd parted. She had seen guilds fall and good men die. She had the scars to speak of the battles she'd won, and lost.

In contrast, Arianna was the same as ever. Her white coat was far more tattered and soiled than Florence had ever allowed it to get previously, and she had to combat the urge to demand Arianna remove the article of clothing so that it could have a proper wash. But Florence had plenty of her own dirty laundry to attend to; she didn't have time for Arianna's any more.

"Florence," Arianna echoed.

What did they do now? How could Florence hope to bridge the gap between them?

"I require a word with Arianna," she announced decisively. It was then that Florence took in the rest of the room, those who had accompanied Ari to Ter.0. Louie opened his mouth to speak but Florence snuck in the first, and second, word. "Louie, I appreciate your *assistance* in helping Arianna get here." The tone of "assistance" had the requisite bite. "I will discuss matters with you later."

"I think—"

"I think if you would like whatever end game you're playing toward, you will vacate this room immediately." Her tone left no room for misinterpretation. There were many whom Florence would defer to. Louie was no longer one of them.

The man merely smirked. "You have grown, haven't you, wayward little crow?"

"One part of that was correct, the other incorrect." Florence pushed aside her smartly tailored jacket, resting her hand on the hilt of one of the revolvers that tugged on a thick belt around her hips.

"Of course. An easy mistake to make." Louie tapped his cheek, referencing the Raven outline on Florence's own.

"I wouldn't test me."

"Nor I, me." The skeletal man gave her a long and piercing stare, but it didn't even scratch the surface of her resolve, much less crack it. She had shot more frightening, powerful people than Louie point-blank. And all she had to do was remind herself of that fact whenever someone—anyone—tried to intimidate her. "We have far more to gain by working together, Florence."

"As does all of Loom." On that point, she could agree with the former king of Mercury Town.

Florence watched Louie and his crew depart down the stairs. They were like specters from a former life, creeping up from the shadows of her past. Eventually, she'd have to catch up with Will and Helen, but there was a sort of understanding there that came with old friends who had endured trials together.

Florence had history with everyone in the group, save Shannra. The moonlight-haired woman glanced back at her and gave Florence a hefty wink. They were still taking their time together, still evolving, and Florence couldn't stop a grin at her newest companion's antics.

Louie was ever unexpected. As loathe as Florence was to admit it, Shannra had been welcome company on Ter.0 while Florence had been organizing the initial structure of the resistance. Plus, the strange little man had brought Arianna back to her.

Her eyes swept back. Arianna had rested her goggles atop her forehead, at last revealing her striking, vermillion eyes—a bold splash of color in their gray world.

She didn't know what to say, and it seemed Ari was equally at a loss.

"Walk with me." The words strummed the tension delicately, rather than snapping it. She didn't know where she'd take Ari just yet, but movement would help. If she could move her feet, her mind might follow.

Arianna continued beside her in silence, peering periodically through the inner windows at the hollow-structured, densely populated core of the five-towered hall.

"You orchestrated all this?" Arianna's tone was thoughtful, almost gentle.

"I—" Florence worked to let go of modesty. "I did." She stopped, resting her hand on the gritty cement of a window sill, looking over Ter.0. Airships never stopped their assault on the skies and the trikes tore up the dust that had settled across the whole of the wasteland. For all the Dragons had killed, there were still more Fenthri left than Florence could've ever imagined. Loom itself was more than Florence could've ever imagined.

"Flor, what do you hope to achieve with this?"

Florence turned, searching Ari's face for some explanation. She had gone from pure admiration to admonishment in a breath.

"Drawing together Loom, the Dragon King only has to attack one place," Arianna continued.

It was an argument Florence had heard before, and she could diffuse it like a simple bomb. "He has no more large-scale weapons to do it with. The Revolvers saw to that." She had never studied in the guild hall proper, but the Revolvers were her own people. The mere idea of their noble sacrifice put a lead slug in her gut. "Separate, we're disorganized, confused. He can pick us off bit by bit, convert those that remain. We're under his thumb. Together, there's strength in numbers. We need all of Loom to see that we are still strong, that we can be one and stand on our own again. We need the king to see that we are not to be underestimated."

She wished she knew what went on in Arianna's head. But, unlike all other times when Florence had awaited her mentor's judgment, she wasn't jittering with nerves, waiting for a verdict. She wanted Arianna's approval as a peer, an equal—not as a pupil or child.

"He's ruthless, Florence. The Dragon King will—"

"You do not need to tell me of his ruthlessness," Florence interrupted. "I was there, Arianna, when the Harvesters' Guild fell. If it weren't for the Vicar Harvester, I would not have made it out alive."

Arianna moved, crossing that seemingly unbreachable gap between them, present the first moment they'd laid eyes on each other. Her arms closed around Florence's shoulders and pulled her close. Frozen shock quickly thawed, warmed by the heat that swelled in Florence's chest at Arianna's closeness.

The woman smelled of cedar . . . and another floral scent that Florence couldn't quite place. Had she always smelled like this? There was a sort of newness to Arianna's embrace that Florence couldn't quite explain.

"I was so worried about you," Arianna whispered. "I thought of you every day on Nova."

Florence's fingers curled fistfuls of Arianna's tired white coat. "I was worried for you too," she confessed easily. "You do have a way of finding trouble."

Arianna snorted and pulled away, resting her palms on Florence's shoulders. "A habit you seem to have inherited."

"There will be a lot more trouble before all this is over." Florence stepped out of the woman's reach. She wasn't a child for Arianna to protect any longer. "Can I count on you, Arianna?"

"Without question."

The lack of hesitation reassured Florence immeasurably. "The first Vicar

Tribunal will assemble in two days' time. At that point, I'll need you to discuss the Philosopher's Box."

Florence watched Arianna's face at the mention of the infamous box. Surely, Arianna had learned by now—from Louie, no doubt—that Florence had outed her ability to make the box. She searched for anger or pain. But whatever emotion Arianna was feeling, she kept it guarded. It was a barrier Florence wanted to break down. She wanted to be as close as they had been in Dortam, but as the women they were now.

"About that . . . Louie has requested unbridled access to the schematics for the box."

Florence's hand found its way back to the hilt of her gun at the mere mention of the conniving little man. "I assume you refused."

"No."

"What?" Florence hissed. She'd taken Arianna to be much smarter than that. "Ari, you know him, and you know what he intends to use the box for. Furthermore, we must keep the mechanics of the box as secret as possible, at least until—"

"If you wanted it to be secret, Flor, sharing its existence with the world was a strange choice."

"Loom has no other way to stand against the Dragons." She was not going to allow Arianna to make her feel guilty. "As we are, we will die. As Perfect Chimera, we have a chance. Plus, I saw no other way to unite the vicars after the destruction of the guilds." Florence sighed, allowing the tension to defuse. She quickly took her hand off her gun, not wanting Arianna to misinterpret the motion. "But we need to make sure that we don't have splintering factions. That those who are made into Perfect Chimera are loyal to Loom and know what they must do."

Arianna sighed heavily, her eyes glazed with a familiar, faraway look.

"Don't let your vision be clouded by the past." Florence took a step closer to her teacher. Arianna was head and shoulders taller than her, so she had to stand on her tiptoes to be in her field of vision. "I need you here, Arianna."

"And I will be." Arianna's focus was solely on Florence. "You lead, Flor, and I will follow."

"Good." That was how she wanted Arianna to look at her, as an equal. Florence believed her, wholly and completely. "Now, what are we going to do about Louie?"

"He served a purpose." Arianna shrugged. "And as long as he thinks he's getting access to the schematics, he owes me three more requests. Getting me to you was the first. The means justified the ends on this."

Florence shouldn't have doubted her former mentor and couldn't stop herself from noting the fact that she had been Arianna's first request. "And if he actually gets around to requesting those schematics?"

Arianna hummed noncommittally. "We can decide then."

"It's not like you to not have a plan calculated, with every contingency accounted for." Florence half-squinted, quizzical. It had been a short period of time on Nova, but could a few months really change a person so much?

She wondered if Arianna could possibly be feeling the same about her. The world had forced its change on Florence as well.

"There are a lot of moving parts to consider. He's in our pocket for now, and if he comes to demand the schematics . . . Later? Well, war is coming, Flor. There will be casualties."

"Indeed." Florence's mind instantly went to Sophie. "In a world like this, accidents can be quite common." Deeming the matter of Louie settled—for now —Florence's mind shifted. "Did you find what you were looking for on Nova?"

"I did." Arianna nodded. "The Dragon King has two rebellions he'll need to face. One here, and one up there."

"House Xin?"

"They're going to help us," Arianna affirmed. "As long as we help them."

Florence would come back to what that meant in a moment. But first, there was a man she wanted to inquire after. A man whose blood flowed through her veins. The only Dragon Florence could stomach thinking of with any sort of fondness. "And Cvareh?"

Ari stilled, so much that Florence couldn't have been certain even from a hand's width away that she breathed.

"His sister, Petra, leads House Xin . . ." Arianna began.

Florence leaned against the wall, settling in to absorb all the information Arianna saw fit to impart on her. She listened to tales of the sky cities she could hardly imagine, supported on magic and blood sport. But despite her every effort to pay careful attention to each detail that might someday prove important in her fight against the Dragon King, one question continued to creep up in her mind: What, exactly, had happened between Cvareh and Arianna on Nova?

# 12

## COLETTA

Usually, after supper, Coletta preferred to retire to the company of her plants. On rare occasions, she treated herself to chilled mead out of a crystal snifter to sweeten the sunset over Lysip. Tonight, in a rare occasion, Coletta treated herself to blood.

It had been a busy day, but one full of triumphs. Nevertheless, there was no reprieve for the righteous, and Coletta had a few more items of key importance on her agenda to complete before the candle wax burned out for the day. It was a list mostly comprised of what her and Yveun had discussed, and the ideas he'd seeded in the back of her mind.

That, more than anything else, was what she valued him for. Certainly, his other uses were vast and important. But he was the one to inspire great thoughts in her. He was the muse, not the painter. Fortunately for them both, she had skill enough with the brush.

"Ryu, your nightly libation has been set out in the garden." Ulia emerged, hands folded and head bowed, from a side hall.

"Return it to the chill box for tomorrow." The girl had to scamper to keep up when Coletta took an unexpected turn from her usual pathways back to her quarters. "Fetch me Topann. I shall be waiting in the gray receiving room."

"Gray receiving room?" Ulia repeated, clearly confused.

"Topann will know where it is."

The orders given, Coletta continued alone.

Toward the top of the Rok Estate was space to store gliders for Riders, as well as the necessary landing and departure areas that accompanied them. But down the slope of the hill, on the side of the estate that faced the edge of the island, was a series of chambers burrowed into the ground below. There, amid the desolate stone walls and dimly lit halls, was another landing area for gliders. One room was connected to the barren track of stone, aptly named for its decor and function.

The gray receiving room was vacant and dark, the air stale. Coletta left the door to the hall open as she walked over to a thin countertop along one wall. It was barren, save a striker.

She picked up the tool that resembled a pair of shears, steel on one side, flint on the other, and lit the two iron oil lamps bolted into walls on either end of the room. It was barely enough light to scare darkness away from the corners and, if anything, seemed only to accentuate the inky blackness that clung to the edges of the room.

*This will do nicely.*

She leaned against the table and passed the time by inspecting her claws until Topann arrived.

"I apologize for my delay." Topann gave a small bow as she entered the room, shutting the door firmly behind her.

"You were not delayed," Coletta pointed out. She knew how long it took to arrive at the Gray Room from Topann's quarters among the flower fields on the opposite end of the estate. "If anything, you hurried."

"I do not like to keep my lady in wait." Topann crossed the floor, taking Coletta's hand in hers. The woman's red fingers curled around her wrist and she brought Coletta's knuckles to her lips.

"A trait of yours I appreciate." Coletta freed her hand from the prostrating woman. "Tell me, have we heard anything from our Fen traitor?"

"He has acquired information on the stores of gold on Loom."

"Excellent."

"However, he seeks to negotiate before he shares this information."

"Negotiate for what?" she inquired.

"I do not yet know."

Coletta thrummed her fingers against the table, annoyed. Her day had been going so well, so smoothly. She was not about to let a Fen be the blemish upon it.

"Very well . . ." Coletta hummed. "You shall go see what he wants."

"Ryu?"

No, she wouldn't understand. "Yveun will go to Loom himself to bring the Fen to their senses."

"I see." Her tone proved she agreed with Coletta that such a course was inherently foolish.

"Yes, well, I would like you to go with him. Take the opportunity to squeeze this Fen for all the information he's worth, and be my eyes and ears."

"Such a mission would be my honor."

"Before that," Coletta continued, "I require your assistance with something."

"Anything."

Coletta knew it to be true. Topann was the oldest of her little buds and had bloomed into a loyal zealot. Though, zealots were easy enough to create. All it took was saving someone whose desperation to be free of something had reached a critical mass. Whether the shackles took the form of a person or a place, Coletta broke her flowers' chains. Thereafter, they were hers.

In that way, all her little flowers were the same. Buds that had grown on the underside of Lysip. Girls that would have sprouted from nothing, into nothing, and died nothing . . . and yet, they had been saved from their fate, given a taste for greatness.

"I need you to find me an Alchemist from among the Fen."

"Ryu, with every respect, I did not think we kept Alchemists here—only Rivets to maintain the gliders."

Coletta ran her fingertips across her lips in thought. "I once brought an Alchemist from Loom to give me their knowledge on the plants and herbs of their world . . ."

Extracting that knowledge had been bloody, at first. But there was an unsurprisingly direct inverse correlation between the willingness of a person to impart their knowledge and the number of toes they still possessed. So unfortunate for the Fenthri that they could not regrow body parts as a Dragon could. It truly was a wonder the gray race had survived at all.

"But," Coletta continued, "that may have been twenty years ago. He could be dead by now." She sighed heavily. "Oh, the Fenthri and their life spans."

"I shall go to the Fen pens and search." Topann was unswayed. "Should I not find one, I will bring one back for my lady from Loom." She said it as though she were bringing back a souvenir from a leisure trip, not a creature, live and resistant.

"Good. The other thing I require shall be easier to procure." Coletta looked about the room again. Sturdy walls, thick, built to dampen sound. "Go below Lysip, and find me an organ donor."

"Any preferences?" It was not the first time Topann had received such a request. Coletta had been using organs to bargain with powers on Loom, and Nova, for years.

"Yes. Where is your magic, Topann?"

"Mine?"

Coletta nodded.

"Hands. Eyes. Ears."

It was a standard set of magic for a Dragon. Coletta was pleased. It would be simple to measure the effects on one such as Topann, who possessed so little magic to begin with. "Find a stomach."

"Of course." There was the beginning of understanding hovering beneath Topann's words. But the woman was undeterred. Coletta had long-held Topann's life in her claws.

"Good." Coletta walked over to her loyal subject. She stretched out a hand

and cupped the woman's cheek in a sign of affection that was almost never seen. Topann stilled, taking a shallow breath. "You have been with me throughout the years, my flower, and I will reward your loyalty."

"You have given me more than enough," Topann whispered. "You showed me the sun, Coletta'Ryu."

Coletta smiled fondly on her first test subject. "Yes. And now I shall show you what it means to be made perfect."

CVAREH LAY IN BED, DEBATING WITH THE DAWN. WAS IT TOO EARLY, OR NOT early enough? Was the sun duller than normal, or did it shine with its usual strength? He wondered if he could somehow delay time by whittling away the seconds, question by question.

Today, Finnyr would arrive.

Lord Xin's presence was palpable in the manor. Cvareh could feel it in the stillness of his room, in the quiet that seemed to seep into the stones.

He stared at the ceiling above his bed, wanting to scream. But his mouth could no longer make sound. He breathed slow, shallow breaths, until tears fell like tiny waterfalls off his cheeks and onto the pillow.

He realized Petra would never see the Xin Manor completed. She would never see House Xin ascend the ranks of Dragon society. Though the likelihood of either coming to pass now seemed slim.

One bright spot: She wouldn't see their family crumble away to nothingness, either.

Daylight inched its way across his ceiling, creeping in through his windows like an unwelcome guest. His attendants were not long to arrive. Cvareh wiped his face with his palms and sat upright.

He could allow himself this weakness only in private. Among Xin, he was the face of his house. Every man and woman had made that abundantly clear with their silent expectation that he would duel Finnyr.

Cvareh stood and went to his dresser. He pulled open his favorite drawer, running his hand over the silks and satins. All the beautiful colors clashed and complemented each other, a rainbow contained in a wooden box.

"Cvareh'O—Ryu." The attendant in the doorway quickly corrected himself.

Cvareh didn't spare the man a disapproving look. They could *not* call him Cvareh'Oji. "What did you have in mind for today?" the man asked, quickly moving between Cvareh and the dresser of fineries.

What did one wear to meet his sister's murderer . . . who also happened to be his brother?

He rubbed his temples. Cain was right; he had learned a deep and profound sympathy and appreciation for Loom. For as backwards as the idea of not having a family was, at least on Loom they weren't killing their own flesh and blood for power.

Which world, again, was the uncivilized one?

"White," he finally decided on.

"White?"

"Yes."

"I—Well, I'm sure there's something in here . . ."

Cvareh honestly didn't know if there would be. He couldn't recall a time he'd ever worn white. But today, he needed strength. He had lost one woman who he thought was invincible, and wanted to feel closer to the other woman he knew who had the same power of conquest, the same bravery, the same drive.

In the end, it was as he suspected. Nothing in the drawer was white, or black, or grey. He wore a light seafoam color that had a rough-cut lace overlay in white.

While it was a far cry from Arianna's coat, the tight-fitting trousers that hugged his thighs and matching shoulder embellishments accentuated his physique, and seemed to give a deeper, richer hue to his skin—which he hoped also reminded Finnyr of their midnight-skinned sister. It wasn't precisely what he'd had in mind, but as Arianna's coat fit her for conquest, this was his own battle-ready armor.

A woman appeared in the doorway, breathless. "Cvareh'Ryu, bocos have been spotted in the western skies."

Eyes were on him, expectant, waiting for his reaction. Cvareh waited as well, to see what rose within him. But the waters of his soul were dark and calm, concealing much in their depths, concealing his true feelings—concealing *him*.

"Then we should go to the arrival platform," Cvareh said, and strode past the woman to lead the way.

The morning's light had lost its luster. It shone through the windows as gray, bland, like the light filtered down to Loom. Cvareh adjusted his shoulder adornments, the beaded silver that dangled from them clinking softly, then dropped his arms limp at his sides. There was a danger to this dark ocean that House Rok had poured into the pit of his soul; it drowned his heart and overflowed into his mind. He didn't hold anger in balled fists. He kept it coiled in the tense muscles of his wrists, ready to unsheathe his claws in a breath.

More people followed as he ascended the stairs and halls of the Xin Manor toward the wide platform that was used to receive people of importance.

Sculptures laden with rare gemstones and lined with gold rimmed the platform where the other half of the manor waited with Cain.

They formed a wide arc, leaving the open end of the platform barren to the air and bocos off in the distance. Was this a receiving party, or a dueling ring?

Cvareh, himself, did not know.

"What will you do?" Cain asked. The man always seemed to know just where and how to push. There was never a question of Cvareh's insecurities, uncertainties, or weaknesses when Cain was around. That made the man a strong ally. Invaluable.

"Do you trust me, Cain?" Cvareh asked, loud enough for the house to hear. Cain had been a favorite of his sister, and it was not by chance that half the family had chosen to stand behind him.

Cain studied him a long moment. Cvareh knew the man understood what he was asking, what he was saying. If they fractured and broke now, Rok could stab a fatal wedge into the foundation of House Xin.

"I trust you, Cvareh'Ryu," Cain affirmed. He didn't hesitate, but the words betrayed his uncertainty. The truth was clear: Cain trusted him, but questioned his methods.

"Good." The bocos were close enough for him to make out their colors. His claws itched for release. "I will only do what I feel is best for House Xin. It is all Petra ever demanded of me."

Cain said nothing more on the matter, settling instead for a small nod. He looked forward again and couldn't contain a growl. "He means to make war with his mere arrival."

The other man had no doubt seen the detail of Finnyr's boco as well. "He seems to be having trouble doing it." Raku, Petra's trusted mount, was very clearly begrudging the notion of having Finnyr ride him. The bird squawked in protest, ruffling its feathers with every few flaps of its mighty wings.

Cvareh was more focused on Finnyr's companions. Two Riders, with only a handful of beads each, flew both sides, and the hulking form of a Tam woman flew closest to Finnyr. Cvareh recognized one of the Riders as the man who had delivered the news yesterday, and the other he'd seen in the king's entourage . . . but the woman was new.

She had but one bead. It should mean she was as green to combat as the color of her skin.

But Cvareh didn't believe the symbolism for a moment, and every look he took at her as she approached reaffirmed the fact. Yveun was playing one of his games with this one. He wanted them to assume the woman was no one of importance.

Cvareh instinctively knew better.

The party of four landed. Raku immediately bucked, trying to take to the skies again. Finnyr pulled hard on the reigns, only managing to upset the bird more.

The rest of House Xin watched, saying nothing. Not one servant moved to help the Oji as he dismounted.

Raku promptly flew away the first second he was able. Cvareh sympathized with the creature. He too wished to ruffle his feathers, cry indignantly, and take off for the horizon. Eventually, the bird would return; Raku was too loyal not to, and those hard-formed habits had long since turned into instinct.

"Is this all the welcome the *mighty* House Xin can muster for their Oji's arrival?" It was fitting the large Tam—no, she bore a Rok symbol on her cheek —was the first to speak. Finnyr couldn't even muster the strength to look any of them in the eye for longer than a moment.

"Welcome back to Ruana, Finnyr'Oji." Cvareh wouldn't allow himself to be a coward. He was better than his brother. But that didn't mean that he could bring himself to say "home" to the man who had seen their sister, the best among them, die at the hand of Rok.

The moment Finnyr's eyes met his was the moment Cvareh knew that he was, indeed, capable of killing his brother.

"It—" Finnyr coughed, trying to clear his throat. He continued, stronger, "It is good to return home to the land of my forefathers as your Oji."

At the word "Oji," an unspoken tension coursed through House Xin. Every man and woman felt it. Even Cvareh's chest tightened around the sound.

It was a pull to the title, a desire to recognize the rank and file that every element of Dragon society had told them from birth was the only thing separating them from destruction and discord. But it didn't feel right when directed at Finnyr, of all people.

From the corner of his eye, Cvareh saw Cain looking to him.

Cvareh's legs itched to move, but his feet stayed. Something about this still wasn't right.

"I have seen your chambers prepared in advance of your arrival."

"At least someone on this dreary rock has sense." The woman at Finnyr's side sneered at the statues that surrounded them, at the men and woman assembled.

"Thank you, Cvareh."

It was a testament to House Xin's steadfastness that an audible, collective gasp didn't rise like a wind at Finnyr's disrespect. To speak Cvareh's name without a suffix . . . to rob him of the title that had been there for so long . . . Cvareh hardly knew what his name sounded like without it.

Cvareh's hate for his brother worsened by the moment.

Cvareh gave a small bow of his head, forcing the interaction to continue. There was nothing he could do, for now, and he wanted it over with.

The people began to shift. There was a whisper, too quiet to discern clearly. Cvareh felt the weight of his family's eyes on him again. Cain wordlessly heaped expectations on him like shrouds of lead.

Cvareh knew what they wanted, especially now that a whiff of a potential slight was in the air.

Finnyr began to walk forward; Cvareh and Cain both parted to allow him to pass. The woman remained glued at his side, always within half a step of Finnyr. Up close, Cvareh could feel her magic. And he could see her eyes—a beautiful, and unnervingly familiar, shade of lilac.

"Are you going to let him go?" Cain finally snapped. His words were hushed and hurried, but anger distorted volume.

"What's this?" The woman turned. "Is this a challenge I hear?"

Cain balled and uncurled his fingers. Cvareh knew the motion his friend made when trying to fight against unsheathing his claws.

"Not a challenge." Cvareh stepped between Cain and the woman. "Cain'Da is merely curious when Finnyr and I will find time to regroup on the current status of the house and affairs of Xin."

"I see . . ." The woman smiled, wide enough for her fangs to be a challenge in their own right. Her eyes were indeed familiar. Not just in color, shape, and shade . . . but in the level of bloodthirsty ruthlessness he had also seen in Arianna's gaze. It was a lust for revenge he was starting to understand too well. "So good to have one so loyal to your house."

"We are lucky." Cvareh held his position. He didn't want to get into a brawl here—not with two Riders on the ground, with this mysterious woman, with Finnyr being a worthless coward the house could tear limb from limb, and especially not with a Dragon King only a half-day's ride away, who was no doubt itching to unleash his full power and lay waste to House Xin.

"Speaking of great loyalty . . ." The woman looked around at those assembled. "The Dragon King has sent me to stay with Finnyr during his transition as Oji. I am Master Rider Fae Rok'Da To, and I will ensure that there is no conduct unbecoming toward those who are, no doubt, loyal to his supreme rule throughout this trying time."

"We are to be babysat by—"

"Cain, enough." Cvareh hated himself. He hated that the moment his claws were unsheathed, it was to direct them at his friend, the most loyal among them to their name.

But his hand drawn back, claws shining faintly in the sunlight, had the right effect. Cain was stunned into silence. He turned to Cvareh in a rage that was quickly quelled.

Cvareh poured it all into his face now that he was turned away from Finnyr and the woman, and the other two Riders were on the far end of the platform, already mid-departure.

They were all angry. Every member of House Xin was angry and bearing the uncomfortable badge of mourning. But he would not have them act in foolishness that would get them killed.

"Forgive me, Cvareh'Ryu." Cain lowered his eyes.

"Shouldn't you be seeking my forgiveness?" Fae's voice sent shivers up Cvareh's spine. "After all, I stand for Yveun'Dono here."

Cain was silent. Cvareh implored him without words. He didn't want blood on these stones, not Cain's.

"I look forward to the honor of having one whom our Dono holds in such high esteem among us," Cain bit out.

The woman knew he was insincere just by her smile. That much was apparent. But she accepted the platitude and returned to Finnyr's side.

With the tension slightly allayed, for now at least, the other Riders took to the skies, no doubt to report back to Yveun at the first possible moment.

None of the other members of House Xin moved. Once again, they all looked to Cvareh for answers he didn't yet have. The home he so loved was quickly devolving into a battleground.

Cvareh started in first.

A familiar set of footsteps fell in close behind.

Cain followed him all the way back to his room, stalking like some predator. Cvareh kept his hands in plain sight, relaxed, claws sheathed. He hadn't spent so much effort on the receiving platform just to flay Cain in private.

Cvareh started for his dresser first thing. He needed new clothes. These were now soiled with the memory of calling Finnyr "Oji." He looked at the heap of fabric on the floor. He would need to get a new tailor on retainer if he was forced to discard clothing just because he used "Oji" in relation to his brother.

"What was that?" Cain finally spoke from where he leaned against the door.

"I don't know yet," Cvareh admitted quietly. He was still trying to figure out all the moving parts at play, and felt blind with no ears or eyes on Rok.

"You just let him come in here—"

"Cain—"

"—don *her* title and—"

"It was not her title!" Cvareh roared in frustration. "We are Dragons, Cain. We live. We fight. We die. All by each other's hands. Petra knew that, and she loved it. Eventually, someone was going to kill her. She knew that." It was why she prayed every day to Lord Xin, Cvareh realized in that instant. "And her death will mean nothing if we throw away our lives and House Xin by challenging my brother."

"Throw away our lives? You don't think you can beat Finnryr?"

"*Think* about this, Cain." His friend was blinded by his sorrow. But Cvareh could permit it no longer. He had shed his tears and moved on; Cain needed to do the same. "If you or I had challenged, the Riders would have stood for him. Finnyr would approve the duel as Oji."

His friend cursed, turning away with a quick spin.

"That woman, the new Master Rider, Fae . . . She seems . . . different. Surely you felt it, too?"

"She seemed as much trash as everything else Yveun dredges up," Cain growled.

"Trash with fearsome power."

Cain didn't argue the fact.

"Yveun wouldn't have sent her unless he believed she could guard Finnyr. Don't let the lack of beads fool you."

"She can't stop all of us."

"Together? No," Cvareh agreed. "But that would be an act of all-out war, a disregard for duels. It would be a complete affront that would sway Tam to stand behind Yveun in a way they never had, for a crusade across our land. Future generations may not even remember Xin's name. If we are to throw all Dragon law aside and bet everything, we better do it when we think there's a good chance we can win."

Cain cursed again and slammed his fist against the door. "So we are to sit here and tolerate all this? We are to accept it, bow to it, smile in the face of this affront?"

Cvareh wished he had a different answer for his friend, for himself, for their house. But he didn't. The truth changed with work, not wishes.

"Smiling or not is up to you. But you will tolerate it, for now."

"If you insist, Cvareh'Ryu." Cain reached for the door handle.

"Cain."

He stopped, but didn't turn.

"I need you with me. I need you to trust me. I can't do this without your help."

Cain sighed softly. When he turned, Cvareh could've guessed what he was about to say from his expression alone. "I already told you once today, you have it. Nothing has changed since Finnyr's arrival. Hopefully, not even your title."

"Thank you." Cvareh looked to the window. "I will figure out a way for our family to not just survive, but thrive."

"For her?"

Cvareh nodded. "For all of us."

The answer was enough. Cain's anger dissipated, and he gave a small bow before departing. Cvareh stared at the door long after Cain disappeared through it. There was work to be done, much work. But underneath it all, his friend persisted. It was a relationship Cvareh already knew he would need in the coming days.

Cvareh leaned against his dresser. The weight of it all had become too heavy. He needed the support, if just for a moment, when no eyes were on him and no expectations accompanied them.

Petra would know what to do. But Petra wasn't there. It was just him, a vicious king, and a gray world far below that was House Xin's only ally against the rising tide. Cvareh tried to organize his mind and, for the first time, plan his next steps.

A sound summoned him back to reality, and Cvareh walked over to the window. He cracked it, slightly, to better hear the low, sad song that echoed off every rock and crag surrounding the Xin Manor. Cvareh leaned against the window frame, and wondered who else paused to listen to Raku's dirge as the masterless boco cried it into the wind.

# 14

## ARIANNA

 Physically, at least.

There was an actual bed. The mattress was a lumpy mess of collected and questionable fabric, but it somewhat held its shape. It was, dare she even think it, almost comfortable when she nested into it far enough.

The world was cooling for winter, but the day's heat soaked into the stones of the five-towered hall and radiated warmth through the night's chill. It was practical. Nothing unnecessary, nothing out of place. It was a world Arianna was familiar with and was glad she could still find comfort in.

She'd needed a good night's rest before this morning.

A sharp rap on her door revealed Florence, promptly at the time she'd informed Arianna she'd be by the night before.

"Good morning, Flor." Arianna couldn't stop herself from smiling. It was good to see the girl, to know she was near, even under present circumstances.

"I hope it's a good morning." Florence took off her top hat, dusting off some imaginary specks before putting it back on and adjusting it several times over as they started to walk down the stairs. Arianna recognized her nervous tell instantly. "At the very least, we'll be able to stop agonizing over what state the tribunal will be in."

Arianna still couldn't believe the notion. Despite the reasoning behind it, despite the ramshackle location, there was to be a Vicar Tribunal. It was an event she had written off ever seeing in her lifetime.

"What are you expecting?" She put aside the odd excitement at the prospect of the day's events. There was work to be done, and Florence needed her focused.

"I know Vicar Harvester will be here. The Vicar Raven may be a question, with all the help the guild is giving to collect up Loom and bring them here . . . I heard Vicar Rivet and Vicar Alchemist arrived last night."

Arianna grimaced at the very idea of seeing Sophie again.

"What?" Florence didn't miss the distasteful expression. Then again, Arianna had done almost nothing to hide it.

"I went quite a few years without seeing Sophie. I could go quite a few more," she admitted. This was Florence, after all. The one person Arianna would make the Philosopher's Box for. If Arianna couldn't trust Flor with the truth, who could she trust?

"That won't be an issue." Florence adjusted the holster that held her guns on both sides of her ribs.

"It won't? She didn't make it through the Dragon's attack?" Arianna didn't feel bad in the slightest. Sophie was intolerable and, had the roles been reversed, Arianna had no doubt Sophie would be thinking the same thing about her.

"She survived. An accident after did her in, I believe."

"An accident?" The notion was almost delicious. Sophie, with her ability to stubbornly survive anything, done in by some innocuous happenstance. "Of what kind?"

Florence shrugged. "Not sure. You know how the Alchemists are . . . ever the secretive bunch."

Ari knew all too well. It had taken her years to penetrate Eva's shell and get the woman to trust her enough to share her research. So, she let the matter with Flor drop entirely, and put it from her mind as one small, golden lining to the whole madness that had become her world.

They rounded into the entrance hall. Even at this hour, people continued in a steady stream, led by Ravens and ushered into the various towers the Rivets had reinforced enough to be usable.

"What a mess we are," Arianna murmured.

"Maybe so . . . But to be a mess, we have to exist. Which is more than a lot of Loom can say."

Arianna kept quiet from then on, watching Florence interact with the people who seemed to know her already. They greeted her respectfully and bowed their heads and tipped their hats as she passed by.

And the day had only just begun.

"We'll be in here." Florence motioned to an open set of doors. "There are similar halls in the other towers, but this one was in the best condition and still happened to have working doors."

"I remember studying in here, once." Arianna paused to run her hand over the wood of the door. It was dusty and dented, but managed somehow to hold all the memories of her time on Ter.0 as a child and a young adult.

"Did you?" Florence paused as well.

"I was just a girl . . . and it was only for one lecture. This had been the

Alchemists' tower, so the talk took place in here." Arianna could barely remember what was said and hated herself for the fact.

"Perhaps, someday, we will see lectures in here again."

"Perhaps." Such a day seemed so far away given their present circumstances that it was pointless to even think of.

At tight capacity, the room could hold maybe one hundred people. Large, but not the sort of room that would dwarf the speaker on the floor. Arianna and Florence walked down a sloping aisle that stretched along one of the five points of the pentagon-shaped space.

The floor was tiered in traditional lecture hall-style seating, with the occupants intended to sit directly on the edge of the tier, their feet over the edge. At the lowest point, where the lecturer would stand to address the room, the five guild symbols had been painted, one in front of each side of the pentagon.

"Florence?" A man's voice drew the girl's attention.

"Vicar Powell, it's so good to see you again."

Her apprentice, the girl she had pulled from the Underground, shaking and scared, now stood a woman who was bold and brave and capable. Florence was speaking with a vicar as though they were casual friends; Arianna had nothing more to do than stand to the side and watch.

"And good to see you as well." Powell clasped hands with Florence. "I heard there was some turmoil at the Alchemists' Guild shortly after your arrival."

"I heard so as well. Such a shame. Happened just after I left to come to Ter.0. I have yet to meet the new Vicar Alchemist . . ."

Arianna took another step closer as a few Ravens began to trickle in. She was honestly surprised they weren't late. The Ravens were notorious for it.

"And this must be the infamous Rivet."

Arianna knew when she was being spoken about and was pulled immediately back to the conversation.

"Yes, this is Arianna, Master Rivet under Master Oliver," Florence introduced them semi-formally.

Arianna clasped hands. "It's good to meet you, Vicar Powell." At least, she hoped it was.

"I owe a lot to Powell." Arianna took note when Florence dropped his title, and further notice that Powell didn't seem to mind. Arianna wasn't sure if it was a sign of some deep familiarity . . . or if Nova had ruined her when it came to reading into titles too much. "He was the one who helped me escape the Harvesters' Guild when the Dragon King attacked."

Arianna immediately saw the man with the circled sickle tattoo on his cheek in a new light. "Thank you, truly. If anything had happened to Florence . . ." She trailed off, barely able to bring herself to think of the idea.

"A decision that seems to be reaffirmed as wise with every passing moment." Powell looked only at Arianna now. She noticed a shift in him, from when he looked anywhere else to when he looked at her, as if she was *different* than the rest of the room.

These were the eyes of a man who knew what she was.

"And the best thanks you could give me is what Florence has already promised," he continued. "The Philosopher's Box."

Arianna nodded. She didn't have any other words. After all, she had spent most of her life pursuing the box in secret, then fighting to keep its existence carefully guarded. Now that people knew, she had to develop a new toolkit, and fast, for managing the topic.

"Vicars sit on the lowest tier." Florence had the insight to save Arianna from herself. "Then elder masters behind them, younger masters behind that, and every guild is allowed a handful of journeymen to sit along the back."

"I'll take my seat, then." Arianna started for the Rivet's section.

Florence grabbed her arm and her voice dropped to a whisper. "Sit on the edge? I may need you to speak . . ." She glanced around the filling room. "After all, I got them all to agree to come because of you."

"I understand, Flor." The last thing Arianna wanted was to cause Florence to lose esteem with those gathered.

She heeded the girl's advice. She sat four rows back from the floor, at the very end. She didn't want to be in the foreground. She was the White Wraith, a member of the last rebellion. Her whole life had been lived in secret—a quality she realized she no longer shared with Florence.

The room continued to fill and Arianna watched nonchalantly as various masters took their seats.

"You always preferred the back."

Arianna's eyes swung to an elderly man, smartly dressed in all black that blended with his coal-colored skin and accented his steely eyes and closely-cropped silver hair. A thin line of stubble covered his sagging cheeks.

"You always preferred being clean-shaven," Arianna pointed out.

"Well, the end of the world can do a number on one's hygiene." Willard chuckled and held out a hand. "Let me see you, Arianna."

She suddenly felt nine years old again. But this time there was no Master Oliver to stand by her side and do the talking for her. Arianna stood on command, walking down to the man whose filled and circled Rivet tattoo was nearly invisible.

"You have hands, now." He inspected the thin line around her wrists where her ashen Fenthri skin stopped and the steely blue of Finnyr's Dragon flesh began.

"A recent acquisition."

"How many organs are you missing?"

Arianna thought about lying. She didn't want to bare herself to the world. But Florence's attention was on her. Even while keeping up a conversation with

Powell, she observed their exchange periodically; Arianna could feel her eyes on her face like a warm breeze.

"Now . . . only lungs."

Willard whistled low. "Only lungs . . ." He eyed her up and down, finally letting go of her hands. "It appears the Alchemists were right, too, about their postulations on Dragon magic affecting a Fenthri's growth. When did you get the blood? Seven?"

"Yes, seven." The memory was seared into her recollection with the fire of magic hitting her veins for the first time. Killing her. Resurrecting her. Time and time again until her blood ran black.

"And when did you become a Perfect Chimera?"

"Eighteen."

"Was it Oliver's work?"

Arianna couldn't stop a small grin. Willard and Oliver had always been friendly rivals of a sort, two who enjoyed mentally sparring with each other almost a little too much. They had needed each other to thrive, but couldn't stand the other's existence in equal measure. A perfect set of counterweights.

"No, no, the final box was not his work."

"Your own." Willard reached out a hand, resting it on the pin Arianna had affixed to the edge of her white coat by her collarbone. "And he gave you the circle for it."

"Just before he died."

For all the rivalry and competition, there was genuine sorrow to Willard's eyes at the memory of his deceased friend. "How did he die?"

"I killed him."

Arianna expected the reaction. She expected the look of shock, the probing stare for a lie where he would find none. Willard said nothing, no doubt expecting her to fill in the blank of the circumstances that led her to such an extreme action. But that was one line of history she wouldn't fill in, one unbroken stretch for the unrelenting passage of sands in the great hourglass of time to wear away.

They would have her knowledge, her schematics, perhaps even her body for their studies. But she would never give them that memory. She would never share the final moments she had with those she had truly loved. Other than her pin, and the box that pumped away within her, it was all she really had left.

"Well." Willard dropped his hand from the pin. "If what you say is true, then I expect you had a very good reason."

Arianna's mind was blank. She wanted him to rally against her. She wanted to see Willard rage for the death of one of the greatest minds of the last generation.

"Knowing Oliver, he likely commanded it." Willard shook his head with an ironic chuckle, heavy with sorrow. "There would be no way you could've done it otherwise."

She wanted to refute him. She wanted to tell him he was wrong. But it was the most truthful thing anyone had said in a long time, and betrayed the depth of the man's familiarity with her. Before Arianna could find any words, he dismissed himself, taking the seat on the lowest tier—the space reserved for the vicar.

If the Dragons' notion of gods were true, Master Oliver would be in some infinite beyond, watching Willard achieve all the goals they had ever competed over. Oliver would also be looking upon her. Were her achievements enough to bring a smile to his face?

By the time the Vicar Tribunal was called to order, the room wasn't even half-full. No guild, at any point, ever had more than about fifteen masters. The Ravens were almost at capacity; twelve lined the seats behind the vicar. The Rivets had seven, counting Arianna—all fresh faces she didn't recognize. The Alchemists had about the same count.

The most sorrowful sections were the Revolvers, who had four, led by a new vicar who very clearly had no idea what he was doing. And the Harvesters, who had five, including Vicar Powell.

Arianna looked around the room at the tired and unwashed faces. This was the best they now had. This was *all* they had.

"I suppose we should begin with introductions." Florence made her way to the center of the room when none of them did anything more than stare at each other. It seemed no one quite knew what to do at a Vicar Tribunal.

"Vicar Powell, Harvesters." Powell stood first at Florence's motion. The room went around clockwise after him.

"Vicar Ethel, Alchemists."

"Vicar Gregory, Revolvers."

"Vicar Willard, Rivets."

"Vicar Dove, Ravens." The woman with the long black braid put her hand on her hip, tilting it to the side. "And before any of you ask . . . Yes, the name is really Dove. Always has been. Was born before the family law. No, I didn't choose Ravens because of it."

Arianna leaned forward, placing her elbows on her knees. Dove was the only one among them who had an ease about her. She was also the only vicar to survive the attack. Willard was the next-most acclimatized to his role. But even he hesitated with a too-long pause when it came to using "Vicar" in association with his name.

Loom was a candle that kept being sliced into pieces from the bottom as it burned from the top.

"Excellent. Well, then . . . Since we're all introduced, we should begin by focusing on the issues of highest priority." Florence grabbed a ledger she'd been carrying all morning. Arianna wondered how many hours the girl had spent preparing. "Foremost, Vicar Powell informed me of concerns with regards to feeding such a centralized population on ground that has no natural resources. I shall concede the floor—"

"The issue of highest priority is the Philosopher's Box." Vicar Dove stood.

All eyes were on Arianna. Unflinching, unwavering, Arianna stared down at Vicar Dove who stared back at her, trying to draw whatever height she could in intimidation.

It wouldn't work. Vicar Dove may have every experience in functioning as the leader of the Ravens' Guild—the most reckless and freewheeling guild of the five. But the room had turned into a battleground, and no one had the gift of combat quite like Arianna.

"The Philosopher's Box will mean little if all of Loom starves before it can be made." Powell remained on his feet as well.

"*If* it can be made," Dove retorted.

"It certainly can be made." Willard pushed off on his knee, bringing himself into a standing position and fighting for the floor. "I knew Arianna as a girl, and knew her teacher. If there would ever be someone who could make such a thing, it would be her."

She just loved being spoken about as if she weren't there. Maybe if Arianna let them continue, she could actually sneak away and no longer be on display like some prize pig. Her fingers twitched, magic curling around her pinky. It'd be easy to illusion the room in a fog. They'd be none the wiser until she was already on a trike.

"If it so easily can be made, how did none of your guild make it before?" Dove didn't back down. "Or have you? And did you sit on the knowledge for years, locked away in your ticking halls?"

"If anyone had locked it away, it would have been an Alchemist," a master seated behind Dove remarked dryly.

"Certainly not a technology we have had in our possession." Vicar Ethel didn't rise to refute the notion.

"If it exists at all." Dove gave a look back to Arianna.

She knew when she was being goaded. The question was, should she let herself be? Arianna looked to Florence, who was allowing the volley of words from the center of the floor. Florence stared up at her with what Arianna hoped she read correctly as an expectant look.

Arianna rose to her feet.

"When I was seven, I left Ter.0 under the tutelage of Master Oliver. We travelled together around the world and ultimately back to the Rivets' Guild."

"I didn't ask for your life's history." Dove folded her arms over her chest.

"Let her speak." Powell, unnecessarily, came to Arianna's defense.

"Master Oliver, as some of you may or may not know, was the one who occupied the seat of knowledge for the Rivets on the Council of Five for the last rebellion," Arianna continued, as though Dove nor Powell had said anything. There were some whispers at the mention of the Council of Five. "If you think talking on the Council of Five is still taboo, you should leave the room now. You're all complicit in this new rebellion, and that will carry a far greater punishment than speaking on the last."

No one moved, but the room was thoroughly silenced.

"Was the box developed for the last rebellion?" Powell asked.

"Indeed." The metallic contraption that occupied her chest, for the first time, seemed loud, as if it wanted to drown out her words—to conceal itself forever under her skin and harness and coat. Arianna pressed onward. She would utter this once, and then never again. "I worked with other guild journeymen in the rebellion on the box. We struck close a few times, but the difficulty lay in finding a way for the blood to remain clean, and the Fenthri body free of rot.

"That was when Eva—" Arianna touched her wrist where Eva's link mark was dated in ink underneath her skin. "—a fellow Alchemist in the rebellion . . . made a discovery.

"We worked with a Dragon then, one who claimed to seek Loom's liberation. Who claimed to be on our side. He brought a flower from the sky world of Nova."

"A *flower*?" Willard clarified.

"Just so," Arianna affirmed. "Eva noticed that her reagents didn't deteriorate in the presence of the flower."

"Why?" Of course the Vicar Alchemist would be the one to inquire.

"I confess . . . I never fully understood it," Arianna admitted. "But, together, we found a way to temper gold with this particular flower." She withheld the name for now; it was too early yet to give them key details. She and Florence still held power as long as they held pertinent information.

"And how does all this relate to the box?" Dove asked.

"Don't you see?" Willard couldn't stop himself. "A metal that purifies the blood by merely being in its presence." He looked back to her. "Do the qualities imbued by tempering wear off?"

"They haven't yet." Arianna saw his somewhat confused look and knew it was time to elaborate. "It was critical for all blood to pass through the box continually, to be purified and prevent rot. All blood passes through one location."

Arianna brought her thumb to her chest.

It was a dark sort of amusement seeing who in the room could follow the relatively simple logic she was presenting them. Willard was the first to get it, followed by the other Rivets. Dove seemed the first, and one of only two, to get it on the Ravens' behalf. It gave her some faith that all the vicars seemed to put it together.

"Eva performed the surgery, both to implant the box and the subsequent organs to test that I would not fall." Arianna drew the sharper of the two daggers crossed at the small of her back. "Naturally, I cannot show you what the box looks like at this moment, as I vitally need it where it is. But I can assure you that the operation continues to be a success."

Arianna wrapped her fingers around the blade and drew it quickly across her palm. She held up her hand for the room to see. Blood, the color of molten gold, dripped from her palm and, in true Dragon fashion, quickly evaporated when exposed to the air. Her wound magically healed over; just like that, all signs of her being the Perfect Chimera disappeared.

All signs, excluding the shock in every set of eyes around the room.

"Traitor to Loom!" One of the Revolver journeymen was on his feet, finger pointed at Arianna.

That certainly wasn't the reaction she'd been expecting.

"You had this weapon and kept it from us? We could have been fighting the Dragons all along."

"I do not think a Revo should point fingers about concealing weapons from Loom." Helen's biting remark was thrown from the back corner but echoed throughout the whole room.

"Do not speak of what you don't understand, little crow," a master Revo cautioned.

"I kept it from Loom because I did not think we had the capability to unite together to use it effectively." Arianna didn't need to defend her decision, but she couldn't stop either. She looked to the vicars, rather than the boy. She didn't care if some little pistol understood, but the vicars must.

"And look at us proving you right . . ." Her Dragon ears picked up Powell's murmur. She was liking him more and more by the moment.

"Furthermore, Perfect Chimera would mean war—something I didn't think Loom could stand more of."

"That shouldn't have been your call to make." Vicar Ethel gave her a wary stare. "It should have fallen to the vicars."

"And what tribunal? I created the box following the One Year War. There was no effective communication among the vicars, especially none that wasn't monitored by Dragon ears." Arianna met the other woman's gaze. "Furthermore, the Dragon we worked with . . ." Arianna couldn't bring herself to say Finnyr's name. And she wouldn't, not so long as there was any likelihood that they would need to work with House Xin. She wouldn't taint the relationship out the gate. "He was working for the king all along. We had spies from every angle, and that was before the box was even well known.

"He was the one who infiltrated the rebellion and brought the Riders upon us. It was the dying wish of Eva, of Master Oliver, of every other Rivet, Revo, Raven, Harvester, and Alchemist involved that the research we produced be destroyed, rather than sequestered by the Dragon King."

The room was silent, an instinctual mourning toward the mere idea of destroying information.

"But you didn't destroy it?" Willard asked hopefully.

"I did." Arianna stared down at them all. She was only midway up through the room, but felt as though she stood from the parapet of judgment itself. "I torched it. My work, theirs, every last bit of it is gone. And then, before they could fall from over-exposure to magic from imbibing to fight off the Riders, or before the Riders could get their claws on them… I killed them. Every last one."

The air in the room was changing. It was charged with their shock and fear. And Arianna was the conduit for it all. She fed off it. She gleaned power from it.

Below her, Florence wore the smallest of smiles.

"And the box?" Willard seemed to be the only one who could find his voice.

"Just the one." Arianna tapped her chest. "And the schematics for it are here." She moved her fingers up to her temple.

"You're a monster," the Revolver from earlier whispered.

"I am." Arianna made no effort to deny it. Let them be so fearful of her that they left her to the shadows and obscurity she much preferred. "I am not Fenthri and not Dragon. I am not limited by the confines of what Loom knows as a Chimera, either. I am a creature of my own creation, and that is why, if I am to share this knowledge with Loom, it will be when there is a plan for how it will be used."

"What do you have in mind?" It seemed Vicar Dove had come around.

"I—"

"There's only one." An Alchemist was on his feet, a journeyman of little importance, judging from his seating placement in the back row. "There's only one box and it's in her."

"Leo—" Vicar Ethel gave a cautioning tone.

"We just cut her open and see how it works." The Alchemist looked to Willard. "You Rivets can take it apart. If she won't give it to us, we take it from her."

Arianna was not about to feel threatened by a child who looked no older than Helen and had half the manners.

"We are not going to take it by force." Willard defended her. Arianna didn't know if it was because of his instinct as her vicar out of respect for her work. Either way, she appreciated the gesture.

"He has a point." Vicar Gregory finally spoke up. "There is little time before we can expect whatever the Dragon King has next for us, especially grouping like this. We need to defend ourselves."

"A defense will be planned." Florence reminded them all that she was there, raising her voice above the din. "It is why we are here." She turned to the Alchemist journeyman. "Now, take your seat."

"You can't command me."

"Take your seat, Leo," Vicar Ethel ordered with a glare that almost swung to Florence after, for ordering one of her students.

"No, he has a point." The Revolver from earlier stood. "I say we kill the traitor to Loom." He drew his gun, leveling it at her.

"Let's say you can kill me. Which is hard. Trust me, it's *hard*. And you *can* quickly reverse engineer the box." Arianna tilted her head to the side, her mouth curling into a grin. "I haven't told you what type of flower you need from Nova. I haven't told you the process to temper gold to get its properties. I haven't explained the principles of the box. How long do you think Loom will last?" She held out her arms. "Fire, if you think you can discover those things before the Dragon King kills us all."

The journeyman's hand shook, the barrel of the revolver making tiny swings through the air.

"Or sit down, and let the adults figure out a way to make sure there is a Loom for you to inherit." She dropped her hands to her sides.

For a brief moment, the Revolver had sense. But Arianna gave the situation too much credit. She now lived in a bent and broken world, where tensions where high and trigger-happy Revo initiates were elevated to journeymen before their time out of sheer necessity.

The boy took his shot.

Her ears rang, magic quickly healing the hearing damage from the gunshot in the small room. Dust plumed from a pockmark in the stone of the tier behind her. Arianna opened her mouth to speak, but all that came out was the sound of another revolver firing.

Smoke disappeared from the barrel of Florence's gun as the Revolver journeyman's body hit the ground hard, blood pooling around his face from the bullet hole between his eyes. The entire room was silent. Arianna looked at the young woman who had been her apprentice. The girl she had pulled out of the Underground.

One shot, and those images were gone.

She didn't know the woman who stood where Florence had been a moment ago. This woman moved the same as Florence, dressed the same as Florence. She even sounded the same as Florence. But Arianna saw her as if for the first time, and couldn't help but wonder how long she had been there.

"Now is not the time for dissension," Florence spoke softly, holstering her gun. "We stand together, or we don't stand at all."

No one spoke. No one moved. It seemed the whole room held its breath.

"Do you agree, Vicar Gregory?" Florence turned to the vicar of the man whom she had just slain in a blink.

"I do," Gregory spoke after a long pause. "The Revolvers need to remember that for every shot we take, there should be two we hold back. With the power to kill comes the responsibility to protect life."

"Well put." Florence looked back to the room. "And protect life is just what we will do, with the power of the Perfect Chimera. But first, I believe the Vicar Harvester wanted to cover some matters of supplies . . ."

"Y-yes, thank you, Florence." Powell cleared his throat, and launched into a lengthy discussion on their current resources.

Everyone else seemed engrossed, but Arianna's focus was entirely on Florence. She was avoiding Arianna's stare, even though she must have felt the weight of it.

Arianna hadn't questioned the idea of throwing her loyalty entirely behind Florence.

But for the first time, she wondered just what, and *whom*, she was supporting. For the first time, she didn't feel like the most dangerous person in the room.

# 15

## CVAREH

 following his brother's arrival. Cvareh didn't make himself too scarce, at least not obviously so, but the gods looked after him and put his brother elsewhere at all times. When dawn came, he soaked in his bath until the water was cold, changed his clothes several times, and took the longest breakfast he could out on his terrace.

But just as Lord Xin came for all men in time, he eventually had to make his way to his brother.

Cvareh wasn't sure if he was surprised that Finnyr had yet to send for him. Surely, they had much to speak on. Petra had been the brave one of the three of them, the one who tackled problems head on—no situation too uncomfortable or frightening. Now, it was Cvareh's turn to be brave.

So, adorned with bronze pauldrons and a swooping blue cape that covered his left arm as he walked, Cvareh made his way to his brother's quarters.

Servants eyed him cautiously along the way, clearly not sure what to make of the youngest Xin sibling heading for the Oji. He could tell by the wariness in their eyes that they wanted him to challenge, while the hurt and betrayal there revealed that none of them expected him to do so.

Cvareh kept silent, his strides brisk and long. What had become Finnyr's domain was the third wing on the lower floor, comprised of only a handful of interconnecting rooms. By far the nicest of what Petra had designed to be guest and Kin chambers. It was good enough, Cvareh appraised as he took in the decor and careful woodwork.

*It's too good for Finnyr*, a treacherous little voice crept up.

His ears picked up voices several paces before the door. Cvareh stilled, trying to catch the words when the door was suddenly opened from within.

"See, I thought I smelled your brother," Fae said to Finnyr, but kept her eyes on Cvareh.

"Forgive me, brother." It was already hard to speak. His jaw was aching from the anger that kept it clamped shut. "I didn't realize by not taking breakfast with you that you would be forced to break the morning's bread with Rok."

Finnyr looked over dully from the table. It was a very different look than at the one he'd worn at his arrival the day prior. Now, he held the advantage. So he looked on Cvareh only apathy and ambivalence, as though he was appraising his own brother to be worth little and less.

"I have had many a meal with Rok. You would do well to find their company enjoyable also, brother." Finnyr looked back to his plate, ripping through a small, seeded loaf and smearing butter on it liberally.

"I had not meant to imply otherwise." Cvareh looked back to the woman who was still eyeing him with a gleeful grin. "I know better."

The woman strolled back into the room, leaving the door open. With all the hip swaying of a brothel madam, she paraded over to the bed, lounging back on it as though it were hers.

Could he have read this wrong? Was Finnyr merely bringing back a lover? It would make sense for him to find someone to confide in throughout the years he had spent on Lysip. A displaced Tam made as much sense as anything else . . .

Finnyr barely regarded the woman, instead watching Cvareh warily as he entered the room. "What do you want?"

"I wish to speak with you." Cvareh cut right to the chase. Finnyr's tone made it clear that they were not going to find themselves on friendly or casual footing.

"Speak, then." Finnyr shoved a wedge of melon into his mouth, chewing like an animal. Juice dribbled down his chin as his teeth chomped into the pale yellow flesh.

"May we have privacy?" Cvareh glanced over at the woman who was inspecting her claws. Cvareh understood the message clearly: She was ready to strike at any moment.

"Anything you say to me can be said before Master Rider Fae."

It was as though his brother had begun speaking Fennish. No, it was something more confounding than the whispering tones of the gray peoples below the God's Line. He was going to allow a Rok Rider to sit in on House Xin conversations?

"Finnyr, I would—"

"That is Finnyr'Oji, Cvareh." Finnyr demanded Cvareh use his title, yet still kept stripping Cvareh of his. It was equal parts confusing and alarming, and Cvareh had no intention of letting it go for a moment longer.

"Finnyr'*Oji*, I would like to know if I am nameless now?" That wasn't what he'd intended to say originally. But this was the path Finnyr was choosing—one of difficulty.

"I have yet to decide." Finnyr returned to his meal.

"What? Who is the Xin'Ryu then?"

"Presently, no one."

"Who do you intend to ask to be the Xin'Ryu?"

"I have yet to decide."

"Finnyr'Oji—" Spitting out the title of Oji in conjunction with Finnyr's name was like spitting up glass. "—I must encourage you to pick a Ryu. If not me, then *someone*. I could even put forward some names of those who are in the House who have proven their loyalty."

"Typical Cvareh," Finnyr snarled quietly, looking up from his meal like a dog protecting a bone. "Always so worried about *loyalty* for House Xin." Finnyr slowly put down his utensils, punctuating the movement by folding his fingers. "I am House Xin now. Do well to remember it."

"I am merely trying to give you counsel, as your brother, if nothing else."

"My brother?" Finnyr scoffed. "We are no more brothers than I am Tam."

The words blindsided Cvareh, hitting him so hard he nearly staggered. Not brothers? No Ryu? No Petra? His world was collapsing one cornerstone after another.

"Were we brothers, you would have sent for me years ago."

"I could take you from the Dragon King no more than Petra could." Cvareh glanced at Fae, who wore the smallest of smiles. She looked like a sea sponge on the beach's shore, lapping up every wave of words, absorbing them into her memory until it filled to capacity.

"Petra, she was an even worse example."

"Stop." Cvareh wouldn't hear it. He couldn't hear it. It was a load too heavy to bear so soon after her death.

"She spoke of family and usurped our father—"

"Stop."

"—sent me away—"

"Finnyr . . ."

"—used you like a tool—"

"I said stop!" Cvareh punched a fist into the doorframe. Anger escaped through heavy exhales and his heaving chest. Wood splintered into his knuckles and the smell of woodsmoke filled the room from his wounds. Cvareh didn't notice; his eyes were only on Finnyr.

There was the fear he expected to see from his coward of a brother. It was all talk. There was no greatness. It wasn't until the shadow of the giant green woman pulled herself off the bed with a sigh that any resolve returned to Finnyr's stare. He was only brave as long as he sat under the protection of Yveun.

Cvareh slowly pulled his fist from the doorframe, regarding the woman and her claws warily. He raised his hands, showing that his claws had yet to be exposed.

"Forgive me, Oji." He spoke to Finnyr, but looked at the Rider. It was apparent who the true Xin'Oji was. "I am merely emotional given the present trials. I shall work on composing myself."

Fae looked to Finnyr, and Cvareh's gaze followed. Finnyr continued to look at him with that same detached, cold stare.

"See that you do, Cvareh," he cautioned. "If you want any hope of keeping any sort of title to your name."

Cvareh gave a small nod. The meeting had been a failure from the moment the door opened and at the rate things were going, it wasn't impossible for him to wind up dead. It made complete sense to turn his back and leave, and yet, something compelled him to hover a moment longer.

"Remember, brother . . . For however much you hated Petra, and hate me, you are still Xin, and we are Dragons. Your blood flows from Lord Xin. Build your own legacy as you see fit, but at least make it truly yours."

Finnyr's mouth was shut so tightly, his lips weren't even visible. "Get out of my sight."

*With pleasure*, Cvareh barely kept himself from saying as he departed down the hall and away from that miserable room.

Cvareh strode through the Xin Manor with the look of a man on a mission, but it was all a carefully crafted illusion. He had no direction to go in, and what seemed like fewer options available to him by the second. His mind and heart both were heavy with a frustrating, infuriating ache.

He found himself walking up a long staircase. It was a narrow offshoot from one of Petra's lower halls, and wound upward into the heights of the manor. When he was lost, there was one place he'd always gone to for answers.

The viewing chamber was empty and that, for some inexplicable reason, surprised him. Cvareh stared at the far edge of the dais, where his sister had sat facing the large windows that looked out across the Ruana mountains toward the temple of Xin. He sat heavily in that same spot, looking for answers he didn't think he'd find.

It wasn't long before footsteps broke the silence, and Cvareh knew who stopped at the top of the stair without having to turn. He knew it by the smell of the man and the sound of his gait, and because there was only one other Xin Dragon who would dare venture up to one of Petra's most personal and private spaces.

"Sit with me?" Cvareh spoke without turning.

Cain didn't speak. He did as he was told, but in the wrong way. He walked around to the far edge where Cvareh sat, sitting next to him.

Cvareh didn't have it in his heart to correct the man. "How did you know I was here?"

"Dawyn told me," Cain answered softly. There was something about the space that made lowering one's voice in reverence natural. "She saw you headed this way."

Cvareh vaguely recognized the name. "One of my sister's attendants?"

Cain shook his head. "She actually helped see to the Fe— to Ari while she was here." He stopped himself mid-word with a glare from Cvareh at the slur for the people down on Loom.

"What is she doing in Petra's wing?" Cvareh felt protective of the space. He wasn't ready to see it turned over to Finnyr, to anyone.

"Paying her respects . . . looking for answers . . ."

Cvareh heard his friend's meaning without needing it spelled out for him. "I don't have the answers."

"I suggest you find some," Cain said firmly. "House Xin needs you."

"Finnyr has not said if I am to remain Ryu." Cvareh shook his head. "Even if he did, this is not what was intended. I was to help Petra, not become Oji myself."

"Pull yourself together. We need a leader." Cain sighed, looking out through the windows. "Plus, life is made of missed intentions."

"Poetic."

"I heard it at a tea parlor in Napole."

Cvareh chuckled and shook his head. With his friend, he should've known. "I think he will avoid appointing a Ryu." Cvareh whispered what he had been too afraid to even think. "If there is no Ryu, he's less likely to be assassinated from within Xin."

"Because if it's not in a clear duel and there's no Ryu, succession isn't assured." Cain cursed under his breath. "Damn that Yveun."

Cvareh was inclined to agree.

"What's worse is that Finnyr will get away with it. Because he knows you love this house too much not to keep functioning as Ryu, with or without title."

Once more, Cvareh's silence was his agreement. He'd always gone along. He'd spent every moment and every breath in devotion to his house. He'd only done what others had set out for him. But what should he do now, when there was no clear path?

"This is wretched."

Cvareh sighed and leaned back, wishing he had his sibling to lean against.

"What is it?" Cain made note of his shift in demeanor.

"I wonder how much could have been avoided if Petra had just given him some favor."

"Turn sympathetic to Finnyr and I will duel you myself," Cain threatened.

"Twenty gods, no." Cvareh shook his head. "Merely wishing things were different."

"Wishing gets us nothing. We need action." Cain folded his arms over his chest, beginning to pace. "We need to show Yveun that we won't tolerate these slights."

"We need to bide our time." Cvareh tried to use his words as a mental block to slow Cain down, but they only seemed to make him pace faster.

"Until what? Until Rok decides to pick us off one by one?"

"Until we hear from Arianna."

Cain spun to face him in one fluid movement.

"You know I'm right." Cvareh preempted whatever the other man was about to say. "If we are to stand a chance against Rok, we need the help of Loom. We bide our time until then."

Cvareh could almost feel Cain's anger bubbling to the surface. He braced himself for the moment it would explode. But Cain took a slow breath, and his whole demeanor shifted.

"How do you plan on making use of them for House Xin?" his friend asked, finally.

"The same way Petra intended: to make us an army." Cvareh wondered how much Petra had shared of her mind with anyone beyond him. Judging from Cain's almost confused frown, he guessed the circle was small, if it existed at all.

"Make us an army? Of people like *her*."

"Arianna is the first of her kind, a Perfect Chimera. They will make more and stand with us. With that much power, we will defeat Yveun."

"I hope you're right . . ." Cain shook his head, starting for the stairs. While Cvareh considered it a success that his friend could even stomach hearing mention of Loom and Arianna without exploding, it seemed the fuse of tolerance was still quick to burn. "Because if you're not, we're all dead."

"I know I am," Cvareh reassured Cain.

"Then I will leave it to you. Fetch me when I'm needed in your master plans, Cvareh'Oji." The final vowel of the honorific echoed back up to Cvareh, ringing in his ears several times over before it finally faded.

*Cvareh . . . Oji . . .*

He'd never thought of the idea before. That had always been Petra's mantle, Petra's mission.

Now, House Xin expected him to bear its weight—him, who had wanted to carry it least. Cvareh knew the esteem would honor many a Dragon, and it was something so many lusted over. But the notion sat uneasy with him. So uneasy, that he wondered if anything could ever make it settle.

# 16
## FLORENCE

Just once in her life, Florence wanted a well-stocked workshop. She didn't want to buy supplies on a budget, or scavenge in secret, or scrape bottoms of barrels. She wanted a workshop with perfectly level tables, cabinets full of all manner of powders—even some she didn't quite know how best to work with— and a door with a lock that prevented people from entering whenever they pleased and nibbing through her work.

"So, this is where you've been holing up." Will ran his hand along the dusty countertop. "A bit dirty."

"Helping run a rebellion severely limits one's ability to clean." Florence looked up from the one surface she had scrubbed to shining perfection. Gun parts were carefully set upon it in meticulous order. Every screw was lined up, the springs sorted by size—it was an organization unique to her, which meant she'd know instantly if one of her items was missing.

"You always did like to keep things tidy." Will walked over to the table, assessing her layout. He touched nothing, an unspoken respect for another's guild ministrations.

Florence paused, her rag hung off the gun barrel she'd been cleaning. "One thing I could control," she said, finally. "When your life's a mess, it feels a bit better to tidy *something*. Even if it's just a bit of laundry, or a countertop."

"Or all of Loom." Will swiped away the dust on the empty secondary table in her room, hoisting himself up to sit on it.

"Loom is still a mess."

"We're getting better. That last meeting of the vicars was *almost* productive."

Florence couldn't keep in a groan. "I came to my workshop to escape that nonsense."

She'd been all but silenced for the meetings subsequent to the first, relegated to sit behind Vicar Gregory and say as little as possible. Florence knew she didn't have a leg to stand on when it came to actually leading the meetings, so she wasn't sure why she still felt frustrated.

"No rest for the weary."

"What do you want, Will?" Florence picked up a wire brush, working out some caked-on gunpowder from her gun barrel.

"I can't just call on a friend?"

"Are we still friends?" Florence flashed him a small grin. "And here I thought you liked Louie more than me."

"The man flies a few feathers short, that's for sure."

"I think you just said I'm not crazy enough for you." Oh, the stories she could tell him to prove otherwise.

"We're all afflicted with a different sort of madness." Will shrugged. "Louie's sort is more similar to mine and Helen's, though."

"Ravens." Florence had suspected Louie's actual guild for some time. The man was restless, wandering, driven to something unseen just over the horizon, just a few more steps away.

"You think so?"

"Birds of a feather." Florence dipped her rag in gun oil, the familiar tang filling her nose.

"Helen wants to take over his work. The man's on death's doorstep."

"What 'work' is that even?" Florence didn't have the foggiest what Louie considered his magnum opus to be.

"There's always something to steal, someone who will pay for it, and the people who need to broker the transactions." Will put his elbows on his knees. "Plus, it's pretty handy we're here with this rebellion of yours."

"We'll see . . ." Florence had ideas for Louie, but none that had paid out dividends yet. The man was like a rare canister—very few occasions to use it, but when you found one, the resulting reaction was magnificent.

*Speaking of canisters . . .* Florence began reassembling her gun. She should have just enough time to make some additional ammunition.

"We got Ari to you."

Her hands paused. *Ari.* The woman had been the kind of quiet Florence wasn't sure she wanted to break. She'd attended every meeting, sat as directed, said what made sense and anything needed to reinforce the idea that Florence had been right to call the Tribunal. But there was a distance between them, rendering the woman untouchable.

"That was chance." Florence tested the hammer and trigger of her gun, unloaded, with satisfying tension and clicks. "She would've gotten to me without you."

"She was in bad shape."

"I have no doubt." Florence re-holstered her gun. "But you don't know Ari like I do. She would've made it to me."

Will hummed, opened his mouth to speak, and was interrupted by a familiar ghost in the doorway.

"Will, I think Helen is looking for you." Shannra made her way into the small workshop.

"What does she need?" Will half-jumped off the table, waiting for Shannra to pass before he started for the door.

"Who knows? Something about a map?" Shannra shrugged.

"She with Louie?"

"Passed her in the hall." Shannra paused where Will had been sitting, the small of her back against the high workshop table.

"Right, thanks."

Florence set out four hollow canisters in a line, looking up at Shannra expectantly. The other woman's mouth spread into a coy little smile.

"Helen is looking for him?" Florence repeated.

"I may have lied." The woman's face lit up with a wide smile.

She shook her head and laughter escaped.

"I hardly get to see you since everyone arrived." Shannra straightened and stepped over to Florence's table. Delicately, her fingers fell like fall leaves onto the surface; not a grain of powder was blown out of place or a canister disturbed.

"Help me," Florence asked, her eyes traversing the line of the woman's fingers, up her arm, to her face. "I could use an extra set of eyes on this."

"With pleasure, Flor."

Shannra was a capable teacher. She explained things thoroughly and kept her expectations both high and reasonable. It made Florence want to learn, want to earn her esteem. It also helped that she was a Revo as well, a journeyman at that, and contained a wealth of knowledge Florence had only just begun to scratch the surface of when she had last worked with a Revo teacher.

Florence watched the woman's hands carefully, her eyes drifting upward when she knew Shannra wouldn't see, to admire her face. Another beautiful spirit in her life. But beauty didn't change that the woman was one of Louie's minions, a fact Florence had been careful not to forget. Helen, Will, Shannra . . . all had to be kept at arm's length.

"... and then just fill it to top as you would normally." Shannra finished her instruction on the canister.

"Is this standard Revolver knowledge?" Shannra was one of the few Florence felt comfortable asking such questions around. She knew the woman wouldn't belittle her odd guild situation. Anyone in Louie's company was in no position to speak down to others for odd choices.

"Fairly so." Shannra nodded and then tapped Florence's bottle of sulfur. "But you add your own twists to it."

"Have to keep things interesting." Florence shrugged.

"Never a dull moment with you, certainly."

"Speaking of . . ." Florence tugged on the chain connected to one of the buttons of her vest, producing a simple pocket watch. "Almost time for the Tribunal. I should start down."

"You got it working again," Shannra appraised.

Florence had discovered the watch among the ruins of Ter.0, a remnant of some bygone days. The front of the watch had an odd design that was almost reminiscent of a wing and some kind of semicircle, but it was too dented to make out the full image. No doubt it had been some Raven's precious trinket before the world collapsed.

"Arianna," Florence answered simply.

"You two don't seem as close as you'd made it sound." Shannra fell into step.

"Are you probing for Louie?" Florence grabbed her top hat from its peg. "Peg" being a generous descriptor for the bit of gnarled iron that was sticking out from a crumbled section of wall.

"Not this time."

"This time." Florence huffed. "How often do our conversations make it back to that Endwig of a man?"

Shannra played with the ends of a handful of hair in thought. "Wait, you think he looks like an Endwig?"

"Most certainly." The resemblance was a bit of a stretch, if Florence was being fair. But she wasn't inclined to be fair toward Louie. "White, thin skin. Beady eyes. A taste for living flesh."

Shannra's laughter bounced between the walls and straight between Florence's ribs. She had a beautiful laugh. "A nightmare given form?"

"Yes, describes him well, don't you think?" Florence tipped her top hat at a passerby, a more frequent occurrence as they continued to descend the tower toward the Hall of the Vicars—as it had become known.

"Don't be cruel, Flor."

"I'm being truthful," Florence insisted. "It just so happens the truth is also cruel."

"I can't be too upset with him."

"Why is that?" Florence asked delicately. Shannra hadn't spoken much about the circumstances under which she'd come into Louie's service.

"Well, if I'm probing you for information on his behalf, it gives me an excuse to see you." Shannra shrugged, back to playing with her hair. "An excuse to talk."

Her movements combined with her words put a pang of longing in Florence's heart for something she didn't quite comprehend. The woman before her was deadly and beautiful, strong and sturdy, yet possessed a vulnerability Florence couldn't help but be drawn to.

It was all a lie, however. Shannra was Louie's. Florence knew how the old king of Mercury Town enlisted his help—extreme loyalty or death. So when the cards fell, she would do Louie's bidding, not her heart's.

Florence found herself at an impasse, the in-between that seemed to define her life. None of that changed the fact that Shannra was still dodging her question, and Florence had every intention of pointing that out. At least until Arianna appeared.

"Headed down, Flor?" Arianna emerged from the hallway, her violet eyes darting between Florence and Shannra.

"It's about that time." Florence patted the pocket where she kept the watch. "Thank you again for fixing it."

"It was honestly a nice distraction for the evening." Arianna was wearing her white coat and harness—always armed to the teeth, even among friends. It was a trait Florence admired and was already attempting to embody.

"I will let you know if I find any other such distractions." Florence flashed her teacher a smile that was reciprocated, however briefly.

"Were it up to the Vicar Revolver, I would have the distraction of manufacturing the Philosopher's Box." Arianna's expression quickly soured. "The man doesn't seem to understand that creating things is a lot more complex than destroying them."

Florence coughed softly and it served to remind Arianna that she was no longer in the company of Rivets.

"I didn't mean to imply that making explosives and ammunition wasn't complex," Arianna quickly backtracked, only mildly apologetic. The day Florence saw Arianna genuinely apologize for her thoughts was the day the world had, indeed, ended. "Merely that it is not as instantaneous as pulling a trigger."

"Especially not when we have still to sort procuring something from Nova," Florence agreed.

"I heard Louie was asked by the Vicar Raven to look into that." Arianna looked across Florence to Shannra.

"And how did you hear that?" Shannra arched her eyebrows.

"Louie isn't the only one who has his ways." Florence's chest filled with an odd sort of pride for Arianna's ability to uncover information. But there was also a twinge of frustration at the fact that she was only *just* hearing about it. Arianna continued to stare down Shannra. "Well? Does he have a solution for it?"

"Sounds like an excellent discussion for the Tribunal." Shannra smiled at them both. In a display of boldness, she grabbed Florence's hand, squeezing it tightly before stepping away. Then, speaking only to Florence: "I'll see you later, yes?"

Florence could feel Arianna's stare creeping between her vertebrae. "Perhaps. We'll see."

Shannra nodded, and strode ahead into the main atrium.

"Florence . . ." Arianna's voice was full of caution. "We have to be careful about her."

"I know, Ari."

"She's one of Louie's."

"Ari, I know." Florence rearranged her words so maybe they'd sink in better. "What sort of things has she been asking you?"

"Don't worry so much. Louie is on our side."

"Flor—"

"Ari, let it drop," Florence demanded with a hard stare. Arianna opened her mouth to protest but quickly abandoned the idea. "I know what I'm doing. Trust me."

"I do trust you."

*But I don't think you know what you're doing*, Florence finished silently. What did she have to do to prove she was capable of organizing herself and others, of defending Loom, of being an active contributor to their future? The more time that passed, the more Florence began to feel like nothing would do it.

She would forever be a student in Arianna's eyes—a ward.

Florence adjusted her top hat and tilted her face downward. She needed this time to compose herself.

The tribunal room was mostly full by the time she arrived. Florence tugged at her pocket watch as she descended the stairs, popping open the repaired latch to look at the hands within.

"Ah, Florence, what time were we supposed to start again?" Powell asked from where he sat.

She pulled out the pocket watch again. "About another two minutes."

"Like I told you." The Vicar Revolver folded his arms where he sat. "Don't know why you felt the need to ask her."

"Just getting another data point, Vicar Gregory, no need to get so bothered." Powell waved off the other man's short fuse.

"Florence, take your seat," her vicar demanded.

"I had a question about today's agenda." Powell still hadn't sat down.

"A question you can ask me, as another vicar," the Gregory insisted.

Florence glanced between the two men and finally ended with a long look at Powell. She hated the feeling of being relegated to the corner when she had something worthwhile to contribute. At least, she thought she did.

"Very well." Powell spoke as Florence stepped up the risers to where journeymen Revos sat. She should be grateful; technically, she shouldn't even be in the room. "What are we talking about today, Vicar Gregory?"

"There's only one thing we need to discuss." Gregory nodded in Arianna's direction. "The lack of schematics in her hands."

"Perhaps we can discuss the lack of a manufacturing line that would necessitate the need for schematics." Arianna's remark was dry.

"You will need to share them with us eventually." The vicar grew more relentless by the day. Florence could only do so much to quell Arianna's frustration at the fact. If only Gregory would *listen* to her . . . and if not her, then Arianna at least.

"In all my years, I have never seen a Revolver so interested in a Rivet's work," Willard jumped into the fray as he entered the room. "Warms my heart to see you taking such an interest. Now that we are reverting the guilds back to a system of choice, perhaps you wish to come have a seat in the back behind me, and allow another Revolver to assume command? You seem to have a promising student with a talent for uniting us, just there in the back row."

Gregory looked over his shoulder directly at her. Florence leveled her eyes against him and fought every urge to look away. She was not going to be submissive, not when she'd done nothing wrong, and especially not when another vicar was standing up for her.

"Ah, Vicar Dove," Powell spoke loudly the second Gregory opened his mouth, cutting off whatever remark the man had been ready to levy against her. "Not a moment too soon."

The Vicar Raven waved her hand, assuming her seat with a yawn. "Don't wait on my account."

Florence resisted the urge to point out that it wasn't much of a Vicar Tribunal if all the vicars were not present at each meeting.

"Well, I have a question for you, so waiting was a necessity. It's with regards to harvesting these magical flowers . . ." Powell started.

"As I have said previously, the Ravens are glad to assist."

*Assist how?* Florence wanted to ask. She expected some resistance; not everything would go smoothly. But she had foolishly believed that all those present on Loom would band together. It still seemed that the selfish nature of mortals won out from time to time, even in the face of certain devastation.

"I'm a bit curious on the details surrounding the *how*, Vicar Raven?" Florence asked from the back of the room, drawing all eyes to her. She wanted to hear if Arianna was right, and she'd play dumb if she had to. "After all, I left the Ravens' Guild. I'm not sure how it all works, getting something from Nova . . ."

"Florence—" Vicar Gregory's tone had been getting harsher by the day.

"I'm curious about these details as well." Powell came to her aid. She didn't know what she'd done to earn such esteem in the man's eyes, but having the favor of a vicar was priceless.

"Well, since a vicar is asking now . . ." Dove gave Florence a look from the corner of her eyes. "We are currently working on the infrastructure between Loom and Nova, to find a consistent means of transport. Without the ability to pilot a glider, we will need to rely on Dragon intervention. But finding Dragons willing to work against the Dragon King while not endangering our own by drawing attention is difficult."

Florence rightly didn't care if Louie was in any sort of danger. That was the line of work he put himself in. But since Vicar Dove was, for whatever reason, keeping Louie's involvement quiet, Florence couldn't call out the fact.

She turned to Arianna expectantly. If they needed Dragons, surely House Xin would come to their aid. Florence met her teacher's eyes, and the other woman remained glued to her seat—and silent.

"Perhaps the Harvesters have some inroads with the Dragons that we could use?" Vicar Dove continued to speak with Powell, but the words were distant.

*Why wasn't Arianna saying anything?* She looked over to the Vicar Alchemist, and promptly realized that Cvareh had held his meetings with Sophie, not the vicar that Florence had ushered in by creating a sudden vacancy in the position. No one else really knew of the depth of Cvareh's involvement beyond her and Ari.

"Perhaps," Powell replied. "But most of our organ seeds—" he didn't even acknowledge the Dragons as people, Florence noticed. "—were given to us to cultivate legally by the Dragon King. An avenue I do not think is available to us any longer." He turned to the masters behind him. "Would any of you . . ."

Arianna still was immobile. Florence stared down at her teacher, but Arianna was doing an excellent job of ignoring her probing gaze. Why wouldn't she speak? It was for the good of Loom. They had the solution neatly. They could move on from the topic.

*What exactly happened between her and Cvareh on Nova?*

The question from the first time she had laid eyes on her teacher again crept back to her. Now, more than ever, she was sure of it.

Frustration found its way like a billow of steam up the flue of her throat. If Arianna wasn't going to say anything, then she would—Vicar Gregory's growing ire toward her be damned. Somewhere in her, Florence felt bad for outing Arianna, but there wasn't any other choice. If Arianna wouldn't do what was best for Loom, Florence would.

The doors to the room were pulled open and a breathless man ran halfway down the stairs before loudly proclaiming, "Rainbows in the sky!"

No one breathed.

Then, chaos.

"What do we do?" Vicar Powell asked no one in particular. Typical Harvester.

"Revolvers, arm yourselves and to vantages!" Vicar Gregory jumped into motion. "Masters, summon the other journeymen. All Revolvers are to take to positions!"

"Vicar Gregory, can my Ravens assist your guns in flying to their stations?" The prior hesitation to work together melted away from Vicar Dove in a moment.

"Yes, while masters convene." Vicar Gregory gave a firm nod to the other vicar and then continued to bark orders.

Florence stood. She hadn't been given a position, but she was going to fight anyway.

"Where are you going, Florence?" the Vicar Revolver demanded.

"To where I can be of use."

"Just stay here. Only Revos were informed of what to do in such a contingency," Vicar Gregory called back, leaving and taking half the room with him.

*Only Revos.* The words echoed and Florence scowled. She adjusted her hat and started for the door.

"He said to stay here," Powell called after her.

Florence spun in place, looking at the three of the five guilds who had yet to move. "I am not going to sit here, waiting to die, while we are under attack." She drew her gun, pointing it to the doorway. "We all thrive, or we all perish— together. There's no other option for us now."

"You received an order from the Vicar Revolver," one of the still-lingering masters with a revolver chamber tattooed on his cheek cautioned her.

"Good thing I'm, apparently, not a Revolver then." Florence grinned, tapped her own cheek, and left the room behind her.

A pair of hasty footsteps caught up to her, slowing to fall into step with her own strides. Florence looked to her right, instinctively tilting her head upward so that the brim of her hat didn't hide Arianna's face. The other woman gripped her shoulder, stopping her in place. Florence's appreciation quickly melted into the frustration from earlier.

"What will it be, Ari?" Florence looked to the doors before them that led to the waste of Ter.0 in all its crumbling glory. "Are you my enemy or my ally? Will you try to keep me from fighting as well?"

She gave a huff of amusement and lightly took off Florence's top hat. People moved around them, rushing, shouting, cowering, drawing weapons and steeling their resolve. But for a brief moment, everything seemed to slow.

"You'll shoot better if you don't have to tilt your head funny to look up." Arianna deposited the hat on the window ledge of one of the inner stairwells. "You'll be upset if it gets damaged, too. Not too many hatteries around here."

It was madness. The world could be moments from ending, and Florence wore a smile at the gesture of her teacher and friend.

"Let's go fight some Dragons." Florence began moving again.

"Let's hope we don't have to." Arianna murmured under her breath. And, just like that, Florence was once more confused by the woman. Did she want to protect Dragons now? *What had happened on Nova?*

They emerged from the doors of the five-towered hall and into the rubble and chaos of the ground below. Men and women scampered to find places to hide. Revolvers held their backs against stones and beams of steel, loaded guns in hand. Florence looked up behind her at the tower, seeing the glint of gun barrels sticking from windows.

The Vicar Revolver stood atop the sloping road that led into the Hall of Ter.0. His arms folded across his chest and his eyes squinted at the sky. He was not the same man who had occupied the tribunal. Gregory was gone, and only the vicar remained in his place.

"You don't listen, do you?" The man glanced over his shoulder at her.

"I think my petulance is endearing." Florence grinned, selecting a few canisters she had made that morning.

"At least someone does." Gregory frowned disapprovingly. "Get back inside. I can't have you being a liability."

"Don't worry about me. I'm only here to help." Florence drew her gun. She knew she was pushing the limits. But she wasn't about to be ordered away and pushed around. She squinted up at the whitewashed sky, speaking before the vicar could. "What're they doing?"

"Flying out of range," Arianna responded, sparing Florence from having to endure another response from Gregory.

One glider broke away from the other two, veering down and away from the wide loop it had been making. The vicar rose a hand as it descended about halfway, just within range. The world was suddenly so heavy with silence that she could hear the collective chorus of guns cocking.

"Listen to me, girl," the vicar muttered. "Don't get us all killed now."

Florence barely refrained from pointing out that she may have been the one who saved Loom by uniting them all. It was a hard line to walk, being a nobody but aspiring to be a someone.

The Rider looped around a few times, looking down at the terrain, each time a little lower. It started its final descent on a trajectory that had them landing with an explosion of color on the dusty ground as the glider touched down lightly. The Dragon didn't move. She stayed exactly where she was, hands on the golden handles of the glider.

It was those handles that funneled magic strategically through and around the Dragon's body, into her feet, and the gold platform on which she stood. A shimmer of gold, like the scales of one of the great southeastern sea snakes, lit up across the Rider's body, forming a corona. It was only the second time Florence had ever seen one, the first being the last time Riders had descended on Mercury Town and brought chaos with them.

It was a field metal and bullets could not penetrate—a field only broken by the strongest of magic, more than any Fenthri had ever mustered. And just like that, it made them all helpless before the Rider.

Arianna took a half-step closer in her direction. Florence watched with equal parts fascination and discomfort as claws grew from her fingertips. The skin of the Dragon hands she had acquired on Nova was so pale that it could almost be mistaken for gray, and there was a sort of willing blindness Florence had mustered toward them.

She couldn't determine if the blue was identical to Cvareh's color or not.

"Arianna," the Rider finally said. The Dragon did not call for a vicar or the leader. She called for Arianna. "Our king wishes to speak with you."

"Yveun is here?" Arianna's voice was nothing more than a whisper. A whisper that could well be the voice of death.

"Yveun'*Dono*, knave."

"He is not our king." Florence raised her gun. She didn't care if her shot would be pointless. She would distract the woman while Arianna attacked. She would catch the corona the second it exhausted. She would have the satisfaction of *finally* pulling the trigger on a Dragon, if nothing else. "He is yours. And he is not welcome on Loom."

"Florence," the vicar hissed. "Do not act out of turn."

Florence didn't move, keeping her stance. Someone had to threaten the Dragons, had to show Loom's claws.

The woman tilted her head with an unnerving jilt to sweep her eyes from Arianna to Florence. Her mouth spread wide, like a crescent moon, and gleamed with razor-sharp teeth. "What a bold child."

"I am not a child," Florence insisted.

"Spoken like a child." The Rider scoffed and looked back to Arianna. "Tell your warriors to put down their weapons."

"Not my call." Arianna still held up her hand, claws out.

"Interesting . . ." The Rider's attention turned back to Florence, rather than the vicar at her side. "Is it yours?"

"It's mine." Vicar Gregory took a step. Sure, *now* he wanted to be threatening.

The Rider tilted their head in the other direction and made a noise that could be interpreted as a snort at the vicar. "What is your name, girl?"

"Florence." She hated answering to "girl" but the sooner she gave the Rider a name, the sooner she could hope for her to use it.

Without warning, the glider sparked back to life, magic flashing through the air with an array of colors. The Rider took to the sky once more, quickly ascending to where the other two gliders continued their wide, slow loops overtop the guild hall. Florence looked back at the men and women stuck on the ground.

A Dragon could fight against three, four Fenthri without the help of anything. Enabled by a glider, protected by corona, and bolstered by any weaponry pilfered or given from the Revolvers, and Florence suddenly knew why Loom had fallen so quickly—why it took so little for the Dragons to keep them under their thumb.

"Coming back . . ." Gregory muttered.

Sure enough, all three gliders were descending now. The main road was only wide enough for two to land side by side, so the third touched down just behind.

To the right of the Dragon Florence had just been speaking to was possibly the largest Dragon she'd ever seen. Easily twice her height, he was made of pure muscle—if muscle was sculpted from rocks. The Dragon King—or so she assumed—wore next to nothing, so Florence and every other Fenthri could see every stretch of skin across the bulging curves of his arms and legs. His flesh was the color of fire, his eyes molten steel, and his shoulder-length hair as red as Fenthri blood. She hadn't been a Chimera for very long, but he radiated ten times the power she had ever felt, easily double the most powerful person she'd ever known—Arianna.

"Yveun . . ." Arianna whispered.

"Good to see you again, Arianna." The Dragon King pulled his lips back into a smile that was half-snarl. "I have come to offer peace to Loom."

"Peace?" Florence repeated. "You?" She'd never known an anger so vicious. "You who destroyed our world is offering peace?"

His head shifted to look at her. A piercing pang shot right between Florence's eyes the second his met hers. It was a dull ache in the back of her mind that spread like venom. Her whole body felt stiff, succumbing to the pressure. Her jaw locked.

"You are Florence, yes or no?"

"Yes."

"You lead this rebellion, yes or no?"

"Yes," she spoke on command like a trained animal, the word drawn out by force from the well of truth deep within her.

"*What?*" She barely heard Gregory whisper at her audacity, even though he stood right beside her.

Florence tried to peel her eyes away from the Dragon King, but she couldn't. She couldn't do anything unless he told her to first. Even breathing without his blessing was currently laborious.

"Of course," the king chuckled, sending sparks of magic off his corona like raindrops that dissipated before they hit the ground. "It would be a child who would have no memory of the last time Loom fell." Yveun shifted his attention to Gregory. "But you, you're old enough to remember."

The vicar was afflicted with the same sort of rigor mortis that had overcome Florence. She saw the panicked look in his eyes, the stiffness in his limbs. Florence knew the sensation was like taking a visit into a nightmare, but she made no motion to release him from it. Her relief at the Dragon King's attention being off her was too great.

"Tell me true: as Loom is now, can you stand against us in another war?" the king continued.

"As we are now?" The words were forced between tight lips. "No."

The whispering she heard on the wind was the sound of Loom's resolve wavering. She saw Fenthri look to each other in confusion.

"What happened the last time a resistance stood against me, Arianna?" The king turned his attention off Gregory.

Arianna looked off to the horizon. She remained still and easy, her breathing even. *Eyes*, Florence realized. Yveun had magic in his eyes—mind control as long as eye contact was maintained. She put it together faster than Gregory, who was once more under the king's thrall.

"You tell us, then. What happened the last time a resistance stood against me?"

"They were destroyed completely," the vicar responded automatically.

Gun barrels began to waver. A man stood to get a better view, giving up his vantage and his fighting position. Florence looked over the field of lost Fenthri, desperate for a home, longing for the logical order they all craved. They had been broken by the man before them, and, for some reason, they looked to that same hand now to fix their world.

"How many perished?" the king pressed.

"Countless. Loom was never the same," Gregory responded.

Eye contact—she had to break the eye contact or the vicar would undo the threads of Loom's resolve himself. Without warning, she gave the vicar a strong shove. The man was much larger than her in all directions, but he was unbraced and stumbled before falling.

"Don't look him in the eye," she offered by way of explanation at the vicar's scowl.

"Foolish girl, the truth should be heard." The king drew her attention again, but Florence made it a point to look just above his head. His magic kept out of her mind and off her skin as a result. "Every man and woman standing here, brandishing their pathetic weapons at my greatness, should know only death awaits."

"It does not!" Florence took a bold step forward. "Arianna is proof of that."

"Florence, I am not the example to use," Arianna hissed.

She knew Arianna hated having the attention on her. But that was what Loom needed right now. And for all Florence loved Arianna, she loved Loom even more.

"You are right. We cannot stand against your Dragons as we are now. But as Perfect Chimera we are even stronger than your Riders. We can be more complete than even you. We can have all magics, fly gliders, and use corona." Florence took another step forward, raising her gun once more at the giant of a man. She could see in her periphery his muscles twitch with rage. Was it too much to hope she could goad him enough? To cause him to release the glider, relinquish his corona, and lunge for her? Even if she died the most horrible death, someone would get the shot on his head.

"And there are a lot more of us, than there are of you," she continued. "We outnumber you. It's why you regulated our breeding, killed us off."

"Foolish Fenthri. You regulated your own breeding long before I did," he snarled. "I was saving you by regulating your ridiculous expenditure of resources."

"The Harvesters would have seen that soon enough." Florence had every faith as long as men like Powell were in the guild. Plus, it wasn't as if she could be proven wrong. No one could ever know what would have happened to Loom had the Dragons not intervened. "And then, when you caught wind of a Perfect Chimera, of the Philosopher's Box being made, you tried to steal her work and kill them all.

"But she survived." Florence pulled back the hammer of her gun. "And no matter how many times you try to kill her, you just can't seem to land the final blow." She spoke as loud as she could. She hoped everyone would hear her words. Because it was well possible that she was about to die. "That is the power of *one* Perfect Chimera. Now, what do you think will happen if you face an entire world of them? Perhaps you're right in wanting to talk peace, but you shouldn't be offering it—you should be asking us for it."

His mouth twitched, his snarl widened, and for one brief second Florence thought she had him.

But the Dragon King hadn't lorded over them for so long by being clumsy. He eased back on his glider, hands still firmly on the handles. "Shoot me, child. Let it be known to the world that it was your gun that heralded Loom's ultimate demise."

He was bluffing. He had to be. Florence locked her elbow to make sure her hand didn't shake. The revolver felt heavier than it ever had. *All I have to do is squeeze the trigger*, repeated over and over in her head like a mantra. It wound up strength that flowed into her forearm, then her hand, then her fingers.

She didn't know what she thought she would really accomplish. At the very least, she'd show everyone that she did not back down. That Fenthri no longer cowered before Dragons.

"Don't shoot, Florence."

All her focus was broken, and Florence whipped her head around to stare down Arianna.

"You offered us peace?" Arianna addressed the Dragon King.

"No . . ." Florence breathed. What was Arianna doing? Would she even think of handing over Loom to the Dragons?

"Take heed, Fen. Even the woman you deem 'perfect' wishes to talk before war." Florence felt the weight of Yveun's stare as he spoke. But her eyes were on Arianna. She didn't look anywhere else. "Yes, I offer you peace as long as you subject utterly to me."

"Give us three days to destroy our weapons and return to our respective guilds. When you return, you will see us ready to serve you."

This was *not* the Arianna Florence knew. Rage shot through her mind like a cannon ball.

"Very well. Let it be known that I am a most merciful god! You have three days. And should I not find all of you back where you belong, ready to serve, I will burn your world to the ground. I will give no quarter. You will all perish."

From behind, she heard the glider take to the sky again. Florence was aware the Dragon King had left as keenly as she was aware that she would forever regret not taking the shot, not trying everything possible to kill him at the one opportunity she may ever have.

Florence stared at the woman who had been her mentor, her role model, her friend . . . and saw someone she no longer recognized.

# 17
## ARIANNA

Her whole body felt heavy. Phantom pains ached in her joints at the mere sight of Yveun. Her mind echoed with the sounds of her flesh tearing under his claws, and howls of rage at the man she wanted dead more than she wanted to draw breath, more than she wanted to tinker and invent.

Arianna was too eager to turn away from the space the Dragon King had just occupied.

No one impeded her short progress back to the guild hall. Part of her wanted to collapse under the weight of all her memories, every misfortune in her life that the Dragon King had orchestrated. Part of her wanted to personally wait where she had just stood for three days until she could tear apart the Dragon King limb by limb.

If she even could . . .

Doubt tightened around her throat in the shape of Yveun's claws and Arianna didn't know how to dislodge it from her neck, where it was slowly suffocating her.

"Arianna!" Florence's voice was the only thing sharp enough to pierce the shell that encased the vortex of her thoughts.

She turned to see the girl sprinting toward her. Florence skidded and half-skipped to a stop. Her fist shot out, grabbing Arianna's coat, jerking her away from the staircase she'd been about to use for escape. It felt like being thrown back on a stage she had been trying to avoid for days.

"What in the five guilds was that?" Florence panted.

"Let me go, Flor." The machine of her mind was clanking loudly; too many wrenches had been thrown in it from different directions. Arianna couldn't be sure what the output would be if she continued to be pushed.

"No, not until you give me some explanation."

Arianna stared down at the girl who was holding her in place. In half a second, she could wrest herself free by breaking or severing Florence's arm in the process. But Arianna would never intentionally hurt Florence.

"Explanation of what?"

"Why did you tell me not to shoot? Why did you offer peace?" Florence shook her head. Arianna knew she wouldn't like the next words out of Florence's mouth by the look the girl gave her. "Whose side are you on?"

"I'd like to hear this answer as well." Gregory and two other vicars stood with a small but growing group who had made it in from the outside.

"I owe none of you an explanation." They were putting her under a dangerous amount of tension with their demands and their idiocy. "If you can't see the logic behind my actions, then none of you are fit to lead Loom."

When he spoke again, Gregory's voice was loud enough for all those assembled to hear. "How dare you. You've been nothing but unhelpful this entire time. If you're on our side, help us."

Arianna stared stubbornly back at him, her mouth pressed shut.

"As the Vicar Revolver, I want to know why you told a Revo not to take her mark."

Florence's eyes were torn away from Arianna at being called a Revolver by the vicar himself.

"Don't call her a Revolver when it suits you to do so," Arianna sneered. Her rage compounded. "That's low, even for you, Gregory."

"Excuse me?"

"Do you really want to have this conversation? I know the rumors about the shots you take in practice. The faulty canisters you'd claim were made by your colleagues." Arianna had carefully vetted Revolvers from the moment she knew Florence would need a teacher, and Gregory's name had come up as a master with some flexible perceptions of morality—especially when it came to Dragons. He'd been a little too flexible for Arianna's comfort then, and now.

"Lies . . ." the vicar whispered.

"Say it a bit stronger so maybe someone will believe you." Arianna shook her head at the sad little man. "If Florence had fired, it would've done nothing but provoke the king's wrath."

"Something we already had."

"And now we have something more: three days assured when we don't have to worry about a Dragon attack." Powell, ever the voice of reason. Arianna liked him more and more by the second. She used the distraction to jerk free of Florence's grasp. The girl didn't make a move to recover her. "We have a timeline for when our preparations need to be complete."

"'Ready' may be a generous word," Willard interjected. "Nothing can be made in three days with regards to the Philosopher's Box."

"Three days to plan, fortify." She'd have to spell it out, apparently.

"Fortify with what?" Gregory snapped back. "There are no weapons."

Arianna sighed at the lot of them acting like children.

"Let us resume the Tribunal," Florence announced suddenly. She looked around at the crowd that had filled the hall, journeymen and initiates watching the vicars bicker like children. Arianna took a step away and Florence caught her as she was about to turn. "You too."

Arianna was picking her battles, and she chose not to fight the girl on the matter.

Once more, the doors closed on the meeting hall. But the room was significantly less full. Only the vicars—who all stood—and a handful of masters clustered around the lowest floor. Arianna sat herself on the edge of one of the higher rows by the door, more than ready to make her escape at the first possible opportunity.

The vicars continued to squabble. Ethel withdrew from the conversation entirely, whispering to the other Alchemists. Willard tried to appeal to everyone's collective sense of logic; Dove preached action, backed up by Gregory until she refused to agree to let him train all Ravens with a weapon. Powell looked lost and frustrated every time he failed as a peacekeeper.

Arianna rested her elbow on her knee, her chin in her palm, watching the chaos unfold.

"None of this would be an issue if she—" Gregory threw a finger in her direction and with it reminded everyone else that she was still in the room "—had merely given us the schematics for the box from the beginning." Arianna wondered if his accusation was reason enough to kill him where he stood.

"How many times will you take that shot at me before you realize it's missing?" Arianna quipped.

Gregory's hand was at his gun. Let him fight her. She'd taken down Dragons twice his size and skill.

"Even if she had—" Willard started.

"Even if I had we would be in the same spot." Arianna spoke over the man who was well her senior in years and experience. But she had no remorse. She didn't want to be at the forefront, but if she was to be thrust there, then she would speak for herself. Gregory opened his mouth to speak, and she spoke over him as well. "If I had given you the schematics from the first day, it would have taken weeks to set up any kind of manufacturing to roll out on the scale we need. And that's ignoring the fact that a key component cannot even be found on our world. A problem that the Vicar Raven still has not solved."

The room had been effectively silenced, but Arianna didn't want to stop.

"This, this here, is the reason I have held the box for years. This is what I tried to caution you against." Arianna looked down on them all like the children they were. "From the first minute, it was all you focused on, to the neglect of other necessities." She gave a nod to Powell, who seemed surprised to be addressed directly. "The Philosopher's Box is powerful. I can't deny it. Likely more powerful than any of you realize. But the box is a *tool* that strengthens *people*. Loom can have all the power in the world, but if we are divided and squabbling, it will matter little as the Dragon King makes sport of our disorganization. Even a Perfect Chimera can be picked off with little issue by a trained Dragon. There has to be a system around making Perfect Chimera, training them to fight, giving them as many organs as possible. Systems we just don't have."

"She's right." Florence was finally on the same page, and the relief of it was like cool water on fiery flesh. "Here we are, proving her right. Vicar Willard, how long to set up some kind of manufacturing for the box?"

The vicar looked back to her, but Arianna stayed silent. If they wanted her input, they'd have to ask. "Well, Arianna said weeks, so I would estimate . . . two months? But only after we have the flowers. And only if we can use the remaining machinery in Ter.3."

"Vicar Dove, you have three weeks to figure out a secure way to get us flowers, and hopefully some stock."

"Three weeks?" the vicar balked at Florence. "I don't know—"

"I'm not asking you, I'm telling you." Florence silenced the vicar from further objection with a look that Arianna didn't know she could make.

"Vicar Gregory, are there *any* weapons left?" That was the moment Florence's voice softened and the whole atmosphere of the room with it. It would take some time before the mere mention of the Revolvers' Guild would not fill every man and woman on Loom with pangs of loss and sorrow.

"No. Not beyond what every Revolver carries on their person or had stashed in some alternative location." Even the vicar lost some of his anger in reporting the fact. "Not unless there were any in transit through the Ravens' routes?"

"It's possible. There'd be a record at the guild hall."

*A record.* Speaking of, she needed to get the copy of Louie's ledger to Florence.

"Good, we're all headed there anyway." Florence continued in the wake of everyone's surprise. "The king expects to find us here. He knows all of Loom has assembled. I have no doubt that when he comes back, he will do so with force, ready to attack the instant he finds us noncompliant."

"So, we move." Willard finally sat, a hand on his knees as he eased himself down.

"We take Loom underground."

"Underground?" Vicar Dove repeated. "Florence, you cannot possibly mean . . ."

"The Dragons are a threat to us as long as they can use their gliders. If they cannot do that, our bullets can reach them."

Arianna thought back to Leona's glider crashing into the entry to the Underground they had escaped into months ago. It was solid logic grounded in proof, even if no one else knew it.

"That's assuming the Dragons even know the entry point . . ." Vicar Dove murmured.

"The Ravens' Folly? You can't possibly expect us to go there." Willard wiped sweat from the back of his neck.

"I don't expect *you* to. You will go down to Ter.3 and begin to set up manufacturing for the box. It will be faster to use whatever remains at the Rivets' Guild than start from scratch. And we can use the existing train lines for transport. They should mostly be intact."

"Alchemists will be the first to go." Vicar Ethel turned away from the masters she had been whispering with. "Train us to implant the box, and we can complete the organs for each Chimera, should we have enough of a farm to harvest from."

"Can you harvest from Perfect Chimera?" Vicar Powell asked.

Arianna grimaced at the idea but answered anyway. "You can. My organs regrow as a Dragon's would."

"That's convenient." Vicars Ethel and Powell said at nearly the same time. Arianna was no longer going to allow herself to be in a room alone with either of them.

"Who are you to order us?" Vicar Gregory's tone had lost some bite, but the question was still pointed enough.

"Do you have a better idea?" Florence held out her hands, as if to receive some great insight from the vicar. "If so, I'd love to hear it."

Gregory looked to the other vicars and masters. None came to his defense. "It will be easier to fortify the Underground with less," Gregory finally murmured. "Even if we'll be fighting on two flanks. Don't know what I want to tangle with less . . . whatever could come from above, or below."

The other vicars voiced their agreement, each one deferring to Florence. Arianna leaned forward again, inspecting the woman who stood in the center of the room. There it was, that same aura she'd sensed before—the one that showed the shaking girl she'd pulled from the Underground was no more.

And if that role was no longer needed in Florence's life, what did that make them?

As if sensing her stare, and thoughts, Florence turned. They shared a long look full of questions that neither of them could answer.

"You will head to Ter.3 with Vicar Willard."

Arianna knew it was coming because it was logical, and because logic could be used more effectively than the sharpest dagger. She wanted to object, to tell Florence that under no circumstances was she going to let the girl out of her sight again. She had gone to the world above and fell back to Loom below just for Florence.

"Go home, and make sure you know whose side you're on." Florence turned her back to Arianna and focused on the vicars once more. "We begin now. There's no time to waste."

None spoke for her and none objected. Arianna didn't really expect them to. One of them saw her as a weapon foremost, another a traitor, and now two more saw her as their new harvesting experiment.

Arianna stood and excused herself without a word. She wondered if she was the only one who had just witnessed the true leader of the rebellion rise.

# 18

## COLETTA

The Gray Room was progressing nicely. Coletta ran her hand along the back shelf, where all manner of wicked-looking tools had been laid out in careful order. A knife was one of the most beautiful creations that had ever come from a forge. It could kill, it could save—it was both famine and feast. She picked up the item, inspecting it by the firelight of one of the two braziers.

"Will all this do?" she finally asked, turning to the man who stood next to Ulia.

"It should be enough, yes." The Fenthri, Thomas, blended in with the room around him—rock-colored and bland.

"What else will you need to conduct the surgery?"

The man brought his eyes upward from their respectful downward cast. He took one more long look at the shelf in quiet thought. "Nothing more comes to mind. But again, I've never done this before."

"So you repeat to the point of disgust." If she didn't desperately need this little man, she would do away with him on the spot. Coletta had only interacted with him a handful of times, but it was already too many.

"I want my queen to be aware that it is possible there will be failures before we see success," he said. Coletta could appreciate one thing about the Fenthri: Their logical minds didn't allow things like emotions to cloud their resolve, usually. Thomas didn't so much as blink when he said the word "failures," when what he really meant was "deaths."

"*You* will not see success," Coletta said softly. "Any success is mine."

"Forgive me for speaking out of turn, my queen." Gold glinted threateningly from around the man's neck, but the collar was tempered to Yveun, not her.

Nevertheless, Coletta could kill him in a second if she so desired. "I merely do not wish to disappoint you."

"Well, that is wise. You shall have some room for trial and error." Coletta set the knife down. She didn't want to give him that leeway, but even she could recognize it was unreasonable to expect otherwise.

The Alchemist Coletta had brought from Loom years ago was, indeed, deceased. Topann had done well, finding a suitable substitute. He was older, but his black hair was only sprinkled with salt, rather than completely white. Thomas was old enough, however, to be born before the segregation of guilds, and he had spent time in his early years studying with the intent to become an Alchemist. When that no longer interested him, he'd switched to the Rivets. Between his knowledge and the information Coletta could acquire through her contact on Loom, she had faith that their research would yield fruit. How hard could it really be to stitch up some organs in a Dragon? There was no need to worry about decay, and they had ample power to heal.

"When will we begin?"

Coletta eyed the man. The question was awfully bold, almost bold enough for her to give him a warning shot. But she permitted it because she believed it mere curiosity rather than an indication of the false notion he could schedule his own timetable of events.

"Soon." Coletta waved him and her flower away. "Ulia, take him to his room."

"My room?" Thomas repeated, looking between them.

"Yes, I have prepared a room for you." Coletta enjoyed the look of shock on his face.

"M-my own room?"

"Indeed. Ulia will show you there."

His mouth gaped open and he looked between them many times over, as if waiting for one of them to correct the statement and inform him that he wasn't getting his own quarters after all and it was back to the squalor he had known his whole life.

"Of course, my queen." Ulia bowed and escorted the man. Coletta's flower avoided touching him, for which Coletta didn't blame her.

The Fenthri were dirty, rotten creatures that smelled and looked of death. Plus, if he tried to run, any Dragon would be twice as fast and kill him three times more horribly than he could ever imagine. By working with them, he now had his own room away from the cramped quarters Nova's Fenthri were confined within. Any Dragon would look at his accommodations and think them barbaric, but after spending most of his life in the darkness of the Fen barracks, Coletta suspected Thomas would find them palatial.

With her business concluded, Coletta started back through the estate to her gardens. She looked out the windows as she passed them, her eyes scanning the skies for traces of rainbow. Yveun had left early that morning and now the sun was halfway through the sky with still no sign of him.

Coletta didn't want to think of the Fenthri as being able to slay her mate. But with numbers alone, they had him. One mistake, and that would be the end of it.

The garden was catharsis. Her flowers and their many concoctions kept her hands busy through the afternoon and into the evening, when the sun hung low and the sky began to fade into Lord Xin's hour of death. Coletta knew the moment the gliders approached, rainbows arcing through the air with a flash of brilliance.

She finished her careful slices of the plant bulb and wiped her hands on the appropriate rag—one of four set out. Her laboratory was such a dangerous place that even a gesture as small as this, done carelessly, could cause a reaction that might kill her. One of the many reasons why she had been so diligent over the years with poisoning herself and building her immunities.

Coletta tapped on a golden panel embedded in the wall that made up one side of her outdoor laboratory. Not so far away, a discharge point flashed; soon enough, Yeaan appeared on command.

"You summoned?" She gave a deep bow.

"Yes. The Dono has only just returned. Tell the chefs to stop preparing dinner for him. He will need his space before he is ready to eat. They should resume when all light has left the sky. It is possible he will insist he is not hungry. Should he do so, I would like for you to deliver the food personally and inform him it's at my request."

"Understood." Yeaan turned on her heel, quickly departing to execute Coletta's orders.

Yveun would no doubt go to his tiny claw-scratched room and pace for a while. He would act the child and refuse food, thinking this a reasonable way to avoid his failures. She would give him space, and a peace offering, to show that they still stood together, even if his effort to bring Loom neatly under their rule did not go as well as he'd planned.

Coletta continued to clean and tuck away her laboratory. Everything had its place, and everything stayed in pristine order. Success wasn't found in mayhem, but a strict maintenance of structure.

She looked up expectantly, her ears picking up the click of the door that led to Yveun's quarters and the main part of the Rok Estate. Sure enough, Topann appeared from around the corner. Coletta quickly assessed her from head to toe, her eyes falling on the small bound book in the woman's hands.

"Yveun?" she asked first.

"The Dono is well," Topann reported. "In a less-than-pleasurable mood. But there were no shots fired."

"And Loom?"

"He gave them three days to decide if they will agree to peace, or if it will be war, at which point he will wage his first attack."

Coletta sighed. Yveun was growing distracted by daydreams of fanfare and an arrival on Loom met with love, where they cherished him for all his contributions to their industrial world. He didn't just want to be the king in function; he wanted to be it in form as well. He wanted the same affection and devotion that he enjoyed on Nova, which, simply, he would never find from an oppressed people.

"Then it shall be war." She had no doubt.

Loom would fight until the only ones left of their abysmal race were chained in gold and kept in perfect servitude to Dragons who guided them with a firm hand. It's how it should have been done from the start, but there wasn't enough space on Nova for all the Fen. The best solution would be for the Dragons to colonize Loom and manage those that remained. But finding Dragons willing to live on Loom may be just as hard as squelching the spirit of rebellion.

Coletta let go of the thoughts, for now. That was all planning, which needed to occur later, when Loom was once more under their thumb. Now, she needed to remain focused on getting matters firmly in hand.

"Is that from our Fen King?" Coletta held out her hand for the journal.

"It is, but it's . . . odd." Topann's voice was hesitant, but she wasted no time imparting the journal to her queen. Coletta knew exactly what her flower meant from the moment she opened to a page at random. "The little man said it was Raven code. Can you read it?"

She couldn't. Coletta had many areas of expertise, but every manner of language from the Fen was not one of them. She snapped the ledger closed.

"What other information did you get from him?"

"The rebellion is being led by a child named Florence," Topann began. Coletta knew that Loom was in a dire state, but it must be truly on its final threads if they were appointing children as their leaders. "A very petulant girl. She brandished a weapon at the Dono himself."

"Did she?" If the name hadn't been imprinted on her mind previously, it was now. Coletta wanted the satisfaction of orchestrating the girl's ultimate demise herself.

"As I said, the Dono is fine. He did not step off his glider, so his corona protected him the whole time."

But the girl no doubt wanted him to. Knowing Yveun, the Fen's affront had made his kingly blood boil so hot that he was tempted to do so to wring her neck. She could not afford to let Yveun off Nova again, Coletta decided then.

"And Arianna?"

"She was there, but did little." Topann thought a moment. "I heard the Riders say she actually called off Florence."

"Interesting . . ." Perhaps the fall back to Loom had knocked the inventor down in more ways than one.

"The king says weapons are scarce since the Revolvers blew themselves up, but I'm not inclined to believe him."

Coletta wasn't either. *After all . . .* She opened the ledger again. Even if she couldn't understand it, the ledger was a record of where gold was being kept on Loom, moved from secret storehouse to storehouse. If Loom had squirreled away gold, Coletta was certain they'd done the same with weapons, and that meant Yveun should brace himself for a greater attack than anticipated.

"There was one more thing." Topann summoned Coletta's thoughts back from the ledger. "The Fen King was grateful for the organs you provided in exchange for the ledger. But he mentioned something new he would be negotiating for: Flowers of Agendi."

Coletta paused, closing the ledger and setting it aside. Her mind pegged the information as important instantly. It was oddly specific and necessary enough to risk the request. The flowers grew only on Nova, and Coletta didn't think it chance that the man who had only dealt in organs for years was suddenly asking for something new mere weeks after Arianna had returned from the sky world.

"Why these flowers?" They had no medicinal properties and no poisons—that she knew of. They weren't even especially beautiful. Some Dragons held that their pollen made their magic feel stronger. But surely that wouldn't be enough to help Chimeras stand against Dragons?

"He didn't say." Topann bowed her head. "Forgive me, my lady, the gliders were leaving and I had to be subtle."

"Rise, Topann." Coletta extended her hand and the woman scooped it up, kissing it firmly, no doubt grateful to still be in her queen's favor. "You have done well to acquire this information. Now we must act upon it."

Coletta looked out over the leafy foliage that surrounded her outdoor laboratory. "I have none of this particular flower. Head to the fields on the north side of the estate where they grow, and bring me ten."

"Ten, yes."

"Then, when you have done this, I need you and Yeaan to collect all offshoots of our great vine." Coletta herself was the "great vine" and every offshoot was where a tendril crept in the form of one of her flowers. "You will find everywhere this flower grows, and you will destroy them all."

"How would you like them destroyed?" Coletta appreciated so very much that such was the woman's only question.

"Uproot them, and take them to some remote place to burn. Do it with as much discretion as you can muster."

"Always, my queen."

"One more thing, Topann." Coletta thought aloud. "Have them bring wine to my chambers this night. No food. I trust you to pick a worthwhile vintage on my behalf."

"Understood."

"Go now, make it so."

By the time Coletta finished cleaning up her laboratory, the wine was waiting for her on a bronze platter in the central room of her quarters. None dared go beyond that point. For if they did, it was well whispered that they weren't long for service to House Rok—or the world.

Coletta picked up the glass, strolling into her study. The room was rectangular with towers of bookshelves filled with all manner of odd knowledge she'd acquired throughout the years. Some volumes were rare, some commonplace, and some would only be important to the authors whose hands had scribbled the words, believing they would never be read.

At the far end, past a chaise and table with a single chair, was a large desk that matched a second in Yveun's side of the estate. Coletta set the ledger down there, but kept wine in hand as she walked over to the wall of windows. Far beneath her, the God's Line was a swirling sea of gray, masking Loom and all its secrets.

She took a long sip, allowing the crimson nectar to sit on her tongue—one of the few things she could still taste. She debated if she would crack this Raven code, or learn all about the Flowers of Agendi first. Coletta turned back into the room with purpose, heading toward her books on plants and herbology. It didn't matter where she started; it would all be torn apart, secrets exposed, by the time she was done.

# 19
## FLORENCE

It seemed as though she had just managed to gather everyone together, only to see them scattered to the wind once more. At least everyone was moving as a unified force rather than blowing in, one rogue tumbleweed at a time.

Her goal for the Tribunal had been accomplished.

Even still, it was exhausting to take all of Loom—who had only just been transported en masse to Ter.0—and move them again. The Vicar Raven was no doubt no more annoyed than she let on about the great exodus, but if the woman was disgruntled, she did a good job of not betraying the fact.

"Are you really going to stay here?" Shannra asked.

"Only as long as it takes to clear Ter.0," Florence replied.

She was so very tired of cleaning out her laboratories, one after the other. But having done it multiple times in her life made it pretty short work. The experience equipped her to make simple decisions on what was most important to take with her, and what could be left behind, if needed. It was simple logic where everything went, and Florence knew it all by heart by now. Every canister, vial, gun part, and jar went in its place easily.

"I'll wait for you."

"No, you won't." Florence didn't know if it was Louie's influence on the girl, or if she genuinely wanted to stay. It was a question she was unexpectedly afraid of asking—or rather, she feared the answer. "I need you to help organize defenses at the Ravens' Guild."

"There are plenty of people who can help organize defenses. I want to protect you."

"There are not plenty of people, and in fact there are precious few Revos left.

Furthermore, I can protect myself. Despite the tattoo on my cheek, I am no Raven."

"I know that better than anyone, but it doesn't mean you couldn't use someone's help."

"The Dragons won't attack for three days. By that point I will be long on my way to Ter.4. I'll be nothing more than a speck on the map; no Dragon will find me and no Fenthri would attack me." Florence was fairly confident that at this point she had solidified her reputation as one of the deadliest people on all of Loom. How many others could challenge the Dragon King himself at gunpoint? Of course, that was a decision Florence had yet to fully unpack now that the initial fight-or-flight response had left her. Her hands had a tremble since the Vicar Tribunal.

"Florence, why won't you let me help you?" Shannra rounded the table. She rested a gentle hand on Florence's shoulder.

She moved away subtly from the offending touch, using the opportunity to stretch for a high jar and shake Shannra's hand free. But her distractions were growing limited, and soon she would be forced to focus on the other woman in the room.

"Do *you* want to help me? Or do you want to help me because Louie asked you to?" Well, there it was. The question was out and there was no taking it back.

"What kind of question is that?" Shannra almost seemed offended. She walked around the table to position herself between Florence and a narrow set of shelves she had been clearing. "Do you think I have been at your side this whole time because of Louie?"

Florence thought about it for a long moment. Was this woman nothing more than a pawn in the greater scheme? And if she was, why did it matter to Florence? "Have you not been?"

"Five Guilds! That's all you think of me, isn't it?" She seemed torn between laughter and anger. It was a combination that fit her. Light and dark. Happiness and sorrow. Anger and joy. Shannra was all of it wrapped into one.

"I don't know what to think of you," Florence answered honestly, at last looking her in the eye.

"Florence." The woman's whole demeanor changed. "Yes, Louie asked me to come here. I told you that from the beginning. I've never kept my affiliation with him a secret." Shannra shook her head. "And I have no doubt that he asked me specifically because he knew I could be of help to you, because he knew you would want to learn from me. But Louie has been here for weeks now, and I spend more time at your side than with him or any of his other . . . employees. It doesn't matter how I came to you; it matters what we do going forward."

She wanted to believe it was all true. Shannra's silver eyes shone brightly in the fading light of the day. Florence wanted to believe they hid no secrets, that there was nothing within them that could even be the seed of a lie. But she wasn't sure—couldn't be sure, maybe ever.

Still, arguing with the woman would do her no good. If her suspicions were founded, Shannra would never admit to them. If they were unfounded, she only risked alienating a friend. Was it better to risk having a false companion than having no companion at all?

"Even still." Florence sighed softly and let go of the argument. Her focus had to be on other places, her energy devoted to more important things than unpacking the true depths of her feelings for the silvery beauty. "You are far more useful to me getting a head start on fortifying the Ravens' Guild and the Underground than offering protection I won't use and don't actually need. I will not be long behind you; all of Ter.0 will be on the move in two days' time and I will be out with the last of them. All this is for only a day's difference."

It seemed like Shannra was going to put up one more fight, and Florence braced herself for whatever the argument may be. The truth was, neither of them owed the other anything.

"Do me one favor." Shannra paused and reached for Florence a second time. This time, she didn't move away. "Okay, *two* favors . . . One, don't store this powder on the edge of the box. Rattle it too much and it could go."

"Really? But I thought that was why we cut it with sulfur?"

"We did. We cut it enough to prevent it from being a danger when mixed with other chemicals for canisters. But the whole thing in a jar? It's a rather pointless risk." Shannra took the jar and nestled it between some of the others toward the center of the box. For good measure, she even wedged in some leftover rags around the various vessels.

"Okay, and this other favor?"

"Seek me out when you arrive at Ter.4?" Shannra gave a small, delicate smile.

If she was being honest with herself, Florence had planned to do so immediately anyway. "I think I can manage that."

"I'll take this ahead for you." Shannra started for the door with the box still in her arms, speaking over her shoulder, "Think of it as collateral, to make sure you come looking for me."

"Collateral? It looks a lot like theft." Florence leaned against the table.

"Well, as you so aptly pointed out, I *am* on Louie's payroll. Who really knows when I may decide to just up and steal something?" Shannra gave a small wink and left the room with a satisfied swing of her hips.

It was one odd relationship to the next.

The halls were washed in shadows, and every footstep she took toward Arianna's room was elongated by a quiet echo. All the chaos was happening downstairs, people uprooting themselves from what fragile peace they had managed to scrape together in a few days since everyone had amassed at Ter.0. But up here, there was only silence—silence and Florence's thoughts.

She wondered if she should feel guilty for how she had treated Arianna. Because she didn't.

Florence wanted answers. The uncertain world that surrounded her owed her nothing. She feared that if she did not take the chances that presented themselves, as they presented themselves, they would be forever lost. All of life's events, loaded into the chamber of a gun, and it all came down to having the courage to squeeze the trigger before the shot was lost. She would not lose this opportunity to speak with her mentor one more time. She would not be relegated to silence, like when Arianna had up and left for Nova, giving Florence no other choice but to swallow her curiosity and hope not to choke on it.

But Arianna was not in her room, leaving Florence to wander the tower in search of her wayward mentor.

As expected, Florence eventually found Arianna in the remnants of one of the Rivets' workshops. Unlike her own workshop, this one was filled to the brim, all manner of gears and tools lining the walls. The tang of metal was sharp on her nose, cut with the warmer scents of grease and oil.

Arianna looked up promptly when she arrived, her Dragon ears no doubt anticipating her arrival for some time now, which explained the lack of surprise on her mentor's face.

Florence leaned in the door frame, folded her arms over her chest, and waited. Arianna stared back, and neither said anything. Time stretched on and, as much as Florence didn't want to be the first one to speak, she wanted to waste her time a lot less.

"Ari, we should talk," she said with a sigh.

"Do you really think I am not loyal to Loom?"

Another sigh. "No. May I come in?"

Arianna motioned to the stool across from her and Florence accepted it. She didn't touch any of the various tools and parts scattered across the table, keeping her hands folded in her lap instead.

"Why did you tell me not to shoot?"

"You know the answer to that."

"I want to hear it," Florence demanded.

"There will be people, at times, you cannot demand answers from." Arianna was hesitant, but acquiesced to her demand anyway. "Because a shot would've done nothing against his corona."

"You don't think I know that? I was trying to coerce him off the glider. If I had, with that many guns on him, we could've taken him down and then . . ."

"Then what?" Arianna pressed when Florence's thought trailed off. "Then we would win? The war is ended before it begins? Freedom reigns on Loom and we celebrate?" Arianna put her gearbox down, which was open to reveal the guts within. "No, Flor. I told you about the Dragon houses when I first arrived. If you had killed the king, there is another who would inherit his throne. And if you killed her, there is another after that. And another, and another . . . All of Dragon society is based around the idea of someone always being in power. One man or one woman always being on top. It's a pyramid you can't topple."

The words were a bitter potion of truth and they turned Florence's thoughts sour. "Then what are we supposed to do? Roll over and accept them as our masters and oppressors?"

"We must work with them."

Florence's stomach churned at the idea, but she forced herself to think logically. She'd been rash since the moment she'd seen the king. Calmed now, she could see that it was Arianna's composure that had kept things from splintering too soon, that had given them time to organize and flee. Again, it came down to Arianna; she still had much to learn from the snow-haired woman.

"You mean Cvareh and his sister?"

Arianna nodded. "His family, the Xin, is fighting against the Dragon King as best they can. But like Loom, they aren't strong enough."

"Why?" Florence wasn't keen yet on the idea of allying with another faction getting crushed by the king. They needed strength.

"There are three Dragon families," Arianna began, and Florence settled into her stool, listening intently. Everything Arianna said sounded vaguely familiar, but Florence listened as though she was hearing for the first time. "Tam, Rok, and Xin. Rok has remained the leader for hundreds—thousands—of years. Tam seems to be in the middle, their mantra favoring balance over upset. So, as long as the Rok family doesn't do anything too heinous, they work to maintain the status quo and do little else."

Florence instantly knew she would not get along with a Tam Dragon. "And Xin?"

"Houses Xin and Rok seem to be constantly fighting over who will be on top. With Tam de facto in the middle, one of them is always in power with the other in the weakest position on Nova."

"The weakest position? Poor things," Florence remarked sarcastically.

"None of them really see us as anything worth fighting over," Arianna admitted.

"So why would we ally with them?" Cvareh had seemed good enough, but if his family didn't see the value in Loom, then she would no longer see the value in him . . . even if it was his blood in her veins.

"Because they *don't* care about us. Cvareh's sister, and the leader of House Xin, only cares about ruling over Nova. If we help her get to that point—"

"Then she'll let Loom be free?"

"Killing the Dragon King means nothing. It's like severing a Dragon's hand. It *will* grow back time and time again. Not only must we sever the hand, but we must replace it with something that suits us better. Only then will Loom be truly free."

Florence let the information soak in. She took off her top hat, brushed off dust that had settled on the brim while she was cleaning out her laboratory, and returned it to her head. "If everything you say is true . . . we must work with House Xin."

Arianna was quiet, prompting Florence's attention. The woman had that same faraway look.

"Ari, what happened up there? The Dragon King knew you by name." She tried to be gentle, but it was a topic as sharp as a scalpel. "Why?"

Still, Ari was silent.

"How did you crash-land with a glider in Dortam?" Florence pushed a little harder.

Nothing.

"Arianna, please, I need to know." *Why?* Why did she need to know so badly? Why did it keep her up at night and draw her patience thin to think Arianna was keeping yet another secret?

"Yveun captured me. I escaped on a glider. I crashed."

It was the most unsatisfying explanation ever. "Yveun, the Dragon King, captured you?"

Arianna picked up her gearbox again. Florence was on her feet, reaching across the table to put her hand between Arianna's tool and the box. The woman brought her violet eyes to Florence's.

"Why didn't you fight?"

"You don't think I did?" Arianna scowled. "You don't think that, succession be damned, I wouldn't have killed him if given the chance?"

"What did he do to you?" she whispered.

"He made me weak." Arianna cursed, throwing down her tool. It was a fit of passion Florence had never seen from the usually reserved woman. "He made me feel weak, and vulnerable, and helpless. *Again.* Again, I could not stand against him or his agents to defend what and who I love." Arianna looked back to Florence; for the first time ever, her eyes beseeched her student for answers. Answers that no one had. "I am loyal to Loom and our fight with every breath I have. I am loyal to *you,* Flor. But no matter how hard I try, I cannot kill him. If I face him again, I will fall. I fear I will take Loom down with me."

Florence felt a dull ache of sympathy for the woman who clearly harbored so much pain and self-loathing. Slowly, as though she was trying not to startle a wounded animal, Florence stood. She rounded the table and reached to clasp one of Arianna's tall shoulders. Under her fingers, she knew there was a tattoo, a mark signifying the day they'd met, and a bond that would exist no matter what paths they traveled.

"You do not have to strike him down, Arianna. Go to Ter.3. Go home and realize that your strength has not left you. And when you see the truth of that, as I do, give me the greatest canister this world has ever known. Give me the Perfect Chimera, and I will hone it as a weapon to deal the final blow."

Arianna's hand clasped Florence's opposite shoulder.

"And give me House Xin to see that this chain of succession the Dragons so value puts someone we want on their throne," Florence continued. How could Arianna think she needed to have the strength to vanquish their foe when she was already the lynchpin holding the entire fate of Loom in place? The woman who wanted nothing more than to sit locked away in a workshop had saved them time and again. "Load the gun, Arianna, and then rest. I'll pull the trigger."

Florence saw hesitation in the woman's eyes, or maybe it was nostalgia. But it hardened like molten steel into a resolve that would hopefully last long enough for them to abolish the scourge of Dragons that plagued Loom once and for all.

"I will, Flor. I will do this one final act of rebellion, for you."

Florence knew the most important thing was that Arianna had agreed to do what they needed. Which made it all the more confusing that her heart clenched at the notion she was doing it all for her alone.

# 20

## ARIANNA

ARIANNA LEANED BACK AGAINST THE UPPER DECK WINDOWS ON LOUIE'S AIRSHIP. Checking the magic discharge was unnecessary now, but it gave her an excuse to be away from everyone. Up here, there was nothing more than a gray sky, the wind, and the earth slowly changing below.

The last time Arianna had traveled this route, it had been by train. She had sat next to Master Oliver, pressed up against the window of the train car, watching Loom unfold before her in a way it never had before. She had pressed forward, hungry for the vast unknown the world seemed to offer.

But this time was different. This time she watched the spiraling trails of magic fade away into the dusky morning over the back of the airship. The world wasn't unfolding before her but collapsing in her wake; it slipped away like a ribbon running wild, and the spool was nearly out.

She knew her body had changed from becoming a Perfect Chimera at such a young age. It was obvious before any others had pointed it out. She could run faster, endure more injuries; her bones were thicker and her height dwarfed most Fenthri. After being on Nova, she knew she was built more like a Dragon than one of her own gray-skinned race.

Arianna looked at the line that ran around her wrist where the soft blue skin of her hands met her natural, steel-colored flesh. These hands had tried to dismantle her world. She would use those same hands to be that man's downfall —to annihilate all who sought to oppress Loom.

The door to the deck opened.

"Am I taking your spot?" Will asked, from where he hovered on the threshold.

"Yes." Arianna turned her eyes forward, pointedly ignoring the child.

"Sorry about that." He clearly wasn't sorry, and sat down next to her. Will drew his heavy coat tighter around him, pulling up the collar to shield his face from the wind that whipped around them. "How are you not freezing to death out here?"

"If it's too cold for you, perhaps you should return indoors?"

"I just may."

*Victory*, Arianna thought.

"I'll wait just long enough to lose him." Will peered over the window ledge and looking into the upper deckhouse before ducking down again.

"Okay, I'll bite." Wasn't as if she had anything else to do. "Lose who?"

"Vicar Willard. The old man just won't shut up about how to make the engine run more efficiently."

Arianna laughed. "Oh, to be young and stupid—"

"Hey!"

"—and not capitalize on the opportunity to learn from a vicar." Arianna adjusted her goggles. Granted, she had some mixed feelings about Vicar Willard, but she was allowed—they had history.

"At first I did." Will was instantly defensive. "But he corrected *everything*."

"That's because everything in this rig is wrong."

"No, it's not. It runs just fine, thank you," the boy insisted.

"It could be better and you know it." He made it too easy for her to push right on his soft spots. "You've been away from the Ravens' Guild proper for a while. Getting sloppy, Will."

"Sloppy? You're one to talk." Will breathed on his hands, looking out at the magic discharge. "Thought you were supposed to be some great White Wraith, master thief, super sneaky."

Arianna arched her eyebrows, not even dignifying him with a response.

"I overheard you and Florence. I know what you gave her."

"I don't know what you're talking about." Arianna looked him in the eye, challenging him to call her on her bluff.

To her frustration, he did. "Sure. Well, then I heard *some other* Arianna through a crack in a wall talking to *some other* Florence about *some other* copy of a ledger she made of something she stole in Ter.3 before leaving the five-tiered hall."

"You were sent to spy on me?" Arianna mentally cursed herself for not inspecting more carefully the rooms surrounding her laboratory.

"Louie likes to know what's going on."

"That he does," she agreed, training her expression to be void of emotion. "Too bad any reports he gets would be from a bored Raven with an overactive imagination."

"Be careful, Ari. I wasn't the first and won't be the last."

"The irony of you telling me that." She'd been in dangerous situations longer than he'd been alive.

"Fine, ignore me." Will shrugged. "Just saying that if it had been anyone else in Louie's crew, you would've been outed."

"*Anyone* else? Including Helen?" Arianna wondered if she was hearing between his words correctly.

"Helen has her eyes on inheriting all of Louie's operations. She'll do anything to suck up to him." Will had the tone of a friend who'd been chapped by some rather cold treatment.

"Why are you telling me this?" Helen and Will were a matched set. In no world could she imagine Will doing anything that would separate them.

"Because when she *does* inherit Louie's kingdom, we'll need a champion. I hear he has a pretty good one he's been working with. Don't want to see Helen burn any bridges we may need to drive over."

Arianna snorted with laughter at the idea of taking orders from either of the children. But still, fair was fair. The warning he gave her was valuable, almost adult-like, and she appreciated it. "Play your cards right, and maybe you'll be so lucky. If you can pay."

"The business is pretty lucrative." Will glanced through the window into the deck cabin.

"Have you heard anything else?" Arianna asked when they both confirmed no one was observing their clandestine meeting.

"Anything else?"

She didn't know if he was being coy, or just stupid. "Why did Louie want the ledger in the first place?"

Will's mouth turned into a frown. "I don't really know. But I know he speaks to someone on Nova with the red-eared one, Adam."

*Red ears*. Arianna's instincts went off again as they had the first time, apprehensive at anything that resembled Rok.

"Do you know who?"

"That's all I know . . . for now."

"For now?"

"Like I said, I want to work with you." Will shrugged again. Arianna didn't know what she'd done to endear herself to the boy, but she wasn't going to challenge it. The fact that he hadn't gone to Louie—or at least claimed he hadn't —was good faith enough. "Except, can we please do this in the future where it's not freezing? I think I'll brave the vicar and his corrections over losing my fingers."

"It's not that cold."

"Ari, my fingers are turning blue."

Before she could even comment on where, when, why, or how he thought it was acceptable to refer to her as "Ari," Will had pulled open the heavy door to the top-deck cabin and disappeared within. She looked back down at her own hands and realized she wouldn't be able to tell if her fingers turned blue.

Even out of his element, Louie could still be a problem . . . She needed to tread carefully and learn what game he was really playing.

It was, in total, a two-day ride from Ter.0 to Ter.3, thanks to Arianna's contributions with magic, Will and Willard working together on improving the engine, and Helen's keen insights on charting their course.

Thick palm fronds branched out overtop each other. Stronger trees that preferred dryer climates quickly disappeared as the land became more marshy and wet. The bogs in the forests to the south of Garre held dark waters, caged by tree roots.

Garre itself was known as the clockwork city.

Tethered by her cabling and winch box to the heavy door behind her, Arianna crouched atop the cabin roof for the best vantage the airship could offer. She dug her knees and fingers into the metal grooves for stability, but the wind threatened to rip her away. The city of her childhood grew from a speck in the distance to the towering mechanical marvel that rivaled any in the world.

The capital of the Rivets was entirely the guild hall. There were no other elements to the city itself; there were no visitors without specific business for the Rivets.

Even late in the year, humidity crept beneath her coat and made her hair cling to her neck. It was an omnipresent citizen of Garre, rising up from the marshes under the city's stilts. A mechanical haven built atop water, destined to fight an endless war against rust and corrosion. It was the worst place possible for the Rivets to have attempted to build, and it was all the more perfect for the fact.

The airship banked and began its descent.

Closer up, the movements of the guild could be seen. Slowly rotating upper walkways ticked around cores like odd-faced clocks, counting down to something unknown. Steam billowed in jets, piped from the depths of the all-metal guild hall. Giant gears showed their teeth proudly on the outside of walls, perpetually churning against equally sized counterparts within.

Arianna had never seen her guild from the air before, and it was quite the sight. There was an undeniably breathtaking quality to its spectrum of metallic colors and carefully constructed pathways and structures that formed one tight, singular city. A city that changed before her own eyes on their descent, as walkways moved with the groaning of gears and various windows and doorways opened and closed.

It was also a vantage by which she could clearly see the remnants of the Dragons' attack—wounds that could not be healed with the limited hands available. An entire wing seemed to have been hit hard, the metal jagged and oddly bent, pulled apart by blasts that Arianna could still imagine the echoes of.

The whole of Garre was spotted with such damages, but it persisted.

The airship looped three times before finally finding a landing that would fit their wingspan. As soon as they touched down, Arianna leapt from the roof, tumbling into the metal below with a clang. She sprinted for the doorway into the guild.

*Locked.*

This was not like the usual locks she faced. She was back in the Rivets' Guild. Here, everything was designed as a challenge—a mental puzzle where success often hung opposite bodily harm. Right now, she suspected that harm took the form of a collapsing platform beneath their feet if she couldn't open the door in time.

Arianna ran her fingers along the lock. There were a series of pictures and numerals on its spinners. She could either solve the puzzle, or break her way in. The Arianna of the past would have delighted in the former . . .

But she was too old for games.

Arianna unclipped and unrolled a bag of tools from her belt, quickly selecting a narrow, flat-headed screwdriver. Fortunately for her . . . the designer of this particular lock expected her to revel in solving the puzzle, not dismantling the thing entirely. Its seams were well exposed and screws easy to access. Arianna had the box apart in a mere minute, manually unlatching the heavy curved bolt that affixed the lock to the door.

The room within crackled with electricity. Arianna could hear it humming in the wires that draped from the ceiling like moss off swamp trees. She flipped a switch next to her, funneling that energy into a bulb in the center of the room. Arianna blinked at the light. The last time she had been at the guild, electricity was new and only in a few areas.

She looked around the room, finding a series of levers on one of the side walls, nestled between two bookcases.

"Lock, raise, release . . ." She read the labels scribbled on each of the handles. Arianna tugged on the one labeled *lock*. The release lever raised slightly in reply, a soft click engaging it in place.

"You're much faster than I," a weathered voice spoke from the doorway.

"I should be." Arianna turned to face Willard, rolling up her tools. "You have a good fifteen years on me, old man."

"You're back in the hall; you'd think you'd show a little more respect to your vicar."

"Just honoring what would've been the wishes of my Master." Arianna couldn't fight a small smile at the idea of being back in the Rivets' Guild, but her face fell at the thought of Master Oliver. He had never been able to return.

"Your work alone honors him."

Arianna didn't have a chance to comment one way or another, for the door to the inside of the hall opened, revealing a man with a filled bolt and wrench tattoo on his cheek. The journeyman crossed his forearms in an X—a gesture of respect within the guild, for the vicar. Willard promptly settled them in what would become their new quarters.

"Should they require anything, see that they receive it, within reason,"

Willard said after Louie and his crew had been closed away behind the doors of their new rooms. Arianna appreciated the vicar's foresight to add the final caveat. "And go tell Charles to meet me in my office in one hour."

"Understood, Vicar." The journeyman departed promptly.

"This way, Arianna." Willard motioned for her to follow him.

She ran her fingertips along the metal walls that encased her. They pulsed with the omnipresent movement of the hall itself. Behind every wall there were gears churning, shifting, pushing something into a new design. Every panel could be removed and tinkered with, and every Rivet was encouraged to leave their mark by doing so.

"What is it?" Willard paused, noticing her palm flat against the wall.

"It's unlike Holx," she observed. "The Ravens' Guild was so quiet from everyone being gone . . . How many people are still here?"

"I believe about fifty journeymen stayed behind, and I left one Master, Master Charles, to oversee them."

*And in case something happened to you*, Arianna finished mentally. "Nearly empty, and the guild still moves, still lives."

Vicar Willard outstretched his gnarled and age-spotted hand, placing it next to hers. "And it will continue to tick, long after we all are dead."

That much was true.

As they continued, the paths became more and more familiar. It was like an old toolkit, where every wrench and screwdriver was remembered the moment it was seen once more. Ghosts were their only company in the empty halls.

"Wait, Willard, my room is that way." Arianna pointed down a hall at one of the forks.

"Your room has long since been given away." Willard progressed forward, and Arianna did the same, ignoring the stab of pain she felt at his words. She knew there hadn't been a home for her to come back to for some time, but to hear it articulated so clearly wasn't easy. "And even if it hadn't been, you no longer belong in that wing."

Instead, Willard led her into a great hall. Square skylights dotted the ceiling, letting in natural light to blend with the electric sconces that dotted every column of the main stretch. Between the columns, down the center of the room, were sturdy wing-backed chairs, high tables—impromptu meeting areas and spaces to sit and think. On the perimeter, between the columns and the outer walls, doorways adorned with nameplates lined the room.

Arianna adjusted her harness, which suddenly felt too tight and tightening with every step.

The Vicar Rivet led her back to the far corner. Her feet weaved her among the couches and chairs, familiar with the path rutted into the plush carpeting. This was the hall of masters, a place she had visited frequently to consult with a man whose door she now faced.

"You kept it?" Her voice was stunted, and she couldn't quite figure out why.

Her eyes fixated on the plaque that read *Master Oliver*.

"In a way."

"Oddly sentimental for a bunch of Rivets." Arianna buried her hands into her pockets and told herself that Oliver's untouched old quarters meant nothing.

"Sentimentality only had little to do with it." Willard tapped one of the two door locks.

Every master's door had its own lock fused with the metal door. But Oliver had conceived a second addition that he welded into the doorframe himself. It was the most complicated lock Arianna had ever had the privilege of seeing crafted, with multiple tumblers and no clear seams or screws.

"You can't open it." She grinned knowingly. "Why not break the door down?"

"Perhaps that was the sentimentality—violating a master's workshop like that. But now . . ."

"You want me to open it?" Arianna arched her eyebrows.

"Well, of course. You know the combination, don't you?"

"I do." Arianna thought briefly about concealing the fact, but she'd have much more fun watching Willard squirm as he pined for access into the physical manifestation of his rival's mind.

A long moment stretched on. "Well . . .?"

"I'll have to think if I want to open it or not."

"This is going to be your chambers, now." He stopped her with a sentence as she turned away. "Everything within is yours."

The words buzzed between her ears louder than the electricity that hummed throughout the guild. "It's not mine to have," she whispered without facing the vicar.

"It is." Willard patted her shoulder, passing by her and heading for the exit.

"He did not give it to me." She wasn't good enough for it. Arianna knew she was ten times more brilliant than most other Rivets and she was still only half as smart as Oliver was.

"I think, in his way, he did."

"Don't you want to see what's inside?" she called across the room.

"Oh, more than anything." The old man stopped. "I've wondered what things Oliver was working on behind that door for years; I've fantasized over his brilliance. But he imparted his master status to you. He gave you the key to that door. He gave you his tutelage. Whatever is in there is meant for you, not me." The conversation shifted before Arianna could formulate a reply. "In an hour I will meet with Master Charles to discuss outfitting a line for your boxes. I'll need you in attendance. I trust you still remember the way to the vicar's quarters."

She remembered it well, as if she hadn't left the guild at all. "I do."

"I will see you then." Willard nodded and departed, leaving Arianna alone with what suddenly felt like the most important decision she would ever make.

# 21

## COLETTA

Coletta was an excellent judge of other's pain.

She had seen men and women die in combat countless times. She had seen Yveun inflict agony with the grace of a dancer. She had watched hordes of nameless, worthless test subjects die under the influence of her experimental poisons.

So, she knew, from the moment she walked into the Gray Room, that Yeaan was not faring well.

"He has poisoned me." Yeaan pointed a long finger in the direction of a cowering Fen. "He has cut me open and he has poisoned me."

"I highly doubt he would be the one poisoning you." Coletta couldn't resist the bit of levity. Who could blame her? The agony of others put her in such a good mood.

"I did not poison her," the Fen insisted.

"Then why is she in such pain?" Coletta approached Yeaan. The woman was nearly doubled over, clutching her stomach.

"I-I don't quite know."

Coletta ignored the incompetence and pulled Yeaan's hands from where they clutched her gut. Sure enough, there was a long, angry line down her abdomen. The red skin was oozing gold, a pale, almost puss-like color from where the skin was visibly rippling with not quite right magic—the body not quite able to mend itself.

"Why isn't it healing?"

"I don't know that either."

"What do you know?" Coletta asked quietly, letting her whispering tones express every ounce of discontent she felt.

"I tried to implant a stomach, as you asked. I used the organs you provided me." He eased some as he spoke. "I implanted them, clumsily perhaps. But I did everything right. It's fairly straightforward actually. And unlike a Fenthri, I didn't have to adjust other organs' positioning to make the size fit . . ."

Coletta frowned at the incision. "Take it out of her."

"My queen, if I do, she will have to regrow her own."

"I would rather that than this agony." Yeaan bared her teeth in a snarl.

"Do it. She's useless to me like this." Coletta cupped Yeaan's cheek gently—comfort amid pain. *Cling to me*, she wanted the touch to say, *let me be your rock in this storm*. For the more her flowers saw her as their foundation, the less likely they would stray. "I will find you better organs next time, from among the sun. I will not try to force lesser scraps of meat from underneath the island into you."

"Thank you, Coletta'Ryu, thank you." The woman took Coletta's hand from her cheek, bringing it to her mouth, kissing it gently.

"Stay strong for me, my flower." Coletta turned to the Fen. "See that she is stronger than before."

"I—"

"No excuses," Coletta snapped, punctuating the demand with a forceful slam of the door. Her day was filled with flowers. The wilting one that needed attendance had consumed her morning and now she returned to her garden, full of life in many forms. Topann patiently waited by her laboratory, hands folded and back straight, poised.

"How is your progress with the Flowers of Agendi?" Coletta asked, headed right for her work table. There was no time for pleasantries.

"We have almost finished burning all of Lysip," Topann reported. "We shall move to Gwaeru to look for any next."

Coletta paused at the mention of the island where House Tam made its home. "See it done with the utmost caution." If they played their cards right, it shouldn't matter if the flowers of Agendi were on that island or not.

"I will."

"That's not all I need you to see, Topann. I require your attentions elsewhere."

"My queen?" She stood when Coletta motioned for her to approach.

"I have taken the time to translate this ledger for your benefit." She placed the book Louie had acquired on the table between them. "Head to Loom with the Riders Yveun is sending to suss out the location of this resistance, and bring gold back with you."

"How much?"

"All of it."

"All of it?" Topann repeated, surprised.

"We require it." Coletta tapped the table in thought. The last missive from House Tam had not gone well. They were growing impatient, and the refineries on Nova were a grand idea by Yveun but an utter failure in practice. They didn't possess enough resources or manpower to make them effective.

"Then I shall bring as much as I can."

"Leverage the Riders and anyone else you see fit."

"Should this be my priority? Above the flowers?" It was a fair question.

"Yes. I'll see that Yeaan assists with them."

"Very well. I shall begin my preparations with haste." When Coletta said nothing more, Topann gave a bow and departed.

# 22

# FLORENCE

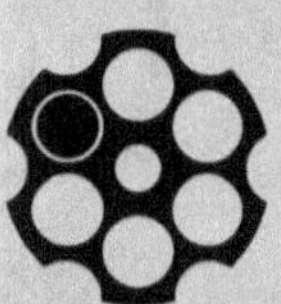


couldn't escape no matter how hard she tried or how far she ran. The force of it
was too much; she kept being drawn back in.

The oppressive blackness and heavy feeling of stone all around her were now
almost like familiar friends. That may have been too strong of a word, but at the
very least, the Underground had become a familiar acquaintance that Florence
was required to interact with by some unspoken law.

Returning this time felt different. This time, the Underground was filled to
the brim with life and noise.

Activity echoed through the caverns, filling every available space and
making the unseen terrors lurking in the shadows slightly less terrifying. Those
terrors were the first thing Florence had asked after when she had arrived at
Ter.4—had there been any Wretch attacks? She had been surprised to hear that
the answer was no. Usually, the Wretches used sound to track easy prey.

The Fenthri that now occupied the tunnels and pathways of the Underground
were anything but. They were armed to the teeth and settling in better than
Florence could have expected. If anything, she wondered if the Wretches were
afraid of *them*. After all, she reasoned, the influx of Fenthri might sound to a
Wretch like one giant beast. If they could be fearsome to Wretches, then perhaps all
of them together might add up to something strong enough to slay Dragons, too.

Florence started up the sloping walkway. The new inhabitants of the
Underground had made fairly quick work of setting up the rocky tunnels and
antechambers as home. Most of the main tunnels had been outfitted with a
patchwork of illumination—from glovis eyes to bioluminescence.

She had been given a lantern that now guided her through the dark tunnel. Those building out the infrastructure—no doubt Rivets—hadn't made it to this corner of the Underground yet. Florence suspected it would take some time, if they ever reached this far at all.

The eerie glow of another lantern winked into existence from the darkness before her. It grew into the shape of a man with a Revolver tattoo on his cheek. He nodded and continued onward; it was the only assurance Florence had that she was headed in the right direction.

After what seemed like forever but was likely only about three minutes—darkness distorted time in weird ways—the tunnel opened into a large cavern. The ceiling was obscured by blackness that clung to it like heavy clouds, but Florence was struck by a sensation of spaciousness above her—a rare commodity in the Underground. In the center of the room there was a giant metal basket, within which countless glowing orbs rested. Florence tried to make sense of what the basket contained—not glovis eyes, nor typical bioluminescence. Whatever it was gave off enough light to bathe most of the cavern in a pale, bluish-green glow.

Light and shadow carved out silhouettes of people hunched over faintly glinting gun parts. Some lay out on bed rolls, perhaps sleeping, or just wiling away the boredom that accompanied waiting for an attack from above or below. A few took notice of her, but none seemed to recognize her. If they did, they didn't seem to care.

Florence progressed through the room, looking for someone familiar. A few of the faces she recognized, though none by name. In that moment, Florence made the decision to move in with the rest of the Revolver journeymen, rather than the more comfortable accommodations above she'd been offered by the vicars. While it was true that her status was unofficial, the Vicar Revolver had called her one of the guild. Even if he'd only done so to manipulate Arianna, she'd twist it to her advantage.

In the far corner, separate from everyone else, torchlight painted a head of white hair a soft blue color. Shannra had set out her own lantern, hunching over it to work on her weapons.

"I'm sorry I'm late for today's lesson." The other woman jolted as if she'd received a physical shock. Her head whipped around and she looked up at Florence. "Careful you don't break your neck."

"Or have a heart attack. Neither are implausible when one sees a ghost." Shannra's mouth cracked into a smile. The woman with the moonlit hair stood, embracing Florence without hesitation. "I was worried about you."

"I told you: You have nothing to worry about." It was awkward to leave her arms by her sides, so Florence wrapped them around Shannra's waist.

"So it would seem," Shannra admitted. "How was the journey here? No issues?"

"No, no issues." It was easy to get lost in the concern so evident in the other woman's eyes—a mix of both elation and relief.

"I have something I need to ask you."

"It sounds important." Shannra sat, motioning for Florence to join her.

"I would like you to tell me if it is." Florence debated where to start. In her satchel, she carried a notebook—one Arianna had meticulously transcribed for her. It was the copy of a ledger Louie had her steal from Holx, a ledger containing information on gold storage across Loom. Florence thought about going directly to the Dove with the information, and she still might. But she first wanted to see if Shannra knew anything about the matter. "How much do you know about Louie's . . . operations?"

"This again?" Shannra's mouth fell into a frown. "Is it too much to ask if you will ever be capable of putting aside my affiliation with Louie?"

"For now, yes," Florence answered honestly. "But how much you help me can only quicken that process."

Shannra sighed. "Very well. What is it?"

"Louie wanted something stolen in Holx, and I want to know why."

"Louie steals lots of things. I can't claim to know the reasoning behind every one." Shannra ran a hand through her wild white hair. "Maybe if you're more specific . . .?"

"He took the most current ledger from the Ravens' Guild that contains information about all the gold storage locations across Loom." Florence studied Shannra's face. Her surprise seemed genuine. "Do you know why he would want this information?"

"For Louie . . . it doesn't seem abnormal for him to go after gold." Shannra shrugged. "I have no doubt that he saw an opportunity and capitalized on it."

The same idea had crossed Florence's mind. While she wanted to believe that Louie would not use the current situation to his advantage if doing so would be detrimental to Loom, she had all evidence to prove otherwise. Still, the request sat uneasy with her. Louie had always been obsessed with organs and magic; he had never once shown much of an interest in gold. Reagents, surely, but never gold.

"Very well. But I will still bring this to the attention of the Vicar Raven."

Shannra sighed. "Do you really want to risk alienating Louie? After all, the Vicar Raven herself knew who she was getting into bed with. She went to him personally to ask him to acquire organs and these magic flowers Arianna seems to need."

"Arianna can take care of herself. And unlike Louie, I believe her when she says she's on our side."

"Very well." Shannra waved away the unappealing notion. "It's not my business anyway."

"Are you still in touch with one of Louie's men through whisper?"

Shannra merely shrugged. The lack of answer was the distance between them embodied.

"I'll take that as a yes." She didn't know what she expected from Shannra, but apparently, she harbored more optimism than she cared to admit.

"One more thing," Florence said as she stood. She needed to go somewhere else to cool down. "By the time you report to Louie, I will have already informed the vicar of his actions against her guild. So, you may want to use whatever means of communication you have at your disposal to let him know. That way, you can try to remain in his good standing."

"It's not like that, you know," she muttered. "I'm not constantly looking for an opportunity to betray you to him."

Florence arched her eyebrows.

"I'm not," the other woman insisted.

"Why does he have your loyalty at all? Why are you involved with him?" Not that it mattered. Whatever her reasons, the fact remained that Shannra was one of Louie's. And that meant Florence should stay well away.

"You wouldn't understand."

"Try me," Florence pressed.

"I was frustrated with the limitations the Revolvers' Guild put on their students." Her voice had dropped to a whisper. "I had all these ideas for projects, but none of them would get approved. They were all deemed too radical, too dangerous."

"So, you found someone who would fund your ideas."

It wasn't a question but Shannra nodded anyway. "By the time I fully realized how he was using my work, it was too late."

"He had enough information on you to get you thrown out of the guild." Under Dragon law, being exiled from your guild meant death. Florence finished the story in her mind, a simple, cautionary tale central to the Revolvers' Guild itself: just because one could, didn't mean one should.

"It doesn't really matter now. The vicar knows of my involvement with Louie because of all this. I suspect the only reason he hasn't kicked me out yet is because Loom is so short on manpower. Especially the Revolvers."

"So why stay with Louie then?" Florence crouched down again so that way she could speak in the quietest voice possible. "He doesn't have anything on you anymore. And even if you do get kicked out, the guilds are reverting back to what they were before the Dragons. There are no more death sentences. There's nothing keeping you to a single guild or location."

"Yes, that may be true. But if I'm kicked out, I have nowhere else to go." Shannra picked up her gun parts, slowly assembling her weapon once more. "And if that's the case, I would rather stay in the company of someone who will actually appreciate my work."

Florence had always thought of Louie's lackeys as greedy bottom-feeders, hungry for the payout that his jobs brought. Or people with such wretched histories that they had no other option than to associate themselves with the gremlin of a man.

But Shannra's story was relatively benign; if anything, it made her association with Louie borderline normal. For a moment, Florence wondered if, under a different set of circumstances, she would've ended up in Louie's service, too.

For all that she'd thought those on Louie's payroll were loyal because of the money, she realized now it was because he offered something far more valuable: a place for wayward souls to call home.

"I appreciate your work." Florence grabbed Shannra's hand. "And many others will, too."

Shannra stared at the initiated contact and gave a small laugh. "You have no idea how good it feels to hear someone say that."

Florence did. In that moment, she was veca away from the dark cavern and back in her and Ari's flat in Old Dortam. She heard Arianna's first praise of her work keenly, felt her chest swell with phantom pride.

"I do, actually," Florence whispered.

"It feels good to hear *you* say that." Shannra turned her head, their noses almost touching. "I want to always be there to appreciate your work, Florence."

*It's not your appreciation I want*, Florence realized suddenly.

She was shaken to her core by the revelation, but in the same instant, so was Loom's fragile reprieve. Gunshots echoed from some faraway location.

Florence was on her feet, ready. The Dragons had made their first attack.

# 23

## ARIANNA

SHE HAD AN HOUR ALL TO HERSELF.

There was no one around her, nowhere to be, no one to interrupt her. Arianna laid out on one of the couches, worn to the perfect softness by countless hours of occupation over the years. She closed her eyes and breathed deeply.

The smell of leather, the size and shape of the furniture, vaguely reminded her of what she had procured for her and Florence's home in Old Dortam. She'd chosen those beaten-up sofas more carefully than she'd ever admit. The hours they'd spent on them, discussing, debating, reading quietly.

Arianna opened her eyes, returning to the here and now. *Here* was the masters' wing of the Rivets' Guild. *Now* saw Florence no longer a girl, nor a wayward student in need of an educational guide and protector.

Sitting, Arianna looked back to the corner where she could still read Master Oliver's name clearly on the door. He, too, had taken in a girl curious about the world and educated her. But Arianna hadn't been ready to give up his tutelage; she would still accept it now if she could.

After the events on Ter.0, she had little doubt Florence did not quite feel the same.

A door down the hall opened unexpectedly. Arianna's feet were on the floor, a hand on her dagger hilt, before the echo of squealing hinges faded from her ears. She coaxed her hand to relax, reminding herself that she was once more around friends and allies.

After spending so much of her life in secret, it was an odd feeling.

"Oh, hello . . ." The coal-skinned man seemed as startled to see her as she was to see him.

"Hello, Master Charles." The name plaque on the door confirmed her suspicion. But it was an easy deduction; Willard had said there was only one other master in the guild presently.

"And you are . . .?" His body was still tense. His light gray eyes scanned her face, no doubt making note of her lack of guild mark.

"Arianna."

"Arianna . . ." he repeated, bringing his fingers to hook his chin in thought.

"Master Arianna." The title was odd on her tongue, unfamiliar. "I was Oliver's pupil."

"Oh . . . *Oh*." Comprehension lit up the man's eyes and he crossed the room to her. His hair was cut short, and shone like an oil slick in the light. "I've heard about you."

"Whatever you've heard, I'm sure it's greatly exaggerated." Arianna leaned back into the sofa.

"It is fairly fantastical to think I'm in the presence of someone who supposedly created the Philosopher's Box."

"I did create it."

"I believe that's what's to be discussed with Mas—Vicar Willard soon." Arianna didn't miss how his instinct was still to refer to Willard as "Master," rather than "Vicar."

"I believe so."

He produced a watch from his pocket, clicking it open. "It's early yet, but I doubt the vicar has many other priorities right now. Would you care to walk with me?"

She stood and fell into step behind him as they wandered through the guild hall toward the vicar's wing. "So, what's been all the rave at Garre while I was gone?"

"Automations along the line," Charles responded easily.

"Sounds interesting."

"It is." Rivets and their "get to the point" nature weren't exactly known for small talk.

"And what happened to Master Oliver?"

"I killed him."

Few statements could stop a conversation as abruptly.

Vicar Willard was in the lavish workshop attached to his private residence. His hands were occupied when they arrived, focusing on making space on the long central table.

"You're early," he observed. "Well, since you're here, help me clean this off."

Arianna and Charles set to work moving the various parts and tools back to their supposed places around the room. Taking over someone else's workshop was like slipping into someone else's shoes. Nothing fit right about it.

"So, I was thinking we would start with building a working model of the

Philosopher's Box that we can use to design the line for mass production," Willard started.

"It really is true?"

"Yes, she has supplied—"

Arianna grabbed one of her daggers and drew it across her palm, showing Charles the same stream of gold she'd displayed to the Vicar Tribunal. Showing was always better than telling. "Proof enough?"

Charles's eyes darted from her palm to her face several times. "Yes."

"As you build, Charles can sketch schematics and I can take notes," Willard instructed as they finished clearing the table. "That'll make it easier to pass on the information to the initiates and journeymen who will be working on and overseeing the line."

Arianna could only nod. The idea of making the Philosopher's Box again put a lump in her throat.

"Let's begin, then."

If she allowed herself to think about how her hands were moving, she risked error. Arianna pushed all else from her mind, beyond the numbers that gave structure to her creations. It had been a long time since she had last made the box, and there were parts that came more slowly to her than others. Still, she worked through them logically; after all, the only other option was allowing Willard to take the only other prototype in existence and build a model based off reverse-engineering. Ari wasn't about to let that happen.

They worked well into the night, tinkering until the box had mostly taken shape—minus one or two essential parts that could be manufactured with ease. Arianna looked at her work, a nearly identical replica of what sat in her chest and kept her alive.

"So now what?" Charles asked.

"It's implanted in place of the heart."

"This . . . it's just a glorified pump. How does it create a Perfect Chimera?" he asked skeptically.

"It's unfinished until it's tempered." Arianna leaned against the table, ignoring what she had just produced. Her eyes swept over the detailed notes and skillful schematics the men had drawn. The greatest thing she had ever done, reduced to a few sheets of paper.

"Tempered?" Charles's confusion reminded her that he hadn't been privy to the Tribunal and that Willard hadn't had time enough to fill him in.

"There's a special flower from Nova that has magic properties. It cleans blood of rot." Judging from Charles's facial shift, she didn't need to explain the rest.

"So, when do we get our hands on it?" He looked to Willard.

"Louie, the man whose airship I arrived on, has been asked by the Vicar Raven to procure it, along with the necessary organs."

Arianna folded her arms over her chest as a physical reminder to keep things close. She wasn't ready to expose her whisper link with Cvareh yet. Not until she had to. Purely because it was an advantage, and those were best kept as secret as possible for as long as possible. There were no other concerns, Arianna assured herself. She'd see if Louie could do it first, and then step in as necessary.

"I see . . ." Charles hummed. "Well, if it's what the Tribunal decided . . ." The man chuckled, shaking his head at himself. "Things I never thought I'd say or hear."

"Indeed, friend, indeed," Willard agreed. "For now, it's been a long day. We'll resume tomorrow, setting up the journeymen on building out a manufacturing line for this. Can the metal be tempered after the fact? Or is it a high-heat tempering that will warp?"

"It can be."

"Good, then we'll produce as many as we can while we're waiting for the supplies to finish them. Rest well, you two. We have a lot of work ahead of us."

Dismissed, she and Charles wandered back through the empty guild. He made no attempts at conversation until they were back at the masters' hall.

"What you said, about killing Oliver . . ." She'd commend him for holding in the need to clarify for as long as he had.

"It's not a lie." Arianna sighed when she saw the spectrum of emotions run across his face. "But it's not entirely the truth, either."

"Why?"

"I had my reasons." *That I will not divulge.* She'd had enough of baring her soul to strangers.

"Well, if the vicar is unconcerned, then I am, too." Charles let the matter go. "After all, no one held Oliver in higher esteem than Willard." Before Arianna could ask him to elaborate, he started for his chambers. "I'll see you in the morning, Master Arianna."

"In the morning, Master Charles," she murmured.

Arianna looked toward the back of the room for a door that was now completely shrouded. She wondered if in that darkness, the ghost of her former master still lingered, watching, waiting. She started for the door.

"I'm here, Master," she whispered. Her fingers hovered over Oliver's lock. "Sorry I'm so late."

Without a second thought, she spun the dials on Oliver's lock in a succession that required a series of clockwise and counterclockwise rotations, pulling on the different dials, and unlatching small parts of the lock itself to reveal secondary push buttons. After a long minute, the lock eventually gave with a *click*. It was a code he hadn't decided to tell her until she'd made the Philosopher's Box.

Now, Arianna wondered if the man had somehow foreseen their betrayal by Finnyr. How much had he accounted for?

Inside, the musty air of the room hit her like the first yawn of a long-slumbering beast. It smelled of oil and grease, metal, aging paper, cracked leather, and the faint tinge of a floral note that was in Oliver's blood, one that Arianna could never quite place. Nostalgia attacked her from every corner.

Understandably, the room hadn't been fitted with electricity. But Arianna knew exactly where he'd kept his oil lamps and matches. Illumination did little to scare away the lingering memories clinging to every wall, book, and unfinished piece of creation that still sat out, waiting for its master to return.

She walked over to his desk, drawn by a familiar set of scribbles. Arianna lifted up her own schematics, done in a rough hand years ago when she was little more than a child.

"Why did you keep these?" she whispered. Her heart knew the answer. It was the same reason why she would always carry a canister marked with the notches of a clumsy Revolver-in-the-making.

*Speaking of Revolvers . . .*

"Letters with the Vicar Revolver . . .?"

She pushed papers aside, skimming through about a month's worth of missives. They went back and forth about ideas, about Dragon bone density and how coronas worked. The words "in a purely hypothetical question for intellectual pursuits" were scrawled multiple times over, safeguarding each page against potential accusations of treason.

"Intellectual pursuits." Arianna scoffed at the idea. This was talk of methods to kill Dragons. She'd always known Oliver to be a revolutionary, but it seemed to extend into his entire history.

Her hand shifted a letter to the side and exposed a very different schematic than the childish one she'd held earlier. This was done with a graceful, steady hand, lines built on each other, coming together to form what Arianna could only describe as a masterpiece of death. And just perhaps, Loom's salvation.

# 24

## FLORENCE

IF THERE WAS SOME TEST IN THE REVOLVERS' GUILD THAT INVOLVED RUNNING through pitch-black corridors towards certain danger, gun in hand, and nothing more than a makeshift plan—Florence would have already achieved master status.

*Nothing good ever comes of the Underground*, she couldn't stop repeating to herself. It was still the most logical place to have collected the majority of Loom. But that didn't change its innate nature: a gaping black hole, filled with nothing but misfortune and bad luck, especially every time she was in it.

More gunfire echoed as her hands counted the canisters that ran along her belts and shoulder harness. She had a good twenty made, ready to go. Those, combined with the one disk bomb she also had tucked away, *should* be enough ammunition. *Should be.* If it wasn't, she would just have to improvise as she had done so many times before.

"All noncombatants," one Raven stood at a crossroads shouting, "head down to the lower halls. This is not a drill! All noncombatants should retreat down to the safety of the lower halls. This is not a drill! Do as you were instructed."

Florence broke free of the startled and cowering masses, and continued to head upward toward the gunfire. The potent smell of sulfur in the air guided her, like a hound attracted to the scent of its quarry. But when she emerged at last into one of the uppermost tunnels—a rare exit topside—ready for a fight, she found none to be had.

A Dragon lay prone on the floor. Gold blood still oozed from his gaping chest and from the forearm that had been torn off at the elbow. Four Fenthri lay dead, scattered around the Dragon. Two Chimera nursed slowly healing wounds;

they bled black, which was lucky, but would be out of commission for however long it took their bodies to mend.

"Press forward," Vicar Gregory ordered from just ahead. "Reseal the doors."

Florence strode past the deceased Dragon, toward the vicar. Just around the bend where he stood, Florence saw two heavy steel doors warped open. Wedged between them, like tree limbs through walls after windstorm, were the remnants of a glider.

"The bloody Rider slammed right into them," Gregory explained unnecessarily.

"Are there more?" Florence asked, trying to catch a glimpse of the sky through the sliver of an opening.

"Likely."

"How did he even get through?" The doors were thick and sturdy. There should have been no way to penetrate them, even sacrificing a glider. What was more, the Dragon shouldn't have known about the entrance at all. Florence only recognized it as the one major access point to the Underground because it was fairly infamous in the Ravens' Guild. But because it was so notable, no one ever used it.

"Came out of nowhere. We didn't even see him until it was too late." Her confusion still apparent, Vicar Gregory continued, "I had taken a small party out through the gates in an effort to help fortify them."

"Oh, the irony." Did it not go without saying that they should not be opening gates and letting the Dragons know of their location?

"Florence, I don't know what you're aspiring for, but do be mindful that I am still the Vicar Revolver," Gregory said in a cautionary tone.

"Yes, you are, and I am grateful that you hold yourself to the highest standard in order to prevent oversight that leads to accidents like this." Her remarks earned some looks from the other Revolvers, but Florence held her ground. Let them see; she wasn't in the wrong here.

"You only just arrived, so I realize you have not yet been informed that the vicars have agreed to collapse tunnels to protect from below and fortify the entrances above." Vicar Gregory ground his teeth. "I think you should head back into the depths of the caverns for safety. With the other noncombatants."

"I don't think that's necessary. After all, you said it yourself: I'm a Revolver, right?" Florence had no inclination to be dismissed and was ready, at last, to use Gregory's words against him. She looked back to the Dragon, then returned her eyes to the sky. There were no rainbow trails, and the sensation of magic did not prickle against her skin. "Plus, I think he was just a scout."

"Why would the Dragons merely send a scout? They made it perfectly clear their attack would come in three days."

"Three days were up two days ago. I'm sure the attack came, but they went to Ter.0 first, expecting to find us waiting and insolent."

"Scouts," Gregory repeated. "They're sending scouts to see where we ran off to."

"That would be my guess. And we can only hope that this Rider was the first."

"And why is that?"

Florence wanted to think his aim was a lot more accurate than his intellect. "Because when this Rider doesn't make it back to Nova, it will be fairly logical for the Dragon King to assume he was killed. And the death of this Rider will lead the Dragon King and his agents directly to us."

"And why would we want that?"

Florence forced herself to sigh mentally, rather than heaving it outward in frustration. "Because we are relatively protected here. And as long as we don't go showing our faces, or get careless, the Dragons will know where we are but not how to get to us. The Rivets' Guild, on the other hand, is not so fortunate."

"We must get a message to them." Gregory had finally caught up with her logic. "I believe Vicar Dove has a means to communicate."

Florence sincerely hoped so, because if they didn't, there was a real possibility that Garre could still fall.

# 25
## ARIANNA

catastrophically wrong.

The peace was nearly unnerving. Whenever it became too much for her, she retreated to Master Oliver's quarters and tinkered with the various projects, the original intentions of which she could only guess. She had yet to figure out how to contact Florence unnoticed about the gun schematics Oliver had been working on. Her solo attempts to complete his renderings only yielded uncertain results.

A Revolver's insight on the mechanics of weaponry would be imperative to finishing her late master's great work. Still, she continued to hope against hope that she would find some way to communicate with Florence privately, rather than involving all the vicars and half the remaining Revolvers.

Arianna wiped soot off her hands from the charcoal pencil she preferred for drafting schematics. It was a pointless gesture, as she was just about to head down to the factory floor that had occupied most of her time in the past week. The factory bustled along with all the impressive noise of a fully operating manufacturing line, but any Rivet who looked upon it would know that it was anything but.

They were grossly understaffed for the technical nature of what they were trying to produce. The tooling workshops had only completed one out of three specialized machines required. And while she had heard from Vicar Willard that more Rivets were on the way, Arianna didn't want to sit on her hands and wait.

So, every day she went down to the factory floor to meet the other journeymen and initiates who had stayed when everyone else had departed for Ter.0.

When she was younger, every initiate of the Rivets' Guild was required to spend a certain amount of time on the factory floor each week. Young Rivets were taught the basics of their trade, and learned that essential quality of a tinkerer: humility. Working the floor inspired respect for how things can come together with elegant sophistication.

But the pedagogy had been abandoned in the wake of the Dragons.

Young men and women—children, really—with soft delicate hands, who had never seen a manufacturing line before, stood before Arianna each day at dawn. Each day, she critiqued their work from the day prior. Even though they had yet to produce a fully functional Philosopher's Box to her specifications, she permitted the better prototypes a place of honor on the shelves along the back wall of the factory for a day or two before getting dismantled and smelted. The gesture served both as an opportunity to raise the spirits of her workers and function as a red herring for Louie. Arianna had no doubt that upon seeing all the yet-imperfect boxes lined up on the shelves the other day, Louie immediately assumed the Rivets were further along in production than they actually were.

It was this assumption that she would use against him. For if knowledge of stockpiled Philosopher's Boxes was to make its way to any third party, Arianna would know immediately who the false information came from. It wasn't as though any of the initiates spoke to Louie; Arianna had gleaned great pleasure so far at seeing the haughty man on the edge of all interactions, never able to penetrate closer.

She glanced up at the catwalk where Louie had appeared the other day. Today, like most days, it was empty. Arianna put it from her mind to focus on the floor. The boxes wouldn't become perfect with her mind busy elsewhere.

They worked until lunch, breaking to head to the mess hall on the floor above.

The food wasn't glamorous, but it was consistent, and it was what Arianna was accustomed to from her childhood.

"It seems like you're doing well with them." Charles sat across from her, startling Arianna from her thoughts. He usually sat with the young Rivets.

"With Louie?" Arianna couldn't imagine what about her relationship with Louie looked remotely positive, let alone qualified as "doing well." It was a sort of peaceful tolerance on the exterior, at best.

"No, no." Charles shook his head as if remembering for the first time in days that the skeletal man and his ragtag followers even existed. "I mean with the initiates. They're doing well learning the line. It's something that many were resistant to, but now they're all taking a liking for it."

Arianna scoffed softly, and refrained from making a comment about how "in her day" all initiates were required to spend time on the line. Instead, she capitalized on the fact that she had someone familiar with what had evolved in the Rivets' Guild while she was away.

"Why is it that the initiates don't work on the line anymore?"

"Ah, that . . . That was a change the Dragons imposed about six years ago.

They wanted most initiates focused on refining." Charles shook his head, expressing in a single gesture that he felt much the same as Arianna on the matter.

"Shortsighted creatures," she muttered. The Dragons had the most use for gold, and they put high value on the difficult-to-craft resource. Converting all manpower to its creation made sense. It was, after all, nearly impossible to produce without a lot of time and manpower.

Well, made sense if a child was the one calling the shots.

Yveun's face appeared in the forefront of her thoughts, and Arianna shook her head to relieve herself of the memory. The Dragon King may be formidable, and may even have had smart insights for Loom—at least regarding the Harvesters—but it seemed he would have driven the true value of the Rivets into dust if he had remained in control much longer. So, a child in only some ways, perhaps.

A giant dais protruding from the ceiling of the cafeteria turned with an audible *click* that silenced the entire room. Everyone looked up at the transformed signal, interpreting it at the same time. Down the tracks not far from Garre, an engine had triggered the pressure switch. Just as Vicar Willard had promised, more Rivets were on their way.

"Well, I suppose lunch is going to be cut short for us." Charles stood, taking note of how little Arianna had eaten. "Have you had enough? I can always greet the newcomers with Vicar Willard alone. You are not required."

"I don't need that much food." Arianna stood as well. "There are a few benefits to being the Perfect Chimera, after all."

"A few? I think I could name several, and I have only known you for two weeks."

The train station for Garre was slightly north of the main guild hall. Steam engines were quite particular about the ground they ran on, and the soft, marshy earth beneath Garre did not do for a train station. The Rivets and Ravens compromised to create a station just beyond the guild hall proper. It was accessible via a short light rail that gently sloped downward to the station. On the way out, the small ferrying rail was powered mostly by gravity and momentum. On the way back in, when it was mostly uphill, the trains were powered by steam—or magic.

Arianna looked with interest toward the large engine that bellowed down the winding track leading from the northern Territory. On it would be extra manpower to set up her manufacturing line, and hopefully new ways to communicate with the rebellion locked beneath the ground of Ter.4. And, in particular, one Raven-tattooed Revolver.

They arrived just before the train did, and the three present leaders of the Rivets' Guild stood alone on the long platform as the engine slowed to a stop. Amid the steam billowing over the platform, the shadows of men and women emerged. They all immediately headed for the light rail without hesitation. All of them were Rivets—knew where to go, what to do. Arianna scanned their cheeks for some sign of any other guilds. But there were none.

"We may want to address our own protection sometime soon with the other vicars," Arianna said to Willard.

"Weaponry is quite tight right now," the old man replied.

As if she didn't already know that. "Yes, and I realize that the majority of it must be used to fortify the Underground and the majority of Loom. But there will be no Loom, should we fail to produce the Philosopher's Box. I doubt it will take long for the Dragon King to check all the other guilds when he returns to Ter.0 and finds no one."

Willard stroked his chin in thought. "You do raise a fair point. I will whisper to the Vicar Raven this night; perhaps we can see some Revolvers on the next train."

Arianna sincerely hoped they would see a next train, period.

A young man jumped from the engine, a filled Raven on his cheek. He looked utterly exhausted, but still determined. "Vicar Rivet." His eyes scanned the three of them, waiting to see who responded, as though he wasn't entirely sure who he was looking for. "I have a message."

"Let me see it." Willard held out his hand.

"It came by whisper a few days after we left Holx." The man produced a hastily scribbled letter, depositing it in Willard's palm. "That's all there was."

"Thank you."

Most of the platform had cleared and, when it was apparent that the train held no more, Charles started to make his way toward the rail as well.

"What does it say?" Arianna wasn't sure if she wanted to know, but when the vicar's face fell, she knew she had to ask.

"What is it, Vicar?" Charles pressed gently, stopping.

Willard looked up from the letter, his attention darting between his companions. Arianna knew she would not like the outcome when his eyes settled on her.

"The Dragons have attacked Ter.4."

# 26

## CVAREH

His knees ached, and his feet had gone numb.

Cvareh knelt before the statue of Lord Agendi in the Temple of Xin. The statue was a spitting image of the mischievous, happy lord; he held his silver box, outstretched, cracked halfway, but his crown of flowers was hidden under a stone veil, the edges of the petals barely protruding from beneath the sculpted fabric.

The temple was the only quiet place he could retreat to now. The only place he could sit and think without his family's questioning eyes, Fae's unyielding presence, or Finnyr in general. But Cvareh's peace was abruptly interrupted when another worshiper knelt beside him.

"Cvareh'Ryu," the man said with a bow of his head. Judging from the man's sky-colored skin and lack of tattoo, he was Xin—though Cvareh didn't recognize him. "I thought that was you. What an honor to kneel before my patron with the Xin'Ryu."

Cvareh did not have the heart to correct the man.

"Simply terrible, isn't it?"

"What is?" Cvareh asked cautiously.

"The flowers. I made it out there today, myself. Sure enough, it's as they say, almost half the island gone."

"Flowers?" Something resembling horror dressed in the trimmings of panic threw its arms around Cvareh's shoulders. The Flowers of Agendi were the one thing Arianna needed from him and his world. The one thing that could offer Xin the future they so desperately needed.

"Is that not why you're praying? So that the dying Lord may find peace?"

"Please, explain. I have not heard this news," Cvareh demanded quickly.

"Oh, no? I suppose not . . . I imagine the manor is still in mourning. It was just rumors at first—that all the Flowers of Agendi had disappeared from the isle of Lysip. Sure enough, there were whispers that Gwaeru was the same. I didn't know what to think, but Agendi is my patron. Perhaps I didn't worship at his temple enough . . ."

"Gone?" Cvareh tried to keep the man on track as his heart began to race. "What do you mean, *gone?*"

"I didn't believe it myself either. Thought it was just gossip with a supernatural twist in the parlors at Napole. But I went out to the lord's temple today and sure enough, half the flowers on the island were missing."

Cvareh jumped to his feet. His knees had turned to gelatin from kneeling for so long and his toes started prickling up to his shins, but he ignored the discomfort. The man blinked up at him, surprised by Cvareh's sudden movement. "Your house needs you. Go to the Xin Manor, and tell Cain Xin'Kin to meet me on the isle."

The man pulled himself to his feet, confused but obedient. "Anything else?"

"No, that's enough." *For now*, Cvareh added in his head.

He was working on a plan as he went. He had been silent in the face of Arianna's demand—holding back, waiting for her signal. It was a natural role for him, the same one Petra had carved for him. But, Arianna was not here. Petra was not here. Which meant if he didn't act, no one would.

Cvareh mounted Saran, who had been perched on one of the high ledges around the Temple of Xin, and took to the skies.

The small pebble islands that floated between outposts and tethered the three main islands of Nova together whizzed under him, blurring into a line. Cvareh squinted ahead, looking against the setting sun for the island he knew well. Even among the howling wind, the buffet of wings, and his own racing thoughts, his heart reminded him that the last time he had flown to this island, Arianna's arms were around him.

A dark speck appeared in the distant sky. Cvareh pushed the boco harder with a short, urging shout. He wanted to be wrong. He wanted to get to the island and see that the man's report had been nothing more than tea parlor gossip.

His shadow crossed over the edge of the island, soaring over greenery until—

Nothing.

The island, once filled completely with the tall stalks of the Flowers of Agendi, was nothing more than bare earth on one side. Cvareh landed his boco on the platform that was now only halfway surrounded by foliage. He dismounted, crossing to the dirt in a few long strides.

The cry of another bird distracted him and Cvareh turned on instinct, claws ready. But he recognized the creature, as well as its rider.

"Raku lets you ride him?" Cvareh phrased it as a question to Cain, but the answer was obvious.

"He does." There was an apologetic note to Cain's voice. "He came to me the other day and began roosting on my balcony . . ."

"I'm glad he returned home, and I'm glad you're the one to ride him," Cvareh said honestly, hoping to allay the guilt Cain clearly felt over being chosen by Petra's mount.

"What is happening?" Cain looked around the island, the question layering in more ways than one.

"Rok." Cvareh scowled.

"Why would Rok attack the Temple of the Lord of Luck? To get back at you?"

"No, Rok isn't quite so small-minded." *Unfortunately.* "The resistance needs these flowers."

"The resistance? On Loom? Needs . . . *flowers*?"

"There's something about them. They're used to make Perfect Chimera." Arianna could've explained it far better than him, but the point seemed to be made well enough. "I didn't want to move for them too early, for fear of identifying them as important. Furthermore, they're needed fresh; if the rebellion isn't ready, we waste this resource."

"Damn Rok is wasting them for us. Yveun must have discovered something during his trip below." The parlors in Napole had been abuzz with rumors of the Dragon King descending to parlay with the Fenthri, but no rumors had mentioned flowers.

"We have to save as many as we can."

"How?"

"We have to move them, replant them somewhere on Ruana where Rok won't find them, but they still can grow." Cvareh was formulating plans as he spoke.

"Do you have an idea for where?" Cain gripped Raku's feathers and Cvareh could sense the ripple of movement about to turn into a wave of feathers.

"No, but it seems you do."

"I'm going to return with help," Cain vowed.

Cvareh gave a solemn nod. "See that you do."

Raku took to the skies and soared higher and higher before becoming nothing more than a speck. The boco was almost as fast as a glider, and they needed that speed now.

Cvareh dropped his eyes back to the earth.

Divots where the flowers had been rooted nestled between ridges of upturned earth. They'd been uprooted, not trampled, not burned. Why? Why would Rok remove them? Why waste the time, when total destruction was so much more efficient?

Cvareh tried to make sense of it. Was it possible that Arianna had negotiated with someone else? He suddenly imagined the flowers already in her possession, acquired via whisper link with some *other* Dragon. He couldn't stop himself from looking to where they had made love on the stone steps of the temple before his patron and the pantheon above.

"She wouldn't," he whispered, needing more than anything to believe it was true. "Saran, take to the skies." Cvareh gave a whistle and gestured the command. The bird took off.

Cvareh raised a hand to his ear, still staring at that spot. She had given herself to him, and he to her.

He uttered a specific, magic word, and felt the tension spring up between them.

"I told you not to contact me." The snappish words were the first he'd heard of her voice in months and somehow, despite their edge, he found them lovely.

"I know. Don't break the link."

The subtle hum of magic filled his ears. There was no retort and the connection between them didn't drop. Cvareh took a deep breath.

"It's important."

"It must be." Her voice had already softened.

"The Flowers of Agendi are being uprooted."

"What? By whom?" Her surprise reassured him that there was no auxiliary method she'd used to acquire them.

"Who else?"

"Rok?"

"I think so. I'm at the temple now. I'll wait and see who comes." Cvareh leaned against one of the pillars at the top of the stone steps, looking over half the barren earth. "Do you know anyone who could've betrayed us?"

There was a long pause that said more than her actual answer. "I'm not sure."

"But you suspect."

"I do."

He was impressed at how well their conversation was going, though everything in him told him not to push things too far. "I'm going to do everything in my power to protect the flowers, but you need to get them sooner rather than later."

"Understood."

There it was: the end of their interaction, the moment when everything was going to drop. "One more thing," he added hastily.

"What?" He was relieved to hear more curiosity than annoyance in her voice.

What was he going to say? *I love you still?* Cvareh knew better; she had no interest in such professions.

"Be careful."

"You too."

The connection ended.

Cvareh walked under the shade of the temple's roof, proceeded to the far wall, and wedged himself in the corner behind the statue of Lord Agendi. He would wait there to discover what force was disrupting the flowers that were so special to them both.

# 27
## ARIANNA

He contacted her.

She had asked him not to. She had told him that if he valued anything about them, he would not.

She had excused herself from the manufacturing line when she felt his whisper and now stood in a small side room adjacent to the floor. Arianna stared at the line through the window. It was beginning to run well. Their defect rate was almost low enough now to call it a proper line. But it would be worth nothing if they didn't have the flowers.

Her Dragon had paid attention to that. As dense and inept as he was at a great many things, he truly understood how critical the flowers were for them. A smile crept on her lips.

She shouldn't be smiling. It betrayed all reason. After all, he'd done what she'd explicitly asked him not to, and the flowers they needed were being destroyed. Not to mention there was still the matter of the Dragon attacks and the schematics she needed to send to Florence.

But her heart was pounding. Her mind was alert and ready. Even as Arianna the Rivet, she experienced the acute sensations normally reserved for Arianna the White Wraith—those that meant something big was coming.

"Charles!" she called, storming back toward the line. "Charles!"

"Yes, here!" A hand waved from the far end of the line and Arianna sprinted to the other master. She gripped his elbow and pulled him to the side. Over all the noise of gears churning and machines whirring, they could barely hear one another, let alone be overheard by anyone else.

"Charles, where do the Rivets keep gliders?"

"Excuse me?"

"I know you keep them here."

"There's a hangar, just outside of Garre proper . . ." His voice trailed off and he gave her a look likely intended to be probing. When she remained silent, he came outright with it. "What do you need it for?"

"Tell Willard I've gone to get him the flowers we need."

"From Nova?"

"The same. We have enough boxes ready; we can begin stage two." Arianna paused, thinking of the gun she'd been working on for weeks. "I'm going to leave out some gun schematics in the masters' hall. See that they're sent to Florence."

"To Florence? Not the Vicar Revolver?" Charles seemed confused. The demand was unorthodox.

"Yes, to Florence—only Florence," she affirmed without hesitation.

"When will you be back?" He glanced nervously at the line.

"When I can," she said. "You're fine. You understand the box."

"The code to the hangar is red, thirty-two, five, orange."

"Heard." Arianna quickly stepped away, betraying the urgency of the situation.

He caught her elbow. "And be careful."

"I—"

"Truly, Arianna, be careful." Charles gripped her arm tightly a moment before letting go. "The world needs you alive right now."

The words "right now" stuck in her mind as she ran up through the halls, back to Master Oliver's room. They echoed like a quiet promise as she grabbed the gun prototype and laid out the schematics for Charles to find later. They continued to replay as she sought out one of the gliders in the far hangar with as much speed as she could manage.

Right now, the world needed her as Arianna the inventor and crafter of the Philosopher's Box. But when the fighting was over, when the rebellion succeeded, she could retire back to obscurity. She could be whomever she wanted and answer to no one, as she'd done all her life in the years leading up to this rebellion.

But before she could slip back between the cracks of time and memory, she needed to see Loom's victory secured. And that meant going back to Nova.

# 28

## CVAREH

HE HAD BEEN WAITING FOR AN HOUR THAT FELT LIKE ETERNITY WHEN CAIN arrived.

His friend and a female Rider unknown to Cvareh landed, dismounted, and started down the path toward the temple. Cvareh stood, emerging from the late hour shadow into the remaining sunlight.

"Send away your boco," he called to them.

"What?"

"Send away your boco," Cvareh repeated, softer now that they were near.

"Why?" Cain asked skeptically. "Aren't we moving flowers?"

"Not yet." Cvareh looked over the horizon for anyone approaching. "We're going to wait to find out who is taking them."

"Cvareh, we should try to save some first."

It was sound advice, but the idea of leaving the island and possibly missing the perpetrators behind the flowers' disappearance was unthinkable.

"We will wait," Cvareh said, weighting the last word with a note of finality. To really drive the point home, he looked to the woman who had been otherwise silent, and changed the topic. "Who are you?"

"Dawyn Xin'Anh Bek," the sapphire-skinned woman answered. She had long golden hair that cascaded in waves, not unlike Petra's curls, but just different enough that it didn't hurt to look on her.

"Do you know why you're here?"

"Cain told me it's to preserve some of the Flowers of Agendi before they all go missing." She kept her eyes down out of respect, but her voice was strong.

"Look at me." Dawyn obliged. Her irises were the color of honey poured into water—yellow on the edge and blue around the iris. "How long have you been in the service of the Xin Manor?"

"All my life."

"How old are you?"

"Thirty-five." She was quite young, but not a child.

"If you are involved in these affairs, I cannot promise your safety."

"Can you promise my safety at the manor?" Cvareh didn't have an answer for her so he remained silent and she continued, instead. "No, you can't really, not anymore." Dawyn looked to Cain, then back to him. "I don't know everything, but I know that Rok killed our Oji and is poisoning our halls as they poisoned our wine. I am not afraid to die, Cvareh'Oji."

There was that title again, chasing him like a beast he didn't want to admit was gaining ground behind him. This time, he didn't outright refute the notion.

"Come, let's talk while we sit." Cvareh wanted to get them out of view. He didn't want the thieves to know that anyone was waiting for them until they landed, until it was too late. The two followed him in, sitting along the back wall. "Why you?"

"Why did I ask for Dawyn's help?" Cain sought clarification and Cvareh nodded. "Because she's as loyal to Xin as anyone could ask, and her family owns a winery on the west coast of Ruana."

Her mention of the poisoned wine made a lot more sense. Cvareh met the woman's unusually colored eyes. This was loyalty to her house, and it was also personal. He didn't need to ask if her family's vintage was some of the wine that had been tampered with.

"There are plots of land at the vineyard where the flowers will thrive," Dawyn explained. "My family will see to them personally with the utmost discretion."

Cvareh hoped she was right.

The conversation kept on with relative ease until it naturally died out. Both the tension and impatience of waiting consumed their focus. Cvareh could hear and feel Cain beginning to stir. But he kept himself still. He would wait days if he had to, and they would wait with him.

When the moon was high in the sky, and wispy clouds cast the world in on-and-off twilight, boco cries cut through the stillness. Cvareh crouched forward, ready to spring into action. Cain and Dawyn did the same.

"Don't move until I do . . . Keep your magic pulled in tight."

Even in the pale moonlight, the approaching Riders' red skin shone brightly, as if by their own light. Three women dismounted their boco. Two went for the flowers, but one stopped mid-step. She held out a ruby-colored hand.

"Come out." She squinted into the temple.

Cvareh stood, and with him, Dawyn and Cain. He walked forward, stepping into the moonlight and stopping on the top stair of the temple.

"Cvareh Xin, you seem to have a habit of being where you shouldn't be and meddling in Rok affairs."

"I don't know what you're talking about," he dead-panned. Why bother trying to mask a lie everyone already knew was false?

"Yveun'Dono will be delighted to have proof of your treachery."

"Yveun'Dono cannot bar me from worshiping at my patron's temple."

"He can do whatever he pleases." The woman narrowed her eyes. "Now, by his order, leave."

Cvareh didn't move. The smart thing to do was to leave. Doing so would be consistent with the role Petra had carved for him: keep his head down, acquire information, be forgotten, be underestimated. She would be the one to plan and execute the attack later. But she was gone, and he had to fight for himself. For Xin.

"By his order? Or Coletta'Ryu's?" Cvareh didn't expect Dawyn to speak, but now that she had, he wanted to hear the answer as well.

"I don't know what you're talking about." The woman's lips curled back, exposing her teeth. "If you do not leave, it will be a refusal of an order from the Dono. We are permitted to kill anyone who demonstrates such impudence."

"Are you?" Cvareh assessed them. "You have no beads, so you're not Riders. I've never heard of anyone but the king's Riders operating with enough authority to duel and kill on his behalf."

"Go, wayward Xin, and you will live out the rest of your god's hour."

"You go, and leave the flowers." Tension rippled through his muscles. "Or I will be forced to defend them on behalf of my patron."

He didn't know if it was excuse enough for a duel, but it was all he had, and the women before him seemed even less concerned than him with the idea of keeping things respectable.

"You, the weakest of the Xin children? Fight us with your pets . . .?" The woman laughed. "Leave, Cvareh."

He didn't need to endure any more disrespect.

Cvareh lunged.

The woman was ready for him and darted forward, claws out, taking the first swipe as they met halfway. Cvareh dodged widely, forced to step back and avoid a second attack from one of the other women. Cain and Dawyn weren't far behind, however, and quickly engaged the other Rok fighters one-to-one.

"This won't last long." The woman before him thrust a clawed hand out. Cvareh side-stepped and quickly pushed off his other foot. A woman's scream rang out nearby; Cvareh turned, expecting to see Dawyn in need of assistance.

"You wretched girl!" The Rok Dragon was on the ground, hand covering a shoulder pouring blood.

Dawyn spat flesh from her mouth. "Look out!"

Cvareh turned back in time to dodge the point of a hairpin slicing downward in a vicious arc.

"Don't let it touch you!" Dawyn shouted, even though they were not very far apart. "They're Coletta's women. Expect poison!"

"Coletta'Ryu, Xin scum." The woman Dawyn was fighting regained her footing and lunged.

Cvareh lost track of Dawyn and Cain, focusing on the fury of attacks at his front. The woman was good, better than she had any right to be. She fought as Cvareh would expect a Rider to, every attack precise and fearless. Her long claws gleamed in the moonlight as Cvareh laced his fingers with hers, gripping her hands in place.

"What do you want with the Flowers of Agendi?" he demanded.

"Wouldn't you like to know?" She kicked out her feet, tumbling backward and pulling Cvareh with her. Her claws dug into his skin as they rolled, swiping at his face and neck, seeking a blow that would incapacitate him long enough to go for his heart.

He twisted, scrambling, and a claw came out of seemingly nowhere, shooting straight through his jugular.

"I will kill you," she snarled, leaning in toward his face.

Cvareh looked at the woman over him, gurgling blood onto the earth as her knees pinned him. He sunk under her weight as though the soft, upturned ground itself was going to engulf him whole. Cvareh saw one imperfection in the moonlight's outline of her hair as she pulled back.

"I will watch you die, just like I watched your sister die."

*Petra.*

Blood spewed from his neck as he mustered a roar that gave voice, at last, to the rage he felt boiling inside. He pushed into the ground until he found something firm enough to brace against and pressed upward. She may have the advantage, but she was off-balance with his sudden movement and he had height on her. His arm, barely long enough, whipped upward.

Her hand caught his wrist, knowing what he had been going for.

Cvareh fought against her. Magic pumped through his veins and fueled his muscles with an energy he shouldn't possess. But she had leverage still, and used it to keep the poisoned hairpin at bay.

Just when he thought the bones in his wrist were about to snap from the woman's grip, it slackened, and her head whipped skyward.

Everything on the island seemed to still as a glider landed, and a large, strawberry-colored Dragon stepped off.

"Yveun'Dono has requested your return," the Rider announced. There was something undeniably familiar about her accent.

"Who are you?" The woman had yet to ease off Cvareh.

"Lesona'Kin."

"I know of no such person."

"Perhaps you are not worthy of such information." The Rok Rider shrugged. "Leave, now."

Finally, the woman eased away. Her claw extracted itself from Cvareh's jugular, but it didn't recess entirely. He felt his tendons beginning to knit . . . but did he dare attack in the presence of another Rider? Looking around, it seemed Cain and Dawyn had the same hesitation.

"I will not be leaving, imposter!" Cvareh's attacker lunged.

The Rider moved with a rustle of clothes she didn't appear to be wearing. Seemingly from nowhere, a gun unlike Cvareh had ever seen materialized. The strangeness of the thing, combined with its presence in a Dragon's hand—and on Nova nonetheless—made Cvareh's brain stutter to find context.

"Die."

He knew the newcomer instantly, the moment he heard the whispered word.

The gun fired, but the discharge exploded by the grip rather than the barrel. What had been a Rok Rider moments before was now a Fenthri woman, clutching the side of her face, doubling over. But she used that motion to grab for the daggers at the small of her back.

Cvareh lunged to action. He sprinted for the Rok woman and the Fenthri— no, the Perfect Chimera—in her sights. She was several steps ahead of him, but his legs had never stepped so wide, his muscles never felt so strong, as they did in when he was working to get to her.

Whoever the Rok woman was, she was not a Rider, because she made a critical error. Cvareh sprung for her, tumbling head over heels. In the process, the hairpin she'd forgotten he still held found its way into her neck.

Cvareh quickly let go, watching as the woman's yelp was cut short by her eyes rolling back in her head. She shuddered violently, collapsing open-mouthed and wide-eyed. Cvareh watched in horror as foam bubbled from between her lips.

He tore his eyes to the Fenthri in their midst. The earth seemed to quiet; he trusted the silence to mean that Cain and Dawyn had won their respective battles, and now stood in as much shock as Cvareh.

"Well, that rescue really blew up in my face." Arianna rubbed her knitting skin, washed white in the pale moonlight.

Cvareh couldn't stop his mirth and roared with laughter for the first time in what felt like forever.

# 29
## ARIANNA

Arianna picked the remaining shrapnel out from her shoulder, flicking it to the ground. Cvareh was busy laughing like a fool and she waited until he stopped to take a breath.

"Are you quite done?" Arianna muttered. "The joke wasn't that funny."

"It was and you know it." Cvareh steadily approached. She could smell him more keenly, see him more clearly, with every confident step. Arianna regarded him warily.

Half of her screamed for him, the other half against. Cvareh was exactly the same as he'd been, the same as he'd always be. He was a Dragon. A few months apart was a not-so-insignificant portion of her life as a Fenthri; for him, it was a blink.

"Cvareh, what're you—"

He cut her short with arms around her, wrapping her up with bone-crushing force. Arianna felt every ripple of his muscles as he tensed against her. She breathed him in as his mouth covered hers. He tasted of daydreams and foolishness. He smelled of sweet nostalgia. The combination silenced the irritated voice trying to remind her that she should be cross with him.

He made her so soft.

"Enough," she whispered across his mouth when he came up for air. Cvareh pulled his head back, noses still touching, questions in his eyes. "That's enough, for now."

"For now?"

"For now."

At that, he finally pulled away, leaving a hulking vacuum of space where his Dragon form once was.

Arianna instantly recognized the two other Dragons in their midst. It had been some time since she'd last seen Dawyn, but she remembered the woman's name keenly from her first affair on Nova. Cain—now there was a face she'd never forget.

"Been awhile." Arianna was nonchalant, confronted with Cain's anger and Dawyn's outright confusion.

"Why are you here?" Cain growled in her direction, looking accusingly at Cvareh.

"He didn't know I was coming either. Heard you might need some help with the flowers, and we can use them on Loom now." Arianna looked to the Dragon corpses. One still frothed bubbles from lips frozen and parted with death. "Poison? Fighting fire with fire now?"

"No." Cvareh turned away from her and looked to Dawyn. Arianna fought the urge to pull his face back to her. She wasn't done having him look at her yet. "Dawyn knew they were Coletta's, because…"

"I found out spending some time on Lysip." Dawyn answered the unspoken question.

"On Lysip?" Arianna narrowed her eyes at the girl. She didn't have much reason to love her, and now she might have a reason to hate her.

"It's not like that." Dawyn shook her head and added hastily, "I went there after the wine incident. I wanted to know what happened and wasn't getting anywhere on Ruana. So, I went to spend time with a relative."

"You're Rok?" The Dragon in front of Arianna was as blue as the sky.

Dawyn shook her head. "My mother's sister mated with a Rok; their son, my cousin, came out red, so she stayed there and joined Rok."

"I'm sorry." Cvareh sounded sincere. Arianna withheld comment that this was the danger of the whole idea of families on Nova. It was so much simpler on Loom without them.

"The situation proved useful enough." Dawyn shrugged but her magic had the sour note of regret all around it. "I heard the rumors of Coletta'Ryu's flowers there. Yveun has his Riders and, while most think she's a disgrace of a Ryu, she has her flowers to act out her nefarious plans."

Arianna looked to the poisoned Dragon, prone on the ground. Sure enough, a lacquered flower sat around her neck. "Who would've thought flowers of all things would be so important," she muttered, and Cvareh hummed his agreement. "We should dispose of the bodies."

"Dispose of them?" Cain looked to Cvareh. "You heard what this wench said." He pointed to the Dragon foaming at the mouth. "She just watched as Petra died. I say we leave their bodies as a message that—"

"We will dispose of them," Cvareh interrupted firmly.

"You're taking her side?" Cain was aghast.

"I'm taking the side of reason. The only message would be that they need to wage war against Xin and now have cause to do it."

"No bodies, no deaths, and no stupid duels," Arianna finished with a nod of affirmation from Cvareh.

Cain looked as if he still wanted to object, but he had the sense to keep it to himself.

One by one, they carried the Rok corpses to the edge of the island, tossing them over like a great offering to the world below.

"The boco, too," Arianna suggested when they were finished.

"The boco?" Dawyn repeated with surprise.

"No trace they even made it to the island tonight." Cvareh unsheathed his claws in agreement with Arianna's suggestion. "We kill the boco, send them over the edge, then we take as many flowers as we can back to your family's vineyard before dawn."

Dawyn and Cain shared a look, then nodded in agreement.

"Whatever you say, not-Oji."

Arianna gave a sideways glance at Cvareh. Of course he wouldn't be the Oji; that role fell to Petra.

"I'm going to take you somewhere safe." He clearly mistook her look as an expectation of attention.

"I was fine on Nova last time." Arianna pressed her fingers together, summoning the guise of Ari Xin'Anh Bek for emphasis.

Cvareh radiated pure happiness. It fluttered from him and soared through his magic. Arianna wasn't used to feeling so much joy from one person, and especially not at the sight of her. She was unsure how to process it, so she ignored it entirely. "We need to move the glider, too."

She hopped back onto the piloting platform, gripping the handles. "If we fly with the dawn, we may be able to hide the trail in your watercolor skies."

"My thoughts exactly." Cvareh brought his fingers to his lips and gave a sharp whistle, summoning his boco. "Follow me, and fly low."

The boco took off with a hop and a flap of its wide wings. Arianna sparked the glider to life, following behind as the bird tucked its feathers and dove toward the clouds below at Cvareh's command. The rising sun lightened the sky from a pale, ethereal gray to the colors of spun candy, brightening almost to white by the time they directed themselves upwards and toward the isle of Ruana.

At first, Arianna thought they were headed for the Xin Manor. But they were too far back; Cvareh pointed at a waterfall ahead of them, pouring between the massive towers and structures carved into the underbelly of Ruana. Whatever he shouted to her was lost, so Arianna was left curious, but followed dutifully behind.

The waterfall was attached to a massive opening into the earth itself. Cvareh went ahead unhindered, but Ariana slowed as she crossed into the vast unknown of the cave beyond the falls. The magic of her glider lit up the darkness, just enough in combination with her magic eyes to make out the path ahead.

Pulling right, pulling left, weaving between columns of stone, stalagmites, and stalactites, there was only one course for her to go and Arianna for once found herself struggling to keep up with Cvareh. He charged ahead with the dexterity of a Raven and just as much disregard for the dangers of how he progressed. Arianna gritted her teeth. Her back felt as though it was going to snap in half from tension.

Light filtered into the blackness, and Arianna breathed a sigh of relief as she heard the squawking of the bird ahead and felt the buffet of wings that usually signaled landing.

The cave had opened up into a small cavern with a wide-ledged mouth. Arianna parked the glider and mentally forced every white-knuckled finger to uncurl.

"Are you trying to kill me?"

"Was it hard to navigate?" Cvareh seemed genuinely concerned.

Arianna sighed heavily. It may not have been hard for a suicidal Raven like Helen or Will, but Arianna had come to start valuing her life, as insane as the notion was. "It'll be fine as a transport route. If I can do it, a Raven can make it twice as fast."

"Careful, Arianna—that sounded like humility." Cvareh extended a hand to her, offering to help her off the glider. Arianna stared at it, but stepped off unassisted thanks to that remark.

"So, where are we?"

"We are at the refinery of Ruana."

"Refinery of Ruana?" Arianna repeated, utterly dumbfounded.

"This way."

Curiosity propelled her to follow Cvareh without further comment around a lip of stone and into a narrow passage that quickly opened up into a cut staircase. The walls transformed from rough and natural to carved, as they ascended into what was clearly a Dragon-built structure.

She watched the back of the man ahead of her, as if the skin between his shoulder blades had some secret to reveal. Not for the first time, Arianna found herself studying him, wondering just what it was about Cvareh that drew her. It was not the depth of his mind, nor the muscle of his frame. Their pull to one another was indescribable; the features she would not usually find her eye drawn toward attracted her like the sheen of a freshly oiled gearbox.

At least, until her eye was pulled in a different direction.

The stairway leveled into an icy hall. Glassless windows welcomed the high snowdrifts of the mountains through their thresholds. Flurries danced on unseen currents, crunching underfoot as they traversed to a large room.

She found herself in a spacious antechamber overlooking an even larger space. Ahead of her, a window of tempered glass—slight imperfections rippled through it—looked down at the core of the refinery. A large vat was suspended by a massive hook off to the side of a grounded tank. They were surrounded by machines and long belts, all cold, waiting for molten steel to be poured down them.

"It's a refinery," she whispered.

There was an odd disconnect between her mind and body. Her eyes told her mind that she looked at a refinery, albeit a small one. But her mind argued back that such a thing was impossible, for she knew she was up on Nova, where paragons of industry did not rightly exist.

"I told you it was." Cvareh was at her side.

"Why?" Arianna was trying to process the idea.

"Yveun is—or at least was—setting them up on Lysip. Started the project a decade back and put Petra in charge of oversight. Naturally, she seized the opportunity to build one here as well."

"So, is your sister here now, then?" Arianna's voice was still a whisper, matching Cvareh's tone. She'd felt a somber shift in Cvareh's magic when he mentioned Petra. Warning bells and alarms sounded in Arianna's mind.

"No. Petra is dead."

Cold.

Detached.

Arianna felt the muscles around her lungs contract and her breathing grow shallow. A feeling deeper than reason and stronger than logic ruled her— empathy. She clutched his hands as though she was pulling him from the unbearable riptide of grief, grabbed him like someone should've grabbed her after Eva.

"You will make it through this," she vowed, acting entirely on impulse.

Cvareh tilted his head to the side and his mouth cracked with a tired smile. He leaned forward and Arianna's eyes closed of their own accord. They, like all other parts of her body, moved in the ocean of this man. He didn't kiss her, but merely rested his forehead against hers and breathed.

"I know." Cvareh took a slow breath. "I have you."

Why did those words make tears prick her eyes? She felt so frustrated by them, so angry, yet so happy. It was like drinking chocolate and licking salt.

"Are you the Oji now?" She had to focus. She couldn't let herself be distracted by the things she'd given away years ago.

"No, but I will be." Arianna opened her mouth to speak, but was interrupted by his movement. "I must go now and see to that. But I will return to you. Make yourself at home until then."

*Oji. Cvareh as the Oji.* Her mind tried to wrap itself around the idea. The prone Dragon she'd found on Loom, leading the rebellion on Nova. He would be pulled from her to change the world, just as Master Oliver had been, just as Eva had been. As Florence was.

The space before her had never felt more cold.

# 30
## FLORENCE

DRAGONS WERE ANNOYING. THEY WEREN'T SCARY, THEY WEREN'T DANGEROUS, and they certainly weren't the fearsome creatures they made themselves out to be.

More than anything, right now, Dragons were simply a nuisance.

Florence sat in an abandoned building on the outer edge of Holx. From her vantage, she could see Dragons swirling around the Ravens' Guild. Every now and again, one would land and its Rider would disappear inside for a few hours. Then they'd eventually return to their glider, having accomplished nothing, and take to the skies again.

She leaned against the wood paneling of the room she'd made her temporary home. Watching the Dragons, recording their movements, keeping track of how far they seemed to get in the guild and how long it took them to do so was a convenient excuse to spend extended time outside the Underground. It had been almost a month since the first Dragon attack, the first unsuccessful one of many, and a month was too long to spend in the dark. Florence felt sorry for the Fenthri who had no other options beyond spending their days confined below. Not sorry enough to pass up the chance to escape the ever-oppressive gloom herself, but sorry still.

Here, her window was cracked. She didn't open it fully because she didn't want her magic to betray even the slightest scent on the wind. But that same wind tickled her cheeks as it whispered of the outside world. Here, Florence could stare up at the sky and watch day turn to night and, more important, night turn to day.

When the Dragons weren't flitting around the guild hall—their forays grew less frequent by the day—she would invent stories about the people who had lived in the apartment she now occupied. When her stories lost their luster, she would wonder how she and Arianna would have redecorated to make things more comfortable. When thinking of Arianna was too painful, or frustrating, she had Shannra to smooth away the rough edges of annoyance.

Shannra was in her arms now. Florence loved the way the light painted the woman's dark skin in graphite hues, like a page from a Rivet's sketchbook. These schematics drew what could be argued as the perfect female proportions.

A soft rapping at the door jarred Florence back to reality. No matter how nice it was to daydream, this was not her home and she was not spending a lazy afternoon with the woman who had somehow become her unorthodox lover. Florence tugged the blankets around them as Shannra began to stir. She loathed disturbing the woman, but the second set of knocks did just that anyway, and Florence worked to preserve their modesty.

"Come in." Florence didn't have to speak loudly to be heard. They were as quiet as possible due to the Dragons' keen hearing.

The door cracked and another Revolver poked her head in. She seemed unsurprised to find Florence and Shannra together.

"I was told to fetch you."

"Fetch me to where?"

"There was a letter for you on the last train from Ter.3. Vicar Gregory wishes to see you regarding it."

"I'll be there in a moment." Florence dismissed the other Revolver with a small nod.

"A letter?" Shannra repeated.

"I know no more than you do." Florence began to button up her clothing once more from naval to neck.

"From Arianna, I'd bet." Shannra straightened and leaned against a window frame. The wind ruffled her hair slightly as Shannra stared at the few Dragons in the sky.

Florence could sense the tension whenever Shannra spoke of Arianna, though they'd never spoken of it, not outright. Florence didn't even know what she'd say if Shannra pressed for clarity. What had she and Arianna been to one another? What were they now? Some questions were best left unanswered or better, unasked.

"Perhaps." Florence leaned forward and kissed Shannra's cheek lightly. "I'll be back as soon as I can. Keep an eye on things for me."

Shannra merely nodded as Florence moved for the door. But before she could reach it, Shannra spoke. "Flor, when all this is over, how about we get a nice little flat in New Dortam, right by the guild hall?"

Florence's mind immediately went to the home she'd shared with Ari in Old Dortam and a melancholy ache filled her chest. "There is no guild hall," she murmured.

"They'll rebuild it." Shannra finally turned her head, her eyes searching, begging. "What do you think of that idea?"

"I think I love sharing my days with you."

Florence left before she could soak in Shannra's reaction and affirm her suspicion that the response was not the one her lover was looking for. Right now, the only thing Florence could let herself think about was seeing Loom survive another day.

Through a back door into a narrow alley, Florence slipped from above ground to under in a mere moment, dropping down through what looked like an open sewage grate. It led her into a tunnel, straight to one of the still-open passages for what had become Loom's unofficial capitol.

She found all the vicars gathered in Ethel's makeshift receiving room, just outside the Vicar Alchemist's sleeping chamber.

"Ah, Florence, thank you for coming." Powell was the first to notice her.

"A Revolver always heeds their vicar's call." Florence wasn't quite sure if Gregory was speaking to her or Powell.

"I heard there was a letter?" She cut right to the chase.

"Yes, here." Powell shifted, passing a carefully sealed envelope. Its thickness was more like a folio than a letter, and Florence looked at the curious marking on its front.

*To Florence*

*From Arianna*

"Vicar Gregory suggested that we open it, but since it was addressed to you specifically, I wanted to make sure it found its way into your hands foremost."

"Thank you, Vicar Powell." Florence could feel the curiosity burning off Gregory to the point that the temperature in the room might have been rising.

Wasting no time, she broke the seal and slid out the papers.

Every leaf was marked over in many places. Layers of text betrayed years of work from different hands. Some, Florence recognized as Arianna's scribbles. Others were foreign to her.

"Don't hold us in such suspense," Vicar Dove practically yawned.

Florence read over the notecard twice. She knew what she was looking at without Arianna's hasty explanation.

"It's schematics for a gun . . . that could fire through a corona."

"Does Arianna now fancy herself a weaponsmith?" Gregory seemed amused, dismissive.

Florence didn't even bother to combat her scowl. "Given what she's accomplished to date, I wouldn't put it past her. Furthermore, it looks like the work wasn't started by her, but the late Master Oliver and the Vicar Revolver I believe you replaced."

Gregory clearly was not pleased with her tone. "Let me see those," he demanded.

Florence had little option but to pass them over.

He read over the papers once, twice. Everyone in the room was attentive, waiting for his assessment.

"Ethel, let me use a pencil?" Gregory dropped to the ground, scraping away pebbles and dust to lay out the schematics on what had now become his work surface. The Vicar Alchemist produced the requested utensil and he set to making hasty smudges and drawing lines across the notes.

"Could such a weapon actually exist?" Powell was the only one who risked breaking the silence.

"I would've said no a few minutes ago. But this . . . this should work."

Florence stepped over, looking at Gregory's sketched calculations. She followed his adjustments, the accounting for an extra feedback of magic, using a canister for priming . . . Her eyes stilled on one line he'd smudged out.

"I think I could make these modifications to something I have currently. It'll make the gun quite large, but I shouldn't need anything too special."

"But that's . . . what about—" Florence tried to point at the spot she'd gotten stuck on.

"Thank you, Florence," Gregory said curtly. "In the future, please inform Arianna to send such things to me directly, as the vicar. Now, we need you to return to your post."

Florence stared at Gregory for three long breaths. She thought about speaking up. She wondered if she should try to make him listen. But this was Loom, where your failures were your own, and you bore the burden of them.

"Should any of the vicars require anything else, you know where to find me."

Florence gave a tip of her hat and left the room, saying nothing about the explosively critical error she'd noticed in Gregory's calculations.

# 31
## CVAREH

world when she was near, yet she made him want to alter everything for the better.

Arianna had come to Nova for him. His boldness had not pushed her away, had in fact brought her to him. Cvareh gripped the feathers of his boco and stared toward the horizon as he raced back toward the Temple of Agendi.

She needed him as the Oji, to fulfill Petra's promises. Petra's memory needed him to defend House Xin. All of Xin needed him to work with Loom. So much rested squarely on his shoulders, and it was time he got to work—starting with arranging transport of the remaining flowers to Dawyn's family's plot.

He didn't even spend half of a day on the task, but when he arrived back at the Xin Manor many hours later, it felt as if he'd been gone an eternity. He had scrubbed himself to bleeding at Dawyn's, but still imagined he could smell the combination of Rok blood and Loom on his skin.

Oddly, Cvareh found it difficult to muster concern over the fact. *Let Finnyr and Fae smell their fallen kin and Loom rising to defeat them*, his mind whispered dangerously.

As soon as he landed his boco, a servant rushed out to greet him.

"Cvareh . . ." There was a long pause following his name, proof the man clearly had no idea how to address him.

"What is it?" The lack of formality suddenly seemed more obvious than it had before—a matter long overdue to be settled.

"I was asked to send you to your brother the moment you returned."

"Did he say what for?" Cvareh had half a mind to ignore the request and attend Finnyr later, just to send the message that he did not jump at his brother's every beck and call.

"No, just that he would be waiting for you in the main hall."

Cvareh trudged down through the manor, exhausted from the lack of sleep and still recovering from combat. But instead of finding every step harder than the last, he found it easier. Life returned to him in the form of anger, frustration, and a small bit of hard-earned triumph. He had shed Rok blood, hidden the fact, and thwarted what was no doubt a very clear plan to put a swift end to Loom's rebellion—and with it, Xin's hopes.

He had done it all before Finnyr had likely even woken for the day.

That anger reached its peak when he entered the hall and his eyes fell on Finnyr, seated on Petra's throne. Where Petra commanded the seat and it cradled her in return, Finnyr was dwarfed by the stone chair. For the first time, Cvareh wondered what he would look like in such a seat.

"Seems an uncomfortable place to wait."

"You did keep us waiting," Finnyr replied curtly.

"I may not have returned at all, and what then? You were planning to sit here all day?" To think, he could have been spending time with Arianna in the refinery *and* making his brother wait. It was truly a missed opportunity.

"Where were you?"

"Worshiping at Lord Xin's temple."

"Do you honestly think that will work on me? I know better."

"I have alibis." Cvareh was glad he had spent so much time there throughout the days prior. "Ask several witnesses, if you'd like." He strode forward before his brother could get in another word. "And you know better? You know *nothing* about me, Finnyr."

"That's Finnyr'Oji." The emerald-skinned Rider stepped forward, her magic blowing like an uncomfortably hot wind. Cvareh ignored the all-too-familiar scent of honeysuckle in it.

"Sorry, *Finnyr'Oji*. New title and all, it slips." Cvareh smiled and didn't even try to make it look sincere.

"You should be more respectful before your Oji." It was a normal thing for a Dragon to say, but the woman looked like she could burst out laughing at any moment. Perhaps she found the idea of Finnyr as Oji as comical as the rest of them.

"And you should be more respectful of the Xin'Ryu, Fae *Rok*'Kin To, and stay out of Xin matters." Cvareh snapped back, rising up onto the lower step.

"The Xin'Ryu? I don't recall Finnyr ever appointing you such." She looked between the two men.

"Finnyr'Oji," Cvareh corrected as he took another step, assuming his position where Petra usually placed him. He looked down at his brother, who seemed utterly stunned to find his little brother standing toe to toe with the Master Rider. "Perhaps he doesn't tell you as much as you'd like to believe?"

Cvareh wasn't backing down now; he'd come too far. "Isn't that right, brother? Tell her, tell this Rok Rider that she is an excellent protector you are most grateful to have, but she doesn't know everything about Xin."

Finnyr seemed at a loss for words, looking between them for something to say. If he wanted lines, Cvareh would feed them to him.

"Tell her that I am the Xin'Ryu."

Finnyr's mouth opened and nothing came out.

"Tell her." Cvareh's hand curled into a fist as he stared down his brother. He searched those familiar golden eyes for any shred of the man Finnyr could have been, for any remaining love he might harbor for his house. Finding none, Cvareh scraped the bottom of Finnyr's pathetic personality for a lingering scrap of self-preservation, and found it.

"He's right. Cvareh is the Xin'Ryu."

Cvareh felt as shocked as Fae looked. Her surprise quickly turned to anger, and she stared down a now-cowering Finnyr. But Cvareh was done; he'd gotten what he wanted, and so had his brother—the oversight of House Rok and all the joys that came with it.

Cvareh walked away, leaving Finnyr alone, and not feeling a speck of regret for the fact.

# 32
## COLETTA

YVEUN NEVER SOUGHT COLETTA OUT IN HER GARDEN UNLESS SOMETHING HAD gone catastrophically wrong.

"Cvareh is moving to gain control of House Xin." Right to the point, her mate wasted no time.

Coletta wiped her hands on a delicately embroidered rag, giving the declaration some thought. "How have you arrived at this conclusion?"

"Fae has whispered this afternoon that the youngest Xin has begun to show signs of ambition. Cvareh, out of everyone, shows ambition! What is this world coming to?" Coletta wasn't sure if he sounded impressed or frustrated.

"It was only a matter of time, and we knew it." Coletta had long suspected there was more to Cvareh than Petra let on. The schematics, and then the events on Loom, followed by the Crimson Court, all confirmed it. This was more of the same, and therefore nothing to be worked into a panic over.

"I would like to bring Fae back to Lysip."

Coletta turned to her ledger, feigning attention to its contents.

"If Xin truly decides to wage war, she will do little alone and—"

"—and we risk losing her," Coletta finished, looking up from her notebook. "I do not disagree with you, Yveun. Fae is far more valuable to us alive. Her presence at Xin would always come to this end."

Yveun nodded. Coletta wondered how much he understood about the delicate play of keeping Fae at House Xin. An opportunity to ensure the house's loyalty just a little longer while they attempted to weaken Loom through demoralizing attacks and weaning their gold, as well as an opportunity to further their organ research.

Even failures could be part of a plan.

"After she has returned and you have had your fun, send her to me," Coletta instructed.

"Have you found more success yet with your experimentations?"

"Not yet," Coletta admitted.

"Then I would not have us carving up our prize stock." Even Yveun referred to the woman as little more than an animal. To them both, Fae was a bitch on a chain, poised to attack, or satiate whatever desires he could conceive.

"She will be fine. Despite our setbacks, there has been no lasting weakness in Yeaan. Even now, my flower seeks out the resources the rebellion on Loom requires, and destroys them." Yveun seemed unconvinced, so Coletta continued. She didn't really need his approval, but things were easier when she had it. "Furthermore, Fae is far stronger, wouldn't you agree? She'll manage without issue, I'm sure."

"I hope you're right, Coletta." And just like that, the hulking monster that was Yveun gave in to his Ryu.

"I usually am." It never hurt to remind him. "Summon her back before House Xin descends into anarchy. Then, contact Tam for a meeting."

"Tam?"

"With Fae gone, I have no doubt Finnyr will be dead within the month. As soon as that happens, we should make sure we have the loyalty of House Tam secured."

"Their tithing?" Yveun asked grimly. Coletta knew he hated Tam's demands; she held no love for them either. But there could be no half measures. Anything less than absolute loyalty to him was a foreign concept.

"I have acquired enough for them to make all things equal in the matter of their assistance for the battles ahead."

"I am a wise man, to leave such important acts in capable hands."

Coletta could not stop the swell of pride that came at his words. "Trust me, Yveun, and I will see us through to a bright future where Rok reigns the worlds above and below unquestioned."

"If anyone can, it is you."

"It is *us*," Coletta reminded him. They would either live together in victory, or perish in failure. No half measures.

# 33

## ARIANNA

"Nevertheless, I don't know how you stomach them," Arianna muttered, having the oddest conversation she'd ever conceived.

"They treat us better than House Rok did." The man across from her, a Fenthri with the Alchemist symbol on his cheek, continued to fiddle with the tubular object they'd been passing between them for the better part of the afternoon.

"So you've said . . ." Arianna mumbled, though she just couldn't imagine it. Fenthri on Nova—not just Nova, but *Ruana*—the whole time she was there. There had been a taste of home hidden right under her nose while she was isolated in the Xin Manor, and Petra never told her. It was almost enough to make Arianna resent the deceased Dragon. "Didn't you want to come home?"

"Of course, but it wasn't an option."

Arianna chewed on her lips and flipped one of her daggers in her free hand. She felt restless, uneasy. Was Xin any better than House Rok if they kept Fenthri? Surely, if conditions were so good, Petra would've mentioned it. Had she been conspiring to put another Yveun in power?

The idea quickly evaporated. Petra was dead and whatever kind of king Cvareh would be, he wouldn't be anything like Yveun.

"Did you try to escape?" She wanted to find a way to make herself feel better about the whole situation.

"To what end? Escape would, at best, require a sympathetic Dragon. I've met Dragons I'd dare call kind, but sympathetic enough to just let me go? Certainly not." The Alchemist, Luther, sighed and leaned back in his chair. "I've been here thirteen years." She believed him, judging by the white streaks in the slate hair running back from his temples. "I don't have that much longer left."

"Hush."

"It's true and you know it." Arianna kept her mouth shut, rather than argue against a fact. The man smiled tiredly at her silence. "I wouldn't know what to do if I returned to Loom. From what you tell me, I doubt I'd recognize it."

"Or maybe you'd know it better. It's moving back to what it was before the Dragons."

He held out the tube and Arianna took it, popping off the bottom and inspecting his work, making her own modifications. "I can't believe you're happy here . . . you *want* to be here."

"I want to be here more than I wanted to be at Rok. I've had my own room, proper food, the ability to work. What more does a Fenthri really want?"

She withheld the word "freedom" for his sake.

"I'm not crammed in a single room like livestock," he continued. "None of us are. None of us are beaten or debased. The ones Petra got out were the lucky ones."

Arianna felt anger rise in her. Anger at herself, at the world she lived in, at the people she'd made into Loom's allies. No matter what happened Arianna was beginning to wonder if Loom was trapped in an endless cycle of subjugation at the hands of Dragons.

It was a dark moment—perhaps one of her darkest—and the least ideal for her to see a Dragon, any Dragon. Naturally, Cvareh rounded the corner of the laboratory at that very instant.

"Ah, I see you've made a friend." He beamed.

Arianna didn't know what expression her face had, but it was enough for Luther to stand from the seat he'd been comfortably occupying for hours and make a swift retreat.

"Xin watch over you, Cvareh'Ryu," the other Fenthri muttered as he passed. Arianna wondered if it had been drilled into him by force or if a Fenthri could actually believe such superstitious nonsense.

Cvareh didn't even motion at the display of respect. His eyes stayed locked with hers, searching. He opened his mouth to speak, but Arianna had already decided she would not give him the liberty of having the first word.

"Were you going to tell me?" She carefully set down the tube she and Luther had been working on to transport the Flowers of Agendi past the clouds without damage.

"Tell you what?" Cvareh frowned.

"Tell me your sister was no better than Yveun."

"*What?*" Cvareh hissed. "You know well and true Petra was not Yveun. Not by any stretch."

"Then what of you?" She practically leapt from the chair. "What of you, Cvareh?" She rammed a finger into his chest, though she couldn't recall crossing the room to get to him. "Are you any better than Yveun?"

"Arianna, what happened?" Cvareh clasped her hand with his. There was no reason why she couldn't wrench herself away; she had the strength. But every part of her suddenly felt weak. Arianna couldn't place why until she felt her eyes burning at their corners.

"Petra, you . . .you kept Fenthri as slaves."

Cvareh's head whipped from her to the door Luther had just exited through. Emotions swept across his face, beckoned by the winds of a truth undeniable to either of them.

Arianna stepped away.

And was tugged closer.

His cheek was against hers, staving off the first prickle of tears by pressing his flesh to her own. His mouth was on her ear, and he uttered promises she didn't know if her heart could hear.

"We never saw them that way, Ari. We couldn't get them home."

"You lie." Her mind knew better, but her heart begged to believe him. It ached for him despite herself.

"I never saw them that way," he clarified.

"Set them free, then."

"Is this your boon?"

"No, this is what you will do for me if you truly care for me."

"And care for you, I do." He moved the corner of his mouth against hers, and then the whole of his lips.

She leaned into him, matched him touch for touch. She hated herself for it, for needing it, for wanting it, for wanting *him*.

*Eva forgive me.*

"Free them," she repeated. It was the only thing she could cling to. She'd lost all other dignity the moment her fingers curled around his.

"I will. When I am Dono, I will," he uttered.

And then, the tears fell.

Not since the death of her master and her last lover had she cried. For what Arianna had just heard was the decree that would separate them; it was the utterance that would tear them apart as the great machine of fate continued to roll over the world.

He would be Dono, and she would be no one. That would be the end of them.

So, for now, she indulged herself. Arianna cast aside all pride. She pulled him by the scraps of fabric he called clothing and pressed herself against him. She felt the curves of that all-too-familiar chest, the swell of his pectorals before they fell to the dips of his abdomen.

Cvareh's hands moved to her face, held her mouth to his, and they breathed together for a blissful moment.

"I will be leaving soon."

"When?" The word was more of a gasp—part groan, into her neck.

"Soon. I must return to Loom. I must bring flowers with me. There are boxes ready for tempering; we shouldn't dally."

"*When?*" he repeated.

"Tomorrow? Soon." She had to return to her world and leave him to his, or else they would fall into that contented state that dulled the pressing needs of all they had become responsible for.

"Then give yourself to me now?"

Like he had given her a choice. "I demand something in exchange."

He laughed darkly against her shoulder. "Of course you do."

"I want your lungs."

"My lungs?" he repeated.

If he were to give them to her, perhaps she could make time stop. In those frozen moments, she could let go of her own harsh judgment for loving such a man. She could savor him, as though he wasn't about to step into a role that prohibited her from standing by his side.

It would be the only part of him she could keep forever.

"Give them to me. Make me Perfect."

He paused and pulled away. His brow furrowed as he inspected her thoughtfully. His long, blue fingers ran through her snow-colored hair and swept it from her brow in thought.

"Arianna, you were perfect long before the Philosopher's Box."

If only it were true.

"Give them to me. Please."

"If that is what you want of me, then it is yours." He kissed her again. "I am yours."

Cvareh crushed her lips with his and encircled her waist with his arms, and Arianna forgot about all reservations as he pushed her against the wall.

# FLORENCE

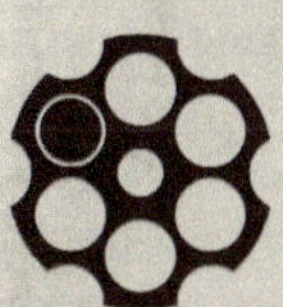

"WITH THIS, WE WILL BE ABLE TO FIGHT DRAGONS HEAD-ON," VICAR GREGORY addressed the Revolvers' Guild. In his hand was a weapon he hoisted up to his shoulder with ease. It had the look of a rifle, only shorter and fatter through the barrel. Wires connected disk-like multipliers, covered in the scratches of Alchemical runes, along its length. "With this, we will no longer be forced to rely on imperfect alchemy or failed negotiations."

"Will there be a Philosopher's Box?" an initiate asked from Florence's left.

It was disturbingly easy to take stock of the guild. All of them now fit into a single cavern in the Underground. There were about twenty-five journeymen, thirty initiates, three masters, and the vicar. Florence would guess the Revolvers were at one-fifth of their previous size, maybe even less.

"The Rivets are still working on the Philosopher's Box. But in the meantime, this will give us a real chance to escape the Underground and fight against the Dragons out in the open." Gregory was back to showing off the weapon. "In fact, the preliminary work on the gun was done by the Master Rivet who designed the Philosopher's Box herself."

As murmurs flew between people assembled in the room, Shannra caught Florence's eyes. There was no mention of Florence, which she could stomach since she hadn't done much other than receive the letter; but there was no mention of Master Oliver—which Florence knew would not sit well with Arianna—or the last Vicar Revolver either.

She wanted to ask herself how such a selfish man could have landed as the head of the Revolvers. But then she remembered they hadn't had many options to choose from. Knowing Gregory, he'd likely strong-armed his way into the position when the rest of the guild was still reeling from grief and terror.

" . . . so I will be taking a select few with me topside this very day. We will go, and we shall use this to cut a Rider from the pack and take them down, so the Dragons know we are working on a weapon that their gliders and coronas won't protect them from."

"I volunteer." An eager journeyman jumped to his feet.

"Take me with you!" A woman joined him, standing tall and resolved.

"I want to see the gun fire!" An initiate was not going to be left out. The Revolvers were nothing if not recklessly curious.

"The masters and I have already decided on the team." Gregory motioned for them to sit down. "It shall be composed of Master Joseph, journeymen Thomas, Willie, Shannra . . ." There was a long pause, audibly separating the last name from the others of journeyman status. " . . . and Florence."

Florence's ears perked up at her name. She rose to her feet, seeing that everyone else who had been called had done so. Shannra's eyes squinted slightly at her. She knew they were both wondering the same thing: What was Gregory up to?

That question was the first thing out of Shannra's mouth as they prepared to go topside in the hour that followed.

"Why would he invite you?" she mumbled, checking her guns for the second time.

"Perhaps he's using me to help navigate the guild hall?" Florence was already on her third check.

"Did he even ask if you could?" Shannra asked. Florence shook her head. Truth was, she wasn't even confident that she could, beyond broad strokes. It'd been so long since she was last there.

"I don't like this, Flor."

"Maybe it's his way of thanking me for giving him the schematics?" Florence's mind immediately jumped back to the vicar's hasty calculations. "Share the glory of its first use?"

Shannra hummed, unconvinced. "Sharing isn't something our vicar is known for." The woman glanced around, but she had maintained her corner away from all the other journeymen. "What Arianna said about Gregory on Ter.0 is true. He's a good Vicar Revolver, but not because he's a renowned teacher."

"It's because he's cutthroat." Florence had figured out that much on her own. It was a strong front for the guild to have right now, especially when the world had gone to pieces and they needed the Vicar Revolver to be a beacon of strength. What was good for the guild, however, was not necessarily the best for Florence.

"He was only ever tolerated because he was effective." Shannra harnessed her weapon.

The word *effective* stuck. Florence grabbed the other woman's wrist, arresting her complete attention. Florence dropped her voice as low as possible.

"When I gave the schematics to him . . . he did some quick calculations, called the problem solved."

"I hear a 'but,'" Shannra whispered, evoking a solemn nod from Florence.

"I noticed the error. He ignored me when I tried to point it out." Shannra's scowl deepened. "He may have since fixed it."

"I doubt it. Gregory was never much known for theory."

"We'll just have to be extra careful."

They each packed an additional box of canisters before setting off to the arranged meeting point. It was a narrow room that had a ladder leading into the Ravens' Guild hall. Vicar Dove had spared one Raven to guide them, inadvertently proving that Florence was not along to navigate. It was a young man who was looking very uncomfortable with the whole idea of what they were about to do.

"Our objective is simple," Gregory instructed the small group. "We will head into the hall and up to a waiting point and wait for a whisper from a lookout. When Thomas gets the signal that a Dragon has landed, we will run to intercept, dispose of the Dragon, and return." He said it as though doing so would be the simplest thing in the world. If Florence had learned one thing, it was that nothing was ever easy when it came to Dragons. "This is nothing more than a test run for the weapon."

"Do you have any reason to believe the weapon may not work?" Florence just couldn't keep her mouth shut.

"Are you questioning my work?"

"Is it not the nature of a journeyman to question?"

"It is. But you are no journeyman."

"What am I, then?" Now was not the time to make such a demand, especially not when they were about to enter a dangerous situation. But Florence didn't hesitate. "You said I was a Revo on Ter.0."

"The masters have not yet discussed your official status, Florence." Master Joseph stepped in to play damage control. "Perhaps that is something we can look into after this test."

Gregory looked at Florence the entire time Joseph spoke. Florence didn't take her eyes away. She refused to allow anyone to think they could intimidate her.

"Let's go." Gregory motioned for the Raven to lead up the ladder.

Florence had entered the Underground through the Ravens' Guild, but this was a different pathway than last. She tried to make sense of where she might be, dredged up old memories of her childhood in the guild, but it wasn't until she saw a level marker along the main helix that she knew. They had a long way to go before they could even be seen by a Dragon, and that assumed any were currently flying around.

"It's odd to see it so quiet," Florence mused softly as they stepped onto the main track.

"I could grab us a trike?" the Raven offered, clearly compelled to fill the space with the sounds of engines churning and wheels spinning.

"Best to keep it quiet," Gregory shot down the idea. "Don't want to draw too much attention."

They continued up the track on foot. Florence adjusted her grip on her gun, peering around corners as they passed. She had seen Dragons landing on the guild hall for stretches of time before taking off again. But it was entirely possible that they had begun to set up operations as they cleared different portions of the building, working their way downward in search of their prey.

There were no markers of Dragons anywhere, however. No markers of any other life, and the silence quickly became uncomfortable. Florence swallowed hard, looking around the group. There was no reason why they should all be so silent. The path they walked had every appearance of being safe and no one—not even Thomas with his Dragon ears—had any reason to believe there were enemies nearby.

Nevertheless, their lips had been sewn shut with invisible strings.

"We're here," the Raven said finally. "Halfway."

"Take us to the closest room with one exit and no windows," Gregory demanded. "We'll wait there."

The Raven led them to a small interior room that was little more than an access for the back panels that supplied electricity to the guild. It was a good thing the Alchemists had been hard at work developing alternatives to electricity, because the generators had long since stopped running and the room would've been completely dark without each of their torches.

"How long do you think it will take?" the man named Willie asked.

"However long it takes." Vicar Gregory settled into a seated position, his prized weapon across his lap.

Florence used the opportunity to inspect it more closely. She scanned the wires, the multipliers, the gold channels that ran along the outside and peeked out from the inside. There was something about it that seemed *off*, but she couldn't quite put her finger on what it was. As a result, she couldn't even be sure there was anything wrong. Perhaps Gregory had seen his error after all and fixed it. Maybe that was why he'd let her come along—a silent nod to her help, however little credit he'd actually give her.

"So, does it use a canister?" Master Joseph made the Revolver's equivalent of small talk.

"Only as a primer to get the reaction going. The rest is magic, after that." Gregory seemed much more inclined to discuss the logistics of his weapon with someone he deemed his equal.

"So the wielder must be a Chimera?"

"Yes, though not a Perfect one."

Florence couldn't deny the merit of the idea. Making Perfect Chimera already felt like it was taking too long, and she was likely the person who would be the most patient with Arianna on the matter. It was also resource-intensive and mostly untested.

But making a gun . . . Most of those still alive on Loom were Chimeras—the healing powers of magic helped many who might not have otherwise survived the attacks on the guilds. If they could perfect this weapon and mass-produce it . . . Between that and Perfect Chimera, Loom would be unstoppable.

The conversation had faded and several of the party were dozing by the time Thomas sat up straight. Florence felt the familiar crackle of magic in the air that heralded a whisper link. Thomas brought his hand to his ear.

"Yes?" Thomas asked the person on the other end of his magical tether. Everyone in the room roused swiftly. "Middle floor . . . landing area . . . by a large crane . . ."

"Airship test pad." The Raven knew the place instantly.

"Is it far?" Gregory stood.

"Not very, up a bit more."

"Master Joseph, you focus on protecting the Raven as he leads us," Gregory commanded. "I will be up running point with them. I want Thomas and Willie watching flanks. Florence and Shannra, take up the rear."

It was an important and sometimes life-saving position, but no Revolver wanted to be put in the back, away from the front line and all the action. Yet again, Florence had no doubt this would come back as some slight against her.

They all voiced their agreement and set off as Gregory had instructed. If the tension was heavy when they ascended the tower, it was multiplied several times over now that they knew a Dragon was present. Everyone kept their breathing low, weapons drawn. Florence wished, not for the first time, that she had sought out an Alchemist for Dragon ears. Not having them suddenly felt like a severe limitation.

Shannra glanced around warily; Florence put her trust in the other woman's magic and long pointed ears. Her head jerked and the Master Revolver held up his hand, looking in the same direction that Shannra was fixated on. Magic pulsed. Thomas raised his hand to his ear.

"Two more have—"

"One incoming!" Shannra announced, leveling her gun in the direction of a side hall. If Florence could feel the pulse of magic from Thomas's whisper link, then surely any Dragon would've been drawn to it.

"I have the bastard in my sights," Gregory proclaimed, hoisting his weapon.

Florence watched as the vicar's gun slowly lit up. She felt his magic spike and the metal began to glow. Magic sparked off the gold in rainbow fractals that shone like embers and disappeared before hitting the ground. Alchemical runes shimmered. Power continued to build in the multipliers, lighting up the gun like a beacon to all Dragons nearby.

All at once, Florence knew why the gun had seemed so *wrong* to her.

She remembered the weapon she had made at the Alchemists' Guild hall. It too had a series of runic multipliers, a series that Florence now knew had been flawed. That, combined with the magic discharge . . .

Florence looked to the door that everyone else had leveled their weapons against. She could hear the footsteps now, closing fast. She was torn between what she ought to do, and what she wanted to do. She wanted to get back at Gregory for every rebuff. She wanted him to bear the responsibility of his haste and hubris. But Florence wasn't inclined to put herself above the best interests of Loom. Not even now.

"Gregory, put the gun down! There's a mistake! The runes are wrong!" Her voice rose, as if to convey the severity of what she was saying.

Gregory did nothing. His eyes remained on the door, his magic pouring into the weapon. It was too late. The proverbial bucket holding his magic had tipped too far into the gun, and there was no way he would be able to disentangle himself from it now.

"Everyone, get back!" Florence could still feel the shrapnel and daze from the gun exploding in the skeleton forest. "It's going to blow!"

Florence ran away. She didn't care how it looked. She didn't give two canisters about Gregory. All she knew was that she had to survive.

The door they had been watching slammed open, but Florence didn't even turn. She threw herself down the hall, hands over head. Her ears filled with the sound of a Dragon's snarl and then the explosion of magic.

Metal and concrete groaned; Florence was slammed into the ground. She tumbled, allowing the momentum to carry her further away along the shock wave. Another body rolled beside her, wheezes betraying life. Florence forced her eyes open and her hands under her shoulders. She pushed upwards, raising her head.

Willie slumped, dazed, against the wall to Florence's right. She would've presumed him dead from the streak of blood that led down to his head, were it not for his groans. Thomas rolled in pain nearby, his lower half burned to a crisp. Even with magical healing, it would likely scar, but the man would live. Shannra was also finding her feet, about as bruised and scraped as Florence. Their position as the rear guard had likely saved them both.

Dragon and Fenthri guts lined the walls, floor, and ceiling out from the epicenter of the blast. Had Florence not known the men who had been standing there moments earlier, she may not have been able to piece together enough flesh to identify them. Gun parts littered the floor.

"More are coming," Shannra warned. "We need to retreat."

Florence stared at Willie and Thomas. She had no attachment to these men, no kinship with them. Most of the journeymen hadn't even given her the time of day while she'd lived among them in the Underground. So, it was surprising to feel her lips form the words, "We can't leave them."

"What?" Shannra hissed. "This is the life of a Revolver; they knew—"

"I won't leave my guildmates behind!" Florence sprung forward into a sprint. She collected up the largest pieces of Gregory's weapon, pulling them together and flicking aside scraps of flesh.

"What are you doing?" Shannra followed her.

"Leave us . . ." Thomas groaned.

"I know what was wrong with it. I saw a similar weapon once before. Riders used it to shoot down the airship Ari and I were on. The magic . . . We think that magic should be colored, split, but if you put all the colors together you get white. The discharge should be white, not rainbow. It's not an airship that diffuses and breaks magic apart for lift . . ."

"What are you going on about?" Shannra was utterly lost.

"I knew this before . . . But I was wrong on the Alchemical runes to multiply without splitting. Gregory made the same mistake, but in a different way, which means . . ." Florence began to frantically sort out the parts.

"Florence, there's no time for this."

"I can fix it." Florence laid out her revolver. The barrel would be shorter. She'd have to account for that when it came to how many multipliers she stacked, and the range it would be effective in before the magic beam unraveled. "I can make it work."

"We're going to die if we stay!"

"Two more, incoming . . ." Thomas moaned.

"Go on without us," Willie wheezed.

"No!" Florence's hands continued to move so quickly that she hardly had time to think between motions.

"Florence, is this about saving guildmembers? Or saving your pride?" Shannra grabbed her elbow. "They knew the risks. Don't insult them. Save yourself. Fix it later."

"I will not be like her!" Florence shouted, tearing her eyes away from the gun parts and bringing them to Shannra's face. "I will not treat my guild like it's expendable!"

"Her? Who? *Your* guild?" Shannra shook her head, standing and letting go of Florence. "What do you think you are?"

"I'm the woman who will save Loom." Florence bent and heated gold, connecting parts with seams that would likely only hold for one or two shots. One or two shots would be all she needed. "Before anything else, I am a Revolver, and I will not let the death of my vicar—however much of an idiot he was—go to waste."

Florence finished etching the runes she needed and stood. The footsteps were close enough now that even she could hear them. She leveled her weapon.

A Dragon bounded around the corner. One or two shots, that was all she had. She couldn't miss. Florence kept her magic even, pouring it in slowly. Consistent, not a burst of power, but a steady stream, like a rope spun from runes and gold and steel.

Gunshots echoed as Shannra panicked. The bullets sheared off the haze of a corona. Florence adjusted her grip slightly and widened her feet. She had to wait until the last moment.

Another female Dragon rounded the corner, gaining speed.

Florence squeezed the trigger.

It wasn't like a normal shot—fire and done. Florence continued to feed her magic into the weapon. *Stay together, stay together*, she repeated in her head as the beam shot out straight and true. The magic impaled the Dragon straight through the chest, his corona cracking and splintering off like an eggshell made of light.

The man fell dead, and Florence already had the other Dragon in her sights. Her magic was depleted from the first shot, and she locked her knees to keep them from buckling. Still, her hands were steady.

Florence waited two breaths after she thought the Dragon was in range.

It felt like the gun demanded every ounce of her, down to the very breath she drew to live. So Florence gave it that, and let the world go black.

# 35
## CVAREH

His chest still ached. There was a sort of phantom pain scraping against his ribs long after his lungs had grown back from where the Alchemist's knife had raked against them. Cvareh rubbed his chest again and thought of how many of his own he had condemned to harvesting. Cvareh had never lost an organ before and, now that he had, he was having a hard time seeing it as anything more than a deeply barbaric process.

For now, the ends still justified the means. But he wondered if the Alchemists in all their madness and wisdom couldn't think of a way to grow organs in their tubes, or harvest from the dead. Something, *anything*, to prevent Dragons from enduring what he just had.

Suffocation. Death without death. Repeating again and again until his tissues had grown and mended enough to hold air again.

He said nothing of his pain. He was the rightful Xin'Oji, the man who would win the war for them all and become Dono, and he had made the choice willingly. Furthermore, Arianna had to endure much the same—at least half of what he had gone through, as she didn't have to regrow—and she had yet to speak a word of discomfort.

It was moments like this one, when he looked at her readying her weapons, not more than one day from undergoing a major operation, that he was ensnared in awe at what she was—something more than he could ever aspire to be. Something different from anyone he'd ever met. And none of it had anything to do with the fact that she was now a true Perfect Chimera.

It was a fundamental construct of her nature, of *her*, that made her an unstoppable enigma. It was the same thing that allowed her to take organs and make them her own, like her hands, or ears, or now his lungs—motley parts that seemed so naturally incorporated into her body, like they'd yearned to be there all along. It was that nature which gave her the wisdom of Dragons four times her age, and kept her going with a profound, insatiable drive.

Cvareh wondered if it was something that could ever be lost. Or if she would forever pursue her ends with the march of a soldier to battle until Lord Xin finally came for her immortal soul.

It was something he wanted to embody as well, something he needed to possess to be worthy of her.

"When will you be back for more?" he asked, picking up the golden tube that would be used not to transport reagents, but flowers.

"I don't know just yet," Arianna said without looking at him. "As I mentioned, the Rivets were growing competent at making the boxes when I left. It's been a few days since then, but there may still be just a few ready for the flowers.

"It may not be me, however, who comes back up." That thought hadn't occurred to Cvareh until the moment she said it. "If all goes according to plan, I won't be the only Perfect Chimera in the world. Whoever comes, I'll have them use that river passage through the island to hide the glider trail."

"Will *you* come back?"

Her motions stopped. She must have heard his heart more than his words, the quiet panic that came at the thought of her leaving him and not returning.

"I'm sure you'll need me to fight at some point." Arianna sheathed her dagger behind her back. "The Perfect Chimera will take some time to train."

"I need you for more than that." He stood over her, looking down. If she could hear that nervousness in his soul at the idea of her trying to vanish from his life again, then she could also hear the truth of his words.

"Are all Dragons this insatiable?"

"Only the ones in love."

Arianna huffed in amusement, shook her head, and stood. She collected her things and carefully loaded the tubes in her bag. But none of it was a gesture of her own feelings toward him, and Cvareh was keenly aware that she had never told him if she reciprocated his affections to the same degree.

"I should be leaving."

He knew it was true. They'd kept each other for three days from the world. Cain had been covering for him, but Cvareh knew it was time to return to the Xin Manor. It was time to assume responsibility for his destiny.

"Whisper to me whenever you come. I will escape the manor to see you."

There was a moment's hesitation when Cvareh rightfully feared she was about to refuse him. But Arianna merely said, "Very well."

"When you return, I will be Oji," he swore. "And I will free them."

Arianna's expression looked as surprised as he felt in that moment. Cvareh had never said anything so bold, never uttered the slightest treason. Furthermore, it was faster than he'd first promised, originally saying he'd keep that vow when he was Dono.

But it felt right.

Right enough for him to know that he had to act on it before the day was done, before he risked losing his resolve.

"You will kill Finnyr?"

"I must." He knew her, and he knew where her mind was.

"I'll consider the lungs a trade for the kill that should be mine." Arianna gave him a stern look, as if warning him not to argue. He wouldn't have anyway. And he would have given her whatever she asked without a trade.

"I will end him," Cvareh vowed.

"Make it terrible. If you let me down in this, I will never forgive you."

Cvareh had never felt more motivated.

The feeling stayed with him the entire ride home. Cvareh knew he would be seen approaching the manor, and word would get back to Finnyr. He made a direct approach for Cain's balcony. It was smaller than his own, and Cvareh ended up making the short leap from his bird as it perched on the ledge before swooping back to the sky.

"The prodigal son returns." Cain opened the doors leading out to the balcony.

"I need you to do something." Cvareh wasted no time. The idea of challenging Finnyr, of assuming the role of Oji, of putting his house knowingly in harm's way by outright starting war against House Rok, was already planting uneasiness in his stomach. If he didn't do this now and seal it in blood, he risked losing his nerve.

"What is it?"

"I need you to find Fae, and keep her from Finnyr and me." Cvareh somehow managed to keep his voice level despite the fear and apprehension that wanted to seep out with every word.

"Cvareh, does this mean—"

"I'm going to challenge him, Cain." Cvareh clasped the shoulder of the man who had been like a brother to him. "I am going to take back House Xin from Rok. But I wish to do it by the laws of the gods. Even if Rok fights with shadows and deceit, I will challenge my brother in a forum befitting the title he claims to hold."

"Then I will distract Fae. I will challenge her if I must." The conviction was unsurprising, but also unwelcome.

"That is the one thing I must ask you not to do. I need you alive, Cain. I need you as my right hand, as my Ryu, should all this come to pass."

He wasn't prepared for the mix of surprise and emotion that crossed his friend's face. But what did Cain think would happen? There was no other choice, as far as Cvareh was concerned, and he wouldn't have chosen another under other less dire circumstances.

"I will do as my Oji commands."

# 36
## COLETTA

Fae had returned, and Yveun had indulged in his dark delights.

There was an easiness that settled over the estate when the king was pleased, not unlike the afterglow of the man himself. It was a collective sigh of relief for them all, none more than Coletta. Yveun wanted results. But he didn't want the practical kind that careful planning and hard work yielded. He wanted fanfare and the kind of victories that would have minstrels singing for centuries to come.

Coletta merely wanted to see their longevity secured.

Fae's arrival set in motion a series of carefully planned steps on Coletta's part. Yveun knew he had his time with the woman. Ulia knew to wait and observe until the Dono was finished with his conquest, and then spirit Fae away to the Gray Room—the room in which Coletta now waited with an Alchemist and a long, glistening tongue centered on a tray like some new delicacy.

"My queen," Ulia announced as she entered the room, Fae trailing behind. The green-skinned woman did little to demonstrate reverence to the Ryu, and Ulia could not contain a disdainful little side-eye. Coletta had the time to deal with neither, so she permitted both.

"Thank you for bringing Fae here. You may leave." Coletta had yet to allow Ulia to watch any of the experiments that went on in the room, and it was an intentional play.

She wanted the youngest flower to fantasize about the possibilities and mull over the potential horrors of the procedure. Even though Ulia would never utter secrets, Coletta knew no one was perfectly tight-lipped. And she wanted just enough truth to seep into the bedrock of Lysip to know that something of a great and terrible nature was happening at the Rok Estate.

"Do you know what is about to happen?" Coletta did not want to mince words with Fae.

"I have some vague idea." The emerald woman combed through her hair, still a nest from Yveun's hands.

"We will begin with your tongue."

"My tongue?"

"I do not believe you have magic there?"

Fae shook her head and sauntered over to the operating table as though she was doing little more than sitting down for a meal. Coletta admired the total lack of self-preserving instinct. It made the woman an ideal warrior to have in her arsenal.

"This will hurt some." The Alchemist regarded Fae warily. She was nearly twice his size.

"Your tiny knives can't hurt me, Fen."

"Open your mouth, then." It was almost as if he had accepted a challenge.

Coletta would never tolerate such boldness from a Fenthri herself, but there was something almost adorable about watching the gray people try to muster strength against their superiors.

Fae obliged and the man set to work. She didn't flinch as he pulled out her tongue with a long pair of metal tongs, the flat paddles at the end indenting the organ he set about removing. Coletta didn't avert her eyes from the moment the scalpel first cut into the flesh of the tongue to the last second before it was entirely severed.

The Alchemist tilted the Dragon's head, allowing blood to pour from the corner of Fae's mouth. Nothing more than a rough stub protruded from where her tongue had been, already beginning to ripple with magic to regrow the absent tissues. Even still, Fae's breaths were even, unlabored, and Coletta was forced to admire her monster yet again.

She watched as the new tongue was stitched into place. Despite having searched for the best organs on Ruana, she could make none take to Yeann or Topann's bodies. They all formed festering, agonizing wounds that her flower's body refused to heal.

But Coletta wasn't one to give up, not when there was so much to explore. It was the one thing she could count on the Fen agreeing with, and the man continued to carve up Dragons at her request.

The Alchemist pulled away, looking at his handiwork. Coletta could tell from his expression alone that something was different this time.

"What is it?" she demanded.

"I can't be sure . . ."

"Out with it, or it's your tongue that will be cut off next," Coletta drawled, not even mustering the energy to threaten him properly.

"This was a success."

"You can tell already?" He nodded. She knew almost instantly when a poison was right and when it was not. But the man's mouth still formed a grim line. "What have you discovered?"

The man looked from Fae to her, as if jarred from thought. He swallowed hard. "I think I know why the other organs didn't take."

Given the amount of fear radiating off the Fen in that moment, Coletta was certain that she was not going to like whatever the explanation was.

# 37
## CVAREH

Cain had gone ahead to distract Fae. Cvareh paced his friend's room for what felt like forever, though he knew it couldn't have been more than a few minutes. When he could wait no longer, he stepped into the hall.

The halls of the Xin Manor seemed alive once more. Even though Cvareh didn't see another soul for the first half of his walk to find Finnyr, the air seemed to pulse with an energy that he hadn't felt since before Petra's death. It was like House Xin was waking up from the grips of mourning at last.

Finnyr wasn't in his room, and neither was Fae. So Cvareh went to the main hall. Again, Finnyr was nowhere to be found, but Cvareh ran into a servant, her hands laden with laundry.

"Have you seen Finnyr?" Cvareh intentionally left off "Oji," an omission that did not go unnoticed.

The woman's eyes widened. "I have not."

He cursed, wheeling for another wing of the manor. Perhaps Finnyr had gone to claim Petra's quarters as his own. Killing him there would be its own kind of pleasure.

"I did, however, hear two men who work with the bocos saying that the Oji had requested a flight. They could not decide which mount to give him."

Cvareh stopped, only sparing a second. "Thank you."

"Good luck," the woman whispered.

If Finnyr was looking for a boco, there was a chance Fae had been called away and he was fleeing until his bodyguard could return. Perhaps he somehow had the instinct to know when death was coming for him. And it *was* coming.

Cvareh paused, turning. He saw the woman at the far end of the hall still, and called back to her. "Leave your task. Round up everyone you can to go to the departure platforms. I need witnesses. And I need to make sure he doesn't escape."

"As you command!" The woman practically threw down her basket of laundry, sprinting away so quickly that Cvareh almost felt a wind kicked up by her feet.

Cvareh thought of Finnyr, his cowardly slip of a brother. If he were Finnyr—which was rightly near impossible to imagine—where would he go? He would want to flee back to the safety of Rok's arms until Fae was no longer indisposed. But he would do so as he did everything else—with a coward's weakness.

So Cvareh headed down through the back passages and thoroughfares to a modest platform. Unlike the one Finnyr arrived on, this had no sculpture, no foliage or design. It was primarily used for quick trips, deliveries, and trysts that were not to be observed by the watchful eyes from the manor.

Here was where he found his brother pacing back and forth, wringing his hands. Cvareh hated that his brother's hands, of all people's, were attached to Arianna. Finnyr didn't deserve the honor. Maybe it was the gods above working in some weird way to see Finnyr's hands put to good use. His brother would have never created anything meaningful with them.

Cvareh waited in the archway leading out to the platform. He knew he didn't have time to waste, but he hadn't thought about what he was going to say. He had to challenge, but he felt there should be more gravity to the situation, more impact.

"Where is my boco?" Finnyr snapped when a servant appeared at the door, two others in tow.

The servant said nothing, looking from Finnyr to Cvareh. That was what finally drew his brother's attention. Cvareh wondered if he was having a waking fantasy, seeing his brother's lip tremble slightly.

"Cvareh, good, I'm glad you're here." Finnyr tried to draw up his height, to make his voice stable. Both failed. Had he always been such a tiny man? "It seems as though we have an issue. They have not yet brought my boco as I commanded. Perhaps as the Xin'Ryu, you can sort this out?"

Three more people appeared from another doorway. Cvareh didn't recognize any of them, but they all hovered with purpose. Their eyes carried a sharpness that seemed to pick at Finnyr with every glance.

"I will not sort it out as the Xin'Ryu."

"I'm your Oji." Finnyr looked around at all of them now, as if to search for someone to affirm the fact. "I'm your Oji!"

"Finnyr Xin'Oji To." It was the one time Cvareh didn't mind saying his brother's name in association with Petra's title. It was something that must be done if he was going to take it. "I challenge you."

"On what grounds?" Finnyr squeaked.

Where should he start? "Neglecting House Xin."

Everyone's eyes volleyed from brother to brother. The outcome would affect each of them in a way that would be forever irreversible. Cvareh's victory would mean war, but his defeat would mean centuries of oppression under House Rok.

"I-I have not—"

"Finnyr, do you accept my duel?" Cvareh pressed.

"Of course I do not!" Finnyr began laughing. "Do you think I'd let you duel me on such unsubstantiated grounds?"

"On what grounds did you duel Petra?" His sister's name was forced out as a snarl. When his brother said nothing, Cvareh asked again, "What grounds, Finnyr? What did you charge her with? Did she cower even though it was a fool's challenge? Or did she stand for it?"

"She challenged me." There was truth in Finnyr's affirmation.

Cvareh took a step forward. "She challenged you? And you killed her?"

"It was a duel!"

"Did you have help?" Cvareh continued his advance. He didn't know what he was going to do yet, but that first step had crossed him over the point of no return. This would end now. One way or another, there would be only one Xin sibling standing when the next morning came.

"N-no."

"Did Rok help you bring down Petra?" Cvareh's claws shot from his hand. "Did you see our sister die a coward's death?"

"Someone stop him!" Finnyr pointed. "He's threatening your Oji."

No one moved.

"Did you kill her?"

"I killed her!"

"Was the fight fair?" Cvareh's voice rose. More people continued to arrive, no doubt drawn by the shouting.

"It was a rightly charged duel," Finnyr insisted.

Cvareh sheathed his claws and reached out for his brother's neck, drawing the man to him with both hands. Had Finnyr always been so weak?

"Don't lie to me," Cvareh growled, pressing his fingertips into Finnyr's squishy flesh. At any moment, his claws could extend right into his brother's pale blue skin. "Don't lie to us."

"I—" Finnyr gasped.

"The eyes of Xin are upon you. Did you kill Petra fairly? Are you the Oji of this house?"

"Help me!" Finnyr's eyes lolled about, looking for salvation. But no one moved. "Fae, help me!"

"She's not coming." Cvareh didn't know what Cain was doing to distract the woman, but it seemed to be working so far.

"What will you do? Kill me without a proper duel?" Finnyr hissed. It only made Cvareh want to squeeze tighter. "Will you be Oji then? No."

"Are you Oji now?" He returned to his earlier line of questioning.

"House Rok recognizes me as such, and they're all that matters in this world."

Cvareh threw his brother aside. Finnyr rolled, scrambling to stop himself before he tumbled dangerously close to the ledge.

"House Rok is all that matters? Your cheek is unmarked, but you are one of them, aren't you?"

Finnyr clambered to his feet, shifting his rumpled clothing back into place. He smoothed his vest over his narrow chest. "House Xin, I command you to slay Cvareh, for assaulting your Oji."

No one moved.

"That's an order!"

"Are you our Oji?" a woman asked.

"Did you kill Petra in a fair duel?" another chimed in.

"W-What?" Finnyr looked around in confusion. "Don't question me. I'm your Oji!"

"Finnyr, you don't understand, do you, what it really means to hold that title?" Cvareh stepped forward.

"Take another step and I-I'll attack you myself."

Cvareh opened his arms, welcoming the first blow. "That's what I wanted from the beginning. If you are our Oji, defend your title. Lord Xin should be on your side."

Finnyr's claws shot out.

It was the final mistake in a lifetime of poor decisions.

Cvareh lunged.

Finnyr tried to guard himself, but the movement was slow and telegraphed. Cvareh swatted the defense away with one hand and plunged the other into his brother's chest. He would waste no time. He would not draw out the fight. As satisfying as the act would be, he had more important things to focus on than bloodlust. It served all of them, even Arianna, for his brother to stop existing as quickly as possible.

Finnyr coughed in shock. "Y-you really did it," he wheezed.

"Salvage her memory." Cvareh's fingers closed around Finnyr's heart. "Did you kill Petra?"

"I did . . . but she was already poisoned." His brother leaned forward, whispering in his ear. "You will never beat her. She is stronger than you all."

"Coletta?" Cvareh asked. It had to be.

Finnyr grinned, grabbed Cvareh's shoulders, and pushed himself away. Cvareh had never seen a Dragon take their own life, but it was a coward's death befitting his brother's existence. Finnyr stumbled backward. One foot had nothing to fall on, and he tumbled lifelessly into the empty air beyond the edge of the balcony.

Cvareh brought his brother's heart to his lips, taking a bite out of it. It was stringy and tough. Even though he knew Arianna had Finnyr's organs, he couldn't find the taste of her in the man himself. It was a relief, and Cvareh cast the unwanted scrap of meat after its owner.

He turned to those gathered, wondering what they thought, what they felt. It was an anticlimactic end that put the title of Oji on a man who had never wanted it and hadn't been trained for it. Were he one of them, he wouldn't feel very confident.

"What now, Cvareh'Oji?" a woman was bold enough to ask.

"Now, we fight." Cvareh took a deep breath. "We fight to end Rok's tyranny."

"How are we to stand against them?" The question wasn't asked to undermine him, but as a genuine concern—a warranted one, Cvareh understood.

"As Xin, we have always placed the end before our ideals. Our patron teaches us that the end is all that matters, for all things march toward the ultimate end—death." Cvareh hoped they would understand, and that his first action as Oji wasn't about to be defending his plan for saving their house from annihilation. "We shall rely on Lord Xin's guidance. We shall set aside our ideals, the pride as Dragons that blinds us from what we must do to gain our victory. We will ally ourselves with the Fenthri on Loom, and we will achieve victory."

The long silence that followed did not encourage him in the slightest.

# 38
## ARIANNA

SHE HATED THAT DRAGON.

She loved him, too.

Cvareh was nothing but raw emotion and conflict that gnawed at her fresh lungs from the inside out. Arianna flew the glider with reckless abandon, plunging into the God's Line and speeding for Garre as though nothing else in the world mattered.

Nothing else did.

She was going to lose the chance to kill Finnyr. She was going to lose the chance to kill Yveun, too, for Cvareh to become Dono. And when he did assume that title, she was going to lose him as well.

Arianna had never wanted to want him in the first place, but now that she did, it was hard to even breathe, thinking about him marching down a path with more conviction than she had ever seen—a path that would ultimately separate them. Just as Florence had found her place in the world, so would Cvareh. And neither of them required a Wraith.

It was night by the time she landed the glider in the far hangar. The room was still, icy with winter, and her breath curled in the air as she relaxed her magic from the glider.

"Good to see our wayward inventor return," a weathered voice spoke, as cold as the darkness itself.

Arianna turned in the direction of the sound. Magic pooled in her eyes and goggles until she could make out the living skeleton lurking in the shadows.

"Garre needs to work on its welcoming committee." Arianna stepped down and started in his direction. Louie stood in front of the entrance to the guild, and there was little else she could do. He didn't budge as she approached. Goggles of his own covered his beady little eyes; Arianna could only assume he stared up at her. She sighed heavily. "What do you want?"

"You don't seem pleased to see me."

"I will never be pleased to see you and am not in the mood for your games." The single sentence used up all the patience she could muster for the man. "Now, step aside."

"We need to speak."

"We have done so. Step aside." Arianna wondered if he was heavier than the tube-filled satchel at her side. She could just lift him up and move him.

"No."

"Do you have a death wish?"

"Not in the slightest. Quite the opposite, actually. The question is, Arianna, do you?"

"Do not threaten me." One warning—that was all he would get.

"The vicars may consider you a threat."

"*What?*"

"Since your little experiment as a weaponsmith blew up in the Vicar Revolver's face." Arianna was instantly reminded of her prototype on Nova. She'd sent the schematics to Florence and—

"I heard Florence was there, too. Fighting Dragons with faulty weapons . . . it's so sad, the outcome."

"Is she alive?" Arianna snapped. She was going to lose Cvareh and Florence; she had accepted that. But she would lose them to their choices and watch them thrive from her place in the shadows. She pushed the small-framed Fenthri against the door. His head banged dully against the metal. "Louie, do not play games with me."

"Then do not play games with me," he growled. "You went to Nova. You conspired to cut me out of the equation. You have yet to produce the schematics for the box . . . And after all I've done for you? After all I am willing to risk to secure your flowers, when Dragons would see them systematically destroyed?"

There was a moment of clarity that cut through the confusion and anger. "What did you say?"

"I will gladly secure the flowers for you." Louie smiled his wretched little grin, thinking he had a leg up on her, not knowing what she carried in her bag.

Arianna's hands loosened their hold, smoothing over the wrinkles thoughtfully, almost gently. She had not told him, or anyone on Loom, about the flowers being destroyed. "How far does your influence reach?"

"Straight to the Dragon Queen."

Those five words sent her into a blind rage. Coletta'Ryu, the woman who had drugged Arianna with her dagger, who had put her under the claws of Yveun —this was who Louie had been in bed with. Leave it to worthless slime like him to deal with such a revolting creature.

With a shout, Arianna swung the frail man to the ground, *hoping* she broke him. Her ears twitched eagerly at the sound of his body breaking and tearing. Arianna was on him, her knees pinning down his arms—as if he needed to be pinned. Louie couldn't put up a fight even if he tried. She felt his bones snap like twigs under her weight.

But Louie didn't cry. He didn't beg for mercy. He didn't even grimace. Instead he grinned like a fool, his crooked yellow teeth winking up at her like dying stars.

"Yes, yes, White Wraith, show me your claws," he urged. "Kill me, go ahead, and never know what I have told her."

"How dare you!" Arianna was glad they were far from the guild, because she was screaming now. There was no reason not to let the dam break, because the only person who could see this jagged, destroyed side of her would be a dead man. "I always knew you were the worst of the worst but this, *this*? You have sold out our world for profit!"

"Indeed," he replied with equal fervor, managing to keep his voice strong despite his position. "And I will do it again, time after time. I'm loyal to the highest bidder. So, you better make your offering more appealing, Arianna, for all of Loom."

"How long?" She couldn't even look at him straight. "How long have you been working with her?"

"*Years*." It made so much sense. The king of the underworld, the man who could seemingly get anything, who always happened to have organs to trade. Of course he did! He had sold his soul to a queen of death for them. "She trusts me, Arianna, and we can use this to our advantage. We can use this to save Loom if—"

"If what?"

"If you do not dare undercut me again," Louie finished.

Arianna reeled back, rolling from the balls of her feet to standing.

"I offered you an opportunity to work together. You went back on that deal."

"We make a new deal, right now. I don't kill you—"

His laughter interrupted her. "You think I care about death? You think I have people I love whom you can threaten? Arianna, you are the most idealistic fool of them all." Arianna watched with disdain as the man continued to lay there, his magic slowly re-growing his muscles and bones, popping his sagging flesh back into place. "If you kill me, you won't have the organs the Alchemists need for the Perfect Chimera. You won't have a means to get those precious flowers off Nova."

Arianna tilted her head to the side. How the tides shifted . . .

"Oh, Louie, *that's* your bargaining chip?" She drew her dagger. She didn't want to do this with Dragon claws. She wanted the tool that took Louie's life to be Fenthri-made. "That queen you so adore has betrayed you. She failed to inform you that her plans have been thwarted and her minions have been killed. That Xin has saved some of the flowers for themselves." Arianna crouched down as Louie's eyes widened with surprise. "Yes, my sweet King of Mercury Town. My friends have not sold me out, unlike yours. And they just so happen to be able to provide organs as well as any other Dragon."

Arianna pointed her dagger at his throat again, thinking back to Cvareh. She wondered if he had killed Finnyr yet. "You know, for most of my life, I've wanted to kill a king. You weren't the man I had in mind, but I think your death may be just as satisfying. Let's find out, shall we?"

"Wait, Arianna, let's not be hasty, I can still—"

"Still what?" She nearly purred with delight. He'd really come alone, thinking his contacts could protect him. He was an old knife, one that would snap if she even tried to put it to whetstone. Only one solution for such a worthless thing. "Be useful? I think there are a few Ravens who have just as much use as you, and they happen to know most of your network."

Arianna leaned forward, sliding a hand around his shoulder. It was an odd sort of embrace. She could feel the pistol he carried in his vest, but he didn't reach for it. He must've known it'd do nothing against her. Even if it alerted someone, he'd be dead before they arrived.

"Did you know it would end like this for you?"

"I couldn't imagine a better death than at the hands of the best thief and killer I've ever had the pleasure of working with." Louie spoke softly, as if to a lover. Arianna wondered if it was the first time the terrible man had been touched by a woman. "Eat my heart, after you cut it out."

"No," she whispered against his ear. "I know it'll taste rotten."

Arianna plunged the dagger between his ribs. She twisted it, the chorus of shattering bones and ripping tissue harmonizing with his final breath. Louie spit black blood that oozed down her shoulder—a stain on her white coat that she'd wear as a badge of honor.

Arianna plunged her hand into his chest, ripped out his heart, and cast it aside.

She stood, leaving the body of the King of Mercury Town oozing black onto the cold floor of the hangar. She left it as a clear warning to any who found it that the White Wraith had returned to Loom.

She slammed open the door Louie had been blocking with a *bang*, not caring who heard. The passage back to the guild was a blur that ended with her yanking another door open without warning. Will and Helen jumped to attention, wide-eyed and startled. Arianna leaned against the doorframe, flipping her knife, blood on her shoulder.

"All of Louie's men—bring them here, now," she demanded cheerfully. "Try to run and I'll flay you alive."

"What?" Helen stuttered.

"We need to do as she says." Will grabbed Helen's arm and dragged her from the room. The boy gave Arianna a sidelong look that she reciprocated. She hadn't forgotten his attempt to warn her on the airship. It may not be enough to save him, but it was enough to keep him alive for the time being.

They returned with three men in tow. Arianna closed the door behind them, appreciating the looks of apprehension each of them wore. She leaned against it, making it clear that no one was getting out without her blessing.

"So, let's talk about loyalty." Arianna pointed her dagger to the man with the red ears. "You first."

"My name is Adam."

"Fantastic Rok ears, those are. They're a whisper link, right?"

"To a woman named Topann."

Continued cooperation would earn him minutes, maybe even hours of life. "And that woman is in the employ of Coletta Rok, the Dragon Queen?"

"Yes."

"Would you sever the whisper link now if I demanded?"

"Yes."

"What's going on?" Helen demanded. "Where's Louie?"

The child wouldn't let herself see the obvious. "I killed him for crimes against Loom."

"You can't do that!" The girl seemed genuinely distraught.

"Occupational hazard for operating outside the law. Louie knew what he was about." There were few laws on Loom—Fenthri laws anyway. Most were unspoken, at that. "Don't commit treason" was a fairly obvious one. Louie's protégé seemed stunned still, so Arianna pressed the point home. "Helen, I am *not* the Master Raven and will never turn a blind eye to treason against Loom. As loathe as I am to kill talent, I dislike those who work against Loom much more."

The child pressed her lips shut.

"Louie liked deals. So how about this? I won't kill you all, and you—and everyone else who was loyal to Louie—work for me now. Whatever he paid you, I'll pay."

"Sounds more than fair, boss." Adam was the first to speak, crossing his arms over his chest and leaning against the wall. The idea clearly didn't bother him the slightest.

"Count us in." Will spoke for himself and Helen. The girl seemed to have a moment of protest, but she had the sense to swallow it.

"Cross me and die—"

Adam held up a hand. She arched her eyebrows at being silenced but permitted him to continue. "We all know what you can do. Would rather work for the Queen of Wraiths than the King of Mercury Town anyway."

*Queen of Wraiths.* That was new. But she'd killed Louie, which meant she'd get his title according to Dragon law. Arianna didn't bother hiding a smirk.

"First things first, then. How was Louie communicating back to Ter.4? I demand word on Florence."

# 39
## CVAREH

Restaurants were quiet enough to lure the rats out in search of food that had been left at tables—unpaid for, uneaten. Gaming parlors were still, decks unshuffled and wheels unspun. The tasting rooms for both wine and tea were, for the first time in the history of the capital city of Ruana, void of patrons.

Cvareh appreciated the reprieve from the chaos that had raged through the night. Hundreds of people, his people, had relocated up the river that ran down the center of Ruana. The order to flee was met with trepidation, but he was surprised by how many people gave him their faith and trusted in his orders.

"Now what?" Cain whispered. There was no need for discretion, but it suited the stillness that pressed in around them.

"Now, we go home." Cvareh took one last look at the building before them.

It was the old Xin Manor, the estate that had once been the most prestigious structure on all of Ruana but had languished in Petra's time as her focus had shifted to the new manor along the Western ridge. This had been his home when he was a boy. It was where his father died; in the calm before the calamity, he could almost pick up the scent of his father's blood from where Petra had ripped his beating heart from his chest.

"That's it?" Cain balked as Cvareh turned away from the old homestead. "You're turning tail and running?"

"Yes," Cvareh affirmed.

"No." Cain grabbed Cvareh's elbow and held his ground, practically yanking him back into place. "I will not let you hand Napole to them. You became Oji to fight."

"And fight I will," Cvareh vowed.

"How do you figure? You're leaving our capital, the Xin jewel, ripe for the taking." Cain snarled at the mere thought. "As your Ryu—"

"As my Ryu I need you above all others to trust me, Cain. Napole is not in the ground, or the buildings. What makes it shine is not the revelries or cafés. It is the people, Cain."

"They will come here."

"I know." Cvareh was counting on it. If Yveun let him down and didn't make a show of taking Ruana, he was in very real trouble. He'd only had time enough to come up with one plan, and this was it.

"You mean to ambush them!" Cain had yet to wrap his mind around not fighting. "The streets will run gold with Rok blood."

"No." Cvareh took Cain's hand, removing it from his person to clutch it tightly in both of his. "I will rob Yveun of his conquest. There will be no victory here. He will land on Ruana and be met with nothing more to claim than dust and rotting food."

"And then you will fight him?"

"I will not duel him yet." Cvareh shook his head and started again for his boco.

Cain fell hastily into step, his feet no doubt trying to make up for the slowness in his mind. "He will certainly challenge you."

"I know."

"You can do it here without fear of others' involvement."

"I know."

"But you won't do it anyway . . ." Cain's voice trailed off, trying to process a concept he had never heard of before. "What are you doing, Cvareh?"

"I am focusing on the end." Cvareh mounted his boco, taking up the reigns and looking toward the breaking dawn. "We've played along with Rok's world order for too long, and for what? If our goal is to build our own, we only have ourselves to answer to."

"This will be war on Tam as well. They will come to Rok's aid," Cain cautioned, finally understanding but still two steps behind.

"I know. So it must be if Xin is to lead. We must earn our victory over both of them." Cvareh squinted, wondering if he imagined the outlines of boco on the horizon. Not wanting to take a chance, he spurred his own mount to the skies. Cain did the same. "We will soon have Perfect Chimera. Only then will we strike."

"And what if she doesn't send them?" Cain called over the wind and flapping of wings. "She will."

"I hope you're right, Oji. All bets are on the table." Cain looked uncertain, but still he followed. Even when his doubts were at their peak, he followed. He had earned every shifting shade of blue his skin took on in the lightening dawn.

"With stakes this high, we have to go all in."

Cvareh gripped the reigns, leaving a city he loved dearly behind him to be ransacked in frustration by Rok and the Dragon King. Instead, he headed for the refinery that had just enough gold to produce the first new glider of what he hoped would be many.

# 40
## FLORENCE

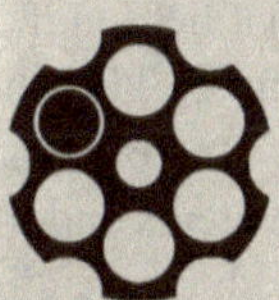



In her mind, she was in that oversized bed in Old Dortam she'd foolishly lamented having to make every morning.

The noise around her was Arianna's. It was a lazy day, one where there was no job and no one in Mercury Town—the sort of day where she could wake slowly and leave the room a bit of a mess. They would quietly sip something hot while their throats woke up, before bundling up to brave the icy winter wind that swept down the mountains, as they set out in search of something more substantial to put in their stomachs.

Florence would ogle the hats on pedestals in the window of her favorite hattery and walk slowly by the one confectionery in all of Old Dortam. It would be Arianna who would insist that they had to keep going. They could stop another day . . . but for now, they had to keep going.

*I have to keep going.*

She cracked her eyes open. The light shining from the other side of her eyelids was not evidence of a bright winter morning, but a buzzing electric bulb. The noise around her was not Arianna, but an Alchemist. The chill was indeed from winter, but it was magnified by the depths of the Underground.

"Shannra? Willie? Thomas?" Florence whispered.

"They're all fine," a familiar voice replied. "Varying states of fine, but all fine, nevertheless."

Florence knew who she was speaking to the moment his face appeared in her vision. "Didn't know you made it to Ter.4, Derek."

"I was one of the last to make it out of Ter.2. You'd already moved by the time I got to Ter.0 and by the time you settled in here . . . Neither Nora or I knew how to approach the infamous Florence."

"Infamous? Has a nice ring to it."

"You would think so." Without warning, he plunged a syringe into her arm and a warm sensation flowed up through her veins.

Silence passed between them as Florence waited for her mind to clear. Things were different now. Perhaps it was because she'd gained "infamy" that she hadn't set out in search of them either. After all, there was a time when he and Nora had been everything to her.

That time was over.

People changed, the world changed, and everyone moved right along.

"How long was I out for?" She looked at her arm, and the large bruise formed around the injection site that her magic had yet to heal.

"Only a day." The Alchemist shook his head. Just like that, their relationship had finished settling into a friendly, but professional comfort. "We could do more if we had access to proper reagents and medicine, but we'll have to let you mend up the old-fashioned way, with magic alone."

Florence wondered how quickly something became "the old-fashioned way" since there had only been magic on Loom for two decades.

"I'm going to fetch the masters."

Derek left, and shortly after two master Revolvers entered the small, makeshift medical room. Florence recognized them as Bernard and Emma. These were the last two Master Revolvers alive and one of them was—or would soon be—vicar.

"Don't bother trying to sit up." One of them raised a hand to stop before she could move. "Save your strength."

If the room wasn't crowded enough, the door opened again and the three other vicars entered. Florence felt like she was some sort of feast laid out for the powerful to devour. It didn't help that her "hospital bed" was an actual table.

"What happened up there?" Dove demanded.

"Give her a moment to catch her breath." Florence appreciated Powell coming to her aid, even when she didn't need it.

"I'm fine, thank you, Vicar Powell." Despite what the masters had told her earlier, Florence pushed herself upright. Her body felt more fatigued than anything else. Her muscles had a dull ache, but it seemed the medicine Derek had given her was taking effect and the pain was a distant whisper in her mind. "Vicar Gregory assigned a group to go into the hall to test the weapon based off the schematics Arianna had discovered in Master Oliver's office . . ."

She tried to summarize everything as succinctly as possible without leaving out any important details. Most important, she tried to expunge the general disdain that she still found herself harboring for Gregory and the incompetence that led to his death—and the deaths and injury of others.

"Why didn't you retreat?" Master Bernard asked when she had finished her story. "Thomas corroborates that he asked you to leave him behind."

Florence thought about it for a long moment, folding and unfolding her hands in her lap. How could she tell the truth without also outing herself as the woman who killed the last Vicar Alchemist? "I know what happened in the Alchemists' Guild." She didn't feel guilty for Sophie in the slightest, just as she didn't feel guilty for not pushing Gregory harder about his mistakes. But she remained intentionally ambiguous. "I know that Vicar Sophie made the decision to leave behind a portion of the guild to die." Florence looked right at Ethel. If anyone knew the truth—it was her. But the vicar's face betrayed nothing. "It has never sat well with me. And there's precious little talent left in Loom."

"You killed a Revolver point-blank in the first Tribunal," Dove pointed out.

"I did. But that was different."

"How so?" Master Emma asked, more curious than threatening.

"Because he made his choice. He stood against Loom, and I stood back. But Thomas, Willie, Shannra, Master Joseph . . ." Florence looked to Dove. "The Raven you sent to guide us." She felt guilty she couldn't remember the lad's name. "They were all following orders. It was a mistake they had no share in making that would cost them their lives."

"How did you know you could make the gun work?" Master Bernard asked. "I saw the equations and details you gave Gregory. How did you arrive at the correct conclusion when he and the rest of us could not?"

Florence wanted to say it was luck, but that wasn't true. "I've worked on magical weapons for the better part of my tutelage. I was the gunsmith for the White Wraith, after all." It felt like such an odd thing to confess now. "I once saw a weapon fired that I can only assume was experimental, possibly stolen, used by a Rider against an airship I was on. I worked on my own guns, tried to recreate what I saw without the benefit of 'proper' guild teaching.

"So, I made up the difference in my lack of education with creativity. Plus —" Florence couldn't stop a small smile from gracing her lips, one that quickly faltered from the severity of the situation. "I know how a Rivet thinks. I know where their minds run into walls and how to step around them."

"Can you recreate it?" Powell asked. "Do you remember what you did?"

"Of course," Florence confirmed. "But I'd want to properly run it by Arianna. She may have improvements to offer."

"With this, we can truly fight back," Bernard murmured. "Regular Chimera can join the fight here on Loom, and we can send the majority of the Perfects directly to Nova."

"More than that, we can *win*." Florence let there be no room for doubt.

"We can win with a strong leader at the helm of the Revolvers." It registered to Florence as a weird thing for Powell of all people to say. The man looked at the two Master Revolvers and wondered who he would pick from between them.

"We are far from a quorum." Emma glanced uncertainly at the room. "I will vote for myself."

"As will I." Bernard side-eyed the woman who was now his competitor. "Perhaps the other vicars can help break the tie."

"I'm not sure I'm qualified." Leave it to the Vicar Alchemist to retreat from the world and its decisions.

"I cast my vote for Florence." Her ears rang as though Powell's words were gunshot.

"What?" Dove squinted her eyes at the Vicar Harvester.

"She is strong because she has learned from many guilds. She is what Loom is working to return to, and what students should strive to be—better versions of themselves through the acquisition of knowledge."

"There's no precedent for this," Ethel cautioned.

"There's no precedent for living in the Underground either." Dove shook her head and pinched the bridge of her nose. She sighed heavily. "I vote for her, too." The Vicar Raven looked to the two shocked Revolvers. "Nothing personal, I just already have a rapport with the girl and I *hate* getting to know new people."

"Do you think the Revolvers would support it?" Ethel was the only one focused on how the guild would receive the news.

"We haven't even heard yet if Florence supports it." Bernard crossed his arms and looked to her.

Florence wondered if she stared down another Gregory, another powerful man who saw her as less because of her age and experience and tutelage. Even if he wasn't, there would always be people like Gregory, seeking to undermine her at every turn.

Florence looked back to Powell. He had risen in an unconventional way as well, and she had witnessed it. Now, she wanted to show him that he had made the right choice in saving her from the wreckage of Ter.1. She wanted to make her life mean something.

"I support it," she affirmed.

"How do you think you can lead the Revolvers without ever truly being one?" Emma asked skeptically.

*It's not an outright no*, Florence thought hopefully. "Respectfully, I have been a Revolver from the day I was born."

The room went silent. Florence wondered if she should say something more, but she let those gathered chew over their own thoughts. It gave her time as well, to think about the position she was about to put herself in. The more she considered, the less afraid she became.

"I change my vote, and cast my support for Florence."

"What?" Bernard gaped at his counterpart.

"She did something the last vicar couldn't do. You saw the gun."

"That's not reason enough to make someone a vicar!"

"She did something more than that," Powell interjected. "She united Loom." The Vicar Harvester held up his hand, drawing a circle in the air around his palm. "Five guilds, once separate like fingers, united once more as a singular entity." He curled his hand into a fist.

The five guilds of Loom—Florence had always imagined them like one great chain, but perhaps they were more like a hand. They could move separately, but their strength came from banding together, from seeing that they were one unified force.

"I support her." Vicar Ethel finally made up her mind. All eyes fell to Bernard.

"I'm outvoted." He shrugged. "My opinion hardly matters."

"It matters to me." Florence waited to continue until she was sure the whole of his attention was on her. "You are one of only two masters. I will need your help, leadership, and insight. I will not take up this mantle surrounded by bad blood."

He squinted at her, and Florence wondered what he was searching for. She knew nothing about the man, so she didn't know what to portray. Even if she did, she was too tired to fabricate anything.

"Had it been you and Gregory alone and you knew his gun was defective, would you still have tried to warn him?"

"Yes." Despite her honest answer, Bernard's eyebrows rose and he looked even more skeptical. "He was the Vicar Revolver. I would have tried to save his life even if it meant pointing out his mistake."

"And if he still didn't listen?"

"Then I would have let him die. As the Vicar Revolver, he must be held responsible for his own mistakes, even if they cost his life."

"And you? Will we hold you accountable with your life?"

"I would have it no other way." A bit of her Raven shone through, and Florence smiled wildly. "Isn't that the way of the Revolver? Taking life in your hands and accepting what happens if you drop it?"

Bernard continued to scrutinize her, but finally gave a nod and left the room. On his way out, he said, "You have my support."

There was a gravity to the way the door clicked closed. It was as if the matter was deemed finished before Florence had even wrapped her mind around it. *Had that really just happened?*

"Let us hold a tribunal tomorrow, when you're feeling stronger," Powell suggested. "We need to go over the status of the Philosopher's Boxes and how we can manufacture your guns, in addition."

"Right. Send me Shannra." Florence tried to keep her voice strong. She felt a tempest of emotions, but none of them was hesitation at being named the Vicar Revolver. "She can whisper to Arianna for me."

The room cleared and Florence found herself alone for one very long minute. She could do nothing more than stare at her hands in shock. Somehow, she'd managed to keep herself level, composed, in control, but now her bones felt like they were trying to rattle her flesh into gelatin.

She curled and uncurled her fingers into fists, thinking of Powell's metaphor. If the guilds were like hands, then she, too, must be. There was a part of her that was scared and it was no less or more than the part of her that was thrilled. Nerves flourished within the confident woman who knew she was about to step into the most important role of her life.

She inhaled through her nose and exhaled through her mouth. Her hands balled into fists. Like the competing parts within her, she would bring all of Loom together as one.

The door opened and Shannra practically bounded in with excitement. "I just heard!"

"News travels fast." Florence smiled faintly.

Shannra sat on the edge of the low table Florence had been laid out on. "I'm sure you wanted to be the first to tell me."

"So don't be upset, hm? Especially because now that you *have* been told, I need you to whisper to Arianna. I must tell her what's happened with the gun."

"I am at your service, Vicar Revolver."

She very much liked the way Shannra purred the words "Vicar Revolver." Florence reached up a hand and cupped the curve of the cheek she so adored.

"I do like the sound of that."

"There's something else you should know." Shannra sat on the edge of her bed, brushing Florence's hair from her face. "There was a whisper while you were out. You're not the only one with a new title."

"What?"

"It seems she's killed Louie. We're all reporting to the Queen of Wraiths now."

"Killed Louie?" Florence repeated, wondering what could've possessed Arianna to go so far. "Don't we need him?"

"She seems to think otherwise."

Florence struggled to make sense of what she was hearing. Just what was Arianna doing?

Shannra raised her hand to her ear, but Florence tugged it away before she could activate the whisper link to one of Louie's—Arianna's—lackeys.

"It can wait one more second," Florence said, pulling the other woman toward her. She claimed Shannra's mouth and felt her lover relax into the kiss. Florence herself relaxed for what felt like the first time in ages, despite the weight of all her new responsibilities. That was Shannra's power, or perhaps the power of them coming together.

Florence would tell Arianna—she must. But vicars did not jump to associate with those who ruled the underworld, and she—Florence, the runaway Raven who had been decreed to die—was a vicar now.

# PART TWO

# 41
## ARIANNA

The clang of gold on metal as her clip slid along the railing came to a hard stop, Arianna swung around a low smokestack at breakneck speeds two seconds after the initial churning of gears ceased. Three seconds after that, a glider whizzed around one of the giant main houses of the refinery hall. To make the jump to the glider, Arianna had to know the glider's approximate rate of speed, her terminal velocity mid-swing, and the cusp where the two would meet.

Numbers like those were all child's play.

She soared through the air on a collision course with the glider. A shining corona coated the Dragon's skin, so Arianna's daggers were sheathed. During her first stint on Nova, a Dragon had pointed out something pivotal to her: The corona was designed to protect from harm, and it was designed by Fenthri. So, the Fenthri engineers—who were geniuses to develop such a magical field—did so to protect from Loom's weaponry: metals, bullets, blasts.

There was never any accounting for bone.

Bone was just what protruded from both of Arianna's fingertips—bone in the shape of giant talons, forged by magic and hardened by the Dragon hands she'd stolen from a man who had worked against Loom until his dying breath. Now, she'd use that same magic to sculpt Loom's future from the flesh that shredded beneath her palms.

The Rider had only a moment to look up in shock as Arianna landed atop him. Her claws dug into his shoulder and neck, shearing flesh from muscle and muscle from bone. Tendons snapped; she savored his look of shock in the moments before he released the handholds, sending them both tumbling through the air.

Wind gusted over her ears, and Arianna knew she had mere breaths before they would both be plastered on the next metal cropping. *Live to fight the next battle*, instinct cried. Arianna relinquished the Rider to the sound of the crashing glider behind her.

She unclipped the golden clip from her harness. The Dragon snarled in rage and flailed his arms, attempting to strike her, or cling to her—whichever he could manage. Her gold line was impervious to his strikes, so she cast it without hesitation. Her stomach was in her throat and shot back down to her lower abdomen as the line snapped to tension.

The Dragon's claws sunk into her calf and Arianna swiped at him with a snarl. She shredded the tendons in his wrist, his hand going lax, and he continued to fall without her. His body met the refinery's rocky foundation with a calamitous *clang*.

Arianna tapped her winch box.

She slowed her descent to nonlethal speeds, keeping the line loose enough that the cabling spun freely off its spools and her stomach shot back into her throat. When she was two pecas from the ground, she pulled the lynchpin on the box and fell the rest of the way.

Dazed and barely conscious, the Dragon Rider blinked up at her. Fools hesitated and sympathizers died. Arianna plunged her claws into the man's chest, perforating his lungs and surrounding his heart. She twisted, ripped, and ended the Dragon's life.

The door to her right burst open.

Arianna sunk her teeth into the soft tissue of the Rider's heart. Blood exploded in her mouth—the taste of blackberries, tart yet sweet. With that sweetness was something all the more savory. Magic flooded her senses. It pulsed within her, bolstered her own. Her wounds healed, her skin regained its strength, and, with a snap of her fingers, her line returned itself to its coil as she turned to face the next enemy.

The Dragon levied a gun against her—one of the reasons she was here to begin with. Arianna dropped into a crouch, ready to dodge the shot. The Dragon snarled and pulled the trigger at the same time as she lunged.

He tried to anticipate her movements; his gun swung right as Arianna pushed forward. He thought she'd move to the side. But Arianna went straight for the jugular.

He swung back. The Dragon pulled the trigger again and Arianna heard a familiar click. She drew her dagger and plunged it into his throat.

"With that style rifle, you need to reload a canister with every shot," she chided softly.

The Dragon threw aside the empty weapon with a shout of frustration. He had fight in him as he gripped her shoulders, making a play for her throat. Arianna tumbled, slid into a crouch, and prepared to lunge anew.

"Witch!" he shouted at her before swiping with his claws.

"Scientist!" Arianna corrected, dodging his slash. She thrust with one dagger and the Dragon moved left, completely ignoring the second blade attached to a golden line at his back.

He fell, and another appeared.

The Dragons here were bleary from sleep, shocked into sluggishness, out of their element in narrow industrial halls. There wasn't a true combatant among them—at least not by the standards of the Queen of Wraiths.

She tore through them, one after the next. Golden daggers floated at the ends of her lines like barbed tentacles shooting from her hips, carving out the hearts of all who dared to oppose her. Arianna killed without question. Man, woman, young or old—if they stood before her, they would be struck down.

Dawn broke over the horizon to find her bathed in slowly evaporating gold. Arianna's chest heaved and her eyes were blurry from exhaustion. She ran on the magic of her conquests, shoving hearts into her mouth in the same unreserved way Florence would indulge herself on an unattended plate of cookies.

Magic from deep below prickled at her senses. Arianna knew what she'd find before she arrived at the heavy, bolted door. Still, when she pulled it open and looked at the squalor within—the men and women blinking nervously at her —her chest felt heavier than all the metal and stone of the refinery that surrounded her.

"I can't save you all." It was where she had to start. "But I can try to give you each the power to save yourselves."

"Who are you?" a woman stammered.

"The Wh—The Queen of Wraiths." Arianna sheathed her daggers. "And I come from the rebellion on Loom."

Shocked rumors rose among the Fenthri slaves.

"House Xin is standing with us, and together we will overthrow the Dragon King and save Loom." For all she believed in Florence and Cvareh, uttering the words was hard. How many times in her lifetime alone would she espouse the end of Yveun's rule? "Help me dismantle this refinery, then flee, hide. Stay out of sight and stay alive until Rok has fallen."

They looked nervously at each other. No one moved. She wondered if Florence would have been able to inspire them to action. Arianna was not meant for rousing speeches or motivating the masses. She was the hired blade in the dark.

"I can take one of you with me," she continued anyway. "Loom needs knowledge of the weaponry and whatever else they're having you make here. I will let you decide who it will be. This is the Fenthri way."

The slaves looked among themselves, and still, no one moved. Then murmurs, speaking, a consensus. Arianna watched them use their minds for themselves for the first time in what may have been decades. They selected one man with the circled symbol of a Rivet on his cheek. He was young enough that

Arianna didn't recognize him from her time in the guild, but old enough that she had no doubt he'd spent most of his life on Nova.

"I'll bring the information back to Loom."

"Good." Arianna gave a curt nod. "Now that that's settled, let's get to work making Rok's life as difficult as possible."

# 42
## COLETTA

Even when the world was at war, Lysip was a beauty to behold. The brown winter grasses against the brilliant reds of the estate created an ethereal elegance that was capped with a bright sky, its blue almost washed into a soft off-white. It was not uncommon for the clouds above the God's Line to deposit rain or snow onto their island. But the winter had been dry so far.

Coletta preferred it this way. She didn't like getting the hems of her clothes muddy, and the only damp she ever wanted to feel on her hands was the blood of her enemies.

As much as Tam flaunted their island's perpetual jewel tones as some kind of superiority, Coletta found the world in stasis several times more stunning than the lushest of gardens—with the exception of her own garden, of course.

It was a day for thinking of Tam, as she'd greeted the viridian house just hours ago. She played the part of the Rok'Ryu they expected—a mysterious woman whose presence often heralded death, but it couldn't be of her own doing, for she was much too frail for that. She didn't have the spine to kill someone; she didn't have a spine at all. Or so Coletta imagined them whispering.

The entourage would take the rumors back to a hungry Gwaeru, where the nobility would eat them up like dogs fighting over the juiciest scrap to bring some satiation to their meaningless lives. House Tam represented balance, "all things equal," as their motto stated. But balance, Coletta found, was a close sibling to complacency, and complacency was the lover of sloth.

While the Dragon in her thought it was always a shame to see her race reduced to something that glorified excess, Tam's taste for finer things and the time to enjoy them suited her. It made the house easy to control, and fairly simple to work with. If there was one thing that didn't suit the comfort of luxury, it was the chaos of rebellion.

The woman walking next to her was one of the few Coletta did not expect to deceive. From the first moment Doriv Tam'Ryu To arrived at the Rok Estate, she saw Coletta as a force to be reckoned with. Coletta saw much the same in her fern-colored counterpart. They each knew who was really in charge at the respective households. So, while the majority of the attendants and upper nobility of both houses sat in on a meeting with Yveun'Oji and Cashi'Oji, the real decisions were being made by the two women who strolled the estate with only a few handpicked attendants many steps behind.

"Lysip in the winter is stunning. The way the sun shines on the browning grasses that adorn your hillsides makes the whole of the island look as though it has been dipped in gold." Doriv'Ryu made no effort to further disguise the remark on their dead foliage as a compliment.

"Gwaeru is equally stunning this time of year. All of your large flowering trees endlessly dumping their petals is quite the spectacle to behold—or so I hear." Coletta responded in kind.

"I didn't know you thought of Gwaeru with such fondness, Rok'Ryu." Doriv'Ryu adjusted the chiming earrings that pulled needle-eye holes into the lobes of her long ears. "Perhaps we'll conduct one of our future meetings on my homeland. Rather than dragging the entirety of House Tam's nobility across the sky."

"Ah, I know how so many speak with fondness of the opportunity to come and try Lysip beef and see the Rok Estate. I'd hate to deny them the opportunity."

"You are a truly charitable woman. I don't know how you give so much away to others while still having enough for yourself, such that you can create the flamboyant lodgings where you house guests." Doriv motioned to the gilding on the columns that supported the roof covering the walkway, which wound through the wild outer fields they roamed.

"It is important to make sure we both take care of our people, while continuing to display Rok's might."

"Indeed . . ." Doriv stopped and half-turned, looking out over the sea of slowly dying greenery between carefully placed statues. Coletta stopped as well, angling her body to mimic the other Ryu.

Neither of them cared about the flowers, or the grasses, or the sun, or the end of the boco mating season, or any of the other pointless topics they had spent the morning discussing. They cared about one thing alone: how close they were to any other living, sentient creature who was not one of their most loyal vassals.

"You like this spot," Coletta observed. "You usually stop here."

"This scuff here—" Doriv answered, running her fingers over an unassuming etching on the column beside her. "—marks the point at which our conversation officially becomes private."

"Indeed." Coletta smiled. She enjoyed the reaction her scarred, gray gums and knobby teeth evoked in other Dragons. It was its own type of terror. "This was a meeting you called. What is so important that you needed to speak with me in person?"

"The wine turned sour at the Crimson Court . . ." Doriv began walking again. "An odd affair, that . . . I don't believe there has ever been a case of deadly mold on wine casks before."

"An odd affair, indeed. Perhaps it was Lord Xin requesting a tithing of his people."

"I certainly hope so." Doriv's hand was back to playing with her earring. "I've heard whispers of some nefarious designs."

"Have you?" Coletta asked earnestly. It was imperative that, at any given time, she knew what the world knew about her. The moment the masses actually saw her as a threat was the moment she lost the vast majority of her effectiveness. Yveun was the visible menace, she the invisible hand holding the dagger from the flanks.

"Only rumors, nothing more, and nothing worth heeding past the gossip parlor doors." The answer wasn't satisfying for Coletta, but she saw no avenue to pursue the matter. Furthermore, she had to trust her alliance with Doriv; if there was something to consider alarming, the woman would tell her. Doriv immediately proved Coletta right. "However, if they are true . . . It would be a grave offense. Ending a Crimson Court before the majority of grievances could be heard would be the least of it, really. To slay Dragons outside of proper duels or cause death on such a mass scale . . . the idea is unprecedented."

Coletta skillfully refrained from pointing out that Xin's mere existence gave her cause to wipe their blue faces off the earth itself.

"And then, there's the matter of Petra Xin'Oji," Doriv continued. "Her death is not sitting well with House Xin. They think that, too, has some darker truth to it. The new Oji dueled the late Finnyr on such grounds. If these accusations prove true, in addition to the other oddities . . . House Tam would need to evaluate, and potentially work to remove a power that acts so far out of Nova's structure."

She heard Doriv's warning clearly. "Well, if such terrible things were to have transpired, it seems the persons involved would have acted with the utmost cunning, if there are only floating rumors. The Xin can hardly be trusted to be unbiased, or logical for that matter. They all have so much to grieve for now. They act like children in their time of mourning."

"One would hope it is just the lunacies of a grieving house . . . It would be a shame to have to forcefully shift the world back into balance so that all things are once more equal."

"Indeed. After all, doing so could result in many of the Tam nobility being forced to give up the titles and the luxuries that come to them from the graciousness of House Rok."

"Rebellion is good for no one," Doriv agreed. "All one needs to do to see it is look at the Fen in the world below."

"Something that should be alleviated soon." It was the only topic Coletta wasn't utterly sure of. The Fen were agents of chaos; no matter how carefully she planned and plotted, the wretched little creatures were determined to prove their insolence. Yveun did the situation no favors, either.

"Let us hope. It's such a nuisance."

"Yes, well, we can only hope the nuisances of the world are put to rest sooner over later."

"I make every effort." Even if half of Coletta's efforts were thwarted by idiocy or incompetence or the foolishness of the system she was forced to navigate.

"Speaking of efforts . . . I hear there is a disgraced Tam babysitting House Xin?"

"There was. Fae Rok," Coletta affirmed.

"How fitting that Rok requires a wayward Tam to keep the balance with House Xin. It is in our blood, after all."

"Rok name, Tam blood—together it's a powerful combination," Coletta answered carefully. She wanted to drive her point with the Tam'Ryu deep. "Our families making a stable balance, equal force . . . We both have much to gain, and much to lose if that balance is disrupted."

"Tam will continue to defend the balance so long as House Rok continues to abide by Dragon law." *Tam and their bloody obsession with the law*, Coletta thought as Doriv spoke. "And so long as we continue to be appropriately compensated for the assistance we give."

They stopped again, now at the apex of the large loop that swept around the outer fields. A pathway split away through the hills, still paved but no longer covered. Usually, their conversation would shift back to veiled threats and jabs as they rounded the curve back to the estate proper.

"How lovely it would be to have some precious gold to adorn Tam's castle." The Tam Ryu turned in a different direction than normal, headed away from the estate.

"Perhaps some could be spared, as a gift between our families—a gesture of thanks." Coletta heard the request clearly. It was a request that all prior conversations with the Ryu had prepared her to hear.

"I said it before, Coletta'Ryu—you are much too generous." Doriv smiled, showing her razor-sharp teeth.

Coletta did the same.

Doriv folded her hands before her. "I hear rumors too that Yveun's refineries are taking shape."

That was the greatest lie of them all. The refineries were a failure. Difficult to maintain, difficult to feed with resources. They were glorified houses for the gold she had stolen from Loom, a façade and nothing more.

"Would you like to see one?" Coletta knew better than to deny the woman, which would only raise suspicion. She knew the request was inevitable, but trusted that her carefully crafted plans would yield the expected result.

Coletta knew something was wrong the moment the wind shifted around them. The air smelled sweet, rather than sharp with the metallic tang of the refinery. She couldn't demand they turn around; to do so would be admitting something had gone awry. But as the refineries nestled in the hills beyond the Rok Estate came into view, Coletta wasn't prepared for what she found.

"It's quiet."

*Damn Doriv and her observations.* "We run it on alternate days, so as not to draw too much attention to it."

The Tam Ryu gave a small hum of amusement.

"I can see the gold transported to you from here," Coletta offered, trying to arrest their progress.

"I'd like to see these operations—temples of industry from the world below."

Coletta had no grounds to object, so she didn't. She continued onward and downward to the main entry. The tangy sweet smell became overwhelming; Coletta had no option to brace herself.

"We'll head straight to the storehouse." Whatever had happened here, Coletta would deal with later. For now, she'd show the gold she'd stolen from Loom, keep the illusion of a strong House Rok, and get Doriv out as quickly as possible.

"Lead on." The woman's smile was knowing, frustratingly so.

Coletta walked through the still passageways, trapped in by lattices of steel and iron, to a small storehouse not far from the outer edge of the refinery grounds. Coletta took a breath, unbarring the door.

Were it not for the dozens, hundreds, thousands of people she'd killed over the years, her face might have cracked. The room that she'd filled to the brim with gold from Loom, stolen from storehouses revealed to her by the self-styled Fen King's notes, was completely vacant. A large pennon hung over a pile of hearts, dull and fraying already with rot.

Coletta read over the brief message, painted with the grease pencils the Fen used to mark various machines and walkways in the refineries.

After a long moment of silence, Doriv was the first to speak. "Coletta'Ryu, who exactly is the Queen of Wraiths?"

# 43
## FLORENCE

Vicar Dove.

"We sent one hundred men and women to be made into Perfect Chimera, and you bring us only three back *and* ask for fifty more."

"Again, just delivering the message."

Florence looked at the delivery summary in question. She knew, better than Powell or Dove, what the request meant. They had precious few Revolvers as it was; to ferry them by the tens to Ter.3 was putting a strain on their ability to defend themselves in Ter.4.

"What are Willard and Ethel thinking?" Dove turned her attention to Powell and Florence.

It was a question Florence knew the other vicar didn't really want to be answered, but answer she would. "They're trying to encourage us to consolidate."

"Then they should outright say it." Dove pushed away from the table where the papers lay strewn, as if she was too disgusted by them to bear another moment in their presence.

The Alchemists had been sent ahead to Garre to learn how to transplant the boxes, and then become Perfect Chimera themselves. At first, due to "tempering issues," the process was painfully slow. But, as was the case with most new technology, things improved quickly and efficiency increased exponentially. From the whispers, it seemed the Alchemists were content to stay in Garre for a while; it was a hard point to argue when that was the site of the boxes.

"I'm fairly sure they have." Florence picked up the letter from Ethel that encouraged the rest of the guilds to come south. "It's not an illogical proposition."

"We cannot keep moving people," Dove objected.

"And there's the issue of Dragon attacks," Powell added.

"If we hadn't already sent so many Revolvers south, that wouldn't be an issue," Dove seethed.

"What's done is done. There's little point in arguing now." Florence couldn't believe she was younger than them both, especially not when they acted like squabbling children. "We should heed Ethel's suggestion and relocate."

"We *just* got to Ter.4," Dove needlessly reminded Florence.

"We arrived at Ter.4 nearly eight months ago. And this move will be far less tedious with established rail lines. We can leave right through the guild hall. It's a fairly straight shot south from Holx."

"But we did just finish fortifying the Underground." As weak as the objection was, it was still an objection and Florence couldn't remember the last time Powell spoke against her. She hoped it wouldn't become a habit.

"Fortifications in the form of blocking tunnels and building some doors," Florence countered. "Hardly any significant investment of time or resources."

"And turrets," Vicar Dove reminded.

"We set up *two* turrets. Though I realize you may have gotten the number confused, since it doesn't directly relate to your Ravens." Florence was almost proud of how nonchalantly she delivered such a scathing remark.

"Careful, Florence, or one might think that you are fostering separation between the guilds."

"I would never." Florence returned them to the topic at hand, not wanting to risk further ire. "In any case . . .we cannot ignore these two attacks on Ter.3. The Dragons have finally realized our manufacturing there."

"Took them long enough," Helen mumbled.

"If only it took them longer," Powell remarked with a pointed look.

"We must protect the factories at all costs," Florence continued, unbothered by the exchanges occurring around her. "They are a far greater priority than staying holed in the Underground."

"We can use those same lines you mentioned earlier to transport what we need here," Dove insisted.

"You can't possibly mean that." Florence was beginning to suspect that Dove was just fighting her for the sake of fighting now.

"I do very much. The trains—"

"The trains run on tracks easily targeted by Dragons." Florence shook her head. "They can destroy the tracks and separate us. Remember the whole reason we banded together?" Florence held up her hand by her shoulder, palms out, fingers upward, mimicking the symbol that had come to represent the sign of their rebellion. "Five guilds, separate but connected, and together strong."

Powell sighed a sound that had a distinct tone of resignation to it. "There *are* more resources in Ter.3 than the Underground. We're running thin on food."

"The Ravens' Guild has storerooms."

"That have all been exhausted."

"Fine." Dove threw her hands into the air. "We shall move again. But we do it slowly, one group at a time."

"No." Florence shot down the idea immediately. "We take out all locomotives at once. We run them one after the other. And we move together, as one unit, safe and strong. That way, if the Dragons should take notice, they can't find a way to block the lines and separate us on opposite ends of the continent."

The room was silent for a long moment. Florence took silence to mean victory, and she turned to Helen and Will. She barely recognized her old friends now. They had gone off to be emissaries of the seedy underbelly of Loom and Florence had become the Vicar Revolver. She wished them well, but there would be little more than that between them as the years progressed—if the years progressed.

"Return to Garre with the requested manpower. Inform Willard, Ethel, and Arianna that we will be moving to Ter.3.2."

"Not Garre?" Powell interrupted.

"No." Florence shook her head and looked back to the edited schematics she and Arianna had been passing between them by way of Helen. "Garre needs to stay focused on making the Philosopher's Box. We will set up in Ter.3.2, close enough that we are nothing more than a stone's throw away and can exchange information, resources, and men with ease. But far enough that we can retrofit our own factories to make the guns. Are there any questions?"

Silence.

"No? Good. Let's get to work."

# 44
## COLETTA

SHE WAS PARTICULARLY GRATEFUL FOR ULIA'S HELP IN UNDOING THE INTRICATE clasping on the front of her jacket that night. Coletta wasn't sure if her hands had ever felt so shaky, and it took all her focus to keep them even, her voice level.

"Is there anything else I can do for you?" Ulia asked as she slung the garment over her hand for proper cleaning. Even the girl, one of the most loyal among them, was nervous now. She had seen the refinery and the look on Doriv's face when the pennon was discovered.

"No, leave." Ulia hovered for a half second, debate written on her face. This was not the night to be insubordinate. But Coletta had every faith that she knew as much; whatever made her falter was of the utmost importance. "Yes?"

"It is perhaps nothing . . ." Ulia kept her eyes downcast. "I do not claim to know the greatness you weave nor would I ever dream of passing judgment—"

"Out with it." Coletta had no patience for floundering. Ulia jumped at the unusual strength in Coletta's voice.

"I noticed that Yeaan's room has been empty for a few days now . . .I merely thought it odd that there has been no sign from her. I wondered, perhaps, if this 'Queen of Wraiths'—"

"How long has it been?" Coletta interrupted, formulating her own theories. She had merely assumed Yeaan had been focused on the eradication of the flowers. But now that she thought of it, it had been some time since one of her more favorite flowers had come before her.

"Since I last saw her . . . a month, maybe more?" Ulia shook her head. "I apologize, my lady, it's merely an estimate."

"You did well to tell me." Coletta forced out the praise. Taking out aggressions on her most loyal for the faults of others was a very certain way to lose that loyalty. "Now, get out."

"Yes." This time, Ulia did depart.

There was truly no rest for the weary. Before Coletta even had a breath to think about Yeaan and the last update she had received on the Flowers of Agendi, another invaded her space.

"Coletta!" Yveun roared.

"I am here." She kept her voice calm, almost monotonous. One of them had to keep it together.

"What happened?" It was such an odd sight to see Yveun in her chambers that Coletta almost overlooked the fact that he was pacing like a wild animal newly freed from its cage. "Everything with the Tam'Oji goes well and then, just as they depart, Doriv'Ryu offers me her condolences for our loss? That there is no gold?" He stopped, and squared off against her. "You assured me there would be gold."

"There was."

"Then what—"

"It was stolen."

"*Stolen?*" Had someone told Coletta what she was currently telling Yveun, her reaction would've been much the same. "Who would dare?"

"The Queen of Wraiths."

Emotions swept across his face, one after the next, swirling until they reached peak speeds, turning the Dono into a twister that was prepared to kill everything in its path. "Queen of Wraiths? I told you that Arianna was dangerous. I told you she was the one we needed to hunt." Yveun drew a finger like a Fenthri gun, casting it at her. "You cautioned against it, sent Fae to Xin. Now see what it has wrought."

Coletta's mouth twitched and she fought to keep her face passive. It was hard to say if Yveun was right, but she also couldn't assert that he was *wrong*.

"These are unfortunate events, but—"

"But? *But?* We are thwarted at every turn on Loom." Yveun snarled out some nasty series of words and set to pacing once more. "Even on Ruana, we are struggling to hold Napole on resolve alone. Our men are dying of skirmishes in the night, or of boredom."

Napole. The "battle"—if it could be called that, as they were met with no resistance from House Xin—was over in a night, which Yveun had interpreted to mean that they could run through the island unhindered. Xin was, unfortunately, too smart for that. They had retreated into their forests and mountains, copying the strategy Loom had been embracing for months.

Hiding was shameful for a Dragon, but it kept them alive.

"That blue scum—" *Cvareh,* Coletta filled in mentally "—will not respond to my demands for a duel."

"Nor will he."

Yveun's claws shot from his fingertips. Coletta allowed the ripple of his magic to send shivers up her spine, dotting it with goosebumps. It was a sickeningly sweet smell, rage ripening her mate.

"He calls himself Oji! If he ever wishes to be recognized properly on Nova, he must respond to my challenge."

"Not if he seeks to topple Nova." Coletta moved with all the grace she possessed, easing herself down on the ottoman in the center of the room.

"He has no hope of toppling Nova. We shall win every duel!"

"There are no duels to be had." Nor would there be. Were she in Cvareh's position, she'd wait until she held all the cards before making a public stand against Yveun.

"This is unheard of. He's acting like . . . like . . . "

"Like a Fenthri." The statement drew Yveun's attention. Finally seeing his eyes clear from anger, enough to listen at least, Coletta continued. "The Fenthri care not for proper society, as we know. They will do anything to survive, and Xin is no better. 'The ends'—*their* ends—will justify the means used to achieve them, even if that means ignoring Dragon law. Why wouldn't they? If they don't, they die. If they do, they have a slim chance of victory."

"You must be truly mad to understand their twisted logic." Yveun shook his head slowly, as if disgust weighted down his movements.

"My madness is why you love me." Coletta stretched her mouth wide, showing her teeth and reminding him of all the poisons she had endured for the sake of their greatness.

"One of the many reasons." Yveun hulked over her like a great mountain casting a long shadow on the ground below it. But Coletta didn't mind being in his shadow—she thrived in it. She conducted her business in his wake, used his greatness to distract from her own, his massive frame her shield. "Our gray wards seek to overthrow us from beneath. The scourge of Dragon society fights against us and is gaining ground. Our key ally has left this day on fragile relations. And yet, you smile."

"I do."

"Why?" At last he asked the right questions. But Coletta didn't know yet if he was ready for the answers.

"Because we, too, can build an army. Xin isn't the only house that can think like the Fen."

"Do you mean . . . ?" Eagerness hovered more potently than his words.

"Xin has looked to the Fenthri to be perfect. Rok, we make our own perfection."

"You have met success." It was not a question.

"Come, my Oji, and allow me to show you my Gray Room." Coletta started for the door, not even bothering to see if he was following. For she knew there was no way Yveun had escaped her mental tether. It was good that she had him enthralled for now. When he learned the bitter truth of her triumph, Coletta knew his rage would be uncontrollable.

# 45
## ARIANNA

Arianna nearly lost her breath pulling the glider upright. She landed it on a platform, albeit roughly, rather than going for the hangar on the edge of Garre. She was in and out so often by glider these days, it had become her own personal landing pad.

"After you."

Xavier, the Master Rivet who'd returned home with her, descended with wonder in his eyes. Arianna couldn't imagine what the homecoming was like for him.

"I never expected to see it again."

"I believe it." Arianna stepped heavily off the glider. Feeding on Dragon hearts was a way to sustain, but not thrive. She needed some time before she went up to Nova again.

There was a click inside the tower her platform was attached to and the entire structure groaned to life. Xavier held his hands out, working to balance himself, unaccustomed to the mechanics of the guild hall. Arianna could hear the grinding of massive gears as an entire segment of the tower turned, connecting with another platform that had been on the opposite side.

Waiting there was a familiar, weathered face.

"I'm beginning to think you have a death wish." It wasn't much of a greeting from the Vicar Rivet. Willard walked over, stopping when his eyes settled on Xavier.

"I brought a master home, liberated from our enemies," Arianna explained. Xavier was overcome with emotion and, given the glistening in his eyes, it would be some time until he could form cohesive sentences.

"I thought you were acquiring more flowers." Willard gave her a long, hard stare.

"Oh, I got those." Arianna patted the satchel at her side. "I just made a detour, working off some intel that Rok had built their own refineries and workshops."

"*What?* How did you find this out?"

"Our Dragon friends." It wasn't entirely a lie. Cvareh had mentioned the refinery project when he had shown her Xin's own structure. But what prompted her to actually investigate was when the Dragon Queen had asked Adam for two more ledgers from Holx, thinking the demand would be passed on to Louie. Arianna recognized the target ingredients as refinery resources.

"Dragon friends?" Xavier was brought back to life with the mention of Dragons. "It's true? Xin?"

"It is." Willard ushered the master toward him. "Come, come, we'll get you inside. I'll summon the Vicar Alchemist to look at you both."

"I'm fine, Willard." Arianna stretched. She knew the cure for her ailments—a good night's rest, rarer than gold now on Loom. "I'm going to head toward the workshops."

"The Vicar Alchemist is here?" Xavier asked, ignoring her. Arianna was hardly offended; she wanted to be forgotten by people as quickly as she appeared before them.

Willard gave Arianna a nod before ushering Xavier away.

"We've come to attend you, oh queen!" Helen burst through a door opposite the one Willard had just departed through. She gave a bow with a mocking flourish.

Arianna was weeks away from trying to fight the foolishness of her unwanted Raven chicks. Instead, she shrugged out of her coat. "Will, follow Willard and tell him that I still need to speak with him when he's done with Xavier." Arianna threw the garment at Helen. "And you, fix my sleeve."

"I am not a tailor!" Helen fumed to the point of nearly stomping her foot like the child she was.

"And I am not a babysitter. You want to remain in my good graces?"

Helen stormed off without another word, thanks to a look of encouragement from Will, who followed close behind. Arianna headed in the opposite direction.

The manufacturing line might be where the boxes were made, but the workshops were where they transformed into functioning Philosopher's Boxes that were then passed along to what had become the Alchemists' wing of the guild hall. They were implanted in Chimera, and after that . . . it was up to the Revolvers for training.

"I'd like to see everyone's progress," Arianna announced the moment she entered the room and set down the tubes of flowers in their storage spot. She was too tired for pleasantries, and focused on the task at hand. It was a mixed bag of successes that launched her into a familiar lecture. " . . . Extracting the properties of the flowers comes more from magic than mechanics. You need to heat the gold using magic, and then pull the magic that lives in the flower into it while it's near-molten.

"Try again." Arianna stood over one particularly focused journeyman and, at the risk of breaking his concentration, said, "Exactly like that . . .You know the magic is transferring properly because the gold will actually begin to cool again. It's very similar to tempering with blood."

"Oh." One journeyman said. "But we're not mixing the molten gold with blood here."

"No, just the magics are mixing," Arianna reiterated. "It's not *identical* to tempering with blood—fundamentally similar, but not the same."

A woman gave a grunt of frustration, hanging her head over like a wilted flower petal. Arianna didn't even need to touch the box in her hands to know that it wasn't tempered properly. She struggled with all her might to stifle a sigh and failed. She was too tired these days to expend much energy on patience.

"Put any boxes you think are successful on the table here." Vicar Willard's voice cut through the room, saving Arianna from herself. "The rest, bring back into the finishing room to be recalibrated so we may try again tomorrow."

Arianna gave the man a severe look, but managed to hold her tongue until they were alone—somehow. "There won't be a tomorrow if they don't get better at this."

"Exactly, so why stress them further and lessen our chances?"

She ground her knuckles into the table next to her.

"You don't really take after Oliver, after all."

"Excuse me?" Arianna arched her eyebrows.

"Well, given how you were at first with the initiates, with Florence, I thought perhaps we had a new great teacher among us."

*Florence.* She knew the woman had departed for Ter.3.2, where they had begun manufacturing the new weapons.

"I just play favorites with the competent. In that way, I'm exactly like Oliver." Arianna shrugged, leaning against the table, completely unashamed of the fact. Willard chuckled at the idea but didn't contest it. "How's our master?"

"With Vicar Ethel, then I think some much-needed rest." Arianna let her silence be her agreement. She could not imagine what the man was going through, having spent his life on Nova until now. Willard returned his attention to the boxes. "Will you be able to do any today?"

Arianna glanced over at the boxes that lined the table. She'd already counted how many they had started with and knew how many more were in the other room waiting to be salvaged. Even more still waited at the end of the line on the factory floor beyond that.

"Ten, maybe fifteen . . ."

"Stick with ten," Willard cautioned. "You have been expending a lot of magic these days with your jaunts up to Nova."

"I'm not a child, old man. I don't need you cautioning me."

"I think you do." Willard stood his ground and Arianna didn't argue the point further. The last thing she wanted was him bringing up the last time she'd pushed herself too hard, and he'd found her completely passed out the next morning on the floor of the workshop. It was an embarrassment he'd spared her publicly, but Arianna was now tempted to tell all of Loom herself so the man couldn't hang it over her head. "We don't have that many flowers, in any case. We're somewhat limited until more Perfect Chimera can confidently fly gliders. We should preserve them for more practice."

"How are things with the Revolvers going?" There was only a small pack of them now, training what few Perfect Chimera had been made. But they were all hoping for more to come, since Loom had moved away from the Underground.

"Progressing. I will ask you to measure the progress of the first class. You know better than any what they need to stand against Dragons."

Arianna folded her arms over her chest. "Speaking of fighting Dragons . . . The refineries on Nova, while utterly pointless as refineries—"

"No resources?"

"No resources." Arianna affirmed. She found it amusing how any Fenthri instantly knew about the issue with refineries on Nova, but none of the Dragons seemed to have figured it out, or heeded the warnings. "In any case, they are making weapons there."

"Dragons armed with weapons. That is not ideal."

"No," she agreed. "But they're rudimentary, and the Dragons don't understand how to use them. We'll still overpower them with Florence's gun and with the Perfect Chimera."

"Oddly optimistic for you," he observed.

Arianna shrugged. "What other choice do I have?"

"A hard spot we've put you in, indeed."

"I don't mind the fighting."

"I didn't just mean the fighting." She stared at the old man, waiting for him to clarify. "You've spent your life in secrecy, Arianna. You've worked in the shadows, functioned mostly alone. Now, so much rests on your shoulders. Too much."

"I'm fine." Arianna herself didn't know if it was a lie. "As I said before, what other choice do I have? I won't abandon Loom."

"That's good to hear."

Arianna searched the vicar's face. Her eyes narrowed. "Did you suspect I would?"

"You were forced into the limelight. Your hand is forced to action. And you were forced to do what no inventor should—share your schematics."

"Sharing them was my choice." The four words were so familiar that Arianna almost believed them.

Willard spared her his protest. "Loom appreciates your loyalty. I, and every Chimera, appreciate you sharing the whole technology of the boxes, unaltered."

That was when she understood him. Arianna couldn't stop a snarl. "I may be a Wraith, but I would not harm my own people."

"You never wanted to share the boxes, and the idea of widespread Perfect Chimera was something you resisted. Forgive me for asking Arianna, but is there anything I should know about them?"

"They are as true as the one in me." Arianna scowled at the man.

"Very well."

"You don't believe me?"

"It doesn't matter if I do or do not. You have or haven't tampered with them. You will or won't. But this wave has crested, Arianna. There is no turning back progress now." He paused, and Arianna had nothing to fill the silence with. "Don't exhaust yourself. We need you alive." With that, the old man departed.

"No turning back progress," she repeated, staring at the boxes that lined the table. Was it really progress? Or was her creation the thing that would drive Loom to its demise?

# 46
## COLETTA

ALONG THE NARROW, DEPRESSINGLY UNADORNED PASSAGE AWAY FROM HER GRAY Room was another receiving area—a collection of holding cells, really—where incoming Fen would be tested on their worth. Rok only had room and resources to support a select few of the wretched creatures, so the pack needed to be thinned. This area had been re-purposed as an observation room for the two women who currently occupied the space.

Topann lay on the table in the center of the room, a book Coletta had granted her open flat. The woman cupped her chin with her palm, lazily flipping the pages as her foot, with a mind of its own, rocked a chair slightly behind her back and forth. Where she was the picture of serenity and patience, the other beast in the room was not.

Fae crouched before the barred door to one of the cells that lined the perimeter and grinned at the cowering Alchemist inside. With one claw, she scratched away at the lock. A deep groove had already formed underneath the harrowing sound of her claw.

At Coletta and Yveun's arrival, the two women were on their feet with varying speeds and levels of decorum. Topann stood straight, head bowed, hands folded demurely before her. Fae leaned heavily against the door of the cell, causing a faint clanking sound as the hinges strained under her bulk. Her purple eyes drifted lustily over to Yveun, the foreplay between them beginning with a mere look.

"How many organs do you each have?" Coletta asked.

"All of them," Topann answered dutifully. "Save for lungs."

"What she said." Fae gave a mocking imitation of Coletta's flower.

"The sickness, the magic rejection . . . You worked through it?" Yveun walked straight for Fae. "I want to see."

"I'll let you see inside me, if it pleases the Dono." Fae made a show of leaning forward to whisper in his ear, but it was really entirely for the titillation of the man before her. Coletta, in turn, gave an approving look to Fae. She needed the woman to smooth over her mate's rough edges at the impending news.

"How did you do it?" Yveun couldn't seem to decide on which head he wanted to let govern his actions, and his body pivoted between her and Fae. Coletta knew his curiosity was great indeed if it pulled him away from the purring sex goddess before him.

"At first, we used like-organs." Coletta motioned to Topann. "A symbol of Rok's strength certainly required the best organs and nothing less. So I scoured the underbelly of Lysip, and then topside when that did not work."

"But you said none of them took," Yveun recalled.

"Indeed. Fae was the key." Having a recklessly accepting test subject had more than proved Fae's worth to Coletta. "She experienced no problem accepting Rok organs, even those from below."

"A particular Dragon, then?" Yveun theorized.

"I thought the same, but Topann still rejected them, even ones regrown from the same stock."

"You said you now have all of them but the rarest?" Yveun looked to her flower. "What did it take?"

Topann looked uncomfortable now. She folded and unfolded her hands firmly, working up her resolve. Coletta spared her flower the difficulty. The agony was needless.

"It took no half measures."

"What does that mean?" The slight edge to Yveun's voice from earlier was returning.

"Well, Fae as a Tam could accept Rok organs without rejection. I assume Xin can accept Tam organs . . ." Coletta wanted to see if he could put it together on his own. She had every faith her mate could, but hate blinded him too much. Prejudice was the true antithesis to progress. "Xin organs. A Perfect Rok Dragon requires Xin organs."

There was a long silence.

Then, an explosion.

"*What?*" Yveun turned his head to the Alchemist in the cage. Coletta knew he hadn't realized at the time that she was locking him in there for his protection. A kindness truly befitting a great ruler like herself. "Explain this, Fen."

"I-I can't!" He scooted away from the opening of his prison. Coletta could almost smell the sour aroma of fear oozing from his pores. "She's right, but I don't know why, it just is."

"Explain!"

Coletta let the exchange drag on a moment. It was good for the Fen to see Yveun in a fearsome role, to reinforce the image of their great and terrible ruler.

"I don't know. I'm not a proper Alchemist. I never received—"

"Do you want to give me excuses?" Yveun's voice dropped, low and deadly, as his hand gripped the lock. Coletta wondered if he could rip it off. She almost wanted to let the situation escalate long enough to see him try.

"Magic rots Fenthri. We know Fenthri bodies aren't made for it, so it rots us out . . . It doesn't matter where the organs come from, it's a property of magic." The man swallowed hard a few times. "Perhaps there are different *types* of magic in different Dragons, in the different houses? There's no way we could've known because it's all magic for a Fenthri—it causes the same issue no matter who it's from, or what type . . . But perhaps it explains why some can have three organs before falling, and some only two. Perhaps different houses have different potencies, or certain organs are noncompatible in a single body . . . " The man trailed off into his own thoughts.

Yveun turned to Coletta. When his world was at its bleakest, its most unstable, he turned to her. It was their balance, their equal parts. "What does this mean?"

"It means that nothing has changed," she said easily. "We hunted Xin before, purely for their deaths. Now, we will hunt them for their organs."

Yveun was quiet a moment, but only just. With a half-snarl, half-roar, he buried his fist into the nearby wall, splintering and cracking the wood. "No, we will not."

"No half measures." Coletta shouldn't have to remind him of their house's motto, of how his failure to embrace it had only led, time and again, to their failure.

"This is not a half measure, this is a matter of our pride! We shall not lower ourselves to Xin for strength." Yveun swung his head toward Topann. For a brief moment, Coletta could feel him considering saying something, but he abandoned the notion, storming out of the room. Even when he was pushed past his limit, he knew better than to disturb her precious flowers.

"Fae." Coletta was unfettered. "Please go see to the Dono."

"With *pleasure*." The woman practically moaned the last word in her carnal excitement.

"Then you will head down to Loom." They didn't have time for dalliances and her mate needed to learn how to be placated without a toy to keep him occupied. If Coletta could teach him that one skill, how much easier would her life be?

"Yes, I remember the deal, what you gave me all this power for. Kill the girl, nab more gold."

"And another, after Florence."

Fae tilted her head as a display of her attention.

"Arianna, Queen of Wraiths."

"Yveun will be pleased." Fae bared her teeth. Clearly the name was already one Yveun had uttered, no doubt time and again.

"Good. Now go." She waited until Fae was gone and they were alone. Well, excluding the Fen. "And you—" she turned to Topann "—you will help me in acquiring Xin organs."

"Whatever you need of me, my lady."

Even if Yveun did not yet agree with her methods, Coletta would charge forward. If they could not find more gold, Tam could not be relied on. Without Tam, and with Xin allying with Loom, the future of Rok looked more uncertain by the hour. But Coletta liked dire situations; they made her creative. And when she was at her most creative, she was also at her most deadly.

# 47
## FLORENCE

THERE WERE A TOTAL OF FOUR ENGINES LEFT IN THE RAVENS' GUILD HALL, BUT only three slowly lurched to a halt at Ter.3.2. The compartments had been cramped, but in the end, there was only enough fuel left at Ter.4 to run three engines. It was a severe oversight on Vicar Dove's part, one that made Florence agitated for nearly the entire trip.

"I'm so ready to be off this train," Shannra muttered. The woman had been dozing off for hours but had perked up slightly when the train began to cut fuel in an effort to conserve their remaining supplies and coast into the station on momentum.

"The ride isn't so bad." Florence stretched her legs forward in the narrow compartment. Her status as vicar—*vicar*! The title still had yet to fully sink in, had earned her a bit of privacy that she shared with Shannra gladly.

"Five days!" Shannra groaned, sinking back into the narrow bed. The cabin was only wide enough for one chair and the bed that was tucked oddly into an alcove that jutted into the hall outside their door. "I forgot what fresh air feels like."

"Then open the window." Florence counted her canisters on a table that was little more than a window ledge and held back a small grin.

"You think you're awfully funny, don't you?" They had discovered the window was broken a day in.

"More than one way to open a window." Florence drew her revolver and brought her arm across her body, the grip exposed on the end as though she was about to smash the window with it.

"Florence, stop!" Shannra lunged, gripping her hands.

Florence grinned, wide and silly. No doubt stir-crazy. "Ask me nicely."

"Oh, I see how it is." Shannra gave a low chuckle that curved her cheek in just the way Florence liked. "You do think you're funny."

"What of it?"

"I'll wipe the smile off that mouth of yours."

"With what?"

Shannra leaned forward, half-laughing into the kiss that set free Florence's own laughter. Florence placed her palms over the other woman's hips, smoothing them against the bone that protruded from her narrow waist. Shannra had never boasted a sturdy frame, but she had begun to shrink before Florence's eyes and hands.

They all had. Being at war, living in hiding—it took a hefty toll on Loom, and rations were scarce as it was. All the more reason to keep moving, follow the remaining resources.

Yes, war was brutal, and it demanded a high price of them all. But Florence wouldn't let that price be Shannra. She indulged herself in what distractions the woman could provide and savored the moments they got to spend together not as Revolvers, but as women.

Instead of tracing the all-too-clear outline of Shannra's lower ribs, Florence kissed them. Instead of focusing on the bony jut of her hips, Florence gave careful mind to the woman's knee resting on the chair right at the apex of her thighs. She reveled in feeling the other woman's hands in her hair and nails on her scalp, and offered the same distraction.

Shannra's hands moved to Florence's back, gripping and smoothing the fabric forward before sliding forward to grace her chest. Florence conceded to the clear desire and rose without forfeiting her lover's mouth. Shannra was taller than Florence, as most were, and she had to crane her neck when standing if Shannra didn't slouch.

Florence carefully worked on the latches of her holster and Shannra was eager to assist. When it came loose, her lover handled the weapons with care, breaking the kiss to set them aside. Despite the fact that it resulted in Shannra's mouth off hers, Florence had never seen anything sexier than this mindfulness of weaponry.

With a soft hum rising in the back of her throat, Florence pulled Shannra back to her, using the height difference to sink her teeth into the woman's skin, scarred and rough with battle. Her white hair tickled Florence's nose and Florence closed her eyes. In the back of her mind, despite all will or conscious effort, another white-haired woman appeared like a dangling loose end, never quite tied off.

Florence pressed her teeth down harder. The flavor of someone else on her tongue was enough to clear her head again, and Florence pursued the distraction. Without much thought, Shannra was on the bed, Florence above her.

Sex had its own power and its own weakness, Florence had learned. It was gaining true vulnerability from another while giving it from yourself at the same time. But there was a guarded look to Shannra's eyes and an echo in all the woman's moans that came from the distance that still lingered between them. Neither was ready to give or take that power.

So they took only pleasure instead.

When the brakes of the train engaged some time later, Florence finally peeled her sweat-slicked body from the sheets. Her clothes hadn't gone far in the small cabin, but she was still stalled by the task of sorting them from Shannra's.

"What's the hurry?" Shannra yawned.

"How can you be sleepy? You've been dozing all day." Florence started with her underthings, dressing up to her skirt, shirt, and vest.

"You wore me out." The woman grinned, forgetting her earlier question entirely. Florence silently applauded herself for the effective distraction.

"Ah, well, that's not very hard." Her statement sent Shannra into a pout that transformed into a retaliation against putting on clothes.

"Where are you off to?"

"Train's almost stopped." Florence looked out their small window. The platform had begun to creep along the sides of the train. They were made of metal and wood, which echoed the architecture of a small town in the distance. Florence saw the marked smokestacks of a refinery and other buildings she didn't recognize.

*Arianna's home.*

It was Florence's first time laying eyes on a proper establishment of Ter.3, and she wondered how different it was from when Arianna was a girl.

"I'll need you to whisper to Arianna," Florence spoke as she adjusted her holster. "Let her know we made it to 3.2."

Shannra's mouth pressed together slightly. The woman was good at a great many things, but hiding her emotions from Florence was not one of them. It was as if Shannra could see through her, straight to that never-quite-defined aspect of her relationship with Arianna.

"Anything else you'd like me to tell her?" Shannra began moving for her clothes.

"No, that should be enough." Florence grabbed her top hat, the final piece of her ensemble. She hoped Arianna would have more to say to her—updates on the Philosopher's Boxes, suggestions for training, a remark on her cleverness for bringing all of Loom south . . . something.

"As you command, Vicar Florence." Shannra raised her hand to her ear.

Florence snatched the appendage by the wrist, quickly bringing it up to press a kiss against Shannra's knuckles. She searched the other woman's eyes. She wanted to offer reassurances, but she didn't quite know for what.

"Thank you, lovely," Florence whispered against Shannra's flesh.

Just like that, her steely eyes eased to wool-soft. "Anything for you, you know."

"Careful on what you offer me . . . I just may take it," she cautioned.

"I hope you do." Florence gave a small smile and moved away. Shannra added, "All of you."

Florence merely nodded, adjusted her hat, and left. She heard Shannra's meaning more clearly than she would've liked, but wasn't inclined to address it. Not yet. There was always tomorrow. For now, she had more important things to focus on than pesky matters of the heart.

For now, she had Loom.

Florence stepped off the yet-moving train, one of the first on the platform. Shannra was right; it had been too long since they had proper fresh air. Florence filled her lungs as if for the first time and relished the filtered sunlight of aboveground Loom. She hoped she had seen the last of the Underground.

After all, she was the Vicar Revolver now. Holx wasn't, and had never been, a place for her.

"Vicar Florence." She shouldn't have been surprised when Dove addressed her; the Vicar Raven would be the other to disembark first. Florence fell into step with the woman as they migrated toward the exit. "I trust your ride was good?"

"The Ravens do an excellent job of maintaining their trains, Vicar."

"They do indeed." Dove was completely oblivious that Florence's compliment held more than a bit of irony. "We should have more than enough coal here to see the rest of the way to Garre, a few routes between . . ."

Dove tried the door of the station master's office. When the handle didn't budge, she didn't even blink, smashing through the window with her pistol and reaching around to unlock it. She descended on the quarters as if she owned them, deftly locating the primary ledger for the station.

"How does it look?" Florence asked.

"More than enough coal . . . Should be a gold storehouse here, too, if I'm not mistaken. Perhaps we could even outfit one engine to focus more on magic and alleviate some of the draw on the resources."

"It'd certainly relieve Powell." Florence looked through the open door back out to the platform, seeing the man in question disembark.

"Anything to quiet him about draining resources," Dove muttered. Florence chose to ignore the remark. She'd seen just how impressive the Harvester's work to manage resources was.

"I'll whisper to Garre, have Arianna speak with Willard about outfitting the next train."

"And I'll look into that storehouse of gold."

Florence said nothing about the copied ledger she still had in her possession. Dove was almost too good at her job, remembering with ease where every outpost for the Ravens was along their trade routes. Plus, if Dove had concealed the state of their coal reserves, Florence could only imagine how she would handle gold. Thus, she kept the means to verify the Vicar Raven to herself.

"I trust you both had a smooth journey?" Powell asked as he joined them, referencing the last time they had spoken on the train a day ago.

"Indeed." Dove closed up the ledger and pushed past the Vicar Harvester. "If you'll both excuse me, I'm going to see to the state of our engines and manage my Ravens."

"Oh, right, very well . . ." Powell was left muttering to a woman who was already out of hearing range. "I don't think she likes me very much," he observed quietly to Florence.

"We don't have to like each other. We merely need to be effective." Florence shrugged and started for the door as well.

"Effective, huh? You like me though, don't you, Florence?"

"You know that's true." She gave Powell an encouraging smile. "We're both young vicars and need to stick together."

"No doubt."

The station had two platforms divided by a turnstile. Powell and Florence emerged opposite the side they'd arrived on, and found themselves on a covered stretch that descended into a cobblestone arc of road lined with small storefronts, completely void of life.

Florence's hand was on her gun before she was even conscious of the prickle up her neck. She looked along the road that led down the sloping hill into the downtown proper, where the smokestacks of the refinery and factories stretched toward the sky.

"It's quiet."

"I was just thinking the same thing," Powell affirmed.

"Revolvers!" Florence called over her shoulder back to the filling platform. The handful of her guild that still remained turned their heads in attention. "We move first, guns at the ready."

There were looks of confusion, but none objected. The Revolvers naturally ordered themselves in small squadrons based on specialization and available weaponry. Bernard was at her right.

"Bernard, I want you to set up roosts with the initiates, there and there." Florence pointed at two balconies down the road. Initiates weren't the best shots, but Florence hoped they could at least lay cover fire.

"Emma, you and I will go with the journeymen." Florence spoke loud enough for everyone to hear, but her eyes caught Shannra's. *Stay close to me*, they said.

"Vicar, we'd like to switch." Bernard spoke before Emma could even open her mouth, setting Florence's eye to twitching. "The Revolvers cannot manage the loss of another Vicar."

"The Revolvers can survive whatever comes our way," Florence said firmly. She'd not have men uttering words that would make the initiates weak. "Furthermore, I will be in good company."

"What are we defending ourselves from?" Emma asked the right question.

"I don't know yet." Florence looked back down the sloping, still road. "But something doesn't feel right."

They walked with guns at the ready down the center of the street. Florence felt the unease from the other Revolvers, but if there was fire to draw, she wanted to draw it. She wanted no chance of going unnoticed by lurking hostiles.

But the silence persisted and, other than its unnerving stillness, it was almost a pleasant walk. The air further south was slightly less bitingly cold and the wind was a gentle breeze. Still, Florence's concern continued to rise like molten steel coming to temperature.

The moment they arrived at the factory's entrance, where the Rivets had gone ahead early to begin manufacturing the corona-blasting guns, Florence knew every sickening concern was founded.

Bodies littered the ground, soaked in black and crimson. Blood formed small rivers in the grooves between the stones of the street. Fenthri and Chimera alike, most bearing Alchemist and Rivet markings, all had the distinct slash marks that came with Dragon talons. A startling few had guns on their person. It was a slaughter of noncombatants that set Florence's mouth into a grim line.

All movement had stilled around her and every living eye was on the large factory doors, pulled shut. Upon them, written with the smear of a large palm, was a message in blood.

"To Florence, with love," Emma read from her side. "What do we do now?"

Florence stared at the door for another long moment, as though it were the Dragon King himself. "We do what Loom is best at. We clean up the mess the Dragons have left us, and we get back to work."

# 48

## CVAREH

looked out onto the refinery floor that wasn't much of a refinery anymore.

"Do you think so?" Cvareh rested his hands on the window sill.

Below, the floor that had been mostly dark since its creation now glowed with life as men and women flitted about from one machine to the next. His eyes tracked over each of the Fenthri, and he silently practiced each of their names. It was something small, but he hoped it would be enough to show Arianna that he had begun to take seriously the idea of Fenthri as equals on Nova.

"Petra wanted to see this place come to life. It was a grand vision that now means something. Yes, I think so."

"Thank you." Cvareh gave his friend a tired smile. His shoulders felt like they sagged a little deeper just from expending the energy to do so. "She wanted it to make gold."

"She couldn't have foreseen that we needed it for a much greater purpose. More than anything, Petra wanted it to be useful." Poiris had a working relationship with his sister that Cvareh had only glimpsed briefly. This had been Petra's pet project; were it not for Poiris, Cvareh would've had a hard time assuming the mantle, going in blind.

"Useful, it is."

"To think, we underestimated them for so long." Poiris's eyes were on the Fenthri. "Thinking them lesser. Thinking we had things to teach them and order to bring. We had a lot more to learn."

"I wouldn't say that . . ." Cvareh's eyes fell on one woman in particular, who nearly stopped all movement on the floor with her white-haired, nearly ethereal presence.

Arianna was a force to be reckoned with. Respected among Fenthri and feared among Dragons alike for her knowledge, she commanded loyalty with an ease Cvareh didn't think she even recognized. With him as Dono and her at his side, they could rule the world together.

*Do I want that?*

It had long since stopped being about what either of them wanted.

"Why is that?" Poiris pulled Cvareh from his thoughts.

"Why is—*oh*, because as much as we have to learn from them, they need to learn from us." Cvareh thought of Arianna when she first landed on Nova, the things she questioned. Was it fair for him to think that she was better off for having her world expanded beyond the cold logic that governed Loom?

"Well, call me greased," Arianna said as she opened the door. "This damn near looks respectable."

"Are you surprised?" Poiris asked, his chest puffing like a bird ruffling its feathers.

"With this one at the helm?" Arianna motioned to Cvareh. "Yes."

"I don't think—"

Cvareh merely chuckled and allowed the sound to diffuse Poiris's tension into confusion. "Poiris, all is well. Please excuse my mate and I."

Arianna arched her eyebrows, a silent question.

Naming her as such extended her all the respect and protections that came with his own status. But he couldn't deny the quiet thrill that hummed through him at the notion.

With Poiris departed, Arianna dropped her bag into a heap by the door, empty. The tubes it carried had already been handed off to be filled anew with flowers. "Your mate. Sounds serious."

"It's not," he lied.

"You're lying."

She could be very frustrating. "It doesn't matter. Nothing does unless we win."

"Until we win," she corrected and stared out down at the Fenthri. "They're doing a good job, seem happy enough."

"When the war is over, every Fenthri who wishes to return home to Loom will be ferried back. The ones who don't will be treated the same as any Dragon."

"None will want to stay."

She sounded as if she had every confidence, but Cvareh wasn't so sure. In the hybrid world that existed just beyond the horizon, there was a place for Fenthri on Nova to maintain the various mechanizations that would no doubt crop up across their landscape. The mere idea brought a smile to Cvareh's mouth.

"What?"

"What?" he echoed.

"That smile."

"Just imagining a Nova with Fenthri, and machines."

Arianna snorted. "The likelihood of that happening is about the same as the Alchemists giving up dissections."

"I don't think so." He leaned against the glass, following her stare. Even now, Dragons were beginning to walk among the Fenthri, work among them. "Plus, for the longevity of one world, we'd better hope that we get along enough to live on land or sky."

"Well, we will be living in both places soon, as Loom is about ready to ferry Perfect Chimera."

"How many?" Cvareh didn't even bother to hide his desperation.

"Ten."

*Ten*, the word echoed. "That's not nearly enough."

"It will have to be."

"Ari—"

"Loom isn't sending anyone who isn't ready to fight. If we send them up here prematurely, they will be slaughtered."

"It's my people who are being slaughtered right now." He knew it was a faulty argument, but he couldn't stop himself. Logic and emotion didn't always work well together.

"Loom could always, instead, just fortify ourselves and leave Xin to fight alone."

Shock started with his mouth and rattled up to his brain. "You'd condemn us to death?"

"That's not what I said."

"Isn't it?" Cvareh pushed off from the sill and stepped into her personal space. He stared down at her, working to ignore the familiar scents of her. "You'd leave me to die by Rok's hand?"

Arianna stared up at him. Her chin stretched forward, as though she was about to fight him. But then her brow softened. What looked like conflict overcame her features, and Cvareh no longer had any idea what was going through the woman's mind. He loathed the distance that had come between them, though he couldn't quite identify when the chasm had started to form.

Cvareh never had the opportunity to find out her answer.

"Attack on the western side of Ruana!" Cain skidded to a stop in the open doorway. His eyes narrowed at Arianna and hers narrowed in reply, the defensive expression instantly back on her face.

How the two most important people in Cvareh's life ended up on opposite sides of the coin, Cvareh did not know. But he appreciated that they could put it all aside for their common enemy.

"It's close to Dawyn's family's vineyards." Cain confirmed Cvareh's worst fear.

"I have to go," he said to them both.

Arianna pushed off from the window sill as well. Her hands went through their motions, an instinctual check of every tool of her trade. She patted her blades, her winch box, her breast pocket where there was, no doubt, some kind of gun or other weapon concealed.

"I will go, too."

"What?" both men said in unison.

She looked directly at Cvareh and he instantly regretted challenging her. For there was nothing more fearsome than an Arianna with something to prove.

"I will go, too," she reiterated. Her attention was solely on Cvareh. "And I will show you just how valuable one Perfect Chimera will be in your fight." Arianna turned to Cain. "Lead on."

Cain obliged and Arianna followed, her focus entirely on Cvareh's Ryu. Cvareh followed close behind, pushing his conflict from his mind. He needed to be focused for whatever battle awaited them. But for now, he felt some pity for whatever Dragons were about to face Arianna.

# 49
## FLORENCE

Florence rose from the bed she shared with Shannra, finally abandoning all hope of sleep. Instead, she tugged on a random shirt and skirt and padded lightly to the large window that overlooked Ter.3.2. Quietly easing open the latch, Florence leaned into the night air.

The world was still. Somewhere, a Revolver kept watch, ready to raise the alarm if gliders were spotted against the darkened sky. But they didn't make their hiding spot known.

Florence rested her elbows on the sill. The metal was like ice under her flesh and shot daggers right to her bones. She inhaled deeply, allowing the cool air to meet the sensation of her arms and finish numbing out her bare toes.

"You're going to catch your death if you let in this weather." Florence half-turned and was met with a blanket slung over her shoulder.

"I didn't hear you stir."

"I know." Shannra nestled herself under the blanket at Florence's side, closing it around them like a great cocoon. She'd thought she wanted to be alone. But Florence was proven wrong by the beautiful woman at her side. Her head gravitated toward Shannra's shoulder, and she pulled the blanket more tightly around them.

"How long do you think it will take?"

"How long do I think what will take?" Shannra followed Florence's gaze, looking at the factory in the distance. "The new weapons? Sooner over later, I'm sure. The revisions didn't seem too complicated, at least according to the Rivets."

"That wasn't what I meant."

"My mind reading must be rusty, then." Florence didn't even bother fighting a small smile at the woman's jest. "What did you mean?"

"All this." Florence nodded to the city sprawled beneath them. The fractured homes, void of occupants. The sloping streets, empty and quiet. "How long until the cities are full again? Until steam clouds the sky at all hours of the day? How long until Loom is alive once more?"

"Loom *is* alive," Shannra insisted. "In no small part thanks to you."

Florence didn't want to be placated. She wanted a real answer. She wanted to know if what she was doing would be enough or if she had only set the target for Loom's revival too far away for anyone to hit.

Ari would've understood what she was trying to say.

"I'm not enough," Florence spoke mostly to herself, to all the flaws she still had and everything that she still wanted to accomplish.

"Where is this coming from? Flor, you can't be discouraged by what happened here."

"I'm not discouraged, I'm motivated," she insisted. "All those people died because someone wanted to leave me a message." Florence scowled at the invisible killer who had laid waste to a factory producing a gun she had an important hand in designing. It was an attack on her even without the words on the doors. "I need to find the person who killed them and shoot them down for Loom. I need to be better for us all—"

It dawned on her in a rush. "I need to be Perfect."

"What are you saying?" Shannra's grip had relaxed some. Despite the blanket being around their shoulders, Florence felt very far out of reach.

"I need to be Perfect." Florence repeated. That was what she was missing. That was what separated everything she was, and everything she could become. It had been Arianna's turning point, the thing that had made her so strong for so many years.

"You don't need to be anything but what you are." Shannra squeezed her tightly again. "You're already enough."

Florence opened her mouth to protest, when the wind shifted and a familiar scent tickled her nose. It was faint, so much that she could've ignored it entirely. Florence looked for the source, turning her face toward the breeze. But Arianna was far away, and the scent was nothing more than a wisp on the wind.

"My mind is made up." Florence kept her eyes on the southwestern horizon, wondering if the smell was all in her mind. She would've known that aroma anywhere: Arianna's magic. Perhaps, it was her mind finally telling her that with Perfection would come an understanding of something greater. She would see the world with eyes like Arianna's and gain insights into all the corners of herself that she seemed to barely understand.

# 50
## COLETTA

Four Dragons snarled from their respective pens in the observation room. Things had changed since Fae and Topann's time. These were not loyal servants who deserved free roam, but bottom-dwellers. Dragons who had never seen the sun couldn't be trusted not to kill each other, let alone leave unharmed the Fenthri charged with observing them for any signs of magic rejection.

She watched as the Alchemist walked the length of the room, purposefully staying out of swiping reach of each of the cages. Coletta wondered what the world looked like to him. The only thing keeping him from certain death was her.

From where she stood, it was a gorgeous world order.

"And how are they?" Coletta inquired, growing impatient with the Fen's endless humming, pen-tapping, and pacing.

"None of them are showing the same signs as Yeann. It seems the Xin organs you have acquired work well."

"If only there were more. You said with one Dragon we could make another Perfect in how long?"

The Alchemist thought a moment. "We'd have to time regrowth . . . too many organs out at once and the body won't heal. One Dragon can make one Perfect Dragon in . . . I'd estimate two weeks? If all the organs aligned."

It was too long. She needed more Xin organs sooner over later. Coletta's eyes settled on the Dragons in their cages once more. Even if there were more to sort, a success would still be a success, and she would do well not to forget it.

Instead of allowing the limitations to frustrate her, she let them bolster her sails.

"My queen." Ulia appeared in the doorway. "Forgive the intrusion, but

Yveun'Dono requests your presence."

"Where is he?" Coletta's voice was impassive toward the summons.

"The sun room."

"Continue as planned," Coletta instructed as a final note to the Fen. Even if they'd only found one Xin Dragon to harvest organs from, Coletta would still have him move forward at whatever snail's pace he could. It was better than nothing.

"Right . . ." The man's agreement trailed off as he looked at the other empty cells in the room, no doubt imagining what it would be like to have them all filled with swiping, snarling, rage-filled Perfect Dragons.

The Fen's greatest fear was Coletta's sweetest wish.

Yveun's temperament had not much improved from their last interaction. The balm of Fae's touch had done little, if anything, to soothe him, and her departure for Loom had only made matters worse.

Coletta dismissed Ulia halfway to the room Yveun had made his center of operations for managing the various battlefronts they faced. She adjusted the beads around her neck, then entered. Yveun sat behind a low desk positioned in front of a great vertical circle, atop a pedestal, overlooking a balcony. Coletta saw it for what it was—fanfare. The real work happened in Gray Rooms and secret gardens.

"That necklace is new," Yveun observed with a glance.

"I thought it fitting." Coletta touched it delicately even though it was likely as sturdy as the bones in her fingers.

"Taking Rider beads for yourself?"

Sure enough, the necklace had been crafted from Dragon bone in the same fashion as the beads the Riders wore to mark their kills. "I think I have earned this many beads and more."

"It's the 'and more' I am most interested in." Yveun hoisted a folio and tossed it toward her feet. The papers scattered across the floor—transcripts of the reports from the Hall of Whispers. "I'm in need of much more from you, Coletta."

Coletta merely arched her eyebrows. "I'm not sure how making a mess of your notes helps me produce it." She folded her hands and stood tall, hoping to convey that she had no interest in collecting up his documents for him.

"We are thwarted at every turn on Loom, Perfect Chimera have begun to fight alongside Xin, and Tam's interest in struggling against the abominations seems to be wearing thin."

Wearing thin because there was no more gold to tip the scales in Rok's favor.

"And you, what have you done?" Yveun approached with purpose. "You have played Alchemist with your Fen toy, doing little for our plight."

"I have given everything for our plight." Coletta stretched her mouth wide, showing her teeth and reminding him of all she had endured for the sake of their dominance.

For the briefest of moments, he softened into the man she was accustomed to seeing when it was just the two of them, alone. Yveun reached out one of his massive hands and ran it almost tenderly across her necklace. "It suits you."

"Thank you. Now, with regards to Tam . . ." Her demeanor shifted and the moment evaporated like fresh blood. She had his levelheaded attention and she needed to capitalize on it while she could. "We do not need them."

"Coletta—"

"Yveun," she interrupted. He had to hear her; everything hinged on him putting aside his prejudice and truly listening to what she said. "You know what Fae has done on Loom. With just her and two other Riders, she took down an entire Fenthri stronghold."

"A feat my Riders could always boast," Yveun countered.

"There were casualties then," Coletta reminded him. "Fae thrives with not so much as a scratch. On Loom, a Perfect Dragon is the perfect predator. *Think* of what we could do with them here, on Nova."

"No."

"Without Tam's assistance we must do something to sway the tides back in our favor." Coletta had always known that pride made men stupid, but she never appreciated *how* stupid until that moment.

"Then acquire more gold and buy back their loyalty."

"There is no more gold," she said for what must have been the hundredth time. "We are sitting atop an army, yet you do not wish to mobilize."

"I will not see Xin organs in my house's Dragons."

"Defeat them with what they are." It would be glorious. The idea of thwarting Xin with their own organs sent shivers up her spine.

"No."

"Yveun—"

"Your Dono has decreed it!" Yveun roared. Coletta didn't even flinch. "You will not put any more Xin organs into Rok bodies. *That* is not perfection; it is an affront to Lord Rok himself."

Coletta started for the door.

"I have not dismissed you," he growled.

"I have dismissed myself." Coletta stood as tall as possible. She was shorter than him, smaller and frailer, yet she could still look down her nose at the short-sighted man who claimed to be her mate. "I will only speak to you again once you are ready to see reason." Her eyes dropped to the papers still scattered on the floor, nothing more than a pathetic list of failures. "I hope it will not be too late by then."

She closed the door gently behind her. Coletta would not give in to sudden outbursts or rage. She was not her mate, who, judging from the crash, promptly set to destroy what remained of his beautiful façade.

*Let him ruin it*, she thought, starting down the hall. Perhaps once he had made a mess of the illusion, he would be ready to face reality.

# 51
## CVAREH

against hers.

"You talk too much," she sighed back in reply. For all the brilliance the woman could craft with her fingers, they seemed to be thwarted every time by the clasps Nova's tailors could conceive.

"What are we?" he repeated.

"What does it matter?"

He heard the fastenings holding up his trousers click open and Cvareh knew there was little more he could do. He was helpless before her, trembling like a mortal before a god whose altar was a small bed in the back of the refinery-turned-factory.

Cvareh pushed her down and heeded her hands. His body swelled, enveloping hers. Arianna pushed and pulled, contorted herself to meet him until that moment when they both could breathe again, when he was fully immersed in her.

It was the greatest feeling he'd ever known, though it would be impossible to attempt to explain to anyone else why it was so wonderful. He didn't try. Cvareh kept them, and whatever they were or weren't, between them. He kept this feeling between them.

This blissful, all-too-short feeling.

It was the fourth time he'd had her in two short months and the wait between each time became harder than the last.

Every time was the same. Every time, she'd arrived to take flowers, bring resources. Every time, she'd ended up fighting alongside Xin men and women against Rok. Every time, she was met with the same apprehension from his people that Arianna would claim didn't weigh on her until the day she died and yet, there was something to it. Some kind of jealousy that came over her like a shadow when those same people praised Cvareh for his actions as their Ryu.

The more others learned of her, the more she withdrew. Her demeanor had even begun to earn praise from Cain, so much that the man had stopped pestering Cvareh at every turn about his fondness for Arianna.

He never thought he'd actually miss Cain's nagging. But at least when his friend complained, it meant things were as they had always been. His silence underscored the distance he felt growing between them.

Cvareh lay at Arianna's side, tracing the outlines of her ashen skin with a long finger. He graced over the scars of her body—the gash where her chest had been cracked open to allow room for his lungs, the ring on her wrists where the hands Finnyr had once carried met her natural flesh, the horizontal slit where her stomach had been scooped out. On and on, her body was pockmarked and flawed. But every curve, every gnarled scar, was *hers*. Her hands belonged to none but her. Even the lungs, still heaving from their lovemaking, he no longer saw as his own.

"Ari . . ." He leaned in to press his nose against her cheek, nuzzling it.

"I should go."

"You've barely caught your breath." He watched her get up, locating her underthings first. Cvareh was proud to say that this time he had not shredded them in his zeal.

"We can't afford time for things like this."

"I object," he said with a chuckle. "We've afforded time, every time."

"And we shouldn't." Arianna buttoned up the fly of her trousers—all seven needless, frustrating, delicate buttons.

"Why?" He watched as she shrugged on her shirt next, back still to him, as her form in all its beauty began to be shrouded from him once more. Arianna located her vest and was buttoning it before he pressed again, realizing she had no intention of answering him. "Why shouldn't we?"

"You're the Xin'Oji."

"Since when have you cared for Dragon titles?" He stood with a soft chuckle and gripped her shoulders, half-turning her to face him. Arianna's eyes were full of all the life and fire he loved in her, even when it was directed toward him. "You are right, I am the Xin'Oji. But that merely means no one will object to me —to us."

"When you kill Yveun . . ."

He appreciated her certainty. "When I kill Yveun, what?" he repeated. It wasn't like her to leave a thought hanging.

"What then?"

"Then I will be Dono." Cvareh searched her face, surprised to find pain there. "I promise you, Arianna, I will be a Dono for Nova. Loom will have their sovereignty."

"I have no doubt." She pulled away from him and snatched up her white coat. Arianna tugged it on with renewed purpose and went right for the door.

"Ari—."

"I have to get back to Loom," she interrupted him curtly, not even bothering to look back. "More Perfect Chimera are ready to send, and guns will soon be ready to ship with them. I need to help train Ravens to run gliders."

Cvareh stared dumbly as she left him to wonder what, exactly, he had said wrong.

Certainly, he could've chased after her, but he didn't. He could've whispered to her in the days that followed, but he didn't do that either. The words that needed to be said, words he was still discovering, needed to be said to her face. And those he wanted to hear, he likewise wanted to see emerge from her mouth.

So, when she whispered a week later that Perfect Chimera were on their way, Cvareh vowed to be ready. He prepared his heart, only to have it sink when he discovered not Arianna making the delivery, but Helen in her stead.

# 5²
# FLORENCE

The Rivets' Guild hall was everything Florence expected after her brief time in Ter.3.2. The clockwork structure of patchwork metal—some dulled with time, greening with age, and other parts fresh like new skin grafts over old wounds—fit with what she'd come to learn was the Rivet sensibility. Steam hissed and gears churned in perpetual motion within the walls.

She was put up in very sensible chambers close to Willard. Florence could tell they were designed especially for guests, as they had different accommodations than usual. Even in comfort, there was something purposeful and methodological about the way the Rivets approached their existence. The whole place echoed of Arianna in the most nostalgic of ways.

Florence had been sequestered from the first moment she'd arrived. Willard and Ethel had greeted her at the platform and talks began almost immediately. How would they allocate their increasing numbers of trained Perfect Chimera? Would they outfit them with Florence's weapon, or would they save the weapon for regular Chimera in effort to double their effective fighting force? Would they be willing to supply the weapon directly to the Dragons? On and on the questions went.

They looked to Florence for answers that she wasn't sure she had. She was the Vicar Revolver, and hadn't ever set foot in the Revolvers' Guild hall—at least, hadn't set foot when she wasn't sneaking. She didn't know the first thing about how to properly train Alchemists to think like fighters. So she made it up as she went, and hoped it all worked out.

Yes, she was exhausted from trying to live up to others' expectations. She was tired of the world looking to her for answers she didn't even know if she had. But Florence knew she wouldn't sleep tonight.

Her mind was heavy, and her heart was knotted. It was a combination that kept sleep at bay and Florence knew better than to fight losing battles. So, instead, she attempted something she hoped would be productive.

She had set out to find Ari and, thanks to Will's help, she knew right where to look.

*Master Oliver*, the name plate on the door still read. She gave a few solid knocks before noticing it was slightly ajar.

"It's open, Flor."

The voice alone shot right to the heart of her. Florence suddenly wondered if she had the courage to enter. She'd done so much, but felt daunted by this small task.

Pulled by an unseen hand, Florence pushed through, and saw, for the first time in months, the visage of the woman she'd admired for years.

Arianna sat behind a large drafting table, where papers weighted by rulers hid under pencils worn down to nibs. Her coat was hung on a peg nailed into one of the bookcases, almost hidden by manuscripts draping half off the overfilled shelves like crooked teeth. Ledgers stuffed in-between threatened to spill out their secrets in protest of their treatment.

Florence's eyes drifted from the worn leather chairs around a table, to the bookshelves, to the doorway to the rooms beyond, and back to Arianna. Any frustration or apprehension she felt melted away the moment she saw the white-haired woman dressed in plain woolen trousers and a rumpled shirt, open at the collar.

It was like finally a piece had been slotted back into place. *This* was where Arianna belonged, not in some dingy flat in Old Dortam.

"So, this is where you grew up?"

Arianna looked around the room, as if with fresh eyes. "Sort of, I suppose . . . Willard found me at seven, and we left due to differences in ideology when I was about ten."

"When he joined the Council of Five and started the rebellion?" Florence helped herself to one of the seats facing Arianna.

"Indeed." Arianna's eyes drifted back to whatever it was she'd been working on and her hand reached for a pencil, no doubt on instinct more than command.

Florence let her work. She knew how Arianna was with an idea; there was no stopping her mind once it was coiled around something. If history had proved anything, it was that the world was better off for letting Ari's ideas run their course.

The chair wrapped her in a cozy embrace, inviting Florence to lean into it. So, she obliged, and tipped her head back. She was going to allow her eyes to flutter closed, perhaps even sneak in a moment of sleep in this tranquil oasis amid a sea of war and questions. But the ceiling captured her focus.

Even there, schematics and equations were plastered. Notes written in multiple hands layered on top of each other, fighting for attention and maybe even supremacy. There was no discernible order, yet Florence knew that if she tried to move a single one, Ari would know instantly.

"You didn't come to the station to greet me," Florence said when the pencil finally stilled.

"By design. I knew Willard and Ethel needed to speak with you."

"We needed you there, too." Florence's eyelids suddenly felt heavy, and she let them close.

"If you had, one of you would've called me." Arianna appeared in Florence's field of view the moment she opened her eyes. Her mentor's hair was awash in the pale orange of the dim lamplight that only stretched a peca away from the desk. "I didn't want to insult your status as a vicar."

Florence wanted to tell Arianna that she still needed her, no matter her title. But she knew that crutch was long gone. She'd been moving away from it for months. So why did she seem to ache so fiercely at the idea of Arianna letting it go, too?

"We may have been able to make an exception for the Queen of Wraiths." Florence grinned lazily.

Arianna chuckled, a deep, rich sound. She stretched out her long legs.

"A foolish moniker."

"An upgrade."

"Who really knows?" Arianna rested her head against the back of the seat in an almost mirror-image of Florence's posture. Florence couldn't help but wonder who had done it first . . . Was it her own habit and Arianna mirrored her? Or was it a trait she'd stolen while growing up with the Rivet? "Perhaps it'll be of use to me when Loom is finally free."

*A free Loom.* Florence had spent so much time fighting that she'd never thought of what she'd do when she had to live after. When the battles were won, what did soldiers become?

"Will you return to Dortam?" Florence was brave enough to ask the question and cowardly enough to fear the answer.

"Who knows?"

"I will be there."

"I assumed so." Arianna straightened with a sincere smile. "You are the Vicar Revolver now, after all. You, Flor! The Vicar Revolver!"

Florence stared at the kind, beaming face of her mentor. It was a gentleness that only she had ever seen, and all her life it had meant something profound. But it was in that moment when she looked into Arianna's brilliant lilac eyes, full of so many emotions—pride, admiration, hope, compassion—that Florence realized they had never seen each other in entirely the same way.

"Ari…" Her throat closed, trapping the words. Florence forced them out; even if the shot missed, she had to pull the trigger or she'd regret leaving the canister in the chamber forever. "I love you."

"And I love you, Flor." Her expression didn't shift in the slightest. Arianna continued to look at her the same way she always had—with the eyes of the proud mentor. Or as Nova would have it, an older sister. It was nothing more or less than that profound connection.

*Not as I love you.*

Surely Arianna knew. Surely she heard it in the crack in her voice and the odd jitter of nerves vibrating across her whole body. Arianna noticed the most minute details in complete strangers, so there was no way she hadn't seen it in Florence.

Which meant every action Arianna took was a careful and measured response. In her own way, Florence's mentor was attempting to communicate her desire for things to remain the same as they'd always been.

Florence didn't know if this had been the response she'd wanted. But it was the response she was going to get. So, she chose not to dwell on "what if" and, instead, focus on how having any response was freeing in its own right.

"Thank you, for everything you ever taught me."

"That is something you don't need to thank me for. What you have accomplished with the rebellion is all the thanks in the world."

"Hopefully, something I continue to accomplish," Florence sighed softly.

"You will." Arianna folded her arms over her chest.

"See this through with me, Arianna?"

"I think I should scold you for having any doubt."

Florence wondered if Arianna felt it, too, the split in their parallel paths drawing near. Florence didn't need a teacher any longer; she needed a partner. One like the woman waiting for her back in Ter.3.2. She couldn't lead if she was constantly following in someone else's shadow.

That night, her heart flipped the switch that would set them, eventually, on their separate paths. They reminisced of their time in Old Dortam, of grand heists and early failures, and Florence began to feel the last cloying hands of childhood and first love release from her soul. When she finally left, it was nearly dawn; Florence had not once brought up the idea of becoming a Perfect Chimera.

Arianna's student-turned-vicar had stopped into the Rivets' Guild for a total of two nights, and they had spent both of them talking into the late hours. But by day, Florence was busy with Willard and Ethel, as well as setting up a new training program under a Master Bernard—one of the two Master Revolvers Florence had left, supposedly. But what were masters worth any more in a world where a Raven-born girl with nothing more than an outline on her cheek could become the Vicar Revolver?

She saw Florence off the morning of the third day.

"Take care of yourself." Florence embraced her tightly but briefly. Her arms didn't seem to linger around Arianna's frame as they once had.

"I should be saying that to you." Arianna righted Florence's hat after it was jostled during their embrace. "Vicar Revolvers aren't well known for their longevity."

"I've already survived longer than the last."

"As if that fact is supposed to make me feel better."

"What will you do, after it's all over?"

Arianna stared down at the girl, the question seeming to curdle time into a sticky weight there was no escaping from. She could keep them here in this moment, if she wanted, but Arianna couldn't even seem to find a breath. Florence was leaving to continue her role as the Vicar Revolver. Cvareh was championing a cause that would make him King of the Dragons. And she . . .

"Will you stay the Queen of Wraiths?" Florence's mouth pulled into a smile. However well the girl knew her, there were still barriers and boundaries her mind wouldn't let her cross, where Arianna wouldn't permit her entry. She wouldn't let Florence know of the turmoil the future presented.

"Perhaps." Arianna tapped her winch box. "I am fairly talented at the whole affair."

"Vicar Willard tells me you're also talented at being a master and teaching students."

"Vicar Willard is a liar," Arianna retorted with mock sweetness, earning a laugh from Florence.

"Come back to Dortam," Florence offered. "I can see a place for you at the Revolvers' home. You could run the refinery there."

"You mean the one I used to steal from?" Arianna arched her eyebrows.

"Who better? You can make it more secure than ever before." The whistle of the train sounded and a Raven scuttled over, giving a light tap to Florence's shoulder.

"We're leaving shortly."

"Yes, I know." Florence tipped her hat, sending the girl away. "In any case, think on it, Ari. I still need you around."

And then she was gone before Arianna could formulate another word.

She disappeared into the curling steam of the engine amid a bustle of men and women loading up the short locomotive with supplies. Arianna, a good head taller than the rest, watched the dark-haired woman go. People parted for her out of respect for the circled Revolver pin she wore on the lapel of her coat.

Arianna was glad Florence hadn't pressed the matter further. *I love you—* she'd heard the girl. Arianna knew all too well the heartache clinging to a lost love could reap, and there would never be anything between them. If not because she was the mentor and Florence the student, then because the girl was a child of the future, and Arianna would always be shrouded in the shadow of the past. It was best for both of them to let go, move on.

Plus, Arianna had her own battles to fight.

"You actually let her go."

Arianna's head whipped to the young man who had suddenly appeared next to her. "Your reward for sneaking up on me is my not lodging a dagger between your eyes."

Will hummed in low amusement at the idea, but continued to drive on the path of his earlier sentiment. "I always thought there was more between you two."

"There was everything between us, in different ways, at different times." The platform had been cleared and Ravens began to shout to each other. The great gears inside the train ground to life. "She needed me, and I needed her. We're both better for what we got out of the arrangement."

"Arrangement?" Will crossed his arms over his chest. "How . . . clinical."

"I'm not an Alchemist."

"How precise, then," he corrected. "Will you go back to her?"

"Just how much did you hear?" Arianna finally peeled her eyes away from the vessel that was taking Florence from her.

"Enough."

"You're getting too good at this job." She was creating monsters left and right. Perfect Chimera and now a competent Will? What next? A tolerable Helen?

"Learning from the best."

She snorted at the idea.

"If you don't want to be Queen of Wraiths, give it to Helen. She wanted to take over for Louie; you'll endear yourself to her if you offer her the same."

"I don't care about endearing myself to her." The potentially harsh statement was void of real bite. She couldn't fault Will for looking after his friend. Nostalgia made her soft. Florence made her soft. All this sentimentality was really beginning to dull her.

"That much is obvious," Will acquiesced. "But she is trying to endear herself to you, nevertheless."

Arianna arched her eyebrows, prompting him to continue.

"She's returned from Nova."

"I was beginning to think she got lost up there." It had been two days since Helen left. Arianna had expected an extra day due to glider exhaustion—all the new Perfect Chimera were becoming accustomed to piloting the machines and managing their magic—but she was also expecting the little crow to be side-tracked by the vast and new lands of Nova. "Take me to her."

Will started for the end of the platform, where the light rail would take them back to the guild proper. "She brought back more flowers and is already preparing for another trip up. It seems the fighting has increased on Nova."

"The Dragons do enjoy their blood sport." Arianna's mind drowned her in images of Cvareh fighting—fighting and losing.

"Something about House Tam no longer assisting Rok—"

"*What?*"

Will repeated himself and, then, added, "Helen said to make sure you knew."

Arianna's eyes turned skyward at the battle that no doubt raged on just beyond the clouds. She'd learned of House Tam's influence on Nova as the silent enforcers; if they were no longer assisting House Rok, that meant power could shift—was, in fact, already shifting.

"Will, see Helen is outfitted with more guns, however many we have. Take the airship to Ter.3.2 and gather any from there as well." Her mouth moved fast, but not as fast as her mind. "Then, bring up all the Perfect Chimera who are ready and willing."

"All of them?"

"A constant stream." They had the manpower. If Tam was backing out from House Rok—for whatever reason—they had the numbers to overwhelm them. "It's time to strike."

"Where are you going?" Will motioned to the trolley approaching down the narrow rail.

"I'm headed up first. It'll be faster for me to get to the gliders this way." She paused on the edge of the platform, her clip already flying toward a far steam pipe. "And tell Helen that if she wants Louie's 'kingdom' then it's hers. But the title is mine."

"More than fair." Will gave a solemn nod.

Arianna returned the gesture a moment before her winch box sprung to life, pulling her in sweeping arcs around the outside of Garre to the hangar where gliders were kept.

# 54
## FLORENCE

“Welcome back, Florence,” Emma greeted her the moment she stepped off the train.

“I should take your presence to mean that something has gone wrong?” Florence asked, barely taking time to sling her bag over her shoulder before they began walking off the platform.

“Quite the contrary, actually. The first batch of weapons have all been tested and not a moment too soon. Will arrived not long before you to pick them up.” Emma seemed pleased to report, and Florence was equally pleased to hear. Her tone shifted, however, on the next note. “It seems the timeline has been pushed forward to get as many Perfect Chimera to Nova as possible.”

“I trust you facilitated this transaction to be as quick and smooth as possible?” Florence gave no indication that she had not heard of nor approved things happening faster. Either Bernard had been included, or he had been told. No matter, it was too late now to change it and Florence silently praised Willard and Ethel for being able to accommodate the change.

“I did.”

“Good. I’m ready to see an end to this war.”

“As we all are.”

Florence gave a nod of agreement and produced a folio from her satchel. “I have new schematics here for the next round of manufacturing.”

“Another round of edits?”

“I have no doubt that there will be some moaning over having to re-tool the line again.” *And I don’t care*, Florence left unsaid. “But there is no point in making something unless we continually strive to make it better, make it right.”

"Agreed." Florence believed Emma stood behind her on the matter. It was the Rivets who would protest.

"Inform the Rivets that these modifications come from Arianna." Florence was still becoming accustomed to Arianna's name meaning something to random strangers, but she'd use it to her benefit without reservation.

"Right away."

"Take it on ahead. I'd like to put my things down and change out of my traveling clothes. I won't be long."

Emma gave a tip of her cap. It had a short, leather, rounded brim with a band over top and, unlike a top hat, the fabric sort of flopped over on one side. Florence had been admiring it since she'd stepped off the train and immediately regretted not asking Emma who had stitched such an interesting headpiece.

*Later.* Right now, her priority was elsewhere. It had nothing to do with changing her clothes or dropping her bag. No, she was on the lookout for a certain someone she had an insatiable urge to see in private.

The door to their adopted abode was unlocked. They had never made a habit of locking it, so Florence thought little of it when she entered the foyer. "Shannra?"

There was a long moment of silence and, just when Florence was about to leave, she heard floorboards creak from an upper floor. The building they had assumed as theirs was three stories. Foyer and living spaces on the first floor, workshops on the second, bedrooms on the third.

"Shannra, it's me." Florence called again as she rounded the first flight of stairs, not wanting to startle the woman if she'd somehow not fully heard the first time. Their respective work tables were vacant, which left the third floor as her only remaining option. She'd been hoping to get the woman in bed, and it seemed Shannra would make it easy on her.

Florence paused halfway up the second flight of stairs, when she heard the floor creaking again. The sound came with a second's worth of hesitation.

Something was off.

The floorboards weren't moving in the rhythms Florence had come to associate with her lover. Their syncopation, combined with the silence and . . .something else . . . something familiar...

Honeysuckle. It was unmistakable after being around Arianna. But where Ari's floral magic was mixed with other scents—there was always the soft hint of something woodsy—this scent was cloying and powerful against the nose. Florence put her finger on the difference immediately as she rounded the last step and into the doorway of the bedroom.

Shannra stood at the double window, just where they'd huddled underneath the blanket the night before Florence left. She turned, greeting Florence with a familiar smile. The fading daylight glinted off her white hair and she opened her arms invitingly.

"It's so good to see you." Florence spread a smile across her face with great effort at the visage that was every bit as familiar as it should be, yet incredibly off-putting. She dropped her bag at the foot of the bed, rummaging through it. "I was hoping I would catch you."

Every hair on Florence's body stood on end. Magic was thick in the air, potent and powerful. It was overwhelming and unlike anything Florence had ever experienced before.

She didn't quite know what specter was before her, but she knew it wasn't Shannra.

Right at the top of her bag, where they should be for any self-respecting Revolver, were her canisters and weapon. "Ari did a great job." Florence held up a canister, putting it on display. "They'll be manufacturing these soon, I'm sure."

Imposter Shannra kept her arms outstretched, motioning in a sort of "come hither" way. Florence popped her spare revolver into the empty slot on the left side of her under-arm hoister.

There was only one entry and exit to the room—the door she had come through. The creature would, no doubt, expect her to flee in the direction she came. Whatever magic this animal possessed, it was a safe assumption to think it could run her down. Until she knew what she was fighting, she wasn't going to waste ammunition fending it off.

Until she knew what she was fighting, she also wasn't going to give it the benefit of predictability.

Florence took a step toward the Shannra-shaped specter. She held out her hands as if to accept its embrace. Every muscle coiled with tension around her bones. At the very last moment, she let it spring.

The specter half-lunged forward, dropping her head. Florence drew her weapon and thrust it to the imposter's chin. Her hand disappeared straight through—an illusion. The muzzle of the gun didn't find the creature's head, as Florence had hoped, but she brought the hilt of the gun hard against its chest, firing in the process.

It roared, a feminine sound, but not like those she'd heard from any Fenthri or Dragon before. She took advantage of the creature's surprise, and bolted.

"Get back here!" Imposter Shannra grabbed for her wrist at the same time Florence's hand twisted the handle of the window. It swung open as she was grabbed back by a hand that felt much larger than what her eyes saw wrapped around her forearm.

Florence used the release of momentum to twist, crossing her arm over her, to draw her second gun. She pressed the muzzle into the air just above the creature's hand, meeting invisible flesh.

Florence pulled the trigger and gold blood flew through the air—a Dragon.

Even still, the monster didn't release its hold on her. Florence yanked her arm, once, twice; on the third time, it snapped free with the Dragon's claws raking across her forearm.

Florence was face-to-face with one of the most unnerving creature she had ever seen. The Dragon was nearly the size of the Dragon King, but lacked the stoicism and composure of the man. She had a hooked nose and narrow jaw, adding to the severity of her overall look.

The eyes were the only familiar part of her. Like the smell of her magic, the woman had a nearly identical set of lilac eyes to Arianna. But the similarities ended there, as these sharp and angry eyes were framed by the rich green skin of a Dragon.

Florence had no doubt this was the animal who had killed everyone at the factory. The one who had called for her demise.

She didn't spare more than that glance. It didn't matter what foe she was up against. She'd kill it, or perish.

Florence launched herself over the windowsill. The roofing over the entryway broke her fall with a clamor. Florence's knee popped painfully as she tried to soften the impact. The pitch of the shingles pulled her downward and she did a quick two-step, landing on the ground with a roll.

She didn't waste time looking back at the Dragon. She had no doubt it would follow, and the loud thud on the ground behind her affirmed the fact. Florence loaded a cartridge into her gun, whirling around a lamppost as magic pushed into her knee, mending the torn ligaments and knitting flesh brutalized in the fall.

With a straight and steady arm, she aimed true at the woman who did little more than jog behind her. *Arrogant Dragon.* She no doubt assumed that it would be a bloodbath like last time. Florence squeezed the trigger. The Dragon was in for a surprise; last time, the Vicar Revolver hadn't been in charge of protecting the factory.

The canister shot forward, the chemicals inside reacting to the sudden motion. It exploded halfway to the Dragon, a plume of thick purple smoke erupting from it. Florence heard coughing but could no longer see her assailant.

She loaded a different canister into her pistol and took aim toward the sky. This was another plume of smoke, but unlike the one before her, it exploded bright red and harmless—a signal, if the gunshots alone weren't enough to alert other Revolvers to her plight.

Just as she was readying her weapon again, the Dragon exploded through the smoke. Florence dodged backward but underestimated the Dragon's long strides. The woman was upon her in a breath, a clawed hand shooting straight for her face. Florence pressed the muzzle of the gun into the Dragon's emerald palm, and pulled the trigger.

At close range, bone splintered and tissue was practically liquefied, exploding in all directions. With golden gore smattering her face, Florence dashed away.

The Dragon didn't cry out in pain, didn't hiss, didn't curse. She began to laugh, so loud it echoed off every building and rattled Florence's brain.

"You are everything I hoped!" the woman screeched, lunging forward again.

A chorus of gunshots alerted Florence that her men and women had joined the fray, stalling the Dragon. The woman brought her hands together, smashing two golden bracelets on her forearms to form a shining barrier that made her impervious to the hail of lead. Florence was almost to the factory and ran as though her life depended on it, because it did.

"I need a corona gun!" she shouted ahead.

A woman with wind-swept hair emerged from the doors. She was a sight to behold—a goddess of weaponry. Shannra was clad in tight-fitting pants and a double-breasted military vest, lined in gold piping. Emma's hat wasn't the only upgrade the Revolvers had received.

Florence let out a small choking noise, relief catching in her throat. She hadn't given much thought to where Shannra had actually been, so she hadn't realized the full power of the subconscious terror in thinking her lover had perished at the hands of the beast.

"Florence, here!" Shannra called. With a grunt, she hoisted the weapon toward Florence.

Florence's hand almost gave out as she caught the gun. Her tendons were shredded still from the Dragon's claws. They'd knitted some, but her magic had been pushed in too many directions at once to have any one singular thing be perfectly mended.

It would've been easier if she'd become a Perfect Chimera. But as Florence rounded once more to face the charging Dragon, she didn't regret her decision. She didn't need Arianna's designs to find her ground and hold it.

"After my shot, you fire," she commanded the men and women who were quick to flank her. "Then hold."

Just as Florence issued the order, the sound of gliders roared through the skies.

"Right flank, to the airships after mark. We take down this one first, and then we take down the ones in the skies." Florence leveled the weapon.

The Dragon continued her rage-filled charge. It was as though she'd gone crazy, like a fallen Chimera.

Florence poured her magic into the gun. She remembered the Skeleton Forest, her early prototype all those months ago. This was different—smooth and easy. It was how a trigger should feel under a trained hand.

She shot a beam of pure energy.

The Dragon hadn't been ready for it, or had vastly underestimated the power Loom now wielded as the shot hit her square in the chest. Florence took a breath as the woman fell and then, the second her body hit the ground, shouted, "Fire!"

Gunfire pelted the ground around the prone Dragon, ceasing when Florence raised her hand.

"Right flank, to airships and higher marks," Florence repeated. "Take down the gliders!" Half the group ran, the other half remained as her cover. Florence charged.

She drew a golden dagger. It was cast in nostalgia—originally crafted as a replica of Arianna's own infamous knives. But this one was entirely her own. She wielded it as an homage—a testament to the woman she had been, and a tribute to the mentor who had helped her become something entirely new.

Florence mounted the dazed Dragon and cut out what remained of her heart, casting it far aside. Florence stood with a sway, looking to the skies. One of the three gliders had already been taken out and the other was under heavy fire.

Relief flooded her, and combined with exhaustion to make her suddenly dizzy. An arm wrapped around her ribs.

"Take it easy."

"Shannra." Florence turned, sloppy and half-delirious, but with all the purpose she'd ever had in the world. Her hand gripped the woman's face and she pulled it to her.

Shannra smelled not of honeysuckle, but of gun oil and sulfur. The tattoo on her face was raised slightly under Florence's thumb as she caressed the familiar lines. *This* was the woman Florence loved. This was her heart's aspiration now— to have a partner, an equal.

"You didn't become a Perfect Chimera." Shannra, still breathless from their kiss, observed Florence's wounds and their thin coating of black blood.

"I'm already the perfect shot; how much more perfect does one woman need to be?" Florence hoped her grin was playful enough to cut the arrogance of the sentiment. She hoped Shannra understood.

"My thoughts exactly."

Gunshots echoed above them, drawing both their attention. The final glider was falling from the sky. Something swelled in her at the sight. This was their turning point. This was the moment when Loom's revolution, at long last, finally took hold.

# 55
## CVAREH

seemed he had no qualms with Dragon or Fenthri.

Men and women littered the ground in shades of red, blue, and gray. But the hand of the Lord of Death wasn't the only thing that unified them. Every corpse oozed gold blood, regardless of skin color.

The age of the Perfect Chimera would be ushered in with blood.

Cvareh pulled on Saran's feathers, banking across the clouds, surveying the battleground below him. Rok continued to make attempts to push further into Ruana. But without the help of Tam, they were continually thwarted. It had been a stalemate for months, but he was beginning to see signs of the momentum shifting.

"Hold your position!" he cried over the winds, swooping low enough for the survivors to hear him. "Another wave comes from the west!"

In the distance, a swath of bocos cut their silhouettes against the skyline. At first, seeing ten to thirty attackers at once would have been cause for concern. But manpower made all the difference. Rok's numbers were dwindling, Cvareh was certain of it. Meanwhile, his numbers were only increasing with every transport of Perfect Chimera.

Cvareh rose higher, squinting against the afternoon light. He saw no rainbow trails. That had been another evolution—the decreasing number of Riders. But from what he heard of the attacks increasing on Loom over the past weeks, he had every suspicion that Yveun was refocusing his minions on the lands below.

The cry of a boco had him twisting in his saddle.

"You looked like you were thinking of doing something reckless," Cain remarked, flying close.

"Never."

"Let them reach the island. We can take them on land."

Cvareh nodded, realizing it to be true. As much as he wanted to cut his enemy right from the sky, they had the advantage on the ground. Perfect Chimera could pilot gliders, but the vessels were in short supply and were primarily allocated to ferrying more soldiers from Loom—not for fighting.

Like an explosion, a plume of clouds tangled in the rainbow tail of a glider breaking through the God's Line far below. It curled upward, chasing after the single-manned vessel that shot toward the sky.

"One of ours?" Cain squinted.

Cvareh didn't need to squint. He saw the tattered flaps of a white coat almost blending in with the clouds and immediately knew. Every muscle in his body tightened in response to the sight. "Arianna."

The glider moved with suicidal speed and reckless agility toward the Rok fighters. They noticed the Fenthri barreling at them like a bullet out of a gun and shifted course. Arianna didn't change her trajectory, continuing head-on.

"We have to help her."

"Cvareh, no." Cain tried to stop him.

Cvareh wasn't about to listen. She had come to fight. There was no world in which he wouldn't do it at her side.

Gunshots echoed over the wind as Arianna sped past the pack of Dragons. One man lunged from his boco at her, only to miss and whistle for his mount to catch him before he was swallowed whole by the God's Line.

"Arianna!" Cvareh shouted, wondering if she could hear him.

If she could, she ignored him.

In a maneuver that would make Helen both jealous and proud, Arianna continued her ascent, high above the pack of Dragons that were now pulling on their floundering boco to try to keep up with the more agile machine. She pulled on the handles, tipping it in a wide arc until she was facing down at the God's Line and the Dragons beneath her.

Arianna let go of the glider and Cvareh's heart went straight to his throat, blocking another scream of concern for the woman's wellbeing. He watched as she seemed to float in the air, falling alongside the vessel, a hair's breadth away. She hoisted a weapon that was strapped to her, holding it with surprising calm given that she was a puppet to gravity and pummeling toward fifteen Dragons all scrambling to kill her.

Cvareh couldn't stop his eyes from closing at the beam of bright light that exploded from the gun.

Another shot rang out and the column of pure magic that punctured through Dragon and boco alike lingered on the wind as though it was trying to draw a line in reality itself.

Arianna reached back for the glider. Another Dragon dove, intending to knock her off-course before she could recover the mechanical safety net.

Cvareh gave a roar and kicked Saran's sides. Faster, he willed the bird to fly faster. He let go of the boco's feathers, feeling the wind whipping his clothing against him as he straightened away from the diving bird. He wouldn't be fast enough if he relied on the boco alone.

His feet pulled from the stirrups, curling under him, and Cvareh launched from the saddle, claws out.

He met the Rok man in a tumble of feathers and blood. Cvareh sought purchase as his enemy's boco squawked and spun through the air, trying to catch the wind once more with the fighting Dragons on its back. He raked his claws across the other man's face as the Rok fighter desperately tried to cast him off.

Petra had always told him that once he used the gift of his lungs on Nova, there would be no turning back. Every Dragon on the entire island would feel the shock wave of his magic. It was his greatest strength, and when Petra had lived, it served her and Xin for Cvareh to never let it be known.

But Cvareh was the Oji now.

He hoped his sister was right in her assumptions, because he wanted every living soul to know that they were up against a force strong enough to command time.

Cvareh sucked in the air through his nose, filling his lungs, and felt the world slow. He looked over and almost lost time in his startle. Arianna's piercing eyes stared back at him. They seemed to look right at him, even though her hair was frozen in a windless world.

She'd recovered herself on the glider, pitched downward, parallel to him.

*Trust me*, those eyes seemed to demand.

And he did.

Cvareh sliced at the Rider's hands and legs with determined swipes. He peeled muscle from bone in deep gashes. He didn't hold time for more than a second—he needed to conserve his magic for the battles ahead—but that was all he needed.

Time snapped back into place as he breathed again. Cvareh was once more in free fall.

Now he spun through the air with a Dragon dazed, confused, and thrown from his boco. Cvareh gripped the man by the throat and plunged his hand into his chest. He took the warm Rok heart and let go of the suddenly still body.

Magic cracked through his mind with a sort of dizzying elasticity. For the first time, Cvareh felt what he'd done to others when he stopped time.

"Hold on!" Arianna cried, coughing blood into the wind.

He closed an arm around her waist, his feet cementing to the glider behind her. Cvareh tore a hunk of heart and shoved the rest into her face. Arianna ate from his hand, and they shared the spoils of their fallen foe.

His lover imbibed like a ravenous beast and turned toward the remaining Rok. With her face half covered in blood, mouth set in a grim line, he felt her lungs expand.

Cvareh watched in wonder as time slowed. She recovered faster, her magic responding to her whims with surgical precision. This was the power of a truly Perfect Chimera. She would always be more than what the Alchemists were splicing together now; she had been crafted by the magic her whole life; with his most recent addition, she had all the power that had ever existed. Arianna raised her arm and pulled the trigger, taking down two Dragons before she nearly collapsed onto the handles, gasping for air between outpourings of gold from her lips.

Cvareh forced the remaining heart into her mouth.

"Let go," he demanded, his hands over hers. "I'll take us to the mainland. There's more who will take them down on Ruana."

"Don't get us killed."

Cvareh felt her magic retreat as her hands slipped from the handles, barely enough to keep her glued to the gold platform beneath them. She turned, grasping him awkwardly, keeping herself in position as he assumed control of the glider.

He was not nearly as graceful as she was with the machine. But he was determined. With Arianna counting on him, there was no world in which he would fail to keep his word.

Cvareh sped past the tiring boco for mainland Ruana. They soared back up to the topside of the island, and he selected a landing spot behind what had become, more or less, the front line.

Perhaps he'd finally had enough practice with the gliders. Or perhaps battle had honed his senses just enough. But Cvareh was half-proud of the landing.

Arianna's magic gave out and she slumped, Cvareh quick to catch her. The sounds of boco on the wind combined with guns cocking; over it all was the ominous announcement from Cain, "More incoming!"

They panted together, and all the things he'd wanted to say and ask were suddenly meaningless. Nothing mattered until victory was assured.

*No.*

Nothing mattered because she was in his arms again.

"I'm going to help." Arianna stood on her own once more. He felt magic swelling in her, already returning at a rate his could not hope to keep pace with.

As much as he wanted to tell her not to, as much as he wanted to flee with her to a safe location to ride out the final throes of the storm, Cvareh knew nothing would stop her. She turned her eyes to the horizon, to their mutual enemy, and adjusted the hulking weapon—a new prototype similar to the guns they'd been sending, but different somehow, too.

"I will come with you."

"Are you sure?" She gave him a quick up and down, no doubt skeptical of the magic she felt—or didn't feel.

Cvareh gave a laugh, skeptical himself. "We are in this together, from now until Rok falls."

"Until Rok falls," she repeated with a solemn nod. "Together until Rok falls."

# 56
## COLETTA

Coletta could smell Ulia before she saw, or even heard her. The woman was coated in a fine gloss of sweat that Coletta knew to associate with fear or nervousness in weaker creatures. Her little flower did well trying to hide it, however. Her strides were even and her hands were still at her sides when she delivered her message.

"The Dono wishes to speak with you."

Coletta thought on the statement a moment. She carefully set down her pruning shears. It seemed today would not be the day she would get to conduct her second set of tests on the Flowers of Agendi. Whatever secrets they held, they did an excellent job of hiding them from her.

"And where is the Dono?"

"The Red Room."

"*Ah*," Coletta murmured softly. That was all the information she needed on the matter. "Thank you for delivering this message, Ulia."

"Is there anything else I can do for you, my lady?" She lowered her head in subservience.

"Not yet." There would be in the coming days; Coletta could feel it. The scales that held the world in balance had already tipped. Equilibrium of power and order had shifted too far out of neutral and now chaos was threatening to reign. The dawn of an age that couldn't be accounted for—that was where the real danger lied.

Ulia left her, heeding the unspoken command. Coletta briefly considered changing her garb before meeting Yveun, but decided to go as she was. Yveun had seen her in all states. He had lifted her up when the poison had wracked her body past the point of brokenness. He had kissed her mouth after her gums had turned black. What had always mattered more than their appearances was their presence for one another. They were there when the cards fell.

Perhaps, her plain attire and immediate attendance of his summons would remind him of that fact. The fact that she had come to him promptly at his command, despite their last disastrous encounter in his war room—a confrontation neither had yet made any motions to reconcile.

The Red Room was on the opposite side of the estate from Coletta's garden. As such, she had ample time to anticipate the mood her Dono might be in. Her general preparation was for bad, worse, and downright volatile.

A Rider posted at the door regarded her warily. It was an uncommon summons to be sure. Coletta gave a tilt of her head and a small uncharacteristic smile, just enough to see the man unnerved by his Ryu's unexpected behavior.

"The Rok'Ryu, Dono," the Rider announced as he opened the door for her.

"Thank you," Coletta said demurely, but still clearly dismissive.

The man nodded and promptly departed. Coletta listened closely to his footsteps, making sure they left his post. She waited until they faded. Only then did she turn her eyes to her mate to see what fate had in store for her.

"It's not enough," he growled.

"What isn't?"

"Everything." Yveun's claws shot from his fingertips. "None of it is enough."

So, it was to remain war between them. Her prompt presence had done nothing to smooth over the agitation of the past, or remind him of the natural roles they'd filled for so long and that had served them so well. "I offered you victory in this war. You would not take it."

"No, you offered me monstrosities made from the skin of our own family." He rose like a thundering god. "I am tasked with protecting House Rok."

"The success of House Rok is all I have ever worked for. It is all I have ever dirtied my hands for and manipulated the shadows for."

Yveun stalked toward her. Coletta wondered if he realized how weak, how out of control, it made him look. Kings never descended. Not for their mates, not for anyone.

"You lost our gold."

It was stolen.

"You lost the loyalty of House Tam."

A loyalty Coletta had bought herself over the years.

"You sent away Fae, splitting our power. There have been no reports from her for over a week. Coletta, if she—"

"Need I remind you that she is a tool, Yveun?" Coletta snarled, no longer able to keep her mouth shut. She was pushed to a rare point, and there was no going back now. "She was a distraction for you, I see now. She did not make us strong, but weak. Good riddance if the Fen have killed her."

"You would do well to not say such things to me." Yveun motioned toward her and Coletta grabbed his wrist with a speed that surprised her mate. His head reared back slightly, like a serpent ready to strike.

"Do not point your claws at me," she whispered dangerously. They sheathed on command. "Better." Coletta released him and Yveun spun away, setting to pace like the pouting child he was. "Fae's death would be tragic. But *we can make more of her* now. What made her strong could be as common as a cherry-skinned Dragon."

"Not this again." He stilled.

"Yveun," she pleaded. Coletta hated begging. But she would beg, bargain, steal, and murder for her House. "I have ten Perfect Dragons—"

"You continued, despite my direct order?" He looked at her with a gaze that was no doubt an attempt to make her feel small.

"I did." His stare had no effect on her. "And we can begin to shift the tides if we set them free. If you bring me three, two, just one Xin, I can produce them faster."

"I needed you to be producing gold for Tam."

"The refineries are a sham!" Coletta's claws plunged into the air. "All knew it from the moment they were commissioned. But I allowed you your fantasies. Refineries are effective on Loom because of their systems and resources. But their gold stores have been tapped dry and my contact tells me that they have not resumed production again with the guilds as they are."

"You." He pointed at her again, without his claws this time. "You told me, you encouraged me, to destroy the guilds."

"And it was the right choice." She stood by the decision without remorse. "But it is still the world we live in, the world we must adapt to."

Yveun growled and set to pacing again. "Tam is useless and disloyal. Xin fights like Fen. The Fen fight worse than Fen. We have three fronts and make headway on none of them!"

"We've made ample headway, if you would only see it as such." Coletta refrained from pointing out that he was making a fourth front by stoking a rift between them.

"It's because I'm not there." Yveun stopped moving, as if punctuating the words. He spoke mostly to himself. "It is because I have been invisible to my people."

"Yveun—" This was dangerous. This was wild autonomy fueled by frustration and blood lust.

"I will go fight."

"My Dono, I implore you to rethink." Coletta felt as though she was scolding a child and not a man nearing ninety.

"You have done enough holding me back."

The words stung. No, not the words—the shock of them, the outright audacity. Anger flashed hot in her blood, a response very few could draw from her, but it was there. Coletta cooled it. If one let it linger, anger was a poison for which there was no antidote.

"I have done everything for the good of our house, for the good of your rule." All reminders were proving futile. Her Dono, her life mate, the man she had worked to see to power and then worked alongside to keep it, suddenly saw her as having no more utility than a set of Fenthri tools.

"I will go to Ruana." Yveun started for the door.

"With more time and just some Xin captives, we will have an army of Perfect Dragons. They will not see it coming. We will blindside them."

"Or we will lose our chance entirely." Yveun's head whipped back to her. "Waiting has given us nothing and the tides are ever shifting against us."

Coletta had one more request of him. One final attempt to save her Dono's life and salvage all they had worked for.

"At least become Perfect first," she implored, knowing the matter futile. "Give yourself the strongest chance."

He stared at her with abject horror, a look that was the final breaking of any love or kindness or even rapport between them. "How dare you suggest your Dono is anything less than perfection. I will not accept Xin organs—not now, or ever. I will not have them in me unless I am sinking my fangs into the hearts of the fallen. And as long as I breathe, I will not stand to see our house sullied by them either."

He strode past her, starting for the door. Coletta merely stood, looking at the lone throne. A seat she knew would never have a master again.

"Yveun—"

"No half measures, Coletta." He paused, briefly, but she refused to look at him. She gave him all the disrespect of her back. "When I return, I will deal with you in the same manner."

Coletta did not cry. She did not scream or shout or rake her claws over the room. She breathed in through her nose, and out through her mouth, three times to regain her composure.

Then, Coletta'Ryu started back for her garden, to prepare for the end of the world.

# 57
## ARIANNA

The reprieve was short-lived, as a frustrated Cain stomped in and disrupted their peace with an endless string of scolding for their recklessness. Cvareh impressed and pleased her in equal measure when he finally stood up for himself, telling off the man.

The break was short-lived, however, as with the dawn came a new swarm of Riders, and a new host of bloodshed.

More fell on both sides, and at long last Arianna was forced to recover her magic. It was like a seemingly never-ending source now. *Seemingly*. For when she hit her limit, it came fast and hard.

"How do you feel?" Cvareh was the only Dragon who would go out of his way to talk to her. No matter how much the Fenthri bled for their cause, the Dragons regarded them with wary eyes. The inverse was also true. Perfect Chimera huddled in groups, avoiding all contact with the Dragons.

"I'm fine." Arianna continued her inspection of the gun in her hands. "This, however . . ."

"Is it broken?" Cvareh sat next to her heavily.

"No, but it's reaching its limit. I thought Flor and I had reached a solution, but it seems not." There were hairline fractures along the barrel that promised years more of testing and dozens of iterations down the line.

"Florence . . ." Cvareh repeated thoughtfully. "How is she?"

"She's found her place." *Not unlike you*, Arianna added for herself alone.

"I suppose we all have."

"Get out of my mind, Dragon."

Cvareh laughed, and Arianna let the sound smooth away her mock ire. She would miss the man, when it was all over. The place he had ultimately found had no room for her. His world, Florence's—neither was Arianna's. As Florence had seen it, so would he, when the time came.

They sat on his balcony at the manor. The glider barely fit and his boco swooped back every now and again, cawing in angry protest at having to share its post. They were away from prying eyes and combat.

Arianna listed to one side, her temple meeting his shoulder.

She closed her eyes the moment his cheek pressed against her head. How she, of all people, had come to enjoy the company of this Dragon, Arianna would never know. But with Florence starting her new life, and Eva and Oliver dead, he was the only one who knew her. He was the only one who'd seen her in her entirety.

"Cvareh," she began, softly. "When you're King—"

"*If*," Cvareh emphasized.

"*When*," she shot right back. Arianna would not tolerate dismissive language now. They'd come too far for it. "Do not forget the promises you made to Loom."

"I would never."

"Because I will hunt you and kill you if you do."

"I wouldn't have it any other way."

She wondered if it was true—if he was sincere in appreciating that some part of their relationship—whatever it was—was strung together with vengeance and inter-world power struggles. It was certainly odd, but she'd lived an odd life. It was only fitting that the only companion she'd found at the end of the road would be the most inconceivable of them all.

"Cvareh—"

Arianna never finished her thought, which was likely a good thing, as she'd suddenly begun to feel dangerously sentimental. Cain bounded onto the balcony, and the expression on his face told them everything. Even still, nothing could've prepared her for his words.

"Yveun approaches."

"What?" they said in unison.

"Are you sure?" Arianna had fully expected the battle against the Dragon King to be drawn out until its bitter end. She never expected the man to make the same mistake she had—to deliver himself neatly to her.

"I don't think I would mistake the Dragon King," Cain replied testily.

Arianna was too distracted by their luck to even think on it. They ascended through the manor to an upper level. Sure enough, a whole flock of boco cluttered the sky, approaching fast. Flanking one man were two Riders with large pennons strapped to their backs bearing the sigil of House Rok.

Arianna adjusted her grip on her weapon. One shot—all she needed was one good shot. The gun had that much left in it, at least. Arianna slowed her breathing as they neared. Just when she was about to take a sharp inhale and lift the barrel—

Cvareh stopped her. "Don't."

"We can kill him right now. We can *end* this."

"You know I must. For Nova to see me as Dono, it must be a proper duel."

Arianna glared at him, the gun, at the approaching king, but more at her circumstances in general. She knew it to be true, though every instinct screamed for her to just end it. Grand acts only created great openings for error.

"A duel?" Cain's hand went slack as he became distracted by Cvareh's words. "You're going to duel him *now*? Why not before?"

"Because now, we can thrive. Tam will undoubtedly side with the victor. With more weapons like the one Arianna is holding, with Perfect Chimera, none will attempt to subvert our victory." Cvareh's eyes drifted back to her. "Because now, time is on my side."

Did she hear him right? Arianna studied his face, searching. She wanted more—needed confirmation of what he was planning. Had his plan all along been to use her lungs against Yveun?

"Cvareh'Ryu," Yveun called out, finally within earshot and hovering just above the platform. "I seek to challenge you. Are you finally done shaming your house with your subversions?"

"I seek to challenge you as well." Cvareh ignored the bait and Arianna silently commended him.

She watched as Yveun landed. Her hands itched—to pull the trigger, to summon claws, to attack. She stood silently, however, forcing herself to stay in place, play her part.

Yveun's eyes found her and then the handful of Perfect Chimera in their midst. "I wouldn't have believed it if I'd not seen it with my own eyes. Xin has stooped so low as to work with Fen. How do you follow such a weak ruler that he must turn to the gray scourge of the earth for power?" Yveun asked the Xin assembled.

"How does Rok follow a man who drives his House to failure because he is too afraid of progress?"

"'Progress,' as you call it, is a threat to all of Nova, as it undermines the foundation of our traditions."

There it was. There was the crux of it. Arianna watched as the other Dragons, both red and blue, considered what side of this line they fell on. Did they stand with an evolving world? Or did they cling to the order that had seemingly served them so well for centuries?

"Progress cannot be stopped once started, not even by a King." Arianna made her voice heard. She made Oliver's voice heard. She made Eva's, and Florence's, and every other Fenthri who had ever worked and died for the idea of a free Loom, heard and accounted for.

"And who would believe a Fen?" he sneered at her.

"Because I am evidence of it." Arianna gave him space to challenge her on the claim, but Yveun's silence was the loudest reply—so loud that the other Rok Dragons exchanged glances. "Because Perfect Chimera are here and will come to Nova in droves. The God's Line will protect none of you. Work with us, or find out what it is like to live beneath a greater race."

Enough Dragons actually seemed to think on her words that Arianna considered the whole claim worth it. Frankly, Loom had no interest in ruling over Nova—at least, she sincerely hoped that sentiment remained unchanged. But the Dragons didn't need to know that. Let it cloud their minds and cast the shadows of doubt on their every movement.

"You lie," someone from Yveun's entourage said.

"Do you really want to take that chance?"

"Enough!" Yveun regained his control the only way he knew how, by shouting it back into place. It was the move of a desperate man. One that had Arianna wondering how she had ever allowed herself to be bested by him. "Will you duel me or not?"

"As the Xin'Oji," Cvareh proclaimed proudly. "I will—for honor of Xin, for my sister, and for the title of Dono of all of Loom."

There was no waiting in Dragon duels.

Arianna watched as both men exploded into motion. Yveun was a stronger, faster, and better fighter than Cvareh. But Cvareh had a weapon that he now deployed.

She felt the strange ache that followed a time stop, and looked on with everyone else as Cvareh moved from where he'd been about to be attacked, to the space just behind the Dragon King.

Yveun looked on in confusion; by the time he realized where his adversary had gone, Cvareh had plunged his teeth into the man's back, drawing blood with fervor.

"Time?" Yveun roared. He bucked backward and Cvareh rolled off. Yveun twisted, lunging for him.

Another snap of magic. Another ache between her temples. Cvareh was holding the Dono's arm, bleeding him from the wrist.

Yveun reached for the man, his hand stopping just before Cvareh's neck. As soon as Cvareh released the Dono's flesh, he took another sharp inhale of air. Arianna's ears barely had time to hear the start of Cvareh's lungs filling before time stopped again.

It was like watching two fighters moving through completely different sequences of events. When Cvareh was in one place, he suddenly appeared in another. It was jarring and sustained purely on Yveun's own magic.

Arianna shifted her gun in her hands, ready to kill. Even by imbibing off the Dragon King, she could see the toll stopping time took on Cvareh's body. He wouldn't last much longer as he was.

Exhaustion lead to mistakes, and Cvareh let go of time a second too early.

His jaw snapped shut on air; Yveun pulled his hand back, plunging his claws forward to Cvareh's chest. Cvareh tumbled backward at the last moment.

Yveun was on the offensive, like a sea monster that had spotted a lone ship. Cvareh dodged and sidestepped, but he did not stop time again. He was conserving his energy.

Arianna caught Cvareh's eye. The distraction was just enough for Yveun to land a clean hit, sending Cvareh reeling, blood pouring from his shoulder. He stumbled backward, and half-fell into her.

By the time she realized what he'd done, time was stopped. Arianna gripped onto him, holding him, so she would not be pulled from the pocket of time he'd created for her. Her eyes met his, and Cvareh looked at her with a mouth pressed shut into a firm line. Cvareh rose his free hand, blood still pouring from his shoulder where his magic was failing to heal him, and pointed at Yveun.

Finally, it clicked.

"Y-You want me to kill him?"

Cvareh nodded.

It was a kindness, a gift unlike any he had ever given her. Together, they walked. Arianna clutched him tightly with one hand and drew her dagger from the other. She'd dreamed about savoring this moment—of what Yveun's face would look like when she killed him slowly, purposefully.

But as she had told Florence, she was not the one destined to kill the Dragon King, at least not in the eyes of the world. So, unceremoniously, just outside time, with Dragons looking on, seeing with unseeing eyes, Arianna carved out the heart of Yveun Rok'Oji Dono.

Cvareh shuddered and quickly yanked her away, half dragging her back to where she'd stood before. Arianna watched as he released her and then—

Time snapped back into place.

There was Cvareh, standing over the fallen corpse of Yveun Dono, heart in hand. He collapsed to his knees over the dead Dragon, coughing blood. Arianna wanted to run to him. She wanted to chew the King's heart herself and spit it into Cvareh's mouth if she must.

But he had given Arianna her moment. Now, she gave him his.

With almost frail weariness, Cvareh raised the heart to his mouth and plunged his teeth into it. He tore off pieces ravenously, snarling at the Rok Riders.

They all watched as their new king bathed in the blood of his predecessor.

# 58
## COLETTA

Coletta was among her flowers when the Riders returned. She stood, feeling frozen in time herself, as they recounted the magic Cvareh had been hiding in him all along. The men and women regarded her as the Rok'Oji now, but they looked on with skeptical eyes even as they said it.

*How could one so frail be the Oji?* she could almost hear them say. She had served a purpose between her and Yveun. He was the visible strength, and she the invisible.

She had never been made for the grand stage.

Coletta went to her laboratory and sat on a bench. She tilted her head back, staring at the blue sky that peeked at her from between the rooftops of the estate and the foliage. It was as if the opulence of the manor threatened to suffocate her. It was as if the vines of her plants wanted to strangle her, for all that she had loved and nurtured them. It was as if the sky itself mocked her, reminding her of the new world order that had been thrust upon them, the future stolen from her claws.

There was no word from Fae, and even if the woman was still alive and somehow proved to be successful, too much momentum was stacked against Rok to have the assassination of one rebel leader deal a crushing blow to Loom. Xin would prevail, which mean Loom would as well, no matter what happened now. A new world was being designed, one that she no longer had a part in crafting.

Coletta sighed softly, and closed her eyes. It had been a good run, while it lasted.

With her by Yveun's side, they had been unstoppable for more than half a century. They were the last in a long line of noble and fearsome Rok leaders. Just over a thousand years of dominance was now coming to an end. But none of Rok's former glory mattered any longer. History was written by those still alive to hold pens. Her magnificent house would be cast as a cruel, tyrannous rule overthrown by a noble insurgence. They would be painted as the last holdover of an era steeped in respect for tradition that was long gone, an era overthrown by engineered perfection.

It was a dishonor too unbearable to conceive.

Coletta moved to the back corner where certain concoctions were locked away. She had one more obligation to her home and house. They would never sing her songs, would never abide by her as Oji. Her life was forfeit. So, before any upstart could challenge and kill her, Coletta would play one final, masterful stroke.

She had been preparing for this inevitability since her final confrontation with Yveun in the Red Room.

She pressed the gold panel, summoning both Topann and Ulia. By the time the two women reported, Coletta had their tools assembled. One look at them told her all she needed to know. They had heard the news of their new "Dono."

"Lord Xin now rules." She did not mince words in life, nor would she in her death. "The great end comes for Rok as we know it."

Both women kept their eyes downcast. Ulia gave a soft sniffle.

"But we will not go quietly. We will not let all we love be consumed by those we hate." Coletta smiled at what had been assembled on the table before her. "We will take that from them. We will make sure that for generations to come, the name Rok is whispered, for fear that we will spring up from underneath our falsely appointed rulers and seek our vengeance."

"What must we do?" Topann's bravery assured Coletta that she was ready for this mission. So, the harder task would go to her.

"You will take this." Coletta motioned to the portion of the table covered with poisoned daggers and vials, enough to take down an entire estate. "And kill all those here."

"My . . . lady?"

Coletta had expected the order to kill her own to be particularly difficult for Topann to stomach. She'd been the most loyal of them all. But it was for that reason that Coletta had chosen her.

"Topann, you will be the only one among us to survive." Coletta took her flower's hands in hers, in a reverse of their usual interactions. "You will plant the seeds of Rok's return. Kill those here, and be the only one to tell the tale. Speak of Loom's savagery and Xin's disregard for our ways. Kill them all in the estate and force Rok to rebuild from the ground up in vengeance, in hate."

There was a brief moment when Coletta thought Topann would refuse, thought she might have to kill the woman and do this most important work herself. But Topann was a warrior, and loyal to her above all else. "I will, my queen. I will unleash every savagery I expect of Loom and Xin on our estate. I will go to the southern cities and tell them of your sacrifices, of the betrayals our house has endured."

"Good." Coletta turned, scooping up a separate dagger from the table. "Ulia, sweet Ulia," she cooed, summoning the girl's attention. Ulia steeled her watering eyes and pressed her mouth into a line. There was anger there, and anger made for sloppy actions. "You will take this, and give the Tam'Oji our regards."

Ulia took the dagger, inspecting what little she could see of the blade at the top of the sheath, by the hilt. "Gold?"

"Because he so loves it. Because his loyalty only extended as far as the gold we provided him."

Ulia's brow furrowed briefly. *Yes, child*, Coletta told her silently, *I have been planning for this for some time*. Granted, in Coletta's plan, Finnyr would have been the Xin'Oji, and once Xin was stabilized under him then they would turn their efforts onto House Tam, replacing *that* Oji with someone far more loyal. But plans adapted and changed. The dagger would gain new purpose.

"I will do this." Ulia took one deep breath that shuddered into stability, and then nodded. She accepted the dagger like it was a boon from a god.

"I bid you both farewell. Topann, any yet living flowers may grow to you." Coletta dismissed them for one final time.

Topann left promptly with a handful of supplies, as though she could not spare one final look for her soon-to-be-dead queen's face. But Ulia lingered. She searched Coletta's posture for answers the Dragon Queen would not allow herself to reveal.

"What will you do?" she whispered.

It was the one time Coletta allowed herself to be questioned, allowed her designs to be known. "If it is chaos the world seeks, then I will see it done." She took up one final dagger and a handful of vials for herself.

Ulia's eyes spoke volumes, but only two words fell from her lips. "Thank you."

Coletta nodded and watched the girl leave. She had done all she could, but it had not been enough. Coletta slung a large pouch over her shoulder and took the last of her supplies.

Perhaps it was not all she could've done. Coletta began to wonder as she started from her garden for the last time. Perhaps she should have been the bold and strong Ryu the house had wanted. If she had been, they would have seen her as the Oji now. She could've continued to lead the charge with Perfect Dragons. But without Yveun at her side, no one would heed her long enough to see the salvation she could offer them.

As she had been in life, in death, she'd be relegated to the shadows.

Coletta walked through the Rok Estate and down to the Gray Room for the final time. She set free the Perfect Dragons. They would live to be fearsome creatures. Rumors of their feats would bubble to the surface of Nova's consciousness until they could no longer be ignored.

Then, amid the growing chaos of the Rok Estate, Coletta'Oji took to the skies one final time, charting her course for Ruana.

# 59
## CVAREH

He could have eaten three more of Yveun's hearts, and it still wouldn't have been enough. Cvareh chewed and tore his way through every last bite. He didn't care much for the taste of Rok blood—even though victory was its own spice—but the magic it brought back to him was essential to merely breathing. His lungs felt in no better state than they had following the Alchemist's removal of them for Arianna. If anything, they could be worse.

His joints ached, and his body was ravaged. But he was Dono. So Cvareh consumed every last bite of Yveun's heart, both for sustenance and for ceremony.

All eyes were on him, and not one Dragon or Fenthri moved. Cvareh wiped his mouth with the back of his hand. He needed to stand, needed to step into his role as Dono.

But the moment he tried, his legs buckled and he struggled to right himself. A strong arm appeared around his waist, connected to a sturdy and familiar form. Arianna had tugged his arm over her shoulder, supporting him before Dragon and Fenthri alike.

*Yes.* The word coursed through his mind at the woman's presence. He wanted her to be seen at his side. He wanted the world to know that she was his and now that he was Dono, there would be no questioning the fact. Cvareh saw the wary eyes from those assembled, but not one Dragon stepped out of place.

"We need to get to Lysip," he wheezed. Cain appeared before him, offering to help support him as well. Cvareh waved away the offer, trying to stand on his own. "We must get a boco—a glider, it will be faster—to Lysip."

"The battle is won, Dono." Hearing the title from Cain's mouth made it all the more real.

"Not yet." Cvareh pulled his arm from Arianna. The moment he tried to step away, however, the world tilted and he lost balance yet again. Cain moved for him, but Arianna was faster.

"Coletta," Arianna finished the thought he couldn't quite seem to get out before.

"Yes."

"What about the Rok'Oji?" Cain hadn't quite kept up. Cain was close, but the Fenthri woman at Cvareh's side was the other half of his mind.

"Do you think she'll accept Cvareh as Dono gracefully?" Arianna spoke loud enough that everyone could hear.

"She doesn't have a choice," Cain insisted.

"Like she didn't have a choice at the Crimson Court?" Arianna fired right back.

Cain floundered.

"Cain Xin'Ryu To," Cvareh announced, elevating Cain to the societal rank of To with a breath. "I request for you to defend my honor on Lysip. See that Coletta assumes her responsibility as the Rok'Oji, under me as Dono, or that she perishes."

Whispers and a few gasps arose from those observing. But there was nothing else he could do. Even if he was the Dragon King, a title alone would not replenish his magic enough to give him the confidence to fly to Lysip. He knew he was sending his friend into the asp's nest. But what else could he do?

"And," Cvareh continued, "you will take Ari Xin'Kin To with you. She will assist however you deem necessary." Whispers and gasps grew louder as Arianna was quickly elevated in both society and House as well.

He locked eyes with the woman at his side. Arianna almost wore a frown. Was she not happy? He'd won, and he could see her forever have a place on Nova.

"We should go." She looked to Cain with renewed purpose. "I'll pilot the glider."

"Lead on," Cain agreed with a nod. To the others assembled, he said, "See your Dono is well cared for and recovers to full strength. We will need him in the months ahead."

Cain's order spurred the scene to life. Arianna disappeared from his side, replaced with a woman that he'd never seen before. Cvareh remained focused on his childhood friend, but mostly his eyes were on his lover.

"Go safe."

He wanted to say so much more. But the woman was strong. Cain was strong. There would be many more opportunities, he assured himself, to say all that needed to be said.

# 60

## ARIANNA

WWIND WHIPPED HER HAIR INTO THE FACE OF THE MAN RIDING THE GLIDER behind her.

"It's there, ahead." Cain pointed over her shoulder and Arianna thought, not for the first time, of dislodging him from his spot with a particularly sudden roll.

"Yes, I can see that. Just focus on staying on." Did he think that she honestly couldn't tell where the isle of Lysip was? There were only three main islands in Nova and, given that they floated nowhere remotely close to each other, she could only assume that they had successfully made it to Lysip when another gigantic land mass came into view.

"I am on." He said it as though the fact should be obvious.

"Stay that way." Arianna ground the words between her teeth. He was very good at acting like he hadn't nearly fallen off twice already. Though Arianna was equally skilled at acting like one of those hadn't been her own attempt to shake him.

"The estate is there." Cain pointed at a massive complex that was unmistakable even to someone who'd never seen it before.

"My eyes still work fine under my goggles." She sighed loudly, wanting to make sure he heard it over the wind. Arianna pulled on the handles and pitched the glider toward the estate.

As they approached, a sharp tang hit her nose and went straight to her head. Her lungs burned, her magic fighting whatever the wind carried. Arianna slowed, making a wide arc and banking away.

"Why aren't you—"

"Can't you smell it?" She pulled on the levers, bringing the glider into a hover.

Cain seemed as though he was going to protest, on principle more than anything else, but when he stopped and took a proper breath his expression changed.

"Coletta." She said the name they were both thinking.

Arianna lowered the glider, moving slowly over the estate. A glimpse of one of the outdoor arcades, corpses lying prone, confirmed her suspicion.

"Twenty above… what did she do?" Cain whispered in horror.

"She refused to let us win." Arianna scowled and tried not to be angry or frustrated at the fact that she would not be the one to kill Yveun's mate. Was one kill really so much to ask for? Her neck ached, reminding her of Coletta's handiwork all too well.

"She killed her own? No that's impossible, even for her . . ."

Arianna finally brought the glider down, bringing a hand over her nose to combat the smell of death, blood, and poison. No one rushed to meet them, no one swarmed in greeting or combat. Their only company was wind. The whole manor was unnervingly still.

"I think you need to come to terms with the impossible," Arianna suggested as she rolled over a corpse with her foot. In the center of the dead woman's chest was a slit, right between her breasts, that had gone a dark gold from the festering poison that oozed from it.

"Why?" Cain muttered, looking at a loss. "Why would she kill her own?"

"She'd lost." Arianna looked in the room attached to the landing area they'd chosen at random. Sure enough, no signs of life. "And she couldn't handle the idea of us besting her house."

"But—"

"It's not a Dragon-like thought, I know. But take it from me, this woman knows no limits."

Cain was silent, respecting the darkness that hovered over her words at the mere mention of Coletta. Arianna knew well enough how low the woman would stoop.

They wandered the estate, looking for signs of life, for any signs of the woman who had reaped such destruction. But none were to be found.

"It's as if she's disappeared into thin air." Cain slammed his fist against a doorframe, splintering the wood and bloodying his hand in anger. "How many bodies have we looked through?"

"Not enough." Arianna crossed her arms over her chest and thought. If she had been in Coletta's position, what would she do?

The realization dawned on her as a Rok man stepped through the doorway.

"I found them!" he shouted, presumably to others. "I found the Xin murderers! They have a Fen!"

"Wait, what?" Cain stalled in his hesitation.

Arianna sprang into motion. She lunged for the man, claws drawn and honed on his chest. Before he even had a chance to react, he was dead.

"We have to get back to Ruana."

"What?" Cain stared at the Dragon she'd just killed, as if debating if he should feel remorse over the death of a Rok.

"We need to go." Arianna grabbed his forearm and tugged him forward. He began running on his own as they sprinted through the manor, toward the glider, and away from the sound of rising voices.

"I don't understand." He skidded to a stop as she jumped on the glider, grabbing both handles firmly.

"Coletta means to pin these murders on Xin. The longer we stay, the more we play into her plans."

"But she—"

"She's not here!" Why couldn't he see that? It had become so painfully obvious to Arianna. It was so objectively clear how stupid they had been.

"Where is she?" The horror in Cain's voice betrayed the fact that he had finally been brought to understanding.

"Get on," Arianna demanded, disturbingly calm. She was going to take off with or without him.

Cain made the smart choice and quickly jumped on behind her.

She yanked the handles and her magic shot into the wings, pulling them upward. Arianna leaned into the movement, as if with force of will alone she could see the glider all but teleport back to Ruana. She ran through everything again in her head, but there was no other option.

"You don't really think she . . ." Cain trailed off, no doubt running through the same probabilities and series of ideas as Arianna.

Coletta was a woman who'd lost everything to one man, who was now not only the Dragon King, but the head of the House she so despised. If she was willing to kill her own for the sake of vengeance against them, what would she do to him?

Arianna swallowed hard and struggled to keep her grip on the handles as her palms grew abnormally slick.

She had to get to Cvareh.

# 61

## CVAREH

One would think that, lying beneath the weight of kingship, one would sink further into the mattress. But he didn't feel any differently. In fact, he felt so very much the same that Cvareh was worried he had somehow missed an important step in becoming the Dono.

It did not feel real yet. He, Cvareh Xin, was the Dono for all of Nova.

Every member of House Xin had begun to fawn over him with renewed intent. Every man and woman seemed to want to get him something. He wished he hadn't sent Arianna and Cain away. House Rok could wait; he needed his two greatest allies to fend off those who would seek to pour praise on him to the point of nausea.

Exhausted and overwhelmed, Cvareh had ultimately sent them all away.

His lungs still ached from the quick successions of stopping time. They'd felt raw from the harvesting; now they felt utterly foreign. They'd been taken out, grown again, ripped apart, and put back together so many times that it was still laborious to breathe.

Yveun's heart had helped exponentially, but even that surge of power wore off. Every inch of his frame had sustained enough wounds and expended enough energy that all he wanted was quiet. All he wanted was sleep.

So, he allowed the attendants to look after him long enough to make minimal treatments to his wounds and then dress him for bed. But it was the silence after they left that he'd truly relished. Silence that now was his only companion in the wake of his ascension to Dono.

Cvareh closed his eyes. His thoughts did not drift to leadership. Nor was he visited by some prophetic vision of Lord Xin blessing him with divine right to rule. Behind his eyelids, he found the face of one woman—Arianna. And with no one to know, or judge him for his daydreams, he indulged the thought.

He saw them sitting together, thrones to match. They would be a beacon for Loom and Nova, a symbol of what their worlds could be, of the partnership that was required for all of them to seek the freedom they had long desired. And, as Dono, he would see that she never wanted for anything.

Dreaming numbed the pain, and soothed him enough that sleep could take its hold.

Movement stirred him. His mind was sluggish, but his body was already feeling much stronger from however much rest he'd gotten. Cvareh groaned softly, trying to dismiss whatever unnecessary helper had disturbed his sleep.

His eyelids fluttered, and he caught a glimpse of red.

*Red.*

Cvareh's eyes shot wide open as he felt a blade plunging between his ribs, straight into his heart. They took in the face of a woman he'd only seen in passing before. Her eyes were dead and emotionless. She could have been sipping tea, rather than killing the Dono in cold blood.

The blade burned as she removed it. The hole closed, magic knitting over the small incision quickly, but the fire remained.

"Coletta," he snarled.

"A gift, for the new Dono." She smiled, exposing teeth that looked more like worn-down knives. Her gums were gnarled and recessed. "I used the same poison on your sister." Coletta's hand cupped his cheek, almost lovingly. "I thought you would want to die as she did."

With a primal scream, Cvareh summoned energy he did not think he possessed, bolting upright. One hand gripped the woman's frail shoulder, feeling bone snap under the force of his fingers as the other hand plunged into her chest. Coletta coughed blood onto his chest, leaning against his cheek. She reeked of death and strawberries.

"Rok will forever seek to regain the throne that is rightfully theirs," she swore darkly.

Cvareh ripped out her heart with ease and pushed her away. Coletta posed no struggle; her triumphant eyes remained wide open even in death. She collapsed onto the floor, and Cvareh discarded her heart across the room, not daring to sink his teeth into the flesh of the poison mistress. Just her blood on his shoulder seemed to burn his skin.

The excitement and exertion quickened his heart. Cvareh collapsed back onto the bed, trying to slow the flow of poison throughout his body. It seared his muscles and sapped his strength.

He stared up at the ceiling above his bed, and wondered what Petra had seen as she lay in an agony that mirrored his.

The door opened and three Xin rushed in, responding to the commotion.

Cvareh didn't know their names, but these would likely be the last faces he saw before he died, so he took them in as though he'd known them all his life.

"I have been poisoned," he whispered, as if speaking too loudly would cause his blood to pump and his body to give out faster. He wanted to slow the take of poison for as long as he could. He wanted to stall the inevitable. He would say only what needed to be said and preserve all remaining words for the one woman he wanted to lay eyes on before the God of Death cast his shroud over Cvareh's form at last.

"Who?" They looked at Coletta's corpse. No doubt, they had never seen the woman before. Coletta avoided public appearances at all costs, since they only sparked rumors of her frailty.

"Coletta Rok'Ryu," he answered. "When—" the word got caught. He thought of Petra again. His sister had endured the same pain as he, likely worse. He would not break down, would not let the pain get the better of him. "When I am gone, Cain is the Xin'Oji, and the Dono."

Cvareh closed his eyes, taking a deep breath. Stasis. Stillness. He had to persevere, had to hang on.

"When Cain'Ryu and Ari'Kin return, send them to me…"

"Dono, what can we do?" one of the men asked hopelessly.

Had he not heard a word Cvareh had said? Death was inevitable.

"Imbibing will sustain me… but not save me." It was the only thing he knew to say.

He shouldn't have been surprised when they returned with a heart in hand a short time later. Cvareh wanted to refuse. It had no doubt been cut from some under-island dweller, someone under the shade of House Xin that he was supposed to protect. But his mind was delirious and focused on only one thing— seeing Arianna again. *He had to see her again.* It was a drive beyond anything else. A drive that could push a man to madness.

He brought the heart to his lips and ate, and when he could no longer eat it himself, it was fed to him. Every bite was smaller than the last, his chewing slower.

But still, he held on.

He held on until he saw white against a colorful world, a peaceful break for eyes overwhelmed by the all-too-bright kaleidoscope he found himself in. He held on until Cain's booming voice summoned his consciousness back toward the surface of the inky darkness he was drowning in. He held on until he felt her hands on him again.

"Ari—"

"Cvareh, I need you to listen to me." Her voice was hurried, thin, frantic.

He smiled tiredly. She had to be forceful up to their very last moment together. Well, call him a romantic, or just insane, but he wouldn't have it any other way.

"Cvareh, listen, stay with me. It won't work if you won't listen." She was talking too quickly for him to really listen, and her voice had an odd pitch he didn't quite recognize. "Cain, help me sit him up. We need him awake—we only have one chance."

Cvareh groaned in protest as they hoisted him upright. The groan turned into a hiss of pain. It was as if jostling his blood reinvigorated the poison, spreading it further through his veins. Their efforts were long past the point of fruitlessness. Three hearts, now cold and void of magic, littered the bed around him.

But still, Arianna clung to him. He felt her arms around him. He felt her strength. His body ached to return the same to her in kind.

"I know what I want my boon to be." She was whispering now. It was soft and low, like a lover, like how he'd always wanted to hear her speak to him. Warmth enveloped him, warmth in the shape of a woman. "Listen closely, Cvareh, because all the magic in the world will be yours to see my boon fulfilled. You will have no choice. You must do this for me."

He leaned against her, let her voice flow through him. This was what he had wanted. This was what he had waited for. This was what kept him clinging to life. To fulfill the contract he had made with a Wraith.

"For my boon, I want . . . I wish . . . I wish for you to heal, stronger than you were before, completely and utterly. Cvareh, for my boon, I wish for you to live."

The words echoed within him, and with them, magic exploded anew.

# 62

## ARIANNA

Magic that normally smelled of woodsmoke took on a new depth. The rich aroma cleared, like a window being opened to some greater beyond, and a crisp smell like rain flooded the room. Arianna continued to cling to him, tighter than she'd ever admit in the future to any who dared recount this moment.

She doubted doing so helped the magic. If anything, it likely hindered him, as she was giving Cvareh new bruises for his magic to heal. But she wasn't exactly thinking logically. All she wanted was for him to return to her. Until that moment her every want and wish had been death—the death of Finnyr, of Yveun, peaceful deaths for her old friends and lover when there were no other options. But now she wished for life. A long and fruitful life, for him.

It was a twitch at first. A movement in his biceps that could have been nothing more than instinct or involuntary reaction. But then it happened again.

His arms found movement, coming back to life. Rain turned back to smoke, and Cvareh breathed normally once more. The sound of his life filled her ears—the shifting of his movement, of his exhales against her cheek. He wrapped her in his embrace, responding with as much fervor as she held him.

Arianna didn't want to open her eyes. What if she was wrong? What if somehow this was all some illusion of a desperate mind too broken to handle the loss of another love?

"Arianna . . ." he breathed, soft enough that she could lie to herself and say she hadn't heard it.

But she did, and the sound had her choking in a sigh of relief. Emotion was raw in her neck and she wanted to scream or cry or laugh, but did none of it. She merely held on to the man she loved, and gulped down her relief. Cain was watching, after all, and there was only so much she'd allow the man to witness.

Cvareh's muscles gained strength, his back straightened, his breathing leveled. He continued to hold her as his heartbeat steadied once more, regular and strong. It was a sound Arianna could listen to for days—years, even.

Finally, he straightened away and merely stared at her with a wonder she'd never seen on anyone before.

"You saved my life."

"Well, it'd be really inconvenient for Loom if the man who has all the deals for our freedom just up and died." She couldn't say what she really felt—not even if she wanted to, which she didn't. It was far too terrifying and grossly romantic to utter aloud. "Plus, I really, really hate that woman." She nodded toward Coletta's corpse, more than a little upset that was yet another death Cvareh had over her. "And I loved the idea of thwarting—"

"I love you too, Arianna," he interrupted boldly.

*Bloody cogs*, he had to up and be the brave one, once again. Here he was professing his love for her in front of his right hand, as the King of the Dragons, and all Arianna could do was muster sarcasm. "That's one way to say thank you, I suppose."

She forced her arms to go slack.

*King of the Dragons*, the words repeated in her head, imprinting as fact. It had all happened so fast, and there was always one more enemy. But now that there were no more standing against them, the future was upon her.

This man was the King of the Dragons, Dono, leader of Nova. He was not just Cvareh anymore; he had a far greater role to play. One dark corner of her heart uttered in reproach for its self-preservation: *you should have let him die in Dortam*.

She'd been the one to save him, to deliver him to the Alchemists, to see his house succeed, to see him become King . . . only to have to let him go.

Arianna stood quickly, before she could allow herself to be trapped by him. He would draw her in and then there would be no escape. She'd damn them both with her sentimentality.

There was practice in her movements. Life had prepared her with an unofficial training to do what needed to be done, even when doing so was impossibly hard. She had dedicated her life to fulfilling her duty, and the dreams of others. It should be instinct, putting her wants second and doing what must be done. But all her preparation wasn't enough now that the moment was upon her. Walking away, what should have been the easiest task of all, had never demanded more strength. For, if she stayed, he would focus on her. He would defer to her. He would hesitate, and pause, and steal moments with her. While his time was what she wanted to steal more than any other thing, it was a heist she wouldn't allow herself to make.

"Where are you going?" His confused, questioning gaze made it all the harder.

"Back to Loom. My job here is done." Arianna attempted to make her escape.

"You can stay."

"I don't belong here." She didn't know why she was indulging argument, but her feet had gone into mutiny against her brain. They were in cahoots with her ears to hear what he'd say next.

"You have a place here," he insisted.

"Cvareh, she's—"

"She's the one we owe the world to," Cvareh snapped at Cain's protest. "I am the Dono and I can decree it."

"You don't get it." She looked back at him and, for the first time ever, was thankful for every hardship she had endured. For it had all hardened her enough to survive this parting. It had given her enough training to turn her face, and her heart, to stone. "Cvareh, this is not something you as a Dragon can decree. I am made of steam. I am hot-blooded, strong and free. I was cast in steel, on Loom, and that maker's mark is not something you can expunge from my soul.

"I don't belong here," she finished. It was said with almost enough conviction to fool herself.

"You belong at my side."

"I do not belong here, and you know it." Arianna watched him deflate with every word, and had to tell herself that what she was doing was for the best.

"What will you do instead?"

"There's always something to steal." Arianna smiled nonchalantly, as if one option was as good as the next. If he dug in his heels now, that carefully crafted façade would crack. She would find some excuse to stay, she knew.

But her bluff was good enough that Cvareh didn't call it. He stared right back at her until she could take it no longer.

Arianna turned and walked out of his room, past all the Xin gathered in the hall, as though nothing in the world were bothering her. Every bit of ease on her exterior hid the heartache inside, as she left behind the Dragon King she loved.

# 63
## FLORENCE

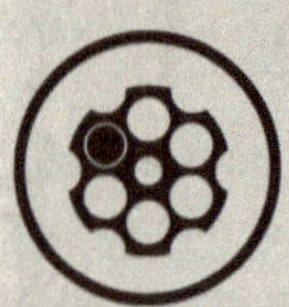



THERE WAS NO WEAPON LIKE HOPE, AND NO AMMUNITION FOR IT LIKE GOOD news.

Word of the victory up on Nova spread faster and thicker than the clouds overhead. Helen, who had been up with Arianna, had whispered back to Will—their decision to get Dragon ears and set up a whisperlink hadn't been the least bit surprising to Florence. Will informed the rest of the Queen's minions, who ultimately dispersed the news to Shannra.

Florence knew the moment Shannra had appeared in her office that there had been victory, just by her expression alone. And because she had already had the information from someone else.

"You already know."

"Emma was here not minutes before you left. Word funneled through the Revolvers who were up with House Xin when it happened." Florence looked back at the list of tasks she'd begun drafting, already several items deep.

"We have claimed victory, and you are still busy at work." Shannra looped around the desk, draping her arms over Florence's shoulders.

"It is only the beginning—freedom is only the beginning for us. Now, we must rebuild Loom, not as it was but as it could be." Florence was having a hard time deciding what to prioritize. Everything seemed like it needed to happen at once. And when everything was a priority, nothing was a priority.

"There is to be another Tribunal?" Shannra had no doubt focused on the first item on Florence's list.

"At Garre. Emma is spreading the word now."

Shannra sighed, though the noise was without any sort of real weight. "What is it with you and Tribunals?"

"I am a vicar, after all." Florence ran a hand up Shannra's arm, starting at where her hand met the desk, helping prop her up, all the way to her shoulder and back.

"You are the Vicar *Revolver*." Shannra turned her head back to Florence. "Your place is in Dortam, not Garre."

"And so it shall be," Florence affirmed. "Once we are all in agreement, every vicar will return to their rightful home to begin rebuilding."

"Will you return home alone?" Shannra asked, staring out the window behind Florence's desk in what had become her makeshift office.

"I think you know the answer to that."

"I want to hear you say it."

Florence didn't bother concealing a smile. "You will accompany me, if you so choose, as a Master Revolver."

"Don't think you can win me over with titles." Shannra tilted her head coyly.

"What can I win you over with then?"

"I asked you once if we could share a flat in Dortam when all this was over. You never answered." Shannra stared her down, as if trying to pin Florence with her eyes. "It's all over now. I need an answer."

Florence stood slowly. She pushed in her chair, and leaned against the desk with Shannra, facing the window, at just one small scrap of the world that was now theirs.

"Let's see . . . A flat in Dortam, right by the Guild hall, I think it was." Shannra hung on her every word. "I'm not sure if, as the Vicar Revolver, I can live outside the hall proper."

"I could be coerced into being flexible on the location."

"Could you?" Florence rounded the woman—her lover, in all her scarred and battle-weary glory. She reached a hand, cupping Shannra's cheek, weaving her fingers in the tangled mess of hair. "What must I do to coerce you?"

"I think you will come up with something creative." Shannra's voice had fallen to a hush, her lids heavy. She leaned forward, ever so slightly, and Florence felt herself moving to meet her.

"I will certainly try, Moonbeam."

Shannra halted, brows furrowed, lips pursed, eyes alert. "Moonbeam?"

"You asked me to be creative." Florence smirked. "I can be dangerous when I'm creative."

"Spoken like a true Vicar Revolver." Shannra was back to whispering. "I like you dangerous, Gunpowder."

Florence smirked at the equally heinous petname. She needed a partner who could roll with the punches and dish it out as well as she took it.

Before either of them could conceive something worse, Florence claimed the woman's mouth with her own. Shannra's tongue was sweeter than any cookie Florence had ever eaten.

"What about all your work?" Shannra asked after several long minutes, gasping for air.

"It will keep."

Florence pushed aside her papers, scattering them to the floor. Yes, there was work to be done, decisions to be made, and things to be settled. But first, she had a woman to hoist onto the desk and more hard-earned flavors of freedom to relish.

# 64

## CVAREH

She had fought at his side. They had made love countless times. He had invited her to stay on Nova and be his queen, his paragon for the new bond between Loom and Nova.

In reply? She couldn't even say that she loved him, even though he knew it was more than true with every beat of his heart.

He wanted to point it out to her. He wanted to demand it from her. But it would mean nothing if he did . . . So, the words were left unsaid in her wake, where he lapped along the shores of all they could've been.

Cvareh stared at where Arianna had just stood. He had done everything Petra had ever dreamed. He had accomplished the dream of hers he had adopted—a Xin'Oji now wore the title of Dono. He, Cvareh, of all Dragons, was now the Dono.

It should have been a cause for celebration. His chest should have swelled with pride so great that his ribs would shatter and be rebuilt with magic now bolstered with the knowledge that he held all of Nova in his palms. But it wasn't.

There was no pride and no fullness. He had achieved everything, but he didn't have the one thing he'd come to want more than anything else. He'd lost the one woman who made everything in his world worthwhile.

"Well, I suppose that makes sense." Cain reminded him of his presence.

Startled, Cvareh half-jumped, as if pulling his feet from the tar of his own thoughts. "What does?"

"You had a boon with her this whole time." Disapproval ran rampant between Cain's words, though his friend didn't pursue it. There wasn't much to be done now about it and the fact that Cvareh had forged such had just saved his life. "Explains your obsession with the woman."

"It's more than that," Cvareh mumbled.

"Is it?" Cain asked, though Cvareh knew he was already aware of the answer so he didn't dignify the question with a response. "Call her back, then. Make her stay."

"I can't."

"Why not? You're the Dono."

"You heard her." Cvareh motioned to where the woman had been standing. "She can't be contained here and I couldn't make her."

"You're the Dono," Cain repeated, as though those three words should explain away everything.

"It means nothing if she doesn't stay of her own will. I can't order her presence just as I can't order her love."

Cain was given pause at the word "love." Surely, his friend must have seen it already. The man's brow knitted, furrowed lines digging over his eyebrows. "And that means something to you?"

It meant more than Cvareh could ever put into words. But all he said was, "It does."

"Then, if you will not command her to stay or order her affections, you must stop giving her your own."

As if it were that simple. As if it had ever been that simple.

He hadn't chosen to love her. He simply did. It had become as undeniable to him as winter's chill and as warming to his soul as summer's sun. Trying to do anything but love her would be like trying to halt the seasons: pointless and impossible.

"I can't do that either," he confessed in a whisper. Cvareh continued to stare after Arianna, the vacant spot where she'd once stood now filling with a new regret that he had not properly imprinted her image on his memory. With her as the Wraith on Loom, and he as the Dono in Nova, their paths were likely to never cross again.

"Then learn how." Cain moved into his field of vision. "Xin needs, *deserves*, an Oji who will celebrate this time and lead with all his heart." Cain shook his head, his tone becoming even more serious. "All of Nova, Cvareh. Not just Xin, but all of Nova needs you now. We are fractured and bleeding, and we need a Dono who will unite us."

"You're right," Cvareh admitted.

"We need someone who knows the Fenthri and is willing to work with them but still defend Nova's interests," Cain continued as if Cvareh hadn't just agreed with everything he'd said. "Someone who can carry on Petra's vision. Someone who has the esteem of our House. We—"

"I know, Cain." Nothing the man had said was untrue. But the whole of it had made Cvareh realize that he was not the only one who fit such a description.

"I will be here for you. It will be my supreme honor to serve as Ryu to the Dono." His friend squeezed his shoulder in a sympathetic display.

"Don't be so sure."

"What?" Cain's brow was back to furrowing. Cvareh could almost feel the panic rising from him.

Cvareh merely smiled at his friend's confusion. "This is a tumultuous time, Cain. Kings are dying left and right…"

# 65

## FLORENCE

---

Dear W.W.,

Shannra tells me that I'm writing to a ghost. Fear not, I corrected her that the proper term is "Wraith."

You've been very good at not being found, this past year. I can only presume it was intentional when all of my efforts to leave no stone unturned left me empty-handed.

At first, I thought perhaps you were worried about my focus not being properly on my duties as Vicar Revolver. I could only imagine though, given the speed at which I've seen the hall and refinery rebuilt, that such was impossible. A distracted vicar does not make for an effective one. And, if I may be so bold, I've been fairly effective.

So, I'm only left to think that you do not want to be found. I attempted to corner Helen on the matter, but she was only slightly less slippery to get a hold of than you. It seems she's settling into her assumed role of rebuilding Mercury Town as well. Perhaps a little too well. (Do not make me send Revolvers down there to clean up any messes.)

In any case, now that I've come to terms with such a realization, I'm left with only one final course of action—this letter.

We are women of action, you and I, not words. Thus, I've toiled over what to put here for weeks now. You are aware, I am sure, of the overall state of affairs in Loom. And judging from the recent report of the "Queen of Wraith's Grand Return to Dortam," I think you're keenly aware of the status in our city. (It's a bit of a flashy title to re-assume, don't you think? For a woman who supposedly died in the battles on Nova.)

I digress, yet again… I want you to know, if nothing else, that I have looked for you. That I will continue to keep my eyes out for a woman in white at every corner I pass, every junction I cross. You, my teacher, my mentor, one of the most talented women I have ever known, will always have a place with me.

And should you never walk through the open door I'm leaving for you, then so be it; know you have my thanks. This runaway Raven will forever be in your debt as the woman who pulled her shaking and scared from the Underground, and once more, showed her the light.

Sincerely,

F.

P.S. I am truly sorry about what happened to Cvareh. However, if you said or did anything to ensure Cain would be so open to keeping positive relationships with Loom, I thank you.

# 66

## ARIANNA

The light was bright enough to cut one's shadow into the cobblestone of the streets, wet and glistening with the night's chill. It was the same moon that had borne witness to the rise of the White Wraith years ago, and was now the sole member of the audience witnessing the rebirth following the metamorphosis of that lone creature.

Arianna darted between back alleys, the hem of her freshly-tailored coat flapping against her legs.

Two Revo grunts were on her tail. They had all the persistence of fresh journeymen let out for the first time to "keep the peace." Yes, they were determined, but Arianna wasn't dissuaded.

Even as rubble and ruin, she knew the pathways and side-streets better than anyone. The farther she got from the center of Dortam, the rougher and more broken things became. It was an area that was still mostly untouched by time—a holdover from the days of Dragons.

She pushed deeper and deeper, knowing she'd lose them eventually. They were already tired of wasting ammunition by taking cheap shots at nothing.

This part of the city had been far enough away from the epicenter of the Revolvers' self-destruction that it had been spared from total ruin. Dortam was a target now; the bullseye was the new metropolis, springing from the ashes of the old. Out from that center was ruin, still in the process of being rebuilt. Further still, a peace of Arianna's heart would always live—Old Dortam. Buildings here jutted at odd angles and collapsed rooftops sagged holes between persistent walls. It was the city of Dortam's criminals and less-than-desirables. It was home for her.

She waited out of sight, tucked in a shaded alcove, listening carefully to the footsteps of the Revos slow. They cursed aloud, debated further pursuit, and eventually decided to let her go. *Smart men*, Arianna applauded. After all, she so hated killing talent. The Revolvers had little and less of it, in their present circumstances.

Arianna reemerged into the moonlight, looking around at the street she'd tracked to for the first time. It was instantly familiar. She remembered the sounds of industry—welding, hammering, the buzz of saws—that filled the air by day, and yielded to the revels of gambling parlors at night. Now, there was only silence, and her footsteps breaking the stillness.

Two streets down, one over, along a back alley, was a stairwell. Some stairs were missing—the iron rusted out and peeling away from itself like rotten flower petals. But the main joints to the building were still strong enough to hold her weight.

She didn't have anywhere else to be tonight. Her patron could wait until morning to get the trinket Arianna carried. For now, she'd rest in what was an all-too-familiar flat.

The door was ajar, but the room showed almost no signs of life.

*Almost no signs.*

Arianna waded through the familiar smells and nostalgic sights over to the kitchen table, where a letter sat among cookie crumbs that had somehow evaded rats for years. It was pristine, fresh, and on it were the letters "W.W." in a familiar hand. Arianna turned it over, and paused.

The floorboards behind her creaked under the weight of another presence. Another ghost reemerging from the memories of past lives she'd given up when Arianna had died.

"It's a bit much don't you think, to have the Dragon King himself hunt me down?"

Arianna turned, setting the letter back down on the table to have her hands free. She didn't know what she should anticipate… a fight? A flight? Or something more?

A Dragon emerged from the bedroom. His hair had grown out in the months since she'd last seen him. It almost brushed his shoulders in its burnt orange disarray. Cvareh wore dark pants and a long-sleeved, high collared shirt in the current fashion—if any of Loom's tailoring could really be called that compared to the pomp of Dragons. It was plain, functional, and everything she'd never associated with him.

"Very much Dragon, not quite King."

Arianna tilted her head curiously.

"You have not heard?" He seemed genuinely surprised.

"When you're a ghost, you don't hear much." Arianna leaned against the wall, folding her arms over her chest. Seeing him was like running her fingers over the dried ink of long-forgotten schematics. She'd not realized just how much she'd missed the familiar designs.

In truth, Arianna had only been truly oblivious until she'd return to Dortam no more than a week ago. Her attempts to fade away had been sincere. She'd secured a cottage in the mountains to the north, far outside the city, that had everything she'd needed.

Or *thought* she'd needed.

For she still found herself drawn back to the city that had been her home following the last rebellion. She'd made the excuse that it was for fresh supplies alone. Then, somehow, a new coat had found its way onto her shoulders, and her feet had found themselves standing before Helen, asking if there were any odd jobs that needed doing.

"Apparently not." He chuckled deeply, a sound that could turn moonlight to sunlight. "Though, I'm coming to realize such myself. We are both ghosts."

"Oh?" She could do little more than make noncommittal noises that encouraged him to continue until he gave her enough information to work with.

"I fear it falls to me to regretfully inform you that the Dragon King you worked so hard to save perished due to poison from Coletta'Ryu."

The words sank into her flesh slowly, seeping through her. They eventually reached her brain and elicited the most ineloquent response of, "What?"

"I hear, however, that his replacement is every inch the man both worlds hoped for in a Dragon King."

"Cvareh, what are you saying?" Arianna truly had been gone too long. No one on Loom had ever said the Dragon King's name; it was always just "Dragon King" or "the king." Surely, Helen had known. Arianna was already fantasizing about how she'd wring the girl's neck for neglecting to mention the "death" of Cvareh.

"Cvareh is dead." He phrased it in a different way, as if she hadn't already figured it out on her own.

"A pity I couldn't kill him. I'd so wanted to kill the Dragon King in the last rebellion." There it was again, the sarcasm that arose in defense of the fragile hope her heart had begun to bleed.

"I have it on good faith that you accomplished that task."

"You should check your sources, as Yveun'Dono was killed by Cvareh'Oji."

They both shared a smile that was quickly stolen by silence. She'd fantasized about seeing him again, but Arianna had never let the thoughts take hold. He was the Dragon King, needed in the sky world, and she had no place there. Now that he was in front of her, she was at an utter loss of what to do.

"You should go back to Nova," she whispered. Arianna knew it was pointless.

"I don't belong there, not any more."

"You're a Dragon. Isn't the only thing that matters to you your place? In society, in the hierarchy?"

"You're right," he affirmed. The man hadn't moved a muscle and she wanted to tackle him for it. Though she had no idea what would happen once she had him on the ground.

"Then why are you here?" And why was she whispering?

"Because this is my place."

Arianna wanted to scream at him for the answer that wasn't an answer. She swallowed hard, but couldn't dislodge the lump in her throat that was blocking all sound. He took a step, and then another. Arianna burned the sight of him into her eyes. The idea that the end of this rebellion, the true end, might not require her to sacrifice everything she loved, rooted itself unbidden in her mind. It was a notion she'd not considered with even the smallest corner of her heart, and now it burrowed so deep, she feared the hole it would leave would have no bottom.

"Is it my place?" he asked, standing toe-to-toe with her.

"I can't choose that for you." It was the only response she could muster. He hadn't forced her to choose, in the end, and so neither could she.

"I long ago made that choice." Cvareh leaned forward with all the slowness of a man who had her daggers shoved at his throat the last time they had occupied this space. His forehead met hers, their noses almost touching. And for a moment, for a brief and blissful moment, they merely breathed. "Do you want me?"

"Yes," she confessed to herself, to him, to his twenty gods, to every maggot and rat and cut-purse that might be listening.

"Do you love me?"

Arianna opened her mouth to respond and closed it. She swallowed once more. She couldn't make this easy for him, not now, not ever.

"Follow me, and find out." Arianna stepped away and locked eyes with him for one deliciously long moment, before she strode out the door, his footsteps close behind.

With the moon watching, the Wraith and the Dragon stepped into the night together.

The Loom Saga was truly a passion project, and it's my sincere hope that you loved reading it as much as I loved writing it.

*If you haven't already,* please consider leaving a review on the individual books, or the complete series, on the retailer of your choice. Honest reviews help both authors and other readers immeasurably.

If you enjoyed the Loom Saga, I invite you to try some of my other epic fantasy works. Keep reading to discover more…

Want even more about the World of Loom than what you find in this appendix?

**Visit: http://elisekova.com/the-world-of-loom/**

*For Character profiles, Concept artwork, Guild history, and more.*

# PRONUNCIATION GUIDE

### PEOPLE
Arianna: *Are-E-ah-nah*
Cvareh: *Suh-var-ay*
Florence: *Floor-in-ss*
Leona: *Lee-oh-nah*
Yveun: *Yeh-vu-n*
Louie: *Loo-EE*
Petra: *Peh-trah*
Sophie: *So-fee*
Agendi: *Again-Dee*
Finnyr: Fihn-er
Dawyn: Dawn
Soph: Sah-f
Luc: Luke
Theodosia: Three-Oh-doh-sha
Faroe: Fuh-row
Topann: Toe-PAh-n

### PLACES
Ter: *(Short for Territory)*
Lysip: *Lisp*
Holx: *Hole-ks*
Keel: *Key-uhl*
Ruana: *Roo-AH-nah*
Easwin: *Ees-win*
Abilla: *Uh-bih-luh*
Venys: *Veh-nis*
Napole: *Nah-pole-Ee*

### THINGS:
Peca: *Peh-kah*
Royuk: *Ree-yook*
Fennish: *Fehn-ish*
Dunca: *Duhn-kah*
Boco: *Boh-Koh*
Endwig: *Ehnd-wihg*
Glovis: *Glow-vihs*
Raku: *Rah-koo*

**Dragon Houses/Titles**

Xin: *Shin*
Rok: *Rock*
Tam: *T-am (same as 'am' in 'I am')*
Oji: *Oh-jee*
Ryu: *Re-you*
Dono: *Dough-no*
To: *Tow*
Bek: *Beck*
Da: *Dah*
Vicar: *Vih-kur*

<u>**FIVE GUILDS OF LOOM**</u>

### ALCHEMISTS
*"Slice and Stich"*
Founded 102 by Vicar Keel
Territory 2

———

### HARVESTERS
*"Sow and Reap"*
Founded 1 by Vicar Faroe
Territory 1

———

### RAVENS
*"Spread Our Wings"*
Founded 474 by Vicar Holx
Territory 4

———

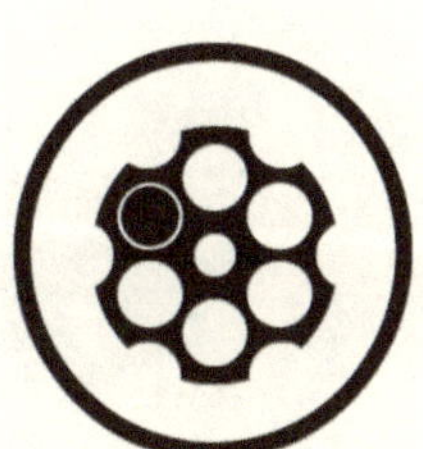

### REVOLVERS
"We are the Spark"
Founded 612 by Vicar Dortam
Territory 5

———

**RIVETS**
Founded 148 by Vicar Garre
Territory 3

**Initiate**

**Journeyman**

**Master**

———

*In Nova, Dragons will also wear brands on their cheeks if they "defect" from the house they are born into to join another house.*

# DRAGON HOUSES

*All members of Dragon society belong to one of three Dragon houses. Ties into the House can be by blood, adoption, mating, or merit.*

**ROK**

**TAM**

# XIN

---

Nova adapted Loom's tradition of placing a circular shape the symbol to designate the highest rank. The shape is a 20 sided polygon representing the 20 gods in the Dragon Pantheon. While this is never branded on a Dragon, it can be used as decoration.

*Sample Oji Symbol:*

# **DRAGON NAMES**

*All Dragon names follow the structure:*
[Given Name] [House Name]'[House Rank] [Societal Rank]

*Shortened names are said as one of the following:*
[Given Name]'[House Rank]
*or*
[Given Name] [Societal Rank]

———

Oji – House Head
Ryu – Second in Command
Kin – Immediate Family to the Oji/Ryu
Da – Extended Family
Anh – Vassals/Lower Members of the Estate

Dono – King/Queen
To – Dono's Advisors/High Nobility
Veh – Nobility Chosen by the Dono
Soh – Upper Common
Bek – Lower Common
(nothing) – Pauper, Slave, Disgraced

# DRAGON MAGIC

Naturally occurring magic in the world of Loom is found in Dragon body parts. Fenthri are not magical by birth. Every organ has its own respective magic:

**Blood** - Healing & Control of Gold

**Hands** - Illusions

**Eyes** - Improved Vision & Mind Control (while in unbroken eye contact)

**Ears** - Improved Hearing & Whispering (Communication over any distance with a single other individual via a secret word)

**Tongue** - Verbal Influence/Persuasion

**Stomach** - Poison & Illness Immunity

**Lungs** - Time Manipulation

**Heart** - Contains all magic found in a Dragon's other body parts, this is the only organ that cannot be regenerated

# CHIMERA

Chimera are not born, they are made by Fenthri who have transplanted Dragon body parts.

The transition to Chimera begins with a painful blood transfusion, replacing all of a Fenthri's blood with Dragon blood. Due to the healing properties in the Dragon blood, the Fenthri does not die, and their body is reprogrammed to produce a hybrid blood from then on. This is what gives Chimera their signature black blood.

Following this, Chimera can obtain transplants of other Dragon body parts. But a Chimera's mind will begin to warp, and eventually "fall" due to magic breaking down their body faster than the blood can regenerate.

A *Perfect Chimera* is the idea of a Chimera that can have all body parts, all magic of a Dragon, without falling.

**Note:** Any Fenthri can temporarily gain magic by ingesting Dragon body parts.

# WORLD CALENDAR

The year's beginning and end is marked by a day of light every twenty cycles of the moon. In this way, both Loom (underneath the cloud barrier) and Nova developed similar 20 month calendars.

———

*Loom*

Loom uses a system where each month and day is only numbered. To write:

[day].[month].[year]

Therefore, 12.1.506 would be the twelfth day of the first month in the year 506.

———

*Nova*

On Nova, months are named after different gods in the pantheon. Days are simply numbered.

# DRAGON PANTHEON

*(In corresponding calendar order)*

Lord Rok - The Life-bringer
Lord Tam - The Balance-keeper
Lady Colwan - The Maker
Lady Luc - The Light-herald
Lady Che - The Honest
Lord Pipa - The Mischievous
Lady Soph - The Destroyer
Lord To - The Wise
Lady Suire - The Warrior
Lord Agendi - The Lucky
Lady Veh - The Bold
Lord Tiand - The Festive
Lady Lei - The Caregiver
Lord Soh - The Loyal
Lady Jeanxi - The Female Lover
Lord Mardu - The Male Lover
Lord Bek - The Dutiful
Lady Tianul - The Peaceful
Lord Pak - The Dark-wielder
Lord Xin - The Death-Giver

# ACKNOWLEDGEMENTS

# BOOK ONE

The Gatekeeper Press Team—I recognize it may be weird to start with the team that helped me bring Air Awakens to market, but I wouldn't be here if it weren't for each of you. The fact that I came across Gatekeeperpress.com at the start of my publishing career was downright serendipitous and it was through the experience, exposure, and partnership that I found there that I was able to get to where I am today. So thank you for your continued professionalism and I hope to work with you all again in the future.

Rob Price—from the bottom of my heart, I thank you. Our partnership began humbly enough, but look at what it has become! When I had nothing but a story and a dream, you helped me through Gatekeeper Press. Then you and Price World Publishing embarked on this journey with me. I hope to continue working with you and your teams in the future.

My editor, Rebecca—it has been an absolute joy to work with you. On a nuts and bolts level, thank you for all the insights you gave me and work you put into this manuscript. But, on a higher level, thank you for being the one to encourage me to take my work beyond the scope of Young Adult. I've grown so much as a writer in a short time working with you and I hope we have many more manuscripts ahead of us.

Nick—thank you for letting me be really bad at listening to you when you said you didn't want to help me conceptualize my work and tolerating all the times I forced you to do it anyway. You are the best beta reader an author could want, and the best friend anyone could ever hope for. I hope you can see all the places you helped change for the better in this manuscript. I will always hold it and think of pacing my living room as I prattled off ideas to you.

My cover artist, Nick D. Grey—thank you so much for bringing the characters of Loom to life. It's been a pleasure working with you and I can't wait to see how you envision Petra and Yveun! I'm so happy that you drew that Bloodborne fan art that brought us together.

Rob—I'm not sure if meeting you when I did was a stroke of luck, or fate, but I know better than to look a gift horse in the mouth. Thank you for all the guidance and help you've given me throughout this process. You offer a unique perspective, a sturdy counterweight when I need it, an expert opinion, and a perpetually patient ear. You are truly one of the best people I have ever had the privilege of meeting.

Jon—your counsel has been invaluable throughout this process. The guidance you have given me has not only been essential in shaping my publication journey, but also sound life advice in general.

Katie—I think it's safe to say that you are the first person who has talked about getting a Loom tattoo! I will always remember with fondness reading over your shoulder the first time you experienced this story and playing just the right music at just the right time. Thank you for always being there to go out with me when I'm going stir crazy!

Doug—thank you for helping me navigate the dollars and cents side of running a business and making sure my books are in order. Your candor and professionalism are always appreciated.

Danielle L. Jensen—our Twitter DMs will live forever in infamy! Thank you for helping me both as an author and as a friend. I can't tell you how much I've appreciated everything from your guidance in why a sentence didn't make sense to you reading the manuscript in advance.

Susan Dennard—your title for the world's most supportive author is only rivalled by the title of most awesome friend. Even when you were deep in the writing cave you allowed me to be random at you. Thank you so much for taking the time to read The Alchemists of Loom when you were so, so busy.

My Tower Guard—even if we are now in a new world, you will always be my dear guard. Near or far, we take care of our own and no one feels that more than me. Thank you so much for all your help in spreading the word about my works. Each and every one of you are so dear to me.

# BOOK TWO

NICK—I wouldn't have made it through this manuscript without you. I push, and you push me harder. Your thoughts, suggestions, insights, were all imperative for me to make it through this story that demanded so much of me. Thank you for having both the strength to demand the world of me and hug me hard enough so I keep it together when I may crack under the pressure.

ROBERT—thank you for all the inspiration you gave to me, however inadvertent. You're an exceptional friend and a role-model for me on how to be a decent human being (even if I'm pretty sure I regularly come up short). Thank you for being a parallel river of temperate waters.

MY EDITOR, REBECCA FAITH HEYMAN—there should be a saying that behind every marginally decent author is an editor who's ten times more amazing. Thank you for working with me on this manuscript and helping me from throwing ideas around to cleaning up my structure when it needed it most. I am so, so glad we met and are getting to have this experience together.

KATIE—as always, thank you for keeping me sane. You give me something no one else does in your unique blend of encouragement and love. I would've long gone crazy if I didn't have you to get turkey clubs and fancy tea with.

ROB and the KEYMASTER PRESS TEAM—thank you for your continued belief in me and, you know, not deciding I'm not worth your time. It's been a delight to work with you and I can only hope we continue to bring worlds into readers hands together.

THE TOWER GUARD—my dear street team, thank you for everything you do! You're always there when I need you and such a great group. I'm so honored to be surrounded with people who really take care of their own.

# BOOK THREE

MY EDITOR, REBECCA FAITH HEYMAN—this book is for you. I couldn't have asked for a better "work wife" and editor and am already looking forward to our next project together.

ROBERT—thank you for giving me shelter, support, and compassion when I needed it most. I wouldn't have survived this manuscript were it not for you.

KATIE—my life would not be the same without you in it. Thank you for your unending support when I need it most.

ROB and the KEYMASTER PRESS TEAM—one more time, thank you for all your help in bringing this story to the world. It wouldn't have reached nearly as many hands without you.

THE TOWER GUARD—without you all this publishing game would be so much more lonely and empty. Thank you for always being there for me!